Joan Didion was born in 1\ in New York City. She is the author of five novels and seven books of non-fiction. Her essays have earned her a reputation as one of the world's greatest living writers. Joan Didion's latest book is the acclaimed memoir *Where I Was From* (2003). She contributes regularly to *The New York Times Review of Books*.

For automatic updates on Joan Didion visit HarperPerennial.co.uk and register for AuthorTracker.

From the reviews of Joan Didion's work:

'Her tough, surgically precise prose is like nothing else I've ever read'
DONNA TARTT

'Because her work, like Hemingway's, is montage . . . she has the same sense of the power of the sentence and the power of the next sentence'
NORMAN MAILER

'All of the essays manifest not only [Didion's] intelligence but an instinct for details that continue to emit pulsations in the reader's memory and a style that is spare, subtly musical in its phrasing and exact . . . the result is a voice like no other in contemporary journalism'
The New York Times Book Review

'An incantation with repetitions and rhythms to entrance the reader, meant to restore full weight to a language made weightless by misuse . . . I should perhaps also mention that I read it twice for pure delight before reading it for review'
Guardian

'Didion manages to make the sorry stuff of troubled times (bike movies, for instance) as interesting and suggestive as the monuments that win her dazzled admiration (Georgia O'Keeffe, the Hoover Dam, the mountains around Bogota) . . . A timely and elegant collection'
New Yorker

'In her portraits of people, Didion is not out to expose but to understand . . . A rich display of some of the best prose written today in this country'   *The New York Times Book Review*

'Didion is an original journalistic talent who can strike at the heart, or the absurdity, of a matter in our contemporary wasteland with quick, graceful strokes'   *San Francisco Chronicle*

'She is one of our true stylists. Her sentences have the wicked precision of a Wodehouse or a Waugh, though she uses them for a different purpose: a cold keening for the times we live in'

RICHARD EDER

'Joan Didion has always held a solitary status as a modern American essayist, her prose defining erudition and cool elegance . . . Her style always belonged more to noir than hip: It suggested a singular integrity, a private struggle with ominous depths. She showed a generation of young American journalists how to make reporting moodily stylish, a personal expression'   *New York Observer*

'Her pages fall like brilliant autumn leaves and arrange themselves as sermons in the stones'   *The New York Times Book Review*

By the same author

Miami
Democracy
Salvador
A Book of Common Prayer
Play It As It Lays
Run River
The Last Thing He Wanted
Where I Was From

JOAN DIDION

Live and Learn

HARPER PERENNIAL
London, New York, Toronto and Sydney

Harper Perennial
An imprint of HarperCollins*Publishers*
77–85 Fulham Palace Road,
Hammersmith, London W6 8JB

www.harperperennial.co.uk

This omnibus edition published by Harper Perennial 2005

Slouching Towards Bethlehem first published in the USA by Farrar,
Straus & Giroux 1968 and in Great Britain by Deutsch 1969
Published as a Flamingo Sixties Classic Edition in 2001
Slouching Towards Bethlehem © Joan Didion 1961, 1964, 1965, 1966, 1967, 1968

The White Album first published in the USA by Simon & Schuster 1979 and
in Great Britain by Weidenfeld & Nicolson 1979
Published by Flamingo in 1993
The White Album © Joan Didion 1979

After Henry first published in the USA by Simon & Schuster 1992 and in
Great Britain as *Sentimental Journeys* by HarperCollins 1993
After Henry © Joan Didion 1992

Joan Didion asserts the moral right to be identified as the author of this work

A catalogue record for this book is available from the British Library

ISBN 978 0 00 720438 0

Thanks are due to the following publishers for permission to reproduce cited excerpts:
in *Slouching Towards Bethlehem*, Mr M. B. Yeats and Macmillan Ltd for
'The Second Coming' from the *Collected Poems* of W. B. Yeats;

in *The White Album*, Farrar, Straus & Giroux for 'Caracas I' from Robert Lowell's
Notebook, Charles Scribner's Sons for James Jones' *From Here to Eternity*,
Wieser & Wieser, Inc., for Karl Shapiro's 'California Winter' from *Collected Poems
1940–1978*, and The Doors Music Company for The Doors' 'Moonlight Drive'

Typeset in Meridien by Rowland Phototypesetting Ltd, Bury St Edmunds, Suffolk

CONTENTS

Slouching Towards Bethlehem

The White Album

I THE WHITE ALBUM

II CALIFORNIA REPUBLIC

III WOMEN

IV SOJOURNS

V ON THE MORNING AFTER THE SIXTIES

After Henry

I AFTER HENRY

II WASHINGTON

III CALIFORNIA

IV NEW YORK

Slouching Towards
Bethlehem

For Quintana

For Ophelia

Acknowledgments

'Where the Kissing Never Stops' appeared first in *The New York Times Magazine* under the title 'Just Folks at a School for Non-Violence.' 'On Keeping a Notebook' and 'Notes from a Native Daughter' appeared first in *Holiday*. 'I Can't Get That Monster out of My Mind' and 'On Morality' first appeared in *The American Scholar*, the latter under the title 'The Insidious Ethic of Conscience.' 'On Self-Respect' and 'Guaymas, Sonora' appeared first in *Vogue*. 'Los Angeles Notebook' includes a section which was published as 'The Santa Ana' in *The Saturday Evening Post*. All the other essays appeared originally in *The Saturday Evening Post*, several under different titles: 'Some Dreamers of the Golden Dream' was published as 'How Can I Tell Them There's Nothing Left'; '7000 Romaine, Los Angeles 38' was published as 'The Howard Hughes Underground'; 'Letter from Paradise, 21° 19' N., 157° 52' W.' was called 'Hawaii: Taps Over Pearl Harbor'; 'Goodbye to All That' was called 'Farewell to the Enchanted City.'

The author is grateful to all these publications for permission to reprint the various essays.

Turning and turning in the widening gyre
The falcon cannot hear the falconer;
Things fall apart; the centre cannot hold;
Mere anarchy is loosed upon the world,
The blood-dimmed tide is loosed, and everywhere
The ceremony of innocence is drowned;
The best lack all conviction, while the worst
Are full of passionate intensity.

Surely some revelation is at hand;
Surely the Second Coming is at hand.
The Second Coming! Hardly are those words out
When a vast image out of Spiritus Mundi
Troubles my sight: somewhere in the sands of the desert
A shape with lion body and the head of a man,
A gaze blank and pitiless as the sun,
Is moving its slow thighs, while all about it
Reel shadows of the indignant desert birds.
The darkness drops again; but now I know
That twenty centuries of stony sleep
Were vexed to nightmare by a rocking cradle,
And what rough beast, its hour come round at last,
Slouches towards Bethlehem to be born?

W. B. YEATS

I learned courage from Buddha, Jesus, Lincoln, Einstein,
and Cary Grant.

MISS PEGGY LEE

A Preface:

This book is called *Slouching Towards Bethlehem* because for several years now certain lines from the Yeats poem which appears two pages back have reverberated in my inner ear as if they were surgically implanted there. The widening gyre, the falcon which does not hear the falconer, the gaze blank and pitiless as the sun; those have been my points of reference, the only images against which much of what I was seeing and hearing and thinking seemed to make any pattern. 'Slouching Towards Bethlehem' is also the title of one piece in the book, and that piece, which derived from some time spent in the Haight-Ashbury district of San Francisco, was for me both the most imperative of all these pieces to write and the only one that made me despondent after it was printed. It was the first time I had dealt directly and flatly with the evidence of atomization, the proof that things fall apart: I went to San Francisco because I had not been able to work in some months, had been paralyzed by the conviction that writing was an irrelevant act, that the world as I had understood it no longer existed. If I was to work again at all, it would be necessary for me to come to terms with disorder. That was why the piece was important to me. And after it was printed I saw that, however directly and flatly I thought I had said it, I had failed to get through to many of the people who read and even liked the piece, failed to suggest that I was talking about something more general than a handful of children wearing mandalas on their foreheads. Disc jockeys telephoned my house and wanted to discuss (on the air) the incidence of 'filth' in the Haight-Ashbury, and acquaintances congratulated me on having finished the piece 'just in time,' because 'the whole fad's dead now, *fini, kaput.*' I suppose almost everyone who writes is afflicted some of the time by the suspicion that nobody out there is listening, but it seemed to me then (perhaps because the piece was important to me) that I had never gotten a feedback so universally beside the point.

Almost all of the pieces here were written for magazines during 1965, 1966, and 1967, and most of them, to get that question out of the way at the outset, were 'my idea.' I was asked to go up to the Carmel Valley and report on Joan Baez's school there; I was asked to go to Hawaii; I think I was asked to write about John Wayne; and I was asked for the short essays on 'morality,' by *The American Scholar*, and on 'self-respect,' by *Vogue*. Thirteen of the twenty pieces were published in *The Saturday Evening Post*. Quite often people write me from places like Toronto and want to know (demand to know) how I can reconcile my conscience with writing for *The Saturday Evening Post*; the answer is quite simple. The *Post* is extremely receptive to what the writer wants to do, pays enough for him to be able to do it right, and is meticulous about not changing copy. I lose a nicety of inflection now and then to the *Post*, but do not count myself compromised. Of course not all of the pieces in this book have to do, in a 'subject' sense, with the general breakup, with things falling apart; that is a large and rather presumptuous notion, and many of these pieces are small and personal. But since I am neither a camera eye nor much given to writing pieces which do not interest me, whatever I do write reflects, sometimes gratuitously, how I feel.

I am not sure what more I could tell you about these pieces. I could tell you that I liked doing some of them more than others, but that all of them were hard for me to do, and took more time than perhaps they were worth; that there is always a point in the writing of a piece when I sit in a room literally papered with false starts and cannot put one word after another and imagine that I have suffered a small stroke, leaving me apparently undamaged but actually aphasic. I was in fact as sick as I have ever been when I was writing 'Slouching Towards Bethlehem'; the pain kept me awake at night and so for twenty and twenty-one hours a day I drank gin-and-hot-water to blunt the pain and took Dexedrine to blunt the gin and wrote the piece. (I would like you to believe that I kept working out of some real professionalism, to meet the deadline, but that would not be entirely true; I did have a deadline, but it was also a troubled time, and working did to the trouble what gin did to the pain.) What else is there to tell? I am bad at interviewing people. I avoid situations in which I have to talk to anyone's press agent. (This precludes doing pieces on most actors, a bonus in itself.) I do not like to make telephone calls, and would not like to count the mornings I have sat on some Best Western motel bed somewhere and tried to force myself to put through the call to the assistant district attorney. My only advantage as a reporter is that I am so physically small, so temperamentally unobtrusive, and so neurotically inarticulate that people tend to forget that my presence runs counter to their best interests. And it always does. That is one last thing to remember: *writers are always selling somebody out.*

I

Life Styles in
the Golden Land

Some Dreamers of the Golden Dream

This is a story about love and death in the golden land, and begins with the country. The San Bernardino Valley lies only an hour east of Los Angeles by the San Bernardino Freeway but is in certain ways an alien place: not the coastal California of the subtropical twilights and the soft westerlies off the Pacific but a harsher California, haunted by the Mojave just beyond the mountains, devastated by the hot dry Santa Ana wind that comes down through the passes at 100 miles an hour and whines through the eucalyptus windbreaks and works on the nerves. October is the bad month for the wind, the month when breathing is difficult and the hills blaze up spontaneously. There has been no rain since April. Every voice seems a scream. It is the season of suicide and divorce and prickly dread, wherever the wind blows.

The Mormons settled this ominous country, and then they abandoned it, but by the time they left the first orange tree had been planted and for the next hundred years the San Bernardino Valley would draw a kind of people who imagined they might live among the talismanic fruit and prosper in the dry air, people who brought with them Midwestern ways of building and cooking and praying and who tried to graft those ways upon the land. The graft took in curious ways. This is the California where it is possible to live and die without ever eating an artichoke, without ever meeting a Catholic or a Jew. This is the California where it is easy to Dial-A-Devotion, but hard to buy a book. This is the country in which a belief in the literal interpretation of Genesis has slipped imperceptibly into a belief

in the literal interpretation of *Double Indemnity*, the country of the
teased hair and the Capris and the girls for whom all life's promise
comes down to a waltz-length white wedding dress and the birth
of a Kimberly or a Sherry or a Debbi and a Tijuana divorce and a
return to hairdressers' school. 'We were just crazy kids,' they say
without regret, and look to the future. The future always looks good
in the golden land, because no one remembers the past. Here is
where the hot wind blows and the old ways do not seem relevant,
where the divorce rate is double the national average and where one
person in every thirty-eight lives in a trailer. Here is the last stop for
all those who come from somewhere else, for all those who drifted
away from the cold and the past and the old ways. Here is where
they are trying to find a new life style, trying to find it in the only
places they know to look: the movies and the newspapers. The case
of Lucille Marie Maxwell Miller is a tabloid monument to that new
life style.

Imagine Banyan Street first, because Banyan is where it hap-
pened. The way to Banyan is to drive west from San Bernardino out
Foothill Boulevard, Route 66: past the Santa Fe switching yards, the
Forty Winks Motel. Past the motel that is nineteen stucco tepees:
'SLEEP IN A WIGWAM – GET MORE FOR YOUR WAMPUM.' Past Fontana Drag City and the Fontana Church of the Nazarene and the Pit
Stop A Go-Go; past Kaiser Steel, through Cucamonga, out to the
Kapu Kai Restaurant-Bar and Coffee Shop, at the corner of Route
66 and Carnelian Avenue. Up Carnelian Avenue from the Kapu Kai,
which means 'Forbidden Seas,' the subdivision flags whip in the
harsh wind. 'HALF-ACRE RANCHES! SNACK BARS! TRAVERTINE
ENTRIES! $95 DOWN.' It is the trail of an intention gone haywire, the
flotsam of the New California. But after a while the signs thin out
on Carnelian Avenue, and the houses are no longer the bright pastels
of the Springtime Home owners but the faded bungalows of the
people who grow a few grapes and keep a few chickens out here,
and then the hill gets steeper and the road climbs and even the
bungalows are few, and here – desolate, roughly surfaced, lined with
eucalyptus and lemon groves – is Banyan Street.

Like so much of this country, Banyan suggests something curious
and unnatural. The lemon groves are sunken, down a three- or
four-foot retaining wall, so that one looks directly into their dense

foliage, too lush, unsettlingly glossy, the greenery of nightmare; the fallen eucalyptus bark is too dusty, a place for snakes to breed. The stones look not like natural stones but like the rubble of some unmentioned upheaval. There are smudge pots, and a closed cistern. To one side of Banyan there is the flat valley, and to the other the San Bernardino Mountains, a dark mass looming too high, too fast, nine, ten, eleven thousand feet, right there above the lemon groves. At midnight on Banyan Street there is no light at all, and no sound except the wind in the eucalyptus and a muffled barking of dogs. There may be a kennel somewhere, or the dogs may be coyotes.

Banyan Street was the route Lucille Miller took home from the twenty-four-hour Mayfair Market on the night of October 7, 1964, a night when the moon was dark and the wind was blowing and she was out of milk, and Banyan Street was where, at about 12:30 a.m., her 1964 Volkswagen came to a sudden stop, caught fire, and began to burn. For an hour and fifteen minutes Lucille Miller ran up and down Banyan calling for help, but no cars passed and no help came. At three o'clock that morning, when the fire had been put out and the California Highway Patrol officers were completing their report, Lucille Miller was still sobbing and incoherent, for her husband had been asleep in the Volkswagen. 'What will I tell the children, when there's nothing left, nothing left in the casket,' she cried to the friend called to comfort her. 'How can I tell them there's nothing left?'

In fact there was something left, and a week later it lay in the Draper Mortuary Chapel in a closed bronze coffin blanketed with pink carnations. Some 200 mourners heard Elder Robert E. Denton of the Seventh-Day Adventist Church of Ontario speak of 'the temper of fury that has broken out among us.' For Gordon Miller, he said, there would be 'no more death, no more heartaches, no more mis-understandings.' Elder Ansel Bristol mentioned the 'peculiar' grief of the hour. Elder Fred Jensen asked 'what shall it profit a man, if he shall gain the whole world, and lose his own soul?' A light rain fell, a blessing in a dry season, and a female vocalist sang 'Safe in the Arms of Jesus.' A tape recording of the service was made for the widow, who was being held without bail in the San Bernardino County Jail on a charge of first-degree murder.

*   *   *

Of course she came from somewhere else, came off the prairie in search of something she had seen in a movie or heard on the radio, for this is a Southern California story. She was born on January 17, 1930, in Winnipeg, Manitoba, the only child of Gordon and Lily Maxwell, both schoolteachers and both dedicated to the Seventh-Day Adventist Church, whose members observe the Sabbath on Saturday, believe in an apocalyptic Second Coming, have a strong missionary tendency, and, if they are strict, do not smoke, drink, eat meat, use makeup, or wear jewelry, including wedding rings. By the time Lucille Maxwell enrolled at Walla Walla College in College Place, Washington, the Adventist school where her parents then taught, she was an eighteen-year-old possessed of unremarkable good looks and remarkable high spirits. 'Lucille wanted to see the world,' her father would say in retrospect, 'and I guess she found out.'

The high spirits did not seem to lend themselves to an extended course of study at Walla Walla College, and in the spring of 1949 Lucille Maxwell met and married Gordon ('Cork') Miller, a twenty-four-year-old graduate of Walla Walla and of the University of Oregon dental school, then stationed at Fort Lewis as a medical officer. 'Maybe you could say it was love at first sight,' Mr Maxwell recalls. 'Before they were ever formally introduced, he sent Lucille a dozen and a half roses with a card that said even if she didn't come out on a date with him, he hoped she'd find the roses pretty anyway.' The Maxwells remember their daughter as a 'radiant' bride.

Unhappy marriages so resemble one another that we do not need to know too much about the course of this one. There may or may not have been trouble on Guam, where Cork and Lucille Miller lived while he finished his Army duty. There may or may not have been problems in the small Oregon town where he first set up private practice. There appears to have been some disappointment about their move to California: Cork Miller had told friends that he wanted to become a doctor, that he was unhappy as a dentist and planned to enter the Seventh-Day Adventist College of Medical Evangelists at Loma Linda, a few miles south of San Bernardino. Instead he bought a dental practice in the west end of San Bernardino County, and the family settled there, in a modest house on the kind of street where there are always tricycles and revolving credit and dreams about bigger houses, better streets. That was 1957. By the summer of 1964 they had achieved the bigger house on the better street and the familiar accouterments of a family on its way up: the $30,000 a year, the three children for the Christmas card, the picture window, the family room, the newspaper photographs that showed 'Mrs Gordon Miller, Ontario Heart Fund Chairman . . .' They were paying the familiar price for it. And they had reached the familiar season of divorce.

It might have been anyone's bad summer, anyone's siege of heat and nerves and migraine and money worries, but this one began particularly early and particularly badly. On April 24 an old friend, Elaine Hayton, died suddenly; Lucille Miller had seen her only the night before. During the month of May, Cork Miller was hospitalized briefly with a bleeding ulcer, and his usual reserve deepened into depression. He told his accountant that he was 'sick of looking at open mouths,' and threatened suicide. By July 8, the conventional tensions of love and money had reached the conventional impasse in the new house on the acre lot at 8488 Bella Vista, and Lucille Miller filed for divorce. Within a month, however, the Millers seemed reconciled. They saw a marriage counselor. They talked about a fourth child. It seemed that the marriage had reached the traditional truce, the point at which so many resign themselves to cutting both their losses and their hopes.

But the Millers' season of trouble was not to end that easily. October 7 began as a commonplace enough day, one of those days that sets the teeth on edge with its tedium, its small frustrations. The temperature reached 102° in San Bernardino that afternoon, and the Miller children were home from school because of Teachers' Institute. There was ironing to be dropped off. There was a trip to pick up a prescription for Nembutal, a trip to a self-service dry cleaner. In the early evening, an unpleasant accident with the Volkswagen: Cork Miller hit and killed a German shepherd, and afterward said that his head felt 'like it had a Mack truck on it.' It was something he often said. As of that evening Cork Miller was $63,479 in debt, including the $29,637 mortgage on the new house, a debt load which seemed oppressive to him. He was a man who wore his responsibilities uneasily, and complained of migraine headaches almost constantly.

He ate alone that night, from a TV tray in the living room. Later the Millers watched John Forsythe and Senta Berger in *See How They Run*, and when the movie ended, about eleven, Cork Miller suggested that they go out for milk. He wanted some hot chocolate. He took a blanket and pillow from the couch and climbed into the passenger seat of the Volkswagen. Lucille Miller remembers reaching over to lock his door as she backed down the driveway. By the time she left the Mayfair Market, and long before they reached Banyan Street, Cork Miller appeared to be asleep.

There is some confusion in Lucille Miller's mind about what happened between 12:30 a.m., when the fire broke out, and 1:50 a.m., when it was reported. She says that she was driving east on Banyan Street at about 35 m.p.h. when she felt the Volkswagen pull sharply to the right. The next thing she knew the car was on the embankment, quite near the edge of the retaining wall, and flames were shooting up behind her. She does not remember jumping out. She does remember prying up a stone with which she broke the window next to her husband, and then scrambling down the retaining wall to try to find a stick. 'I don't know how I was going to push him out,' she says. 'I just thought if I had a stick, I'd push him out.' She could not, and after a while she ran to the intersection of Banyan and Carnelian Avenue. There are no houses at that corner, and almost no traffic. After one car had passed without stopping, Lucille Miller ran back down Banyan toward the burning Volkswagen. She did not stop, but she slowed down, and in the flames she could see her husband. He was, she said, 'just black.'

At the first house up Sapphire Avenue, half a mile from the Volkswagen, Lucille Miller finally found help. There Mrs Robert Swenson called the sheriff, and then, at Lucille Miller's request, she called Harold Lance, the Millers' lawyer and their close friend. When Harold Lance arrived he took Lucille Miller home to his wife, Joan. Twice Harold Lance and Lucille Miller returned to Banyan Street and talked to the Highway Patrol officers. A third time Harold Lance returned alone, and when he came back he said to Lucille Miller, 'O.K. . . . you don't talk any more.'

When Lucille Miller was arrested the next afternoon, Sandy Slagle was with her. Sandy Slagle was the intense, relentlessly loyal medical student who used to baby-sit for the Millers, and had been living as a member of the family since she graduated from high school in 1959. The Millers took her away from a difficult home situation, and she thinks of Lucille Miller not only as 'more or less a mother or a sister' but as 'the most wonderful character' she has ever known. On the night of the accident, Sandy Slagle was in her dormitory at Loma Linda University, but Lucille Miller called her early in the morning and asked her to come home. The doctor was there when Sandy Slagle arrived, giving Lucille Miller an injection of Nembutal. 'She was crying as she was going under,' Sandy Slagle recalls. 'Over and over she'd say, "Sandy, all the hours I spent trying to save him and now what are they trying to *do* to me?"'

At 1:30 that afternoon, Sergeant William Paterson and Detectives Charles Callahan and Joseph Karr of the Central Homicide Division arrived at 8488 Bella Vista. 'One of them appeared at the bedroom door,' Sandy Slagle remembers, 'and said to Lucille, "You've got ten minutes to get dressed or we'll take you as you are." She was in her nightgown, you know, so I tried to get her dressed.'

Sandy Slagle tells the story now as if by rote, and her eyes do not waver. 'So I had her panties and bra on her and they opened the door again, so I got some Capris on her, you know, and a scarf.' Her voice drops. 'And then they just took her.'

The arrest took place just twelve hours after the first report that there had been an accident on Banyan Street, a rapidity which would later prompt Lucille Miller's attorney to say that the entire case was an instance of trying to justify a reckless arrest. Actually what first caused the detectives who arrived on Banyan Street toward dawn that morning to give the accident more than routine attention were certain apparent physical inconsistencies. While Lucille Miller had said that she was driving about 35 m.p.h. when the car swerved to a stop, an examination of the cooling Volkswagen showed that it was in low gear, and that the parking rather than the driving lights were on. The front wheels, moreover, did not seem to be in exactly the position that Lucille Miller's description of the accident would suggest, and the right rear wheel was dug in deep, as if it had been spun in place. It seemed curious to the detectives, too, that a sudden stop from 35 m.p.h. – the same jolt which was presumed to have knocked over a gasoline can in the back seat and somehow started the fire – should have left two milk cartons upright on the back floorboard, and the remains of a Polaroid camera box lying apparently undisturbed on the back seat.

No one, however, could be expected to give a precise account of what did and did not happen in a moment of terror, and none of these inconsistencies seemed in themselves incontrovertible evidence of criminal intent. But they did interest the Sheriff's Office, as did Gordon Miller's apparent unconsciousness at the time of the accident, and the length of time it had taken Lucille Miller to get help. Something, moreover, struck the investigators as wrong about Harold Lance's attitude when he came back to Banyan Street the third time and found the investigation by no means over. 'The way Lance was acting,' the prosecuting attorney said later, 'they thought maybe they'd hit a nerve.'

And so it was that on the morning of October 8, even before the doctor had come to give Lucille Miller an injection to calm her, the San Bernardino County Sheriff's Office was trying to construct another version of what might have happened between 12:30 and 1:50 a.m. The hypothesis they would eventually present was based on the somewhat tortuous premise that Lucille Miller had undertaken a plan which failed: a plan to stop the car on the lonely road, spread gasoline over her presumably drugged husband, and, with a stick on the accelerator, gently 'walk' the Volkswagen over the embankment, where it would tumble four feet down the retaining wall into the lemon grove and almost certainly explode. If this happened, Lucille Miller might then have somehow negotiated the two miles up Carnelian to Bella Vista in time to be home when the accident was discovered. This plan went awry, according to the Sheriff's Office hypothesis, when the car would not go over the rise of the embankment. Lucille Miller might have panicked then – after she had killed the engine the third or fourth time, say, out there on the dark road with the gasoline already spread and the dogs baying and the wind blowing and the unspeakable apprehension that a pair of headlights would suddenly light up Banyan Street and expose her there – and set the fire herself.

Although this version accounted for some of the physical evidence – the car in low because it had been started from a dead stop, the parking lights on because she could not do what needed doing without some light, a rear wheel spun in repeated attempts to get the car over the embankment, the milk cartons upright because there had been no sudden stop – it did not seem on its own any more or less credible than Lucille Miller's own story. Moreover, some of the physical evidence did seem to support her story: a nail in a front tire, a nine-pound rock found in the car, presumably the one with which she had broken the window in an attempt to save her husband. Within a few days an autopsy had established that Gordon Miller was alive when he burned, which did not particularly help the State's case, and that he had enough Nembutal and Sandoptal in his blood to put the average person to sleep, which did: on the other hand Gordon Miller habitually took both Nembutal and Fiorinal (a common headache prescription which contains Sandoptal), and had been ill besides.

It was a spotty case, and to make it work at all the State was going to have to find a motive. There was talk of unhappiness, talk of another man. That kind of motive, during the next few weeks, was what they set out to establish. They set out to find it in accountants' ledgers and double-indemnity clauses and motel registers, set out to determine what might move a woman who believed in all the promises of the middle class – a woman who had been chairman of the Heart Fund and who always knew a reasonable little dressmaker and who had come out of the bleak wild of prairie fundamentalism to find what she imagined to be the good life – what should drive such a woman to sit on a street called Bella Vista and look out her new picture window into the empty California sun and calculate how to burn her husband alive in a Volkswagen. They found the wedge they wanted closer at hand than they might have at first expected, for, as testimony would reveal later at the trial, it seemed that in December of 1963 Lucille Miller had begun an affair with the husband of one of her friends, a man whose daughter called her 'Auntie Lucille,' a man who might have seemed to have the gift for people and money and the good life that Cork Miller so noticeably lacked. The man was Arthwell Hayton, a well-known San Bernardino attorney and at one time a member of the district attorney's staff.

In some ways it was the conventional clandestine affair in a place like San Bernardino, a place where little is bright or graceful, where

it is routine to misplace the future and easy to start looking for it in
bed. Over the seven weeks that it would take to try Lucille Miller
for murder, Assistant District Attorney Don A. Turner and defense
attorney Edward P. Foley would between them unfold a curiously
predictable story. There were the falsified motel registrations. There
were the lunch dates, the afternoon drives in Arthwell Hayton's red
Cadillac convertible. There were the interminable discussions of the
wronged partners. There were the confidantes ('I knew everything,'
Sandy Slagle would insist fiercely later. 'I knew every time, places,
everything') and there were the words remembered from bad magazine stories ('Don't kiss me, it will trigger things,' Lucille Miller
remembered telling Arthwell Hayton in the parking lot of Harold's
Club in Fontana after lunch one day) and there were the notes, the
sweet exchanges: 'Hi Sweetie Pie! You are my cup of tea! Happy
Birthday – you don't look a day over 29!! Your baby, Arthwell.'

And, toward the end, there was the acrimony. It was April 24,
1964, when Arthwell Hayton's wife, Elaine, died suddenly, and nothing good happened after that. Arthwell Hayton had taken his cruiser,
Captain's Lady, over to Catalina that weekend; he called home at nine
o'clock Friday night, but did not talk to his wife because Lucille
Miller answered the telephone and said that Elaine was showering.
The next morning the Haytons' daughter found her mother in bed,
dead. The newspapers reported the death as accidental, perhaps the
result of an allergy to hair spray. When Arthwell Hayton flew home
from Catalina that weekend, Lucille Miller met him at the airport,
but the finish had already been written.

It was in the breakup that the affair ceased to be in the conventional mode and began to resemble instead the novels of James M.
Cain, the movies of the late 1930s, all the dreams in which violence
and threats and blackmail are made to seem commonplaces of
middle-class life. What was most startling about the case that the
State of California was preparing against Lucille Miller was something that had nothing to do with law at all, something that never
appeared in the eight-column afternoon headlines but was always
there between them: the revelation that the dream was teaching the
dreamers how to live. Here is Lucille Miller talking to her lover
sometime in the early summer of 1964, after he had indicated that,
on the advice of his minister, he did not intend to see her any more:

'First, I'm going to go to that dear pastor of yours and tell him a few things ... When I do tell him that, you won't be in the Redlands Church any more ... Look, Sonny Boy, if you think your reputation is going to be ruined, your life won't be worth two cents.' Here is Arthwell Hayton, to Lucille Miller: 'I'll go to Sheriff Frank Bland and tell him some things that I know about you until you'll wish you'd never heard of Arthwell Hayton.' For an affair between a Seventh-Day Adventist dentist's wife and a Seventh-Day Adventist personal-injury lawyer, it seems a curious kind of dialogue.

'Boy, I could get that little boy coming and going,' Lucille Miller later confided to Erwin Sprengle, a Riverside contractor who was a business partner of Arthwell Hayton's and a friend to both the lovers. (Friend or no, on this occasion he happened to have an induction coil attached to his telephone in order to tape Lucille Miller's call.) 'And he hasn't got one thing on me that he can prove. I mean, I've got concrete – he has nothing concrete.' In the same taped conversation with Erwin Sprengle, Lucille Miller mentioned a tape that she herself had surreptitiously made, months before, in Arthwell Hayton's car.

'I said to him, I said "Arthwell, I just feel like I'm being used." ' ... He started sucking his thumb and he said "I love you ... This isn't something that happened yesterday. I'd marry you tomorrow if I could. I don't love Elaine." He'd love to hear that played back, wouldn't he?'

'Yeah,' drawled Sprengle's voice on the tape. 'That would be just a little incriminating, wouldn't it?'

'Just a *little* incriminating,' Lucille Miller agreed. 'It really *is*.'

Later on the tape, Sprengle asked where Cork Miller was.

'He took the children down to the church.'

'You didn't go?'

'No.'

'You're naughty.'

It was all, moreover, in the name of 'love'; everyone involved placed a magical faith in the efficacy of the very word. There was the significance that Lucille Miller saw in Arthwell's saying that he 'loved' her, that he did not 'love' Elaine. There was Arthwell insisting, later, at the trial, that he had never said it, that he may have 'whispered sweet nothings in her ear' (as her defense hinted

that he had whispered in many ears), but he did not remember
bestowing upon her the special seal, saying the word, declaring 'love.'
There was the summer evening when Lucille Miller and Sandy Slagle
followed Arthwell Hayton down to his new boat in its mooring at
Newport Beach and untied the lines with Arthwell aboard, Arthwell
and a girl with whom he later testified he was drinking hot chocolate and watching television. 'I did that on purpose,' Lucille Miller
told Erwin Sprengle later, 'to save myself from letting my heart do
something crazy.'

January 11, 1965, was a bright warm day in Southern California,
the kind of day when Catalina floats on the Pacific horizon and the
air smells of orange blossoms and it is a long way from the bleak and
difficult East, a long way from the cold, a long way from the past.
A woman in Hollywood staged an all-night sit-in on the hood of her
car to prevent repossession by a finance company. A seventy-year-
old pensioner drove his station wagon at five miles an hour past
three Gardena poker parlors and emptied three pistols and a twelve-
gauge shotgun through their windows, wounding twenty-nine people.
'Many young women become prostitutes just to have enough money
to play cards,' he explained in a note. Mrs Nick Adams said that she
was 'not surprised' to hear her husband announce his divorce plans
on the Les Crane Show, and, farther north, a sixteen-year-old
jumped off the Golden Gate Bridge and lived.

And, in the San Bernardino County Courthouse, the Miller trial
opened. The crowds were so bad that the glass courtroom doors were
shattered in the crush, and from then on identification disks were
issued to the first forty-three spectators in line. The line began form-
ing at 6 a.m., and college girls camped at the courthouse all night,
with stores of graham crackers and No-Cal.

All they were doing was picking a jury, those first few days, but
the sensational nature of the case had already suggested itself. Early
in December there had been an abortive first trial, a trial at which
no evidence was ever presented because on the day the jury was
seated the San Bernardino *Sun-Telegram* ran an 'inside' story quoting
Assistant District Attorney Don Turner, the prosecutor, as saying,
'We are looking into the circumstances of Mrs Hayton's death. In

view of the current trial concerning the death of Dr Miller, I do not feel I should comment on Mrs Hayton's death.' It seemed that there had been barbiturates in Elaine Hayton's blood, and there had seemed some irregularity about the way she was dressed on that morning when she was found under the covers, dead. Any doubts about the death at the time, however, had never gotten as far as the Sheriff's Office. 'I guess somebody didn't want to rock the boat,' Turner said later. 'These were prominent people.'

Although all of that had not been in the *Sun-Telegram*'s story, an immediate mistrial had been declared. Almost as immediately, there had been another development: Arthwell Hayton had asked newspapermen to an 11 a.m. Sunday morning press conference in his office. There had been television cameras, and flash bulbs popping. 'As you gentlemen may know,' Hayton had said, striking a note of stiff bonhomie, 'there are very often women who become amorous toward their doctor or lawyer. This does not mean on the physician's or lawyer's part that there is any romance toward the patient or client.'

'Would you deny that you were having an affair with Mrs Miller?' a reporter had asked.

'I would deny that there was any romance on my part whatsoever.'

It was a distinction he would maintain through all the wearing weeks to come.

So they had come to see Arthwell, these crowds who now milled beneath the dusty palms outside the courthouse, and they had also come to see Lucille, who appeared as a slight, intermittently pretty woman, already pale from lack of sun, a woman who would turn thirty-five before the trial was over and whose tendency toward haggardness was beginning to show, a meticulous woman who insisted, against her lawyer's advice, on coming to court with her hair piled high and lacquered. 'I would've been happy if she'd come in with it hanging loose, but Lucille wouldn't do that,' her lawyer said. He was Edward P. Foley, a small, emotional Irish Catholic who several times wept in the courtroom. 'She has a great honesty, this woman,' he added, 'but this honesty about her appearance always worked against her.'

By the time the trial opened, Lucille Miller's appearance included

maternity clothes, for an official examination on December 18 had
revealed that she was then three and a half months pregnant, a fact
which made picking a jury even more difficult than usual, for Turner
was asking the death penalty. 'It's unfortunate but there it is,' he
would say of the pregnancy to each juror in turn, and finally twelve
were seated, seven of them women, the youngest forty-one, an
assembly of the very peers – housewives, a machinist, a truck driver,
a grocery-store manager, a filing clerk – above whom Lucille Miller
had wanted so badly to rise.

That was the sin, more than the adultery, which tended to
reinforce the one for which she was being tried. It was implicit in
both the defense and the prosecution that Lucille Miller was an
erring woman, a woman who perhaps wanted too much. But to the
prosecution she was not merely a woman who would want a new
house and want to go to parties and run up high telephone bills
($1,152 in ten months), but a woman who would go so far as to
murder her husband for his $80,000 in insurance, making it appear
an accident in order to collect another $40,000 in double indemnity
and straight accident policies. To Turner she was a woman who did
not want simply her freedom and a reasonable alimony (she could
have had that, the defense contended, by going through with her
divorce suit), but wanted everything, a woman motivated by 'love
and greed.' She was a 'manipulator.' She was a 'user of people.'

To Edward Foley, on the other hand, she was an impulsive woman
who 'couldn't control her foolish little heart.' Where Turner skirted
the pregnancy, Foley dwelt upon it, even calling the dead man's
mother down from Washington to testify that her son had told her
they were going to have another baby because Lucille felt that it
would 'do much to weld our home again in the pleasant relations
that we used to have.' Where the prosecution saw a 'calculator,' the
defense saw a 'blabbermouth,' and in fact Lucille Miller did emerge
as an ingenuous conversationalist. Just as, before her husband's
death, she had confided in her friends about her love affair, so she
chatted about it after his death, with the arresting sergeant. 'Of
course Cork lived with it for years, you know,' her voice was heard
to tell Sergeant Paterson on a tape made the morning after her arrest.
'After Elaine died, he pushed the panic button one night and just
asked me right out, and that, I think, was when he really – the first

time he really faced it.' When the sergeant asked why she had agreed to talk to him, against the specific instructions of her lawyers, Lucille Miller said airily, 'Oh, I've always been basically quite an honest person . . . I mean I can put a hat in the cupboard and say it cost ten dollars less, but basically I've always kind of just lived my life the way I wanted to, and if you don't like it you can take off.'

The prosecution hinted at men other than Arthwell, and even, over Foley's objections, managed to name one. The defense called Miller suicidal. The prosecution produced experts who said that the Volkswagen fire could not have been accidental. Foley produced witnesses who said that it could have been. Lucille's father, now a junior-high-school teacher in Oregon, quoted Isaiah to reporters: '*Every tongue that shall rise against thee in judgment thou shalt condemn.*' 'Lucille did wrong, her affair,' her mother said judiciously. 'With her it was love. But with some I guess it's just passion.' There was Debbie, the Millers' fourteen-year-old, testifying in a steady voice about how she and her mother had gone to a supermarket to buy the gasoline can the week before the accident. There was Sandy Slagle, in the courtroom every day, declaring that on at least one occasion Lucille Miller had prevented her husband not only from committing suicide but from committing suicide in such a way that it would appear an accident and ensure the double-indemnity payment. There was Wenche Berg, the pretty twenty-seven-year-old Norwegian governess to Arthwell Hayton's children, testifying that Arthwell had instructed her not to allow Lucille Miller to see or talk to the children.

Two months dragged by, and the headlines never stopped. Southern California's crime reporters were headquartered in San Bernardino for the duration: Howard Hertel from the *Times*, Jim Bennett and Eddy Jo Bernal from the *Herald Examiner*. Two months in which the Miller trial was pushed off the *Examiner's* front page only by the Academy Award nominations and Stan Laurel's death. And finally, on March 2, after Turner had reiterated that it was a case of 'love and greed,' and Foley had protested that his client was being tried for adultery, the case went to the jury.

They brought in the verdict, guilty of murder in the first degree, at 4:50 p.m. on March 5. 'She didn't do it,' Debbie Miller cried, jumping up from the spectators' section. 'She didn't *do* it.' Sandy Slagle collapsed in her seat and began to scream. 'Sandy, for God's sake please *don't*,' Lucille Miller said in a voice that carried across the courtroom, and Sandy Slagle was momentarily subdued. But as the jurors left the courtroom she screamed again: 'You're murderers . . . Every last one of you is a *murderer*.' Sheriff's deputies moved in then, each wearing a string tie that read '1965 SHERIFF'S RODEO,' and Lucille Miller's father, that sad-faced junior-high-school teacher who believed in the word of Christ and the dangers of wanting to see the world, blew her a kiss off his fingertips.

The California Institution for Women at Frontera, where Lucille Miller is now, lies down where Euclid Avenue turns into country road, not too many miles from where she once lived and shopped and organized the Heart Fund Ball. Cattle graze across the road, and Rainbirds sprinkle the alfalfa. Frontera has a softball field and tennis courts, and looks as if it might be a California junior college, except that the trees are not yet high enough to conceal the concertina wire around the top of the Cyclone fence. On visitors' day there are big cars in the parking area, big Buicks and Pontiacs that belong to grandparents and sisters and fathers (not many of them belong to husbands), and some of them have bumper stickers that say 'SUPPORT YOUR LOCAL POLICE.'

A lot of California murderesses live here, a lot of girls who somehow misunderstood the promise. Don Turner put Sandra Garner here (and her husband in the gas chamber at San Quentin) after the 1959 desert killings known to crime reporters as 'the soda-pop murders.' Carole Tregoff is here, and has been ever since she was convicted of conspiring to murder Dr Finch's wife in West Covina, which is not too far from San Bernardino. Carole Tregoff is in fact a nurse's aide in the prison hospital, and might have attended Lucille Miller had her baby been born at Frontera; Lucille Miller chose instead to have it outside, and paid for the guard who stood outside the delivery room in St Bernardine's Hospital. Debbie Miller came to take the baby home from the hospital, in a white dress with pink ribbons, and Debbie was allowed to choose a name. She named the baby Kimi Kai. The children live with Harold and Joan Lance now, because Lucille Miller will probably spend ten years at Frontera. Don Turner waived his original request for the death penalty (it was generally agreed that he had demanded it only, in Edward Foley's words, 'to get anybody with the slightest trace of human kindness in their veins off the jury'), and settled for life imprisonment with the possibility of parole. Lucille Miller does not like it at Frontera, and has had trouble adjusting. 'She's going to have to learn humility,' Turner says. 'She's going to have to use her ability to charm, to manipulate.'

The new house is empty now, the house on the street with the sign that says

PRIVATE ROAD
BELLA VISTA
DEAD END

The Millers never did get it landscaped, and weeds grow up around the fieldstone siding. The television aerial has toppled on the roof, and a trash can is stuffed with the debris of family life: a cheap suitcase, a child's game called 'Lie Detector.' There is a sign on what would have been the lawn, and the sign reads 'ESTATE SALE.' Edward Foley is trying to get Lucille Miller's case appealed, but there have been delays. 'A trial always comes down to a matter of sympathy,' Foley says wearily now. 'I couldn't create sympathy for her.' Everyone is a little weary now, weary and resigned, everyone except Sandy Slagle, whose bitterness is still raw. She lives in an apartment near the medical school in Loma Linda, and studies reports of the case in *True Police Cases* and *Official Detective Stories*. 'I'd much rather we not talk about the Hayton business too much,' she tells visitors, and she keeps a tape recorder running. 'I'd rather talk about Lucille and what a wonderful person she is and how her rights were violated.' Harold Lance does not talk to visitors at all. 'We don't want to give away what we can sell,' he explains pleasantly; an attempt was made to sell Lucille Miller's personal story to *Life*, but *Life* did not want to buy it. In the district attorney's offices they are prosecuting other murders now, and do not see why the Miller trial attracted so much attention. 'It wasn't a very interesting murder as murders go,' Don Turner says laconically. Elaine Hayton's death is no longer under investigation. 'We know everything we want to know,' Turner says.

Arthwell Hayton's office is directly below Edward Foley's. Some

people around San Bernardino say that Arthwell Hayton suffered;
others say that he did not suffer at all. Perhaps he did not, for time
past is not believed to have any bearing upon time present or future,
out in the golden land where every day the world is born anew.
In any case, on October 17, 1965, Arthwell Hayton married again,
married his children's pretty governess, Wenche Berg, at a service in
the Chapel of the Roses at a retirement village near Riverside. Later
the newlyweds were feted at a reception for seventy-five in the
dining room of Rose Garden Village. The bridegroom was in black
tie, with a white carnation in his buttonhole. The bride wore a long
white *peau de soie* dress and carried a shower bouquet of sweetheart
roses with stephanotis streamers. A coronet of seed pearls held her
illusion veil.

1966

John Wayne: A Love Song

In the summer of 1943 I was eight, and my father and mother and small brother and I were at Peterson Field in Colorado Springs. A hot wind blew through that summer, blew until it seemed that before August broke, all the dust in Kansas would be in Colorado, would have drifted over the tar-paper barracks and the temporary strip and stopped only when it hit Pikes Peak. There was not much to do, a summer like that: there was the day they brought in the first B-29, an event to remember but scarcely a vacation program. There was an Officers' Club, but no swimming pool; all the Officers' Club had of interest was artificial blue rain behind the bar. The rain interested me a good deal, but I could not spend the summer watching it, and so we went, my brother and I, to the movies.

We went three and four afternoons a week, sat on folding chairs in the darkened Quonset hut which served as a theater, and it was there, that summer of 1943 while the hot wind blew outside, that I first saw John Wayne. Saw the walk, heard the voice. Heard him tell the girl in a picture called *War of the Wildcats* that he would build her a house, 'at the bend in the river where the cottonwoods grow.' As it happened I did not grow up to be the kind of woman who is the heroine in a Western, and although the men I have known have had many virtues and have taken me to live in many places I have come to love, they have never been John Wayne, and they have never taken me to that bend in the river where the cottonwoods grow. Deep in that part of my heart where the artificial rain forever falls, that is still the line I wait to hear.

I tell you this neither in a spirit of self-revelation nor as an exercise in total recall, but simply to demonstrate that when John Wayne rode through my childhood, and perhaps through yours, he determined forever the shape of certain of our dreams. It did not seem possible that such a man could fall ill, could carry within him that most inexplicable and ungovernable of diseases. The rumor struck some obscure anxiety, threw our very childhoods into question. In John Wayne's world, John Wayne was supposed to give the orders. 'Let's ride,' he said, and 'Saddle up.' 'Forward *ho*,' and 'A man's gotta do what he's got to do.' 'Hello, there,' he said when he first saw the girl, in a construction camp or on a train or just standing around on the front porch waiting for somebody to ride up through the tall grass. When John Wayne spoke, there was no mistaking his intentions; he had a sexual authority so strong that even a child could perceive it. And in a world we understood early to be characterized by venality and doubt and paralyzing ambiguities, he suggested another world, one which may or may not have existed ever but in any case existed no more: a place where a man could move free, could make his own code and live by it; a world in which, if a man did what he had to do, he could one day take the girl and go riding through the draw and find himself home free, not in a hospital with something going wrong inside, not in a high bed with the flowers and the drugs and the forced smiles, but there at the bend in the bright river, the cottonwoods shimmering in the early morning sun.

'Hello, there.' Where did he come from, before the tall grass? Even his history seemed right, for it was no history at all, nothing to intrude upon the dream. Born Marion Morrison in Winterset, Iowa, the son of a druggist. Moved as a child to Lancaster, California, part of the migration to that promised land sometimes called 'the west coast of Iowa.' Not that Lancaster was the promise fulfilled; Lancaster was a town on the Mojave where the dust blew through. But Lancaster was still California, and it was only a year from there to Glendale, where desolation had a different flavor: antimacassars among the orange groves, a middle-class prelude to Forest Lawn. Imagine Marion Morrison in Glendale. A Boy Scout, then a student at Glendale High. A tackle for U.S.C., a Sigma Chi. Summer vacations, a job moving props on the old Fox lot. There, a meeting with John

Ford, one of the several directors who were to sense that into this perfect mold might be poured the inarticulate longings of a nation wondering at just what pass the trail had been lost. 'Dammit,' said Raoul Walsh later, 'the son of a bitch looked like a man.' And so after a while the boy from Glendale became a star. He did not become an actor, as he has always been careful to point out to interviewers ('How many times do I gotta tell you, I don't act at all, I *re*-act'), but a star, and the star called John Wayne would spend most of the rest of his life with one or another of those directors, out on some forsaken location, in search of the dream.

> *Out where the skies are a trifle bluer*
> *Out where friendship's a little truer*
> *That's where the West begins.*

Nothing very bad could happen in the dream, nothing a man could not face down. But something did. There it was, the rumor, and after a while the headlines. 'I licked the Big C,' John Wayne announced, as John Wayne would, reducing those outlaw cells to the level of any other outlaws, but even so we all sensed that this would be the one unpredictable confrontation, the one shoot-out Wayne could lose. I have as much trouble as the next person with illusion and reality, and I did not much want to see John Wayne when he must be (or so I thought) having some trouble with it himself, but I did, and it was down in Mexico when he was making the picture his illness had so long delayed, down in the very country of the dream.

It was John Wayne's 165th picture. It was Henry Hathaway's 84th. It was number 34 for Dean Martin, who was working off an old contract to Hal Wallis, for whom it was independent production number 65. It was called *The Sons of Katie Elder*, and it was a Western, and after the three-month delay they had finally shot the exteriors up in Durango, and now they were in the waning days of interior shooting at Estudio Churubusco outside Mexico City, and the sun was hot and the air was clear and it was lunchtime. Out under the pepper trees the boys from the Mexican crew sat around sucking caramels, and down the road some of the technical men sat around a place which served a stuffed lobster and a glass of tequila for one dollar American, but it was inside the cavernous empty commissary where the talent sat around, the reasons for the exercise, all sitting around the big table picking at *huevos con queso* and Carta Blanca beer. Dean Martin, unshaven. Mack Gray, who goes where Martin goes. Bob Goodfried, who was in charge of Paramount publicity and who had flown down to arrange for a trailer and who had a delicate stomach. 'Tea and toast,' he warned repeatedly. 'That's the ticket. You can't trust the lettuce.' And Henry Hathaway, the director, who did not seem to be listening to Goodfried. And John Wayne, who did not seem to be listening to anyone.

'This week's gone slow,' Dean Martin said, for the third time.

'How can you say that?' Mack Gray demanded.

'*This . . . week's . . . gone . . . slow*, that's how I can say it.'

'You don't mean you want it to end.'

'I'll say it right out, Mack, I want it to *end*. Tomorrow night I shave this beard, I head for the airport, I say *adiós amigos!* Bye-bye *muchachos!*'

Henry Hathaway lit a cigar and patted Martin's arm fondly. 'Not tomorrow, Dino.'

'Henry, what are you planning to add? A World War?'

Hathaway patted Martin's arm again and gazed into the middle distance. At the end of the table someone mentioned a man who, some years before, had tried unsuccessfully to blow up an airplane.

'He's still in jail,' Hathaway said suddenly.

'In jail?' Martin was momentarily distracted from the question whether to send his golf clubs back with Bob Goodfried or consign them to Mack Gray. 'What's he in jail for if nobody got killed?'

'Attempted murder, Dino,' Hathaway said gently. 'A felony.'

'You mean some guy just *tried* to kill me he'd end up in jail?'

Hathaway removed the cigar from his mouth and looked across the table. 'Some guy just tried to kill *me* he wouldn't end up in jail. How about you, Duke?'

Very slowly, the object of Hathaway's query wiped his mouth, pushed back his chair, and stood up. It was the real thing, the authentic article, the move which had climaxed a thousand scenes on 165 flickering frontiers and phantasmagoric battlefields before, and it was about to climax this one, in the commissary at Estudio Churubusco outside Mexico City. 'Right,' John Wayne drawled. 'I'd kill him.'

Almost all the cast of *Katie Elder* had gone home, that last week; only the principals were left, Wayne, and Martin, and Earl Holliman, and Michael Anderson, Jr, and Martha Hyer. Martha Hyer was not around much, but every now and then someone referred to her, usually as 'the girl.' They had all been together nine weeks, six of them in Durango. Mexico City was not quite Durango; wives like to come along to places like Mexico City, like to shop for handbags, go to parties at Merle Oberon Pagliai's, like to look at her paintings. But Durango. The very name hallucinates. Man's country. Out where the West begins. There had been ahuehuete trees in Durango; a waterfall, rattlesnakes. There had been weather, nights so cold that they had postponed one or two exteriors until they could shoot inside at Churubusco. 'It was the girl,' they explained. 'You couldn't keep the girl out in cold like that.' Henry Hathaway had cooked in Durango, *gazpacho* and ribs and the steaks that Dean Martin had ordered flown down from the Sands; he had wanted to cook in Mexico City, but the management of the Hotel Bamer refused to let him set up a brick barbecue in his room. 'You really missed something, *Durango*,' they would say, sometimes joking and sometimes not, until it became a refrain, Eden lost.

But if Mexico City was not Durango, neither was it Beverly Hills. No one else was using Churubusco that week, and there inside the big sound stage that said LOS HIJOS DE KATIE ELDER on the door, there with the pepper trees and the bright sun outside, they could still, for just so long as the picture lasted, maintain a world peculiar to men who like to make Westerns, a world of loyalties and fond raillery, of sentiment and shared cigars, of interminable desultory recollections; campfire talk, its only point to keep a human voice raised against the night, the wind, the rustlings in the brush.

'Stuntman got hit accidentally on a picture of mine once,' Hathaway would say between takes of an elaborately choreographed fight scene. 'What was his name, married Estelle Taylor, met her down in Arizona.'

The circle would close around him, the cigars would be fingered. The delicate art of the staged fight was to be contemplated.

'I only hit one guy in my life,' Wayne would say. 'Accidentally, I mean. That was Mike Mazurki.'

'Some guy. Hey, Duke says he only hit one guy in his life, Mike Mazurki.'

'Some choice.' Murmurings, assent.

'It wasn't a choice, it was an accident.'

'I can believe it.'

'You bet.'

'Oh boy. Mike Mazurki.'

And so it would go. There was Web Overlander, Wayne's makeup man for twenty years, hunched in a blue Windbreaker, passing out sticks of Juicy Fruit. '*Insect spray*,' he would say. 'Don't tell us about insect spray. We saw insect spray in Africa, all right. Remember Africa?' Or, '*Steamer* clams. Don't tell us about steamer clams. We got our fill of steamer clams all right, on the *Hatari!* appearance tour. Remember Bookbinder's?' There was Ralph Volkie, Wayne's trainer for eleven years, wearing a red baseball cap and carrying around a clipping from Hedda Hopper, a tribute to Wayne. 'This Hopper's some lady,' he would say again and again. 'Not like some of these guys, all they write is sick, sick, sick, how can you call that guy *sick*, when he's got pains, coughs, works all day, *never complains*. That guy's got the best hook since Dempsey, not *sick*.'

And there was Wayne himself, fighting through number 165. There was Wayne, in his thirty-three-year-old spurs, his dusty neckerchief, his blue shirt. 'You don't have too many worries about what to wear in these things,' he said. 'You can wear a blue shirt, or, if you're down in Monument Valley, you can wear a yellow shirt.' There was Wayne, in a relatively new hat, a hat which made him look curiously like William S. Hart. 'I had this old cavalry hat I loved, but I lent it to Sammy Davis. I got it back, it was unwearable. I think they all pushed it down on his head and said *O.K., John Wayne* – you know, a joke.'

There was Wayne, working too soon, finishing the picture with a bad cold and a racking cough, so tired by late afternoon that he kept an oxygen inhalator on the set. And still nothing mattered but the Code. 'That guy,' he muttered of a reporter who had incurred his displeasure. 'I admit I'm balding. I admit I got a tire around my middle. What man fifty-seven doesn't? Big news. Anyway, that guy.'

He paused, about to expose the heart of the matter, the root of the distaste, the fracture of the rules that bothered him more than the alleged misquotations, more than the intimation that he was no longer the Ringo Kid. 'He comes down, uninvited, but I ask him over anyway. So we're sitting around drinking mescal out of a water jug.'

He paused again and looked meaningfully at Hathaway, readying him for the unthinkable denouement. 'He had to be *assisted* to his room.'

They argued about the virtues of various prizefighters, they argued about the price of J & B in pesos. They argued about dialogue.

'As rough a guy as he is, Henry, I still don't think he'd raffle off his mother's *Bible*.'

'I like a shocker, Duke.'

They exchanged endless training-table jokes. 'You know why they call this memory sauce?' Martin asked, holding up a bowl of chili.

'Why?'

'Because you *remember it in the morning*.'

'Hear that, Duke? Hear why they call this memory sauce?'

They delighted one another by blocking out minute variations in the free-for-all fight which is a set piece in Wayne pictures; motivated or totally gratuitous, the fight sequence has to be in the picture, because they so enjoy making it. 'Listen – this'll really be funny. Duke picks up the kid, see, and then it takes both Dino and Earl to throw him out the door – *how's that?*'

They communicated by sharing old jokes; they sealed their cama-raderie by making gentle, old-fashioned fun of wives, those civilizers, those tamers. 'So Señora Wayne takes it into her head to stay up and have one brandy. So for the rest of the night it's "Yes, Pilar, you're right, dear. I'm a bully, Pilar, you're right, I'm impossible."'

'You hear that? Duke says Pilar threw a table at him.'

'Hey, Duke, here's something funny. That finger you hurt today, get the Doc to bandage it up, go home tonight, show it to Pilar, tell her she did it when she threw the table. You know, make her think she was really cutting up.'

They treated the oldest among them respectfully; they treated the youngest fondly. 'You see that kid?' they said of Michael Anderson, Jr. 'What a kid.'

'He don't act, it's right from the heart,' said Hathaway, patting his heart.

'Hey kid,' Martin said. 'You're gonna be in my next picture. We'll have the whole thing, no beards. The striped shirts, the girls, the hi-fi, the eye lights.'

They ordered Michael Anderson his own chair, with 'BIG MIKE' tooled on the back. When it arrived on the set, Hathaway hugged him. 'You see that?' Anderson asked Wayne, suddenly too shy to look him in the eye. Wayne gave him the smile, the nod, the final accolade. 'I saw it, kid.'

On the morning of the day they were to finish *Katie Elder*, Web Overlander showed up not in his Windbreaker but in a blue blazer. 'Home, Mama,' he said, passing out the last of his Juicy Fruit. 'I got on my getaway clothes.' But he was subdued. At noon, Henry Hathaway's wife dropped by the commissary to tell him that she might fly over to Acapulco. 'Go ahead,' he told her. 'I get through here, all I'm gonna do is take Seconal to a point just this side of suicide.' They were all subdued. After Mrs Hathaway left, there were desultory attempts at reminiscing, but man's country was receding fast; they were already halfway home, and all they could call up was the 1961 Bel Air fire, during which Henry Hathaway had ordered the Los Angeles Fire Department off his property and saved the place himself by, among other measures, throwing everything flammable into the swimming pool. 'Those fire guys might've just given it up,' Wayne said. 'Just let it burn.' In fact this was a good story, and one incorporating several of their favorite themes, but a Bel Air story was still not a Durango story.

In the early afternoon they began the last scene, and although they spent as much time as possible setting it up, the moment finally came when there was nothing to do but shoot it. 'Second team out, first team in, *doors closed*,' the assistant director shouted one last time. The stand-ins walked off the set, John Wayne and Martha Hyer walked on. 'All right, boys, *silencio*, this is a picture.' They took it twice. Twice the girl offered John Wayne the tattered Bible. Twice

John Wayne told her that 'there's a lot of places I go where that wouldn't fit in.' Everyone was very still. And at 2:30 that Friday afternoon Henry Hathaway turned away from the camera, and in the hush that followed he ground out his cigar in a sand bucket. 'O.K.,' he said. 'That's it.'

Since that summer of 1943 I had thought of John Wayne in a number of ways. I had thought of him driving cattle up from Texas, and bringing airplanes in on a single engine, thought of him telling the girl at the Alamo that 'Republic is a beautiful word.' I had never thought of him having dinner with his family and with me and my husband in an expensive restaurant in Chapultepec Park, but time brings odd mutations, and there we were, one night that last week in Mexico. For a while it was only a nice evening, an evening anywhere. We had a lot of drinks and I lost the sense that the face across the table was in certain ways more familiar than my husband's.

And then something happened. Suddenly the room seemed suffused with the dream, and I could not think why. Three men appeared out of nowhere, playing guitars. Pilar Wayne leaned slightly forward, and John Wayne lifted his glass almost imperceptibly toward her. 'We'll need some Pouilly-Fuissé for the rest of the table,' he said, 'and some red Bordeaux for the Duke.' We all smiled, and drank the Pouilly-Fuissé for the rest of the table and the red Bordeaux for the Duke, and all the while the men with the guitars kept playing, until finally I realized what they were playing, what they had been playing all along: 'The Red River Valley' and the theme from *The High and the Mighty*. They did not quite get the beat right, but even now I can hear them, in another country and a long time later, even as I tell you this.

1965

Where the Kissing Never Stops

Outside the Monterey County Courthouse in Salinas, California, the Downtown Merchants' Christmas decorations glittered in the thin sunlight that makes the winter lettuce grow. Inside, the crowd blinked uneasily in the blinding television lights. The occasion was a meeting of the Monterey County Board of Supervisors, and the issue, on this warm afternoon before Christmas 1965, was whether or not a small school in the Carmel Valley, the Institute for the Study of Nonviolence, owned by Miss Joan Baez, was in violation of Section 32-C of the Monterey County Zoning Code, which prohibits land use 'detrimental to the peace, morals, or general welfare of Monterey County.' Mrs Gerald Petkuss, who lived across the road from the school, had put the problem another way. 'We wonder what kind of people would go to a school like this,' she asked quite early in the controversy. 'Why they aren't out working and making money.'

Mrs Petkuss was a plump young matron with an air of bewildered determination, and she came to the rostrum in a strawberry-pink knit dress to say that she had been plagued 'by people associated with Miss Baez's school coming up to ask where it was although they knew perfectly *well* where it was – one gentleman I remember had a beard.'

'Well I don't *care*,' Mrs Petkuss cried when someone in the front row giggled. 'I have three small children, that's a big responsibility, and I don't like to have to worry about . . .' Mrs Petkuss paused delicately. 'About who's around.'

The hearing lasted from two until 7:15 p.m., five hours and fifteen minutes of participatory democracy during which it was suggested, on the one hand, that the Monterey County Board of Supervisors was turning our country into Nazi Germany, and, on the other, that the presence of Miss Baez and her fifteen students in the Carmel Valley would lead to 'Berkeley-type' demonstrations, demoralize trainees at Fort Ord, paralyze Army convoys using the Carmel Valley road, and send property values plummeting throughout the county. 'Frankly, I can't conceive of anyone buying property near such an operation,' declared Mrs Petkuss's husband, who is a veterinarian. Both Dr and Mrs Petkuss, the latter near tears, said that they were particularly offended by Miss Baez's presence on her property during weekends. It seemed that she did not always stay inside. She sat out under trees, and walked around the property.

'We don't start until one,' someone from the school objected. 'Even if we did make noise, which we don't, the Petkusses could sleep until one, I don't see what the problem is.'

The Petkusses' lawyer jumped up. 'The *problem* is that the Petkusses happen to have a very beautiful swimming pool, they'd like to have guests out on weekends, like to use the pool.'

'They'd have to stand up on a table to see the school.'

'They will, too,' shouted a young woman who had already indicated her approval of Miss Baez by reading aloud to the supervisors a passage from John Stuart Mill's *On Liberty*. 'They'll be out with spyglasses.'

'That is not true,' Mrs Petkuss keened. 'We see the school out of three bedroom windows, out of one living-room window, it's the only direction we can *look*.'

Miss Baez sat very still in the front row. She was wearing a long-sleeved navy-blue dress with an Irish lace collar and cuffs, and she kept her hands folded in her lap. She is extraordinary looking, far more so than her photographs suggest, since the camera seems to emphasize an Indian cast to her features and fails to record either the startling fineness and clarity of her bones and eyes or, her most striking characteristic, her absolute directness, her absence of guile. She has a great natural style, and she is what used to be called a lady. 'Scum,' hissed an old man with a snap-on bow tie who had identified himself as 'a veteran of two wars' and who is a regular at such meetings. '*Spaniel*.' He seemed to be referring to the length of

Miss Baez's hair, and was trying to get her attention by tapping with his walking stick, but her eyes did not flicker from the rostrum. After a while she got up, and stood until the room was completely quiet. Her opponents sat tensed, ready to spring up and counter whatever defense she was planning to make of her politics, of her school, of beards, of 'Berkeley-type' demonstrations and disorder in general.

'Everybody's talking about their forty- and fifty-thousand-dollar houses and their property values going down,' she drawled finally, keeping her clear voice low and gazing levelly at the supervisors. 'I'd just like to say one thing. I have more than one *hundred* thousand dollars invested in the Carmel Valley, and I'm interested in protecting my property too.' The property owner smiled disingenuously at Dr and Mrs Petkuss then, and took her seat amid complete silence.

She is an interesting girl, a girl who might have interested Henry James, at about the time he did Verena Tarrant, in *The Bostonians*. Joan Baez grew up in the more evangelistic thickets of the middle class, the daughter of a Quaker physics teacher, the granddaughter of two Protestant ministers, an English-Scottish Episcopalian on her mother's side, a Mexican Methodist on her father's. She was born on Staten Island, but raised on the edges of the academic community all over the country; until she found Carmel, she did not really come from anywhere. When it was time to go to high school, her father was teaching at Stanford, and so she went to Palo Alto High School, where she taught herself 'House of the Rising Sun' on a Sears, Roebuck guitar, tried to achieve a vibrato by tapping her throat with her finger, and made headlines by refusing to leave the school during a bomb drill. When it was time to go to college, her father was at M.I.T. and Harvard, and so she went a month to Boston University, dropped out, and for a long while sang in coffee bars around Harvard Square. She did not much like the Harvard Square life ('They just lie in their pads, smoke pot, and do stupid things like that,' said the ministers' granddaughter of her acquaintances there), but she did not yet know another.

In the summer of 1959, a friend took her to the first Newport Folk Festival. She arrived in Newport in a Cadillac hearse with 'JOAN BAEZ' painted on the side, sang a few songs to 13,000 people, and there it was, the new life. Her first album sold more copies than the work of any other female folksinger in record history. By the end of 1961 Vanguard had released her second album, and her total sales were behind those of only Harry Belafonte, the Kingston Trio, and the Weavers. She had finished her first long tour, had given a concert at Carnegie Hall which was sold out two months in advance, and had turned down $100,000 worth of concert dates because she would work only a few months a year.

She was the right girl at the right time. She had only a small repertory of Child ballads ('What's Joanie still doing with this Mary Hamilton?' Bob Dylan would fret later), never trained her pure soprano and annoyed some purists because she was indifferent to the origins of her material and sang everything 'sad.' But she rode in with the folk wave just as it was cresting. She could reach an audience in a way that neither the purists nor the more commercial folksingers seemed to be able to do. If her interest was never in the money, neither was it really in the music: she was interested instead in something that went on between her and the audience. 'The easiest kind of relationship for me is with ten thousand people,' she said. 'The hardest is with one.'

She did not want, then or ever, to entertain; she wanted to move people, to establish with them some communion of emotion. By the end of 1963 she had found, in the protest movement, something upon which she could focus the emotion. She went into the South. She sang at Negro colleges, and she was always there where the barricade was, Selma, Montgomery, Birmingham. She sang at the Lincoln Memorial after the March on Washington. She told the Internal Revenue Service that she did not intend to pay the sixty percent of her income tax that she calculated went to the defense establishment. She became the voice that meant protest, although she would always maintain a curious distance from the movement's more ambiguous moments. ('I got pretty sick of those Southern marches after a while,' she could say later. 'All these big entertainers renting little planes and flying down, always about 35,000 people in town.') She had recorded only a handful of albums, but she had seen her face on the cover of *Time*. She was just twenty-two.

Joan Baez was a personality before she was entirely a person, and, like anyone to whom that happens, she is in a sense the hapless victim of what others have seen in her, written about her, wanted her to be and not to be. The roles assigned to her are various, but variations on a single theme. She is the Madonna of the disaffected. She is the pawn of the protest movement. She is the unhappy analysand. She is the singer who would not train her voice, the rebel who drives the Jaguar too fast, the Rima who hides with the birds and the deer. Above all, she is the girl who 'feels' things, who has hung on to the freshness and pain of adolescence, the girl ever wounded, ever young. Now, at an age when the wounds begin to heal whether one wants them to or not, Joan Baez rarely leaves the Carmel Valley.

Although all Baez activities tend to take on certain ominous overtones in the collective consciousness of Monterey County, what actually goes on at Miss Baez's Institute for the Study of Nonviolence, which was allowed to continue operating in the Carmel Valley by a three-two vote of the supervisors, is so apparently ingenuous as to disarm even veterans of two wars who wear snap-on bow ties. Four days a week, Miss Baez and her fifteen students meet at the school for lunch: potato salad, Kool-Aid, and hot dogs broiled on a portable barbecue. After lunch they do ballet exercises to Beatles records, and after that they sit around on the bare floor beneath a photomural of Cypress Point and discuss their reading: *Gandhi on Nonviolence*, Louis Fischer's *Life of Mahatma Gandhi*, Jerome Frank's *Breaking the Thought Barrier*, Thoreau's *On Civil Disobedience*, Krishnamurti's *The First and Last Freedom* and *Think on These Things*, C. Wright Mills's *The Power Elite*, Huxley's *Ends and Means*, and Marshall McLuhan's *Understanding Media*. On the fifth day, they meet as usual but spend the afternoon in total silence, which involves not only not talking but also not reading, not writing, and not smoking. Even on discussion days, this silence is invoked for regular twenty-minute or hour intervals, a regimen described by one student as 'invaluable for clearing your mind of personal hangups' and by Miss Baez as 'just about the most important thing about the school.'

There are no admission requirements, other than that applicants must be at least eighteen years old; admission to each session is granted to the first fifteen who write and ask to come. They come from all over, and they are on the average very young, very earnest, and not very much in touch with the larger scene, less refugees from it than children who do not quite apprehend it. They worry a great deal about 'responding to one another with beauty and tenderness,' and their response to one another is in fact so tender that an afternoon at the school tends to drift perilously into the never-never. They debate whether or not it was a wise tactic for the Vietnam Day Committee at Berkeley to try to reason with Hell's Angels 'on the hip level.'

'O.K.,' someone argues. 'So the Angels just shrug and say "our thing's violence." How can the V.D.C. guy answer that?'

They discuss a proposal from Berkeley for an International Nonviolent Army: 'The idea is, we go to Vietnam and we go into these villages, and then if they burn them, we burn too.'

'It has a beautiful simplicity,' someone says.

Most of them are too young to have been around for the memorable events of protest, and the few who have been active tell stories to those who have not, stories which begin 'One night at the Scranton Y . . .' or 'Recently when we were sitting in at the A.E.C. . . .' and 'We had this eleven-year-old on the Canada-to-Cuba march who was at the time corresponding with a Ghandian, and he . . .' They talk about Allen Ginsberg, 'the only one, the only beautiful voice, the only one talking.' Ginsberg had suggested that the V.D.C. send women carrying babies and flowers to the Oakland Army Terminal.

'Babies and flowers,' a pretty little girl breathes. 'But that's so *beautiful*, that's the whole *point*.'

'Ginsberg was down here one weekend,' recalls a dreamy boy with curly golden hair. 'He brought a copy of the *Fuck Songbag*, but we burned it.' He giggles. He is holding a clear violet marble up to the window, turning it in the sunlight. 'Joan gave it to me,' he says. 'One night at her house, when we all had a party and gave each other presents. It was like Christmas but it wasn't.'

The school itself is an old whitewashed adobe house quite far out among the yellow hills and dusty scrub oaks of the Upper Carmel Valley. Oleanders support a torn wire fence around the school, and

there is no sign, no identification at all. The adobe was a one-room
county school until 1950; after that it was occupied in turn by the
So Help Me Hannah Poison Oak Remedy Laboratory and by a small
shotgun-shell manufacturing business, two enterprises which apparently did not present the threat to property values that Miss Baez
does. She bought the place in the fall of 1965, after the County
Planning Commission told her that zoning prohibited her from running the school in her house, which is on a ten-acre piece a few
miles away. Miss Baez is the vice president of the Institute, and its
sponsor; the $120 fee paid by each student for each six-week session
includes lodging, at an apartment house in Pacific Grove, and does
not meet the school's expenses. Miss Baez not only has a $40,000
investment in the school property but is responsible as well for the
salary of Ira Sandperl, who is the president of the Institute, the leader
of the discussions, and in fact the *éminence grise* of the entire project.
'You might think we're starting in a very small way,' Ira Sandperl
says. 'Sometimes the smallest things can change the course of history.
Look at the Benedictine order.'

In a way it is impossible to talk about Joan Baez without talking about Ira Sandperl. 'One of the men on the Planning Commission said I was being led down the primrose path by the lunatic
fringe,' Miss Baez giggles. 'Ira said maybe he's the lunatic and his
beard's the fringe.' Ira Sandperl is a forty-two-year-old native of
St Louis who has, besides the beard, a shaved head, a large nuclear-
disarmament emblem on his corduroy jacket, glittering and slightly
messianic eyes, a high cracked laugh and the general look of a man
who has, all his life, followed some imperceptibly but fatally askew
rainbow. He has spent a good deal of time in pacifist movements
around San Francisco, Berkeley, and Palo Alto, and was, at the time
he and Miss Baez hit upon the idea of the Institute, working in a
Palo Alto bookstore.

Ira Sandperl first met Joan Baez when she was sixteen and was
brought by her father to a Quaker meeting in Palo Alto. 'There
was something magic, something different about her even then,' he
recalls. 'I remember once she was singing at a meeting where I
was speaking. The audience was so responsive that night that I said
"Honey, when you grow up we'll have to be an evangelical team."'
He smiles, and spreads his hands.

The two became close, according to Ira Sandperl, after Miss Baez's father went to live in Paris as a UNESCO advisor. 'I was the oldest friend around, so naturally she turned to me.' He was with her at the time of the Berkeley demonstrations in the fall of 1964. 'We were actually the outside agitators you heard so much about,' he says. 'Basically we wanted to turn an *un*violent movement into a *non*violent one. Joan was *enor*mously instrumental in pulling the movement out of its slump, although the boys may not admit it now.'

A month or so after her appearance at Berkeley, Joan Baez talked to Ira Sandperl about the possibility of tutoring her for a year. 'She found herself among politically knowledgeable people,' he says, 'and while she had strong *feelings*, she didn't know any of the socio-economic-political-historical terms of nonviolence.'

'It was all vague,' she interrupts, nervously brushing her hair back. 'I want it to be less vague.'

They decided to make it not a year's private tutorial but a school to go on indefinitely, and enrolled the first students late in the summer of 1965. The Institute aligns itself with no movements ('Some of the kids are just leading us into another long, big, violent mess,' Miss Baez says), and there is in fact a marked distrust of most activist organizations. Ira Sandperl, for example, had little use for the V.D.C., because the V.D.C. believed in nonviolence only as a limited tactic, accepted conventional power blocs, and even ran one of its leaders for Congress, which is anathema to Sandperl. 'Darling, let me put it this way. In civil rights, now, the President signs a bill, who does he call to witness it? Adam Powell? No. He calls Rustin, Farmer, King, *none* of them in the conventional power structure.' He pauses, as if envisioning a day when he and Miss Baez will be called upon to witness the signing of a bill outlawing violence. 'I'm not optimistic, darling, but I'm hopeful. There's a difference. I'm hopeful.'

The gas heater sputters on and off and Miss Baez watches it, her duffel coat drawn up around her shoulders. 'Everybody says I'm politically naïve, and I am,' she says after a while. It is something she says frequently to people she does not know. 'So are the people running politics, or we wouldn't be in wars, would we.'

The door opens and a short middle-aged man wearing handmade sandals walks in. He is Manuel Greenhill, Miss Baez's manager, and although he has been her manager for five years, he has never before visited the Institute, and he has never before met Ira Sandperl.

'At last!' Ira Sandperl cries, jumping up. 'The disembodied voice on the telephone is here at last! There *is* a Manny Greenhill! There *is* an Ira Sandperl! Here I am! Here's the villain!'

It is difficult to arrange to see Joan Baez, at least for anyone not tuned to the underground circuits of the protest movement. The New York company for which she records, Vanguard, will give only Manny Greenhill's number, in Boston. 'Try Area Code 415, prefix DA 4, number 4321,' Manny Greenhill will rasp. Area Code 415, DA 4-4321 will connect the caller with Keppler's Bookstore in Palo Alto, which is where Ira Sandperl used to work. Someone at the bookstore will take a number, and, after checking with Carmel to see if anyone there cares to hear from the caller, will call back, disclosing a Carmel number. The Carmel number is not, as one might think by now, for Miss Baez, but for an answering service. The service will take a number, and, after some days or weeks, a call may or may not be received from Judy Flynn, Miss Baez's secretary. Miss Flynn says that she will 'try to contact' Miss Baez. 'I don't see people,' says the heart of this curiously improvised web of wrong numbers, disconnected telephones, and unreturned calls. 'I lock the gate and hope nobody comes, but they come anyway. Somebody's been telling them where I live.'

She lives quietly. She reads, and she talks to the people who have been told where she lives, and occasionally she and Ira Sandperl go to San Francisco, to see friends, to talk about the peace movement. She sees her two sisters and she sees Ira Sandperl. She believes that her days at the Institute talking and listening to Ira Sandperl are bringing her closer to contentment than anything she has done so far. 'Certainly than the singing. I used to stand up there and think I'm getting so many thousand dollars, and for what?' She is defensive about her income ('Oh, I have some money from somewhere'), vague about her plans. 'There are some things I want to do. I want to try some rock 'n' roll and some classical music. But I'm not going to start worrying about the charts and the sales because then where are you?'

Exactly where it is she wants to be seems an open question, bewildering to her and even more so to her manager. If he is asked what his most celebrated client is doing now and plans to do in the future, Manny Greenhill talks about 'lots of plans,' 'other areas,' and 'her own choice.' Finally he hits upon something: 'Listen, she just did a documentary for Canadian television, *Variety* gave it a great review, let me read you.'

Manny Greenhill reads. 'Let's see. Here *Variety* says "*planned only a twenty-minute interview but when CBC officials in Toronto saw the film they decided to go with a special –* "' He interrupts himself. 'That's pretty newsworthy right there. Let's see now. Here they quote her ideas on peace . . . you know those . . . here she says "*every time I go to Hollywood I want to throw up*" . . . let's not get into that . . . here now, "*her impersonations of Ringo Starr and George Harrison were dead-on,*" get that, that's good.'

Manny Greenhill is hoping to get Miss Baez to write a book, to be in a movie, and to get around to recording the rock 'n' roll songs. He will not discuss her income, although he will say, at once jaunty and bleak, 'but it won't be much *this* year.' Miss Baez let him schedule only one concert for 1966 (down from an average of thirty a year), has accepted only one regular club booking in her entire career, and is virtually never on television. 'What's she going to do on Andy Williams?' Manny Greenhill shrugs. 'One time she sang one of Pat Boone's songs with him,' he adds, 'which proves she can get along, but still. We don't want her up there with some dance routine behind her.' Greenhill keeps an eye on her political appearances, and tries to prevent the use of her name. 'We say, if they use her name it's a concert. The point is, if they haven't used her name, then if she doesn't like the looks of it she can get out.' He is resigned to the school's cutting into her schedule. 'Listen,' he says. 'I've always encouraged her to be political. I may not be active, but let's say I'm concerned.' He squints into the sun. 'Let's say maybe I'm just too old.'

To encourage Joan Baez to be 'political' is really only to encourage Joan Baez to continue 'feeling' things, for her politics are still, as she herself said, 'all vague.' Her approach is instinctive, pragmatic, not too far from that of any League of Women Voters member. 'Frankly, I'm down on Communism,' is her latest word on that subject. On recent events in the pacifist movement, she has this to say: 'Burning draft cards doesn't make sense, and burning themselves makes even less.' When she was at Palo Alto High School and refused to leave the building during a bomb drill, she was not motivated by theory; she did it because 'it was the practical thing to do, I mean it seemed to me this drill was impractical, all these people thinking they could get into some kind of little shelter and be saved with canned water.' She has made appearances for Democratic administrations, and is frequently quoted as saying: 'There's never been a good Republican folksinger'; it is scarcely the diction of the new radicalism. Her concert program includes some of her thoughts about 'waiting on the eve of destruction,' and her thoughts are these:

> *My life is a crystal teardrop. There are snowflakes falling in the teardrop and little figures trudging around in slow motion. If I were to look into the teardrop for the next million years, I might never find out who the people are, and what they are doing. Sometimes I get lonesome for a storm. A full-blown storm where everything changes. The sky goes through four days in an hour, the trees wail, little animals skitter in the mud and everything gets dark and goes completely wild. But it's really God – playing music in his favorite cathedral in heaven – shattering stained glass – playing a gigantic organ – thundering on the keys – perfect harmony – perfect joy.*

Although Miss Baez does not actually talk this way when she is kept from the typewriter, she does try, perhaps unconsciously, to hang on to the innocence and turbulence and capacity for wonder, however ersatz or shallow, of her own or of anyone's adolescence. This openness, this vulnerability, is of course precisely the reason why she is so able to 'come through' to all the young and lonely and inarticulate, to all those who suspect that no one else in the world understands about beauty and hurt and love and brotherhood. Perhaps because she is older now, Miss Baez is sometimes troubled that she means, to a great many of her admirers, everything that is beautiful and true.

'I'm not very happy with my thinking about it,' she says. 'Sometimes I tell myself, "Come on, Baez, you're just like everybody else," but then I'm not happy with that either.'

'Not everybody else has the voice,' Ira Sandperl interrupts dotingly.

'Oh, it's all right to have the *voice*, the *voice* is all right . . .'

She breaks off and concentrates for a long while on the buckle of her shoe.

So now the girl whose life is a crystal teardrop has her own place, a place where the sun shines and the ambiguities can be set aside a little while longer, a place where everyone can be warm and loving and share confidences. 'One day we went around the room and told a little about ourselves,' she confides, 'and I discovered that *boy*, I'd had it pretty easy.' The late afternoon sun streaks the clean wooden floor and the birds sing in the scrub oaks and the beautiful children sit in their coats on the floor and listen to Ira Sandperl.

'Are you a vegetarian, Ira?' someone asks idly.

'Yes. Yes, I am.'

'Tell them, Ira,' Joan Baez says. 'It's nice.'

He leans back and looks toward the ceiling. 'I was in the Sierra once.' He pauses, and Joan Baez smiles approvingly. 'I saw this magnificent tree *growing* out of bare rock, *thrusting* itself . . . and I thought *all right, tree*, if you want to live that much, *all right!* All *right!* O.K.! I won't chop you! I won't eat you! The one thing we all have in common is that we all want to *live!*'

'But what about vegetables,' a girl murmurs.

'Well, I realized, of course, that as long as I was in *this flesh* and *this blood* I couldn't be *per*fectly nonviolent.'

It is getting late. Fifty cents apiece is collected for the next day's lunch, and someone reads a request from the Monterey County Board of Supervisors that citizens fly American flags to show that 'Kooks, Commies, and Cowards do not represent our County,' and someone else brings up the Vietnam Day Committee, and a dissident member who had visited Carmel.

'Marv's an honest-to-God nonviolenter,' Ira Sandperl declares. 'A man of honesty and love.'

'He said he's an anarchist,' someone interjects doubtfully.

'Right,' Ira Sandperl agrees. 'Absolutely.'

'Would the V.D.C. call Gandhi bourgeois?'

'Oh, they must know better, but they lead such bourgeois lives themselves . . .'

'That's so true,' says the dreamy blond boy with the violet marble. 'You walk into their office, they're so unfriendly, so unfriendly and cold . . .'

Everyone smiles lovingly at him. By now the sky outside is the color of his marble, but they are all reluctant about gathering up their books and magazines and records, about finding their car keys and ending the day, and by the time they are ready to leave Joan Baez is eating potato salad with her fingers from a bowl in the refrigerator, and everyone stays to share it, just a little while longer where it is warm.

1966

Comrade Laski, C.P.U.S.A. (M.-L.)

Michael Laski, also known as M. I. Laski, is a relatively obscure young man with deep fervent eyes, a short beard, and a pallor which seems particularly remarkable in Southern California. With his striking appearance and his relentlessly ideological diction, he looks and talks precisely like the popular image of a professional revolutionary, which in fact he is. He was born twenty-six years ago in Brooklyn, moved as a child to Los Angeles, dropped out of U.C.L.A. his sophomore year to organize for the Retail Clerks, and now, as General Secretary of the Central Committee of the Communist Party U.S.A. (Marxist-Leninist), a splinter group of Stalinist-Maoists who divide their energies between Watts and Harlem, he is rigidly committed to an immutable complex of doctrine, including the notions that the traditional American Communist Party is a 'revisionist bourgeois clique,' that the Progressive Labor Party, the Trotskyites, and 'the revisionist clique headed by Gus Hall' prove themselves opportunistic bourgeois lackeys by making their peace appeal not to the 'workers' but to the liberal imperialists; and that H. Rap Brown is the tool, if not the conscious agent, of the ruling imperialist class.

Not long ago I spent some time with Michael Laski, down at the Workers' International Bookstore in Watts, the West Coast headquarters of the C.P.U.S.A. (M.-L.). We sat at a kitchen table beneath the hammer-and-sickle flag and the portraits of Marx, Engels, Mao Tse-tung, Lenin, and Stalin (Mao in the favored center position), and we discussed the revolution necessary to bring about the dictatorship

of the proletariat. Actually I was interested not in the revolution but
in the revolutionary. He had with him a small red book of Mao's
poems, and as he talked he squared it on the table, aligned it with
the table edge first vertically and then horizontally. To understand
who Michael Laski is you must have a feeling for that kind of compulsion. One does not think of him eating, or in bed. He has nothing
in common with the passionate personalities who tend to turn up
on the New Left. Michael Laski scorns deviationist reformers. He
believes with Mao that political power grows out of the barrel of a
gun, a point he insists upon with blazing and self-defeating candor.
His place in the geography of the American Left is, in short, an almost
impossibly lonely and quixotic one, unpopular, unpragmatic. He
believes that there are 'workers' in the United States, and that, when
the time comes, they will 'arise,' not in anarchy but in conscious
concert, and he also believes that 'the ruling class' is self-conscious,
and possessed of demonic powers. He is in all ways an idealist.

As it happens I am comfortable with the Michael Laskis of this
world, with those who live outside rather than in, those in whom
the sense of dread is so acute that they turn to extreme and doomed
commitments; I know something about dread myself, and appreciate
the elaborate systems with which some people manage to fill the
void, appreciate all the opiates of the people, whether they are as
accessible as alcohol and heroin and promiscuity or as hard to come
by as faith in God or History.

But of course I did not mention dread to Michael Laski, whose
particular opiate is History. I did suggest 'depression,' did venture
that it might have been 'depressing' for him to see only a dozen or
so faces at his last May Day demonstration, but he told me that
depression was an impediment to the revolutionary process, a disease
afflicting only those who do not have ideology to sustain them.
Michael Laski, you see, did not feel as close to me as I did to him.
'I talk to you at all,' he said, 'only as a calculated risk. Of course
your function is to gather information for the intelligence services.
Basically you want to conduct the same probe the F.B.I. would carry
out if they could put us in a chair.' He paused and tapped the small
red book with his fingernails. 'And yet,' he said finally, 'there's a
definite advantage to me in talking to you. Because of one fact: these
interviews provide a public record of my existence.'

Still, he was not going to discuss with me what he called 'the underground apparatus' of the C.P.U.S.A. (M.-L.), any more than he would tell me how many members constituted the cadre. 'Obviously I'm not going to give you that kind of information,' he said. 'We know as a matter of course that we'll be outlawed.' The Workers' International Bookstore, however, was 'an open facility,' and I was free to look around. I leafed through some of the literature out of Peking (*Vice-Premier Chen Yi Answers Questions Put by Correspondents*), Hanoi (*President Ho Chi Minh Answers President L. B. Johnson*), and Tirana, Albania (*The Hue and Cry About a Change in Tito's Policy and the Undeniable Truth*), and I tried to hum, from a North Vietnamese song book, 'When the Party Needs Us Our Hearts Are Filled with Hatred.' The literature was in the front of the store, along with a cash register and the kitchen table; in back, behind a plywood partition, were a few cots and the press and mimeograph machine on which the Central Committee prints its 'political organ,' *People's Voice*, and its 'theoretical organ,' *Red Flag*. 'There's a cadre assigned to this facility in order to guarantee the security,' Michael Laski said when I mentioned the cots. 'They have a small arsenal in back, a couple of shotguns and a number of other items.'

So much security may seem curious when one considers what the members of the cadre actually do, which is, aside from selling the *People's Voice* and trying to set up People's Armed Defense Groups, largely a matter of perfecting their own ideology, searching out 'errors' and 'mistakes' in one another's attitudes. 'What we do may seem a waste of time to some people,' Michael Laski said suddenly. 'Not having any ideology yourself, you might wonder what the Party offers. It offers nothing. It offers thirty or forty years of putting the Party above everything. It offers beatings. Jail. On the high levels, assassination.'

But of course that was offering a great deal. The world Michael Laski had constructed for himself was one of labyrinthine intricacy and immaculate clarity, a world made meaningful not only by high purpose but by external and internal threats, intrigues and apparatus, an immutably ordered world in which things mattered. Let me tell you about another day at the Workers' International Bookstore. The Marxist-Leninists had been out selling the *People's Voice*, and now Michael Laski and three other members of the cadre were going over the proceeds, a ceremony as formal as a gathering of the Morgan partners.

'Mr – *Comrade* – Simmons – what was the total income?' Michael Laski asked.

'Nine dollars and ninety-one cents.'

'Over what period of time?'

'Four hours.'

'What was the total number of papers sold?'

'Seventy-five.'

'And the average per hour?'

'Nineteen.'

'The average contribution?'

'Thirteen and a half cents.'

'The largest contribution?'

'Sixty cents.'

'The smallest?'

'Four cents.'

'It was not a very good day, Comrade Simmons. Can you explain?'

'It's always bad the day before welfare and unemployment checks arrive.'

'Very good, Comrade Simmons.'

You see what the world of Michael Laski is: a minor but perilous triumph of being over nothingness.

1967

7000 Romaine, Los Angeles 38

Seven thousand Romaine Street is in that part of Los Angeles familiar to admirers of Raymond Chandler and Dashiell Hammett: the underside of Hollywood, south of Sunset Boulevard, a middle-class slum of 'model studios' and warehouses and two-family bungalows. Because Paramount and Columbia and Desilu and the Samuel Goldwyn studios are nearby, many of the people who live around here have some tenuous connection with the motion-picture industry. They once processed fan photographs, say, or knew Jean Harlow's manicurist. 7000 Romaine looks itself like a faded movie exterior, a pastel building with chipped *art moderne* detailing, the windows now either boarded or paned with chicken-wire glass and, at the entrance, among the dusty oleander, a rubber mat that reads WELCOME.

Actually no one is welcome, for 7000 Romaine belongs to Howard Hughes, and the door is locked. That the Hughes 'communications center' should lie here in the dull sunlight of Hammett-Chandler country is one of those circumstances that satisfy one's suspicion that life is indeed a scenario, for the Hughes empire has been in our time the only industrial complex in the world – involving, over the years, machinery manufacture, foreign oil-tool subsidiaries, a brewery, two airlines, immense real-estate holdings, a major motion-picture studio, and an electronics and missile operation – run by a man whose *modus operandi* most closely resembles that of a character in *The Big Sleep*.

As it happens, I live not far from 7000 Romaine, and I make a point of driving past it every now and then, I suppose in the same

spirit that Arthurian scholars visit the Cornish coast. I am interested
in the folklore of Howard Hughes, in the way people react to him,
in the terms they use when they talk about him. Let me give you an
example. A few weeks ago I lunched with an old friend at the Beverly
Hills Hotel. One of the other guests was a well-married woman in
her thirties who had once been a Hughes contract starlet, and another was a costume designer who had worked on a lot of Hughes
pictures and who still receives a weekly salary from 7000 Romaine,
on the understanding that he work for no one else. He has done
nothing but cash that weekly check for some years now. They sat
there in the sun, the one-time starlet and the sometime costume
designer for a man whose public appearances are now somewhat
less frequent than those of The Shadow, and they talked about him.
They wondered how he was and why he was devoting 1967 to
buying up Las Vegas.

'You can't tell me it's like they say, that he bought the Desert Inn
just because the high rollers were coming in and they wouldn't let
him keep the penthouse,' the ex-starlet mused, fingering a diamond
as big as the Ritz. 'It must be part of some larger mission.'

The phrase was exactly right. Anyone who skims the financial
press knows that Hughes never has business 'transactions,' or 'negotiations'; he has 'missions.' His central mission, as *Fortune* once put
it in a series of love letters, has always been 'to preserve his power
as the proprietor of the largest pool of industrial wealth still under
the absolute control of a single individual.' Nor does Hughes have
business 'associates'; he has only 'adversaries.' When the adversaries
'appear to be' threatening his absolute control, Hughes 'might or
might not' take action. It is such phrases as 'appear to be' and 'might
or might not,' peculiar to business reportage involving Hughes, that
suggested the special mood of a Hughes mission. And here is what
the action might or might not be: Hughes might warn, at the critical
moment, 'You're holding a gun to my head.' If there is one thing
Hughes dislikes, it is a gun to his head (generally this means a request
for an appearance, or a discussion of policy), and at least one president of T.W.A., a company which, as Hughes ran it, bore an operational similarity only to the government of Honduras, departed on
this note.

The stories are endless, infinitely familiar, traded by the faithful like baseball cards, fondled until they fray around the edges and blur into the apocryphal. There is the one about the barber, Eddie Alexander, who was paid handsomely to remain on 'day and night standby' in case Hughes wanted a haircut. 'Just checking, Eddie,' Hughes once said when he called Alexander at two in the morning. 'Just wanted to see if you were standing by.' There was the time Convair wanted to sell Hughes 340 transports and Hughes insisted that, to insure 'secrecy,' the mission be discussed only between midnight and dawn, by flashlight, in the Palm Springs Municipal Dump. There was the evening when both Hughes and Greg Bautzer, then his lawyer, went incommunicado while, in the conference room of the Chemical Bank in New York, the money men waited to lend T.W.A. $165 million. There they were, $165 million in hand, the men from two of the country's biggest insurance companies and nine of its most powerful banks, all waiting, and it was 7 p.m. of the last day the deal could be made and the bankers found themselves talking by phone not to Hughes, not even to Bautzer, but to Bautzer's wife, the movie star Dana Wynter. 'I hope he takes it in pennies,' a Wall Street broker said when Hughes, six years later, sold T.W.A. for $546 million, 'and drops it on his toes.'

Then there are the more recent stories. Howard Hughes is en route to Boston aboard the Super Chief with the Bel Air Patrol riding shotgun. Howard Hughes is in Peter Bent Brigham Hospital. Howard Hughes commandeers the fifth floor of the Boston Ritz. Howard Hughes is or is not buying 37½ percent of Columbia Pictures through the Swiss Banque de Paris. Howard Hughes is ill. Howard Hughes is dead. No, Howard Hughes is in Las Vegas. Howard Hughes pays $13 million for the Desert Inn. $15 million for the Sands. Gives the State of Nevada $6 million for a medical school. Negotiates for ranches, Alamo Airways, the North Las Vegas Air Terminal, more ranches, the rest of the Strip. By July of 1967 Howard Hughes is the largest single landholder in Clark County, Nevada. 'Howard likes Las Vegas,' an acquaintance of Hughes's once explained, 'because he likes to be able to find a restaurant open in case he wants a sandwich.'

Why do we like those stories so? Why do we tell them over and over? Why have we made a folk hero of a man who is the antithesis of all our official heroes, a haunted millionaire out of the West, trailing a legend of desperation and power and white sneakers? But

then we have always done that. Our favorite people and our favorite stories become so not by any inherent virtue, but because they
illustrate something deep in the grain, something unadmitted. Shoeless Joe Jackson, Warren Gamaliel Harding, the *Titanic: how the mighty
are fallen.* Charles Lindbergh, Scott and Zelda Fitzgerald, Marilyn
Monroe: *the beautiful and damned.* And Howard Hughes. That we
have made a hero of Howard Hughes tells us something interesting
about ourselves, something only dimly remembered, tells us that the
secret point of money and power in America is neither the things
that money can buy nor power for power's sake (Americans are
uneasy with their possessions, guilty about power, all of which is
difficult for Europeans to perceive because they are themselves so
truly materialistic, so versed in the uses of power), but absolute
personal freedom, mobility, privacy. It is the instinct which drove
America to the Pacific, all through the nineteenth century, the desire
to be able to find a restaurant open in case you want a sandwich, to
be a free agent, live by one's own rules.

Of course we do not admit that. The instinct is socially suicidal,
and because we recognize that this is so we have developed workable
ways of saying one thing and believing quite another. A long time
ago, Lionel Trilling pointed out what he called 'the fatal separation'
between 'the ideas of our educated liberal class and the deep places
of the imagination.' 'I mean only,' he wrote, 'that our educated class
has a ready if mild suspiciousness of the profit motive, a belief in
progress, science, social legislation, planning and international co-
operation . . . Those beliefs do great credit to those who hold them.
Yet it is a comment, if not on our beliefs then on our way of holding
them, that not a single first-rate writer has emerged to deal with
these ideas, and the emotions that are consonant with them, in a
great literary way.' Officially we admire men who exemplify those
ideas. We admire the Adlai Stevenson character, the rational man,
the enlightened man, the man not dependent upon the potentially
psychopathic mode of action. Among rich men, we officially admire
Paul Mellon, a socially responsible inheritor in the European mold.
There has always been that divergence between our official and our
unofficial heroes. It is impossible to think of Howard Hughes without seeing the apparently bottomless gulf between what we say we
want and what we do want, between what we officially admire and

secretly desire, between, in the largest sense, the people we marry and the people we love. In a nation which increasingly appears to prize social virtues, Howard Hughes remains not merely antisocial but grandly, brilliantly, surpassingly, asocial. He is the last private man, the dream we no longer admit.

1967

California Dreaming

Every weekday morning at eleven o'clock, just about the time the sun burns the last haze off the Santa Barbara hills, fifteen or twenty men gather in what was once the dining room of a shirt manufacturer's mansion overlooking the Pacific Ocean and begin another session of what they like to call 'clarifying the basic issues.' The place is the Center for the Study of Democratic Institutions, the current mutation of the Fund for the Republic, and since 1959, when the Fund paid $250,000 for the marble villa and forty-one acres of eucalyptus, a favored retreat for people whom the Center's president, Robert M. Hutchins, deems controversial, stimulating, and, perhaps above all, cooperative, or *our kind*. 'If they just want to work on their own stuff,' Hutchins has said, 'then they ought not to come here. Unless they're willing to come in and work with the group as a group, then this place is not for them.'

Those invited to spend time at the Center get an office (there are no living quarters at the Center) and a salary, the size of which is reportedly based on the University of California pay scale. The selection process is usually described as 'mysterious,' but it always involves 'people we know.' Paul Hoffman, who was at one time president of the Ford Foundation and then director of the Fund for the Republic, is now the Center's honorary chairman, and his son is there quite a bit, and Robert Hutchins's son-in-law. Rexford Tugwell, one of the New Deal 'brain trust,' is there ('Why not?' he asked me. 'If I weren't here I'd be in a rest home'), and Harvey Wheeler, the co-author of *Fail-Safe*. Occasionally someone might be asked to the

Center because he has built-in celebrity value, *e.g.*, Bishop James Pike. 'What we are is a group of highly skilled public-relations experts,' Harry Ashmore says. Harry Ashmore is a fixture at the Center, and he regards Hutchins – or, as the president of the Center is inflexibly referred to in the presence of outsiders, Dr Hutchins – as 'a natural intellectual resource.' What these highly skilled public-relations experts do, besides clarifying the basic issues and giving a lift to Bennett Cerf ('My talk with Paul Hoffman on the Coast gave me a lift I won't forget,' Bennett Cerf observed some time ago), is to gather every weekday for a few hours of discussion, usually about one of several broad areas that the Center is concentrating upon at any given time – The City, say, or The Emerging Constitution. Papers are prepared, read, revised, reread, and sometimes finally published. This process is variously described by those who participate in it as 'pointing the direction for all of us toward a greater understanding' and 'applying human reason to the complex problems of our brand-new world.'

I have long been interested in the Center's rhetoric, which has about it the kind of ectoplasmic generality that always makes me sense I am on the track of the real soufflé, the genuine American *kitsch*, and so not long ago I arranged to attend a few sessions in Santa Barbara. It was in no sense time wasted. The Center is the most perfectly indigenous cultural phenomenon since the Encyclopaedia Britannica's *Syntopicon*, which sets forth 'The 102 Great Ideas of Western Man' and which we also owe to Robert, or Dr, Hutchins. 'Don't make the mistake of taking a chair at the big table,' I was warned *sotto voce* on my first visit to the Center. 'The talk there is pretty high-powered.'

'Is there any evidence that living in a violent age encourages violence?' someone was asking at the big table.

'That's hard to measure.'

'I think it's the Westerns on television.'

'I tend [*pause*] to agree.'

Every word uttered at the Center is preserved on tape, and not only colleges and libraries but thousands of individuals receive Center tapes and pamphlets. Among the best-selling pamphlets have been A. A. Berle, Jr's *Economic Power and the Free Society*, Clark Kerr's *Unions and Union Leaders of Their Own Choosing*, Donald Michael's

Cybernation: The Silent Conquest, and Harrison Brown's *Community of Fear.* Seventy-five thousand people a year then write fan letters to the Center, confirming the staff in its conviction that everything said around the place mystically improves the national, and in fact the international, weal. From a Colorado country-day-school teacher: 'I use the Center's various papers in my U.S. history-current events course. It seems to me that there is no institution in the U.S. today engaged in more valuable and first-rate work than the Center.' From a California mother: 'Now my fifteen-year-old daughter has discovered your publications. This delights me as she is one of those regular teenagers. But when she curls up to read, it is with your booklets.'

The notion that providing useful papers for eighth-grade current-events classes and reading for regular teenagers might not be at all times compatible with establishing 'a true intellectual community' (another Hutchins aim) would be considered, at the Center, a downbeat and undemocratic cavil. 'People are entitled to learn what we're thinking,' someone there told me. The place is in fact avidly anti-intellectual, the deprecatory use of words like 'egghead' and 'ivory tower' reaching heights matched only in a country-club locker room. Hutchins takes pains to explain that by 'an intellectual community' he does not mean a community 'whose members regard themselves as "intellectuals."' Harry Ashmore frets particularly that 'men of affairs' may fail to perceive the Center's 'practical utility.' Hutchins likes to quote Adlai Stevenson on this point: 'The Center can be thought of as a kind of national insurance plan, a way of making certain that we will deserve better and better.'

Although one suspects that this pragmatic Couéism as a mode of thought comes pretty naturally to most of the staff at the Center, it is also vital to the place's survival. In 1959 the Fund for the Republic bequeathed to the Center the $4 million left of its original $15 million Ford Foundation grant, but that is long gone, and because there was never any question of more Ford money, the Center must pay its own way. Its own way costs about a million dollars a year. Some twelve thousand contributors provide the million a year, and it helps if they can think of a gift to the Center not as a gift to support some visionaries who never met a payroll but 'as an investment [tax-exempt] in the preservation of our free way of life.' It helps, too, to present the donor with a fairly broadstroke picture of how the Center is besieged by the forces of darkness, and in this effort the Center has had an invaluable, if unintentional, ally in the Santa Barbara John Birch Society. 'You can't let the fascists drive them out of town,' I was advised by an admirer of the Center.

Actually, even without the Birch Society as a foil, Hutchins has evolved the $E=mc^2$ of all fund-raising formulae. The Center is supported on the same principle as a vanity press. People who are in a position to contribute large sums of money are encouraged to participate in clarifying the basic issues. Dinah Shore, a founding member, is invited up to discuss civil rights with Bayard Rustin. Steve Allen talks over 'Ideology and Intervention' with Senator Fulbright and Arnold Toynbee, and Kirk Douglas, a founding member, speaks his piece on 'The Arts in a Democratic Society.' Paul Newman, in the role of 'concerned citizen,' is on hand to discuss 'The University in America' with Dr Hutchins, Supreme Court Justice William O. Douglas, Arnold Grant, Rosemary Park, and another concerned citizen, Jack Lemmon. 'Apropos of absolutely nothing,' Mr Lemmon says, pulling on a pipe, 'just for my own amazement – I don't *know*, but I *want* to know – ' At this juncture he wants to know about student unrest, and, at another, he worries that government contracts will corrupt 'pure research.'

'You mean maybe they get a grant to develop some new kind of *plastic*,' Mr Newman muses, and Mr Lemmon picks up the cue: 'What happens then to the humanities?'

Everyone goes home flattered, and the Center prevails. Well, why not? One morning I was talking with the wife of a big contributor as we waited on the terrace for one of the Center's ready-mixed martinis and a few moments' chat with Dr Hutchins. 'These sessions are way over my head,' she confided, 'but I go out floating on air.'

1967

Marrying Absurd

To be married in Las Vegas, Clark County, Nevada, a bride must swear that she is eighteen or has parental permission and a bridegroom that he is twenty-one or has parental permission. Someone must put up five dollars for the license. (On Sundays and holidays, fifteen dollars. The Clark County Courthouse issues marriage licenses at any time of the day or night except between noon and one in the afternoon, between eight and nine in the evening, and between four and five in the morning.) Nothing else is required. The State of Nevada, alone among these United States, demands neither a premarital blood test nor a waiting period before or after the issuance of a marriage license. Driving in across the Mojave from Los Angeles, one sees the signs way out on the desert, looming up from that moonscape of rattlesnakes and mesquite, even before the Las Vegas lights appear like a mirage on the horizon: 'GETTING MARRIED? Free License Information First Strip Exit.' Perhaps the Las Vegas wedding industry achieved its peak operational efficiency between 9:00 p.m. and midnight of August 26, 1965, an otherwise unremarkable Thursday which happened to be, by Presidential order, the last day on which anyone could improve his draft status merely by getting married. One hundred and seventy-one couples were pronounced man and wife in the name of Clark County and the State of Nevada that night, sixty-seven of them by a single justice of the peace, Mr James A. Brennan. Mr Brennan did one wedding at the Dunes and the other sixty-six in his office, and charged each couple eight dollars. One bride lent her veil to six others. 'I got it down from five to three minutes,' Mr Brennan said later of his feat. 'I could've married them *en masse*, but they're people, not cattle. People expect more when they get married.'

What people who get married in Las Vegas actually do expect – what, in the largest sense, their 'expectations' are – strikes one as a curious and self-contradictory business. Las Vegas is the most extreme and allegorical of American settlements, bizarre and beautiful in its venality and in its devotion to immediate gratification, a place the tone of which is set by mobsters and call girls and ladies' room attendants with amyl nitrite poppers in their uniform pockets. Almost everyone notes that there is no 'time' in Las Vegas, no night and no day and no past and no future (no Las Vegas casino, however, has taken the obliteration of the ordinary time sense quite so far as Harold's Club in Reno, which for a while issued, at odd intervals in the day and night, mimeographed 'bulletins' carrying news from the world outside); neither is there any logical sense of where one is. One is standing on a highway in the middle of a vast hostile desert looking at an eighty-foot sign which blinks 'STARDUST' or 'CAESAR'S PALACE.' Yes, but what does that explain? This geographical implausibility reinforces the sense that what happens there has no connection with 'real' life; Nevada cities like Reno and Carson are ranch towns, Western towns, places behind which there is some historical imperative. But Las Vegas seems to exist only in the eye of the beholder. All of which makes it an extraordinarily stimulating and interesting place, but an odd one in which to want to wear a candlelight satin Priscilla of Boston wedding dress with Chantilly lace insets, tapered sleeves and a detachable modified train.

And yet the Las Vegas wedding business seems to appeal to precisely that impulse. 'Sincere and Dignified Since 1954,' one wedding chapel advertises. There are nineteen such wedding chapels in Las Vegas, intensely competitive, each offering better, faster, and, by implication, more sincere services than the next: Our Photos Best Anywhere, Your Wedding on A Phonograph Record, Candlelight with Your Ceremony, Honeymoon Accommodations, Free Transportation from Your Motel to Courthouse to Chapel and Return to Motel, Religious or Civil Ceremonies, Dressing Rooms, Flowers, Rings, Announcements, Witnesses Available, and Ample Parking. All of these services, like most others in Las Vegas (sauna baths, payroll-check cashing, chinchilla coats for sale or rent) are offered twenty-four hours a day, seven days a week, presumably on the premise that marriage, like craps, is a game to be played when the table seems hot.

But what strikes one most about the Strip chapels, with their wishing wells and stained-glass paper windows and their artificial bouvardia, is that so much of their business is by no means a matter of simple convenience, of late-night liaisons between show girls and baby Crosbys. Of course there is some of that. (One night about eleven o'clock in Las Vegas I watched a bride in an orange minidress and masses of flame-colored hair stumble from a Strip chapel on the arm of her bridegroom, who looked the part of the expendable nephew in movies like *Miami Syndicate*. 'I gotta get the kids,' the bride whimpered. 'I gotta pick up the sitter, I gotta get to the midnight show.' 'What you gotta get,' the bridegroom said, opening the door of a Cadillac Coupe de Ville and watching her crumple on the seat, 'is sober.') But Las Vegas seems to offer something other than 'convenience'; it is merchandising 'niceness,' the facsimile of proper ritual, to children who do not know how else to find it, how to make the arrangements, how to do it 'right.' All day and evening long on the Strip, one sees actual wedding parties, waiting under the harsh lights at a crosswalk, standing uneasily in the parking lot of the Frontier while the photographer hired by The Little Church of the West ('Wedding Place of the Stars') certifies the occasion, takes the picture: the bride in a veil and white satin pumps, the bridegroom usually in a white dinner jacket, and even an attendant or two, a sister or a best friend in hot-pink *peau de soie*, a flirtation veil, a carnation nosegay. 'When I Fall in Love It Will Be Forever,' the organist plays, and then a few bars of Lohengrin. The mother cries; the stepfather, awkward in his role, invites the chapel hostess to join them for a drink at the Sands. The hostess declines with a professional smile; she has already transferred her interest to the group waiting outside. One bride out, another in, and again the sign goes up on the chapel door: 'One moment please – Wedding.'

I sat next to one such wedding party in a Strip restaurant the last time I was in Las Vegas. The marriage had just taken place; the bride still wore her dress, the mother her corsage. A bored waiter poured out a few swallows of pink champagne ('on the house') for everyone but the bride, who was too young to be served. 'You'll need something with more kick than that,' the bride's father said with heavy jocularity to his new son-in-law; the ritual jokes about the wedding night had a certain Panglossian character, since the bride was clearly several months pregnant. Another round of pink champagne, this time not on the house, and the bride began to cry. 'It was just as nice,' she sobbed, 'as I hoped and dreamed it would be.'

1967

Slouching Towards Bethlehem

The center was not holding. It was a country of bankruptcy notices and public-auction announcements and commonplace reports of casual killings and misplaced children and abandoned homes and vandals who misspelled even the four-letter words they scrawled. It was a country in which families routinely disappeared, trailing bad checks and repossession papers. Adolescents drifted from city to torn city, sloughing off both the past and the future as snakes shed their skins, children who were never taught and would never now learn the games that had held the society together. People were missing. Children were missing. Parents were missing. Those left behind filed desultory missing-persons reports, then moved on themselves.

It was not a country in open revolution. It was not a country under enemy siege. It was the United States of America in the cold late spring of 1967, and the market was steady and the G.N.P. high and a great many articulate people seemed to have a sense of high social purpose and it might have been a spring of brave hopes and national promise, but it was not, and more and more people had the uneasy apprehension that it was not. All that seemed clear was that at some point we had aborted ourselves and butchered the job, and because nothing else seemed so relevant I decided to go to San Francisco. San Francisco was where the social hemorrhaging was showing up. San Francisco was where the missing children were gathering and calling themselves 'hippies.' When I first went to San Francisco in that cold late spring of 1967 I did not even know what

I wanted to find out, and so I just stayed around awhile, and made a few friends.

A sign on Haight Street, San Francisco:

> *Last Easter Day*
> *My Christopher Robin wandered away.*
> *He called April 10th*
> *But he hasn't called since*
> *He said he was coming home*
> *But he hasn't shown.*
>
> *If you see him on Haight*
> *Please tell him not to wait*
> *I need him now*
> *I don't care how*
> *If he needs the bread*
> *I'll send it ahead.*
>
> *If there's hope*
> *Please write me a note*
> *If he's still there*
> *Tell him how much I care*
> *Where he's at I need to know*
> *For I really love him so!*
>
> > *Deeply,*
> > *Marla*
>
> *Marla Pence*
> *12702 NE. Multnomah*
> *Portland, Ore. 97230*
> *503/252-2720.*

I am looking for somebody called Deadeye and I hear he is on the Street this afternoon doing a little business, so I keep an eye out for him and pretend to read the signs in the Psychedelic Shop on Haight

Street when a kid, sixteen, seventeen, comes in and sits on the floor
beside me.

'What are you looking for,' he says.

I say nothing much.

'I been out of my mind for three days,' he says. He tells me he's
been shooting crystal, which I already pretty much know because
he does not bother to keep his sleeves rolled down over the needle
tracks. He came up from Los Angeles some number of weeks ago,
he doesn't remember what number, and now he'll take off for New
York, if he can find a ride. I show him a sign offering a ride to
Chicago. He wonders where Chicago is. I ask where he comes from.
'Here,' he says. I mean before here. 'San Jose, Chula Vista, I dunno.
My mother's in Chula Vista.'

A few days later I run into him in Golden Gate Park when the
Grateful Dead are playing. I ask if he found a ride to New York. 'I
hear New York's a bummer,' he says.

Deadeye never showed up that day on the Street, and somebody
says maybe I can find him at his place. It is three o'clock and Deadeye
is in bed. Somebody else is asleep on the living-room couch, and a
girl is sleeping on the floor beneath a poster of Allen Ginsberg, and
there are a couple of girls in pajamas making instant coffee. One of
the girls introduces me to the friend on the couch, who extends one
arm but does not get up because he is naked. Deadeye and I have a
mutual acquaintance, but he does not mention his name in front of
the others. 'The man you talked to,' he says, or 'that man I was
referring to earlier.' The man is a cop.

The room is overheated and the girl on the floor is sick. Deadeye
says she has been sleeping for twenty-four hours now. 'Lemme ask
you something,' he says. 'You want some grass?' I say I have to be
moving on. 'You want it,' Deadeye says, 'it's yours.' Deadeye used
to be an Angel around Los Angeles but that was a few years ago.
'Right now,' he says, 'I'm trying to set up this groovy religious group
– "Teenage Evangelism."'

*   *   *

Don and Max want to go out to dinner but Don is only eating macrobiotic so we end up in Japantown again. Max is telling me how he lives free of all the old middle-class Freudian hang-ups. 'I've had this old lady for a couple of months now, maybe she makes something special for my dinner and I come in three days late and tell her I've been balling some other chick, well, maybe she shouts a little but then I say "That's me, baby," and she laughs and says "That's you, Max." ' Max says it works both ways. 'I mean if she comes in and tells me she wants to ball Don, maybe, I say "O.K., baby, it's your trip." '

Max sees his life as a triumph over 'don'ts.' Among the don'ts he had done before he was twenty-one were peyote, alcohol, mescaline, and Methedrine. He was on a Meth trip for three years in New York and Tangier before he found acid. He first tried peyote when he was in an Arkansas boys' school and got down to the Gulf and met 'an Indian kid who was doing a don't. Then every weekend I could get loose I'd hitchhike seven hundred miles to Brownsville, Texas, so I could cop peyote. Peyote went for thirty cents a button down in Brownsville on the street.' Max dropped in and out of most of the schools and fashionable clinics in the eastern half of America, his standard technique for dealing with boredom being to leave. Example: Max was in a hospital in New York and 'the night nurse was a groovy spade, and in the afternoon for therapy there was a chick from Israel who was interesting, but there was nothing much to do in the morning, so I left.'

We drink some more green tea and talk about going up to Malakoff Diggings in Nevada County because some people are starting a commune there and Max thinks it would be a groove to take acid in the diggings. He says maybe we could go next week, or the week after, or anyway sometime before his case comes up. Almost everybody I meet in San Francisco has to go to court at some point in the middle future. I never ask why.

I am still interested in how Max got rid of his middle-class Freudian hang-ups and I ask if he is now completely free.

'Nah,' he says. 'I got acid.'

Max drops a 250- or 350-microgram tab every six or seven days.

Max and Don share a joint in the car and we go over to North Beach to find out if Otto, who has a temporary job there, wants to go to Malakoff Diggings. Otto is pitching some electronics engineers. The engineers view our arrival with some interest, maybe, I think, because Max is wearing bells and an Indian headband. Max has a low tolerance for straight engineers and their Freudian hang-ups. 'Look at 'em,' he says. 'They're always yelling "queer" and then they come sneaking down to the Haight-Ashbury trying to get the hippie chick because she fucks.'

We do not get around to asking Otto about Malakoff Diggings because he wants to tell me about a fourteen-year-old he knows who got busted in the Park the other day. She was just walking through the Park, he says, minding her own, carrying her school-books, when the cops took her in and booked her and gave her a pelvic. *Fourteen years old,* Otto says. 'A *pelvic.*'

'Coming down from acid,' he adds, 'that could be a real bad trip.'

I call Otto the next afternoon to see if he can reach the fourteen-year-old. It turns out she is tied up with rehearsals for her junior-high-school play, *The Wizard of Oz*. 'Yellow-brick-road time,' Otto says. Otto was sick all day. He thinks it was some cocaine-and-wheat somebody gave him.

There are always little girls around rock groups – the same little girls who used to hang around saxophone players, girls who live on the celebrity and power and sex a band projects when it plays – and there are three of them out here this afternoon in Sausalito where the Grateful Dead rehearse. They are all pretty and two of them still have baby fat and one of them dances by herself with her eyes closed.

I ask a couple of the girls what they do.

'I just kind of come out here a lot,' one of them says.

'I just sort of know the Dead,' the other says.

The one who just sort of knows the Dead starts cutting up a loaf of French bread on the piano bench. The boys take a break and one of them talks about playing the Los Angeles Cheetah, which is in the old Aragon Ballroom. 'We were up there drinking beer where Lawrence Welk used to sit,' Jerry Garcia says.

The little girl who was dancing by herself giggles. 'Too much,' she says softly. Her eyes are still closed.

Somebody said that if I was going to meet some runaways I better pick up a few hamburgers and Cokes on the way, so I did, and we are eating them in the Park together, me, Debbie who is fifteen, and Jeff who is sixteen. Debbie and Jeff ran away twelve days ago, walked out of school one morning with $100 between them. Because a missing-juvenile is out on Debbie – she was already on probation because her mother had once taken her down to the police station and declared her incorrigible – this is only the second time they have been out of a friend's apartment since they got to San Francisco. The first time they went over to the Fairmont Hotel and rode the outside elevator, three times up and three times down. 'Wow,' Jeff says, and that is all he can think to say, about that.

I ask why they ran away.

'My parents said I had to go to church,' Debbie says. 'And they wouldn't let me dress the way I wanted. In the seventh grade my skirts were longer than anybody's – it got better in the eighth grade, but still.'

'Your mother was kind of a bummer,' Jeff agrees.

'They didn't like Jeff. They didn't like my girlfriends. My father thought I was cheap and he told me so. I had a C average and he told me I couldn't date until I raised it, and that bugged me too.'

'My mother was just a genuine all-American bitch,' Jeff says. 'She was really troublesome about hair. Also she didn't like boots. It was really weird.'

'Tell about the chores,' Debbie says.

'For example I had chores. If I didn't finish ironing my shirts for the week I couldn't go out for the weekend. It was weird. Wow.'

Debbie giggles and shakes her head. 'This year's gonna be wild.'

'We're just gonna let it all happen,' Jeff says. 'Everything's in the future, you can't pre-plan it. First we get jobs, then a place to live. Then, I dunno.'

Jeff finishes off the French fries and gives some thought to what kind of job he could get. 'I always kinda dug metal shop, welding, stuff like that.' Maybe he could work on cars, I say. 'I'm not too mechanically minded,' he says. 'Anyway you can't pre-plan.'

'I could get a job baby-sitting,' Debbie says. 'Or in a dime store.'

'You're always talking about getting a job in a dime store,' Jeff says.

'That's because I worked in a dime store already.'

Debbie is buffing her fingernails with the belt to her suède jacket. She is annoyed because she chipped a nail and because I do not have any polish remover in the car. I promise to get her to a friend's apartment so that she can redo her manicure, but something has been bothering me and as I fiddle with the ignition I finally ask it. I ask them to think back to when they were children, to tell me what they had wanted to be when they were grown up, how they had seen the future then.

Jeff throws a Coca-Cola bottle out the car window. 'I can't remember I ever thought about it,' he says.

'I remember I wanted to be a veterinarian once,' Debbie says. 'But now I'm more or less working in the vein of being an artist or a model or a cosmetologist. Or something.'

I hear quite a bit about one cop, Officer Arthur Gerrans, whose name has become a synonym for zealotry on the Street. 'He's our Officer Krupke,' Max once told me. Max is not personally wild about Officer Gerrans because Officer Gerrans took Max in after the Human Be-In last winter, that's the big Human Be-In in Golden Gate Park where 20,000 people got turned on free, or 10,000 did, or some number did, but then Officer Gerrans has busted almost everyone in the District at one time or another. Presumably to forestall a cult of personality, Officer Gerrans was transferred out of the District not long ago, and when I see him it is not at the Park Station but at the Central Station on Greenwich Avenue.

We are in an interrogation room, and I am interrogating Officer Gerrans. He is young and blond and wary and I go in slow. I wonder what he thinks 'the major problems' in the Haight are.

Officer Gerrans thinks it over. 'I would say the major problems there,' he says finally, 'the major problems are narcotics and juveniles. Juveniles and narcotics, those are your major problems.'

I write that down.

'Just one moment,' Officer Gerrans says, and leaves the room. When he comes back he tells me that I cannot talk to him without permission from Chief Thomas Cahill.

'In the meantime,' Officer Gerrans adds, pointing at the notebook in which I have written *major problems: juveniles, narcotics,* 'I'll take those notes.'

The next day I apply for permission to talk to Officer Gerrans and also to Chief Cahill. A few days later a sergeant returns my call.

'We have finally received clearance from the Chief per your request,' the sergeant says, 'and that is taboo.'

I wonder why it is taboo to talk to Officer Gerrans.

Officer Gerrans is involved in court cases coming to trial.

I wonder why it is taboo to talk to Chief Cahill.

The Chief has pressing police business.

I wonder if I can talk to anyone at all in the Police Department.

'No,' the sergeant says, 'not at the particular moment.'

Which was my last official contact with the San Francisco Police Department.

Norris and I are standing around the Panhandle and Norris is telling me how it is all set up for a friend to take me to Big Sur. I say what I really want to do is spend a few days with Norris and his wife and the rest of the people in their house. Norris says it would be a lot easier if I'd take some acid. I say I'm unstable. Norris says all right, anyway, *grass,* and he squeezes my hand.

One day Norris asks how old I am. I tell him I am thirty-two. It takes a few minutes, but Norris rises to it. 'Don't worry,' he says at last. 'There's old hippies too.'

It is a pretty nice evening and nothing much happening and Max brings his old lady, Sharon, over to the Warehouse. The Warehouse, which is where Don and a floating number of other people live, is not actually a warehouse but the garage of a condemned hotel. The Warehouse was conceived as total theater, a continual happening, and I always feel good there. What happened ten minutes ago or what is going to happen a half hour from now tends to fade from

mind in the Warehouse. Somebody is usually doing something interesting, like working on a light show, and there are a lot of interesting
things around, like an old Chevrolet touring car which is used as a
bed and a vast American flag fluttering up in the shadows and an
overstuffed chair suspended like a swing from the rafters, the point
of that being that it gives you a sensory-deprivation high.

One reason I particularly like the Warehouse is that a child named
Michael is staying there now. Michael's mother, Sue Ann, is a sweet
wan girl who is always in the kitchen cooking seaweed or baking
macrobiotic bread while Michael amuses himself with joss sticks or
an old tambourine or a rocking horse with the paint worn off. The
first time I ever saw Michael was on that rocking horse, a very blond
and pale and dirty child on a rocking horse with no paint. A blue
theatrical spotlight was the only light in the Warehouse that afternoon, and there was Michael in it, crooning softly to the wooden
horse. Michael is three years old. He is a bright child but does not
yet talk.

This particular night Michael is trying to light his joss sticks and
there are the usual number of people floating through and they all
drift into Don's room and sit on the bed and pass joints. Sharon is
very excited when she arrives.

'Don,' she cries, breathless. 'We got some STP today.' At this time
STP is a pretty big deal, remember; nobody yet knew what it was and
it was relatively, although just relatively, hard to come by. Sharon is
blond and scrubbed and probably seventeen, but Max is a little vague
about that since his court case comes up in a month or so and he
doesn't need statutory rape on top of it. Sharon's parents were living
apart when last she saw them. She does not miss school or anything
much about her past, except her younger brother. 'I want to turn
him on,' she confided one day. 'He's fourteen now, that's the perfect
age. I know where he goes to high school and someday I'll just go
get him.'

Time passes and I lose the thread and when I pick it up again Max
seems to be talking about what a beautiful thing it is the way Sharon
washes dishes.

'Well it *is* beautiful,' Sharon says. '*Everything* is. I mean you watch
that blue detergent blob run on the plate, watch the grease cut –
well, it can be a real trip.'

Pretty soon now, maybe next month, maybe later, Max and Sharon plan to leave for Africa and India, where they can live off the land. 'I got this little trust fund, see,' Max says, 'which is useful in that it tells cops and border patrols I'm O.K., but living off the land is the thing. You can get your high and get your dope in the city, O.K., but we gotta get out somewhere and live organically.'

'Roots and things,' Sharon says, lighting another joss stick for Michael. Michael's mother is still in the kitchen cooking seaweed. 'You can eat them.'

Maybe eleven o'clock, we move from the Warehouse to the place where Max and Sharon live with a couple named Tom and Barbara. Sharon is pleased to get home ('I hope you got some hash joints fixed in the kitchen,' she says to Barbara by way of greeting) and everybody is pleased to show off the apartment, which has a lot of flowers and candles and paisleys. Max and Sharon and Tom and Barbara get pretty high on hash, and everyone dances a little and we do some liquid projections and set up a strobe and take turns getting a high on that. Quite late, somebody called Steve comes in with a pretty, dark girl. They have been to a meeting of people who practice a Western yoga, but they do not seem to want to talk about that. They lie on the floor awhile, and then Steve stands up.

'Max,' he says, 'I want to say one thing.'

'It's your trip.' Max is edgy.

'I found love on acid. But I lost it. And now I'm finding it again. With nothing but grass.'

Max mutters that heaven and hell are both in one's karma.

'That's what bugs me about psychedelic art,' Steve says.

'What about psychedelic art,' Max says. 'I haven't seen much psychedelic art.'

Max is lying on a bed with Sharon, and Steve leans down to him. 'Groove, baby,' he says. 'You're a groove.'

Steve sits down then and tells me about one summer when he was at a school of design in Rhode Island and took thirty trips, the last ones all bad. I ask why they were bad. 'I could tell you it was my neuroses,' he says, 'but fuck that.'

A few days later I drop by to see Steve in his apartment. He paces nervously around the room he uses as a studio and shows me some paintings. We do not seem to be getting to the point.

'Maybe you noticed something going on at Max's,' he says abruptly.

It seems that the girl he brought, the dark pretty one, had once been Max's girl. She had followed him to Tangier and now to San Francisco. But Max has Sharon. 'So she's kind of staying around here,' Steve says.

Steve is troubled by a lot of things. He is twenty-three, was raised in Virginia, and has the idea that California is the beginning of the end. 'I feel it's insane,' he says, and his voice drops. 'This chick tells me there's no meaning to life but it doesn't matter, we'll just flow right out. There've been times I felt like packing up and taking off for the East Coast again, at least there I had a *target*. At least there you expect that it's going to *happen*.' He lights a cigarette for me and his hands shake. 'Here you know it's not going to.'

I ask what it is that is supposed to happen.

'I don't know,' he says. 'Something. Anything.'

Arthur Lisch is on the telephone in his kitchen, trying to sell VISTA a program for the District. 'We already *got* an emergency,' he says into the telephone, meanwhile trying to disentangle his daughter, age one and a half, from the cord. 'We don't get help here, nobody can guarantee what's going to happen. We've got people sleeping in the streets here. We've got people starving to death.' He pauses. 'All right,' he says then, and his voice rises. 'So they're doing it by choice. So what.'

By the time he hangs up he has limned what strikes me as a pretty Dickensian picture of life on the edge of Golden Gate Park, but then this is my first exposure to Arthur Lisch's 'riot-on-the-Street-unless' pitch. Arthur Lisch is a kind of leader of the Diggers, who, in the official District mythology, are supposed to be a group of anonymous good guys with no thought in their collective head but to lend a helping hand. The official District mythology also has it that the Diggers have no 'leaders,' but nonetheless Arthur Lisch is one. Arthur Lisch is also a paid worker for the American Friends' Service Committee and he lives with his wife, Jane, and their two small children in a railroad flat, which on this particular day lacks organization. For one thing the telephone keeps ringing. Arthur promises to attend a hearing at city hall. Arthur promises to 'send Edward, he's O.K.' Arthur promises to get a good group, maybe the Loading Zone, to play free for a Jewish benefit. For a second thing the baby is crying, and she does not stop until Jane Lisch appears with a jar of Gerber's Junior Chicken Noodle Dinner. Another confusing element is somebody named Bob, who just sits in the living room and looks at his toes. First he looks at the toes on one foot, then at the toes on the other. I make several attempts to include Bob in the conversation before I realize he is on a bad trip. Moreover, there are two people hacking up what looks like a side of beef on the kitchen floor, the idea being that when it gets hacked up, Jane Lisch can cook it for the daily Digger feed in the Park.

Arthur Lisch does not seem to notice any of this. He just keeps talking about cybernated societies and the guaranteed annual wage and riot on the Street, unless.

I call the Lisches a day or so later and ask for Arthur. Jane Lisch says he's next door taking a shower because somebody is coming down from a bad trip in their bathroom. Besides the freak-out in the bathroom they are expecting a psychiatrist in to look at Bob. Also a doctor for Edward, who is not O.K. at all but has the flu. Jane says maybe I should talk to Chester Anderson. She will not give me his number.

Chester Anderson is a legacy of the Beat Generation, a man in his middle thirties whose peculiar hold on the District derives from his possession of a mimeograph machine, on which he prints communiqués signed 'the communication company.' It is another tenet of the official District mythology that the communication company will print anything anybody has to say, but in fact Chester Anderson prints only what he writes himself, agrees with, or considers harmless or dead matter. His statements, which are left in piles and pasted on windows around Haight Street, are regarded with some apprehension in the District and with considerable interest by outsiders, who study them, like China watchers, for subtle shifts in obscure ideologies. An Anderson communiqué might be doing something as specific as fingering someone who is said to have set up a marijuana bust, or it might be working in a more general vein:

Pretty little 16-year-old middle-class chick comes to the Haight
to see what it's all about & gets picked up by a 17-year-old
street dealer who spends all day shooting her full of speed
again & again, then feeds her 3,000 mikes & raffles off her
temporarily unemployed body for the biggest Haight Street
gangbang since the night before last. The politics and ethics of
ecstasy. Rape is as common as bullshit on Haight Street. Kids
are starving on the Street. Minds and bodies are being maimed
as we watch, a scale model of Vietnam.

Somebody other than Jane Lisch gave me an address for Chester
Anderson, 443 Arguello, but 443 Arguello does not exist. I telephone
the wife of the man who gave me 443 Arguello and she says it's 742
Arguello.

'But don't go up there,' she says.

I say I'll telephone.

'There's no number,' she says. 'I can't give it to you.'

'742 Arguello,' I say.

'No,' she says. 'I don't know. And don't go there. And don't use
either my name or my husband's name if you do.'

She is the wife of a full professor of English at San Francisco State
College. I decide to lie low on the question of Chester Anderson for
awhile.

> *Paranoia strikes deep –*
> *Into your life it will creep –*
>   is a song the Buffalo
>   Springfield sings.

The appeal of Malakoff Diggings has kind of faded out but Max says
why don't I come to his place, just be there, the next time he takes
acid. Tom will take it too, probably Sharon, maybe Barbara. We can't
do it for six or seven days because Max and Tom are in STP space
now. They are not crazy about STP but it has advantages. 'You've
still got your forebrain,' Tom says. 'I could write behind STP, but not
behind acid.' This is the first time I have heard of anything you can't
do behind acid, also the first time I have heard that Tom writes.

                    *   *   *

Otto is feeling better because he discovered it wasn't the cocaine-and-wheat that made him sick. It was the chicken pox, which he caught baby-sitting for Big Brother and the Holding Company one night when they were playing. I go over to see him and meet Vicki, who sings now and then with a group called the Jook Savages and lives at Otto's place. Vicki dropped out of Laguna High 'because I had mono,' followed the Grateful Dead up to San Francisco one time and has been here 'for a while.' Her mother and father are divorced, and she does not see her father, who works for a network in New York. A few months ago he came out to do a documentary on the District and tried to find her, but couldn't. Later he wrote her a letter in care of her mother urging her to go back to school. Vicki guesses maybe she will sometime but she doesn't see much point in it right now.

We are eating a little tempura in Japantown, Chet Helms and I, and he is sharing some of his insights with me. Until a couple of years ago Chet Helms never did much besides hitchhiking, but now he runs the Avalon Ballroom and flies over the Pole to check out the London scene and says things like 'Just for the sake of clarity I'd like to categorize the aspects of primitive religion as I see it.' Right now he is talking about Marshall McLuhan and how the printed word is finished, out, over. 'The *East Village Other* is one of the few papers in America whose books are in the black,' he says. 'I know that from reading *Barron's*.'

A new group is supposed to play in the Panhandle today but they are having trouble with the amplifier and I sit in the sun listening to a couple of little girls, maybe seventeen years old. One of them has a lot of makeup and the other wears Levi's and cowboy boots. The boots do not look like an affectation, they look like she came up off a ranch about two weeks ago. I wonder what she is doing here in the Panhandle trying to make friends with a city girl who is snubbing her but I do not wonder long, because she is homely and awkward and I think of her going all the way through the consolidated union high school out there where she comes from and nobody ever asking

her to go into Reno on Saturday night for a drive-in movie and a
beer on the riverbank, so she runs. 'I know a thing about dollar bills,'
she is saying now. 'You get one that says "1111" in one corner and
"1111" in another, you take it down to Dallas, Texas, they'll give
you $15 for it.'

'Who will?' the city girl asks.

'I don't know.'

'There are only three significant pieces of data in the world today,'
is another thing Chet Helms told me one night. We were at the
Avalon and the big strobe was going and the colored lights and the
Day-Glo painting and the place was full of high-school kids trying to
look turned on. The Avalon sound system projects 126 decibels at
100 feet but to Chet Helms the sound is just there, like the air, and
he talks through it. 'The first is,' he said, 'God died last year and was
obited by the press. The second is, fifty percent of the population is
or will be under twenty-five.' A boy shook a tambourine toward us
and Chet smiled benevolently at him. 'The third,' he said, 'is that
they got twenty billion irresponsible dollars to spend.'

Thursday comes, some Thursday, and Max and Tom and Sharon and
maybe Barbara are going to take some acid. They want to drop it
about three o'clock. Barbara has baked fresh bread, Max has gone to
the Park for fresh flowers, and Sharon is making a sign for the door
which reads 'DO NOT DISTURB, RING, KNOCK, OR IN ANY OTHER WAY
DISTURB. LOVE.' This is not how I would put it to either the health
inspector, who is due this week, or any of the several score narcotics
agents in the neighborhood, but I figure the sign is Sharon's trip.

Once the sign is finished Sharon gets restless. 'Can I at least play
the new record?' she asks Max.

'Tom and Barbara want to save it for when we're high.'

'I'm getting bored, just sitting around here.'

Max watches her jump up and walk out. 'That's what you call
pre-acid uptight jitters,' he says.

Barbara is not in evidence. Tom keeps walking in and out. 'All
these innumerable last-minute things you have to do,' he mutters.

'It's a tricky thing, acid,' Max says after a while. He is turning the stereo on and off. 'When a chick takes acid, it's all right if she's alone, but when she's living with somebody this edginess comes out. And if the hour-and-a-half process before you take the acid doesn't go smooth . . .' He picks up a roach and studies it, then adds, 'They're having a little thing back there with Barbara.'

Sharon and Tom walk in.

'You pissed off too?' Max asks Sharon.

Sharon does not answer.

Max turns to Tom. 'Is she all right?'

'Yeh.'

'Can we take acid?' Max is on edge.

'I don't know what she's going to do.'

'What do you want to do?'

'What I want to do depends on what she wants to do.' Tom is rolling some joints, first rubbing the papers with a marijuana resin he makes himself. He takes the joints back to the bedroom, and Sharon goes with him.

'Something like this happens every time people take acid,' Max says. After a while he brightens and develops a theory around it. 'Some people don't like to go out of themselves, that's the trouble. You probably wouldn't. You'd probably like only a quarter of a tab. There's still an ego on a quarter tab, and it wants things. Now if that thing is balling – and your old lady or your old man is off somewhere flashing and doesn't want to be touched – well, you get put down on acid, you can be on a bummer for months.'

Sharon drifts in, smiling. 'Barbara might take some acid, we're all feeling better, we smoked a joint.'

At three-thirty that afternoon Max, Tom, and Sharon placed tabs under their tongues and sat down together in the living room to wait for the flash. Barbara stayed in the bedroom, smoking hash. During the next four hours a window banged once in Barbara's room, and about five-thirty some children had a fight on the street. A curtain billowed in the afternoon wind. A cat scratched a beagle in Sharon's lap. Except for the sitar music on the stereo there was no other sound or movement until seven-thirty, when Max said 'Wow.'

*   *   *

I spot Deadeye on Haight Street, and he gets in the car. Until we get off the Street he sits very low and inconspicuous. Deadeye wants me to meet his old lady, but first he wants to talk to me about how he got hip to helping people.

'Here I was, just a tough kid on a motorcycle,' he says, 'and suddenly I see that young people don't have to walk alone.' Deadeye has a clear evangelistic gaze and the reasonable rhetoric of a car salesman. He is society's model product. I try to meet his gaze directly because he once told me he could read character in people's eyes, particularly if he has just dropped acid, which he did, about nine o'clock this morning. 'They just have to remember one thing,' he says. 'The Lord's Prayer. And that can help them in more ways than one.'

He takes a much-folded letter from his wallet. The letter is from a little girl he helped. 'My loving brother,' it begins. 'I thought I'd write you a letter since I'm a part of you. Remember that: When you feel happiness, I do, when you feel . . .'

'What I want to do now,' Deadeye says, 'is set up a house where a person of any age can come, spend a few days, talk over his problems. *Any age*. People your age, they've got problems too.'

I say a house will take money.

'I've found a way to make money,' Deadeye says. He hesitates only a few seconds. 'I could've made eighty-five dollars on the Street just then. See, in my pocket I had a hundred tabs of acid. I had to come up with twenty dollars by tonight or we're out of the house we're in, so I knew somebody who had acid, and I knew somebody who wanted it, so I made the connection.'

Since the Mafia moved into the LSD racket, the quantity is up and the quality is down . . . Historian Arnold Toynbee celebrated his 78th birthday Friday night by snapping his fingers and tapping his toes to the Quicksilver Messenger Service . . . are a couple of items from Herb Caen's column one morning as the West declined in the spring of 1967.

When I was in San Francisco a tab, or a cap, of LSD-25 sold for three to five dollars, depending upon the seller and the district. LSD was slightly cheaper in the Haight-Ashbury than in the Fillmore, where it was used rarely, mainly as a sexual ploy, and sold by pushers of hard drugs, *e.g.*, heroin, or 'smack.' A great deal of acid was being cut with Methedrine, which is the trade name for an amphetamine, because Methedrine can simulate the flash that low-quality acid lacks. Nobody knows how much LSD is actually in a tab, but the standard trip is supposed to be 250 micrograms. Grass was running ten dollars a lid, five dollars a matchbox. Hash was considered 'a luxury item.' All the amphetamines, or 'speed' – Benzedrine, Dexedrine, and particularly Methedrine – were in far more common use in the late spring than they had been in the early spring. Some attributed this to the presence of the Syndicate; others to a general deterioration of the scene, to the incursions of gangs and younger part-time, or 'plastic,' hippies, who like the amphetamines and the illusions of action and power they give. Where Methedrine is in wide use, heroin tends to be available, because, I was told, 'You can get awful damn high shooting crystal, and smack can be used to bring you down.'

Deadeye's old lady, Gerry, meets us at the door of their place. She is a big, hearty girl who has always counseled at Girl Scout camps during summer vacations and was 'in social welfare' at the University of Washington when she decided that she 'just hadn't done enough living' and came to San Francisco. 'Actually the heat was bad in Seattle,' she adds.

'The first night I got down here,' she says, 'I stayed with a gal I met over at the Blue Unicorn. I looked like I'd just arrived, had a knapsack and stuff.' After that, Gerry stayed at a house the Diggers were running, where she met Deadeye. 'Then it took time to get my bearings, so I haven't done much work yet.'

I ask Gerry what work she does. 'Basically I'm a poet,' she says, 'but I had my guitar stolen right after I arrived, and that kind of hung up my thing.'

'Get your books,' Deadeye orders. 'Show her your books.'

Gerry demurs, then goes into the bedroom and comes back with several theme books full of verse. I leaf through them but Deadeye is still talking about helping people. 'Any kid that's on speed,' he says, 'I'll try to get him off it. The only advantage to it from the kids' point of view is that you don't have to worry about sleeping or eating.'

'Or sex,' Gerry adds.

'That's right. When you're strung out on crystal you don't need *nothing*.'

'It can lead to the hard stuff,' Gerry says. 'Take your average Meth freak, once he's started putting the needle in his arm, it's not too hard to say, well, let's shoot a little smack.'

All the while I am looking at Gerry's poems. They are a very young girl's poems, each written out in a neat hand and finished off with a curlicue. Dawns are roseate, skies silver-tinted. When Gerry writes 'crystal' in her books, she does not mean Meth.

'You gotta get back to your writing,' Deadeye says fondly, but Gerry ignores this. She is telling about somebody who propositioned her yesterday. 'He just walked up to me on the Street, offered me six hundred dollars to go to Reno and do the thing.'

'You're not the only one he approached,' Deadeye says.

'If some chick wants to go with him, fine,' Gerry says. 'Just don't bum my trip.' She empties the tuna-fish can we are using for an ashtray and goes over to look at a girl who is asleep on the floor. It is the same girl who was sleeping on the floor the first day I came to Deadeye's place. She has been sick a week now, ten days. 'Usually when somebody comes up to me on the Street like that,' Gerry adds, 'I hit him for some change.'

When I saw Gerry in the Park the next day I asked her about the sick girl, and Gerry said cheerfully that she was in the hospital, with pneumonia.

Max tells me about how he and Sharon got together. 'When I saw her the first time on Haight Street, I flashed. I mean flashed. So I started some conversation with her about her beads, see, but I didn't care about her beads.' Sharon lived in a house where a friend of Max's lived, and the next time he saw her was when he took the friend some bananas. 'It was during the great banana bubble. You had to kind of force your personality and the banana peels down their throats. Sharon and I were like kids – we just smoked bananas and looked at each other and smoked more bananas and looked at each other.'

But Max hesitated. For one thing he thought Sharon was his friend's girl. 'For another I didn't know if I wanted to get hung up with an old lady.' But the next time he visited the house, Sharon was on acid.

'So everybody yelled "Here comes the banana man,"' Sharon interrupts, 'and I got all excited.'

'She was living in this crazy house,' Max continues. 'There was this one kid, all he did was scream. His whole trip was to practice screams. It was too much.' Max still hung back from Sharon. 'But then she offered me a tab, and I knew.'

Max walked to the kitchen and back with the tab, wondering whether to take it. 'And then I decided to flow with it, and that was that. Because once you drop acid with somebody you flash on, you see the whole world melt in her eyes.'

'It's stronger than anything in the world,' Sharon says.

'Nothing can break it up,' Max says. 'As long as it lasts.'

> *No milk today –*
> *My love has gone away . . .*
> *The end of my hopes –*
> *The end of all my dreams –*
> is a song I heard every morning in the
> cold late spring of 1967 on KFRC, the
> Flower Power Station, San Francisco.

Deadeye and Gerry tell me they plan to be married. An Episcopal priest in the District has promised to perform the wedding in Golden Gate Park, and they will have a few rock groups there, 'a real community thing.' Gerry's brother is also getting married, in Seattle. 'Kind of interesting,' Gerry muses, 'because, you know, his is the traditional straight wedding, and then you have the contrast with ours.'

'I'll have to wear a tie to his,' Deadeye says.

'Right,' Gerry says.

'Her parents came down to meet me, but they weren't ready for me,' Deadeye notes philosophically.

'They finally gave it their blessing,' Gerry says. 'In a way.'

'They came to me and her father said, "Take care of her,"' Dead-eye reminisces. 'And her mother said, "Don't let her go to jail."'

Barbara baked a macrobiotic apple pie and she and Tom and Max and Sharon and I are eating it. Barbara tells me how she learned to find happiness in 'the woman's thing.' She and Tom had gone somewhere to live with the Indians, and although she first found it hard to be shunted off with the women and never to enter into any of the men's talk, she soon got the point. 'That was where the *trip* was,' she says.

Barbara is on what is called the woman's trip to the exclusion of almost everything else. When she and Tom and Max and Sharon need money, Barbara will take a part-time job, modeling or teaching kindergarten, but she dislikes earning more than ten or twenty dollars a week. Most of the time she keeps house and bakes. 'Doing something that shows your love that way,' she says, 'is just about the most beautiful thing I know.' Whenever I hear about the woman's trip, which is often, I think a lot about nothin'-says-lovin'-like-something-from-the-oven and the Feminine Mystique and how it is possible for people to be the unconscious instruments of values they would strenuously reject on a conscious level, but I do not mention this to Barbara.

It is a pretty nice day and I am just driving down the Street and I see Barbara at a light.

What am I doing, she wants to know.

I am just driving around.

'Groovy,' she says.

It's a beautiful day, I say.

'Groovy,' she agrees.

She wants to know if I will come over. Sometime soon, I say.

'Groovy,' she says.

I ask if she wants to drive in the Park but she is too busy. She is out to buy wool for her loom.

* * *

Arthur Lisch gets pretty nervous whenever he sees me now because the Digger line this week is that they aren't talking to 'media poisoners,' which is me. So I still don't have a tap on Chester Anderson, but one day in the Panhandle I run into a kid who says he is Chester's 'associate.' He has on a black cape, black slouch hat, mauve Job's Daughters sweatshirt and dark glasses, and he says his name is Claude Hayward, but never mind that because I think of him just as The Connection. The Connection offers to 'check me out.'

I take off my dark glasses so he can see my eyes. He leaves his on.

'How much you get paid for doing this kind of media poisoning?' he says for openers.

I put my dark glasses back on.

'There's only one way to find out where it's at,' The Connection says, and jerks his thumb at the photographer I'm with. 'Dump him and get out on the Street. Don't take money. You won't need money.' He reaches into his cape and pulls out a mimeographed sheet announcing a series of classes at the Digger Free Store on How to Avoid Getting Busted, Gangbangs, VD, Rape, Pregnancy, Beatings, and Starvation. 'You oughta come,' The Connection says. 'You'll need it.'

I say maybe, but meanwhile I would like to talk to Chester Anderson.

'If we decide to get in touch with you at all,' The Connection says, 'we'll get in touch with you real quick.' He kept an eye on me in the Park after that but never called the number I gave him.

It is twilight and cold and too early to find Deadeye at the Blue Unicorn so I ring Max's bell. Barbara comes to the door.

'Max and Tom are seeing somebody on a kind of business thing,' she says. 'Can you come back a little later?'

I am hard put to think what Max and Tom might be seeing somebody about in the way of business, but a few days later in the Park I find out.

'Hey,' Max calls. 'Sorry you couldn't come up the other day, but *business* was being done.' This time I get the point. 'We got some great stuff,' he says, and begins to elaborate. Every third person in the Park this afternoon looks like a narcotics agent and I try to change the subject. Later I suggest to Max that he be more wary in public. 'Listen, I'm very cautious,' he says. 'You can't be too careful.'

By now I have an unofficial taboo contact with the San Francisco Police Department. What happens is that this cop and I meet in various late-movie ways, like I happen to be sitting in the bleachers at a baseball game and he happens to sit down next to me, and we exchange guarded generalities. No information actually passes between us, but after a while we get to kind of like each other.

'The kids aren't too bright,' he is telling me on this particular day. 'They'll tell you they can always spot an undercover, they'll tell you about "the kind of car he drives." They aren't talking about undercovers, they're talking about plainclothesmen who just happen to drive unmarked cars, like I do. They can't tell an undercover. An undercover doesn't drive some black Ford with a two-way radio.'

He tells me about an undercover who was taken out of the District because he was believed to be overexposed, too familiar. He was transferred to the narcotics squad, and by error was sent immediately back into the District as a narcotics undercover.

The cop plays with his keys. 'You want to know how smart these kids are?' he says finally. 'The first week, this guy makes forty-three cases.'

The Jook Savages are supposed to be having a May Day party in Larkspur and I go by the Warehouse and Don and Sue Ann think it would be nice to drive over there because Sue Ann's three-year-old, Michael, hasn't been out lately. The air is soft and there is a sunset haze around the Golden Gate and Don asks Sue Ann how many flavors she can detect in a single grain of rice and Sue Ann tells Don maybe she better learn to cook *yang*, maybe they are all too *yin* at the Warehouse, and I try to teach Michael 'Frère Jacques.' We each have our own trip and it is a nice drive. Which is just as well because there is nobody at all at the Jook Savages' place, not even the Jook Savages. When we get back Sue Ann decides to cook up a lot of apples they have around the Warehouse and Don starts working with his light show and I go down to see Max for a minute. 'Out of sight,' Max says about the Larkspur caper. 'Somebody thinks it would be groovy to turn on five hundred people the first day in May, and it would be, but then they turn on the last day in April instead, so it doesn't happen. If it happens, it happens. If it doesn't, it doesn't. Who cares. Nobody cares.'

Some kid with braces on his teeth is playing his guitar and boasting that he got the last of the STP from Mr O. himself and somebody else is talking about how five grams of acid will be liberated within the next month and you can see that nothing much is happening this afternoon around the *San Francisco Oracle* office. A boy sits at a drawing board drawing the infinitesimal figures that people do on speed, and the kid with the braces watches him. '*I'm gonna shoot my wo-man*,' he sings softly. '*She been with a-noth-er man.*' Someone works out the numerology of my name and the name of the photographer I'm with. The photographer's is all white and the sea ('If I were to make you some beads, see, I'd do it mainly in white,' he is told), but mine has a double death symbol. The afternoon does not seem to be getting anywhere, so it is suggested that we go over to Japantown and find somebody named Sandy who will take us to the Zen temple.

Four boys and one middle-aged man are sitting on a grass mat at Sandy's place, sipping anise tea and watching Sandy read Laura Huxley's *You Are Not the Target*.

We sit down and have some anise tea. 'Meditation turns us on,' Sandy says. He has a shaved head and the kind of cherubic face usually seen in newspaper photographs of mass murderers. The middle-aged man, whose name is George, is making me uneasy because he is in a trance next to me and stares at me without seeing me.

I feel that my mind is going – George is *dead*, or we *all* are – when the telephone rings.

'It's for George,' Sandy says.

'George, *tele*phone.'

'*George.*'

Somebody waves his hand in front of George and George finally gets up, bows, and moves toward the door on the balls of his feet.

'I think I'll take George's tea,' somebody says. 'George – are you coming back?'

George stops at the door and stares at each of us in turn. 'In a moment,' he snaps.

> *Do you know who is the first eternal spaceman of this universe?*
> *The first to send his wild wild vibrations*
> *To all those cosmic superstations?*
> *For the song he always shouts*
> *Sends the planets flipping out . . .*
> *But I'll tell you before you think me loony*
> *That I'm talking about Narada Muni . . .*
> *Singing*
> HARE KRISHNA   HARE KRISHNA
> KRISHNA KRISHNA HARE HARE
> HARE RAMA   HARE RAMA
> RAMA RAMA   HARE HARE
> is a Krishna song. Words by
> Howard Wheeler and music by
> Michael Grant.

Maybe the trip is not in Zen but in Krishna, so I pay a visit to Michael Grant, the Swami A.C. Bhaktivedanta's leading disciple in San Francisco. Michael Grant is at home with his brother-in-law and his wife, a pretty girl wearing a cashmere pullover, a jumper, and a red caste mark on her forehead.

'I've been associated with the Swami since about last July,' Michael says. 'See, the Swami came here from India and he was at this ashram in upstate New York and he just kept to himself and chanted a lot. For a couple of months. Pretty soon I helped him get his storefront in New York. Now it's an international movement, which we spread by teaching this chant.' Michael is fingering his red wooden beads and I notice that I am the only person in the room with shoes on. 'It's catching on like wildfire.'

'If everybody chanted,' the brother-in-law says, 'there wouldn't be any problem with the police or anybody.'

'Ginsberg calls the chant ecstasy, but the Swami says that's not exactly it.' Michael walks across the room and straightens a picture of Krishna as a baby. 'Too bad you can't meet the Swami,' he adds. 'The Swami's in New York now.'

'Ecstasy's not the right word at all,' says the brother-in-law, who has been thinking about it. 'It makes you think of some . . . mun*dane* ecstasy.'

The next day I drop by Max and Sharon's, and find them in bed smoking a little morning hash. Sharon once advised me that half a joint even of grass would make getting up in the morning a beautiful thing. I ask Max how Krishna strikes him.

'You can get a high on a mantra,' he says. 'But I'm holy on acid.' Max passes the joint to Sharon and leans back. 'Too bad you couldn't meet the Swami,' he says. 'The Swami was the turn-on.'

Anybody who thinks this is all about drugs has his head in a bag. It's a social movement, quintessentially romantic, the kind that recurs in times of real social crisis. The themes are always the same. A return to innocence. The invocation of an earlier authority and control. The mysteries of the blood. An itch for the transcendental, for purification. Right there you've got the ways that romanticism historically ends up in trouble, lends itself to authoritarianism. When the direction appears. How long do you think it'll take for that to happen? is a question a San Francisco psychiatrist asked me.

At the time I was in San Francisco the political potential of what was then called the movement was just becoming clear. It had always been clear to the revolutionary core of the Diggers, whose every guerrilla talent was now bent toward open confrontations and the creation of a summer emergency, and it was clear to many of the straight doctors and priests and sociologists who had occasion to work in the District, and it could rapidly become clear to any outsider who bothered to decode Chester Anderson's call-to-action communiqués or to watch who was there first at the street skirmishes which now set the tone for life in the District. One did not have to be a political analyst to see it; the boys in the rock groups saw it, because they were often where it was happening. 'In the Park there are always twenty or thirty people below the stand,' one of the Dead complained to me. 'Ready to take the crowd on some militant trip.'

But the peculiar beauty of this political potential, as far as the activists were concerned, was that it remained not clear at all to most of the inhabitants of the District, perhaps because the few seventeen-year-olds who are political realists tend not to adopt romantic idealism as a life style. Nor was it clear to the press, which at varying levels of competence continued to report 'the hippie phenomenon' as an extended panty raid; an artistic avant-garde led by such comfortable YMHA regulars as Allen Ginsberg; or a thoughtful protest, not unlike joining the Peace Corps, against the culture which had produced Saran-Wrap and the Vietnam War. This last, or they're-trying-to-tell-us-something approach, reached its apogee in a *Time* cover story which revealed that hippies 'scorn money – they call it "bread"' and remains the most remarkable, if unwitting, extant evidence that the signals between the generations are irrevocably jammed.

Because the signals the press was getting were immaculate of political possibilities, the tensions of the District went unremarked upon, even during the period when there were so many observers on Haight Street from *Life* and *Look* and CBS that they were largely observing one another. The observers believed roughly what the children told them: that they were a generation dropped out of political action, beyond power games, that the New Left was just another ego trip. *Ergo*, there really were no activists in the Haight-Ashbury, and those things which happened every Sunday were spontaneous demonstrations because, just as the Diggers say, the police are brutal and juveniles have no rights and runaways are deprived of their right to self-determination and people are starving to death on Haight Street, a scale model of Vietnam.

Of course the activists – not those whose thinking had become rigid, but those whose approach to revolution was imaginatively anarchic – had long ago grasped the reality which still eluded the press: we were seeing something important. We were seeing the desperate attempt of a handful of pathetically unequipped children to create a community in a social vacuum. Once we had seen these children, we could no longer overlook the vacuum, no longer pretend that the society's atomization could be reversed. This was not a traditional generational rebellion. At some point between 1945 and 1967 we had somehow neglected to tell these children the rules of the game we happened to be playing. Maybe we had stopped believing in the rules ourselves, maybe we were having a failure of nerve about the game. Maybe there were just too few people around to do the telling. These were children who grew up cut loose from the web of cousins and great-aunts and family doctors and lifelong neighbors who had traditionally suggested and enforced the society's values. They are children who have moved around a lot, *San Jose, Chula Vista, here*. They are less in rebellion against the society than ignorant of it, able only to feed back certain of its most publicized self-doubts, *Vietnam, Saran-Wrap, diet pills, the Bomb*.

They feed back exactly what is given them. Because they do not believe in words – words are for 'typeheads,' Chester Anderson tells them, and a thought which needs words is just one more of those ego trips – their only proficient vocabulary is in the society's platitudes. As it happens I am still committed to the idea that the ability to think for one's self depends upon one's mastery of the language, and I am not optimistic about children who will settle for saying, to indicate that their mother and father do not live together, that they come from 'a broken home.' They are sixteen, fifteen, fourteen years old, younger all the time, an army of children waiting to be given the words.

Peter Berg knows a lot of words.

'Is Peter Berg around?' I ask.

'Maybe.'

'Are you Peter Berg?'

'Yeh.'

The reason Peter Berg does not bother sharing too many words with me is because two of the words he knows are 'media poisoning.' Peter Berg wears a gold earring and is perhaps the only person in the District on whom a gold earring looks obscurely ominous. He belongs to the San Francisco Mime Troupe, some of whose members started the Artist's Liberation Front for 'those who seek to combine their creative urge with socio-political involvement.' It was out of the Mime Troupe that the Diggers grew, during the 1966 Hunter's

Point riots, when it seemed a good idea to give away food and do puppet shows in the streets making fun of the National Guard. Along with Arthur Lisch, Peter Berg is part of the shadow leadership of the Diggers, and it was he who more or less invented and first introduced to the press the notion that there would be an influx into San Francisco during the summer of 1967 of 200,000 indigent adolescents. The only conversation I ever have with Peter Berg is about how he holds me personally responsible for the way *Life* captioned Henri Cartier-Bresson's pictures out of Cuba, but I like to watch him at work in the Park.

Janis Joplin is singing with Big Brother in the Panhandle and almost everybody is high and it is a pretty nice Sunday afternoon between three and six o'clock, which the activists say are the three hours of the week when something is most likely to happen in the Haight-Ashbury, and who turns up but Peter Berg. He is with his wife and six or seven other people, along with Chester Anderson's associate The Connection, and the first peculiar thing is, they're in blackface.

I mention to Max and Sharon that some members of the Mime Troupe seem to be in blackface.

'It's street theater,' Sharon assures me. 'It's supposed to be really groovy.'

The Mime Troupers get a little closer, and there are some other peculiar things about them. For one thing they are tapping people on the head with dime-store plastic nightsticks, and for another they are wearing signs on their backs. 'HOW MANY TIMES YOU BEEN RAPED, YOU LOVE FREAKS?' and 'WHO STOLE CHUCK BERRY'S MUSIC?', things like that. Then they are distributing communication company fliers which say:

> & this summer thousands of un-white un-suburban boppers are going to want to know why you've given up what they can't get & how you get away with it & how come you not a faggot with hair so long & they want haight street one way or the other. IF YOU DON'T KNOW, BY AUGUST HAIGHT STREET WILL BE A CEMETERY.

Max reads the flier and stands up. 'I'm getting bad vibes,' he says, and he and Sharon leave.

I have to stay around because I'm looking for Otto so I walk over to where the Mime Troupers have formed a circle around a Negro. Peter Berg is saying if anybody asks that this is street theater, and I figure the curtain is up because what they are doing right now is jabbing the Negro with the nightsticks. They jab, and they bare their teeth, and they rock on the balls of their feet and they wait.

'I'm beginning to get annoyed here,' the Negro says. 'I'm gonna get mad.'

By now there are several Negroes around, reading the signs and watching.

'Just beginning to get annoyed, are you?' one of the Mime Troupers says. 'Don't you think it's about time?'

'Nobody *stole* Chuck Berry's music, man,' says another Negro who has been studying the signs. 'Chuck Berry's music belongs to *every*body.'

'Yeh?' a girl in blackface says. 'Everybody *who*?'

'Why,' he says, confused. 'Everybody. In America.'

'In *America*,' the blackface girl shrieks. 'Listen to him talk about *America*.'

'Listen,' he says helplessly. 'Listen here.'

'What'd *America* ever do for you?' the girl in blackface jeers. 'White kids here, they can sit in the Park all summer long, listening to the music they stole, because their bigshot parents keep sending them money. Who ever sends you money?'

'Listen,' the Negro says, his voice rising. 'You're gonna start something here, this isn't right – '

'You tell us what's right, black boy,' the girl says.

The youngest member of the blackface group, an earnest tall kid about nineteen, twenty, is hanging back at the edge of the scene. I offer him an apple and ask what is going on. 'Well,' he says, 'I'm new at this, I'm just beginning to study it, but you see the capitalists are taking over the District, and that's what Peter – well, ask Peter.'

I did not ask Peter. It went on for a while. But on that particular Sunday between three and six o'clock everyone was too high and the weather was too good and the Hunter's Point gangs who usually come in between three and six on Sunday afternoon had come in on Saturday instead, and nothing started. While I waited for Otto I asked a little girl I knew slightly what she had thought of it. 'It's something groovy they call street theater,' she said. I said I had wondered if it might not have political overtones. She was seventeen years old and she worked it around in her mind awhile and finally she remembered a couple of words from somewhere. 'Maybe it's some John Birch thing,' she said.

When I finally find Otto he says 'I got something at my place that'll blow your mind,' and when we get there I see a child on the living-room floor, wearing a reefer coat, reading a comic book. She keeps licking her lips in concentration and the only off thing about her is that she's wearing white lipstick.

'Five years old,' Otto says. 'On acid.'

The five-year-old's name is Susan, and she tells me she is in High Kindergarten. She lives with her mother and some other people, just got over the measles, wants a bicycle for Christmas, and particularly likes Coca-Cola, ice cream, Marty in the Jefferson Airplane, Bob in the Grateful Dead, and the beach. She remembers going to the beach once a long time ago, and wishes she had taken a bucket. For a year now her mother has given her both acid and peyote. Susan describes it as getting stoned.

I start to ask if any of the other children in High Kindergarten get stoned, but I falter at the key words.

'She means do the other kids in your class turn on, *get stoned*,' says the friend of her mother's who brought her to Otto's.

'Only Sally and Anne,' Susan says.

'What about Lia?' her mother's friend prompts.

'Lia,' Susan says, 'is not in High Kindergarten.'

Sue Ann's three-year-old Michael started a fire this morning before anyone was up, but Don got it out before much damage was done. Michael burned his arm though, which is probably why Sue Ann was so jumpy when she happened to see him chewing on an electric cord. 'You'll fry like rice,' she screamed. The only people around were Don and one of Sue Ann's macrobiotic friends and somebody who was on his way to a commune in the Santa Lucias, and they didn't notice Sue Ann screaming at Michael because they were in the kitchen trying to retrieve some very good Moroccan hash which had dropped down through a floorboard damaged in the fire.

1967

II

Personals

II

Personals

On Keeping a Notebook

' "That woman Estelle," ' the note reads, ' "is partly the reason why George Sharp and I are separated today." *Dirty crepe-de-Chine wrapper, hotel bar, Wilmington RR, 9:45 a.m. August Monday morning.*'

Since the note is in my notebook, it presumably has some meaning to me. I study it for a long while. At first I have only the most general notion of what I was doing on an August Monday morning in the bar of the hotel across from the Pennsylvania Railroad station in Wilmington, Delaware (waiting for a train? missing one? 1960? 1961? why Wilmington?), but I do remember being there. The woman in the dirty crepe-de-Chine wrapper had come down from her room for a beer, and the bartender had heard before the reason why George Sharp and she were separated today. 'Sure,' he said, and went on mopping the floor. 'You told me.' At the other end of the bar is a girl. She is talking, pointedly, not to the man beside her but to a cat lying in the triangle of sunlight cast through the open door. She is wearing a plaid silk dress from Peck & Peck, and the hem is coming down.

Here is what it is: the girl has been on the Eastern Shore, and now she is going back to the city, leaving the man beside her, and all she can see ahead are the viscous summer sidewalks and the 3 a.m. long-distance calls that will make her lie awake and then sleep drugged through all the steaming mornings left in August (1960? 1961?). Because she must go directly from the train to lunch in New York, she wishes that she had a safety pin for the hem of the plaid silk dress, and she also wishes that she could forget about the hem and the lunch and stay in the cool bar that smells of disinfectant and malt and make friends with the woman in the crepe-de-Chine wrapper. She is afflicted by a little self-pity, and she wants to compare Estelles. That is what that was all about.

Why did I write it down? In order to remember, of course, but exactly what was it I wanted to remember? How much of it actually happened? Did any of it? Why do I keep a notebook at all? It is easy to deceive oneself on all those scores. The impulse to write things down is a peculiarly compulsive one, inexplicable to those who do not share it, useful only accidentally, only secondarily, in the way that any compulsion tries to justify itself. I suppose that it begins or does not begin in the cradle. Although I have felt compelled to write things down since I was five years old, I doubt that my daughter ever will, for she is a singularly blessed and accepting child, delighted with life exactly as life presents itself to her, unafraid to go to sleep and unafraid to wake up. Keepers of private notebooks are a different breed altogether, lonely and resistant rearrangers of things, anxious malcontents, children afflicted apparently at birth with some pre-sentiment of loss.

My first notebook was a Big Five tablet, given to me by my mother with the sensible suggestion that I stop whining and learn to amuse myself by writing down my thoughts. She returned the tablet to me a few years ago; the first entry is an account of a woman who believed herself to be freezing to death in the Arctic night, only to find, when day broke, that she had stumbled onto the Sahara Desert, where she would die of the heat before lunch. I have no idea what turn of a five-year-old's mind could have prompted so insistently 'ironic' and exotic a story, but it does reveal a certain predilection for the extreme which has dogged me into adult life; perhaps if I were analytically inclined I would find it a truer story than any I might have told about Donald Johnson's birthday party or the day my cousin Brenda put Kitty Litter in the aquarium.

So the point of my keeping a notebook has never been, nor is it now, to have an accurate factual record of what I have been doing or thinking. That would be a different impulse entirely, an instinct for reality which I sometimes envy but do not possess. At no point have

I ever been able successfully to keep a diary; my approach to daily life ranges from the grossly negligent to the merely absent, and on those few occasions when I have tried dutifully to record a day's events, boredom has so overcome me that the results are mysterious at best. What is this business about 'shopping, typing piece, dinner with E, depressed'? Shopping for what? Typing what piece? Who is E? Was this 'E' depressed, or was I depressed? Who cares?

In fact I have abandoned altogether that kind of pointless entry; instead I tell what some would call lies. 'That's simply not true,' the members of my family frequently tell me when they come up against my memory of a shared event. 'The party was *not* for you, the spider was *not* a black widow, *it wasn't that way at all.'* Very likely they are right, for not only have I always had trouble distinguishing between what happened and what merely might have happened, but I remain unconvinced that the distinction, for my purposes, matters. The cracked crab that I recall having for lunch the day my father came home from Detroit in 1945 must certainly be embroidery, worked into the day's pattern to lend verisimilitude; I was ten years old and would not now remember the cracked crab. The day's events did not turn on cracked crab. And yet it is precisely that fictitious crab that makes me see the afternoon all over again, a home movie run all too often, the father bearing gifts, the child weeping, an exercise in family love and guilt. Or that is what it was to me. Similarly, perhaps it never did snow that August in Vermont; perhaps there never were flurries in the night wind, and maybe no one else felt the ground hardening and summer already dead even as we pretended to bask in it, but that was how it felt to me, and it might as well have snowed, could have snowed, did snow.

How it felt to me: that is getting closer to the truth about a notebook. I sometimes delude myself about why I keep a notebook, imagine that some thrifty virtue derives from preserving everything observed. See enough and write it down, I tell myself, and then some morning when the world seems drained of wonder, some day when I am only going through the motions of doing what I am supposed to do, which is write – on that bankrupt morning I will simply open my notebook and there it will all be, a forgotten account with accumulated interest, paid passage back to the world out there: dialogue overheard in hotels and elevators and at the hat-check counter in Pavillon (one middle-aged man shows his hat check to another and says, 'That's my old football number'); impressions of Bettina Aptheker and Benjamin Sonnenberg and Teddy ('Mr Acapulco') Stauffer; careful *aperçus* about tennis bums and failed fashion models and Greek shipping heiresses, one of whom taught me a significant lesson (a lesson I could have learned from F. Scott Fitzgerald, but perhaps we all must meet the very rich for ourselves) by asking, when I arrived to interview her in her orchid-filled sitting room on the second day of a paralyzing New York blizzard, whether it was snowing outside.

I imagine, in other words, that the notebook is about other people. But of course it is not. I have no real business with what one stranger said to another at the hat-check counter in Pavillon; in fact I suspect that the line 'That's my old football number' touched not my own imagination at all, but merely some memory of something once read, probably 'The Eighty-Yard Run.' Nor is my concern with a woman in a dirty crepe-de-Chine wrapper in a Wilmington bar. My stake is always, of course, in the unmentioned girl in the plaid silk dress. *Remember what it was to be me:* that is always the point.

It is a difficult point to admit. We are brought up in the ethic that others, any others, all others, are by definition more interesting than ourselves; taught to be diffident, just this side of self-effacing. ('You're the least important person in the room and don't forget it,' Jessica Mitford's governess would hiss in her ear on the advent of any social occasion; I copied that into my notebook because it is only recently that I have been able to enter a room without hearing some such phrase in my inner ear.) Only the very young and the very old may recount their dreams at breakfast, dwell upon self, interrupt with memories of beach picnics and favorite Liberty lawn dresses and the rainbow trout in a creek near Colorado Springs. The rest of us are expected, rightly, to affect absorption in other people's favorite dresses, other people's trout.

And so we do. But our notebooks give us away, for however dutifully we record what we see around us, the common denominator of all we see is always, transparently, shamelessly, the implacable 'I.' We are not talking here about the kind of notebook that is patently for public consumption, a structural conceit for binding together a series of graceful *pensées*; we are talking about something private, about bits of the mind's string too short to use, an indiscriminate and erratic assemblage with meaning only for its maker.

And sometimes even the maker has difficulty with the meaning. There does not seem to be, for example, any point in my knowing for the rest of my life that, during 1964, 720 tons of soot fell on every square mile of New York City, yet there it is in my notebook, labeled 'FACT.' Nor do I really need to remember that Ambrose Bierce liked to spell Leland Stanford's name '£eland $tanford' or that 'smart women almost always wear black in Cuba,' a fashion hint without much potential for practical application. And does not the relevance of these notes seem marginal at best?:

In the basement museum of the Inyo County Courthouse in Independence, California, sign pinned to a mandarin coat: 'This MANDARIN COAT was often worn by Mrs Minnie S. Brooks when giving lectures on her TEAPOT COLLECTION.'

Redhead getting out of car in front of Beverly Wilshire Hotel, chinchilla stole, Vuitton bags with tags reading:

MRS LOU FOX
HOTEL SAHARA
VEGAS

Well, perhaps not entirely marginal. As a matter of fact, Mrs Minnie S. Brooks and her MANDARIN COAT pull me back into my own childhood, for although I never knew Mrs Brooks and did not visit Inyo County until I was thirty, I grew up in just such a world, in houses cluttered with Indian relics and bits of gold ore and ambergris and the souvenirs my Aunt Mercy Farnsworth brought back from the Orient. It is a long way from that world to Mrs Lou Fox's world, where we all live now, and is it not just as well to remember that? Might not Mrs Minnie S. Brooks help me to remember what I am? Might not Mrs Lou Fox help me to remember what I am not?

*   *   *

But sometimes the point is harder to discern. What exactly did I have in mind when I noted down that it cost the father of someone I know $650 a month to light the place on the Hudson in which he lived before the Crash? What use was I planning to make of this line by Jimmy Hoffa: 'I may have my faults, but being wrong ain't one of them'? And although I think it interesting to know where the girls who travel with the Syndicate have their hair done when they find themselves on the West Coast, will I ever make suitable use of it? Might I not be better off just passing it on to John O'Hara? What is a recipe for sauerkraut doing in my notebook? What kind of magpie keeps this notebook? *'He was born the night the Titanic went down.'* That seems a nice enough line, and I even recall who said it, but is it not really a better line in life than it could ever be in fiction?

But of course that is exactly it: not that I should ever use the line, but that I should remember the woman who said it and the afternoon I heard it. We were on her terrace by the sea, and we were finishing the wine left from lunch, trying to get what sun there was, a California winter sun. The woman whose husband was born the night the *Titanic* went down wanted to rent her house, wanted to go back to her children in Paris. I remember wishing that I could afford the house, which cost $1,000 a month. 'Someday you will,' she said lazily. 'Someday it all comes.' There in the sun on her terrace it seemed easy to believe in someday, but later I had a low-grade afternoon hangover and ran over a black snake on the way to the supermarket and was flooded with inexplicable fear when I heard the checkout clerk explaining to the man ahead of me why she was finally divorcing her husband. 'He left me no choice,' she said over and over as she punched the register. 'He has a little seven-month-old baby by her, he left me no choice.' I would like to believe that my dread then was for the human condition, but of course it was for me, because I wanted a baby and did not then have one and because I wanted to own the house that cost $1,000 a month to rent and because I had a hangover.

It all comes back. Perhaps it is difficult to see the value in having one's self back in that kind of mood, but I do see it; I think we are well advised to keep on nodding terms with the people we used to be, whether we find them attractive company or not. Otherwise they turn up unannounced and surprise us, come hammering on the mind's door at 4 a.m. of a bad night and demand to know who deserted them, who betrayed them, who is going to make amends. We forget all too soon the things we thought we could never forget. We forget the loves and the betrayals alike, forget what we whispered and what we screamed, forget who we were. I have already lost touch with a couple of people I used to be; one of them, a seventeen-year-old, presents little threat, although it would be of some interest to me to know again what it feels like to sit on a river levee drinking vodka-and-orange-juice and listening to Les Paul and Mary Ford and their echoes sing 'How High the Moon' on the car radio. (You see I still have the scenes, but I no longer perceive myself among those present, no longer could even improvise the dialogue.) The other one, a twenty-three-year-old, bothers me more. She was always a good deal of trouble, and I suspect she will reappear when I least want to see her, skirts too long, shy to the point of aggravation, always the injured party, full of recriminations and little hurts and stories I do not want to hear again, at once saddening me and angering me with her vulnerability and ignorance, an apparition all the more insistent for being so long banished.

It is a good idea, then, to keep in touch, and I suppose that keeping in touch is what notebooks are all about. And we are all on our own when it comes to keeping those lines open to ourselves: your notebook will never help me, nor mine you. '*So what's new in the whiskey business?*' What could that possibly mean to you? To me it means a blonde in a Pucci bathing suit sitting with a couple of fat men by the pool at the Beverly Hills Hotel. Another man approaches, and they all regard one another in silence for a while. 'So what's new in the whiskey business?' one of the fat men finally says by way of welcome, and the blonde stands up, arches one foot and dips it in the pool, looking all the while at the cabaña where Baby Pignatari is talking on the telephone. That is all there is to that, except that several years later I saw the blonde coming out of Saks Fifth Avenue in New York with her California complexion and a voluminous mink coat. In the harsh wind that day she looked old and irrevocably tired to me, and even the skins in the mink coat were not worked the way they were doing them that year, not the way she would have wanted them done, and there is the point of the story. For a while after that I did not like to look in the mirror, and my eyes would

skim the newspapers and pick out only the deaths, the cancer victims, the premature coronaries, the suicides, and I stopped riding the
Lexington Avenue IRT because I noticed for the first time that all
the strangers I had seen for years – the man with the seeing eye dog,
the spinster who read the classified pages every day, the fat girl who
always got off with me at Grand Central – looked older than they
once had.

It all comes back. Even that recipe for sauerkraut: even that brings
it back. I was on Fire Island when I first made that sauerkraut, and
it was raining, and we drank a lot of bourbon and ate the sauerkraut
and went to bed at ten, and I listened to the rain and the Atlantic
and felt safe. I made the sauerkraut again last night and it did not
make me feel any safer, but that is, as they say, another story.

1966

On Self-Respect

Once, in a dry season, I wrote in large letters across two pages of a notebook that innocence ends when one is stripped of the delusion that one likes oneself. Although now, some years later, I marvel that a mind on the outs with itself should have nonetheless made painstaking record of its every tremor, I recall with embarrassing clarity the flavor of those particular ashes. It was a matter of misplaced self-respect.

I had not been elected to Phi Beta Kappa. This failure could scarcely have been more predictable or less ambiguous (I simply did not have the grades), but I was unnerved by it; I had somehow thought myself a kind of academic Raskolnikov, curiously exempt from the cause-effect relationships which hampered others. Although even the humorless nineteen-year-old that I was must have recognized that the situation lacked real tragic stature, the day that I did not make Phi Beta Kappa nonetheless marked the end of something, and innocence may well be the word for it. I lost the conviction that lights would always turn green for me, the pleasant certainty that those rather passive virtues which had won me approval as a child automatically guaranteed me not only Phi Beta Kappa keys but happiness, honor, and the love of a good man; lost a certain touching faith in the totem power of good manners, clean hair, and proven competence on the Stanford-Binet scale. To such doubtful amulets had my self-respect been pinned, and I faced myself that day with the nonplused apprehension of someone who has come across a vampire and has no crucifix at hand.

Although to be driven back upon oneself is an uneasy affair at best, rather like trying to cross a border with borrowed credentials, it seems to me now the one condition necessary to the beginnings of real self-respect. Most of our platitudes notwithstanding, self-deception remains the most difficult deception. The tricks that work on others count for nothing in that very well-lit back alley where one keeps assignations with oneself: no winning smiles will do here, no prettily drawn lists of good intentions. One shuffles flashily but in vain through one's marked cards – the kindness done for the wrong reason, the apparent triumph which involved no real effort, the seemingly heroic act into which one had been shamed. The dismal fact is that self-respect has nothing to do with the approval of others – who are, after all, deceived easily enough; has nothing to do with reputation, which, as Rhett Butler told Scarlett O'Hara, is something people with courage can do without.

To do without self-respect, on the other hand, is to be an unwilling audience of one to an interminable documentary that details one's failings, both real and imagined, with fresh footage spliced in for every screening. *There's the glass you broke in anger, there's the hurt on X's face; watch now, this next scene, the night Y came back from Houston, see how you muff this one.* To live without self-respect is to lie awake some night, beyond the reach of warm milk, phenobarbital, and the sleeping hand on the coverlet, counting up the sins of commission and omission, the trusts betrayed, the promises subtly broken, the gifts irrevocably wasted through sloth or cowardice or carelessness. However long we postpone it, we eventually lie down alone in that notoriously uncomfortable bed, the one we make ourselves. Whether or not we sleep in it depends, of course, on whether or not we respect ourselves.

To protest that some fairly improbable people, some people who *could not possibly respect themselves*, seem to sleep easily enough is to miss the point entirely, as surely as those people miss it who think that self-respect has necessarily to do with not having safety pins in one's underwear. There is a common superstition that 'self-respect' is a kind of charm against snakes, something that keeps those who have it locked in some unblighted Eden, out of strange beds, ambivalent conversations, and trouble in general. It does not at all. It has nothing to do with the face of things, but concerns instead a separate peace, a private reconciliation. Although the careless, suicidal Julian English in *Appointment in Samarra* and the careless, incurably dishonest Jordan Baker in *The Great Gatsby* seem equally improbable candidates for self-respect, Jordan Baker had it, Julian English did not. With that genius for accommodation more often seen in women than in men, Jordan took her own measure, made her own peace, avoided threats to that peace: 'I hate careless people,' she told Nick Carraway. 'It takes two to make an accident.'

Like Jordan Baker, people with self-respect have the courage of their mistakes. They know the price of things. If they choose to commit adultery, they do not then go running, in an access of bad conscience, to receive absolution from the wronged parties; nor do they complain unduly of the unfairness, the undeserved embarrassment, of being named co-respondent. In brief, people with self-respect exhibit a certain toughness, a kind of moral nerve; they display what was once called *character*, a quality which, although approved in the abstract, sometimes loses ground to other, more instantly negotiable virtues. The measure of its slipping prestige is that one tends to think of it only in connection with homely children and United States senators who have been defeated, preferably in the primary, for reelection. Nonetheless, character – the willingness to accept responsibility for one's own life – is the source from which self-respect springs.

Self-respect is something that our grandparents, whether or not they had it, knew all about. They had instilled in them, young, a certain discipline, the sense that one lives by doing things one does not particularly want to do, by putting fears and doubts to one side, by weighing immediate comforts against the possibility of larger, even intangible, comforts. It seemed to the nineteenth century admirable, but not remarkable, that Chinese Gordon put on a clean white suit and held Khartoum against the Mahdi; it did not seem unjust that the way to free land in California involved death and difficulty and dirt. In a diary kept during the winter of 1846, an emigrating twelve-year-old named Narcissa Cornwall noted coolly: 'Father was busy reading and did not notice that the house was being filled with strange Indians until Mother spoke about it.' Even lacking any clue as to what Mother said, one can scarcely fail to be impressed by the entire incident: the father reading, the Indians filing in, the mother choosing the words that would not alarm, the child duly recording the event and noting further that those particular Indians were not, 'fortunately for us,' hostile. Indians were simply part of the *donnée*.

In one guise or another, Indians always are. Again, it is a question of recognizing that anything worth having has its price. People who respect themselves are willing to accept the risk that the Indians will be hostile, that the venture will go bankrupt, that the liaison may not turn out to be one in which *every day is a holiday because you're married to me*. They are willing to invest something of themselves; they may not play at all, but when they do play, they know the odds.

That kind of self-respect is a discipline, a habit of mind that can never be faked but can be developed, trained, coaxed forth. It was once suggested to me that, as an antidote to crying, I put my head in a paper bag. As it happens, there is a sound physiological reason, something to do with oxygen, for doing exactly that, but the psychological effect alone is incalculable: it is difficult in the extreme to continue fancying oneself Cathy in *Wuthering Heights* with one's head in a Food Fair bag. There is a similar case for all the small disciplines, unimportant in themselves; imagine maintaining any kind of swoon, commiserative or carnal, in a cold shower.

But those small disciplines are valuable only insofar as they represent larger ones. To say that Waterloo was won on the playing fields of Eton is not to say that Napoleon might have been saved by a crash program in cricket; to give formal dinners in the rain forest would be pointless did not the candlelight flickering on the liana call forth deeper, stronger disciplines, values instilled long before. It is a kind of ritual, helping us to remember who and what we are. In order to remember it, one must have known it.

To have that sense of one's intrinsic worth which constitutes self-respect is potentially to have everything: the ability to discriminate, to love and to remain indifferent. To lack it is to be locked within oneself, paradoxically incapable of either love or indifference. If we do not respect ourselves, we are on the one hand forced to despise those who have so few resources as to consort with us, so little perception as to remain blind to our fatal weaknesses. On the other, we are peculiarly in thrall to everyone we see, curiously determined to live out – since our self-image is untenable – their false notions of us. We flatter ourselves by thinking this compulsion to please others an attractive trait: a gist for imaginative empathy, evidence of our willingness to give. *Of course* I will play Francesca to your Paolo, Helen Keller to anyone's Annie Sullivan: no expectation is too misplaced, no role too ludicrous. At the mercy of those we cannot but hold in contempt, we play roles doomed to failure before they are begun, each defeat generating fresh despair at the urgency of divining and meeting the next demand made upon us.

It is the phenomenon sometimes called 'alienation from self.' In its advanced stages, we no longer answer the telephone, because someone might want something; that we could say *no* without drowning in self-reproach is an idea alien to this game. Every encounter demands too much, tears the nerves, drains the will, and the specter of something as small as an unanswered letter arouses such disproportionate guilt that answering it becomes out of the question. To assign unanswered letters their proper weight, to free us from the expectations of others, to give us back to ourselves – there lies the great, the singular power of self-respect. Without it, one eventually discovers the final turn of the screw: one runs away to find oneself, and finds no one at home.

1961

I Can't Get That Monster out of My Mind

Quite early in the action of an otherwise unmemorable monster movie (I do not even remember its name), having to do with a mechanical man who walks underwater down the East River as far as Forty-ninth Street and then surfaces to destroy the United Nations, the heroine is surveying the grounds of her country place when the mechanical monster bobs up from a lake and attempts to carry off her child. (Actually we are aware that the monster wants only to make friends with the little girl, but the young mother, who has presumably seen fewer monster movies than we have, is not. This provides pathos, and dramatic tension.) Later that evening, as the heroine sits on the veranda reflecting upon the day's events, her brother strolls out, tamps his pipe, and asks: 'Why the brown study, Deborah?' Deborah smiles, ruefully. 'It's nothing, Jim, really,' she says. 'I just can't get that monster out of my mind.'

I just can't get that monster out of my mind. It is a useful line, and one that frequently occurs to me when I catch the tone in which a great many people write or talk about Hollywood. In the popular imagination, the American motion-picture industry still represents a kind of mechanical monster, programmed to stifle and destroy all that is interesting and worthwhile and 'creative' in the human spirit. As an adjective, the very word 'Hollywood' has long been pejorative and suggestive of something referred to as 'the System,' a phrase delivered with the same sinister emphasis that James Cagney once lent to 'the Syndicate.' The System not only strangles talent but poisons the soul, a fact supported by rich webs of lore. Mention

Hollywood, and we are keyed to remember Scott Fitzgerald, dying at Malibu, attended only by Sheilah Graham while he ground out college-weekend movies (he was also writing *The Last Tycoon*, but that is not part of the story); we are conditioned to recall the brightest minds of a generation, deteriorating around the swimming pool at the Garden of Allah while they waited for calls from the Thalberg Building. (Actually it takes a fairly romantic sensibility to discern why the Garden of Allah should have been a more insidious ambiance than the Algonquin, or why the Thalberg Building, and Metro-Goldwyn-Mayer, should have been more morally debilitating than the Graybar Building, and *Vanity Fair*. Edmund Wilson, who has this kind of sensibility, once suggested that it has something to do with the weather. Perhaps it does.)

Hollywood the Destroyer. It was essentially a romantic vision, and before long Hollywood was helping actively to perpetuate it: think of Jack Palance, as a movie star finally murdered by the System in *The Big Knife*; think of Judy Garland and James Mason (and of Janet Gaynor and Fredric March before them), their lives blighted by the System, or by the Studio – the two phrases were, when the old major studios still ran Hollywood, more or less interchangeable – in *A Star Is Born*. By now, the corruption and venality and restrictiveness of Hollywood have become such firm tenets of American social faith – and of Hollywood's own image of itself – that I was only mildly surprised, not long ago, to hear a young screenwriter announce that Hollywood was 'ruining' him. 'As a writer,' he added. 'As a writer,' he had previously written, over a span of ten years in New York, one comedy (as opposed to 'comic') novel, several newspaper reviews of other people's comedy novels, and a few years' worth of captions for a picture magazine.

Now. It is not surprising that the specter of Hollywood the Destroyer still haunts the rote middle intelligentsia (the monster lurks, I understand, in the wilds between the Thalia and the Museum of Modern Art), or at least those members of it who have not yet perceived the *chic* conferred upon Hollywood by the *Cahiers du Cinema* set. (Those who have perceived it adopt an equally extreme position, speculating endlessly about what Vincente Minnelli was up to in *Meet Me in St Louis*, attending seminars on Nicholas Ray, that kind of thing.) What is surprising is that the monster still haunts Hollywood itself – and Hollywood knows better, knows that the monster was laid to rest, dead of natural causes, some years ago. The Fox back lot is now a complex of office buildings called Century City; Paramount makes not forty movies a year but 'Bonanza.' What was once The Studio is now a releasing operation, and even the Garden of Allah is no more. Virtually every movie made is an independent production – and is that not what we once wanted? Is that not what we once said could revolutionize American movies? The millennium is here, the era of 'fewer and better' motion pictures, and what have we? We have fewer pictures, but not necessarily better pictures. Ask Hollywood why, and Hollywood resorts to murmuring about the monster. It has been, they say, impossible to work 'honestly' in Hollywood. Certain things have prevented it. The studios, or what is left of the studios, thwart their every dream. The moneymen conspire against them. New York spirits away their prints before they have finished cutting. They are bound by clichés. There is something wrong with 'the intellectual climate.' If only they were allowed some freedom, if only they could exercise an individual voice . . .

If only. These protests have about them an engaging period optimism, depending as they do upon the Rousseauean premise that most people, left to their own devices, think not in clichés but with originality and brilliance; that most individual voices, once heard, turn out to be voices of beauty and wisdom. I think we would all agree that a novel is nothing if it is not the expression of an individual voice, of a single view of experience – and how many good or even interesting novels, of the thousands published, appear each year? I doubt that more can be expected of the motion-picture industry. Men who do have interesting individual voices have for some time now been making movies in which those voices are heard; I think of Elia Kazan's *America America*, and, with a good deal less enthusiasm for the voice, of Stanley Kubrick's *Dr Strangelove*.

But it is not only the 'interesting' voices who now have the opportunity to be heard. John Frankenheimer was quoted in *Life* as admitting: 'You can't call Hollywood "The Industry" any more. Today we have a chance to put our personal fantasies on film.' Frankenheimer's own personal fantasies have included *All Fall Down*, in which we learned that Warren Beatty and Eva Marie Saint were in love when Frankenheimer dissolved to some swans shimmering on a lake, and *Seven Days in May*, which, in its misapprehension of the way the American power elite thinks and talks and operates (the movie's United States Senator from California, as I recall, drove a Rolls-Royce), appeared to be fantasy in the most clinical sense of that word. Carl Foreman, who, before he was given a chance to put his personal fantasies on film, worked on some very good (of their type) movies – *High Noon* and *The Guns of Navarone*, for two – later released what he called his 'personal statement': *The Victors*, a phenomenon which suggests only that two heads are perhaps better than one, if that one is Foreman's.

One problem is that American directors, with a handful of exceptions, are not much interested in style; they are at heart didactic. Ask what they plan to do with their absolute freedom, with their chance to make a personal statement, and they will pick an 'issue,' a 'problem.' The 'issues' they pick are generally no longer real issues, if indeed they ever were – but I think it a mistake to attribute this to any calculated venality, to any conscious playing it safe. (I am reminded of a screenwriter who just recently discovered dwarfs – although he, like the rest of us, must have lived through that period when dwarfs turned up on the fiction pages of the glossier magazines with the approximate frequency that Suzy Parker turned up on the advertising pages. This screenwriter sees dwarfs as symbols of modern man's crippling anomie. There is a certain cultural lag.) Call it instead – this apparent calculation about what 'issues' are now safe – an absence of imagination, a sloppiness of mind in some ways encouraged by a comfortable feedback from the audience, from the bulk of the reviewers, and from some people who ought to know better. Stanley Kramer's *Judgment at Nuremberg*, made in 1961, was an intrepid indictment not of authoritarianism in the abstract, not of the trials themselves, not of the various moral and legal issues involved, but of Nazi war atrocities, about which there would have seemed already to be some consensus. (You may remember that *Judgment at Nuremberg* received an Academy Award, which the screenwriter Abby Mann accepted on the behalf of 'all intellectuals.') Later, Kramer and Abby Mann collaborated on *Ship of Fools*, into which they injected 'a little more compassion and humor' and in which they advanced the action from 1931 to 1933 – the better to register another defiant protest against the National Socialist Party.

Foreman's *The Victors* set forth, interminably, the proposition that war defeats the victors equally with the vanquished, a notion not exactly radical. (Foreman is a director who at first gives the impression of having a little style, but the impression is entirely spurious, and prompted mostly by his total recall for old Eisenstein effects.) Stanley Kubrick's *Dr Strangelove*, which did have a little style, was scarcely a picture of relentless originality; rarely have we seen so much made over so little. John Simon, in the *New Leader*, declared that the 'altogether admirable thing' about *Dr Strangelove* was that it managed to be 'thoroughly irreverent about everything the Establishment takes seriously: atomic war, government, the army, international relations, heroism, sex, and what not.' I don't know who John Simon thinks makes up the Establishment, but skimming back at random from 'what not,' sex is our most durable communal joke; Billy Wilder's *One, Two, Three* was a boffo (*cf. Variety*) spoof of international relations; the army as a laugh line has filtered right down to Phil Silvers and 'Sergeant Bilko'; and, if 'government' is something about which the American Establishment is inflexibly reverent, I seem to have been catching some pretty underground material on prime time television. And what not. *Dr Strangelove* was essentially a one-line gag, having to do with the difference between all other wars and nuclear war. By the time George Scott had said 'I think I'll mosey on over to the War Room' and Sterling Hayden had said 'Looks like we got ourselves a shootin' war' and the SAC bomber had begun heading for its Soviet targets to the tune of 'When Johnny Comes Marching Home Again,' Kubrick had already developed a full fugue upon the theme, and should have started counting the minutes until it would begin to pall.

What we have, then, are a few interesting minds at work; and a great many less interesting ones. The European situation is not all that different. Antonioni, among the Italians, makes beautiful, intelligent, intricately and subtly built pictures, the power of which lies entirely in their structure; Visconti, on the other hand, has less sense of form than anyone now directing. One might as well have viewed a series of stills, in no perceptible order, as his *The Leopard*. Federico Fellini and Ingmar Bergman share a stunning visual intelligence and a numbingly banal view of human experience; Alain Resnais, in *Last Year at Marienbad* and *Muriel*, demonstrated a style so intrusive that one suspected it to be a smoke screen, suspected that it was intruding upon a vacuum. As for the notion that European movies tend to be more original than American movies, no one who saw *Boccaccio '70* could ever again automatically modify the word 'formula' with 'Hollywood.'

So. With perhaps a little prodding from abroad, we are all grown up now in Hollywood, and left to set out in the world on our own. We are no longer in the grip of a monster; Harry Cohn no longer runs Columbia like, as the saying went, a concentration camp. Whether or not a picture receives a Code seal no longer matters much at the box office. No more curfew, no more Daddy, *anything goes*. Some of us do not quite like this permissiveness; some of us would like to find 'reasons' why our pictures are not as good as we know in our hearts they might be. Not long ago I met a producer who complained to me of the difficulties he had working within what I recognized as the System, although he did not call it that. He longed, he said, to do an adaptation of a certain Charles Jackson short story. 'Some really terrific stuff,' he said. 'Can't touch it, I'm afraid. About masturbation.'

1964

On Morality

As it happens I am in Death Valley, in a room at the Enterprise Motel and Trailer Park, and it is July, and it is hot. In fact it is 119°. I cannot seem to make the air conditioner work, but there is a small refrigerator, and I can wrap ice cubes in a towel and hold them against the small of my back. With the help of the ice cubes I have been trying to think, because *The American Scholar* asked me to, in some abstract way about 'morality,' a word I distrust more every day, but my mind veers inflexibly toward the particular.

Here are some particulars. At midnight last night, on the road in from Las Vegas to Death Valley Junction, a car hit a shoulder and turned over. The driver, very young and apparently drunk, was killed instantly. His girl was found alive but bleeding internally, deep in shock. I talked this afternoon to the nurse who had driven the girl to the nearest doctor, 185 miles across the floor of the Valley and three ranges of lethal mountain road. The nurse explained that her husband, a talc miner, had stayed on the highway with the boy's body until the coroner could get over the mountains from Bishop, at dawn today. 'You can't just leave a body on the highway,' she said. 'It's immoral.'

It was one instance in which I did not distrust the word, because she meant something quite specific. She meant that if a body is left alone for even a few minutes on the desert, the coyotes close in and eat the flesh. Whether or not a corpse is torn apart by coyotes may seem only a sentimental consideration, but of course it is more: one of the promises we make to one another is that we will try to retrieve our casualties, try not to abandon our dead to the coyotes. If we have been taught to keep our promises – if, in the simplest terms, our upbringing is good enough – we stay with the body, or have bad dreams.

I am talking, of course, about the kind of social code that is sometimes called, usually pejoratively, 'wagon-train morality.' In fact that is precisely what it is. For better or worse, we are what we learned as children: my own childhood was illuminated by graphic litanies of the grief awaiting those who failed in their loyalties to each other. The Donner-Reed Party, starving in the Sierra snows, all the ephemera of civilization gone save that one vestigial taboo, the provision that no one should eat his own blood kin. The Jayhawkers, who quarreled and separated not far from where I am tonight. Some of them died in the Funerals and some of them died down near Badwater and most of the rest of them died in the Panamints. A woman who got through gave the Valley its name. Some might say that the Jayhawkers were killed by the desert summer, and the Donner Party by the mountain winter, by circumstances beyond control; we were taught instead that they had somewhere abdicated their responsibilities, somehow breached their primary loyalties, or they would not have found themselves helpless in the mountain winter or the desert summer, would not have given way to acrimony, would not have deserted one another, would not have *failed*. In brief, we heard such stories as cautionary tales, and they still suggest the only kind of 'morality' that seems to me to have any but the most potentially mendacious meaning.

You are quite possibly impatient with me by now; I am talking, you want to say, about a 'morality' so primitive that it scarcely deserves the name, a code that has as its point only survival, not the attainment of the ideal good. Exactly. Particularly out here tonight, in this country so ominous and terrible that to live in it is to live with antimatter, it is difficult to believe that 'the good' is a knowable quantity. Let me tell you what it is like out here tonight. Stories travel at night on the desert. Someone gets in his pickup and drives a couple of hundred miles for a beer, and he carries news of what is happening, back wherever he came from. Then he drives another hundred miles for another beer, and passes along stories from the last place as well as from the one before; it is a network kept alive by people whose instincts tell them that if they do not keep moving at night on the desert they will lose all reason. Here is a story that is going around the desert tonight: over across the Nevada line, sheriff's deputies are diving in some underground pools, trying to retrieve a couple of bodies known to be in the hole. The widow of one of the drowned boys is over there; she is eighteen, and pregnant, and is said not to leave the hole. The divers go down and come up, and she just stands there and stares into the water. They have been diving for ten days but have found no bottom to the caves, no bodies and no trace of them, only the black 90° water going down and down and down, and a single translucent fish, not classified. The story tonight is that one of the divers has been hauled up incoherent, out of his head, shouting – until they got him out of there so that the widow could not hear – about water that got hotter instead of cooler as he went down, about light flickering through the water, about magma, about underground nuclear testing.

That is the tone stories take out here, and there are quite a few of them tonight. And it is more than the stories alone. Across the road at the Faith Community Church a couple of dozen old people, come here to live in trailers and die in the sun, are holding a prayer sing. I cannot hear them and do not want to. What I can hear are occasional coyotes and a constant chorus of 'Baby the Rain Must Fall' from the jukebox in the Snake Room next door, and if I were also to hear those dying voices, those Midwestern voices drawn to this lunar country for some unimaginable atavistic rites, *rock of ages cleft for me*, I think I would lose my own reason. Every now and then I imagine I hear a rattlesnake, but my husband says that it is a faucet, a paper rustling, the wind. Then he stands by a window, and plays a flashlight over the dry wash outside.

What does it mean? It means nothing manageable. There is some sinister hysteria in the air out here tonight, some hint of the monstrous perversion to which any human idea can come. 'I followed my own conscience.' 'I did what I thought was right.' How many madmen have said it and meant it? How many murderers? Klaus Fuchs said it, and the men who committed the Mountain Meadows Massacre said it, and Alfred Rosenberg said it. And, as we are rotely and rather presumptuously reminded by those who would say it now, Jesus said it. Maybe we have all said it, and maybe we have been wrong. Except on that most primitive level – our loyalties to those we love – what could be more arrogant than to claim the primacy of personal conscience? ('Tell me,' a rabbi asked Daniel Bell when he said, as a child, that he did not believe in God. 'Do you think God cares?') At least some of the time, the world appears to me as a painting by Hieronymous Bosch; were I to follow my conscience then, it would lead me out onto the desert with Marion Faye, out to where he stood in *The Deer Park* looking east to Los Alamos and praying, as if for rain, that it would happen: '. . . *let it come and clear the rot and the stench and the stink, let it come for all of everywhere, just so it comes and the world stands clear in the white dead dawn.*'

Of course you will say that I do not have the right, even if I had the power, to inflict that unreasonable conscience upon you; nor do I want you to inflict your conscience, however reasonable, however enlightened, upon me. ('We must be aware of the dangers which lie in our most generous wishes,' Lionel Trilling once wrote. 'Some paradox of our nature leads us, when once we have made our fellow men the objects of our enlightened interest, to go on to make them the objects of our pity, then of our wisdom, ultimately of our coercion.') That the ethic of conscience is intrinsically insidious seems scarcely a revelatory point, but it is one raised with increasing infrequency; even those who do raise it tend to *segue* with troubling readiness into the quite contradictory position that the ethic of conscience is dangerous when it is 'wrong,' and admirable when it is 'right.'

You see I want to be quite obstinate about insisting that we have no way of knowing – beyond that fundamental loyalty to the social code – what is 'right' and what is 'wrong,' what is 'good' and what 'evil.' I dwell so upon this because the most disturbing aspect of 'morality' seems to me to be the frequency with which the word now appears; in the press, on television, in the most perfunctory kinds of conversation. Questions of straightforward power (or survival) politics, questions of quite indifferent public policy, questions of almost anything: they are all assigned these factitious moral burdens. There is something facile going on, some self-indulgence at work. Of course we would all like to 'believe' in something, like to assuage our private guilts in public causes, like to lose our tiresome selves; like, perhaps, to transform the white flag of defeat at home into the brave white banner of battle away from home. And of course it is all right to do that; that is how, immemorially, things have gotten done. But I think it is all right only so long as we do not delude ourselves about what we are doing, and why. It is all right only so long as we remember that all the *ad hoc* committees, all the picket lines, all the brave signatures in *The New York Times*, all the tools of agitprop straight across the spectrum, do not confer upon anyone any *ipso facto* virtue. It is all right only so long as we recognize that the end may or may not be expedient, may or may not be a good idea, but in any case has nothing to do with 'morality.' Because when we start deceiving ourselves into thinking not that we want something or need something, not that it is a pragmatic necessity for us to have it, but that it is a *moral imperative* that we have it, then is when we join the fashionable madmen, and then is when the thin whine of hysteria is heard in the land, and then is when we are in bad trouble. And I suspect we are already there.

1965

On Going Home

I am home for my daughter's first birthday. By 'home' I do not mean the house in Los Angeles where my husband and I and the baby live, but the place where my family is, in the Central Valley of California. It is a vital although troublesome distinction. My husband likes my family but is uneasy in their house, because once there I fall into their ways, which are difficult, oblique, deliberately inarticulate, not my husband's ways. We live in dusty houses ('D-U-S-T,' he once wrote with his finger on surfaces all over the house, but no one noticed it) filled with mementos quite without value to him (what could the Canton dessert plates mean to him? how could he have known about the assay scales, why should he care if he did know?), and we appear to talk exclusively about people we know who have been committed to mental hospitals, about people we know who have been booked on drunk-driving charges, and about property, particularly about property, land, price per acre and C-2 zoning and assessments and freeway access. My brother does not understand my husband's inability to perceive the advantage in the rather common real-estate transaction known as 'sale-leaseback,' and my husband in turn does not understand why so many of the people he hears about in my father's house have recently been committed to mental hospitals or booked on drunk-driving charges. Nor does he understand that when we talk about sale-leasebacks and right-of-way condemnations we are talking in code about the things we like best, the yellow fields and the cottonwoods and the rivers rising and falling and the mountain roads closing when the heavy snow comes in. We miss each other's points, have another drink and regard the fire. My brother refers to my husband, in his presence, as 'Joan's husband.' Marriage is the classic betrayal.

Or perhaps it is not any more. Sometimes I think that those of us who are now in our thirties were born into the last generation to carry the burden of 'home,' to find in family life the source of all tension and drama. I had by all objective accounts a 'normal' and a 'happy' family situation, and yet I was almost thirty years old before I could talk to my family on the telephone without crying after I had hung up. We did not fight. Nothing was wrong. And yet some name-less anxiety colored the emotional charges between me and the place that I came from. The question of whether or not you could go home again was a very real part of the sentimental and largely literary bag-gage with which we left home in the fifties; I suspect that it is irrelevant to the children born of the fragmentation after World War II. A few weeks ago in a San Francisco bar I saw a pretty young girl on crystal take off her clothes and dance for the cash prize in an 'amateur-topless' contest. There was no particular sense of moment about this, none of the effect of romantic degradation, of 'dark journey,' for which my generation strived so assiduously. What sense could that girl possibly make of, say, *Long Day's Journey into Night*? Who is beside the point?

That I am trapped in this particular irrelevancy is never more apparent to me than when I am home. Paralyzed by the neurotic lassitude engendered by meeting one's past at every turn, around every corner, inside every cupboard, I go aimlessly from room to room. I decide to meet it head-on and clean out a drawer, and I spread the contents on the bed. A bathing suit I wore the summer I was seventeen. A letter of rejection from *The Nation*, an aerial photo-graph of the site for a shopping center my father did not build in 1954. Three teacups hand-painted with cabbage roses and signed 'E.M.,' my grandmother's initials. There is no final solution for letters of rejection from *The Nation* and teacups hand-painted in 1900. Nor is there any answer to snapshots of one's grandfather as a young man on skis, surveying around Donner Pass in the year 1910. I smooth out the snapshot and look into his face, and do and do not see my own. I close the drawer, and have another cup of coffee with my mother. We get along very well, veterans of a guerrilla war we never understood.

Days pass. I see no one. I come to dread my husband's evening call, not only because he is full of news of what by now seems to me our remote life in Los Angeles, people he has seen, letters which require attention, but because he asks what I have been doing, suggests uneasily that I get out, drive to San Francisco or Berkeley. Instead I drive across the river to a family graveyard. It has been vandalized since my last visit and the monuments are broken, overturned in the dry grass. Because I once saw a rattlesnake in the grass I stay in the car and listen to a country-and-Western station. Later I drive with my father to a ranch he has in the foothills. The man who runs his cattle on it asks us to the roundup, a week from Sunday, and although I know that I will be in Los Angeles I say, in the oblique way my family talks, that I will come. Once home I mention the broken monuments in the graveyard. My mother shrugs.

I go to visit my great-aunts. A few of them think now that I am my cousin, or their daughter who died young. We recall an anecdote about a relative last seen in 1948, and they ask if I still like living in New York City. I have lived in Los Angeles for three years, but I say that I do. The baby is offered a horehound drop, and I am slipped a dollar bill 'to buy a treat.' Questions trail off, answers are abandoned, the baby plays with the dust motes in a shaft of afternoon sun.

It is time for the baby's birthday party: a white cake, strawberry-marshmallow ice cream, a bottle of champagne saved from another party. In the evening, after she has gone to sleep, I kneel beside the crib and touch her face, where it is pressed against the slats, with mine. She is an open and trusting child, unprepared for and unaccustomed to the ambushes of family life, and perhaps it is just as well that I can offer her little of that life. I would like to give her more. I would like to promise her that she will grow up with a sense of her cousins and of rivers and of her great-grandmother's teacups, would like to pledge her a picnic on a river with fried chicken and her hair uncombed, would like to give her *home* for her birthday, but we live differently now and I can promise her nothing like that. I give her a xylophone and a sundress from Madeira, and promise to tell her a funny story.

1967

III

Seven Places
of the Mind

Notes from a Native Daughter

It is very easy to sit at the bar in, say, La Scala in Beverly Hills, or Ernie's in San Francisco, and to share in the pervasive delusion that California is only five hours from New York by air. The truth is that La Scala and Ernie's are only five hours from New York by air. California is somewhere else.

Many people in the East (or 'back East,' as they say in California, although not in La Scala or Ernie's) do not believe this. They have been to Los Angeles or to San Francisco, have driven through a giant redwood and have seen the Pacific glazed by the afternoon sun off Big Sur, and they naturally tend to believe that they have in fact been to California. They have not been, and they probably never will be, for it is a longer and in many ways a more difficult trip than they might want to undertake, one of those trips on which the destination flickers chimerically on the horizon, ever receding, ever diminishing. I happen to know about that trip because I come from California, come from a family, or a congeries of families, that has always been in the Sacramento Valley.

You might protest that no family has been in the Sacramento Valley for anything approaching 'always.' But it is characteristic of Californians to speak grandly of the past as if it had simultaneously begun, *tabula rasa*, and reached a happy ending on the day the wagons started west. *Eureka* – 'I Have Found It' – as the state motto has it. Such a view of history casts a certain melancholia over those who participate in it; my own childhood was suffused with the conviction that we had long outlived our finest hour. In fact that is what

I want to tell you about: what it is like to come from a place like Sacramento. If I could make you understand that, I could make you understand California and perhaps something else besides, for Sacramento *is* California, and California is a place in which a boom mentality and a sense of Chekhovian loss meet in uneasy suspension; in which the mind is troubled by some buried but ineradicable suspicion that things had better work here, because here, beneath that immense bleached sky, is where we run out of continent.

In 1847 Sacramento was no more than an adobe enclosure, Sutter's Fort, standing alone on the prairie; cut off from San Francisco and the sea by the Coast Range and from the rest of the continent by the Sierra Nevada, the Sacramento Valley was then a true sea of grass, grass so high a man riding into it could tie it across his saddle. A year later gold was discovered in the Sierra foothills, and abruptly Sacramento was a town, a town any moviegoer could map tonight in his dreams – a dusty collage of assay offices and wagonmakers and saloons. Call that Phase Two. Then the settlers came – the farmers, the people who for two hundred years had been moving west on the frontier, the peculiar flawed strain who had cleared Virginia, Kentucky, Missouri; they made Sacramento a farm town. Because the land was rich, Sacramento became eventually a rich farm town, which meant houses in town, Cadillac dealers, a country club. In that gentle sleep Sacramento dreamed until perhaps 1950, when something happened. What happened was that Sacramento woke to the fact that the outside world was moving in, fast and hard. At the moment of its waking Sacramento lost, for better or for worse, its character, and that is part of what I want to tell you about.

But the change is not what I remember first. First I remember running a boxer dog of my brother's over the same flat fields that our great-great-grandfather had found virgin and had planted; I remember swimming (albeit nervously, for I was a nervous child, afraid of sinkholes and afraid of snakes, and perhaps that was the beginning of my error) the same rivers we had swum for a century: the Sacramento, so rich with silt that we could barely see our hands a few inches beneath the surface; the American, running clean and fast with melted Sierra snow until July, when it would slow down, and rattlesnakes would sun themselves on its newly exposed rocks. The Sacramento, the American, sometimes the Cosumnes, occasionally the Feather. Incautious children died every day in those rivers; we read about it in the paper, how they had miscalculated a current or stepped into a hole down where the American runs into the Sacramento, how the Berry Brothers had been called in from Yolo County to drag the river but how the bodies remained unrecovered. 'They were from away,' my grandmother would extrapolate from the newspaper stories. 'Their parents had no *business* letting them in the river. They were visitors from Omaha.' It was not a bad lesson, although a less than reliable one; children we knew died in the rivers too.

When summer ended – when the State Fair closed and the heat broke, when the last green hop vines had been torn down along the H Street road and the tule fog began rising off the low ground at night – we would go back to memorizing the Products of Our Latin American Neighbors and to visiting the great-aunts on Sunday, dozens of great-aunts, year after year of Sundays. When I think now of those winters I think of yellow elm leaves wadded in the gutters outside the Trinity Episcopal Pro-Cathedral on M Street. There are actually people in Sacramento now who call M Street Capitol Avenue, and Trinity has one of those featureless new buildings, but perhaps children still learn the same things there on Sunday mornings:

Q. In what way does the Holy Land resemble the Sacramento Valley?
A. In the type and diversity of its agricultural products.

And I think of the rivers rising, of listening to the radio to hear at what height they would crest and wondering if and when and where the levees would go. We did not have as many dams in those years. The bypasses would be full, and men would sandbag all night. Sometimes a levee would go in the night, somewhere upriver; in the morning the rumor would spread that the Army Engineers had dynamited it to relieve the pressure on the city.

After the rains came spring, for ten days or so; the drenched fields would dissolve into a brilliant ephemeral green (it would be yellow and dry as fire in two or three weeks) and the real-estate business would pick up. It was the time of year when people's grandmothers went to Carmel; it was the time of year when girls who could not even get into Stephens or Arizona or Oregon, let alone Stanford or Berkeley, would be sent to Honolulu, on the *Lurline*. I have no recollection of anyone going to New York, with the exception of a cousin who visited there (I cannot imagine why) and reported that the shoe salesmen at Lord & Taylor were 'intolerably rude.' What happened in New York and Washington and abroad seemed to impinge not at all upon the Sacramento mind. I remember being taken to call upon a very old woman, a rancher's widow, who was reminiscing (the favored conversational mode in Sacramento) about the son of some contemporaries of hers. 'That Johnston boy never did amount to much,' she said. Desultorily, my mother protested: Alva Johnston, she said, had won the Pulitzer Prize, when he was working for *The New York Times*. Our hostess looked at us impassively. 'He never amounted to anything in Sacramento,' she said.

Hers was the true Sacramento voice, and, although I did not realize it then, one not long to be heard, for the war was over and the boom was on and the voice of the aerospace engineer would be heard in the land. VETS NO DOWN! EXECUTIVE LIVING ON LOW FHA!

Later, when I was living in New York, I would make the trip back to Sacramento four and five times a year (the more comfortable the flight, the more obscurely miserable I would be, for it weighs heavily upon my kind that we could perhaps not make it by wagon), trying to prove that I had not meant to leave at all, because in at least one respect California – the California we are talking about – resembles Eden: it is assumed that those who absent themselves from its blessings have been banished, exiled by some perversity of heart. Did not the Donner-Reed Party, after all, eat its own dead to reach Sacramento?

I have said that the trip back is difficult, and it is – difficult in a way that magnifies the ordinary ambiguities of sentimental journeys. Going back to California is not like going back to Vermont, or Chicago; Vermont and Chicago are relative constants, against which one measures one's own change. All that is constant about the California of my childhood is the rate at which it disappears. An instance: on Saint Patrick's Day of 1948 I was taken to see the legislature 'in action,' a dismal experience; a handful of florid assemblymen, wearing green hats, were reading Pat-and-Mike jokes into the record. I still think of the legislators that way – wearing green hats, or sitting around on the veranda of the Senator Hotel fanning themselves and being entertained by Artie Samish's emissaries. (Samish was the lobbyist who said, 'Earl Warren may be the governor of the state, but I'm the governor of the legislature.') In fact there is no longer a veranda at the Senator Hotel – it was turned into an airline ticket office, if you want to embroider the point – and in any case the legislature has largely deserted the Senator for the flashy motels north of town, where the tiki torches flame and the steam rises off the heated swimming pools in the cold Valley night.

It is hard to *find* California now, unsettling to wonder how much of it was merely imagined or improvised; melancholy to realize how much of anyone's memory is no true memory at all but only the traces of someone else's memory, stories handed down on the family network. I have an indelibly vivid 'memory,' for example, of how Prohibition affected the hop growers around Sacramento: the sister of a grower my family knew brought home a mink coat from San Francisco, and was told to take it back, and sat on the floor of the parlor cradling that coat and crying. Although I was not born until a year after Repeal, that scene is more 'real' to me than many I have played myself.

I remember one trip home, when I sat alone on a night jet from New York and read over and over some lines from a W. S. Merwin poem I had come across in a magazine, a poem about a man who had been a long time in another country and knew that he must go home:

> . . . *But it should be*
> *Soon. Already I defend hotly*
> *Certain of our indefensible faults,*
> *Resent being reminded; already in my mind*
> *Our language becomes freighted with a richness*
> *No common tongue could offer, while the mountains*
> *Are like nowhere on earth, and the wide rivers.*

You see the point. I want to tell you the truth, and already I have
told you about the wide rivers.

It should be clear by now that the truth about the place is elusive,
and must be tracked with caution. You might go to Sacramento
tomorrow and someone (although no one I know) might take you
out to Aerojet-General, which has, in the Sacramento phrase, 'something to do with rockets.' Fifteen thousand people work for Aerojet,
almost all of them imported; a Sacramento lawyer's wife told me,
as evidence of how Sacramento was opening up, that she believed
she had met one of them, at an open house two Decembers ago.
('Couldn't have been nicer, actually,' she added enthusiastically. 'I
think he and his wife bought the house next *door* to Mary and Al,
something like that, which of course was how *they* met him.') So
you might go to Aerojet and stand in the big vendors' lobby where
a couple of thousand components salesmen try every week to sell
their wares and you might look up at the electrical wallboard that
lists Aerojet personnel, their projects and their location at any given
time, and you might wonder if I have been in Sacramento lately.
MINUTEMAN, POLARIS, TITAN, the lights flash, and all the coffee tables
are littered with airline schedules, very now, very much in touch.

But I could take you a few miles from there into towns where
the banks still bear names like The Bank of Alex Brown, into towns
where the one hotel still has an octagonal-tile floor in the dining
room and dusty potted palms and big ceiling fans; into towns where
everything – the seed business, the Harvester franchise, the hotel,
the department store and the main street – carries a single name,
the name of the man who built the town. A few Sundays ago I was
in a town like that, a town smaller than that, really, no hotel, no
Harvester franchise, the bank burned out, a river town. It was the
golden anniversary of some of my relatives and it was 110° and the
guests of honor sat on straight-backed chairs in front of a sheaf of
gladioluses in the Rebekah Hall. I mentioned visiting Aerojet-General
to a cousin I saw there, who listened to me with interested disbelief.
Which is the true California? That is what we all wonder.

*   *   *

Let us try out a few irrefutable statements, on subjects not open to interpretation. Although Sacramento is in many ways the least typical of the Valley towns, it *is* a Valley town, and must be viewed in that context. When you say 'the Valley' in Los Angeles, most people assume that you mean the San Fernando Valley (some people in fact assume that you mean Warner Brothers), but make no mistake: we are talking not about the valley of the sound stages and the ranchettes but about the real Valley, the Central Valley, the fifty thousand square miles drained by the Sacramento and the San Joaquin Rivers and further irrigated by a complex network of sloughs, cutoffs, ditches, and the Delta-Mendota and Friant-Kern Canals.

A hundred miles north of Los Angeles, at the moment when you drop from the Tehachapi Mountains into the outskirts of Bakersfield, you leave Southern California and enter the Valley. 'You look up the highway and it is straight for miles, coming at you, with the black line down the center coming at you and at you . . . and the heat dazzles up from the white slab so that only the black line is clear, coming at you with the whine of the tires, and if you don't quit staring at that line and don't take a few deep breaths and slap yourself hard on the back of the neck you'll hypnotize yourself.'

Robert Penn Warren wrote that about another road, but he might have been writing about the Valley road, U.S. 99, three hundred miles from Bakersfield to Sacramento, a highway so straight that when one flies on the most direct pattern from Los Angeles to Sacramento one never loses sight of U.S. 99. The landscape it runs through never, to the untrained eye, varies. The Valley eye can discern the point where miles of cotton seedlings fade into miles of tomato seedlings, or where the great corporation ranches – Kern County Land, what is left of DiGiorgio – give way to private operations (somewhere on the horizon, if the place is private, one sees a house and a stand of scrub oaks), but such distinctions are in the long view irrelevant. All day long, all that moves is the sun, and the big Rainbird sprinklers.

Every so often along 99 between Bakersfield and Sacramento there is a town: Delano, Tulare, Fresno, Madera, Merced, Modesto, Stockton. Some of these towns are pretty big now, but they are all the same at heart, one- and two- and three-story buildings artlessly arranged, so that what appears to be the good dress shop stands

beside a W. T. Grant store, so that the big Bank of America faces a
Mexican movie house. *Dos Peliculas, Bingo Bingo Bingo*. Beyond the
downtown (pronounced *down*town, with the Okie accent that now
pervades Valley speech patterns) lie blocks of old frame houses –
paint peeling, sidewalks cracking, their occasional leaded amber
windows overlooking a Foster's Freeze or a five-minute car wash or
a State Farm Insurance office; beyond those spread the shopping
centers and the miles of tract houses, pastel with redwood siding,
the unmistakable signs of cheap building already blossoming on those
houses which have survived the first rain. To a stranger driving 99
in an air-conditioned car (he would be on business, I suppose, any
stranger driving 99, for 99 would never get a tourist to Big Sur or
San Simeon, never get him to the California he came to see), these
towns must seem so flat, so impoverished, as to drain the imagination. They hint at evenings spent hanging around gas stations, and
suicide pacts sealed in drive-ins.

But remember:

Q. In what way does the Holy Land resemble the Sacramento Valley?
A. In the type and diversity of its agricultural products.

U.S. 99 in fact passes through the richest and most intensely
cultivated agricultural region in the world, a giant outdoor hothouse
with a billion-dollar crop. It is when you remember the Valley's
wealth that the monochromatic flatness of its towns takes on a curious meaning, suggests a habit of mind some would consider perverse.
There is something in the Valley mind that reflects a real indifference
to the stranger in his air-conditioned car, a failure to perceive even
his presence, let alone his thoughts or wants. An implacable insularity is the seal of these towns. I once met a woman in Dallas, a
most charming and attractive woman accustomed to the hospitality
and social hypersensitivity of Texas, who told me that during the
four war years her husband had been stationed in Modesto, she had
never once been invited inside anyone's house. No one in Sacramento would find this story remarkable ('She probably had no relatives there,' said someone to whom I told it), for the Valley towns
understand one another, share a peculiar spirit. They think alike and
they look alike. I can tell Modesto from Merced, but I have visited

there, gone to dances there; besides, there is over the main street of Modesto an arched sign which reads:

WATER – WEALTH
CONTENTMENT – HEALTH

There is no such sign in Merced.

I said that Sacramento was the least typical of the Valley towns, and it is – but only because it is bigger and more diverse, only because it has had the rivers and the legislature; its true character remains the Valley character, its virtues the Valley virtues, its sadness the Valley sadness. It is just as hot in the summertime, so hot that the air shimmers and the grass bleaches white and the blinds stay drawn all day, so hot that August comes on not like a month but like an affliction; it is just as flat, so flat that a ranch of my family's with a slight rise on it, perhaps a foot, was known for the hundred some years which preceded this year as 'the hill ranch.' (It is known this year as a subdivision in the making, but that is another part of the story.) Above all, in spite of its infusions from outside, Sacramento retains the Valley insularity.

To sense that insularity a visitor need do no more than pick up a copy of either of the two newspapers, the morning *Union* or the afternoon *Bee*. The *Union* happens to be Republican and impoverished and the *Bee* Democratic and powerful ('THE VALLEY OF THE BEES!' as the McClatchys, who own the Fresno, Modesto, and Sacramento *Bees*, used to headline their advertisements in the trade press. 'ISOLATED FROM ALL OTHER MEDIA INFLUENCE'), but they read a good deal alike, and the tone of their chief editorial concerns is strange and wonderful and instructive. The *Union*, in a county heavily and reliably Democratic, frets mainly about the possibility of a local takeover by the John Birch Society; the *Bee*, faithful to the letter of its founder's will, carries on overwrought crusades against phantoms it still calls 'the power trusts.' Shades of Hiram Johnson, whom the *Bee* helped elect governor in 1910. Shades of Robert La Follette, to whom the *Bee* delivered the Valley in 1924. There is something about the Sacramento papers that does not quite connect with the way

Sacramento lives now, something pronouncedly beside the point. The aerospace engineers, one learns, read the San Francisco *Chronicle*.

The Sacramento papers, however, simply mirror the Sacramento peculiarity, the Valley fate, which is to be paralyzed by a past no longer relevant. Sacramento is a town which grew up on farming and discovered to its shock that land has more profitable uses. (The chamber of commerce will give you crop figures, but pay them no mind – what matters is the feeling, the knowledge that where the green hops once grew is now Larchmont Riviera, that what used to be the Whitney ranch is now Sunset City, thirty-three thousand houses and a country-club complex.) It is a town in which defense industry and its absentee owners are suddenly the most important facts; a town which has never had more people or more money, but has lost its *raison d'être*. It is a town many of whose most solid citizens sense about themselves a kind of functional obsolescence. The old families still see only one another, but they do not see even one another as much as they once did; they are closing ranks, preparing for the long night, selling their rights-of-way and living on the proceeds. Their children still marry one another, still play bridge and go into the real-estate business together. (There is no other business in Sacramento, no reality other than land – even I, when I was living and working in New York, felt impelled to take a University of California correspondence course in Urban Land Economics.) But late at night when the ice has melted there is always somebody now, some Julian English, whose heart is not quite in it. For out there on the outskirts of town are marshaled the legions of aerospace engineers, who talk their peculiar condescending language and tend their dichondra and plan to stay in the promised land; who are raising a new generation of native Sacramentans and who do not care, really do not care, that they are not asked to join the Sutter Club. It makes one wonder, late at night when the ice is gone; introduces some air into the womb, suggests that the Sutter Club is perhaps not, after all, the Pacific Union or the Bohemian; that Sacramento is not *the city*. In just such self-doubts do small towns lose their character.

I want to tell you a Sacramento story. A few miles out of town is a place, six or seven thousand acres, which belonged in the beginning to a rancher with one daughter. That daughter went abroad and married a title, and when she brought the title home to live on the ranch, her father built them a vast house – music rooms, conservatories, a ballroom. They needed a ballroom because they entertained: people from abroad, people from San Francisco, house parties that lasted weeks and involved special trains. They are long dead, of course, but their only son, aging and unmarried, still lives on the place. He does not live in the house, for the house is no longer there. Over the years it burned, room by room, wing by wing. Only the chimneys of the great house are still standing, and its heir lives in their shadow, lives by himself on the charred site, in a house trailer.

That is a story my generation knows; I doubt that the next will know it, the children of the aerospace engineers. Who would tell it to them? Their grandmothers live in Scarsdale, and they have never met a great-aunt. 'Old' Sacramento to them will be something colorful, something they read about in *Sunset*. They will probably think that the Redevelopment has always been there, that the Embarcadero, down along the river, with its amusing places to shop and its picturesque fire houses turned into bars, has about it the true flavor of the way it was. There will be no reason for them to know that in homelier days it was called Front Street (the town was not, after all, settled by the Spanish) and was a place of derelicts and missions and itinerant pickers in town for a Saturday-night drunk: VICTORIOUS LIFE MISSION, JESUS SAVES, BEDS 25¢ A NIGHT, CROP INFORMATION HERE. They will have lost the real past and gained a manufactured one, and there will be no way for them to know, no way at all, why a house trailer should stand alone on seven thousand acres outside town.

But perhaps it is presumptuous of me to assume that they will be missing something. Perhaps in retrospect this has been a story not about Sacramento at all, but about the things we lose and the promises we break as we grow older; perhaps I have been playing out unawares the Margaret in the poem:

> *Margaret, are you grieving*
> *Over Goldengrove unleaving? . . .*
> *It is the blight man was born for,*
> *It is Margaret you mourn for.*

1965

Letter from Paradise, 21° 19' N., 157° 52' W.

Because I had been tired too long and quarrelsome too much and too often frightened of migraine and failure and the days getting shorter, I was sent, a recalcitrant thirty-one-year-old child, to Hawaii, where winter does not come and no one fails and the median age is twenty-three. There I could become a new woman, there with the life-insurance salesmen on million-dollar-a-year incentive trips, there with the Shriners and the San Francisco divorcées and the splurging secretaries and the girls in the string bikinis and the boys in search of the perfect wave, children who understood the insouciant economy of buying a Honda or a surfboard for one dollar down and $2.50 a week and then abandoning it, children who have never been told, as I was told, that golden lads and girls all must as chimney sweepers come to dust. I was to lie beneath the same sun that had kept Doris Duke and Henry Kaiser forever hopeful. I was to play at sipping frozen daiquiris and wear flowers in my hair as if ten years had never happened. I was to see for myself that just beyond the end of the line lay not Despond but Diamond Head.

I went, a wary visitor. I do not believe that the stories told by lovely hula hands merit extensive study. I have never heard a Hawaiian word, including and perhaps most particularly *aloha*, which accurately expressed anything I had to say. I have neither enough capacity for surprise nor enough heart for twice-told tales to make you listen again to tedious vignettes about Midwesterners in souvenir shirts and touring widows in muumuus and simulated pearls, about the Kodak Hula Show or the Sunday Night Luau or the Schoolteacher and the Beach Boy. And so, now that it is on the line between us that I lack all temperament for paradise, real or facsimile, I am going to find it difficult to tell you precisely how and why Hawaii moves me, touches me, saddens and troubles and engages my imagination, what it is in the air that will linger long after I have forgotten the smell of pikake and pineapple and the way the palms sound in the trade winds.

Perhaps because I grew up in California, Hawaii figured large in my fantasies. I sat as a child on California beaches and imagined that I saw Hawaii, a certain shimmer in the sunset, a barely perceptible irregularity glimpsed intermittently through squinted eyes. The curious void in this fantasy was that I had not the slightest idea what Hawaii would look like if I did see it, for in my child's mind there were three distant Hawaiis, and I could perceive no connections among the three.

There was, to begin with, the Hawaii first shown to me in an atlas on December 7, 1941, the pastel pinpoints that meant war and my father going away and makeshift Christmases in rented rooms near Air Corps bases and nothing the same ever again. Later, when the war was over, there was another Hawaii, a big rock candy mountain in the Pacific which presented itself to me in newspaper photographs of well-fed Lincoln-Mercury dealers relaxing beside an outrigger at the Royal Hawaiian Hotel or disembarking *en famille* from the *Lurline*, a Hawaii where older cousins might spend winter vacations learning to surfboard (for that is what it was called in those simpler days, surfboarding, and it was peculiar to Hawaii) and where godmothers might repair to rest and to learn all the lyrics to 'My Little Grass Shack in Kealakekua Hawaii.' I do not remember how many nights I lay awake in bed and listened to someone downstairs singing 'My Little Grass Shack in Kealakekua Hawaii,' but I do remember that I made no connection between that Hawaii and the Hawaii of December 7, 1941.

And then, always, there was a third Hawaii, a place which seemed to have to do neither with war nor with vacationing godmothers but only with the past, and with loss. The last member of my direct family ever to live in Hawaii was a great-great-grandfather who taught there as a young missionary in 1842, and I was given to understand that life in the Islands, as we called Hawaii on the West

Coast, had been declining steadily since. My aunt married into a family which had lived for generations in the Islands, but they did not even visit there any more; 'Not since Mr *Kaiser*,' they would say, as if the construction of the Hawaiian Village Hotel on a few acres of reclaimed tidal flat near Fort De Russy had in one swing of the builder's crane wiped out their childhoods and their parents' childhoods, blighted forever some subtropical cherry orchard where every night in the soft blur of memory the table was set for forty-eight in case someone dropped by; as if Henry Kaiser had personally condemned them to live out their lives in California exile among only their token mementos, the calabashes and the carved palace chairs and the flat silver for forty-eight and the diamond that had been Queen Liliuokalani's and the heavy linens embroidered on all the long golden afternoons that were no more.

Of course as I grew older I recognized that the name 'Henry Kaiser' carried more symbolic than literal freight, but even then I missed the point, imagined that it was merely the proliferation of hotels and hundred-dollar thrift flights that had disturbed the old order, managed to dismiss the Hawaii of my first memory, the Hawaii which meant war, as an accident of history, a freak relevant neither to the gentle idyll that must have been the past nor to the frenetic paean to middle-income leisure that must be the present. In so doing I misapprehended Hawaii completely, for if there is a single aura which pervades Honolulu, one mood which lends the lights a feverish luster and the pink catamarans a heartbreaking absurdity and which engages the imagination as mere paradise never could, that mood is, inescapably, one of war.

It begins, of course, in what we remember.

> *Hawaii is our Gibraltar, and almost our Channel Coast. Planes, their eyes sharpened by the year-round clearness of blue Pacific days, can keep easy watch over an immense sea-circle, of which Hawaii is the centre. With Hawaii on guard, a surprise attack on us from Asia, the experts believe, would be quite impossible. So long as the great Pearl Harbor Naval Base, just down the road from Honolulu, is ours, American warships and submarines can run their un-Pacific errands*

with a maximum of ease. Pearl Harbor is one of the greatest, if not the very greatest, maritime fortresses in the world. Pearl Harbor has immense reserves of fuel and food, and huge and clanging hospitals for the healing of any wounds which steel can suffer. It is the one sure sanctuary in the whole of the vast Pacific both for ships and men.

John W. Vandercook, in
Vogue, January 1, 1941

Every afternoon now, twenty-five years after the fact, the bright pink tour boats leave Kewalo Basin for Pearl Harbor. It has a kind of sleazy festivity at first, the prospect of an outing on a fine day, the passengers comparing complaints about their tour directors and their accommodations and the food at Canlis' Charcoal Broiler, the boys diving for coins around the boats; 'Hey Mister Big,' they scream. 'How's about a coin.' Sometimes a woman will throw a bill, and then be outraged when the insolent brown bodies pluck it from the air and jeer at her expectations. As the boat leaves the basin the boys swim back, their cheeks stuffed with money, and the children pout that they would rather be at the beach, and the women in their new Liberty House shifts and leftover leis sip papaya juice and study a booklet billed as *An Ideal Gift – Picture Story of December 7.*

It is, after all, a familiar story that we have come to hear – familiar even to the children, for of course they have seen John Wayne and John Garfield at Pearl Harbor, have spent countless rainy afternoons watching Kirk Douglas and Spencer Tracy and Van Johnson wonder out loud why Hickam does not answer this morning – and no one listens very closely to the guide. Sugar cane now blows where the *Nevada* went aground. An idle figure practices putting on Ford Island. The concessionaire breaks out more papaya juice. It is hard to remember what we came to remember.

And then something happens. I took that bright pink boat to Pearl Harbor on two afternoons, but I still do not know what I went to find out, which is how other people respond a quarter of a century later. I do not know because there is a point at which I began to cry, and to notice no one else. I began to cry at the place where the *Utah* lies in fifty feet of water, water neither turquoise nor bright blue here but the gray of harbor waters everywhere, and I did not stop until after the pink boat had left the *Arizona*, or what is visible of the *Arizona*: the rusted after-gun turret breaking the gray water, the flag at full mast because the Navy considers the *Arizona* still in commission, a full crew aboard, 1,102 men from forty-nine states. All I know about how other people respond is what I am told: that everyone is quiet at the *Arizona*.

A few days ago someone just four years younger than I am told me that he did not see why a sunken ship should affect me so, that John Kennedy's assassination, not Pearl Harbor, was the single most indelible event of what he kept calling 'our generation.' I could tell him only that we belonged to different generations, and I did not tell him what I want to tell you, about a place in Honolulu that is quieter still than the *Arizona*: the National Memorial Cemetery of the Pacific. They all seem to be twenty years old, the boys buried up there in the crater of an extinct volcano named Punchbowl, twenty and nineteen and eighteen and sometimes not that old. 'SAMUEL FOSTER HARMON,' one stone reads. 'PENNSYLVANIA. PVT 27 REPL DRAFT 5 MARINE DIV. WORLD WAR II. APRIL 10 1928–MARCH 25 1945.' Samuel Foster Harmon died, at Iwo Jima, fifteen days short of his seventeenth birthday. Some of them died on December 7 and some of them died after the *Enola Gay* had already bombed Hiroshima and some of them died on the dates of the landings at Okinawa and Iwo Jima and Guadalcanal and one whole long row of them, I am told, died on the beach of an island we no longer remember. There are 19,000 graves in the vast sunken crater above Honolulu.

I would go up there quite a bit. If I walked to the rim of the crater I could see the city, look down over Waikiki and the harbor and the jammed arterials, but up there it was quiet, and high enough into the rain forest so that a soft mist falls most of the day. One afternoon a couple came and left three plumeria leis on the grave of a California boy who had been killed, at nineteen, in 1945. The leis were already wilting by the time the woman finally placed them on the grave, because for a long time she only stood there and twisted them in her hands. On the whole I am able to take a very long view of death, but I think a great deal about what there is to remember, twenty-one years later, of a boy who died at nineteen. I saw no one else there but the men who cut the grass and the men who dig new graves, for they are bringing in bodies now from Vietnam. The graves filled last week and the week before that and even last month do not yet have stones, only plastic identification cards, streaked by the mist and splattered with mud. The earth is raw and trampled in that part of the crater, but the grass grows fast, up there in the rain cloud.

It is not very far from the crater down to Hotel Street, which is to Honolulu what Market Street is to San Francisco, the bright night street in a port city. The carrier *Coral Sea* was in Honolulu that week, and 165 men in from Vietnam on rest-and-recuperation leave, and 3,500 Marines on their way to Okinawa and then to Vietnam (they were part of the reactivated 5th Marine Division, and it was the 5th, if you will remember, to which the sixteen-year-old Samuel Foster Harmon belonged), and besides that there was the regular complement of personnel for Pearl and Hickam and Camp H. M. Smith and Fort Shafter and Fort De Russy and Bellows A.F.B. and the Kaneohe Marine Air Station and Schofield Barracks, and sooner or later they all got downtown to Hotel Street. They always have. The Navy cleaned out the red-light houses at the end of World War II, but the Hotel Streets of this world do not change perceptibly from war to war. The girls with hibiscus in their hair stroll idly in front of the penny arcades and the Japanese pool halls and the massage studios. 'GIRLS WANTED FOR MASSAGE WORK,' the signs say. 'WHAT A REFRESHING NEW TINGLE.' The fortunetellers sit and file their nails behind flowered paper curtains. The boys from the cast of the Boys Will Be Girls Revue stand out on the sidewalk in lamé evening dresses, smoking cigarettes and looking the sailors over.

And the sailors get drunk. They all seem to be twenty years old on Hotel Street, too, twenty and nineteen and eighteen and drunk because they are no longer in Des Moines and not yet in Danang. They look in at the taxi-dance places and they look in at the strip places with the pictures of Lili St Cyr and Tempest Storm outside (Lili St Cyr was in California and Tempest Storm in Baltimore, but never mind, they all look alike on Saturday night in Honolulu) and they fish in their pockets for quarters to see the Art Movie in the back of the place that sells *Sunshine* and *Nude* and all the paperbacks with chained girls on the cover. They have snapshots laminated.

They record their own voices (*Hi, Sweetheart, I'm in Honolulu tonight*) and they talk to the girls with hibiscus in their hair.

But mostly they just get a little drunker, and jostle around on the sidewalk avoiding the Hawaii Armed Forces Patrol and daring one another to get tattooed. In a show of bravado they rip off their shirts a half block before they reach Lou Normand's Tattoo Parlor and then they sit with glazed impassivity while the needle brands them with a heart or an anchor or, if they are particularly flush or particularly drunk, a replica of Christ on the cross with the stigmata in red. Their friends cluster outside the glass cubicle watching the skin redden and all the while, from a country-and-western bar on the corner, 'King of the Road' reverberates down Hotel Street. The songs change and the boys come and go but Lou Normand has been Thirty Years in the Same Location.

Perhaps it seems not surprising that there should be a mood of war at the scenes of famous defeats and at the graves of seventeen-year-olds and downtown in a port city. But the mood is not only there. War is in the very fabric of Hawaii's life, ineradicably fixed in both its emotions and its economy, dominating not only its memory but its vision of the future. There is a point at which every Honolulu conversation refers back to war. People sit in their gardens up on Makiki Heights among their copa de oro and their star jasmine and they look down toward Pearl Harbor and get another drink and tell you about the morning it happened. Webley Edwards was on the radio, they remember that, and what he said that morning again and again was 'This is an air raid, take cover, *this is the real McCoy.*' That is not a remarkable thing to say, but it is a remarkable thing to have in one's memory. And they remember how people drove up into the hills and parked to watch the fires, just as they do now when a tsunami wave is due. They remember emergency wards in school auditoriums and how the older children were dispatched to guard reservoirs with unloaded guns. They laugh about trying to drive over the Pali in the fog after the 9 p.m. blackout, and about how their wives took thick books and large handkerchiefs down to the Y.W.C.A. and used them to show girls from the outer islands how to make a hospital bed, and they remember how it was when there were only three hotels on all two miles of Waikiki, the Royal for the Navy, the Halekulani for the press, and the Moana. In fact they contrive to leave an indistinct impression that it was in 1945, or perhaps '46, that they last got down to Waikiki. 'I suppose the Royal hasn't changed,' one Honolulan who lives within eight minutes of the Royal remarked to me. 'The Halekulani,' another said, as if it had just flickered into memory and she was uncertain it still existed. '*That* used to be kind of fun for drinks.' Everyone was younger then, and in the telling a certain glow suffuses those years.

And then, if they have a stake in selling Hawaii, and there are very few people left in Hawaii who refuse to perceive that they do have a stake in selling it, they explain why Hawaii's future is so bright. In spite of what might be considered a classic false economy, based first upon the military, next upon the tourist, and third upon subsidized sugar, Hawaii's future is bright because Hawaii is the hub of the Pacific, a phrase employed in Honolulu only slightly less frequently than 'our wonderful *aloha* spirit.' They point out that Hawaii is the hub of the Pacific as far as the travel industry goes, and that Hawaii is also the hub of the Pacific as far as – they pause, and perhaps pick up a glass and study it before continuing. 'And, well, frankly, if it goes the other way, what I mean by that is if the *situation* goes the other way, we're in the right spot for that, too.' Perhaps nowhere else in the United States is the prospect of war regarded with so much equanimity.

Of course it is easy to suggest reasons, to say that after all Hawaii has already lived through one war, or to point out that Honolulu is even now in a war zone, steeped in the vocabulary of the military, deeply committed to the business of war. But it runs deeper than that. War is viewed with a curious ambivalence in Hawaii because the largest part of its population interprets war, however unconsciously, as a force for good, an instrument of social progress. And of course it was precisely World War II which cracked the spine of sugar feudalism, opened up a contracting economy and an immobile society, shattered forever the pleasant but formidable colonial world in which a handful of families controlled everything Hawaii did, where it shopped, how it shipped its goods, who could come in and how far they could go and at what point they would be closed out.

We have, most of us, some image of prewar Hawaii. We have

heard the phrase 'Big Five,' and we have a general notion that certain families acquired a great deal of money and power in Hawaii and kept that money and that power for a very long while. The reality of Hawaiian power was at once more obvious and more subtle than one might imagine it to have been. The Big Five companies – C. Brewer, Theo. H. Davies, American Factors, Castle & Cooke, and Alexander & Baldwin – began as 'factors' for the sugar planters; in effect they were plantation management. Over the years, the Big Five families and a few others – the Dillinghams, say, who were descended from a stranded sailor who built Hawaii's first railroad – intermarried, sat on one another's boards, got into shipping and insurance and money, and came to comprise a benevolent oligarchy unlike any on the mainland.

For almost half a century this interlocking directorate extended into every area of Hawaiian life, and its power could be exercised immediately and personally. American Factors, for example, owned (and still owns) the major Hawaiian department store, Liberty House. In 1941, Sears, Roebuck, working secretly through intermediaries, bought land for a store in suburban Honolulu. Sears finally opened its store, but not until the Sears president, Robert E. Wood, had threatened to buy his own ship; there had been some question as to whether Matson Navigation, controlled by Castle & Cooke and Alexander & Baldwin, would ship merchandise for anyone so baldly attempting to compete with a Big Five enterprise.

That was Hawaii. And then World War II came. Island boys went to war, and came home with new ideas. Mainland money came in, against all Island opposition. After World War II, the late Walter Dillingham could come down to a public hearing from his house on Diamond Head and cast at Henry Kaiser the most meaningful epithet of antebellum Hawaii – '*visitor*' – and have its significance lost on perhaps half his audience. In spirit if never quite in fact, World War II made everyone a Dillingham, and anyone in Hawaii too slow to perceive this for himself was constantly told it, by politicians and by labor leaders and by mainland observers.

The extent of the change, of course, has often been overstated, for reasons sometimes sentimental and sometimes strategic, but it is true that Hawaii is no more what it once was. There is still only one 'Lowell' in Honolulu, and that is Lowell Dillingham, still only one 'Ben,' and that is his brother – but Ben Dillingham was over-whelmingly defeated in his 1962 campaign for the United States Senate by Daniel Inouye, a Nisei. (In the 1920s, when a congressional committee asked Ben Dillingham's father and Henry Baldwin why so few Japanese voted in Hawaii, they could suggest only that perhaps the Japanese were under instructions from Tokyo not to register.) There is still a strong feeling in old-line Honolulu that the Big Five 'caved in' to labor – but Jack Hall, the tough I.L.W.U. leader who was once convicted under the Smith Act for conspiring to teach the overthrow of the United States Government by force and violence, now sits on the board of the Hawaii Visitors' Bureau and commends the ladies of the Outdoor Circle for their efforts in 'preserving the loveliness that is Hawaii.' And Chinn Ho, who as a schoolboy used to chalk up quotations for a downtown broker, now owns not only a few score million dollars' worth of real estate but also that broker's own house, out on Diamond Head, hard by Ben Dillingham's. 'The thing is,' the broker's niece told me, 'I suppose he wanted it when he was fourteen.'

But perhaps there is no clearer way to understand the change than to visit Punahou School, the school the missionaries founded 'for their children and their children's children,' a statement of pur-pose interpreted rather literally until quite recently. To leaf through Punahou's old class books is a briefing in Hawaiian oligarchy, for the same names turn up year after year, and the names are the same as those which appear in cut stone or discreet brass letters down around what Honolulu calls The Street, Merchant Street, down on those corners where the Big Five have their offices and most Island business is done. In 1881 an Alexander delivered the commencement address and a Dillingham the commencement poem; at the 1882 graduation a Baldwin spoke on 'Chinese Immigration,' an Alexander on 'Labor Ipse Voluptas,' and a Bishop on 'Sunshine.' And although high-caste Hawaiians have always coexisted with and in fact inter-married with the white oligarchy, their Punahou classmates usually visualized them, when it came time for class prophecies, 'playing in a band.'

It is not that Punahou is not still the school of the Island power elite; it is. 'There will always be room at Punahou for those children who belong here,' Dr John Fox, headmaster since 1944, assured alumni in a recent bulletin. But where in 1944 there were 1,100 students and they had a median IQ of 108, now there are 3,400 with a median IQ of 125. Where once the enrollment was ten percent Oriental, now it is a fraction under thirty percent. And so it is that outside Punahou's new Cooke Library, where the archives are kept by a great-great-granddaughter of the Reverend Hiram Bingham, there sit, among the plumeria blossoms drifted on the steps, small Chinese boys with their books in Pan American flight bags.

'John Fox is rather controversial, I guess you know,' old-family alumni will sometimes say now, but they do not say exactly where-in the controversy lies. Perhaps because Hawaii sells itself so assiduously as the very model of a modern melting pot, the entire area of race relations is conversationally delicate. 'I wouldn't exactly say we had discrimination here,' one Honolulu woman explained tactfully. 'I'd say we had a wonderful, wonderful competitive feeling.' Another simply shrugs. 'It's just something that's never pressed. The Orientals are – well, discreet's not really the word, but they aren't like the Negroes and the Jews, they don't push in where they're not wanted.'

Even among those who are considered Island liberals, the question of race has about it, to anyone who has lived through these hypersensitive past years on the mainland, a curious and rather engaging ingenuousness. 'There are very definitely people here who know the Chinese socially,' one woman told me. 'They have them to their houses. The uncle of a friend of mine, for example, has Chinn Ho to his house all the time.' Although this seemed a statement along the lines of 'Some of my best friends are Rothschilds,' I accepted it in the spirit in which it was offered – just as I did the primitive progressivism of an Island teacher who was explaining, as we walked down a corridor of her school, about the miracles of educational integration the war had wrought. 'Look,' she said suddenly, grabbing a pretty Chinese girl by the arm and wheeling her around to face me. 'You wouldn't have seen this here before the war. Look at those eyes.'

And so, in the peculiar and still insular mythology of Hawaii, the dislocations of war became the promises of progress. Whether or not the promises have been fulfilled depends of course upon who is talking, as does whether or not progress is a virtue, but in any case it is war that is pivotal to the Hawaiian imagination, war that fills the mind, war that seems to hover over Honolulu like the rain clouds on Tantalus. Not very many people talk about that. They talk about freeways on Oahu and condominiums on Maui and beer cans at the Sacred Falls and how much wiser it is to bypass Honolulu altogether in favor of going directly to Laurance Rockefeller's Mauna Kea, on Hawaii. (In fact the notion that the only place to go in the Hawaiian Islands is somewhere on Maui or Kauai or Hawaii has by now filtered down to such wide acceptance that one can only suspect Honolulu to be due for a revival.) Or, if they are of a more visionary turn, they talk, in a kind of James Michener rhetoric, about how Hawaii is a multiracial paradise and a labor-management paradise and a progressive paradise in which the past is now reconciled with the future, where the I.LW.U.'s Jack Hall lunches at the Pacific Club and where that repository of everything old-line in Hawaii, the Bishop Estate, works hand in hand with Henry Kaiser to transform Koko Head into a $350 million development named Hawaii Kai. If they are in the travel business they talk about The Million Visitor Year (1970) and The Two Million Visitor Year (1980) and twenty thousand Rotarians convening in Honolulu in 1969 and they talk about The Product. 'The reports show what we need,' one travel man told me. 'We need more attention to shaping and molding the product.' The product is the place they live.

If they are from Honolulu but a little *arriviste* – say if they have been here only thirty years – they drop the name 'Lowell' and talk about their charity work. If they are from Honolulu but not at all *arriviste* they talk about opening boutiques and going into the real-estate business and whether or not it was rude for Jacqueline Kennedy to appear for dinner at Henry Kaiser's in a muumuu and bare feet. ('I mean I *know* people come here to relax and not get dressed up, but still . . .') They get to the mainland quite often but not often enough to be well-informed about what is going on there. They like to entertain and to be entertained and to have people coming through. ('What would it be like without them?' one woman asked me rhetorically. 'It'd be Saturday night at the club in Racine, Wisconsin.') They are very gracious and very enthusiastic, and give such an appearance of health and happiness and hope that I

sometimes find it difficult to talk to them. I think that they would
not understand why I came to Hawaii, and I think that they will
perhaps not understand what I am going to remember.

                                                                    1966

Rock of Ages

Alcatraz Island is covered with flowers now: orange and yellow nasturtiums, geraniums, sweet grass, blue iris, black-eyed Susans. Candytuft springs up through the cracked concrete in the exercise yard. Ice plant carpets the rusting catwalks. 'WARNING! KEEP OFF! U.S. PROPERTY,' the sign still reads, big and yellow and visible for perhaps a quarter of a mile, but since March 21, 1963, the day they took the last thirty or so men off the island and sent them to prisons less expensive to maintain, the warning has been only *pro forma*, the gun turrets empty, the cell blocks abandoned. It is not an unpleasant place to be, out there on Alcatraz with only the flowers and the wind and a bell buoy moaning and the tide surging through the Golden Gate, but to like a place like that you have to want a moat.

I sometimes do, which is what I am talking about here. Three people live on Alcatraz Island now. John and Marie Hart live in the same apartment they had for the sixteen years that he was a prison guard; they raised five children on the island, back when their neighbors were the Birdman and Mickey Cohen, but the Birdman and Mickey Cohen are gone now and so are the Harts' children, moved away, the last married in a ceremony on the island in June 1966. One other person lives on Alcatraz, a retired merchant seaman named Bill Doherty, and, between them, John Hart and Bill Doherty are responsible to the General Services Administration for maintaining a twenty-four-hour watch over the twenty-two-acre island. John Hart has a dog named Duffy, and Bill Doherty has a dog named Duke, and although the dogs are primarily good company they are also the first line of defense on Alcatraz Island. Marie Hart has a corner window which looks out to the San Francisco skyline, across a mile and a half of bay, and she sits there and paints 'views' or plays her organ, songs like 'Old Black Joe' and 'Please Go 'Way and Let Me Sleep.' Once a week the Harts take their boat to San Francisco to pick up their mail and shop at the big Safeway in the Marina, and occasionally Marie Hart gets off the island to visit her children. She likes to keep in touch with them by telephone, but for ten months recently, after a Japanese freighter cut the cable, there was no telephone service to or from Alcatraz. Every morning the KGO traffic reporter drops the San Francisco *Chronicle* from his helicopter, and when he has time he stops for coffee. No one else comes out there except a man from the General Services Administration named Thomas Scott, who brings out an occasional congressman or somebody who wants to buy the island or, once in a while, his wife and small son, for a picnic. Quite a few people would like to buy the island, and Mr Scott reckons that it would bring about five million dollars in a sealed-bid auction, but the General Services Administration is powerless to sell it until Congress acts on a standing proposal to turn the island into a 'peace park.' Mr Scott says that he will be glad to get Alcatraz off his hands, but the charge of a fortress island could not be something a man gives up without ambivalent thoughts.

I went out there with him a while ago. Any child could imagine a prison more like a prison than Alcatraz looks, for what bars and wires there are seem perfunctory, beside the point; the island itself was the prison, and the cold tide its wall. It is precisely what they called it: the Rock. Bill Doherty and Duke lowered the dock for us, and in the station wagon on the way up the cliff Bill Doherty told Mr Scott about small repairs he had made or planned to make. Whatever repairs get made on Alcatraz are made to pass the time, a kind of caretaker's scrimshaw, because the government pays for no upkeep at all on the prison; in 1963 it would have cost five million dollars to repair, which is why it was abandoned, and the $24,000 a year that it costs to maintain Alcatraz now is mostly for surveillance, partly to barge in the 400,000 gallons of water that Bill Doherty and the Harts use every year (there is no water at all on Alcatraz, one impediment to development), and the rest to heat two apartments and keep some lights burning. The buildings seem quite literally abandoned. The key locks have been ripped from the cell doors and the big electrical locking mechanisms disconnected. The tear-gas vents in the cafeteria are empty and the paint is buckling everywhere, corroded by the sea air, peeling off in great scales of pale green and ocher. I stood for a while in Al Capone's cell, five by nine feet, number 200 on the second tier of B Block, not one of the view cells, which were awarded on seniority, and I walked through the solitary block, totally black when the doors were closed. 'Snail Mitchel,' read a pencil scrawl on the wall of Solitary 14. 'The only man that ever got shot for walking too slow.' Beside it was a calendar, the months penciled on the wall with the days scratched off, May, June, July, August of some unnumbered year.

Mr Scott, whose interest in penology dates from the day his office acquired Alcatraz as a potential property, talked about escapes and security routines and pointed out the beach where Ma Barker's son Doc was killed trying to escape. (They told him to come back up, and he said he would rather be shot, and he was.) I saw the shower room with the soap still in the dishes. I picked up a yellowed program from an Easter service (*Why seek ye the living among the dead? He is not here, but is risen*) and I struck a few notes on an upright piano with the ivory all rotted from the keys and I tried to imagine the prison as it had been, with the big lights playing over the windows all night long and the guards patrolling the gun galleries and the silverware clattering into a bag as it was checked in after meals, tried dutifully to summon up some distaste, some night terror of the doors locking and the boat pulling away. But the fact of it was that I liked it out there, a ruin devoid of human vanities, clean of human illusions, an empty place reclaimed by the weather where a woman plays an organ to stop the wind's whining and an old man plays ball with a dog named Duke. I could tell you that I came back because I had promises to keep, but maybe it was because nobody asked me to stay.

1967

The Seacoast of Despair

I went to Newport not long ago, to see the great stone *fin-de-siècle* 'cottages' in which certain rich Americans once summered. The places loom still along Bellevue Avenue and Cliff Walk, one after another, silk curtains frayed but gargoyles intact, monuments to something beyond themselves; houses built, clearly, to some transcendental point. No one had made clear to me exactly what that point was. I had been promised that the great summer houses were museums and warned that they were monstrosities, had been assured that the way of life they suggested was graceful beyond belief and that it was gross beyond description, that the very rich were different from you and me and yes, they had lower taxes, and if 'The Breakers' was perhaps not entirely tasteful, still, *où sont les croquet wickets d'antan*. I had read Edith Wharton and I had read Henry James, who thought that the houses should stand there always, reminders 'of the peculiarly awkward vengeances of affronted proportion and discretion.'

But all that turns out to be beside the point, all talk of taxes and taste and affronted proportion. If, for example, one pursues the course, as Mrs Richard Gambrill did in 1900, of engaging the architect who did the New York Public Library, approving plans for an eighteenth-century French château on a Rhode Island beach, ordering the garden copied after one Henry VIII gave to Anne Boleyn, and naming the result 'Vernon Court,' one moves somehow beyond the charge of breached 'discretion.' Something else is at work here. No aesthetic judgment could conceivably apply to the Newport of

Bellevue Avenue, to those vast follies behind their hand-wrought gates; they are products of the metastasis of capital, the Industrial Revolution carried to its logical extreme, and what they suggest is how recent are the notions that life should be 'comfortable,' that those who live it should be 'happy.'

'Happiness' is, after all, a consumption ethic, and Newport is the monument of a society in which production was seen as the moral point, the reward if not exactly the end, of the economic process. The place is devoid of the pleasure principle. To have had the money to build 'The Breakers' or 'Marble House' or 'Ochre Court' and to choose to build at Newport is in itself a denial of possibilities; the island is physically ugly, mean without the saving grace of extreme severity, a landscape less to be enjoyed than dominated. The prevalence of topiary gardening in Newport suggests the spirit of the place. And it was not as if there were no other options for these people: William Randolph Hearst built not at Newport but out on the edge of the Pacific. San Simeon, whatever its peculiarities, is in fact *la cuesta encantada*, swimming in golden light, sybaritic air, a deeply romantic place. But in Newport the air proclaims only the sources of money. Even as the sun dapples the great lawns and the fountains plash all around, there is something in the air that has nothing to do with pleasure and nothing to do with graceful tradition, a sense not of how prettily money can be spent but of how harshly money is made, an immediate presence of the pits and the rails and the foundries, of turbines and pork-belly futures. So insistent is the presence of money in Newport that the mind springs ineluctably to the raw beginnings of it. A contemplation of 'Rosecliff' dissolves into the image of Big Jim Fair, digging the silver out of a mountain in Nevada so that his daughter might live in Newport. 'Old Man Berwind, he'd turn in his grave to see that oil truck parked in the driveway,' a guard at 'The Elms' said to me as we surveyed the sunken garden there. 'He made it in coal, soft coal.' It had been on my mind as well as on the guard's, even as we stood in the sunlight outside the marble summer house, coal, soft coal, words like *bituminous* and *anthracite*, not the words of summer fancy.

In that way Newport is curiously Western, closer in spirit to Virginia City than to New York, to Denver than to Boston. It has the stridency usually credited to the frontier. And, like the frontier, it was not much of a game for women. Men paid for Newport, and granted to women the privilege of living in it. Just as gilt vitrines could be purchased for the correct display of biscuit Sèvres, so marble stairways could be bought for the advantageous display of women. In the filigreed gazebos they could be exhibited in a different light; in the French sitting rooms, in still another setting. They could be cajoled, flattered, indulged, given pretty rooms and Worth dresses, allowed to imagine that they ran their own houses and their own lives, but when it came time to negotiate, their freedom proved *trompe l'oeil*. It was the world of Bailey's Beach which made a neurasthenic of Edith Wharton, and, against her will, the Duchess of Marlborough of Consuelo Vanderbilt. The very houses are men's houses, factories, undermined by tunnels and service railways, shot through with plumbing to collect salt water, tanks to store it, devices to collect rain water, vaults for table silver, equipment inventories of china and crystal and 'Tray cloths – fine' and 'Tray cloths – ordinary.' Somewhere in the bowels of 'The Elms' is a coal bin twice the size of Julia Berwind's bedroom. The mechanics of such houses take precedence over all desires or inclinations; neither for great passions nor for morning whims can the factory be shut down, can production – of luncheons, of masked balls, of *marrons glacés* – be slowed. To stand in the dining room of 'The Breakers' is to imagine fleeing from it, pleading migraine.

What Newport turns out to be, then, is homiletic, a fantastically elaborate stage setting for an American morality play in which money and happiness are presented as antithetical. It is a curious theatrical for these particular men to have conceived, but then we all judge ourselves sometime; it is hard for me to believe that Cornelius Vanderbilt did not sense, at some point in time, in some dim billiard room of his unconscious, that when he built 'The Breakers' he damned himself. The world must have seemed greener to all of them, out there when they were young and began laying the rails or digging for high-grade ore in the Comstock or daring to think that they might corner copper. More than anyone else in the society, these men had apparently dreamed the dream and made it work. And what they did then was to build a place which seems to illustrate, as in a child's primer, that the production ethic led step by step to unhappiness, to restrictiveness, to entrapment in the mechanics of living. In that way the lesson of Bellevue Avenue is more seriously radical than the idea of Brook Farm. Who could fail to read the sermon in the stones of Newport? Who could think that the building of a railroad could guarantee salvation, when there on the lawns of the men who built the railroad nothing is left but the shadows of migrainous women, and the pony carts waiting for the long-dead children?

1967

Guaymas, Sonora

It had rained in Los Angeles until the cliff was crumbling into the surf and I did not feel like getting dressed in the morning, so we decided to go to Mexico, to Guaymas, where it was hot. We did not go for marlin. We did not go to skin-dive. We went to get away from ourselves, and the way to do that is to drive, down through Nogales some day when the pretty green places pall and all that will move the imagination is some place difficult, some desert. The desert, any desert, is indeed the valley of the shadow of death; come back from the desert and you feel like Alcestis, reborn. After Nogales on Route 15 there is nothing but the Sonoran desert, nothing but mesquite and rattlesnakes and the Sierra Madre floating to the east, no trace of human endeavor but an occasional Pemex truck hurtling north and once in a while in the distance the dusty Pullman cars of the Ferrocarril del Pacifico. Magdalena is on Route 15, and then Hermosillo, where the American ore and cattle buyers gather in the bar at the Hotel San Alberto. There is an airport in Hermosillo, and Hermosillo is only eighty-five miles above Guaymas, but to fly is to miss the point. The point is to become disoriented, shriven, by the heat and the deceptive perspectives and the oppressive sense of carrion. The road shimmers. The eyes want to close.

And then, just past that moment when the desert has become the only reality, Route 15 hits the coast and there is Guaymas, a lunar thrust of volcanic hills and islands with the warm Gulf of California lapping idly all around, lapping even at the cactus, the water glassy as a mirage, the ships in the harbor whistling unsettlingly, moaning, ghost schooners, landlocked, lost. That is Guaymas. As far as the town goes, Graham Greene might have written it: a shadowy square with a filigree pergola for the Sunday band, a racket of birds, a cathedral in bad repair with a robin's-egg-blue tile dome, a turkey buzzard on the cross. The wharves are piled with bales of Sonoran cotton and mounds of dark copper concentrates; out on the freighters with the Panamanian and Liberian flags the Greek and German boys stand in the hot twilight and stare sullenly at the grotesque and claustrophobic hills, at the still town, a curious limbo at which to call.

Had we really been intent upon losing ourselves we might have stayed in town, at a hotel where faded and broken turquoise-blue shutters open onto the courtyard, where old men sit in the doorways and nothing moves, but instead we stayed outside town, at the Playa de Cortés, the big old hotel built by the Southern Pacific before the railways were nationalized. That place was a mirage, too, lovely and cool with thick whitewashed walls and dark shutters and bright tiles, tables made from ebony railroad ties, pale appliquéd muslin curtains, shocks of corn wrapped around the heavy beams. Pepper trees grew around the swimming pool, and lemons and bananas in the court-yard. The food was unremarkable, but after dinner one could lie in a hammock on the terrace and listen to the fountains and the sea. For a week we lay in hammocks and fished desultorily and went to bed early and got very brown and lazy. My husband caught eight sharks, and I read an oceanography textbook, and we did not talk much. At the end of the week we wanted to do something, but all there was to do was visit the tracking station for an old space program or go see John Wayne and Claudia Cardinale in *Circus World*, and we knew it was time to go home.

1965

Los Angeles Notebook

1

There is something uneasy in the Los Angeles air this afternoon, some unnatural stillness, some tension. What it means is that tonight a Santa Ana will begin to blow, a hot wind from the northeast whining down through the Cajon and San Gorgonio Passes, blowing up sandstorms out along Route 66, drying the hills and the nerves to the flash point. For a few days now we will see smoke back in the canyons, and hear sirens in the night. I have neither heard nor read that a Santa Ana is due, but I know it, and almost everyone I have seen today knows it too. We know it because we feel it. The baby frets. The maid sulks. I rekindle a waning argument with the telephone company, then cut my losses and lie down, given over to whatever it is in the air. To live with the Santa Ana is to accept, consciously or unconsciously, a deeply mechanistic view of human behavior.

I recall being told, when I first moved to Los Angeles and was living on an isolated beach, that the Indians would throw themselves into the sea when the bad wind blew. I could see why. The Pacific turned ominously glossy during a Santa Ana period, and one woke in the night troubled not only by the peacocks screaming in the olive trees but by the eerie absence of surf. The heat was surreal. The sky had a yellow cast, the kind of light sometimes called 'earthquake weather.' My only neighbor would not come out of her house for days, and there were no lights at night, and her husband roamed the place with a machete. One day he would tell me that he had heard a trespasser, the next a rattlesnake.

'On nights like that,' Raymond Chandler once wrote about the Santa Ana, 'every booze party ends in a fight. Meek little wives feel the edge of the carving knife and study their husbands' necks. Anything can happen.' That was the kind of wind it was. I did not know then that there was any basis for the effect it had on all of us, but it turns out to be another of those cases in which science bears out folk wisdom. The Santa Ana, which is named for one of the canyons it rushes through, is a *foehn* wind, like the *foehn* of Austria and Switzerland and the *hamsin* of Israel. There are a number of persistent malevolent winds, perhaps the best known of which are the mistral of France and the Mediterranean sirocco, but a *foehn* wind has distinct characteristics: it occurs on the leeward slope of a mountain range and, although the air begins as a cold mass, it is warmed as it comes down the mountain and appears finally as a hot dry wind. Whenever and wherever a *foehn* blows, doctors hear about headaches and nausea and allergies, about 'nervousness,' about 'depression.' In Los Angeles some teachers do not attempt to conduct formal classes during a Santa Ana, because the children become unmanageable. In Switzerland the suicide rate goes up during the *foehn*, and in the courts of some Swiss cantons the wind is considered a mitigating circumstance for crime. Surgeons are said to watch the wind, because blood does not clot normally during a *foehn*. A few years ago an Israeli physicist discovered that not only during such winds, but for the ten or twelve hours which precede them, the air carries an unusually high ratio of positive to negative ions. No one seems to know exactly why that should be; some talk about friction and others suggest solar disturbances. In any case the positive ions are there, and what an excess of positive ions does, in the simplest terms, is make people unhappy. One cannot get much more mechanistic than that.

Easterners commonly complain that there is no 'weather' at all in Southern California, that the days and the seasons slip by relentlessly, numbingly bland. That is quite misleading. In fact the climate is characterized by infrequent but violent extremes: two periods of torrential subtropical rains which continue for weeks and wash out the hills and send subdivisions sliding toward the sea; about twenty scattered days a year of the Santa Ana, which, with its incendiary dryness, invariably means fire. At the first prediction of a Santa Ana, the Forest Service flies men and equipment from northern California into the southern forests, and the Los Angeles Fire Department cancels its ordinary non-firefighting routines. The Santa Ana caused Malibu to burn the way it did in 1956, and Bel Air in 1961, and Santa Barbara in 1964. In the winter of 1966–67 eleven men were killed fighting a Santa Ana fire that spread through the San Gabriel Mountains.

Just to watch the front-page news out of Los Angeles during a Santa Ana is to get very close to what it is about the place. The longest single Santa Ana period in recent years was in 1957, and it lasted not the usual three or four days but fourteen days, from November 21 until December 4. On the first day 25,000 acres of the San Gabriel Mountains were burning, with gusts reaching 100 miles an hour. In town, the wind reached Force 12, or hurricane force, on the Beaufort Scale; oil derricks were toppled and people ordered off the downtown streets to avoid injury from flying objects. On November 22 the fire in the San Gabriels was out of control. On November 24 six people were killed in automobile accidents, and by the end of the week the Los Angeles *Times* was keeping a box score of traffic deaths. On November 26 a prominent Pasadena attorney, depressed about money, shot and killed his wife, their two sons, and himself. On November 27 a South Gate divorcée, twenty-two, was murdered and thrown from a moving car. On November 30 the San Gabriel fire was still out of control, and the wind in town was blowing eighty miles an hour. On the first day of December four people died violently, and on the third the wind began to break.

It is hard for people who have not lived in Los Angeles to realize how radically the Santa Ana figures in the local imagination. The city burning is Los Angeles's deepest image of itself: Nathanael West perceived that, in *The Day of the Locust*; and at the time of the 1965 Watts riots what struck the imagination most indelibly were the fires. For days one could drive the Harbor Freeway and see the city on fire, just as we had always known it would be in the end. Los Angeles weather is the weather of catastrophe, of apocalypse, and, just as the reliably long and bitter winters of New England determine the way life is lived there, so the violence and the unpredictability of the Santa Ana affect the entire quality of life in Los Angeles, accentuate its impermanence, its unreliability. The wind shows us how close to the edge we are.

2

'Here's why I'm on the beeper, Ron,' said the telephone voice on the all-night radio show. 'I just want to say that this *Sex for the Secretary* creature – whatever her name is – certainly isn't contributing anything to the morals in this country. It's pathetic. Statistics *show.*'

'It's *Sex and the Office*, honey,' the disc jockey said. 'That's the title. By Helen Gurley Brown. Statistics show what?'

'I haven't got them right here at my fingertips, naturally. But they *show.*'

'I'd be interested in hearing them. Be constructive, you Night Owls.'

'All right, let's take *one* statistic,' the voice said, truculent now. 'Maybe I haven't read the book, but what's this business she recommends about going *out with married men for lunch?*'

So it went, from midnight until 5 a.m., interrupted by records and by occasional calls debating whether or not a rattlesnake can swim. Misinformation about rattlesnakes is a leitmotiv of the insomniac imagination in Los Angeles. Toward 2 a.m. a man from 'out Tarzana way' called to protest. 'The Night Owls who called earlier must have been thinking about, uh, *The Man in the Gray Flannel Suit* or some other book,' he said, 'because Helen's one of the few authors trying to tell us what's really going *on*. Hefner's another, and he's also controversial, working in, uh, another area.'

An old man, after testifying that he 'personally' had seen a swimming rattlesnake, in the Delta-Mendota Canal, urged 'moderation' on the Helen Gurley Brown question. 'We shouldn't get on the beeper to call things pornographic before we've read them,' he complained, pronouncing it porn-ee-oh-graphic. 'I say, get the book. Give it a chance.' The original *provocateur* called back to agree that she would get the book. 'And then I'll burn it,' she added.

'Book burner, eh?' laughed the disc jockey good-naturedly.

'I wish they still burned witches,' she hissed.

3

It is three o'clock on a Sunday afternoon and 105° and the air so thick with smog that the dusty palm trees loom up with a sudden and rather attractive mystery. I have been playing in the sprinklers with the baby and I get in the car and go to Ralph's Market on the corner of Sunset and Fuller wearing an old bikini bathing suit. That is not a very good thing to wear to the market but neither is it, at Ralph's on the corner of Sunset and Fuller, an unusual costume. Nonetheless a large woman in a cotton muumuu jams her cart into mine at the butcher counter. *'What a thing to wear to the market,'* she says in a loud but strangled voice. Everyone looks the other way and I study a plastic package of rib lamb chops and she repeats it. She follows me all over the store, to the Junior Foods, to the Dairy Products, to the Mexican Delicacies, jamming my cart whenever she can. Her husband plucks at her sleeve. As I leave the check-out counter she raises her voice one last time: *'What a thing to wear to Ralph's,'* she says.

4

A party at someone's house in Beverly Hills: a pink tent, two orchestras, a couple of French Communist directors in Cardin evening jackets, chili and hamburgers from Chasen's. The wife of an English actor sits at a table alone; she visits California rarely although her husband works here a good deal. An American who knows her slightly comes over to the table.

'Marvelous to see you here,' he says.

'Is it,' she says.

'How long have you been here?'

'Too long.'

She takes a fresh drink from a passing waiter and smiles at her husband, who is dancing.

The American tries again. He mentions her husband.

'I hear he's marvelous in this picture.'

She looks at the American for the first time. When she finally speaks she enunciates every word very clearly. 'He . . . is . . . also . . . a . . . fag,' she says pleasantly.

5

The oral history of Los Angeles is written in piano bars. 'Moon River,' the piano player always plays, and 'Mountain Greenery.' 'There's a Small Hotel' and 'This Is Not the First Time.' People talk to each other, tell each other about their first wives and last husbands. 'Stay funny,' they tell each other, and 'This is to die over.' A construction man talks to an unemployed screenwriter who is celebrating, alone, his tenth wedding anniversary. The construction man is on a job in Montecito: 'Up in Montecito,' he says, 'they got one square mile with 135 millionaires.'

'Putrescence,' the writer says.

'That's all you got to say about it?'

'Don't read me wrong, I think Santa Barbara's one of the most – Christ, *the* most – beautiful places in the world, but it's a beautiful place that contains a . . . *putrescence*. They just live on their putrescent millions.'

'So give me putrescent.'

'No, no,' the writer says. 'I just happen to think millionaires have some sort of lacking in their . . . in their elasticity.'

A drunk requests 'The Sweetheart of Sigma Chi.' The piano player says he doesn't know it. 'Where'd you learn to play the piano?' the drunk asks. 'I got two degrees,' the piano player says. 'One in musical education.' I go to a coin telephone and call a friend in New York. 'Where are you?' he says. 'In a piano bar in Encino,' I say. 'Why?' he says. 'Why not,' I say.

1965–1967

Goodbye to All That

How many miles to Babylon?
Three score miles and ten —
Can I get there by candlelight?
Yes, and back again —
If your feet are nimble and light
You can get there by candlelight.

It is easy to see the beginnings of things, and harder to see the ends. I can remember now, with a clarity that makes the nerves in the back of my neck constrict, when New York began for me, but I cannot lay my finger upon the moment it ended, can never cut through the ambiguities and second starts and broken resolves to the exact place on the page where the heroine is no longer as optimistic as she once was. When I first saw New York I was twenty, and it was summertime, and I got off a DC-7 at the old Idlewild temporary terminal in a new dress which had seemed very smart in Sacramento but seemed less smart already, even in the old Idlewild temporary terminal, and the warm air smelled of mildew and some instinct, programmed by all the movies I had ever seen and all the songs I had ever heard sung and all the stories I had ever read about New York, informed me that it would never be quite the same again. In fact it never was. Some time later there was a song on all the juke-boxes on the upper East Side that went 'but where is the schoolgirl who used to be me,' and if it was late enough at night I used to wonder that. I know now that almost everyone wonders something like that, sooner or later and no matter what he or she is doing, but one of the mixed blessings of being twenty and twenty-one and even twenty-three is the conviction that nothing like this, all evidence to the contrary notwithstanding, has ever happened to anyone before.

Of course it might have been some other city, had circumstances been different and the time been different and had I been different, might have been Paris or Chicago or even San Francisco, but because I am talking about myself I am talking here about New York. That first night I opened my window on the bus into town and watched for the skyline, but all I could see were the wastes of Queens and the big signs that said MIDTOWN TUNNEL THIS LANE and then a flood of summer rain (even that seemed remarkable and exotic, for I had come out of the West where there was no summer rain), and for the next three days I sat wrapped in blankets in a hotel room air-conditioned to 35° and tried to get over a bad cold and a high fever. It did not occur to me to call a doctor, because I knew none, and although it did occur to me to call the desk and ask that the air conditioner be turned off, I never called, because I did not know how much to tip whoever might come – was anyone ever so young? I am here to tell you that someone was. All I could do during those three days was talk long-distance to the boy I already knew I would never marry in the spring. I would stay in New York, I told him, just six months, and I could see the Brooklyn Bridge from my window. As it turned out the bridge was the Triborough, and I stayed eight years.

In retrospect it seems to me that those days before I knew the names of all the bridges were happier than the ones that came later, but perhaps you will see that as we go along. Part of what I want to tell you is what it is like to be young in New York, how six months can become eight years with the deceptive ease of a film dissolve, for that is how those years appear to me now, in a long sequence of sentimental dissolves and old-fashioned trick shots – the Seagram Building fountains dissolve into snowflakes, I enter a revolving door at twenty and come out a good deal older, and on a different street. But most particularly I want to explain to you, and in the process

perhaps to myself, why I no longer live in New York. It is often said
that New York is a city for only the very rich and the very poor. It is
less often said that New York is also, at least for those of us who
came there from somewhere else, a city for only the very young.

I remember once, one cold bright December evening in New York,
suggesting to a friend who complained of having been around too
long that he come with me to a party where there would be, I assured
him with the bright resourcefulness of twenty-three, 'new faces.' He
laughed literally until he choked, and I had to roll down the taxi
window and hit him on the back. 'New faces,' he said finally, 'don't
tell me about *new faces.*' It seemed that the last time he had gone to
a party where he had been promised 'new faces,' there had been
fifteen people in the room, and he had already slept with five of the
women and owed money to all but two of the men. I laughed with
him, but the first snow had just begun to fall and the big Christmas
trees glittered yellow and white as far as I could see up Park Avenue
and I had a new dress and it would be a long while before I would
come to understand the particular moral of the story.

It would be a long while because, quite simply, I was in love with
New York. I do not mean 'love' in any colloquial way, I mean that I
was in love with the city, the way you love the first person who ever
touches you and never love anyone quite that way again. I remember
walking across Sixty-second Street one twilight that first spring, or
the second spring, they were all alike for a while. I was late to meet
someone but I stopped at Lexington Avenue and bought a peach and
stood on the corner eating it and knew that I had come out of the
West and reached the mirage. I could taste the peach and feel the
soft air blowing from a subway grating on my legs and I could smell
lilac and garbage and expensive perfume and I knew that it would
cost something sooner or later – because I did not belong there, did
not come from there – but when you are twenty-two or twenty-
three, you figure that later you will have a high emotional balance,
and be able to pay whatever it costs. I still believed in possibilities
then, still had the sense, so peculiar to New York, that something
extraordinary would happen any minute, any day, any month. I was
making only $65 or $70 a week then ('Put yourself in Hattie Carnegie's hands,' I was advised without the slightest trace of irony by
an editor of the magazine for which I worked), so little money that

some weeks I had to charge food at Bloomingdale's gourmet shop in order to eat, a fact which went unmentioned in the letters I wrote to California. I never told my father that I needed money because then he would have sent it, and I would never know if I could do it by myself. At that time making a living seemed a game to me, with arbitrary but quite inflexible rules. And except on a certain kind of winter evening – six-thirty in the Seventies, say, already dark and bitter with a wind off the river, when I would be walking very fast toward a bus and would look in the bright windows of brownstones and see cooks working in clean kitchens and imagine women lighting candles on the floor above and beautiful children being bathed on the floor above that – except on nights like those, I never felt poor; I had the feeling that if I needed money I could always get it. I could write a syndicated column for teenagers under the name 'Debbi Lynn' or I could smuggle gold into India or I could become a $100 call girl, and none of it would matter.

Nothing was irrevocable; everything was within reach. Just around every corner lay something curious and interesting, something I had never before seen or done or known about. I could go to a party and meet someone who called himself Mr Emotional Appeal and ran The Emotional Appeal Institute or Tina Onassis Blandford or a Florida cracker who was then a regular on what he called 'the Big C,' the Southampton-El Morocco circuit ('I'm well-connected on the Big C, honey,' he would tell me over collard greens on his vast borrowed terrace), or the widow of the celery king of the Harlem market or a piano salesman from Bonne Terre, Missouri, or someone who had already made and lost two fortunes in Midland, Texas. I could make promises to myself and to other people and there would be all the time in the world to keep them. I could stay up all night and make mistakes, and none of it would count.

You see I was in a curious position in New York: it never occurred to me that I was living a real life there. In my imagination I was always there for just another few months, just until Christmas or Easter or the first warm day in May. For that reason I was most comfortable in the company of Southerners. They seemed to be in New York as I was, on some indefinitely extended leave from wherever they belonged, disinclined to consider the future, temporary exiles who always knew when the flights left for New Orleans or

Memphis or Richmond or, in my case, California. Someone who lives always with a plane schedule in the drawer lives on a slightly different calendar. Christmas, for example, was a difficult season. Other people could take it in stride, going to Stowe or going abroad or going for the day to their mothers' places in Connecticut; those of us who believed that we lived somewhere else would spend it making and canceling airline reservations, waiting for weatherbound flights as if for the last plane out of Lisbon in 1940, and finally comforting one another, those of us who were left, with the oranges and mementos and smoked-oyster stuffings of childhood, gathering close, colonials in a far country.

Which is precisely what we were. I am not sure that it is possible for anyone brought up in the East to appreciate entirely what New York, the idea of New York, means to those of us who came out of the West and the South. To an Eastern child, particularly a child who has always had an uncle on Wall Street and who has spent several hundred Saturdays first at F. A. O. Schwarz and being fitted for shoes at Best's and then waiting under the Biltmore clock and dancing to Lester Lanin, New York is just a city, albeit *the* city, a plausible place for people to live. But to those of us who came from places where no one had heard of Lester Lanin and Grand Central Station was a Saturday radio program, where Wall Street and Fifth Avenue and Madison Avenue were not places at all but abstractions ('Money,' and 'High Fashion,' and 'The Hucksters'), New York was no mere city. It was instead an infinitely romantic notion, the mysterious nexus of all love and money and power, the shining and perishable dream itself. To think of 'living' there was to reduce the miraculous to the mundane; one does not 'live' at Xanadu.

In fact it was difficult in the extreme for me to understand those young women for whom New York was not simply an ephemeral Estoril but a real place, girls who bought toasters and installed new cabinets in their apartments and committed themselves to some reasonable future. I never bought any furniture in New York. For a year or so I lived in other people's apartments; after that I lived in the Nineties in an apartment furnished entirely with things taken from storage by a friend whose wife had moved away. And when I left the apartment in the Nineties (that was when I was leaving everything, when it was all breaking up) I left everything in it, even my winter clothes and the map of Sacramento County I had hung on the bedroom wall to remind me who I was, and I moved into a monastic four-room floor-through on Seventy-fifth Street. 'Monastic' is perhaps misleading here, implying some chic severity; until after I was married and my husband moved some furniture in, there was nothing at all in those four rooms except a cheap double mattress and box springs, ordered by telephone the day I decided to move, and two French garden chairs lent me by a friend who imported them. (It strikes me now that the people I knew in New York all had curious and self-defeating sidelines. They imported garden chairs which did not sell very well at Hammacher Schlemmer or they tried to market hair straighteners in Harlem or they ghosted exposés of Murder Incorporated for Sunday supplements. I think that perhaps none of us was very serious, *engagé* only about our most private lives.)

All I ever did to that apartment was hang fifty yards of yellow theatrical silk across the bedroom windows, because I had some idea that the gold light would make me feel better, but I did not bother to weight the curtains correctly and all that summer the long panels of transparent golden silk would blow out the windows and get tangled and drenched in the afternoon thunderstorms. That was the year, my twenty-eighth, when I was discovering that not all of the promises would be kept, that some things are in fact irrevocable and that it had counted after all, every evasion and every procrastination, every mistake, every word, all of it.

That is what it was all about, wasn't it? Promises? Now when New York comes back to me it comes in hallucinatory flashes, so clinically detailed that I sometimes wish that memory would effect the distortion with which it is commonly credited. For a lot of the time I was in New York I used a perfume called *Fleurs de Rocaille*, and then *L'Air du Temps*, and now the slightest trace of either can short-circuit my connections for the rest of the day. Nor can I smell Henri Bendel jasmine soap without falling back into the past, or the particular mixture of spices used for boiling crabs. There were barrels of crab boil in a Czech place in the Eighties where I once shopped. Smells, of course, are notorious memory stimuli, but there are other things

which affect me the same way. Blue-and-white striped sheets. Ver-
mouth cassis. Some faded nightgowns which were new in 1959 or
1960, and some chiffon scarves I bought about the same time.

I suppose that a lot of us who have been young in New York have
the same scenes on our home screens. I remember sitting in a lot of
apartments with a slight headache about five o'clock in the morning.
I had a friend who could not sleep, and he knew a few other people
who had the same trouble, and we would watch the sky lighten and
have a last drink with no ice and then go home in the early morning
light, when the streets were clean and wet (had it rained in the
night? we never knew) and the few cruising taxis still had their
headlights on and the only color was the red and green of traffic
signals. The White Rose bars opened very early in the morning; I
recall waiting in one of them to watch an astronaut go into space,
waiting so long that at the moment it actually happened I had my
eyes not on the television screen but on a cockroach on the tile floor.
I liked the bleak branches above Washington Square at dawn, and
the monochromatic flatness of Second Avenue, the fire escapes and
the grilled storefronts peculiar and empty in their perspective.

It is relatively hard to fight at six-thirty or seven in the morning
without any sleep, which was perhaps one reason we stayed up all
night, and it seemed to me a pleasant time of day. The windows
were shuttered in that apartment in the Nineties and I could sleep a
few hours and then go to work. I could work then on two or three
hours' sleep and a container of coffee from Chock Full O' Nuts. I
liked going to work, liked the soothing and satisfactory rhythm of
getting out a magazine, liked the orderly progression of four-color
closings and two-color closings and black-and-white closings and
then The Product, no abstraction but something which looked effortlessly glossy and could be picked up on a news-stand and weighed
in the hand. I liked all the minutiae of proofs and layouts, liked
working late on the nights the magazine went to press, sitting and
reading *Variety* and waiting for the copy desk to call. From my office
I could look across town to the weather signal on the Mutual of New
York Building and the lights that alternately spelled out TIME and
LIFE above Rockefeller Plaza; that pleased me obscurely, and so did
walking uptown in the mauve eight o'clocks of early summer
evenings and looking at things, Lowestoft tureens in Fifty-seventh

Street windows, people in evening clothes trying to get taxis, the trees just coming into full leaf, the lambent air, all the sweet promises of money and summer.

Some years passed, but I still did not lose that sense of wonder about New York. I began to cherish the loneliness of it, the sense that at any given time no one need know where I was or what I was doing. I liked walking, from the East River over to the Hudson and back on brisk days, down around the Village on warm days. A friend would leave me the key to her apartment in the West Village when she was out of town, and sometimes I would just move down there, because by that time the telephone was beginning to bother me (the canker, you see, was already in the rose) and not many people had that number. I remember one day when someone who did have the West Village number came to pick me up for lunch there, and we both had hangovers, and I cut my finger opening him a beer and burst into tears, and we walked to a Spanish restaurant and drank Bloody Marys and *gazpacho* until we felt better. I was not then guilt-ridden about spending afternoons that way, because I still had all the afternoons in the world.

And even that late in the game I still liked going to parties, all parties, bad parties, Saturday-afternoon parties given by recently married couples who lived in Stuyvesant Town, West Side parties given by unpublished or failed writers who served cheap red wine and talked about going to Guadalajara, Village parties where all the guests worked for advertising agencies and voted for Reform Democrats, press parties at Sardi's, the worst kinds of parties. You will have perceived by now that I was not one to profit by the experience of others, that it was a very long time indeed before I stopped believing in new faces and began to understand the lesson in that story, which was that it is distinctly possible to stay too long at the Fair.

I could not tell you when I began to understand that. All I know is that it was very bad when I was twenty-eight. Everything that was said to me I seemed to have heard before, and I could no longer listen. I could no longer sit in little bars near Grand Central and listen to someone complaining of his wife's inability to cope with the help while he missed another train to Connecticut. I no longer had any

interest in hearing about the advances other people had received
from their publishers, about plays which were having second-act
trouble in Philadelphia, or about people I would like very much if
only I would come out and meet them. I had already met them,
always. There were certain parts of the city which I had to avoid. I
could not bear upper Madison Avenue on weekday mornings (this
was a particularly inconvenient aversion, since I then lived just fifty
or sixty feet east of Madison), because I would see women walking
Yorkshire terriers and shopping at Gristede's, and some Veblenesque
gorge would rise in my throat. I could not go to Times Square in
the afternoon, or to the New York Public Library for any reason
whatsoever. One day I could not go into a Schrafft's; the next day it
would be Bonwit Teller.

I hurt the people I cared about, and insulted those I did not. I cut
myself off from the one person who was closer to me than any other.
I cried until I was not even aware when I was crying and when I
was not, cried in elevators and in taxis and in Chinese laundries, and
when I went to the doctor he said only that I seemed to be depressed,
and should see a 'specialist.' He wrote down a psychiatrist's name
and address for me, but I did not go.

Instead I got married, which as it turned out was a very good
thing to do but badly timed, since I still could not walk on upper
Madison Avenue in the mornings and still could not talk to people
and still cried in Chinese laundries. I had never before understood
what 'despair' meant, and I am not sure that I understand now, but
I understood that year. Of course I could not work. I could not
even get dinner with any degree of certainty, and I would sit in the
apartment on Seventy-fifth Street paralyzed until my husband would
call from his office and say gently that I did not have to get dinner,
that I could meet him at Michael's Pub or at Toots Shor's or at
Sardi's East. And then one morning in April (we had been married
in January) he called and told me that he wanted to get out of New
York for a while, that he would take a six-month leave of absence,
that we would go somewhere.

It was three years ago that he told me that, and we have lived in
Los Angeles since. Many of the people we knew in New York think
this a curious aberration, and in fact tell us so. There is no possible,
no adequate answer to that, and so we give certain stock answers,

the answers everyone gives. I talk about how difficult it would be for us to 'afford' to live in New York right now, about how much 'space' we need. All I mean is that I was very young in New York, and that at some point the golden rhythm was broken, and I am not that young any more. The last time I was in New York was in a cold January, and everyone was ill and tired. Many of the people I used to know there had moved to Dallas or had gone on Antabuse or had bought a farm in New Hampshire. We stayed ten days, and then we took an afternoon flight back to Los Angeles, and on the way home from the airport that night I could see the moon on the Pacific and smell jasmine all around and we both knew that there was no longer any point in keeping the apartment we still kept in New York. There were years when I called Los Angeles 'the Coast,' but they seem a long time ago.

1967

The White Album

For Earl McGrath,
and for Lois Wallace

Acknowledgments

Most of these pieces appeared, in various forms and at various times, in the following magazines, and I would like to thank the editors of each: *Esquire*, *The Saturday Evening Post*, *Life* (more specifically the 'old' *Saturday Evening Post* and the 'old' *Life*), *Travel & Leisure*, the *LA Times*, *The New York Times*, *New West*, and *The New York Review of Books*.

I

The White Album

The White Album

1

We tell ourselves stories in order to live. The princess is caged in the consulate. The man with the candy will lead the children into the sea. The naked woman on the ledge outside the window on the sixteenth floor is a victim of accidie, or the naked woman is an exhibitionist, and it would be 'interesting' to know which. We tell ourselves that it makes some difference whether the naked woman is about to commit a mortal sin or is about to register a political protest or is about to be, the Aristophanic view, snatched back to the human condition by the fireman in priest's clothing just visible in the window behind her, the one smiling at the telephoto lens. We look for the sermon in the suicide, for the social or moral lesson in the murder of five. We interpret what we see, select the most workable of the multiple choices. We live entirely, especially if we are writers, by the imposition of a narrative line upon disparate images, by the 'ideas' with which we have learned to freeze the shifting phantasmagoria which is our actual experience.

Or at least we do for a while. I am talking here about a time when I began to doubt the premises of all the stories I had ever told myself, a common condition but one I found troubling. I suppose this period began around 1966 and continued until 1971. During those five years I appeared, on the face of it, a competent enough member of some community or another, a signer of contracts and Air Travel cards, a citizen: I wrote a couple of times a month for one magazine or another, published two books, worked on several motion pictures; participated in the paranoia of the time, in the raising of a small child, and in the entertainment of large numbers of people passing through my house; made gingham curtains for spare bedrooms, remembered to ask agents if any reduction of points would be *pari passu* with the financing studio, put lentils to soak on Saturday night for lentil soup on Sunday, made quarterly F.I.C.A. payments and renewed my driver's license on time, missing on the written examination only the question about the financial responsibility of California drivers. It was a time of my life when I was frequently 'named.' I was named godmother to children. I was named lecturer and panelist, colloquist and conferee. I was even named, in 1968, a *Los Angeles Times* 'Woman of the Year,' along with Mrs Ronald Reagan, the Olympic swimmer Debbie Meyer, and ten other California women who seemed to keep in touch and do good works. I did no good works but I tried to keep in touch. I was responsible. I recognized my name when I saw it. Once in a while I even answered letters addressed to me, not exactly upon receipt but eventually, particularly if the letters had come from strangers. 'During my absence from the country these past eighteen months,' such replies would begin.

This was an adequate enough performance, as improvisations go. The only problem was that my entire education, everything I had ever been told or had told myself, insisted that the production was never meant to be improvised: I was supposed to have a script, and had mislaid it. I was supposed to hear cues, and no longer did. I was meant to know the plot, but all I knew was what I saw: flash pictures in variable sequence, images with no 'meaning' beyond their temporary arrangement, not a movie but a cutting-room experience. In what would probably be the middle of my life I wanted still to believe in the narrative and in the narrative's intelligibility, but to know that one could change the sense with every cut was to begin to perceive the experience as rather more electrical than ethical.

During this period I spent what were for me the usual proportions of time in Los Angeles and New York and Sacramento. I spent what seemed to many people I knew an eccentric amount of time in Honolulu, the particular aspect of which lent me the illusion that I could any minute order from room service a revisionist theory of my own history, garnished with a vanda orchid. I watched Robert

Kennedy's funeral on a verandah at the Royal Hawaiian Hotel in Honolulu, and also the first reports from My Lai. I reread all of George Orwell on the Royal Hawaiian Beach, and I also read, in the papers that came one day late from the mainland, the story of Betty Lansdown Fouquet, a 26-year-old woman with faded blond hair who put her five-year-old daughter out to die on the center divider of Interstate 5 some miles south of the last Bakersfield exit. The child, whose fingers had to be pried loose from the Cyclone fence when she was rescued twelve hours later by the California Highway Patrol, reported that she had run after the car carrying her mother and stepfather and brother and sister for 'a long time.' Certain of these images did not fit into any narrative I knew.

Another flash cut:

'In June of this year patient experienced an attack of vertigo, nausea, and a feeling that she was going to pass out. A thorough medical evaluation elicited no positive findings and she was placed on Elavil, Mg 20, tid ... The Rorschach record is interpreted as describing a personality in process of deterioration with abundant signs of failing defenses and increasing inability of the ego to mediate the world of reality and to cope with normal stress ... Emotionally, patient has alienated herself almost entirely from the world of other human beings. Her fantasy life appears to have been virtually completely preempted by primitive, regressive libidinal preoccupations many of which are distorted and bizarre ... In a technical sense basic affective controls appear to be intact but it is equally clear that they are insecurely and tenuously maintained for the present by a variety of defense mechanisms including intellectualization, obsessive-compulsive devices, projection, reaction-formation, and somatization, all of which now seem inadequate to their task of controlling or containing an underlying psychotic process and are therefore in process of failure. The content of patient's responses is highly unconventional and frequently bizarre, filled with sexual and anatomical preoccupations, and basic reality contact is obviously and seriously impaired at times. In quality and level of sophistication patient's responses are characteristic of those of individuals of high average or superior intelligence but she is now functioning intellectually in impaired fashion at barely average level.

Patient's thematic productions on the Thematic Apperception Test emphasize her fundamentally pessimistic, fatalistic, and depressive view of the world around her. It is as though she feels deeply that all human effort is foredoomed to failure, a conviction which seems to push her further into a dependent, passive withdrawal. In her view she lives in a world of people moved by strange, conflicted, poorly comprehended, and, above all, devious motivations which commit them inevitably to conflict and failure . . .'

The patient to whom this psychiatric report refers is me. The tests mentioned – the Rorschach, the Thematic Apperception Test, the Sentence Completion Test and the Minnesota Multiphasic Personality Index – were administered privately, in the outpatient psychiatric clinic at St John's Hospital in Santa Monica, in the summer of 1968, shortly after I suffered the 'attack of vertigo and nausea' mentioned in the first sentence and shortly before I was named a *Los Angeles Times* 'Woman of the Year.' By way of comment I offer only that an attack of vertigo and nausea does not now seem to me an inappropriate response to the summer of 1968.

2

In the years I am talking about I was living in a large house in a part of Hollywood that had once been expensive and was now described by one of my acquaintances as a 'senseless-killing neighborhood.' This house on Franklin Avenue was rented, and paint peeled inside and out, and pipes broke and window sashes crumbled and the tennis court had not been rolled since 1933, but the rooms were many and high-ceilinged and, during the five years that I lived there, even the rather sinistral inertia of the neighborhood tended to suggest that I should live in the house indefinitely.

In fact I could not, because the owners were waiting only for a zoning change to tear the house down and build a high-rise apartment building, and for that matter it was precisely this anticipation of imminent but not exactly immediate destruction that lent the neighborhood its particular character. The house across the street had been built for one of the Talmadge sisters, had been the Japanese consulate in 1941, and was now, although boarded up, occupied by a number of unrelated adults who seemed to constitute some kind of therapy group. The house next door was owned by Synanon. I recall looking at a house around the corner with a rental sign on it: this house had once been the Canadian consulate, had 28 large rooms and two refrigerated fur closets, and could be rented, in the spirit of the neighborhood, only on a month-to-month basis, unfurnished. Since the inclination to rent an unfurnished 28-room house for a month or two is a distinctly special one, the neighborhood was peopled mainly by rock-and-roll bands, therapy groups, very old women wheeled down the street by practical nurses in soiled uniforms, and by my husband, my daughter and me.

Q. *And what else happened, if anything . . .*

A. *He said that he thought that I could be a star, like, you know, a young Burt Lancaster, you know, that kind of stuff.*

Q. *Did he mention any particular name?*

A. *Yes, sir.*

Q. *What name did he mention?*

A. *He mentioned a lot of names. He said Burt Lancaster. He said Clint Eastwood. He said Fess Parker. He mentioned a lot of names . . .*

Q. *Did you talk after you ate?*

A. *While we were eating, after we ate. Mr Novarro told our fortunes with some cards and he read our palms.*

Q. *Did he tell you you were going to have a lot of good luck or bad luck or what happened?*

A. *He wasn't a good palm reader.*

These are excerpts from the testimony of Paul Robert Ferguson and Thomas Scott Ferguson, brothers, ages 22 and 17 respectively, during their trial for the murder of Ramon Novarro, age 69, at his house in Laurel Canyon, not too far from my house in Hollywood, on the night of October 30, 1968. I followed this trial quite closely, clipping reports from the newspapers and later borrowing a transcript from one of the defense attorneys. The younger of the brothers, 'Tommy Scott' Ferguson, whose girl friend testified that she had stopped being in love with him 'about two weeks after Grand Jury,' said that he had been unaware of Mr Novarro's career as a silent film actor until he was shown, at some point during the night of the murder, a photograph of his host as Ben-Hur. The older brother, Paul Ferguson, who began working carnivals when he was 12 and described himself at 22 as having had 'a fast life and a good one,' gave the jury, upon request, his definition of a hustler: 'A hustler is someone who can talk – not just to men, to women, too. Who can cook. Can keep company. Wash a car. Lots of things make up a hustler. There are a lot of lonely people in this town, man.' During the course of the trial each of the brothers accused the other of the murder. Both were convicted. I read the transcript several times, trying to bring the picture into some focus which did not suggest that I lived, as my psychiatric report had put it, 'in a world of people moved by strange, conflicted, poorly comprehended and, above all, devious motivations'; I never met the Ferguson brothers.

I did meet one of the principals in another Los Angeles County murder trial during those years: Linda Kasabian, star witness for the prosecution in what was commonly known as the Manson Trial. I once asked Linda what she thought about the apparently chance sequence of events which had brought her first to the Spahn Movie Ranch and then to the Sybil Brand Institute for Women on charges, later dropped, of murdering Sharon Tate Polanski, Abigail Folger, Jay Sebring, Voytek Frykowski, Steven Parent, and Rosemary and Leno LaBianca. 'Everything was to teach me something,' Linda said. Linda did not believe that chance was without pattern. Linda operated on what I later recognized as dice theory, and so, during the years I am talking about, did I.

It will perhaps suggest the mood of those years if I tell you that during them I could not visit my mother-in-law without averting my eyes from a framed verse, a 'house blessing,' which hung in a hallway of her house in West Hartford, Connecticut.

> God bless the corners of this house,
> And be the lintel blest –
> And bless the hearth and bless the board
> And bless each place of rest –
> And bless the crystal windowpane that lets the starlight in
> And bless each door that opens wide, to stranger as to kin.

This verse had on me the effect of a physical chill, so insistently did it seem the kind of 'ironic' detail the reporters would seize upon, the morning the bodies were found. In my neighborhood in California we did not bless the door that opened wide to stranger as to kin. Paul and Tommy Scott Ferguson were the strangers at Ramon Novarro's door, up on Laurel Canyon. Charles Manson was the stranger at Rosemary and Leno LaBianca's door, over in Los Feliz. Some strangers at the door knocked, and invented a reason to come inside: a call, say, to the Triple A, about a car not in evidence. Others just opened the door and walked in, and I would come across them in the entrance hall. I recall asking one such stranger what he wanted. We looked at each other for what seemed a long time, and then he saw my husband on the stair landing. 'Chicken Delight,' he said finally, but we had ordered no Chicken Delight, nor was he carrying any. I took the license number of his panel truck. It seems to me now that during those years I was always writing down the license numbers of panel trucks, panel trucks circling the block, panel trucks parked across the street, panel trucks idling at the intersection. I put these license numbers in a dressing-table drawer where they could be found by the police when the time came.

That the time would come I never doubted, at least not in the inaccessible places of the mind where I seemed more and more to be living. So many encounters in those years were devoid of any logic save that of the dreamwork. In the big house on Franklin Avenue many people seemed to come and go without relation to what I did. I knew where the sheets and towels were kept but I did not always know who was sleeping in every bed. I had the keys but not the key. I remember taking a 25-mg. Compazine one Easter Sunday and making a large and elaborate lunch for a number of people, many of whom were still around on Monday. I remember walking barefoot all day on the worn hardwood floors of that house and I remember 'Do You Wanna Dance' on the record player, 'Do You Wanna Dance' and 'Visions of Johanna' and a song called 'Midnight Confessions.' I remember a babysitter telling me that she saw death in my aura. I remember chatting with her about reasons why this might be so, paying her, opening all the French windows and going to sleep in the living room.

It was hard to surprise me in those years. It was hard to even get my attention. I was absorbed in my intellectualization, my obsessive-compulsive devices, my projection, my reaction-formation, my somatization, and in the transcript of the Ferguson trial. A musician I had met a few years before called from a Ramada Inn in Tuscaloosa to tell me how to save myself through Scientology. I had met him once in my life, had talked to him for maybe half an hour about brown rice and the charts, and now he was telling me from Alabama about E-meters, and how I might become a Clear. I received a telephone call from a stranger in Montreal who seemed to want to enlist me in a narcotics operation. 'Is it cool to talk on this telephone?' he asked several times. 'Big Brother isn't listening?'

I said that I doubted it, although increasingly I did not.

'Because what we're talking about, basically, is applying the Zen philosophy to money and business, dig? And if I say we are going to finance the underground, and if I mention major money, you know what I'm talking about because you know what's going down, right?'

Maybe he was not talking about narcotics. Maybe he was talking about turning a profit on M-1 rifles: I had stopped looking for the logic in such calls. Someone with whom I had gone to school in Sacramento and had last seen in 1952 turned up at my house in Hollywood in 1968 in the guise of a private detective from West Covina, one of very few licensed women private detectives in the State of California. 'They call us Dickless Tracys,' she said, idly but definitely fanning out the day's mail on the hall table. 'I have a lot of very close friends in law enforcement,' she said then. 'You might want to meet them.' We exchanged promises to keep in touch but never met again: a not atypical encounter of the period. The Sixties were over before it occurred to me that this visit might have been less than entirely social.

3

It was six, seven o'clock of an early spring evening in 1968 and I was sitting on the cold vinyl floor of a sound studio on Sunset Boulevard, watching a band called The Doors record a rhythm track. On the whole my attention was only minimally engaged by the preoccupations of rock-and-roll bands (I had already heard about acid as a transitional stage and also about the Maharishi and even about Universal Love, and after a while it all sounded like marmalade skies to me), but The Doors were different, The Doors interested me. The Doors seemed unconvinced that love was brotherhood and the Kama Sutra. The Doors' music insisted that love was sex and sex was death and therein lay salvation. The Doors were the Norman Mailers of the Top Forty, missionaries of apocalyptic sex. *Break on through*, their lyrics urged, and *Light my fire*, and:

> *Come on baby, gonna take a little ride*
> *Goin' down by the ocean side*
> *Gonna get real close*
> *Get real tight*
> *Baby gonna drown tonight –*
> *Goin' down, down, down.*

On this evening in 1968 they were gathered together in uneasy symbiosis to make their third album, and the studio was too cold and the lights were too bright and there were masses of wires and banks of the ominous blinking electronic circuitry with which musicians live so easily. There were three of the four Doors. There was a bass player borrowed from a band called Clear Light. There were the producer and the engineer and the road manager and a couple of girls and a Siberian husky named Nikki with one gray eye and one gold. There were paper bags half filled with hard-boiled eggs and chicken livers and cheeseburgers and empty bottles of apple juice and California rosé. There was everything and everybody The Doors needed to cut the rest of this third album except one thing, the fourth Door, the lead singer, Jim Morrison, a 24-year-old graduate of U.C.L.A. who wore black vinyl pants and no underwear and tended to suggest some range of the possible just beyond a suicide pact. It was Morrison who had described The Doors as 'erotic politicians.' It was Morrison who had defined the group's interests as 'anything about revolt, disorder, chaos, about activity that appears to have no meaning.' It was Morrison who got arrested in Miami in December of 1967 for giving an 'indecent' performance. It was Morrison who wrote most of The Doors' lyrics, the peculiar character of which was to reflect either an ambiguous paranoia or a quite unambiguous insistence upon the love-death as the ultimate high. And it was Morrison who was missing. It was Ray Manzarek and Robby Krieger and John Densmore who made The Doors sound the way they sounded, and maybe it was Manzarek and Krieger and Densmore who made seventeen out of twenty interviewees on *American Bandstand* prefer The Doors over all other bands, but it was Morrison who got up there in his black vinyl pants with no underwear and projected the idea, and it was Morrison they were waiting for now.

'Hey listen,' the engineer said. 'I was listening to an FM station on the way over here, they played three Doors songs, first they played "Back Door Man" and then "Love Me Two Times" and "Light My Fire." '

'I heard it,' Densmore muttered. 'I heard it.'

'So what's wrong with somebody playing three of your songs?'

'This cat dedicates it to his family.'

'Yeah? To his family?'

'To his family. Really crass.'

Ray Manzarek was hunched over a Gibson keyboard. 'You think *Morrison's* going to come back?' he asked to no one in particular.

No one answered.

'So we can do some *vocals?*' Manzarek said.

The producer was working with the tape of the rhythm track they had just recorded. 'I hope so,' he said without looking up.

'Yeah,' Manzarek said. 'So do I.'

My leg had gone to sleep, but I did not stand up; unspecific tensions seemed to be rendering everyone in the room catatonic. The producer played back the rhythm track. The engineer said that he wanted to do his deep-breathing exercises. Manzarek ate a hard-boiled egg. 'Tennyson made a mantra out of his own name,' he said to the engineer. 'I don't know if he said "Tennyson Tennyson Tennyson" or "Alfred Alfred Alfred" or "Alfred Lord Tennyson," but anyway, he did it. Maybe he just said "Lord Lord Lord." '

'Groovy,' the Clear Light bass player said. He was an amiable enthusiast, not at all a Door in spirit.

'I wonder what Blake said,' Manzarek mused. 'Too bad *Morrison's* not here. *Morrison* would know.'

*   *   *

It was a long while later. Morrison arrived. He had on his black vinyl pants and he sat down on a leather couch in front of the four big blank speakers and he closed his eyes. The curious aspect of Morrison's arrival was this: no one acknowledged it. Robby Krieger continued working out a guitar passage. John Densmore tuned his drums. Manzarek sat at the control console and twirled a corkscrew and let a girl rub his shoulders. The girl did not look at Morrison, although he was in her direct line of sight. An hour or so passed, and still no one had spoken to Morrison. Then Morrison spoke to Manzarek. He spoke almost in a whisper, as if he were wresting the words from behind some disabling aphasia.

'It's an hour to West Covina,' he said. 'I was thinking maybe we should spend the night out there after we play.'

Manzarek put down the corkscrew. 'Why?' he said.

'Instead of coming back.'

Manzarek shrugged. 'We were planning to come back.'

'Well, I was thinking, we could rehearse out there.'

Manzarek said nothing.

'We could get in a rehearsal, there's a Holiday Inn next door.'

'We could do that,' Manzarek said. 'Or we could rehearse Sunday, in town.'

'I guess so.' Morrison paused. 'Will the place be ready to rehearse Sunday?'

Manzarek looked at him for a while. 'No,' he said then.

I counted the control knobs on the electronic console. There were seventy-six. I was unsure in whose favor the dialogue had been resolved, or if it had been resolved at all. Robby Krieger picked at his guitar, and said that he needed a fuzz box. The producer suggested that he borrow one from the Buffalo Springfield, who were recording in the next studio. Krieger shrugged. Morrison sat down again on the leather couch and leaned back. He lit a match. He studied the flame awhile and then very slowly, very deliberately, lowered it to the fly of his black vinyl pants. Manzarek watched him. The girl who was rubbing Manzarek's shoulders did not look at anyone. There was a sense that no one was going to leave the room, ever. It would be some weeks before The Doors finished recording this album. I did not see it through.

4

Someone once brought Janis Joplin to a party at the house on Franklin Avenue: she had just done a concert and she wanted brandy-and-Benedictine in a water tumbler. Music people never wanted ordinary drinks. They wanted sake, or champagne cocktails, or tequila neat. Spending time with music people was confusing, and required a more fluid and ultimately a more passive approach than I ever acquired. In the first place time was never of the essence: we would have dinner at nine unless we had it at eleven-thirty, or we could order in later. We would go down to U.S.C. to see the Living Theater if the limo came at the very moment when no one had just made a drink or a cigarette or an arrangement to meet Ultra Violet at the Montecito. In any case David Hockney was coming by. In any case Ultra Violet was not at the Montecito. In any case we would go down to U.S.C. and see the Living Theater tonight or we would see the Living Theater another night, in New York, or Prague. First we wanted sushi for twenty, steamed clams, vegetable vindaloo and many rum drinks with gardenias for our hair. First we wanted a table for twelve, fourteen at the most, although there might be six more, or eight more, or eleven more: there would never be one or two more, because music people did not travel in groups of 'one' or 'two.' John and Michelle Phillips, on their way to the hospital for the birth of their daughter Chynna, had the limo detour into Hollywood in order to pick up a friend, Anne Marshall. This incident, which I often embroider in my mind to include an imaginary second detour, to the Luau for gardenias, exactly describes the music business to me.

5

Around five o'clock on the morning of October 28, 1967, in the desolate district between San Francisco Bay and the Oakland estuary that the Oakland police call Beat 101A, a 25-year-old black militant named Huey P. Newton was stopped and questioned by a white police officer named John Frey, Jr. An hour later Huey Newton was under arrest at Kaiser Hospital in Oakland, where he had gone for emergency treatment of a gunshot wound in his stomach, and a few weeks later he was indicted by the Alameda County Grand Jury on charges of murdering John Frey, wounding another officer, and kidnapping a bystander.

In the spring of 1968, when Huey Newton was awaiting trial, I went to see him in the Alameda County Jail. I suppose I went because I was interested in the alchemy of issues, for an issue is what Huey Newton had by then become. To understand how that had happened you must first consider Huey Newton, who he was. He came from an Oakland family, and for a while he went to Merritt College. In October of 1966 he and a friend named Bobby Seale organized what they called the Black Panther Party. They borrowed the name from the emblem used by the Freedom Party in Lowndes County, Alabama, and, from the beginning, they defined themselves as a revolutionary political group. The Oakland police knew the Panthers, and had a list of the twenty or so Panther cars. I am telling you neither that Huey Newton killed John Frey nor that Huey Newton did not kill John Frey, for in the context of revolutionary politics Huey Newton's guilt or innocence was irrelevant. I am telling you only how Huey Newton happened to be in the Alameda County Jail, and why rallies were held in his name, demonstrations organized whenever he appeared in court. LET'S SPRING HUEY, the buttons read (fifty cents each), and here and there on the courthouse steps, among the Panthers with their berets and sunglasses, the chants would go up:

> Get your M-.
> 31
> 'Cause baby we gonna
> Have some fun.
> BOOM BOOM. BOOM BOOM.

'Fight on, brother,' a woman would add in the spirit of a good-natured amen. 'Bang-bang.'

> *Bullshit bullshit*
> *Can't stand the game*
> *White man's playing.*
> *One way out, one way out.*
> *BOOM BOOM. BOOM BOOM.*

In the corridor downstairs in the Alameda County Courthouse there was a crush of lawyers and CBC correspondents and cameramen and people who wanted to 'visit Huey.'

'Eldridge doesn't mind if I go up,' one of the latter said to one of the lawyers.

'If Eldridge doesn't mind, it's all right with me,' the lawyer said. 'If you've got press credentials.'

'I've got kind of dubious credentials.'

'I can't take you up then. *Eldridge* has got dubious credentials. One's bad enough. I've got a good working relationship up there, I don't want to blow it.' The lawyer turned to a cameraman. 'You guys rolling yet?'

On that particular day I was allowed to go up, and a *Los Angeles Times* man, and a radio newscaster. We all signed the police register and sat around a scarred pine table and waited for Huey Newton. 'The only thing that's going to free Huey Newton,' Rap Brown had said recently at a Panther rally in Oakland Auditorium, 'is gunpowder.' 'Huey Newton laid down his life for us,' Stokely Carmichael had said the same night. But of course Huey Newton had not yet laid down his life at all, was just here in the Alameda County Jail waiting to be tried, and I wondered if the direction these rallies were taking ever made him uneasy, ever made him suspect that in many ways he was more useful to the revolution behind bars than on the street. He seemed, when he finally came in, an extremely likable young man, engaging, direct, and I did not get the sense that he had intended to become a political martyr. He smiled at us all and waited for his lawyer, Charles Garry, to set up a tape recorder, and he chatted softly with Eldridge Cleaver, who was then the Black Panthers' Minister of Information. (Huey Newton was still the Minister of Defense.) Eldridge Cleaver wore a black sweater and one gold earring and spoke in an almost inaudible drawl and was allowed to see Huey Newton because he had those 'dubious credentials,' a press card from

Ramparts. Actually his interest was in getting 'statements' from Huey Newton, 'messages' to take outside; in receiving a kind of prophecy to be interpreted as needed.

'We need a statement, Huey, about the ten-point program,' Eldridge Cleaver said, 'so I'll ask you a question, see, and you answer it . . .'

'How's Bobby,' Huey Newton asked.

'He's got a hearing on his misdemeanors, see . . .'

'I thought he had a felony.'

'Well, that's another thing, the felony, he's also got a couple of misdemeanors . . .'

Once Charles Garry had set up the tape recorder Huey Newton stopped chatting and started lecturing, almost without pause. He talked, running the words together because he had said them so many times before, about 'the American capitalistic-materialistic system' and 'so-called free enterprise' and 'the fight for the liberation of black people throughout the world.' Every now and then Eldridge Cleaver would signal Huey Newton and say something like, 'There are a lot of people interested in the Executive Mandate Number Three you've issued to the Black Panther Party, Huey. Care to comment?'

And Huey Newton would comment. 'Yes. Mandate Number Three is this demand from the Black Panther Party speaking for the black community. Within the Mandate we admonish the racist police force . . .' I kept wishing that he would talk about himself, hoping to break through the wall of rhetoric, but he seemed to be one of those autodidacts for whom all things specific and personal present themselves as mine fields to be avoided even at the cost of coherence, for whom safety lies in generalization. The newspaperman, the radio man, they tried:

Q. *Tell us something about yourself, Huey, I mean your life before the Panthers.*

A. *Before the Black Panther Party my life was very similar to that of most black people in this country.*

Q. *Well, your family, some incidents you remember, the influences that shaped you —*

A. *Living in America shaped me.*

Q. *Well, yes, but more specifically —*

A. *It reminds me of a quote from James Baldwin: 'To be black and conscious in America is to be in a constant state of rage.'*

'To be black and conscious in America is to be in a constant state of rage,' Eldridge Cleaver wrote in large letters on a pad of paper, and then he added: '*Huey P. Newton quoting James Baldwin.*' I could see it emblazoned above the speakers' platform at a rally, imprinted on the letterhead of an ad hoc committee still unborn. As a matter of fact almost everything Huey Newton said had the ring of being a 'quotation,' a 'pronouncement' to be employed when the need arose. I had heard Huey P. Newton On Racism ('The Black Panther Party is against racism'), Huey P. Newton On Cultural Nationalism ('The Black Panther Party believes that the only culture worth holding on to is revolutionary culture'), Huey P. Newton On White Radicalism, On Police Occupation of the Ghetto, On the European Versus the African. 'The European started to be sick when he denied his sexual nature,' Huey Newton said, and Charles Garry interrupted then, bringing it back to first principles. 'Isn't it true, though, Huey,' he said, 'that racism got its start for *economic* reasons?'

This weird interlocution seemed to take on a life of its own. The small room was hot and the fluorescent light hurt my eyes and I still did not know to what extent Huey Newton understood the nature of the role in which he was cast. As it happened I had always appreciated the logic of the Panther position, based as it was on the proposition that political power began at the end of the barrel of a gun (exactly what gun had even been specified, in an early memorandum from Huey P. Newton: '*Army .45; carbine; 12-gauge Magnum shotgun with 18″ barrel, preferably the brand of High Standard; M-16; .357 Magnum pistols; P-38*'), and I could appreciate as well the particular beauty in Huey Newton as 'issue.' In the politics of revolution everyone was expendable, but I doubted that Huey Newton's political sophistication extended to seeing himself that way: the value of a Scottsboro case is easier to see if you are not yourself the Scottsboro boy. 'Is there anything else you want to ask Huey?' Charles Garry asked. There did not seem to be. The lawyer adjusted his tape recorder. 'I've had a request, Huey,' he said, 'from a high-school student, a reporter on his school paper, and he wanted a statement from you, and he's going to call me tonight. Care to give me a message for him?'

Huey Newton regarded the microphone. There was a moment in which he seemed not to remember the name of the play, and then he brightened. 'I would like to point out,' he said, his voice gaining volume as the memory disks clicked, *high school, student, youth, message to youth*, 'that America is becoming a very young nation . . .'

I heard a moaning and a groaning, and I went over and it was – this Negro fellow was there. He had been shot in the stomach and at the time he didn't appear in any acute distress and so I said I'd see, and I asked him if he was a Kaiser, if he belonged to Kaiser, and he said, 'Yes, yes. Get a doctor. Can't you see I'm bleeding? I've been shot. Now get someone out here.' And I asked him if he had his Kaiser card and he got upset at this and he said, 'Come on, get a doctor out here, I've been shot.' I said, 'I see this, but you're not in any acute distress.' . . . So I told him we'd have to check to make sure he was a member . . . And this kind of upset him more and he called me a few nasty names and said, 'Now get a doctor out here right now, I've been shot and I'm bleeding.' And he took his coat off and his shirt and he threw it on the desk there and he said, 'Can't you see all this blood?' And I said, 'I see it.' And it wasn't that much, and so I said, 'Well, you'll have to sign our admission sheet before you can be seen by a doctor.' And he said, 'I'm not signing anything.' And I said, 'You cannot be seen by a doctor unless you sign the admission sheet,' and he said, 'I don't have to sign anything' and a few more choice words . . .

This is an excerpt from the testimony before the Alameda County Grand Jury of Corrine Leonard, the nurse in charge of the Kaiser Foundation Hospital emergency room in Oakland at 5:30 A.M. on October 28, 1967. The 'Negro fellow' was of course Huey Newton, wounded that morning during the gunfire which killed John Frey. For a long time I kept a copy of this testimony pinned to my office wall, on the theory that it illustrated a collision of cultures, a classic instance of an historical outsider confronting the established order at its most petty and impenetrable level. This theory was shattered when I learned that Huey Newton was in fact an enrolled member of the Kaiser Foundation Health Plan, i.e., in Nurse Leonard's words, 'a Kaiser.'

6

One morning in 1968 I went to see Eldridge Cleaver in the San
Francisco apartment he then shared with his wife, Kathleen. To be
admitted to this apartment it was necessary to ring first and then
stand in the middle of Oak Street, at a place which could be observed
clearly from the Cleavers' apartment. After this scrutiny the visitor
was, or was not, buzzed in. I was, and I climbed the stairs to find
Kathleen Cleaver in the kitchen frying sausage and Eldridge Cleaver
in the living room listening to a John Coltrane record and a number
of other people all over the apartment, people everywhere, people
standing in doorways and people moving around in one another's
peripheral vision and people making and taking telephone calls.
'When can you move on that?' I would hear in the background, and
'You can't bribe me with a dinner, man, those *Guardian* dinners are
all Old Left, like a wake.' Most of these other people were members
of the Black Panther Party, but one of them, in the living room, was
Eldridge Cleaver's parole officer. It seems to me that I stayed about
an hour. It seems to me that the three of us – Eldridge Cleaver, his
parole officer and I – mainly discussed the commercial prospects of
Soul on Ice, which, it happened, was being published that day. We
discussed the advance ($5,000). We discussed the size of the first
printing (10,000 copies). We discussed the advertising budget and
we discussed the bookstores in which copies were or were not available. It was a not unusual discussion between writers, with the
difference that one of the writers had his parole officer there and the
other had stood out on Oak Street and been visually frisked before
coming inside.

7

TO PACK AND WEAR:
    2 skirts
    2 jerseys or leotards
    1 pullover sweater

2 pair shoes
stockings
bra
nightgown, robe, slippers
cigarettes
bourbon
bag with:
    shampoo
    toothbrush and paste
    Basis soap
    razor, deodorant
    aspirin, prescriptions, Tampax
    face cream, powder, baby oil

TO CARRY:
    mohair throw
    typewriter
    2 legal pads and pens
    files
    house key

This is a list which was taped inside my closet door in Hollywood during those years when I was reporting more or less steadily. The list enabled me to pack, without thinking, for any piece I was likely to do. Notice the deliberate anonymity of costume: in a skirt, a leotard, *and stockings*, I could pass on either side of the culture. Notice the mohair throw for trunk-line flights (i.e., no blankets) and for the motel room in which the air conditioning could not be turned off. Notice the bourbon for the same motel room. Notice the typewriter for the airport, coming home: the idea was to turn in the Hertz car, check in, find an empty bench, and start typing the day's notes.

It should be clear that this was a list made by someone who prized control, yearned after momentum, someone determined to play her role as if she had the script, heard her cues, knew the narrative. There is on this list one significant omission, one article I needed and never had: a watch. I needed a watch not during the day, when I could turn on the car radio or ask someone, but at night, in the motel. Quite often I would ask the desk for the time every half hour or so, until finally, embarrassed to ask again, I would call Los Angeles and ask my husband. In other words I had skirts, jerseys, leotards, pullover sweater, shoes, stockings, bra, nightgown, robe, slippers, cigarettes, bourbon, shampoo, toothbrush and paste, Basis soap, razor, deodorant, aspirin, prescriptions, Tampax, face cream, powder, baby oil, mohair throw, typewriter, legal pads, pens, files and a house key, but I didn't know what time it was. This may be a parable, either of my life as a reporter during this period or of the period itself.

8

Driving a Budget Rent-A-Car between Sacramento and San Francisco one rainy morning in November of 1968 I kept the radio on very loud. On this occasion I kept the radio on very loud not to find out what time it was but in an effort to erase six words from my mind, six words which had no significance for me but which seemed that year to signal the onset of anxiety or fright. The words, a line from Ezra Pound's 'In a Station of the Metro,' were these: *Petals on a wet black bough*. The radio played 'Wichita Lineman' and 'I Heard It on the Grapevine.' *Petals on a wet black bough*. Somewhere between the Yolo Causeway and Vallejo it occurred to me that during the course of any given week I met too many people who spoke favorably about bombing power stations. Somewhere between the Yolo Causeway and Vallejo it also occurred to me that the fright on this particular morning was going to present itself as an inability to drive this Budget Rent-A-Car across the Carquinas Bridge. *The Wichita Lineman was still on the job*. I closed my eyes and drove across the Carquinas Bridge, because I had appointments, because I was working, because I had promised to watch the revolution being made at San Francisco State College and because there was no place in Vallejo to turn in a Budget Rent-A-Car and because nothing on my mind was in the script as I remembered it.

9

At San Francisco State College on that particular morning the wind was blowing the cold rain in squalls across the muddied lawns and against the lighted windows of empty classrooms. In the days before there had been fires set and classes invaded and finally a confrontation with the San Francisco Police Tactical Unit, and in the weeks to come the campus would become what many people on it were pleased to call 'a battlefield.' The police and the Mace and the noon arrests would become the routine of life on the campus, and every night the combatants would review their day on television: the waves of students advancing, the commotion at the edge of the frame, the riot sticks flashing, the instant of jerky camera that served to suggest at what risk the film was obtained; then a cut to the weather map. In the beginning there had been the necessary 'issue,' the suspension of a 22-year-old instructor who happened as well to be Minister of Education for the Black Panther Party, but that issue, like most, had soon ceased to be the point in the minds of even the most dense participants. Disorder was its own point.

I had never before been on a campus in disorder, had missed even Berkeley and Columbia, and I suppose I went to San Francisco State expecting something other than what I found there. In some not at all trivial sense, the set was wrong. The very architecture of California state colleges tends to deny radical notions, to reflect instead a modest and hopeful vision of progressive welfare bureaucracy, and as I walked across the campus that day and on later days the entire San Francisco State dilemma – the gradual politicization, the 'issues' here and there, the obligatory 'Fifteen Demands,' the continual arousal of the police and the outraged citizenry – seemed increasingly off-key, an instance of the *enfants terribles* and the Board of Trustees unconsciously collaborating on a wishful fantasy (Revolution on Campus) and playing it out in time for the six o'clock news. 'Adjet-prop committee meeting in the Redwood Room,' read a scrawled note on the cafeteria door one morning; only someone who needed very badly to be alarmed could respond with force to a guerrilla band that not only announced its meetings on the enemy's bulletin board but seemed innocent of the spelling, and so the meaning, of the words it used. 'Hitler Hayakawa,' some of the faculty had begun calling S. I. Hayakawa, the semanticist who had become the college's third president in a year and had incurred considerable displeasure by trying to keep the campus open. *'Eichmann,'* Kay Boyle had screamed at him at a rally. In just such broad strokes was the picture being painted in the fall of 1968 on the pastel campus at San Francisco State.

The place simply never seemed serious. The headlines were dark that first day, the college had been closed 'indefinitely,' both Ronald Reagan and Jesse Unruh were threatening reprisals; still, the climate inside the Administration Building was that of a musical comedy about college life. 'No *chance* we'll be open tomorrow,' secretaries informed callers. 'Go skiing, have a good time.' Striking black militants dropped in to chat with the deans; striking white radicals exchanged gossip in the corridors. 'No interviews, no press,' announced a student strike leader who happened into a dean's office where I was sitting; in the next moment he was piqued because no one had told him that a Huntley-Brinkley camera crew was on campus. 'We can still plug into that,' the dean said soothingly. Everyone seemed joined in a rather festive camaraderie, a shared jargon, a shared sense of moment: the future was no longer arduous and indefinite but immediate and programmatic, aglow with the prospect of problems to be 'addressed,' plans to be 'implemented.' It was agreed all around that the confrontations could be 'a very healthy development,' that maybe it took a shutdown 'to get something done.' The mood, like the architecture, was 1948 functional, a model of pragmatic optimism.

Perhaps Evelyn Waugh could have gotten it down exactly right: Waugh was good at scenes of industrious self-delusion, scenes of people absorbed in odd games. Here at San Francisco State only the black militants could be construed as serious: they were at any rate picking the games, dictating the rules, and taking what they could from what seemed for everyone else just an amiable evasion of routine, of institutional anxiety, of the tedium of the academic calendar. Meanwhile the administrators could talk about programs. Meanwhile the white radicals could see themselves, on an investment of virtually nothing, as urban guerrillas. It was working out well for everyone, this game at San Francisco State, and its peculiar virtues had never been so clear to me as they became one afternoon when I sat in on a meeting of fifty or sixty SDS members. They had called a press conference for later that day, and now they were discussing 'just what the format of the press conference should be.'

'This has to be on our terms,' someone warned. 'Because they'll ask very leading questions, they'll ask *questions*.'

'Make them submit any questions in writing,' someone else suggested. 'The Black Student Union does that very successfully, then they just don't answer anything they don't want to answer.'

'That's it, don't fall into their trap.'

'Something we should stress at this press conference is *who owns the media*.'

'You don't think it's common knowledge that the papers represent corporate interests?' a realist among them interjected doubtfully.

'I don't think it's *understood*.'

Two hours and several dozen hand votes later, the group had selected four members to tell the press who owned the media, had decided to appear *en masse* at an opposition press conference, and had debated various slogans for the next day's demonstration. 'Let's see, first we have "Hearst Tells It Like It Ain't", then "Stop Press Distortion" – that's the one there was some political controversy about . . .'

And, before they broke up, they had listened to a student who had driven up for the day from the College of San Mateo, a junior college down the peninsula from San Francisco. 'I came up here today with some Third World students to tell you that we're with you, and we hope you'll be with *us* when we try to pull off a strike next week, because we're really into it, we carry our motorcycle helmets all the time, can't think, can't go to class.'

He had paused. He was a nice-looking boy, and fired with his task. I considered the tender melancholy of life in San Mateo, which is one of the richest counties per capita in the United States of America, and I considered whether or not the Wichita Lineman and the petals on the wet black bough represented the aimlessness of the bourgeoisie, and I considered the illusion of aim to be gained by holding a press conference, the only problem with press conferences being that the press asked questions. 'I'm here to tell you that at College of San Mateo we're living like *revolutionaries*,' the boy said then.

10

We put 'Lay Lady Lay' on the record player, and 'Suzanne.' We went down to Melrose Avenue to see the Flying Burritos. There was a jasmine vine grown over the verandah of the big house on Franklin Avenue, and in the evenings the smell of jasmine came in through all the open doors and windows. I made bouillabaisse for people who did not eat meat. I imagined that my own life was simple and sweet, and sometimes it was, but there were odd things going around town. There were rumors. There were stories. Everything was unmentionable but nothing was unimaginable. This mystical flirtation with the idea of 'sin' – this sense that it was possible to go 'too far,' and that many people were doing it – was very much with us in Los Angeles in 1968 and 1969. A demented and seductive vortical tension was building in the community. The jitters were setting in. I recall a time when the dogs barked every night and the moon was always full. On August 9, 1969, I was sitting in the shallow end of my sister-in-law's swimming pool in Beverly Hills when she received a telephone call from a friend who had just heard about the murders at Sharon Tate Polanski's house on Cielo Drive. The phone rang many times during the next hour. These early reports were garbled and contradictory. One caller would say hoods, the next would say chains. There were twenty dead, no, twelve, ten, eighteen. Black masses were imagined, and bad trips blamed. I remember all of the day's misinformation very clearly, and I also remember this, and wish I did not: *I remember that no one was surprised.*

11

When I first met Linda Kasabian in the summer of 1970 she was wearing her hair parted neatly in the middle, no makeup, Elizabeth Arden 'Blue Grass' perfume, and the unpressed blue uniform issued to inmates at the Sybil Brand Institute for Women in Los Angeles. She was at Sybil Brand in protective custody, waiting out the time until she could testify about the murders of Sharon Tate Polanski,

Abigail Folger, Jay Sebring, Voytek Frykowski, Steven Parent, and Rosemary and Leno LaBianca, and, with her lawyer, Gary Fleischman, I spent a number of evenings talking to her there. Of these evenings I remember mainly my dread at entering the prison, at leaving for even an hour the infinite possibilities I suddenly perceived in the summer twilight. I remember driving downtown on the Hollywood Freeway in Gary Fleischman's Cadillac convertible with the top down. I remember watching a rabbit graze on the grass by the gate as Gary Fleischman signed the prison register. Each of the half-dozen doors that locked behind us as we entered Sybil Brand was a little death, and I would emerge after the interview like Persephone from the underworld, euphoric, elated. Once home I would have two drinks and make myself a hamburger and eat it ravenously.

'Dig it,' Gary Fleischman was always saying. One night when we were driving back to Hollywood from Sybil Brand in the Cadillac convertible with the top down he demanded that I tell him the population of India. I said that I did not know the population of India. 'Take a guess,' he prompted. I made a guess, absurdly low, and he was disgusted. He had asked the same question of his niece ('a college girl'), of Linda, and now of me, and none of us had known. It seemed to confirm some idea he had of women, their essential ineducability, their similarity under the skin. Gary Fleischman was someone of a type I met only rarely, a comic realist in a porkpie hat, a business traveler on the far frontiers of the period, a man who knew his way around the courthouse and Sybil Brand and remained cheerful, even jaunty, in the face of the awesome and impenetrable mystery at the center of what he called 'the case.' In fact we never talked about 'the case,' and referred to its central events only as 'Cielo Drive' and 'LaBianca.' We talked instead about Linda's childhood pastimes and disappointments, her high-school romances and her concern for her children. This particular juxtaposition of the spoken and the unspeakable was eerie and unsettling, and made my notebook a litany of little ironies so obvious as to be of interest only to dedicated absurdists. An example: Linda dreamed of opening a combination restaurant-boutique and pet shop.

12

Certain organic disorders of the central nervous system are characterized by periodic remissions, the apparent complete recovery of the afflicted nerves. What happens appears to be this: as the lining of a nerve becomes inflamed and hardens into scar tissue, thereby blocking the passage of neural impulses, the nervous system gradually changes its circuitry, finds other, unaffected nerves to carry the same messages. During the years when I found it necessary to revise the circuitry of my mind I discovered that I was no longer interested in whether the woman on the ledge outside the window on the sixteenth floor jumped or did not jump, or in why. I was interested only in the picture of her in my mind: her hair incandescent in the floodlights, her bare toes curled inward on the stone ledge.

In this light all narrative was sentimental. In this light all connections were equally meaningful, and equally senseless. Try these: on the morning of John Kennedy's death in 1963 I was buying, at Ransohoff's in San Francisco, a short silk dress in which to be married. A few years later this dress of mine was ruined when, at a dinner party in Bel-Air, Roman Polanski accidentally spilled a glass of red wine on it. Sharon Tate was also a guest at this party, although she and Roman Polanski were not yet married. On July 27, 1970, I went to the Magnin-Hi Shop on the third floor of I. Magnin in Beverly Hills and picked out, at Linda Kasabian's request, the dress in which she began her testimony about the murders at Sharon Tate Polanski's house on Cielo Drive. 'Size 9 Petite,' her instructions read. 'Mini but not extremely mini. In velvet if possible. Emerald green or gold. Or: A Mexican peasant-style dress, smocked or embroidered.' She needed a dress that morning because the district attorney, Vincent Bugliosi, had expressed doubts about the dress she had planned to wear, a long white homespun shift. 'Long is for evening,' he had advised Linda. Long was for evening and white was for brides. At her own wedding in 1965 Linda Kasabian had worn a white brocade suit. Time passed, times changed. Everything was to teach us something. At 11:20 on that July morning in 1970 I delivered the dress in which she would testify to Gary Fleischman, who was waiting in front of his office on Rodeo Drive in Beverly Hills. He was wearing his porkpie hat and he was standing with Linda's second husband, Bob Kasabian, and their friend Charlie Melton, both of whom were wearing long white robes. Long was for Bob and Charlie, the dress in the I. Magnin box was for Linda. The three of them took the I. Magnin box and got into Gary Fleischman's Cadillac convertible with the top down and drove off in the sunlight toward the freeway downtown, waving back at me. I believe this to be an authentically senseless chain of correspondences, but in the jingle-jangle morning of that summer it made as much sense as anything else did.

13

I recall a conversation I had in 1970 with the manager of a motel in which I was staying near Pendleton, Oregon. I had been doing a piece for *Life* about the storage of VX and GB nerve gas at an Army arsenal in Umatilla County, and now I was done, and trying to check out of the motel. During the course of checking out I was asked this question by the manager, who was a Mormon: *If you can't believe you're going to heaven in your own body and on a first-name basis with all the members of your family, then what's the point of dying?* At that time I believed that my basic affective controls were no longer intact, but now I present this to you as a more cogent question than it might at first appear, a kind of koan of the period.

14

Once I had a rib broken, and during the few months that it was painful to turn in bed or raise my arms in a swimming pool I had, for the first time, a sharp apprehension of what it would be like to be old. Later I forgot. At some point during the years I am talking about here, after a series of periodic visual disturbances, three electroencephalograms, two complete sets of skull and neck X-rays, one five-hour glucose tolerance test, two electromyelograms, a battery of chemical tests and consultations with two ophthalmologists, one internist and three neurologists, I was told that the disorder was not really in my eyes, but in my central nervous system. I might or might not experience symptoms of neural damage all my life. These symptoms, which might or might not appear, might or might not involve my eyes. They might or might not involve my arms or legs, they might or might not be disabling. Their effects might be lessened by cortisone injections, or they might not. It could not be predicted. The condition had a name, the kind of name usually associated with telethons, but the name meant nothing and the neurologist did not like to use it. The name was multiple sclerosis, but the name had no meaning. This was, the neurologist said, an exclusionary diagnosis, and meant nothing.

I had, at this time, a sharp apprehension not of what it was like to be old but of what it was like to open the door to the stranger and find that the stranger did indeed have the knife. In a few lines of dialogue in a neurologist's office in Beverly Hills, the improbable had become the probable, the norm: things which happened only to other people could in fact happen to me. I could be struck by lightning, could dare to eat a peach and be poisoned by the cyanide in the stone. The startling fact was this: my body was offering a precise physiological equivalent to what had been going on in my mind. 'Lead a simple life,' the neurologist advised. 'Not that it makes any difference we know about.' In other words it was another story without a narrative.

15

Many people I know in Los Angeles believe that the Sixties ended abruptly on August 9, 1969, ended at the exact moment when word of the murders on Cielo Drive traveled like brushfire through the community, and in a sense this is true. The tension broke that day. The paranoia was fulfilled. In another sense the Sixties did not truly end for me until January of 1971, when I left the house on Franklin Avenue and moved to a house on the sea. This particular house on the sea had itself been very much a part of the Sixties, and for some months after we took possession I would come across souvenirs of that period in its history – a piece of Scientology literature beneath a drawer lining, a copy of *Stranger in a Strange Land* stuck deep on a closet shelf – but after a while we did some construction, and between the power saws and the sea wind the place got exorcized.

I have known, since then, very little about the movements of the people who seemed to me emblematic of those years. I know of course that Eldridge Cleaver went to Algeria and came home an entrepreneur. I know that Jim Morrison died in Paris. I know that Linda Kasabian fled in search of the pastoral to New Hampshire, where I once visited her; she also visited me in New York, and we took our children on the Staten Island Ferry to see the Statue of Liberty. I also know that in 1975 Paul Ferguson, while serving a life sentence for the murder of Ramon Novarro, won first prize in a PEN fiction contest and announced plans to 'continue my writing.' Writing had helped him, he said, to 'reflect on experience and see what it means.' Quite often I reflect on the big house in Hollywood, on 'Midnight Confessions' and on Ramon Novarro and on the fact that Roman Polanski and I are godparents to the same child, but writing has not yet helped me to see what it means.

1968–1978

II

California Republic

James Pike, American

It is a curious and arrogantly secular monument, Grace Episcopal Cathedral in San Francisco, and it imposes its tone on everything around it. It stands directly upon the symbolic nexus of all old California money and power, Nob Hill. Its big rose window glows at night and dominates certain views from the Mark Hopkins and the Fairmont, as well as from Randolph and Catherine Hearst's apartment on California Street. In a city dedicated to the illusion that all human endeavor tends mystically west, toward the Pacific, Grace Cathedral faces resolutely east, toward the Pacific Union Club. As a child I was advised by my grandmother that Grace was 'unfinished,' and always would be, which was its point. In the years after World War I my mother had put pennies for Grace in her mite box but Grace would never be finished. In the years after World War II I would put pennies for Grace in my mite box but Grace would never be finished. In 1964 James Albert Pike, who had come home from St John the Divine in New York and *The Dean Pike Show* on ABC to be Bishop of California, raised three million dollars, installed images of Albert Einstein, Thurgood Marshall and John Glenn in the clerestory windows, and, in the name of God (James Albert Pike had by then streamlined the Trinity, eliminating the Son and the Holy Ghost), pronounced Grace 'finished.' This came to my attention as an odd and unsettling development, an extreme missing of the point – at least as I had understood the point in my childhood – and it engraved James Albert Pike on my consciousness more indelibly than any of his previous moves.

What was one to make of him. Five years after he finished Grace,
James Albert Pike left the Episcopal Church altogether, detailing his
pique in the pages of *Look*, and drove into the Jordanian desert in a
white Ford Cortina rented from Avis. He went with his former
student and bride of nine months, Diane. Later she would say that
they wanted to experience the wilderness as Jesus had. They equipped themselves for this mission with an Avis map and two bottles of
Coca-Cola. The young Mrs Pike got out alive. Five days after James
Albert Pike's body was retrieved from a canyon near the Dead Sea a
Solemn Requiem Mass was offered for him at the cathedral his own
hubris had finished in San Francisco. Outside on the Grace steps the
cameras watched the Black Panthers demonstrating to free Bobby
Seale. Inside the Grace nave Diane Kennedy Pike and her two prede-
cessors, Jane Alvies Pike and Esther Yanovsky Pike, watched the
cameras and one another.

That was 1969. For some years afterward I could make nothing
at all of this peculiar and strikingly 'now' story, so vast and atavistic
was my irritation with the kind of man my grandmother would have
called 'just a damn old fool,' the kind of man who would go into the
desert with the sappy Diane and two bottles of Coca-Cola, but I see
now that Diane and the Coca-Cola are precisely the details which
lift the narrative into apologue. James Albert Pike has been on my
mind quite a bit these past few weeks, ever since I read a biography
of him by William Stringfellow and Anthony Towne, *The Death and
Life of Bishop Pike*, an adoring but instructive volume from which
there emerges the shadow of a great literary character, a literary
character in the sense that Howard Hughes and Whittaker Chambers
were literary characters, a character so ambiguous and driven and
revealing of his time and place that his gravestone in the Protestant Cemetery in Jaffa might well have read only *JAMES PIKE,
AMERICAN*.

Consider his beginnings. He was the only child of an ambitious
mother and an ailing father who moved from Kentucky a few years
before his birth in 1913 to homestead forty acres of mesquite in
Oklahoma. There had been for a while a retreat to a one-room shack
in Alamogordo, New Mexico, there had been always the will of the
mother to improve the family's prospects. She taught school. She
played piano with a dance band, she played piano in a silent-movie

theater. She raised her baby James a Catholic and she entered him in the Better Babies Contest at the Oklahoma State Fair and he took first prize, two years running. 'I thought you would like that,' she told his biographers almost sixty years later. 'He started out a winner.'

He also started out dressing paper dolls in priests' vestments. The mother appears to have been a woman of extreme determination. Her husband died when James was two. Six years later the widow moved to Los Angeles, where she devoted herself to maintaining a world in which nothing 'would change James' life or thwart him in any way,' a mode of upbringing which would show in the son's face and manner all his life. 'Needless to say this has all been a bit tedious for me to relive,' he complained when the question of his first divorce and remarriage seemed to stand between him and election as Bishop of California; his biography is a panoply of surprised petulance in the face of other people's attempts to 'thwart' him by bringing up an old marriage or divorce or some other 'long-dead aspect of the past.'

In Los Angeles there was Hollywood High, there was Mass every morning at Blessed Sacrament on Sunset Boulevard. After Hollywood High there was college with the Jesuits, at Santa Clara, at least until James repudiated the Catholic Church and convinced his mother that she should do the same. He was eighteen at the time, but it was characteristic of both mother and son to have taken this adolescent 'repudiation' quite gravely: they give the sense of having had no anchor but each other, and to have reinvented their moorings every day. After Santa Clara, for the freshly invented agnostic, there was U.C.L.A., then U.S.C., and finally the leap east. Back East. Yale Law. A job in Washington with the Securities and Exchange Commission. 'You have to understand that he was very lonely in Washington,' his mother said after his death. 'He really wanted to come home. I wish he had.' And yet it must have seemed to such a western child that he had at last met the 'real' world, the 'great' world, the world to beat. The world in which, as the young man who started out a winner soon discovered and wrote to his mother, 'practically every churchgoer you meet in our level of society is Episcopalian, and an R.C. or straight Protestant is as rare as hen's teeth.'

One thinks of Gatsby, coming up against the East. One also thinks of Tom Buchanan, and his vast carelessness. (Some 25 years later, in Santa Barbara, when the Bishop of California's mistress swallowed

55 sleeping pills, he appears to have moved her from his apartment into her own before calling an ambulance, and to have obscured certain evidence before she died.) One even thinks of Dick Diver, who also started out a winner, and who tried to embrace the essence of the American continent in Nicole as James Albert Pike would now try to embrace it in the Episcopal Church. *'Practically every churchgoer you meet in our level of society is Episcopalian.'*

It is an American Adventure of Barry Lyndon, this Westerner going East to seize his future, equipped with a mother's love and with what passed in the makeshift moorage from which he came as a passion for knowledge. As evidence of this passion his third wife, Diane, would repeat this curious story: he 'had read both the dictionary and the phone book from cover to cover by the time he was five, and a whole set of the Encyclopaedia Britannica before he was ten.' Diane also reports his enthusiasm for the Museum of Man in Paris, which seemed to him to offer, in the hour he spent there, 'a complete education,' the 'entire history of the human race . . . in summary form.'

In summary form. One gets a sense of the kind of mindless fervor that a wife less rapt than Diane might find unhinging. In the late thirties, as Communion was about to be served at the first Christmas Mass of James Albert Pike's new career as an Episcopalian, his first wife, Jane, another transplanted Californian, is reported to have jumped up and run screaming from the church. There would have been nothing in the phone book to cover that, or in the Britannica either. Later he invented an ecclesiastical annulment to cover his divorce from Jane, although no such annulment was actually granted. 'In his mind,' his biographers explain, 'the marriage was not merely a mistake, but a nullity in the inception.' In his mind. He needed to believe in the annulment because he wanted to be Bishop of California. 'At heart he was a Californian,' a friend said. 'He had grown up with the idea that San Francisco was it . . . he was obsessed with the idea of being Bishop of California. Nothing in heaven or hell could have stopped him.' In his mind. 'Tom and Gatsby, Daisy and Jordan and I, were all Westerners,' as Nick Carraway said, 'and perhaps we possessed some deficiency in common which made us subtly unadaptable to Eastern life.'

*   *   *

In his mind. I recall standing in St Thomas Church in New York one Monday morning in 1964 debating whether or not to steal a book by James Albert Pike, a pastoral tract called *If You Marry Outside Your Faith*. I had only a twenty-dollar bill and could not afford to leave it in the box but I wanted to read the book more closely, because a few weeks before I had in fact married a Catholic, which was what Bishop Pike seemed to have in mind. I had not been brought up to think it made much difference what I married, as long as I steered clear of odd sects where they didn't drink at the wedding (my grandmother was an Episcopalian only by frontier chance; her siblings were Catholics but there was no Catholic priest around the year she needed christening), and I was struck dumb by Bishop Pike's position, which appeared to be that I had not only erred but had every moral right and obligation to erase this error by regarding my marriage as null, and any promises I had made as invalid. In other words the way to go was to forget it and start over.

In the end I did not steal *If You Marry Outside Your Faith*, and over the years I came to believe that I had doubtless misread it. After considering its source I am no longer so sure. 'Jim never cleaned up after himself,' a friend notes, recalling his habit of opening a shirt and letting the cardboards lie where they fell, and this *élan* seems to have applied to more than his laundry. Here was a man who moved through life believing that he was entitled to forget it and start over, to shed women when they became difficult and allegiances when they became tedious and simply *move on*, dismissing those who quibbled as petty and 'judgmental' and generally threatened by his superior and more dynamic view of human possibility. That there was an ambivalence and a speciousness about this moral frontiersmanship has not gone unnoticed, but in the rush to call the life 'only human' I suspect we are overlooking its real interest, which is as social history. The man was a Michelin to his time and place. At the peak of his career James Albert Pike carried his peace cross (he had put away his pectoral cross for the duration of the Vietnam War, which outlived him) through every charlatanic thicket in American life, from the Center for the Study of Democratic Institutions to the Aspen Institute of Humanistic Studies to Spiritual Frontiers, which was at the time the Ford Foundation of the spirit racket. James Albert Pike was everywhere at the right time. He was in Geneva for *Pacem in Terris*. He was in Baltimore for the trial of the Catonsville Nine, although he had to be briefed on the issue in the car from the airport. He was in the right room at the right time to reach his son, Jim Jr, an apparent suicide on Romilar, via séance. The man kept moving. If death was troubling then start over, and reinvent it as 'The Other Side.' If faith was troubling then leave the Church, and reinvent it as 'The Foundation for Religious Transition.'

This sense that the world can be reinvented smells of the Sixties in this country, those years when no one at all seemed to have any memory or mooring, and in a way the Sixties were the years for which James Albert Pike was born. When the man who started out a winner was lying dead in the desert his brother-in-law joined the search party, and prayed for the assistance of God, Jim Jr, and Edgar Cayce. I think I have never heard a more poignant trinity.

1976

Holy Water

Some of us who live in arid parts of the world think about water with a reverence others might find excessive. The water I will draw tomorrow from my tap in Malibu is today crossing the Mojave Desert from the Colorado River, and I like to think about exactly where that water is. The water I will drink tonight in a restaurant in Hollywood is by now well down the Los Angeles Aqueduct from the Owens River, and I also think about exactly where that water is: I particularly like to imagine it as it cascades down the 45-degree stone steps that aerate Owens water after its airless passage through the mountain pipes and siphons. As it happens my own reverence for water has always taken the form of this constant meditation upon where the water is, of an obsessive interest not in the politics of water but in the waterworks themselves, in the movement of water through aqueducts and siphons and pumps and forebays and afterbays and weirs and drains, in plumbing on the grand scale. I know the data on water projects I will never see. I know the difficulty Kaiser had closing the last two sluiceway gates on the Guri Dam in Venezuela. I keep watch on evaporation behind the Aswan in Egypt. I can put myself to sleep imagining the water dropping a thousand feet into the turbines at Churchill Falls in Labrador. If the Churchill Falls Project fails to materialize, I fall back on waterworks closer at hand – the tailrace at Hoover on the Colorado, the surge tank in the Tehachapi Mountains that receives California Aqueduct water pumped higher than water has ever been pumped before – and finally I replay a morning when I was seventeen years old and caught, in a military-surplus life raft, in the construction of the Nimbus Afterbay Dam on the American River near Sacramento. I remember that at the moment it happened I was trying to open a tin of anchovies with capers. I recall the raft spinning into the narrow chute through which the river had been temporarily diverted. I recall being deliriously happy.

I suppose it was partly the memory of that delirium that led me to visit, one summer morning in Sacramento, the Operations Control Center for the California State Water Project. Actually so much water is moved around California by so many different agencies that maybe only the movers themselves know on any given day whose water is where, but to get a general picture it is necessary only to remember that Los Angeles moves some of it, San Francisco moves some of it, the Bureau of Reclamation's Central Valley Project moves some of it and the California State Water Project moves most of the rest of it, moves a vast amount of it, moves more water farther than has ever been moved anywhere. They collect this water up in the granite keeps of the Sierra Nevada and they store roughly a trillion gallons of it behind the Oroville Dam and every morning, down at the Project's headquarters in Sacramento, they decide how much of their water they want to move the next day. They make this morning decision according to supply and demand, which is simple in theory but rather more complicated in practice. In theory each of the Project's five field divisions – the Oroville, the Delta, the San Luis, the San Joaquin and the Southern divisions – places a call to headquarters before nine A.M. and tells the dispatchers how much water is needed by its local water contractors, who have in turn based their morning estimates on orders from growers and other big users. A schedule is made. The gates open and close according to schedule. The water flows south and the deliveries are made.

In practice this requires prodigious coordination, precision, and the best efforts of several human minds and that of a Univac 418. In practice it might be necessary to hold large flows of water for power production, or to flush out encroaching salinity in the Sacramento-San Joaquin Delta, the most ecologically sensitive point on the system. In practice a sudden rain might obviate the need for a delivery when that delivery is already on its way. In practice what is being delivered here is an enormous volume of water, not quarts of milk or spools of thread, and it takes two days to move such a delivery down through Oroville into the Delta, which is the great pooling place for California water and has been for some years alive with electronic sensors and telemetering equipment and men blocking channels and diverting flows and shoveling fish away from the pumps. It takes perhaps another six days to move this same water down the California Aqueduct from the Delta to the Tehachapi and put it over the hill to Southern California. 'Putting some over the hill' is what they say around the Project Operations Control Center when they want to indicate that they are pumping Aqueduct water from the floor of the San Joaquin Valley up and over the Tehachapi Mountains. 'Pulling it down' is what they say when they want to indicate that they are lowering a water level somewhere in the system. They can put some over the hill by remote control from this room in Sacramento with its Univac and its big board and its flashing lights. They can pull down a pool in the San Joaquin by remote control from this room in Sacramento with its locked doors and its ringing alarms and its constant print-outs of data from sensors out there in the water itself. From this room in Sacramento the whole system takes on the aspect of a perfect three-billion-dollar hydraulic toy, and in certain ways it is. 'LET'S START DRAINING QUAIL AT 12:00' was the 10:51 A.M. entry on the electronically recorded communications log the day I visited the Operations Control Center. 'Quail' is a reservoir in Los Angeles County with a gross capacity of 1,636,018,000 gallons. 'OK' was the response recorded in the log. I knew at that moment that I had missed the only vocation for which I had any instinctive affinity: I wanted to drain Quail myself.

Not many people I know carry their end of the conversation when I want to talk about water deliveries, even when I stress that these deliveries affect their lives, indirectly, every day. 'Indirectly' is not quite enough for most people I know. This morning, however, several people I know were affected not 'indirectly' but 'directly' by the way the water moves. They had been in New Mexico shooting a picture, one sequence of which required a river deep enough to sink a truck, the kind with a cab and a trailer and fifty or sixty wheels. It so happened that no river near the New Mexico location was running

that deep this year. The production was therefore moved today to
Needles, California, where the Colorado River normally runs, depending upon releases from Davis Dam, eighteen to twenty-five feet
deep. Now. Follow this closely: yesterday we had a freak tropical
storm in Southern California, two inches of rain in a normally dry
month, and because this rain flooded the fields and provided more
irrigation than any grower could possibly want for several days, no
water was ordered from Davis Dam.

No orders, no releases.

Supply and demand.

As a result the Colorado was running only seven feet deep past
Needles today, Sam Peckinpah's desire for eighteen feet of water in
which to sink a truck not being the kind of demand anyone at Davis
Dam is geared to meet. The production closed down for the weekend.
Shooting will resume Tuesday, providing some grower orders water
and the agencies controlling the Colorado release it. Meanwhile many
gaffers, best boys, cameramen, assistant directors, script supervisors,
stunt drivers and maybe even Sam Peckinpah are waiting out the
weekend in Needles, where it is often 110 degrees at five P.M. and
hard to get dinner after eight. This is a California parable, but a true
one.

I have always wanted a swimming pool, and never had one. When
it became generally known a year or so ago that California was
suffering severe drought, many people in water-rich parts of the
country seemed obscurely gratified, and made frequent reference
to Californians having to brick up their swimming pools. In fact a
swimming pool requires, once it has been filled and the filter has
begun its process of cleaning and recirculating the water, virtually
no water, but the symbolic content of swimming pools has always
been interesting: a pool is misapprehended as a trapping of affluence,
real or pretended, and of a kind of hedonistic attention to the body.
Actually a pool is, for many of us in the West, a symbol not of
affluence but of order, of control over the uncontrollable. A pool is
water, made available and useful, and is, as such, infinitely soothing
to the western eye.

It is easy to forget that the only natural force over which we have any control out here is water, and that only recently. In my memory California summers were characterized by the coughing in the pipes that meant the well was dry, and California winters by all-night watches on rivers about to crest, by sandbagging, by dynamite on the levees and flooding on the first floor. Even now the place is not all that hospitable to extensive settlement. As I write a fire has been burning out of control for two weeks in the ranges behind the Big Sur coast. Flash floods last night wiped out all major roads into Imperial County. I noticed this morning a hairline crack in a living-room tile from last week's earthquake, a 4.4 I never felt. In the part of California where I now live aridity is the single most prominent feature of the climate, and I am not pleased to see, this year, cactus spreading wild to the sea. There will be days this winter when the humidity will drop to ten, seven, four. Tumbleweed will blow against my house and the sound of the rattlesnake will be duplicated a hundred times a day by dried bougainvillea drifting in my driveway. The apparent ease of California life is an illusion, and those who believe the illusion real live here in only the most temporary way. I know as well as the next person that there is considerable transcendent value in a river running wild and undammed, a river running free over granite, but I have also lived beneath such a river when it was running in flood, and gone without showers when it was running dry.

'The West begins,' Bernard DeVoto wrote, 'where the average annual rainfall drops below twenty inches.' This is maybe the best definition of the West I have ever read, and it goes a long way toward explaining my own passion for seeing the water under control, but many people I know persist in looking for psychoanalytical implications in this passion. As a matter of fact I have explored, in an amateur way, the more obvious of these implications, and come up with nothing interesting. A certain external reality remains, and resists interpretation. The West begins where the average annual rainfall drops below twenty inches. Water is important to people who do not have it, and the same is true of control. Some fifteen years ago I tore a poem by Karl Shapiro from a magazine and pinned it on my kitchen wall. This fragment of paper is now on the wall of a sixth kitchen, and crumbles a little whenever I touch it, but I keep it there for the last stanza, which has for me the power of a prayer:

> *It is raining in California, a straight rain*
> *Cleaning the heavy oranges on the bough,*
> *Filling the gardens till the gardens flow,*
> *Shining the olives, tiling the gleaming tile,*
> *Waxing the dark camellia leaves more green,*
> *Flooding the daylong valleys like the Nile.*

I thought of those lines almost constantly on the morning in Sacramento when I went to visit the California State Water Project Operations Control Center. If I had wanted to drain Quail at 10:51 that morning, I wanted, by early afternoon, to do a great deal more. I wanted to open and close the Clifton Court Forebay intake gate. I wanted to produce some power down at the San Luis Dam. I wanted to pick a pool at random on the Aqueduct and pull it down and then refill it, watching for the hydraulic jump. I wanted to put some water over the hill and I wanted to shut down all flow from the Aqueduct into the Bureau of Reclamation's Cross Valley Canal, just to see how long it would take somebody over at Reclamation to call up and complain. I stayed as long as I could and watched the system work on the big board with the lighted checkpoints. The Delta salinity report was coming in on one of the teletypes behind me. The Delta tidal report was coming in on another. The earthquake board, which has been desensitized to sound its alarm (a beeping tone for Southern California, a high-pitched tone for the north) only for those earthquakes which register at least 3.0 on the Richter Scale, was silent. I had no further business in this room and yet I wanted to stay the day. I wanted to be the one, that day, who was shining the olives, filling the gardens, and flooding the daylong valleys like the Nile. I want it still.

1977

Many Mansions

The new official residence for governors of California, unlandscaped, unfurnished, and unoccupied since the day construction stopped in 1975, stands on eleven acres of oaks and olives on a bluff overlooking the American River outside Sacramento. This is the twelve-thousand-square-foot house that Ronald and Nancy Reagan built. This is the sixteen-room house in which Jerry Brown declined to live. This is the vacant house which cost the State of California one-million-four, not including the property, which was purchased in 1969 and donated to the state by such friends of the Reagans as Leonard K. Firestone of Firestone Tire and Rubber and Taft Schreiber of the Music Corporation of America and Holmes Tuttle, the Los Angeles Ford dealer. All day at this empty house three maintenance men try to keep the bulletproof windows clean and the cobwebs swept and the wild grass green and the rattlesnakes down by the river and away from the thirty-five exterior wood and glass doors. All night at this empty house the lights stay on behind the eight-foot chain-link fence and the guard dogs lie at bay and the telephone, when it rings, startles by the fact that it works. 'Governor's Residence,' the guards answer, their voices laconic, matter-of-fact, quite as if there were some phantom governor to connect. Wild grass grows where the tennis court was to have been. Wild grass grows where the pool and sauna were to have been. The American is the river in which gold was discovered in 1848, and it once ran fast and full past here, but lately there have been upstream dams and dry years. Much of the bed is exposed. The far bank has been dredged and graded. That the river is running low is of no real account, however, since one of the many peculiarities of the new Governor's Residence is that it is so situated as to have no clear view of the river.

It is an altogether curious structure, this one-story one-million-four dream house of Ronald and Nancy Reagan's. Were the house on the market (which it will probably not be, since, at the time it was costing a million-four, local real estate agents seemed to agree on $300,000 as the top price ever paid for a house in Sacramento County), the words used to describe it would be 'open' and 'contemporary,' although technically it is neither. 'Flow' is a word that crops up quite a bit when one is walking through the place, and so is 'resemble.' The walls 'resemble' local adobe, but they are not: they are the same concrete blocks, plastered and painted a rather stale yellowed cream, used in so many supermarkets and housing projects and Coca-Cola bottling plants. The door frames and the exposed beams 'resemble' native redwood, but they are not: they are construction-grade lumber of indeterminate quality, stained brown. If anyone ever moves in, the concrete floors will be carpeted, wall to wall. If anyone ever moves in, the thirty-five exterior wood and glass doors, possibly the single distinctive feature in the house, will be, according to plan, 'draped.' The bathrooms are small and standard. The family bedrooms open directly onto the nonexistent swimming pool, with all its potential for noise and distraction. To one side of the fireplace in the formal living room there is what is known in the trade as a 'wet bar,' a cabinet for bottles and glasses with a sink and a long vinyl-topped counter. (This vinyl 'resembles' slate.) In the entire house there are only enough bookshelves for a set of the World Book and some Books of the Month, plus maybe three Royal Doulton figurines and a back file of *Connoisseur*, but there is $90,000 worth of other teak cabinetry, including the 'refreshment center' in the 'recreation room.' There is that most ubiquitous of all 'luxury features,' a bidet in the master bathroom. There is one of those kitchens which seem designed exclusively for defrosting by microwave and compacting trash. It is a house built for a family of snackers.

And yet, appliances notwithstanding, it is hard to see where the million-four went. The place has been called, by Jerry Brown, a 'Taj Mahal.' It has been called a 'white elephant,' a 'resort,' a 'monument to the colossal ego of our former governor.' It is not exactly any of these things. It is simply and rather astonishingly an enlarged version of a very common kind of California tract house, a monument not to colossal ego but to a weird absence of ego, a case study in the architecture of limited possibilities, insistently and malevolently 'democratic,' flattened out, mediocre and 'open' and as devoid of privacy or personal eccentricity as the lobby area in a Ramada Inn. It is the architecture of 'background music,' decorators, 'good taste.' I recall once interviewing Nancy Reagan, at a time when her husband was governor and the construction on this house had not yet begun. We drove down to the State Capitol Building that day, and Mrs Reagan showed me how she had lightened and brightened offices there by replacing the old burnished leather on the walls with the kind of beige burlap then favored in new office buildings. I mention this because it was on my mind as I walked through the empty house on the American River outside Sacramento.

From 1903 until Ronald Reagan, who lived in a rented house in Sacramento while he was governor ($1,200 a month, payable by the state to a group of Reagan's friends), the governors of California lived in a large white Victorian Gothic house at 16th and H Streets in Sacramento. This extremely individual house, three stories and a cupola and the face of Columbia the Gem of the Ocean worked into the molding over every door, was built in 1877 by a Sacramento hardware merchant named Albert Gallatin. The state paid $32,500 for it in 1903 and my father was born in a house a block away in 1908. This part of town has since run to seed and small business, the kind of place where both Squeaky Fromme and Patricia Hearst could and probably did go about their business unnoticed, but the Governor's Mansion, unoccupied and open to the public as State Historical Landmark Number 823, remains Sacramento's premier example of eccentric domestic architecture.

As it happens I used to go there once in a while, when Earl Warren was governor and his daughter Nina was a year ahead of me at C. K. McClatchy Senior High School. Nina was always called 'Honey Bear' in the papers and in *Life* magazine but she was called 'Nina' at C. K. McClatchy Senior High School and she was called 'Nina' (or sometimes 'Warren') at weekly meetings of the Mañana Club, a local institution to which we both belonged. I recall being initiated into the Mañana Club one night at the old Governor's Mansion, in a ceremony which involved being blindfolded and standing around Nina's bedroom in a state of high apprehension about secret rites which never materialized. It was the custom for the members to hurl mild insults at the initiates, and I remember being dumbfounded to hear Nina, by my fourteen-year-old lights the most glamorous and unapproachable fifteen-year-old in America, characterize me as 'stuck on herself.' There in the Governor's Mansion that night I learned for the first time that my face to the world was not necessarily the face in my mirror. 'No smoking on the third floor,' everyone kept saying. 'Mrs Warren *said*. No smoking on the third floor *or else*.'

Firetrap or not, the old Governor's Mansion was at that time my favorite house in the world, and probably still is. The morning after I was shown the new 'Residence' I visited the old 'Mansion,' took the public tour with a group of perhaps twenty people, none of whom seemed to find it as ideal as I did. 'All those stairs,' they murmured, as if stairs could no longer be tolerated by human physiology. 'All those stairs,' and 'all that waste space.' The old Governor's Mansion does have stairs and waste space, which is precisely why it remains the kind of house in which sixty adolescent girls might gather and never interrupt the real life of the household. The bedrooms are big and private and high-ceilinged and they do not open on the swimming pool and one can imagine reading in one of them, or writing a book, or closing the door and crying until dinner. The bathrooms are big and airy and they do not have bidets but they do have room for hampers, and dressing tables, and chairs on which to sit and read a story to a child in the bathtub. There are hallways wide and narrow, stairs front and back, sewing rooms, ironing rooms, secret rooms. On the gilt mirror in the library there is worked a bust of Shakespeare, a pretty fancy for a hardware merchant in a California farm town in 1877. In the kitchen there is no trash compactor and there is no 'island' with the appliances built in but there are two pantries, and a nice old table with a marble top for rolling out pastry and making divinity fudge and chocolate leaves. The morning I took the tour our guide asked if anyone could think why the old table had a marble top. There were a dozen or so other women in the group, each of an age to have cooked unnumbered meals, but not one of them could think of a single use for a slab of marble in the kitchen. It occurred to me that we had finally evolved a society in which knowledge of a pastry marble, like a taste for stairs and closed doors, could be construed as 'elitist,' and as I left the Governor's Mansion I felt very like the heroine of Mary McCarthy's *Birds of America*, the one who located America's moral decline in the disappearance of the first course.

A guard sleeps at night in the old mansion, which has been condemned as a dwelling by the state fire marshal. It costs about $85,000 a year to keep guards at the new official residence. Meanwhile the current governor of California, Edmund G. Brown, Jr, sleeps on a mattress on the floor in the famous apartment for which he pays $275 a month out of his own $49,100 annual salary. This has considerable and potent symbolic value, as do the two empty houses themselves, most particularly the house the Reagans built on the river. It is a great point around the Capitol these days to have 'never seen' the house on the river. The governor himself has 'never seen' it. The governor's press secretary, Elisabeth Coleman, has 'never seen' it. The governor's chief of staff, Gray Davis, admits to having seen it, but only once, when 'Mary McGrory wanted to see it.' This unseen house on the river is, Jerry Brown has said, 'not my style.'

As a matter of fact this is precisely the point about the house on the river – the house is not Jerry Brown's style, not Mary McGrory's style, *not our style* – and it is a point which presents a certain problem, since the house so clearly is the style not only of Jerry Brown's predecessor but of millions of Jerry Brown's constituents. Words are chosen carefully. Reasonable objections are framed. One hears about how the house is too far from the Capitol, too far from the Legislature. One hears about the folly of running such a lavish establishment for an unmarried governor and one hears about the governor's temperamental austerity. One hears every possible reason for not living in the house except the one that counts: it is the kind of house that has a wet bar in the living room. It is the kind of house that has a refreshment center. It is the kind of house in which one does not live, but there is no way to say this without getting into

touchy and evanescent and finally inadmissible questions of taste,
and ultimately of class. I have seldom seen a house so evocative of
the unspeakable.

1977

The Getty

The place might have been commissioned by The Magic Christian. Mysteriously and rather giddily splendid, hidden in a grove of syca- mores just above the Pacific Coast Highway in Malibu, a commem- oration of high culture so immediately productive of crowds and jammed traffic that it can now be approached by appointment only, the seventeen-million-dollar villa built by the late J. Paul Getty to house his antiquities and paintings and furniture manages to strike a peculiar nerve in almost everyone who sees it. From the beginning, the Getty was said to be vulgar. The Getty was said to be 'Disney.' The Getty was even said to be Jewish, if I did not misread the subtext in 'like a Beverly Hills nouveau-riche dining room' (*Los Angeles Times*, January 6, 1974) and 'gussied up like a Bel-Air dining room' (*New York Times*, May 28, 1974).

The Getty seems to stir up social discomforts at levels not easily plumbed. To mention this museum in the more enlightened of those very dining rooms it is said to resemble is to invite a kind of nervous derision, as if the place were a local hoax, a perverse and deliberate affront to the understated good taste and general class of everyone at the table. The Getty's intricately patterned marble floors and walls are 'garish.' The Getty's illusionistic portico murals are 'back lot.' The entire building, an informed improvisation on a villa buried by mud from Vesuvius in 79 A.D. and seen again only dimly during some eighteenth-century tunneling around Herculaneum, is ritually dis- missed as 'inauthentic,' although what 'authentic' could mean in this context is hard to say.

Something about the place embarrasses people. The collection itself is usually referred to as 'that kind of thing,' as in 'not even the best of that kind of thing,' or 'absolutely top-drawer if you like that kind of thing,' both of which translate 'not our kind of thing.' The Getty's damask-lined galleries of Renaissance and Baroque paintings are distinctly that kind of thing, there being little in the modern temperament that responds immediately to popes and libertine babies, and so are the Getty's rather unrelenting arrangements of French furniture. A Louis XV writing table tends to please the modern eye only if it has been demystified by a glass of field flowers and some silver-framed snapshots, as in a Horst photograph for *Vogue*. Even the Getty's famous antiquities are pretty much that kind of thing, evoking as they do not their own period but the eighteenth- and nineteenth-century rage for antiquities. The sight of a Greek head depresses many people, strikes an unliberated chord, reminds them of books in their grandmother's parlor and of all they were supposed to learn and never did. This note of 'learning' pervades the entire Getty collection. Even the handful of Impressionists acquired by Getty were recently removed from the public galleries, put away as irrelevant. The Getty collection is in certain ways unremittingly reproachful, and quite inaccessible to generations trained in the conviction that a museum is meant to be fun, with Calder mobiles and Barcelona chairs.

In short the Getty is a monument to 'fine art,' in the old-fashioned didactic sense, which is part of the problem people have with it. The place resists contemporary notions about what art is or should be or ever was. A museum is now supposed to kindle the untrained imagination, but this museum does not. A museum is now supposed to set the natural child in each of us free, but this museum does not. This was art acquired to teach a lesson, and there is also a lesson in the building which houses it: the Getty tells us that the past was perhaps different from the way we like to perceive it. Ancient marbles were not always attractively faded and worn. Ancient marbles once appeared just as they appear here: as strident, opulent evidence of imperial power and acquisition. Ancient murals were not always bleached and mellowed and 'tasteful.' Ancient murals once looked as they do here: as if dreamed by a Mafia don. Ancient fountains once worked, and drowned out that very silence we have come to expect and want from the past. Ancient bronze once gleamed ostentatiously. The old world was once discomfitingly new, or even nouveau, as people like to say about the Getty. (I have never been sure what the word 'nouveau' can possibly mean in America, implying as it does that the speaker is gazing down six hundred years of rolled lawns.) At a time when all our public conventions remain rooted in a kind of knocked-down romanticism, when the celebration of natural man's capacity for moving onward and upward has become a kind of official tic, the Getty presents us with an illustrated lesson in classical doubt. The Getty advises us that not much changes. The Getty tells us that we were never any better than we are and will never be any better than we were, and in so doing makes a profoundly unpopular political statement.

The Getty's founder may or may not have had some such statement in mind. In a way he seems to have wanted only to do something no one else could or would do. In his posthumous book, *As I See It*, he advises us that he never wanted 'one of those concrete-bunker-type structures that are the fad among museum architects.' He refused to pay for any 'tinted-glass-and-stainless-steel monstrosity.' He assures us that he was 'neither shaken nor surprised' when his villa was finished and 'certain critics sniffed.' He had 'calculated the risks.' He knew that he was flouting the 'doctrinaire and elitist' views he believed endemic in 'many Art World (or should I say Artsy-Craftsy?) quarters.'

Doctrinaire and elitist. Artsy-craftsy. On the surface the Getty would appear to have been a case of he-knew-what-he-liked-and-he-built-it, a tax dodge from the rather louche world of the international rich, and yet the use of that word 'elitist' strikes an interesting note. The man who built himself the Getty never saw it, although it opened a year and a half before his death. He seems to have liked the planning of it. He personally approved every paint sample. He is said to have taken immense pleasure in every letter received from anyone who visited the museum and liked it (such letters were immediately forwarded to him by the museum staff), but the idea of the place seems to have been enough, and the idea was this: here was a museum built not for those elitist critics but for 'the public.' Here was a museum that would be forever supported by its founder alone, a museum that need never depend on any city or state or federal funding, a place forever 'open to the public and free of all charges.'

As a matter of fact large numbers of people who do not ordinarily visit museums like the Getty a great deal, just as its founder knew they would. There is one of those peculiar social secrets at work here. On the whole 'the critics' distrust great wealth, but 'the public' does not. On the whole 'the critics' subscribe to the romantic view of man's possibilities, but 'the public' does not. In the end the Getty stands above the Pacific Coast Highway as one of those odd monuments, a palpable contract between the very rich and the people who distrust them least.

1977

Bureaucrats

The closed door upstairs at 120 South Spring Street in downtown Los Angeles is marked OPERATIONS CENTER. In the windowless room beyond the closed door a reverential hush prevails. From six A.M. until seven P.M. in this windowless room men sit at consoles watching a huge board flash colored lights. 'There's the heart attack,' someone will murmur, or 'we're getting the gawk effect.' 120 South Spring is the Los Angeles office of Caltrans, or the California Department of Transportation, and the Operations Center is where Caltrans engineers monitor what they call 'the 42-Mile Loop.' The 42-Mile Loop is simply the rough triangle formed by the intersections of the Santa Monica, the San Diego and the Harbor freeways, and 42 miles represents less than ten per cent of freeway mileage in Los Angeles County alone, but these particular 42 miles are regarded around 120 South Spring with a special veneration. The Loop is a 'demonstration system,' a phrase much favored by everyone at Caltrans, and is part of a 'pilot project,' another two words carrying totemic weight on South Spring.

The Loop has electronic sensors embedded every half-mile out there in the pavement itself, each sensor counting the crossing cars every twenty seconds. The Loop has its own mind, a Xerox Sigma V computer which prints out, all day and night, twenty-second readings on what is and is not moving in each of the Loop's eight lanes. It is the Xerox Sigma V that makes the big board flash red when traffic out there drops below fifteen miles an hour. It is the Xerox Sigma V that tells the Operations crew when they have an 'incident' out there. An 'incident' is the heart attack on the San Diego, the jackknifed truck on the Harbor, the Camaro just now tearing out the Cyclone fence on the Santa Monica. 'Out there' is where incidents happen. The windowless room at 120 South Spring is where incidents get 'verified.' 'Incident verification' is turning on the closed-circuit TV on the console and watching the traffic slow down to see (this is 'the gawk effect') where the Camaro tore out the fence.

As a matter of fact there is a certain closed-circuit aspect to the entire mood of the Operations Center. 'Verifying' the incident does not after all 'prevent' the incident, which lends the enterprise a kind of tranced distance, and on the day recently when I visited 120 South Spring it took considerable effort to remember what I had come to talk about, which was that particular part of the Loop called the Santa Monica Freeway. The Santa Monica Freeway is 16.2 miles long, runs from the Pacific Ocean to downtown Los Angeles through what is referred to at Caltrans as 'the East-West Corridor,' carries more traffic every day than any other freeway in California, has what connoisseurs of freeways concede to be the most beautiful access ramps in the world, and appeared to have been transformed by Caltrans, during the several weeks before I went downtown to talk about it, into a 16.2-mile parking lot.

The problem seemed to be another Caltrans 'demonstration,' or 'pilot,' a foray into bureaucratic terrorism they were calling 'The Diamond Lane' in their promotional literature and 'The Project' among themselves. That the promotional literature consisted largely of schedules for buses (or 'Diamond Lane Expresses') and invitations to join a car pool via computer ('Commuter Computer') made clear not only the putative point of The Project, which was to encourage travel by car pool and bus, but also the actual point, which was to eradicate a central Southern California illusion, that of individual mobility, without anyone really noticing. This had not exactly worked out. 'FREEWAY FIASCO,' the *Los Angeles Times* was head-lining page-one stories. 'THE DIAMOND LANE: ANOTHER BUST BY CALTRANS.' 'CALTRANS PILOT EFFORT ANOTHER IN LONG LIST OF FAILURES.' 'OFFICIAL DIAMOND LANE STANCE: LET THEM HOWL.'

All 'The Diamond Lane' theoretically involved was reserving the fast inside lanes on the Santa Monica for vehicles carrying three or

more people, but in practice this meant that 25 per cent of the
freeway was reserved for 3 per cent of the cars, and there were other
odd wrinkles here and there suggesting that Caltrans had dedicated
itself to making all movement around Los Angeles as arduous as
possible. There was for example the matter of surface streets. A
'surface street' is anything around Los Angeles that is not a freeway
('going surface' from one part of town to another is generally
regarded as idiosyncratic), and surface streets do not fall directly
within the Caltrans domain, but now the engineer in charge of surface streets was accusing Caltrans of threatening and intimidating
him. It appeared that Caltrans wanted him to create a 'confused and
congested situation' on his surface streets, so as to force drivers back
to the freeway, where they would meet a still more confused and
congested situation and decide to stay home, or take a bus. 'We are
beginning a process of deliberately making it harder for drivers to
use freeways,' a Caltrans director had in fact said at a transit conference some months before. 'We are prepared to endure considerable
public outcry in order to pry John Q. Public out of his car . . . I
would emphasize that this is a political decision, and one that can be
reversed if the public gets sufficiently enraged to throw us rascals
out.'

Of course this political decision was in the name of the greater
good, was in the interests of 'environmental improvement' and 'con-
servation of resources,' but even there the figures had about them a
certain Caltrans opacity. The Santa Monica normally carried 240,000
cars and trucks every day. These 240,000 cars and trucks normally
carried 260,000 people. What Caltrans described as its ultimate goal
on the Santa Monica was to carry the same 260,000 people, 'but in
7,800 fewer, or 232,200 vehicles.' The figure '232,200' had a visionary precision to it that did not automatically create confidence,
especially since the only effect so far had been to disrupt traffic
throughout the Los Angeles basin, triple the number of daily accidents on the Santa Monica, prompt the initiation of two lawsuits
against Caltrans, and cause large numbers of Los Angeles County
residents to behave, most uncharacteristically, as an ignited and conscious proletariat. Citizen guerrillas splashed paint and scattered nails
in the Diamond Lanes. Diamond Lane maintenance crews expressed
fear of hurled objects. Down at 120 South Spring the architects of the

Diamond Lane had taken to regarding 'the media' as the architects of their embarrassment, and Caltrans statements in the press had been cryptic and contradictory, reminiscent only of old communiqués out of Vietnam.

To understand what was going on it is perhaps necessary to have participated in the freeway experience, which is the only secular communion Los Angeles has. Mere driving on the freeway is in no way the same as participating in it. Anyone can 'drive' on the freeway, and many people with no vocation for it do, hesitating here and resisting there, losing the rhythm of the lane change, thinking about where they came from and where they are going. Actual participants think only about where they are. Actual participation requires a total surrender, a concentration so intense as to seem a kind of narcosis, a rapture-of-the-freeway. The mind goes clean. The rhythm takes over. A distortion of time occurs, the same distortion that characterizes the instant before an accident. It takes only a few seconds to get off the Santa Monica Freeway at National-Overland, which is a difficult exit requiring the driver to cross two new lanes of traffic streamed in from the San Diego Freeway, but those few seconds always seem to me the longest part of the trip. The moment is dangerous. The exhilaration is in doing it. 'As you acquire the special skills involved,' Reyner Banham observed in an extraordinary chapter about the freeways in his 1971 *Los Angeles: The Architecture of Four Ecologies*, 'the freeways become a special way of being alive . . . the extreme concentration required in Los Angeles seems to bring on a state of heightened awareness that some locals find mystical.'

Indeed some locals do, and some nonlocals too. Reducing the number of lone souls careering around the East-West Corridor in a state of mechanized rapture may or may not have seemed socially desirable, but what it was definitely not going to seem was easy. 'We're only seeing an initial period of unfamiliarity,' I was assured the day I visited Caltrans. I was talking to a woman named Eleanor Wood and she was thoroughly and professionally grounded in the diction of 'planning' and it did not seem likely that I could interest her in considering the freeway as regional mystery. 'Any time you try to rearrange people's daily habits, they're apt to react impetuously. All this project requires is a certain rearrangement of people's daily planning. That's really all we want.'

It occurred to me that a certain rearrangement of people's daily planning might seem, in less rarefied air than is breathed at 120 South Spring, rather a great deal to want, but so impenetrable was the sense of higher social purpose there in the Operations Center that I did not express this reservation. Instead I changed the subject, mentioned an earlier 'pilot project' on the Santa Monica: the big electronic message boards that Caltrans had installed a year or two before. The idea was that traffic information transmitted from the Santa Monica to the Xerox Sigma V could be translated, here in the Operations Center, into suggestions to the driver, and flashed right back out to the Santa Monica. This operation, in that it involved telling drivers electronically what they already knew empirically, had the rather spectral circularity that seemed to mark a great many Caltrans schemes, and I was interested in how Caltrans thought it worked.

'Actually the message boards were part of a larger pilot project,' Mrs Wood said. 'An ongoing project in incident management. With the message boards we hoped to learn if motorists would modify their behavior according to what we told them on the boards.'

I asked if the motorists had.

'Actually no,' Mrs Wood said finally. 'They didn't react to the signs exactly as we'd hypothesized they would, no. *But.* If we'd *known* what the motorist would do ... then we wouldn't have needed a pilot project in the first place, would we.'

The circle seemed intact. Mrs Wood and I smiled, and shook hands. I watched the big board until all lights turned green on the Santa Monica and then I left and drove home on it, all 16.2 miles of it. All the way I remembered that I was watched by the Xerox Sigma V. All the way the message boards gave me the number to call for CAR POOL INFO. As I left the freeway it occurred to me that they might have their own rapture down at 120 South Spring, and it could be called Perpetuating the Department. Today the California Highway Patrol reported that, during the first six weeks of the Diamond Lane, accidents on the Santa Monica, which normally range between 49 and 72 during a six-week period, totaled 204. Yesterday plans were announced to extend the Diamond Lane to other freeways at a cost of $42,500,000.

1976

Good Citizens

1

I was once invited to a civil rights meeting at Sammy Davis, Jr's house, in the hills above the Sunset Strip. 'Let me tell you how to get to Sammy's,' said the woman to whom I was talking. 'You turn left at the old Mocambo.' I liked the ring of this line, summing up as it did a couple of generations of that peculiar vacant fervor which is Hollywood political action, but acquaintances to whom I repeated it seemed uneasy. Politics are not widely considered a legitimate source of amusement in Hollywood, where the borrowed rhetoric by which political ideas are reduced to choices between the good (equality is good) and the bad (genocide is bad) tends to make even the most casual political small talk resemble a rally. 'Those who cannot remember the past are condemned to repeat it,' someone said to me at dinner not long ago, and before we had finished our *fraises des bois* he had advised me as well that 'no man is an island.' As a matter of fact I hear that no man is an island once or twice a week, quite often from people who think they are quoting Ernest Hemingway. 'What a sacrifice on the altar of nationalism,' I heard an actor say about the death in a plane crash of the president of the Philippines. It is a way of talking that tends to preclude further discussion, which may well be its intention: the public life of liberal Hollywood comprises a kind of dictatorship of good intentions, a social contract in which actual and irreconcilable disagreement is as taboo as failure or bad teeth, a climate devoid of irony. 'Those men are our unsung heroes,' a quite charming and intelligent woman once said to me at a party in Beverly Hills. She was talking about the California State Legislature.

I remember spending an evening in 1968, a week or so before the California primary and Robert Kennedy's death, at Eugene's in Beverly Hills, one of the 'clubs' opened by supporters of Eugene McCarthy. The Beverly Hills Eugene's, not unlike Senator McCarthy's campaign itself, had a certain *déjà vu* aspect to it, a glow of 1952 humanism: there were Ben Shahn posters on the walls, and the gesture toward a strobe light was nothing that might interfere with 'good talk,' and the music was not 1968 rock but the kind of jazz people used to have on their record players when everyone who believed in the Family of Man bought Scandinavian stainless-steel flatware and voted for Adlai Stevenson. There at Eugene's I heard the name 'Erich Fromm' for the first time in a long time, and many other names cast out for the sympathetic magic they might work ('I saw the Senator in San Francisco, where I was with Mrs Leonard Bernstein . . .'), and then the evening's main event: a debate between William Styron and the actor Ossie Davis. It was Mr Davis' contention that in writing *The Confessions of Nat Turner* Mr Styron had encouraged racism ('Nat Turner's love for a white maiden, I feel my country can become psychotic about this'), and it was Mr Styron's contention that he had not. (David Wolper, who had bought the motion picture rights to *Nat Turner*, had already made his position clear: 'How can anyone protest a book,' he had asked in the trade press, 'that has withstood the critical test of time since last October?') As the evening wore on, Mr Styron said less and less, and Mr Davis more and more ('So you might ask, why didn't *I* spend five years and write *Nat Turner?* I won't go into my reasons why, but . . .'), and James Baldwin sat between them, his eyes closed and his head thrown back in understandable but rather theatrical agony. Mr Baldwin summed up: 'If Bill's book does no more than what it's done tonight, it's a very important event.' 'Hear, hear,' cried someone sitting on the floor, and there was general agreement that it had been a stimulating and significant evening.

Of course there was nothing crucial about that night at Eugene's in 1968, and of course you could tell me that there was certainly no harm and perhaps some good in it. But its curious vanity and irrelevance stay with me, if only because those qualities characterize so many of Hollywood's best intentions. Social problems present themselves to many of these people in terms of a scenario, in which, once certain key scenes are licked (the confrontation on the court-house steps, the revelation that the opposition leader has an anti-Semitic past, the presentation of the bill of particulars to the President, a Henry Fonda cameo), the plot will proceed inexorably to an upbeat fade. Marlon Brando does not, in a well-plotted motion picture, picket San Quentin in vain: what we are talking about here is faith in a dramatic convention. Things 'happen' in motion pictures. There is always a resolution, always a strong cause-effect dramatic line, and to perceive the world in those terms is to assume an ending for every social scenario. If Budd Schulberg goes into Watts and forms a Writers' Workshop, then 'Twenty Young Writers' must emerge from it, because the scenario in question is the familiar one about how the ghetto teems with raw talent and vitality. If the poor people march on Washington and camp out, there to receive bundles of clothes gathered on the Fox lot by Barbra Streisand, then some good must come of it (the script here has a great many dramatic staples, not the least of them a sentimental notion of Washington as an open forum, *cf. Mr Deeds Goes to Washington*), and doubts have no place in the story.

There are no bit players in Hollywood politics: everyone makes things 'happen.' As it happens I live in a house in Hollywood in which, during the late Thirties and early Fifties, a screenwriters' cell of the Communist Party often met. Some of the things that are in the house now were in it then: a vast Stalinist couch, the largest rag rug I have ever seen, cartons of *New Masses*. Some of the people who came to meetings in the house were blacklisted, some of them never worked again and some of them are now getting several hundred thousand dollars a picture; some of them are dead and some of them are bitter and most of them lead very private lives. Things did change, but in the end it was not they who made things change, and their enthusiasms and debates sometimes seem very close to me in this house. In a way the house suggests the particular vanity of perceiving social life as a problem to be solved by the good will of individuals, but I do not mention that to many of the people who visit me here.

2

Pretty Nancy Reagan, the wife then of the governor of California, was standing in the dining room of her rented house on 45th Street in Sacramento, listening to a television newsman explain what he wanted to do. She was listening attentively. Nancy Reagan is a very attentive listener. The television crew wanted to watch her, the newsman said, while she was doing precisely what she would ordinarily be doing on a Tuesday morning at home. Since I was also there to watch her doing precisely what she would ordinarily be doing on a Tuesday morning at home, we seemed to be on the verge of exploring certain media frontiers: the television newsman and the two cameramen could watch Nancy Reagan being watched by me, or I could watch Nancy Reagan being watched by the three of them, or one of the cameramen could step back and do a *cinéma vérité* study of the rest of us watching and being watched by one another. I had the distinct sense that we were on the track of something revelatory, the truth about Nancy Reagan at 24 frames a second, but the television newsman opted to overlook the moment's peculiar essence. He suggested that we watch Nancy Reagan pick flowers in the garden. 'That's something you might ordinarily do, isn't it?' he asked. 'Indeed it is,' Nancy Reagan said with spirit. Nancy Reagan says almost everything with spirit, perhaps because she was once an actress and has the beginning actress's habit of investing even the most casual lines with a good deal more dramatic emphasis than is ordinarily called for on a Tuesday morning on 45th Street in Sacramento. 'Actually,' she added then, as if about to disclose a delightful surprise, 'actually, I really *do* need flowers.'

She smiled at each of us, and each of us smiled back. We had all been smiling quite a bit that morning. 'And then,' the television newsman said thoughtfully, surveying the dining-room table, 'even though you've got a beautiful arrangement right now, we could set up the pretense of your arranging, you know, the flowers.'

We all smiled at one another again, and then Nancy Reagan walked resolutely into the garden, equipped with a decorative straw basket about six inches in diameter. 'Uh, Mrs Reagan,' the newsman called after her. 'May I ask what you're going to select for flowers?'

'Why, I don't know,' she said, pausing with her basket on a garden step. The scene was evolving its own choreography.

'Do you think you could use rhododendrons?'

Nancy Reagan looked critically at a rhododendron bush. Then she turned to the newsman and smiled. 'Did you know there's a Nancy Reagan rose now?'

'Uh, no,' he said. 'I didn't.'

'It's awfully pretty, it's a kind of, of, a kind of coral color.'

'Would the . . . the Nancy Reagan rose be something you might be likely to pick now?'

A silvery peal of laughter. 'I could certainly *pick* it. But I won't be *using* it.' A pause. 'I *can* use the rhododendron.'

'Fine,' the newsman said. 'Just fine. Now I'll ask a question, and if you could just be nipping a bud as you answer it . . .'

'Nipping a bud,' Nancy Reagan repeated, taking her place in front of the rhododendron bush.

'Let's have a dry run,' the cameraman said.

The newsman looked at him. 'In other words, by a dry run, you mean you want her to fake nipping the bud.'

'Fake the nip, yeah,' the cameraman said. 'Fake the nip.'

3

Outside the Miramar Hotel in Santa Monica a hard subtropical rain had been falling for days. It scaled still more paint from the faded hotels and rooming houses that front the Pacific along Ocean Avenue. It streamed down the blank windows of unleased offices, loosened the soft coastal cliffs and heightened the most characteristic Santa Monica effect, that air of dispirited abandon which suggests that the place survives only as illustration of a boom gone bankrupt, evidence of some irreversible flaw in the laissez-faire small-business ethic. In any imaginative sense Santa Monica seemed an eccentric place for the United States Junior Chamber of Commerce to be holding a national congress, but there they were, a thousand delegates and wives, gathered in the Miramar Hotel for a relentless succession of keynote banquets and award luncheons and prayer breakfasts and outstanding-young-men forums. Now it was the President's Luncheon and everyone was listening to an animated singing group called The New Generation and I was watching the pretty young wife of one delegate pick sullenly at her lunch. 'Let someone else eat this slop,' she said suddenly, her voice cutting through not only the high generalities of the occasion but The New Generation's George M. Cohan medley as well. Her husband looked away, and she repeated it. To my left another delegate was urging me to ask every man in the room how the Jaycees had changed his life. I watched the girl down the table and asked the delegate how the Jaycees had changed his life. 'It saved my marriage and it built my business,' he whispered. 'You could find a thousand inspirational stories right here at this President's Luncheon.' Down the table the young wife was sobbing into a pink napkin. The New Generation marched into 'Supercalifragilisticexpialidocious.' In many ways the Jaycees' 32nd Annual Congress of America's Ten Outstanding Young Men was a curious and troubling way to spend a few days in the opening weeks of 1970.

I suppose I went to Santa Monica in search of the abstraction lately called 'Middle America,' went to find out how the Jaycees, with their Couéistic emphasis on improving one's world and one's self simultaneously, had weathered these past several years of cultural shock. In a very real way the Jaycees have exemplified, usually so ingenuously that it was popular to deride them, certain ideas shared by almost all of the people in America's small cities and towns and by at least some of the people in America's large cities, ideas shared in an unexamined way even by those who laughed at the Jaycees' boosterism and pancake breakfasts and safe-driving Road-e-os. There was the belief in business success as a transcendent ideal. There was the faith that if one transforms oneself from an 'introvert' into an 'extrovert,' if one learns to 'speak effectively' and 'do a job,' success and its concomitant, spiritual grace, follow naturally. There was the approach to international problems which construed the underdeveloped world as a temporarily depressed area in need mainly of People-to-People programs. ('Word of Operation Brotherhood swept through the teeming masses of Asia like a fresh wind from the sea,' reads a Jaycee report on one such program in the late Fifties.) If only because these ideas, these last rattles of Social Darwinism, had in fact been held in common by a great many people who never bothered to articulate them, I wondered what the Jaycees were thinking now, wondered what their mood might be at a time when, as their national president put it one day at the Miramar, 'so much of America seems to be looking at the negative.'

At first I thought I had walked out of the rain into a time warp: the Sixties seemed not to have happened. All these Jaycees were, by definition, between 21 and 35 years old, but there was a disquieting tendency among them to have settled foursquare into middle age. There was the heavy jocularity, the baroque rhetoric of another generation entirely, a kind of poignant attempt to circumnavigate social conventions that had in fact broken down in the Twenties. Wives were lovely and forbearing. Getting together for drinks was having a cocktail reception. Rain was liquid sunshine and the choice of a table for dinner was making an executive decision. They knew that this was a brave new world and they said so. It was time to 'put brotherhood into action,' to 'open our neighborhoods to those of all colors.' It was time to 'turn attention to the cities,' to think about youth centers and clinics and the example set by a black policeman-preacher in Philadelphia who was organizing a decency rally patterned after Miami's. It was time to 'decry apathy.'

The word 'apathy' cropped up again and again, an odd word to use in relation to the past few years, and it was a while before I realized what it meant. It was not simply a word remembered from the Fifties, when most of these men had frozen their vocabularies: it was a word meant to indicate that not enough of 'our kind' were speaking out. It was a cry in the wilderness, and this resolute determination to meet 1950 head-on was a kind of refuge. Here were some people who had been led to believe that the future was always a rational extension of the past, that there would ever be world enough and time for 'turning attention,' for 'problems' and 'solutions.' Of course they would not admit their inchoate fears that the world was not that way any more. Of course they would not join the 'fashionable doubters.' Of course they would ignore the 'pessimistic pundits.' Late one afternoon I sat in the Miramar lobby, watching the rain fall and the steam rise off the heated pool outside and listening to a couple of Jaycees discussing student unrest and whether the 'solution' might not lie in on-campus Jaycee groups. I thought about this astonishing notion for a long time. It occurred to me finally that I was listening to a true underground, to the voice of all those who have felt themselves not merely shocked but personally betrayed by recent history. It was supposed to have been their time. It was not.

1968–1970

Notes Toward a Dreampolitik

1

Elder Robert J. Theobold, pastor of what was until October 12, 1968, the Friendly Bible Apostolic Church in Port Hueneme, California, is twenty-eight years old, born and bred in San Jose, a native Californian whose memory stream could encompass only the boom years; in other words a young man who until October 12, 1968, had lived his entire life in the nerve center of the most elaborately technological and media-oriented society in the United States, and so the world. His looks and to some extent his background are indistinguishable from those of a legion of computer operators and avionics technicians. Yet this is a young man who has remained immaculate of the constant messages with which a technological society bombards itself, for at the age of sixteen he was saved, received the Holy Spirit in a Pentecostal church. Brother Theobold, as the eighty-some members of his congregation call him, now gets messages only from the Lord, 'forcible impressions' instructing him, for example, to leave San Jose and start a church in Port Hueneme, or, more recently, to lead his congregation on the 12th of October, 1968, from Port Hueneme to Murfreesboro, Tennessee, in order to avoid destruction by earthquake.

'We're leaving the 12th but I don't have any message that it's going to happen before the end of 1968,' Brother Theobold told me one morning a few weeks before he and his congregation piled their belongings into campers and cars and left California for Tennessee.

He was minding the children that morning, and his two-year-old walked around sucking on a plastic bottle while Brother Theobold talked to me and fingered the pages of a tooled-leather Bible. 'This one minister I heard, he definitely said it would happen before the end of 1970, but as far as I'm concerned, the Lord has shown me that it's definitely coming but he hasn't shown me *when*.'

I mentioned to Brother Theobold that most seismologists were predicting an imminent major earthquake on the San Andreas Fault, but he did not seem unduly interested: Brother Theobold's perception of the apocalypse neither began with nor depended upon the empirical. In a way the Pentecostal mind reveals itself most clearly in something like Brother Theobold's earthquake prophecy. Neither he nor the members of his congregation to whom I talked had ever been particularly concerned by reports in the newspapers that an earthquake was overdue. 'Of course we'd *heard* of earthquakes,' a soft-voiced woman named Sister Mosley told me. 'Because the Bible mentions there'll be more and more toward the end of time.' Nor was there any need to think twice about pulling up stakes and joining a caravan to a small town few of them had ever seen. I kept asking Brother Theobold how he had chosen Murfreesboro, and over and over he tried to tell me: he had 'received a telephone call from a man there,' or 'God had directed this particular man to call on this particular day.' The man did not seem to have made a direct entreaty to Brother Theobold to bring his flock to Tennessee, but there had been no question in Brother Theobold's mind that God's intention was exactly that. 'From the natural point of view I didn't care to go to Murfreesboro at all,' he said. 'We just bought this place, it's the nicest place we ever had. But I put it up to the Lord, and the Lord said *put it up for sale*. Care for a Dr Pepper?'

We might have been talking in different languages, Brother Theobold and I; it was as if I knew all the words but lacked the grammar, and so kept questioning him on points that seemed to him ineluctably clear. He seemed to be one of those people, so many of whom gravitate to Pentecostal sects, who move around the West and the South and the Border States forever felling trees in some interior wilderness, secret frontiersmen who walk around right in the ganglia of the fantastic electronic pulsing that is life in the United States and continue to receive information only through the most tenuous

chains of rumor, hearsay, haphazard trickledown. In the social conventions by which we now live there is no category for people like
Brother Theobold and his congregation, most of whom are young
and white and nominally literate; they are neither the possessors
nor the dispossessed. They participate in the national anxieties only
through a glass darkly. They teach their daughters to eschew makeup
and to cover their knees, and they believe in divine healing, and in
speaking in tongues. Other people leave towns like Murfreesboro,
and they move into them. To an astonishing extent they keep themselves unviolated by common knowledge, by the ability to make
routine assumptions; when Brother Theobold first visited Murfreesboro he was dumbfounded to learn that the courthouse there had
been standing since the Civil War. 'The *same building*,' he repeated
twice, and then he got out a snapshot as corroboration. In the interior
wilderness no one is bloodied by history, and it is no coincidence
that the Pentecostal churches have their strongest hold in places
where Western civilization has its most superficial hold. There are
more than twice as many Pentecostal as Episcopal churches in Los
Angeles.

2

The scene is quite near the end of Roger Corman's 1966 *The Wild
Angels*, which was the first and in many ways the classic exploitation
bike movie. Here it is: the Angels, led by Peter Fonda, are about to
bury one of their number. They have already torn up the chapel,
beaten and gagged the preacher, and held a wake, during which the
dead man's girl was raped on the altar and the corpse itself, propped
up on a bench in full biker colors, dark goggles over the eyes and a
marijuana cigarette between the lips, was made an object of necro-
philia. Now they stand at the grave, and, uncertain how to mark the
moment, Peter Fonda shrugs. 'Nothing to say,' he says.

What we have here is an obligatory bike-movie moment, the
outlaw-hero embracing man's fate: I tell you about it only to suggest
the particular mood of these pictures. Many of them are extraordinarily beautiful in their instinct for the real look of the American

West, for the faded banners fluttering over abandoned gas stations
and for the bleached streets of desert towns. These are the movies
known to the trade as 'programmers,' and very few adults have ever
seen one. Most of them are made for less than $200,000. They are
shown in New York only occasionally. Yet for several years bike
movies have constituted a kind of underground folk literature for
adolescents, have located an audience and fabricated a myth to
exactly express that audience's every inchoate resentment, every
yearning for the extreme exhilaration of death. To die violently is
'righteous,' a flash. To keep on living, as Peter Fonda points out in
The Wild Angels, is just to keep on paying rent. A successful bike
movie is a perfect Rorschach of its audience.

I saw nine of them recently, saw the first one almost by accident
and the rest of them with a notebook. I saw *Hell's Angels on Wheels*
and *Hell's Angels '69*. I saw *Run Angel Run* and *The Glory Stompers* and
The Losers. I saw *The Wild Angels*, I saw *Violent Angels*, I saw *The Savage
Seven* and I saw *The Cycle Savages*. I was not even sure why I kept
going. To have seen one bike movie is to have seen them all, so
meticulously observed are the rituals of getting the bikers out of
town and onto the highway, of 'making a run,' of terrorizing the
innocent 'citizens' and fencing with the Highway Patrol and, finally,
meeting death in a blaze, usually quite a literal blaze, of romantic
fatalism. There is always that instant in which the outlaw leader
stands revealed as existential hero. There is always that 'perverse'
sequence in which the bikers batter at some psychic sound barrier,
degrade the widow, violate the virgin, defile the rose and the cross
alike, break on through to the other side and find, once there, 'nothing to say.' The brutal images glaze the eye. The senseless insouciance
of all the characters in a world of routine stompings and casual death
takes on a logic better left unplumbed.

I suppose I kept going to these movies because there on the screen
was some news I was not getting from *The New York Times*. I began
to think I was seeing ideograms of the future. To watch a bike movie
is finally to apprehend the extent to which the toleration of small
irritations is no longer a trait much admired in America, the extent
to which a nonexistent frustration threshold is seen not as psychopathic but as a 'right.' A biker is goaded on the job about the swastika
on his jacket, so he picks up a wrench, threatens the foreman, and

later describes the situation as one in which the foreman 'got
uptight.' A biker runs an old man off the road: the old man was 'in
the way,' and his subsequent death is construed as further 'hassling.'
A nurse happens into a hospital room where a biker beats her unconscious and rapes her: that she later talks to the police is made
to seem a betrayal, evidence only of some female hysteria, vindic-
tiveness, sexual deprivation. Any girl who 'acts dumb' deserves what
she gets, and what she gets is beaten and turned out from the group.
Anything less than instant service in a restaurant constitutes intolerable provocation, or 'hassling': tear the place apart, leave the owner
for dead, gangbang the waitress. Rev up the Harleys and ride.

To imagine the audience for whom these sentiments are tailored,
maybe you need to have sat in a lot of drive-ins yourself, to have
gone to school with boys who majored in shop and worked in gas
stations and later held them up. Bike movies are made for all these
children of vague 'hill' stock who grow up absurd in the West and
Southwest, children whose whole lives are an obscure grudge against
a world they think they never made. These children are, increasingly,
everywhere, and their style is that of an entire generation.

3

Palms, California, is a part of Los Angeles through which many
people drive on their way from 20th Century-Fox to Metro-
Goldwyn-Mayer, and vice versa. It is an area largely unnoticed by
those who drive through it, an invisible prairie of stucco bungalows
and two-story 'units,' and I mention it at all only because it is in
Palms that a young woman named Dallas Beardsley lives. Dallas
Beardsley has spent all of her twenty-two years on this invisible
underside of the Los Angeles fabric, living with her mother in places
like Palms and Inglewood and Westchester: she went to Airport
Junior High School, out near Los Angeles International Airport, and
to Westchester High School, where she did not go out with boys
but did try out for cheerleader. She remembers not being chosen
cheerleader as her 'biggest discouragement.' After that she decided
to become an actress, and one morning in October of 1968 she

bought the fifth page of *Daily Variety* for an advertisement which read in part: 'There is no one like me in the world. I'm going to be a movie star.'

It seemed an anachronistic ambition, wanting to be a movie star; girls were not supposed to want that in 1968. They were supposed to want only to perfect their *karma*, to give and get what were called good vibrations and to renounce personal ambition as an ego game. They were supposed to know that wanting things leads in general to grief, and that wanting to be a movie star leads in particular to U.C.L.A. Neuropsychiatric. Such are our conventions. But here was Dallas Beardsley, telling the world what she wanted for $50 down and $35 a month on an eight-month contract with *Variety*. *I'm going to be a movie star.*

I called Dallas, and one hot afternoon we drove around the Hollywood hills and talked. Dallas had long blond hair and a sundress and she was concerned about a run in her stocking and she did not hesitate when I asked what it meant to be a movie star. 'It means being known all over the world,' she said. 'And bringing my family a bunch of presents on Christmas Day, you know, like carloads, and putting them by the tree. And it means happiness, and living by the ocean in a huge house.' She paused. 'But being *known*. It's important to me to be *known*.' That morning she had seen an agent, and she was pleased because he had said that his decision not to handle her was 'nothing personal.' 'The big agents are nice,' she said. 'They answer letters, they return your calls. It's the little ones who're nasty. But I understand, I really do.' Dallas believes that all people, even agents, are 'basically good inside,' and that 'when they hurt you, it's because they've been hurt themselves, and anyway maybe God means for you to be hurt, so some beautiful thing can happen later.' Dallas attends the Unity Church in Culver City, the general thrust of which is that everything works out for the best, and she described herself as 'pretty religious' and 'politically less on the liberal side than most actors.'

Her dedication to the future is undiluted. The jobs she takes to support herself – she has been a Kelly Girl, and worked in restaurants – do not intrude upon her ambitions. She does not go out to parties or on dates. 'I work till six-thirty, then I have a dance lesson, then I rehearse at the workshop – when would I have time? Anyway I'm not interested in that.' As I drove home that day through the somnolent back streets of Hollywood I had the distinct sense that everyone I knew had some fever which had not yet infected the invisible city. In the invisible city girls were still disappointed at not being chosen cheerleader. In the invisible city girls still got discovered at Schwab's and later met their true loves at the Mocambo or the Troc, still dreamed of big houses by the ocean and carloads of presents by the Christmas tree, still prayed to be known.

4

Another part of the invisible city.

'Speaking for myself,' the young woman said, 'in this seven months since I been on the program it's been real good. I was strictly a Gardena player, lowball. I'd play in the nighttime after I got my children to bed, and of course I never got home before five A.M., and my problem was, I couldn't sleep then, I'd replay every hand, so the next day I'd be, you know, tired. Irritable. With the children.'

Her tone was that of someone who had adapted her mode of public address from analgesic commercials, but she was not exactly selling a product. She was making a 'confession' at a meeting of Gamblers Anonymous: nine o'clock on a winter evening in a neighborhood clubhouse in Gardena, California. Gardena is the draw-poker capital of Los Angeles County (no stud, no alcoholic beverages, clubs closed between five A.M. and nine A.M. and all day on Christmas Day), and the proximity of the poker clubs hung over this meeting like a paraphysical substance, almost as palpable as the American flag, the portraits of Washington and Lincoln, and the table laid by the Refreshments Committee. There it was, just around the corner, the action, and here in this overheated room were forty people, shifting uneasily on folding chairs and blinking against the cigarette smoke, who craved it. 'I never made this Gardena meeting before,' one of them said, 'for one simple reason only, which is I break out in a cold sweat every time I pass Gardena on the freeway even, but I'm here tonight because every night I make a meeting is a night I don't place a bet, which with the help of God and you people is 1,223 nights now.' Another: 'I started out for a Canoga Park meeting and turned around on the freeway, that was last Wednesday, I ended up in Gardena and now I'm on the verge of divorce again.' And a third: 'I didn't lose no fortune, but I lost all the money I could get my hands on, it began in the Marine Corps, I met a lot of pigeons in Vietnam, I was making easy money and it was, you might say, this period in my life that, uh, led to my downfall.' This last speaker was a young man who said that he had done OK in mechanical drawing at Van Nuys High School. He wore his hair in a sharp 1951 ducktail. He was, like Dallas Beardsley, twenty-two years old. Tell me the name of the elected representative from the invisible city.

1968–1970

III

Women

The Women's Movement

To make an omelette you need not only those broken eggs but someone 'oppressed' to break them: every revolutionist is presumed to understand that, and also every woman, which either does or does not make fifty-one per cent of the population of the United States a potentially revolutionary class. The creation of this revolutionary 'class' was from the virtual beginning the 'idea' of the women's movement, and the tendency for popular discussion of the movement to center for so long around day-care centers is yet another instance of that studied resistance to political ideas which characterizes our national life.

'The new feminism is not just the revival of a serious political movement for social equality,' the feminist theorist Shulamith Firestone announced flatly in 1970. 'It is the second wave of the most important revolution in history.' This was scarcely a statement of purpose anyone could find cryptic, and it was scarcely the only statement of its kind in the literature of the movement. Nonetheless, in 1972, in a 'special issue' on women, *Time* was still musing genially that the movement might well succeed in bringing about 'fewer diapers and more Dante.'

That was a very pretty image, the idle ladies sitting in the gazebo and murmuring *lasciate ogni speranza*, but it depended entirely upon the popular view of the movement as some kind of collective inchoate yearning for 'fulfillment,' or 'self-expression,' a yearning absolutely devoid of ideas and capable of engendering only the most *pro forma* benevolent interest. In fact there was an idea, and the idea was Marxist, and it was precisely to the extent that there was this Marxist idea that the curious historical anomaly known as the women's movement would have seemed to have any interest at all. Marxism in this country had ever been an eccentric and quixotic passion. One oppressed class after another had seemed finally to miss the point. The have-nots, it turned out, aspired mainly to having. The minorities seemed to promise more, but finally disappointed: it developed that they actually cared about the issues, that they tended to see the integration of the luncheonette and the seat in the front of the bus as real goals, and only rarely as ploys, counters in a larger game. They resisted that essential inductive leap from the immediate reform to the social ideal, and, just as disappointingly, they failed to perceive their common cause with other minorities, continued to exhibit a self-interest disconcerting in the extreme to organizers steeped in the rhetoric of 'brotherhood.'

And then, at that exact dispirited moment when there seemed no one at all willing to play the proletariat, along came the women's movement, and the invention of women as a 'class.' One could not help admiring the radical simplicity of this instant transfiguration. The notion that, in the absence of a cooperative proletariat, a revolutionary class might simply be invented, made up, 'named' and so brought into existence, seemed at once so pragmatic and so visionary, so precisely Emersonian, that it took the breath away, exactly confirmed one's idea of where nineteenth-century transcendental instincts, crossed with a late reading of Engels and Marx, might lead. To read the theorists of the women's movement was to think not of Mary Wollstonecraft but of Margaret Fuller at her most high-minded, of rushing position papers off to mimeo and drinking tea from paper cups in lieu of eating lunch; of thin raincoats on bitter nights. If the family was the last fortress of capitalism, then let us abolish the family. If the necessity for conventional reproduction of the species seemed unfair to women, then let us transcend, via technology, 'the very organization of nature,' the oppression, as Shulamith Firestone saw it, 'that goes back through recorded history to the animal kingdom itself.' *I accept the universe*, Margaret Fuller had finally allowed: Shulamith Firestone did not.

It seemed very New England, this febrile and cerebral passion. The solemn *a priori* idealism in the guise of radical materialism somehow bespoke old-fashioned self-reliance and prudent sacrifice. The clumsy torrent of words became a principle, a renunciation of style as unserious. The rhetorical willingness to break eggs became, in practice, only a thrifty capacity for finding the sermon in every stone. Burn the literature, Ti-Grace Atkinson said in effect when it was suggested that, even come the revolution, there would still remain the whole body of 'sexist' Western literature. But of course no books would be burned: the women of this movement were perfectly capable of crafting didactic revisions of whatever apparently intractable material came to hand. 'As a parent you should become an interpreter of myths,' advised Letty Cottin Pogrebin in the preview issue of *Ms*. 'Portions of any fairy tale or children's story can be salvaged during a critique session with your child.' Other literary analysts devised ways to salvage other books: Isabel Archer in *The Portrait of a Lady* need no longer be the victim of her own idealism. She could be, instead, the victim of a sexist society, a woman who had 'internalized the conventional definition of wife.' The narrator of Mary McCarthy's *The Company She Keeps* could be seen as 'enslaved because she persists in looking for her identity in a man.' Similarly, Miss McCarthy's *The Group* could serve to illustrate 'what happens to women who have been educated at first-rate women's colleges – taught philosophy and history – and then are consigned to breast-feeding and gourmet cooking.'

The idea that fiction has certain irreducible ambiguities seemed never to occur to these women, nor should it have, for fiction is in most ways hostile to ideology. They had invented a class; now they had only to make that class conscious. They seized as a political technique a kind of shared testimony at first called a 'rap session,' then called 'consciousness-raising,' and in any case a therapeutically oriented American reinterpretation, according to the British feminist Juliet Mitchell, of a Chinese revolutionary practice known as 'speaking bitterness.' They purged and regrouped and purged again, worried out one another's errors and deviations, the 'elitism' here, the 'careerism' there. It would have been merely sententious to call some of their thinking Stalinist: of course it was. It would have been pointless even to speak of whether one considered these women 'right' or 'wrong,' meaningless to dwell upon the obvious, upon the coarsening of moral imagination to which such social idealism so often leads. To believe in 'the greater good' is to operate, necessarily, in a certain ethical suspension. Ask anyone committed to Marxist analysis how many angels on the head of a pin, and you will be asked in return to never mind the angels, tell me who controls the production of pins.

To those of us who remain committed mainly to the exploration of moral distinctions and ambiguities, the feminist analysis may have seemed a particularly narrow and cracked determinism. Nonetheless it was serious, and for these high-strung idealists to find themselves out of the mimeo room and onto the Cavett show must have been in certain ways more unsettling to them than it ever was to the viewers. They were being heard, and yet not really. Attention was finally being paid, and yet that attention was mired in the trivial. Even the brightest movement women found themselves engaged in sullen public colloquies about the inequities of dishwashing and the intolerable humiliations of being observed by construction workers on Sixth Avenue. (This grievance was not atypic in that discussion of it seemed always to take on unexplored Ms Scarlett overtones, suggestions of fragile cultivated flowers being 'spoken to,' and therefore violated, by uppity proles.) They totted up the pans scoured, the towels picked off the bathroom floor, the loads of laundry done in a lifetime. Cooking a meal could only be 'dogwork,' and to claim any pleasure from it was evidence of craven acquiescence in one's own forced labor. Small children could only be odious mechanisms for the spilling and digesting of food, for robbing women of their 'freedom.' It was a long way from Simone de Beauvoir's grave and awesome recognition of woman's role as 'the Other' to the notion that the first step in changing that role was Alix Kates Shulman's marriage contract ('wife strips beds, husband remakes them'), a document reproduced in *Ms*, but it was toward just such trivialization that the women's movement seemed to be heading.

Of course this litany of trivia was crucial to the movement in the beginning, a key technique in the politicizing of women who had perhaps been conditioned to obscure their resentments even from themselves. Mrs Shulman's discovery that she had less time than her husband seemed to have was precisely the kind of chord the movement had hoped to strike in all women (the 'click! of recognition,' as Jane O'Reilly described it), but such discoveries could

be of no use at all if one refused to perceive the larger point, failed
to make that inductive leap from the personal to the political.
Splitting up the week into hours during which the children were
directed to address their 'personal questions' to either one parent or
another might or might not have improved the quality of Mr and
Mrs Shulman's marriage, but the improvement of marriages would
not a revolution make. It could be very useful to call housework, as
Lenin did, 'the most unproductive, the most barbarous and the most
arduous work a woman can do,' but it could be useful only as the
first step in a political process, only in the 'awakening' of a class to
its position, useful only as a metaphor: to believe, during the late
Sixties and early Seventies in the United States of America, that the
words had literal meaning was not only to stall the movement in the
personal but to seriously delude oneself.

More and more, as the literature of the movement began to reflect
the thinking of women who did not really understand the movement's ideological base, one had the sense of this stall, this delusion,
the sense that the drilling of the theorists had struck only some
psychic hardpan dense with superstitions and little sophistries, wish
fulfillment, self-loathing and bitter fancies. To read even desultorily
in this literature was to recognize instantly a certain dolorous phantasm, an imagined Everywoman with whom the authors seemed to
identify all too entirely. This ubiquitous construct was everyone's
victim but her own. She was persecuted even by her gynecologist,
who made her beg in vain for contraceptives. She particularly needed
contraceptives because she was raped on every date, raped by her
husband, and raped finally on the abortionist's table. During the
fashion for shoes with pointed toes, she, like 'many women,' had
her toes amputated. She was so intimidated by cosmetics advertising
that she would sleep 'huge portions' of her day in order to forestall
wrinkling, and when awake she was enslaved by detergent commercials on television. She sent her child to a nursery school where the
little girls huddled in a 'doll corner,' and were forcibly restrained
from playing with building blocks. Should she work she was paid
'three to ten times less' than an (always) unqualified man holding
the same job, was prevented from attending business lunches
because she would be 'embarrassed' to appear in public with a man
not her husband, and, when she traveled alone, faced a choice

between humiliation in a restaurant and 'eating a doughnut' in her hotel room.

The half-truths, repeated, authenticated themselves. The bitter fancies assumed their own logic. To ask the obvious – why she did not get herself another gynecologist, another job, why she did not get out of bed and turn off the television set, or why, the most eccentric detail, she stayed in hotels where only doughnuts could be obtained from room service – was to join this argument at its own spooky level, a level which had only the most tenuous and unfortunate relationship to the actual condition of being a woman. That many women are victims of condescension and exploitation and sex-role stereotyping was scarcely news, but neither was it news that other women are not: nobody forces women to buy the package.

But of course something other than an objection to being 'discriminated against' was at work here, something other than an aversion to being 'stereotyped' in one's sex role. Increasingly it seemed that the aversion was to adult sexual life itself: how much cleaner to stay forever children. One is constantly struck, in the accounts of lesbian relationships which appear from time to time in movement literature, by the emphasis on the superior 'tenderness' of the relationship, the 'gentleness' of the sexual connection, as if the participants were wounded birds. The derogation of assertiveness as 'machismo' has achieved such currency that one imagines several million women too delicate to deal at any level with an overtly heterosexual man. Just as one had gotten the unintended but inescapable suggestion, when told about the 'terror and revulsion' experienced by women in the vicinity of construction sites, of creatures too 'tender' for the abrasiveness of daily life, too fragile for the streets, so now one was getting, in the later literature of the movement, the impression of women too 'sensitive' for the difficulties of adult life, women unequipped for reality and grasping at the movement as a rationale for denying that reality. The transient stab of dread and loss which accompanies menstruation simply never happens: we only thought it happened, because a male-chauvinist psychiatrist told us so. No woman need have bad dreams after an abortion: she has only been told she should. The power of sex is just an oppressive myth, no longer to be feared, because what the sexual connection really amounts to, we learn in one woman's account of a postmarital affair presented as liberated and liberating, is 'wise-cracking and laughing' and 'lying together and then leaping up to play and sing the entire *Sesame Street Songbook.*' All one's actual apprehension of what it is like to be a woman, the irreconcilable difference of it – that sense of living one's deepest life underwater, that dark involvement with blood and birth and death – could now be declared invalid, unnecessary, *one never felt it at all.*

One was only told it, and now one is to be reprogrammed, fixed up, rendered again as inviolate and unstained as the 'modern' little girls in the Tampax advertisements. More and more we have been hearing the wishful voices of just such perpetual adolescents, the voices of women scarred not by their class position as women but by the failure of their childhood expectations and misapprehensions. 'Nobody ever so much as mentioned' to Susan Edmiston 'that when you say "I do," what you are doing is not, as you thought, vowing your eternal love, but rather subscribing to a whole system of rights, obligations and responsibilities that may well be anathema to your most cherished beliefs.' To Ellen Peck 'the birth of children too often means the dissolution of romance, the loss of freedom, the abandonment of ideals to economics.' A young woman described on the cover of *New York* as 'The Suburban Housewife Who Bought the Promises of Women's Lib and Came to the City to Live Them' tells us what promises she bought: 'The chance to respond to the bright lights and civilization of the Big Apple, yes. The chance to compete, yes. But most of all, the chance to have some fun. Fun is what's been missing.'

Eternal love, romance, fun. The Big Apple. These are relatively rare expectations in the arrangements of consenting adults, although not in those of children, and it wrenches the heart to read about these women in their brave new lives. An ex-wife and mother of three speaks of her plan to 'play out my college girl's dream. I am going to New York to become this famous writer. Or this working writer. Failing that, I will get a job in publishing.' She mentions a friend, another young woman who 'had never had any other life than as a daughter or wife or mother' but who is 'just discovering herself to be a gifted potter.' The childlike resourcefulness – to get a job in publishing, to become a gifted potter! – bewilders the imagination. The astral discontent with actual lives, actual men, the denial of the real generative possibilities of adult sexual life, somehow touches beyond words. 'It is the right of the oppressed to organize around their oppression *as they see and define it*,' the movement theorists insist doggedly in an effort to solve the question of these women, to convince themselves that what is going on is still a political process, but the handwriting is already on the wall. These are converts who want not a revolution but 'romance,' who believe not in the oppression of women but in their own chances for a new life in exactly the mold of their old life. In certain ways they tell us sadder things about what the culture has done to them than the theorists ever did, and they also tell us, I suspect, that the movement is no longer a cause but a symptom.

1972

Doris Lessing

To read a great deal of Doris Lessing over a short span of time is to feel that the original hound of heaven has commandeered the attic. She holds the mind's other guests in ardent contempt. She appears for meals only to dismiss as decadent the household's own preoccupations with writing well. For more than twenty years now she has been registering, in a torrent of fiction that increasingly seems conceived in a stubborn rage against the very idea of fiction, every tremor along her emotional fault system, every slippage in her self-education. *Look here*, she is forever demanding, a missionary devoid of any but the most didactic irony: *The Communist Party is not the answer. There is a life beyond vaginal orgasm. St John of the Cross was not as dotty as certain Anglicans would have had you believe.* She comes hard to ideas, and, once she has collared one, worries it with Victorian doggedness.

That she is a writer of considerable native power, a 'natural' writer in the Dreiserian mold, someone who can close her eyes and 'give' a situation by the sheer force of her emotional energy, seems almost a stain on her conscience. She views her real gift for fiction much as she views her own biology, as another trick to entrap her. She does not want to 'write well.' Her leaden disregard for even the simplest rhythms of language, her arrogantly bad ear for dialogue – all of that is beside her own point. More and more, Mrs Lessing writes exclusively in the service of immediate cosmic reform: she wants to write, as the writer Anna in *The Golden Notebook* wanted to write, only to 'create a new way of looking at life.'

Consider *Briefing for a Descent into Hell*. Here Mrs Lessing gave us a novel exclusively of 'ideas,' not a novel about the play of ideas in the lives of certain characters but a novel in which the characters exist only as markers in the presentation of an idea. The situation in the novel was this: a well-dressed but disheveled man is found wandering, an amnesiac, on the embankment near the Waterloo Bridge in London. He is taken by the police to a psychiatric hospital where, in the face of total indifference on his part, attempts are made to identify him. He is Charles Watkins, a professor of classics at Cambridge. An authority in his field, an occasional lecturer on more general topics. Lately a stammerer. Lately prone to bad evenings during which he condemns not only his own but all academic disciplines as 'pigswill.' A fifty-year-old man who finally cracked, and in cracking personified Mrs Lessing's conviction that 'the millions who have cracked' were 'making cracks where the light could shine through at last.' For of course the 'nonsense' that Charles Watkins talks in the hospital makes, to the reader although not to the doctors, unmistakable 'sense.'

So pronounced was Charles Watkins' acumen about the inner reality of those around him that much of the time *Briefing for a Descent into Hell* read like a selective case study from an R. D. Laing book. The reality Charles Watkins describes is familiar to anyone who has ever had a high fever, or been exhausted to the point of breaking, or is just on the whole only marginally engaged in the dailiness of life. He experiences the loss of ego, the apprehension of the cellular nature of all matter, the 'oneness' of things that seems always to lie just past the edge of controlled conscious thought. He hallucinates, or 'remembers,' the nature of the universe. He 'remembers' – or is on the verge of remembering, before electroshock obliterates the memory and returns him to 'sanity' – something very like a 'briefing' for life on earth.

The details of this briefing were filled in by Mrs Lessing, only too relieved to abandon the strain of creating character and slip into her own rather more exhortative voice. Imagine an interplanetary conference, convened on Venus to discuss once again the problem of the self-destructive planet Earth. (The fancy that extraterrestrial life is by definition of a higher order than our own is one that soothes all children, and many writers.) The procedure is this: certain

superior beings descend to Earth brainprinted with the task of arous-
ing the planet to its folly. These emissaries have, once on Earth, no
memory of their more enlightened life. They wake slowly to their
mission. They recognize one another only vaguely, and do not
remember why. We are to understand, of course, that Charles Watkins is among those who have made the Descent, whether literal or
metaphorical, and is now, for just so long as he can resist therapy,
awake. This is the initial revelation in the book, and it is also the
only one.

Even given Mrs Lessing's tendency to confront all ideas *tabula
rasa*, we are dealing here with less than astonishing stuff. The idea
that there is sanity in insanity, that truth lies on the far side of
madness, informs not only a considerable spread of Western literature but also, so commonly is it now held, an entire generation's
experiment with hallucinogens. Most of Mrs Lessing's thoughts
about the cultural definition of insanity reflect or run parallel to
those of Laing, and yet the idea was already so prevalent that Laing
cannot even be said to have popularized it: his innovation was only
to have taken it out of the realm of instinctive knowledge and into
the limited context of psychiatric therapy. Although Mrs Lessing
apparently thought the content of *Briefing for a Descent into Hell* so
startling that she was impelled to add an explanatory afterword, a
two-page parable about the ignorance of certain psychiatrists at large
London teaching hospitals, she had herself dealt before with this
very material. In *The Golden Notebook* Anna makes this note for a
story: 'A man whose "sense of reality" has gone; and because of it,
has a deeper sense of reality than "normal" people.' By the time Mrs
Lessing finished *The Four-Gated City* she had refined the proposition:
Lynda Coldridge's deeper sense of reality is not the result but the
definition of her madness. So laboriously is this notion developed in
the closing three hundred pages of *The Four-Gated City* that one would
have thought that Mrs Lessing had more or less exhausted its literary
possibilities.

But she was less and less interested in literary possibilities, which
is where we strike the faultline. 'If I saw it in terms of an artistic
problem, then it'd be easy, wouldn't it,' Anna tells her friend Molly,
in *The Golden Notebook*, as explanation of her disinclination to write
another book. 'We could have ever such intelligent chats about the

modern novel.' This may seem a little on the easy side, even to the reader who is willing to overlook Anna's later assertion that she cannot write because 'a Chinese peasant' is looking over her shoulder. ('Or one of Castro's guerrilla fighters. Or an Algerian fighting in the F.L.N.') *Madame Bovary* told us more about bourgeois life than several generations of Marxists have, but there does not seem much doubt that Flaubert saw it as an artistic problem.

That Mrs Lessing does not suggests her particular dilemma. What we are witnessing here is a writer undergoing a profound and continuing cultural trauma, a woman of determinedly utopian and distinctly teleological bent assaulted at every turn by fresh evidence that the world is not exactly improving as promised. And, because such is the particular quality of her mind, she is compelled in the face of this evidence to look even more frenetically for the final cause, the unambiguous answer.

In the beginning her search was less frenzied. She came out of Southern Rhodesia imprinted ineradicably by precisely the kind of rigid agrarian world that most easily makes storytellers of its exiled children. What British Africa gave her, besides those images of a sky so empty and a society so inflexible as to make the slightest tremor in either worth remarking upon, was a way of perceiving the rest of her life: for a long time to come she could interpret all she saw in terms of 'injustice,' not merely the injustice of white man to black, of colonizer to colonized, but the more general injustices of class and particularly of sex. She grew up knowing not only what hard frontiers do to women but what women then do to the men who keep them there. She could hear in all her memories that 'voice of the suffering female' passed on from mothers to daughters in a chain broken only at great cost.

Of these memories she wrote a first novel, *The Grass Is Singing*, entirely traditional in its conventions. Reality was *there*, waiting to be observed by an omniscient third person. *The Grass Is Singing* was neat in its construction, relatively scrupulous in its maintenance of tone, predicated upon a world of constants. Its characters moved through that world unconscious of knowledge shared by author and reader. The novel was, in brief, everything Mrs Lessing was to reject as 'false' and 'evasive' by the time she wrote *The Golden Notebook*. 'Why not write down, simply, what happened between Molly and her son today?' Anna demands of herself. 'Why do I never write down, simply, what happens? Why don't I keep a diary? Obviously, my changing everything into fiction is simply a means of concealing something from myself . . . I shall keep a diary.'

It would be hard to imagine a character more unrelievedly self-conscious, or more insistently the author's surrogate, than Anna Gould in *The Golden Notebook*. The entire intention of the novel is to shatter the conventional distance of fiction, to deny all distinction between toad and garden, to 'write down, simply, what happens.' Call the writer Anna Gould or call her Doris Lessing, *The Golden Notebook* is the diary of a writer in shock. There she is in London, 1950. A young woman determined to forge a life as a 'free woman,' as an 'intellectual,' she has come out of a simple society into what Robert Penn Warren once called the convulsion of the world, and she is finding some equivocation in the answers so clear to her in Africa. Her expectations give off a bright and dated valiance. Her disenchantments are all too familiar. The sheer will, the granitic ambitiousness of *The Golden Notebook* overrides everything else about it. Great raw hunks of undigested experience, unedited transcripts of what happened between Molly and her son today, overwhelming memories and rejections of those memories as sentimental, the fracturing of a sensibility beginning for the first time to doubt its perceptions: all of it runs out of the teller's mind and into the reader's with deliberate disregard for the nature of the words in between. The teller creates 'characters' and 'scenes' only to deny their validity. She berates herself for clinging to the 'certainty' of her memories in the face of the general uncertainty. Mrs Lessing looms through *The Golden Notebook* as a woman driven by doubts not only about what to tell but about the validity of telling it at all.

Yet she continued to write, and to write fiction. Not until the end of the five-volume *Children of Violence* series did one sense a weakening of that compulsion to remember, and a metastasis of that cognitive frenzy for answers. She had seen, by then, a great deal go, had seized a great many answers and lost them. Organized politics went early. Freudian determinism seemed incompatible. The Africa of her memory was another country. The voice she felt most deeply, that of women trying to define their relationships to one another and to men, first went shrill and then, appropriated by and reduced to a 'movement,' slipped below the range of her attention. She had been betrayed by all those answers and more, and yet, increasingly possessed, her only response has been to look for another. That she is scarcely alone in this possession is what lends her quest its great interest: the impulse to final solutions has been not only Mrs Lessing's dilemma but the guiding delusion of her time. It is not an impulse I hold high, but there is something finally very moving about her tenacity.

1971

Georgia O'Keeffe

'Where I was born and where and how I have lived is unimportant,' Georgia O'Keeffe told us in the book of paintings and words published in her ninetieth year on earth. She seemed to be advising us to forget the beautiful face in the Stieglitz photographs. She appeared to be dismissing the rather condescending romance that had attached to her by then, the romance of extreme good looks and advanced age and deliberate isolation. 'It is what I have done with where I have been that should be of interest.' I recall an August afternoon in Chicago in 1973 when I took my daughter, then seven, to see what Georgia O'Keeffe had done with where she had been. One of the vast O'Keeffe 'Sky Above Clouds' canvases floated over the back stairs in the Chicago Art Institute that day, dominating what seemed to be several stories of empty light, and my daughter looked at it once, ran to the landing, and kept on looking. 'Who drew it,' she whispered after a while. I told her. 'I need to talk to her,' she said finally.

My daughter was making, that day in Chicago, an entirely unconscious but quite basic assumption about people and the work they do. She was assuming that the glory she saw in the work reflected a glory in its maker, that the painting was the painter as the poem is the poet, that every choice one made alone – every word chosen or rejected, every brush stroke laid or not laid down – betrayed one's character. *Style is character*. It seemed to me that afternoon that I had rarely seen so instinctive an application of this familiar principle, and I recall being pleased not only that my daughter responded to style

as character but that it was Georgia O'Keeffe's particular style to
which she responded: this was a hard woman who had imposed her
192 square feet of clouds on Chicago.

'Hardness' has not been in our century a quality much admired in
women, nor in the past twenty years has it even been in official
favor for men. When hardness surfaces in the very old we tend to
transform it into 'crustiness' or eccentricity, some tonic pepperiness
to be indulged at a distance. On the evidence of her work and what
she has said about it, Georgia O'Keeffe is neither 'crusty' nor eccentric. She is simply hard, a straight shooter, a woman clean of received
wisdom and open to what she sees. This is a woman who could early
on dismiss most of her contemporaries as 'dreamy,' and would later
single out one she liked as 'a very poor painter.' (And then add,
apparently by way of softening the judgment: 'I guess he wasn't a
painter at all. He had no courage and I believe that to create one's
own world in any of the arts takes courage.') This is a woman who
in 1939 could advise her admirers that they were missing her point,
that their appreciation of her famous flowers was merely sentimental. 'When I paint a red hill,' she observed coolly in the catalogue for
an exhibition that year, 'you say it is too bad that I don't always
paint flowers. A flower touches almost everyone's heart. A red hill
doesn't touch everyone's heart.' This is a woman who could describe
the genesis of one of her most well-known paintings – the 'Cow's
Skull: Red, White and Blue' owned by the Metropolitan – as an act
of quite deliberate and derisive orneriness. 'I thought of the city men
I had been seeing in the East,' she wrote. 'They talked so often of
writing the Great American Novel – the Great American Play – the
Great American Poetry . . . So as I was painting my cow's head on
blue I thought to myself, "I'll make it an American painting. They
will not think it great with the red stripes down the sides – Red,
White and Blue – but they will notice it."'

The city men. The men. They. The words crop up again and again as
this astonishingly aggressive woman tells us what was on her mind
when she was making her astonishingly aggressive paintings. It was
those city men who stood accused of sentimentalizing her flowers:
'I made you take time to look at what I saw and when you took time

to really notice my flower you hung all your associations with flowers on my flower and you write about my flower as if I think and see what you think and see – and I don't.' *And I don't.* Imagine those words spoken, and the sound you hear is *don't tread on me.* 'The men' believed it impossible to paint New York, so Georgia O'Keeffe painted New York. 'The men' didn't think much of her bright color, so she made it brighter. The men yearned toward Europe so she went to Texas, and then New Mexico. The men talked about Cézanne, 'long involved remarks about the "plastic quality" of his form and color,' and took one another's long involved remarks, in the view of this angelic rattlesnake in their midst, altogether too seriously. 'I can paint one of those dismal-colored paintings like the men,' the woman who regarded herself always as an outsider remembers thinking one day in 1922, and she did: a painting of a shed 'all low-toned and dreary with the tree beside the door.' She called this act of rancor 'The Shanty' and hung it in her next show. 'The men seemed to approve of it,' she reported fifty-four years later, her contempt undimmed. 'They seemed to think that maybe I was beginning to paint. That was my only low-toned dismal-colored painting.'

Some women fight and others do not. Like so many successful guerrillas in the war between the sexes, Georgia O'Keeffe seems to have been equipped early with an immutable sense of who she was and a fairly clear understanding that she would be required to prove it. On the surface her upbringing was conventional. She was a child on the Wisconsin prairie who played with china dolls and painted watercolors with cloudy skies because sunlight was too hard to paint and, with her brother and sisters, listened every night to her mother read stories of the Wild West, of Texas, of Kit Carson and Billy the Kid. She told adults that she wanted to be an artist and was embarrassed when they asked what kind of artist she wanted to be: she had no idea 'what kind.' She had no idea what artists did. She had never seen a picture that interested her, other than a pen-and-ink Maid of Athens in one of her mother's books, some Mother Goose illustrations printed on cloth, a tablet cover that showed a little girl with pink roses, and the painting of Arabs on horseback that hung in her grandmother's parlor. At thirteen, in a Dominican convent, she was mortified when the sister corrected her drawing. At Chatham Episcopal Institute in Virginia she painted lilacs and sneaked time

alone to walk out to where she could see the line of the Blue Ridge
Mountains on the horizon. At the Art Institute in Chicago she was
shocked by the presence of live models and wanted to abandon
anatomy lessons. At the Art Students League in New York one of
her fellow students advised her that, since he would be a great
painter and she would end up teaching painting in a girls' school,
any work of hers was less important than modeling for him. Another
painted over her work to show her how the Impressionists did trees.
She had not before heard how the Impressionists did trees and she
did not much care.

At twenty-four she left all those opinions behind and went for
the first time to live in Texas, where there were no trees to paint and
no one to tell her how not to paint them. In Texas there was only
the horizon she craved. In Texas she had her sister Claudia with her
for a while, and in the late afternoons they would walk away from
town and toward the horizon and watch the evening star come out.
'That evening star fascinated me,' she wrote. 'It was in some way
very exciting to me. My sister had a gun, and as we walked she
would throw bottles into the air and shoot as many as she could
before they hit the ground. I had nothing but to walk into nowhere
and the wide sunset space with the star. Ten watercolors were made
from that star.' In a way one's interest is compelled as much by the
sister Claudia with the gun as by the painter Georgia with the star,
but only the painter left us this shining record. Ten watercolors were
made from that star.

1976

IV

Sojourns

In the Islands

1969: I had better tell you where I am, and why. I am sitting in a
high-ceilinged room in the Royal Hawaiian Hotel in Honolulu watching the long translucent curtains billow in the trade wind and trying
to put my life back together. My husband is here, and our daughter,
age three. She is blond and barefoot, a child of paradise in a frangipani lei, and she does not understand why she cannot go to the
beach. She cannot go to the beach because there has been an earthquake in the Aleutians, 7.5 on the Richter scale, and a tidal wave is
expected. In two or three minutes the wave, if there is one, will hit
Midway Island, and we are awaiting word from Midway. My husband watches the television screen. I watch the curtains, and imagine
the swell of the water.

The bulletin, when it comes, is a distinct anticlimax: Midway
reports no unusual wave action. My husband switches off the television set and stares out the window. I avoid his eyes, and brush the
baby's hair. In the absence of a natural disaster we are left again to
our own uneasy devices. We are here on this island in the middle of
the Pacific in lieu of filing for divorce.

I tell you this not as aimless revelation but because I want you to
know, as you read me, precisely who I am and where I am and what
is on my mind. I want you to understand exactly what you are
getting: you are getting a woman who for some time now has felt
radically separated from most of the ideas that seem to interest other
people. You are getting a woman who somewhere along the line
misplaced whatever slight faith she ever had in the social contract,

in the meliorative principle, in the whole grand pattern of human endeavor. Quite often during the past several years I have felt myself a sleepwalker, moving through the world unconscious of the moment's high issues, oblivious to its data, alert only to the stuff of bad dreams, the children burning in the locked car in the super-market parking lot, the bike boys stripping down stolen cars on the captive cripple's ranch, the freeway sniper who feels 'real bad' about picking off the family of five, the hustlers, the insane, the cunning Okie faces that turn up in military investigations, the sullen lurkers in doorways, the lost children, all the ignorant armies jostling in the night. Acquaintances read *The New York Times*, and try to tell me the news of the world. I listen to call-in shows.

You will perceive that such a view of the world presents diffi-culties. I have trouble making certain connections. I have trouble maintaining the basic notion that keeping promises matters in a world where everything I was taught seems beside the point. The point itself seems increasingly obscure. I came into adult life equipped with an essentially romantic ethic, holding always before me the examples of Axel Heyst in *Victory* and Milly Theale in *The Wings of the Dove* and Charlotte Rittenmayer in *The Wild Palms* and a few dozen others like them, believing as they did that salvation lay in extreme and doomed commitments, promises made and somehow kept outside the range of normal social experience. I still believe that, but I have trouble reconciling salvation with those ignorant armies camped in my mind. I could indulge here in a little idle generalization, could lay off my own state of profound emotional shock on the larger cultural breakdown, could talk fast about con-vulsions in the society and alienation and anomie and maybe even assassination, but that would be just one more stylish shell game. I am not the society in microcosm. I am a thirty-four-year-old woman with long straight hair and an old bikini bathing suit and bad nerves sitting on an island in the middle of the Pacific waiting for a tidal wave that will not come.

We spend, my husband and I and the baby, a restorative week in paradise. We are each the other's model of consideration, tact, restraint at the very edge of the precipice. He refrains from noticing when I am staring at nothing, and in turn I refrain from dwelling at length upon a newspaper story about a couple who apparently threw their infant and then themselves into the boiling crater of a live volcano on Maui. We also refrain from mentioning any kicked-down doors, hospitalized psychotics, any chronic anxieties or packed suit-cases. We lie in the sun, drive out through the cane to Waimea Bay. We breakfast on the terrace, and gray-haired women smile benevolently at us. I smile back. Happy families are all alike on the terrace of the Royal Hawaiian Hotel in Honolulu. My husband comes in from Kalakaua Avenue one morning and tells me that he has seen a six-foot-two drag queen we know in Los Angeles. Our acquaint-ance was shopping, my husband reports, for a fishnet bikini and did not speak. We both laugh. I am reminded that we laugh at the same things, and read him this complaint from a very old copy of *Honolulu* magazine I picked up in someone's office: 'When President Johnson recently came to Honolulu, the morning paper's banner read some-thing like "PICKETS TO GREET PRESIDENT." Would it not have been just as newsworthy to say "WARM ALOHA TO GREET PRESIDENT"?' At the end of the week I tell my husband that I am going to try harder to make things matter. My husband says that he has heard that before, but the air is warm and the baby has another frangipani lei and there is no rancor in his voice. Maybe it can be all right, I say. Maybe, he says.

1970: Quite early every morning in Honolulu, on that stretch of Waikiki Beach which fronts the Royal Hawaiian Hotel, an employee of the hotel spends fifteen or twenty minutes raking the sand within a roped enclosure reserved for registered guests. Since this 'private' beach differs from the 'public' beach only by its raked sand, its rope, and its further remove from the water, it is at first difficult to see why anyone would sit there, but people do. They sit there all day long and in great numbers, facing the sea in even rows.

I had been an occasional visitor to Honolulu for several years before I entirely perceived that the roped beach was central to the essence of the Royal Hawaiian, that the point of sitting there was not at all exclusivity, as is commonly supposed on Waikiki, but inclu-sivity. Anyone behind the rope is presumed to be, by tacit definition, 'our kind.' Anyone behind the rope will watch over our children as we will watch over theirs, will not palm room keys or smoke dope

or listen to Creedence Clearwater on a transistor when we are awaiting word from the Mainland on the prime rate. Anyone behind the
rope, should we venture conversation, will 'know people we know':
the Royal's roped beach is an enclave of apparent strangers ever on
the verge of discovering that their nieces roomed in Lagunita at
Stanford the same year, or that their best friends lunched together
during the last Crosby. The fact that anyone behind the rope would
understand the word 'Crosby' to signify a golf tournament at Pebble
Beach suggests the extent to which the Royal Hawaiian is not merely
a hotel but a social idea, one of the few extant clues to a certain kind
of American life.

Of course great hotels have always been social ideas, flawless
mirrors to the particular societies they service. Had there never been
an Empire there would not have been a Raffles. To understand what
the Royal is now you must first understand what it was, from 1927
through the Thirties, the distant and mildly exotic 'pink palace' of
the Pacific, the resort built by the Matson Line to rival and surpass
such hotels as the Coronado, the Broadmoor, Del Monte. Standing
then almost alone on Waikiki, the Royal made Honolulu a place to
go, made all things 'Hawaiian' – leis, ukuleles, luaus, coconut-leaf
hats and the singing of 'I Wanna Learn to Speak Hawaiian' – a
decade's craze at country-club dances across the United States.
During the fourteen years between the Royal's opening and Pearl
Harbor people came in on the Matson Line's *Malolo* and *Lurline*
and they brought with them not only steamer trunks but children
and grandchildren and valets and nurses and silver Rolls-Royces and
ultramarine-blue Packard roadsters. They 'wintered' at the Royal,
or 'summered' there, or 'spent several months.' They came to the
Royal to rest 'after hunting in South Africa.' They went home 'by
way of Banff and Lake Louise.' In Honolulu there was polo, golf,
bowling on the green. Every afternoon the Royal served tea on rattan
tables. The maids wove leis for every guest. The chefs constructed,
as table decoration, the United States Capitol Building in Hawaiian
sugar.

The Royal's scrapbooks for those years survive as an index to
America's industrial fortunes, large and small. Mellons and Du Ponts
and Gettys and the man who had just patented the world's largest
incubator (47,000-egg capacity) seem to differ not at all from one

another, photographed at the Royal in 1928. Dorothy Spreckels strums a ukulele on the verandah. Walter P. Chrysler, Jr, arrives with his mother and father for a season at the Royal. A figure on the beach is described as 'a Colorado Springs society woman,' a young couple as 'prominently identified with the young-married set in Akron.' At the Royal they met not only one another but a larger world as well: Australian station owners, Ceylonese tea planters, Cuban sugar operators.

In the faded photographs one sees mostly mothers and daughters. The men, when they are present, display in the main an affecting awkwardness, an awareness that they have harsher roles, say as mayor of Seattle or president of the Overland Motor Company, a resistance to the world of summering and wintering. In 1931 the son of President Hoover spent time at the Royal, was widely entertained, caught thirty-eight fish off the Kona coast of Hawaii, and had his picture taken on the Royal beach shaking hands with Duke Kahanamoku. This photograph appeared in *Town and Country*, which also reported in 1931 that 'the diving boys in Honolulu harbor say that fishing has been good and there are no indications of hard times in the denominations of coins flipped to them as bait from incoming steamers.'

Nor did the turnings of the Sixties effect much change at the Royal. What the place reflected in the Thirties it reflects still, in less flamboyant mutations: a kind of life lived always on the streets where the oldest trees grow. It is a life so secure in its traditional concerns that the cataclysms of the larger society disturb it only as surface storms disturb the sea's bottom, a long time later and in oblique ways. It is a life lived by millions of people in this country and largely forgotten by most of us. Sometimes I think I remember it only at the Royal Hawaiian. There in the warm early evenings, the women in turquoise-blue and buttercup-yellow chiffons seem, as they wait for cars under the pink porte-cochere, the natural inheritors of a style later seized upon by Patricia Nixon and her daughters. In the mornings, when the beach is just raked and the air damp and sweet from the dawn rain, I see the same women, now in printed silks and lined cashmere cardigans, eating papaya on the terrace just as they have done every few seasons since they were young girls, in the late Twenties, and came to the Royal with their mothers and sisters. Their

husbands scan the San Francisco and Los Angeles papers with the
practiced disinterest of men who believe their lives safe in municipal
bonds. These papers arrive at the Royal one and sometimes two days
late, which lends the events of the day a peculiar and unsettling
distance. I recall overhearing a conversation at the Royal's newsstand
on the morning after the California primary in June 1968, the morning Robert Kennedy lay dying in Good Samaritan Hospital in Los
Angeles. 'How'd the primary go?' a man buying cigarettes asked his
wife. She studied the day-old headlines. '"Early Turnout Heavy,'"
she said. Later in the morning I overheard this woman discussing
the assassination: her husband had heard the news when he dropped
by a brokerage office to get the day's New York closings.

To sit by the Royal pool and read *The New York Review of Books* is
to feel oneself an asp, disguised in a voile beach robe, in the very
bosom of the place. I put *The New York Review of Books* aside and talk
to a pretty young woman who has honeymooned at the Royal,
because honeymoons at the Royal are a custom in her family, with
each of her three husbands. My daughter makes friends at the pool
with another four-year-old, Jill, from Fairbanks, Alaska, and it is
taken for granted by Jill's mother and aunt that the two children
will meet again, year after year, in the immutable pleasant rhythms
of a life that used to be, and at the Royal Hawaiian seems still to be.
I sit in my voile beach robe and watch the children and wish, against
all the evidence I know, that it might be so.

1970: To look down upon Honolulu from the high rain forest that
divides windward Oahu from the leeward city is to see, in the center
of an extinct volcano named Puowaina, a place so still and private
that once seen it is forever in the mind. There are banyan trees in
the crater, and rain trees, and 19,500 graves. Yellow primavera blazes
on the hills above. Whole slopes seem clouded in mauve jacaranda.
This is the place commonly called Punchbowl, the National Memorial
Cemetery of the Pacific, and 13,000 of the dead in its crater were
killed during World War II. Some of the rest died in Korea. For
almost a decade now, in the outer sections just inside the rim of the
crater, they have been digging graves for Americans killed in Vietnam, not many, a fraction of the total, one, two, three a week, most

of them Island boys but some of them carried here by families who live thousands of miles across the Pacific, a gesture that touches by its very difficulty. Because the Vietnam dead are shipped first to Travis A.F.B. in California and then to the next of kin, those Mainland families burying their sons or husbands in Honolulu must bring the bodies back over the Pacific one last time. The superintendent of Punchbowl, Martin T. Corley, refers to such burials as his 'ship-in Vietnams.'

'A father or an uncle calls me from the Mainland and he says they're bringing their boy here, I don't ask why,' Mr Corley said when I talked to him not long ago. We were sitting in his office in the crater and on the wall hung the Bronze Star and Silver Star citations he had received in Europe in 1944, Martin T. Corley, a man in an aloha shirt who had gone from South Ozone Park in Queens to the Battle of the Bulge to a course in cemetery management at Fort Sam Houston and finally, twenty-some years later, to an office in an extinct volcano in the Pacific from which he could watch the quick and the dead in still another war.

I watched him leafing through a stack of what he called 'transmittals,' death forms from Vietnam. There in Martin T. Corley's office Vietnam seemed considerably less chimerical than it had seemed on the Mainland for some months, less last year's war, less successfully consigned to that limbo of benign neglect in which any mention of continuing casualties was made to seem a little counterproductive, a little démodé. There in the crater it seemed less easy to believe that weekly killed-in-action figures under 100 might by some sleight-of-hand add up to zero, a nonexistent war. There in sight of the automatic gravediggers what the figures added up to, for the first twelve weeks of 1970, was 1,078 dead. Martin T. Corley gets a transmittal on each of them. He holds these transmittal forms for fifteen or twenty days before throwing them away, just in case a family wants to bring its dead to Punchbowl. 'See, we had a family bring a boy in from Oregon a few days ago,' he said. 'We've got a California coming in now. We figure they've got their reasons. We pick the plot, open the grave. These ship-in families, we don't see them until the hearse comes through the gate.'

*   *   *

On a warm windy afternoon a few days later I stood with Mr Corley on the soft grass up in Section K of the crater and waited for one such family to come through the gate. They had flown out from the Mainland with the body the night before, six of them, the mother and father and a sister and her husband and a couple of other relatives, and they would bury their boy in the afternoon sun and fly back a few hours later. We waited, and we watched, and then, on the road below, the six Air Force pallbearers snapped to attention. The bugler jumped up from beneath a banyan tree and took his place behind the honor guard. We could see the hearse then, winding up and around the circular road to Section K, the hearse and two cars, their headlights dim in the tropical sun. 'Two of us from the office come to all the Vietnams,' Mr Corley said suddenly. 'I mean in case the family breaks down or something.'

All I can tell you about the next ten minutes is that they seemed a very long time. We watched the coffin being carried to the grave and we watched the pallbearers lift the flag, trying to hold it taut in the warm trade wind. The wind was blowing hard, toppling the vases of gladioli set by the grave, obliterating some of the chaplain's words. 'If God is for us then who can be against us,' the chaplain said, a red-headed young major in suntans, and then I did not hear any more for a while. I was standing behind the six canvas chairs where the family sat, standing there with Mr Corley and an Air Force survival assistance officer, and I was looking beyond the chaplain to a scattering of graves so fresh they had no headstones, just plastic markers stuck in the ground. 'We tenderly commit this body to the ground,' the chaplain said then. The men in the honor guard raised their rifles. Three shots cracked out. The bugler played taps. The pallbearers folded the flag until only the blue field and a few stars showed, and one of them stepped forward to present the flag to the father. For the first time the father looked away from the coffin, looked away from the pallbearers and out across the expanse of graves. A slight man with his face trembling and his eyes wet, he stood facing Mr Corley and me, and for a moment we looked directly at each other, but he was seeing not me, not Mr Corley, not anyone.

It was not quite three o'clock. The father, transferring the flag from hand to hand as if it burned, said a few halting words to the pallbearers. I walked away from the grave then, down to my car, and waited for Mr Corley to talk to the father. He wanted to tell the father that if he and his wife wanted to come back before their plane left, the grave would be covered by four o'clock. 'Sometimes it makes them feel better to see it,' Mr Corley said when he caught up with me. 'Sometimes they get on the plane and they worry, you know, it didn't get covered.' His voice trailed off. 'We cover within thirty minutes,' he said finally. 'Fill, cover, get the marker on. That's one thing I remember from my training.' We stood there a moment in the warm wind, then said goodbye. The pallbearers filed onto the Air Force bus. The bugler walked past, whistling 'Raindrops Keep Fallin' on My Head.' Just after four o'clock the father and mother came back and looked for a long while at the covered grave, then took a night flight back to the Mainland. Their son was one of 101 Americans killed that week in Vietnam.

1975: The 8:45 A.M. Pan American to Honolulu this morning was delayed half an hour before takeoff from Los Angeles. During this delay the stewardesses served orange juice and coffee and two children played tag in the aisles and, somewhere behind me, a man began screaming at a woman who seemed to be his wife. I say that the woman seemed to be his wife only because the tone of his invective sounded practiced, although the only words I heard clearly were these: 'You are driving me to murder.' After a moment I was aware of the door to the plane being opened a few rows behind me, and of the man rushing off. There were many Pan American employees rushing on and off then, and considerable confusion. I do not know whether the man reboarded the plane before takeoff or whether the woman came on to Honolulu alone, but I thought about it all the way across the Pacific. I thought about it while I was drinking a sherry-on-the-rocks and I thought about it during lunch and I was still thinking about it when the first of the Hawaiian Islands appeared off the left wing tip. It was not until we had passed Diamond Head and were coming in low over the reef for landing at Honolulu, however, that I realized what I most disliked about this incident: I disliked it because it had the aspect of a short story, one of those 'little epiphany' stories in which the main character glimpses a crisis in a stranger's life – a woman weeping in a tearoom, often, or an accident seen from the window of a train, 'tearooms' and 'trains' still being fixtures of short stories although not of real life – and is moved to see his or her own life in a new light. I was not going to Honolulu because I wanted to see life reduced to a short story. I was going to Honolulu because I wanted to see life expanded to a novel, and I still do. I wanted room for flowers, and reef fish, and people who may or may not be driving one another to murder but in any case are not impelled, by the demands of narrative convention, to say so out loud on the 8:45 A.M. Pan American to Honolulu.

1977: I have never seen a postcard of Hawaii that featured Schofield Barracks. Schofield is off the track, off the tour, hard by the shadowy pools of the Wahiawa Reservoir, and to leave Honolulu and drive inland to Schofield is to sense a clouding of the atmosphere, a darkening of the color range. The translucent pastels of the famous coast give way to the opaque greens of interior Oahu. Crushed white coral gives way to red dirt, sugar dirt, deep red laterite soil that crumbles soft in the hand and films over grass and boots and hubcaps. Clouds mass over the Waianae Range. Cane fires smoke on the horizon and rain falls fitfully. BUY SOME COLLARD GREENS, reads a sign on a weathered frame grocery in Wahiawa, just across the two-lane bridge from the Schofield gate. MASSAGE PARLOR, CHECKS CASHED, 50TH STATE POOLROOM, HAPPY HOUR, CASH FOR CARS. Schofield Loan. Schofield Pawn. Schofield Sands Motor Lodge. Then, finally, Schofield itself, the Schofield we all know from James Jones's *From Here to Eternity*, the Schofield that is Home of the 25th 'Tropic Lightning' Infantry Division, formerly the Hawaii Division, James Jones's own division, Robert E. Lee Prewitt's division, Maggio's and Warden's and Stark's and Dynamite Holmes's division, *Fit to Fight, Trained to Win, Ready to Go. All Wars Are Won in the End by the Infantryman. Through These Portals Pass the Finest Soldiers in the World – 25TH INFANTRY DIVISION SOLDIERS. TROPIC LIGHTNING REENLISTMENT.* I have never driven into Schofield and seen those words without hearing the blues that end *From Here to Eternity*:

Got paid out on Monday
Not a dog soldier no more
They gimme all that money
So much my pockets is sore
More dough than I can use. Reenlistment Blues.
Ain't no time to lose. Reenlistment Blues.

Certain places seem to exist mainly because someone has written about them. Kilimanjaro belongs to Ernest Hemingway. Oxford, Mississippi, belongs to William Faulkner, and one hot July week in Oxford I was moved to spend an afternoon walking the graveyard looking for his stone, a kind of courtesy call on the owner of the property. A place belongs forever to whoever claims it hardest, remembers it most obsessively, wrenches it from itself, shapes it, renders it, loves it so radically that he remakes it in his image, and not only Schofield Barracks but a great deal of Honolulu itself has always belonged for me to James Jones. The first time I ever saw Hotel Street in Honolulu was on a Saturday night in 1966 when all the bars and tattoo parlors were full of military police and girls looking for a dollar and nineteen-year-olds, on their way to or from Saigon, looking for a girl. I recall looking that night for the particular places that had figured in *From Here to Eternity*: the Black Cat, the Blue Anchor, the whorehouse Jones called the New Congress Hotel. I remember driving up Wilhemina Rise to look for Alma's house and I remember walking out of the Royal Hawaiian Hotel and expecting to see Prewitt and Maggio sitting on the curb and I remember walking the Waialae Country Club golf course, trying to figure exactly where Prewitt died. I think it was in the trap near the fifth green.

It is hard to see one of these places claimed by fiction without a sudden blurring, a slippage, a certain vertiginous occlusion of the imagined and the real, and this slippage was particularly acute the last time I arrived in Honolulu, on a June day when the author of *From Here to Eternity* had been dead just a few weeks. In New York the death of James Jones had been the occasion for many considerations and reconsiderations. Many mean guilts had been recalled and exorcized. Many lessons had been divined, in both the death and the life. In Honolulu the death of James Jones had been marked by the publication, in the *Honolulu Star-Bulletin*, of an excerpt from the author's *Viet Journal*, the epilogue, the part in which he talked about returning to Honolulu in 1973 and looking for the places he had remembered in *From Here to Eternity* but had last seen in 1942, when he was twenty-one years old and shipped out for Guadalcanal with the 25th Division. In 1973 the five pillboxes on Makapuu Head had seemed to James Jones exactly as he had left them in 1942. In 1973 the Royal Hawaiian Hotel had seemed to James Jones less formidably rich than he had left it in 1942, and it had occurred to him with considerable poignance that he was a man in his fifties who could walk into the Royal Hawaiian and buy whatever he wanted.

He had bought a beer and gone back to Paris. In June of 1977 he was dead and it was not possible to buy a copy of his great novel, his living novel, the novel in which he so loved Honolulu that he remade it in his image, in any of Honolulu's largest bookstores. 'Is it a best-seller?' I was asked in one, and the golden child in charge of another suggested that I try the psychic-science shelf. In that instant I thought I grieved for James Jones, a man I never met, but I think I grieved for all of us: for Jones, for myself, for the sufferers of mean guilts and for their exorcists, for Robert E. Lee Prewitt, for the Royal Hawaiian Hotel and for this golden nitwit who believed eternity to be a psychic science.

I have never been sure whether the extreme gravity of *From Here to Eternity* is an exact reflection of the light at Schofield Barracks or whether I see the light as grave because I have read James Jones. 'It had rained all morning and then suddenly cleared at noon, and the air, freshly washed today, was like dark crystal in the sharp clarity and sombre focus it gave to every image.' It was in this sombre focus that James Jones rendered Schofield, and it was in this sombre focus that I last saw Schofield, one Monday during that June. It had rained in the morning and the smell of eucalyptus was sharp in the air and I had again that familiar sense of having left the bright coast and entered a darker country. The black outline of the Waianae Range seemed obscurely oppressive. A foursome on the post golf course seemed to have been playing since 1940, and to be doomed to continue. A soldier in fatigues appeared to be trimming a bougain-villea hedge, swinging at it with a scythe, but his movements were hypnotically slowed, and the scythe never quite touched the hedge. Around the tropical frame bungalows where the families of Schofield officers have always lived there was an occasional tricycle but no child, no wife, no sign of life but one: a Yorkshire terrier yapping on the lawn of a colonel's bungalow. As it happens I have spent time around Army posts in the role of an officer's child, have even played with lap dogs on the lawns of colonels' quarters, but I saw this Yorkshire with Prewitt's eyes, and I hated it.

I had driven out to Schofield in other seasons, but this trip was different. I was making this trip for the same reason I had walked the Oxford graveyard, a courtesy call on the owner. This trip I made appointments, spoke to people, asked questions and wrote down answers, had lunch with my hosts at the Aloha Lightning NCO Club and was shown the regimental trophies and studied the portraits of commanding officers in every corridor I walked down. Unlike the golden children in the Honolulu bookstores these men I met at Schofield, these men in green fatigues, all knew exactly who James Jones was and what he had written and even where he had slept and eaten and probably gotten drunk during the three years he spent at Schofield. They recalled the incidents and locations of *From Here to Eternity* in minute detail. They anticipated those places that I would of course want to see: D Quad, the old stockade, the stone quarry, Kolekole Pass. Some weeks before, there had been at the post theater a special screening of the movie *From Here to Eternity*, an event arranged by the Friends of the Tropic Lightning Historical Society, and everyone to whom I spoke at Schofield had turned out for this screening. Many of these men were careful to qualify their obvious attachment to James Jones's view of their life by pointing out that the Army had changed. Others did not mention the change. One, a young man who had re-upped once and now wanted out, mentioned that it had not changed at all. We were standing on the lawn in D Quad, Jones's quad, Robert E. Lee Prewitt's quad, and I was watching the idle movement around the square, a couple of soldiers dropping a basketball through a hoop, another cleaning an M-16, a desultory argument at the Dutch door of the supply room – when he volunteered a certain inchoate dissatisfaction with his six years in the 25th Division. 'I read this book *From Here to Eternity*,' he said, 'and they still got the same little games around here.'

I suppose everything had changed and nothing had. A mess hall was now called a 'dining facility,' but they still served chipped beef on toast and they still called it 'S.O.S.' A stockade was now called a 'confinement facility,' and the confinement facility for all military installations on Oahu was now at Pearl Harbor, but the old stockade at Schofield was now the headquarters for the military police, and during the time I was there the M.P.s brought in a handcuffed soldier, bare to the waist and shoeless. Investigators in aloha shirts chatted in the exercise yard. Office supplies were stored in some of the 'close confinement' cells, but there were still the plain wooden bunks, 'plate beds,' beds for those occasions, it was explained to me by a major who had once been in charge of the Schofield stockade, 'when a guy is completely berserk and starts ripping up his mattress.' On the wall there were still the diagrams detailing the order in which belongings were to be arranged: WHITE TOWEL, SOAP WITH DISH, DEODORANT, TOOTHPASTE, TOOTHBRUSH, COMB, SHAVING CREAM, RAZOR.

In many ways I found it difficult to leave Schofield that day. I had fallen into the narcoleptic movements of the Army day. I had picked up the liquid speech patterns of the Army voice. I took a copy of the *Tropic Lightning News* back into Honolulu with me, and read it that night in my hotel room. During the month of May the Schofield military police had reported 32 arrests for driving under the influence of alcohol, 115 arrests for possession of marijuana, and the theft of a number of items, including one Sansui amplifier, one Sansui pre-amp and tuner, one Kenwood receiver and turntable, two Bose speakers and the tachometer from a 1969 Ford Mustang. One private, two spec fours and one sergeant were asked in the 'Troop Talk' column to name their ideal, or favorite, post. One chose Fort Hood. Another chose Fort Sam Houston. None chose Schofield Barracks. In the letters column one correspondent advised a WAC who had objected to the shows at the NCO Club to stay home ('We once had it set up where you girls didn't have to see the entertainment, but the loverly libbers put an end to that'), and another advised 'barracks rats' to stop limiting their lives to 'erasing Army hatred by indulging in smoke or drink or listening to Peter Frampton at eighty decibels.' I thought about barracks rats and I thought about Prewitt and Maggio and I thought about Army hatred and it seemed to me that night in

Honolulu that only the details had changed, that James Jones had known a great simple truth: the Army was nothing more or less than life itself. I wish I could tell you that on the day in May when James Jones died someone had played a taps for him at Schofield Barracks, but I think this is not the way life goes.

1969–1977

In Hollywood

'You can take Hollywood for granted like I did,' Cecilia Brady tells the reader in *The Last Tycoon*, 'or you can dismiss it with the contempt we reserve for what we don't understand. It can be understood, too, but only dimly and in flashes. Not half a dozen men have ever been able to keep the whole equation of pictures in their heads.' To the extent that *The Last Tycoon* is 'about' Hollywood it is about not Monroe Stahr but Cecilia Brady, as anyone who understands the equation of pictures even dimly or in flashes would apprehend immediately: the Monroe Stahrs come and go, but the Cecilia Bradys are the second generation, the survivors, the inheritors of a community as intricate, rigid, and deceptive in its mores as any devised on this continent. At midwinter in the survivors' big houses off Benedict Canyon the fireplaces blaze all day with scrub oak and eucalyptus, the French windows are opened wide to the subtropical sun, the rooms filled with white phalaenopsis and cymbidium orchids and needlepoint rugs and the requisite scent of Rigaud candles. Dinner guests pick with vermeil forks at broiled fish and limestone lettuce *vinaigrette*, decline dessert, adjourn to the screening room, and settle down to *The Heartbreak Kid* with a little seltzer in a Baccarat glass.

After the picture the women, a significant number of whom seem to have ascended through chronic shock into an elusive dottiness, discuss for a ritual half-hour the transpolar movements of acquaintances and the peace of spirit to be derived from exercise class, ballet class, the use of paper napkins at the beach. Quentin Bell's *Virginia*

Woolf was an approved event this winter, as were the Chinese acrobats, the recent visits to Los Angeles of Bianca Jagger, and the opening in Beverly Hills of a branch of Bonwit Teller. The men talk pictures, grosses, the deal, the morning line on the talent. 'Face it,' I heard someone say the other night of a director whose current picture had opened a few days before to tepid business. 'Last week he was bankable.'

Such evenings end before midnight. Such couples leave together. Should there be marital unhappiness it will go unmentioned until one of the principals is seen lunching with a lawyer. Should there be illness it will go unadmitted until the onset of the terminal coma. Discretion is 'good taste,' and discretion is also good business, since there are enough imponderables in the business of Hollywood without handing the dice to players too distracted to concentrate on the action. This is a community whose notable excesses include virtually none of the flesh or spirit: heterosexual adultery is less easily tolerated than respectably settled homosexual marriages or well-managed liaisons between middle-aged women. 'A nice lesbian relationship, the most common thing in the world,' I recall Otto Preminger insisting when my husband and I expressed doubt that the heroine of the Preminger picture we were writing should have one. 'Very easy to arrange, does not threaten the marriage.'

Flirtations between men and women, like drinks after dinner, remain largely the luxury of character actors out from New York, one-shot writers, reviewers being courted by Industry people, and others who do not understand the *mise* of the local *scène*. In the houses of the inheritors the preservation of the community is paramount, and it is also Universal, Columbia, Fox, Metro, and Warner's. It is in this tropism toward survival that Hollywood sometimes presents the appearance of the last extant stable society.

One afternoon not long ago, at a studio where my husband was doing some work, the director of a picture in production collapsed of cardiac arrest. At six o'clock the director's condition was under discussion in the executives' steam room.

'I called the hospital,' the head of production for the studio said. 'I talked to his wife.'

'Hear what Dick did,' one of the other men in the steam room commanded. 'Wasn't that a nice thing for Dick to do.'

This story illustrates many elements of social reality in Hollywood, but few of the several non-Industry people to whom I have told it have understood it. For one thing it involves a 'studio,' and many people outside the Industry are gripped by the delusion that 'studios' have nothing to do with the making of motion pictures in modern times. They have heard the phrase 'independent production,' and have fancied that the phrase means what the words mean. They have been told about 'runaways,' about 'empty sound stages,' about 'death knell' after 'death knell' sounding for the Industry.

In fact the byzantine but very efficient economics of the business render such rhetoric even more meaningless than it sounds: the studios still put up almost all the money. The studios still control all effective distribution. In return for financing and distributing the average 'independent' picture, the studio gets not only the largest share (at least half) of any profit made by the picture, but, more significantly, 100 per cent of what the picture brings in up to a point called the 'break,' or break-even, an arbitrary figure usually set at 2.7 or 2.8 times the actual, or 'negative,' cost of the picture.

Most significant of all, the 'break-even' never represents the point at which the studio actually breaks even on any given production: that point occurs, except on paper, long before, since the studio has already received 10 to 25 per cent of the picture's budget as an 'overhead' charge, has received additional rental and other fees for any services actually rendered the production company, and continues to receive, throughout the picture's release, a fee amounting to about a third of the picture's income as a 'distribution' charge. In other words there is considerable income hidden in the risk itself, and the ideal picture from the studio's point of view is often said to be the picture that makes one dollar less than break-even. More perfect survival book-keeping has been devised, but mainly in Chicago and Las Vegas.

Still, it is standard for anyone writing about Hollywood to slip out of the economic reality and into a catchier metaphor, usually paleontological, *vide* John Simon: 'I shall not rehearse here the well-known facts of how the industry started dying from being too bulky, toothless, and dated – just like all those other saurians of a few aeons ago . . .' So pervasive is this vocabulary of extinction (Simon forgot the mandatory allusion to the La Brea Tar Pits) that I am frequently assured by visitors that the studios are 'morgues,' that they are 'shuttered up,' that in 'the new Hollywood' the 'studio has no power.' The studio has.

January in the last extant stable society. I know that it is January for an empirical fact only because wild mustard glazes the hills an acid yellow, and because there are poinsettias in front of all the bungalows down around Goldwyn and Technicolor, and because many people from Beverly Hills are at La Costa and Palm Springs and many people from New York are at the Beverly Hills Hotel.

'This whole town's dead,' one such New York visitor tells me. 'I dropped into the Polo Lounge last night, the place was a wasteland.' He tells me this every January, and every January I tell him that people who live and work here do not frequent hotel bars either before or after dinner, but he seems to prefer his version. On reflection I can think of only three non-Industry people in New York whose version of Hollywood corresponds at any point with the reality of the place, and they are Johanna Mankiewicz Davis, Jill Schary Robinson and Jean Stein vanden Heuvel, the daughters respectively of the late screenwriter Herman Mankiewicz; the producer and former production chief at Metro, Dore Schary; and the founder of the Music Corporation of America and Universal Pictures, Jules Stein. 'We don't go for strangers in Hollywood,' Cecilia Brady said.

Days pass. Visitors arrive, scout the Polo Lounge, and leave, confirmed in their conviction that they have penetrated an artfully camouflaged disaster area. The morning mail contains a statement from 20th Century-Fox on a picture in which my husband and I are supposed to have 'points,' or a percentage. The picture cost $1,367,224.57. It has so far grossed $947,494.86. The statement might suggest to the casual subtracter that the picture is about $400,000 short of breaking even, but this is not the case: the statement reports that the picture is $1,389,112.72 short of breaking even. '$1,389,112.72 unrecovered' is, literally, the bottom line.

In lieu of contemplating why a venture that cost a million-three and has recovered almost a million remains a million-three in the red, I decide to get my hair cut, pick up the trades, learn that *The Poseidon Adventure* is grossing four million dollars a week, that Adolph 'Papa' Zukor will celebrate his 100th birthday at a dinner sponsored by Paramount, and that James Aubrey, Ted Ashley and Freddie Fields rented a house together in Acapulco over Christmas. At this moment in the action, James Aubrey is Metro-Goldwyn-Mayer. Ted Ashley is Warner Brothers. Freddie Fields is Creative Management Associates, First Artists and the Directors Company. The players will change but the game will stay the same. The bottom line seems clear on the survival of Adolph 'Papa' Zukor, but not yet on that of James Aubrey, Ted Ashley and Freddie Fields.

'Listen, I got this truly beautiful story,' the man who cuts my hair says to me. 'Think about some new Dominique-Sanda-type unknown. *Comprenez* so far?'

So far *comprends*. The man who cuts my hair, like everyone else in the community, is looking for the action, the game, a few chips to lay down. Here in the grand casino no one needs capital. One needs only this truly beautiful story. Or maybe if no truly beautiful story comes to mind one needs $500 to go halves on a $1,000 option payment for someone else's truly beautiful but (face it) three-year-old property. (A book or a story is a 'property' only until the deal; after that it is 'the basic material,' as in 'I haven't read the basic material on *Gatsby*.') True, the casino is not now so wide open as it was in '69, summer and fall of '69 when every studio in town was narcotized by *Easy Rider*'s grosses and all that was needed to get a picture off the ground was the suggestion of a $750,000 budget, a low-cost NABET or even a nonunion crew, and this terrific 22-year-old kid director. As it turned out most of these pictures were shot as usual by IATSE rather than NABET crews and they cost as usual not seven-fifty but a million-two and many of them ended up unreleased, shelved. And so there was one very bad summer there, the hangover summer of 1970, when nobody could get past the gate without a commitment from Barbra Streisand.

That was the summer when all the terrific 22-year-old directors went back to shooting television commercials and all the creative 24-year-old producers used up the leases on their office space at

Warner Brothers by sitting out there in the dull Burbank sunlight smoking dope before lunch and running one another's unreleased pictures after lunch. But that period is over and the game is back on, development money available, the deal dependent only upon the truly beautiful story and the right elements. The elements matter. 'We like the *elements*,' they say at studios when they are maybe going to make the deal. That is why the man who cuts my hair is telling me his story. A writer might be an element. I listen because in certain ways I am a captive but willing audience, not only to the hairdresser but at the grand casino.

The place makes everyone a gambler. Its spirit is speedy, obsessive, immaterial. The action itself is the art form, and is described in aesthetic terms: 'A very imaginative deal,' they say, or, 'He writes the most creative deals in the business.' There is in Hollywood, as in all cultures in which gambling is the central activity, a lowered sexual energy, an inability to devote more than token attention to the preoccupations of the society outside. The action is everything, more consuming than sex, more immediate than politics; more important always than the acquisition of money, which is never, for the gambler, the true point of the exercise.

I talk on the telephone to an agent, who tells me that he has on his desk a check made out to a client for $1,275,000, the client's share of first profits on a picture now in release. Last week, in someone's office, I was shown another such check, this one made out for $4,850,000. Every year there are a few such checks around town. An agent will speak of such a check as being 'on my desk,' or 'on Guy McElwaine's desk,' as if the exact physical location lent the piece of paper its credibility. One year they might be the *Midnight Cowboy* and *Butch Cassidy* checks, another year the *Love Story* and *Godfather* checks.

In a curious way these checks are not 'real,' not real money in the sense that a check for a thousand dollars can be real money; no one 'needs' $4,850,000, nor is it really disposable income. It is instead the unexpected payoff on dice rolled a year or two before, and its reality is altered not only by the time lapse but by the fact that no one ever counted on the payoff. A four-million-dollar windfall has the aspect only of Monopoly money, but the actual pieces of paper which bear such figures have, in the community, a totemic significance. They are totems of the action. When I hear of these totems I think reflexively of Sergius O'Shaugnessy, who sometimes believed what he said and tried to take the cure in the very real sun of Desert D'Or with its cactus, its mountain, and the bright green foliage of its love and its money.

Since any survivor is believed capable in the community of conferring on others a ritual and lucky kinship, the birthday dinner for Adolph 'Papa' Zukor turns out also to have a totemic significance. It is described by Robert Evans, head of production at Paramount, as 'one of the memorable evenings in our Industry . . . There's never been anyone who's reached one hundred before.' Hit songs from old Paramount pictures are played throughout dinner. Jack Valenti speaks of the guest of honor as 'the motion picture world's living proof that there is a connection between us and our past.'

Zukor himself, who is described in Who's Who as a 'motion picture mfr.' and in Daily Variety as a 'firm believer in the philosophy that today is the first day of the rest of your life,' appears after dinner to express his belief in the future of motion pictures and his pleasure at Paramount's recent grosses. Many of those present have had occasion over the years to regard Adolph 'Papa' Zukor with some rancor, but on this night there is among them a resigned warmth, a recognition that they will attend one another's funerals. This ceremonial healing of old and recent scars is a way of life among the survivors, as is the scarring itself. 'Having some fun' is what the scarring is called. 'Let's go see Nick, I think we'll have some fun,' David O. Selznick remembered his father saying to him when the elder Selznick was on his way to tell Nick Schenk that he was going to take 50 per cent of the gross of Ben-Hur away from him.

The winter progresses. My husband and I fly to Tucson with our daughter for a few days of meetings on a script with a producer on location. We go out to dinner in Tucson: the sitter tells me that she has obtained, for her crippled son, an autographed picture of Paul Newman. I ask how old her son is. 'Thirty-four,' she says.

We came for two days, we stay for four. We rarely leave the Hilton

Inn. For everyone on the picture this life on location will continue for twelve weeks. The producer and the director collect Navajo belts and speak every day to Los Angeles, New York, London. They are setting up other deals, other action. By the time this picture is released and reviewed they will be on location in other cities. A picture in release is gone. A picture in release tends to fade from the minds of the people who made it. As the four-million-dollar check is only the totem of the action, the picture itself is in many ways only the action's by-product. 'We can have some fun with this one,' the producer says as we leave Tucson. 'Having some fun' is also what the action itself is called.

I pass along these notes by way of suggesting that much of what is written about pictures and about picture people approaches reality only occasionally and accidentally. At one time the assurance with which many writers about film palmed off their misconceptions puzzled me a good deal. I used to wonder how Pauline Kael, say, could slip in and out of such airy subordinate clauses as 'now that the studios are collapsing,' or how she could so misread the labyrinthine propriety of Industry evenings as to characterize 'Hollywood wives' as women 'whose jaws get a hard set from the nights when they sit soberly at parties waiting to take their sloshed geniuses home.' (This fancy, oddly enough, cropped up in a review of *Alex in Wonderland*, a Paul Mazursky picture which, whatever its faults, portrayed with meticulous accuracy that level of 'young' Hollywood on which the average daily narcotic intake is one glass of a three-dollar Mondavi white and two marijuana cigarettes shared by six people.) These 'sloshed' husbands and 'collapsing' studios derive less from Hollywood life than from some weird West Side *Playhouse 90* about Hollywood life, presumably the same one Stanley Kauffmann runs on his mind's screen when he speaks of a director like John Huston as 'corrupted by success.'

What is there to be said about this particular cast of mind? Some people who write about film seem so temperamentally at odds with what both Fellini and Truffaut have called the 'circus' aspect of making film that there is flatly no question of their ever apprehending the social or emotional reality of the process. In this connection I think particularly of Kauffmann, whose idea of a nasty disclosure about the circus is to reveal that the aerialist is up there to get our attention. I recall him advising his readers that Otto Preminger (the same Otto Preminger who cast Joseph Welch in *Anatomy of a Murder* and engaged Louis Nizer to write a script about the Rosenbergs) was a 'commercial showman,' and also letting them know that he was wise to the 'phoniness' in the chase sequence in *Bullitt*: 'Such a chase through the normal streets of San Francisco would have ended in deaths much sooner than it does.'

A curious thing about Kauffmann is that in both his dogged right-mindedness and his flatulent diction he is indistinguishable from many members of the Industry itself. He is a man who finds R. D. Laing 'blazingly humane.' Lewis Mumford is 'civilized and civilizing' and someone to whom we owe a 'long debt,' Arthur Miller a 'tragic agonist' hampered in his artistry only by 'the shackles of our time.' It is the vocabulary of the Jean Hersholt Humanitarian Award. Kauffmann divined in *Bullitt* not only its 'phoniness' but a 'possible propagandistic motive': 'to show (particularly to the young) that law and order are not necessarily Dullsville.' The 'motive' in *Bullitt* was to show that several million people would pay three dollars apiece to watch Steve McQueen drive fast, but Kauffmann, like my acquaintance who reports from the Polo Lounge, seems to prefer his version. 'People in the East pretend to be interested in how pictures are made,' Scott Fitzgerald observed in his notes on Hollywood. 'But if you actually tell them anything, you find . . . they never see the ventriloquist for the doll. Even the intellectuals, who ought to know better, like to hear about the pretensions, extravagances and vulgarities – tell them pictures have a private grammar, like politics or automobile production or society, and watch the blank look come into their faces.'

Of course there is good reason for this blank look, for this almost queasy uneasiness with pictures. To recognize that the picture is but the by-product of the action is to make rather more arduous the task of maintaining one's self-image as (Kauffmann's own job definition) 'a critic of new works.' Making judgments on films is in many ways so peculiarly vaporous an occupation that the only question is why, beyond the obvious opportunities for a few lecture fees and a little careerism at a dispiritingly self-limiting level, anyone does it in the first place. A finished picture defies all attempts to analyze what makes it work or not work: the responsibility for its every frame is clouded not only in the accidents and compromises of production but in the clauses of its financing. *The Getaway* was Sam Peckinpah's picture, but Steve McQueen had the 'cut,' or final right to edit. *Up the Sandbox* was Irvin Kershner's picture, but Barbra Streisand had the cut. In a series of interviews with directors, Charles Thomas Samuels asked Carol Reed why he had used the same cutter on so many pictures. 'I had no control,' Reed said. Samuels asked Vittorio De Sica if he did not find a certain effect in one of his Sophia Loren films a bit artificial. 'It was shot by the second unit,' De Sica said. 'I didn't direct it.' In other words, Carlo Ponti wanted it.

Nor does calling film a 'collaborative medium' exactly describe the situation. To read David O. Selznick's instructions to his directors, writers, actors and department heads in *Memo from David O. Selznick* is to come very close to the spirit of actually making a picture, a spirit not of collaboration but of armed conflict in which one antagonist has a contract assuring him nuclear capability. Some reviewers make a point of trying to understand whose picture it is by 'looking at the script': to understand whose picture it is one needs to look not particularly at the script but at the deal memo.

About the best a writer on film can hope to do, then, is to bring an engaging or interesting intelligence to bear upon the subject, a kind of *petit-point*-on-Kleenex effect which rarely stands much scrutiny. 'Motives' are inferred where none existed; allegations spun out of thin speculation. Perhaps the difficulty of knowing who made which choices in a picture makes this airiness so expedient that it eventually infects any writer who makes a career of reviewing; perhaps the initial error is in making a career of it. Reviewing motion pictures, like reviewing new cars, may or may not be a useful consumer service (since people respond to a lighted screen in a dark room in the same secret and powerfully irrational way they respond to most sensory stimuli, I tend to think much of it beside the point, but never mind that); the review of pictures has been, as well, a traditional diversion for writers whose actual work is somewhere else. Some 400 mornings spent at press screenings in the late Thirties were, for Graham Greene, an 'escape,' a way of life 'adopted quite voluntarily from a sense of fun.' Perhaps it is only when one inflates this sense of fun into (Kauffmann again) 'a continuing relation with an art' that one passes so headily beyond the reality principle.

February in the last extant stable society. A few days ago I went to lunch in Beverly Hills. At the next table were an agent and a director who should have been, at that moment, on his way to a location to begin a new picture. I knew what he was supposed to be doing because this picture had been talked about around town: six million dollars above the line. There was two million for one actor. There was a million and a quarter for another actor. The director was in for $800,000. The property had cost more than half a million; the first-draft screenplay $200,000, the second draft a little less. A third writer had been brought in, at $6,000 a week. Among the three writers were two Academy Awards and one New York Film Critics Award. The director had an Academy Award for his last picture but one.

And now the director was sitting at lunch in Beverly Hills and he wanted out. The script was not right. Only 38 pages worked, the director said. The financing was shaky. 'They're in breach, we all recognize your right to pull out,' the agent said carefully. The agent represented many of the principals, and did not want the director to pull out. On the other hand he also represented the director, and the director seemed unhappy. It was difficult to ascertain what anyone involved did want, except for the action to continue. 'You pull out,' the agent said, 'it dies right here, not that I want to influence your decision.' The director picked up the bottle of Margaux they were drinking and examined the label.

'Nice little red,' the agent said.

'Very nice.'

I left as the Sanka was being served. No decision had been reached. Many people have been talking these past few days about this aborted picture, always with a note of regret. It had been a very creative deal and they had run with it as far as they could run and they had had some fun and now the fun was over, as it also would have been had they made the picture.

1973

In Bed

Three, four, sometimes five times a month, I spend the day in bed with a migraine headache, insensible to the world around me. Almost every day of every month, between these attacks, I feel the sudden irrational irritation and the flush of blood into the cerebral arteries which tell me that migraine is on its way, and I take certain drugs to avert its arrival. If I did not take the drugs, I would be able to function perhaps one day in four. The physiological error called migraine is, in brief, central to the given of my life. When I was 15, 16, even 25, I used to think that I could rid myself of this error by simply denying it, character over chemistry. 'Do you have headaches *sometimes? frequently? never?*' the application forms would demand. 'Check one.' Wary of the trap, wanting whatever it was that the successful circumnavigation of that particular form could bring (a job, a scholarship, the respect of mankind and the grace of God), I would check one. '*Sometimes,*' I would lie. That in fact I spent one or two days a week almost unconscious with pain seemed a shameful secret, evidence not merely of some chemical inferiority but of all my bad attitudes, unpleasant tempers, wrongthink.

For I had no brain tumor, no eyestrain, no high blood pressure, nothing wrong with me at all: I simply had migraine headaches, and migraine headaches were, as everyone who did not have them knew, imaginary. I fought migraine then, ignored the warnings it sent, went to school and later to work in spite of it, sat through lectures in Middle English and presentations to advertisers with involuntary tears running down the right side of my face, threw up in washrooms, stumbled home by instinct, emptied ice trays onto my bed and tried to freeze the pain in my right temple, wished only for a neurosurgeon who would do a lobotomy on house call, and cursed my imagination.

It was a long time before I began thinking mechanistically enough to accept migraine for what it was: something with which I would be living, the way some people live with diabetes. Migraine is something more than the fancy of a neurotic imagination. It is an essentially hereditary complex of symptoms, the most frequently noted but by no means the most unpleasant of which is a vascular headache of blinding severity, suffered by a surprising number of women, a fair number of men (Thomas Jefferson had migraine, and so did Ulysses S. Grant, the day he accepted Lee's surrender), and by some unfortunate children as young as two years old. (I had my first when I was eight. It came on during a fire drill at the Columbia School in Colorado Springs, Colorado. I was taken first home and then to the infirmary at Peterson Field, where my father was stationed. The Air Corps doctor prescribed an enema.) Almost anything can trigger a specific attack of migraine: stress, allergy, fatigue, an abrupt change in barometric pressure, a contretemps over a parking ticket. A flashing light. A fire drill. One inherits, of course, only the predisposition. In other words I spent yesterday in bed with a headache not merely because of my bad attitudes, unpleasant tempers and wrongthink, but because both my grandmothers had migraine, my father has migraine and my mother has migraine.

No one knows precisely what it is that is inherited. The chemistry of migraine, however, seems to have some connection with the nerve hormone named serotonin, which is naturally present in the brain. The amount of serotonin in the blood falls sharply at the onset of migraine, and one migraine drug, methysergide, or Sansert, seems to have some effect on serotonin. Methysergide is a derivative of lysergic acid (in fact Sandoz Pharmaceuticals first synthesized LSD-25 while looking for a migraine cure), and its use is hemmed about with so many contraindications and side effects that most doctors prescribe it only in the most incapacitating cases. Methysergide, when it is prescribed, is taken daily, as a preventive; another preventive which works for some people is old-fashioned ergotamine tartrate, which helps to constrict the swelling blood vessels during the 'aura,' the period which in most cases precedes the actual headache.

Once an attack is under way, however, no drug touches it. Migraine gives some people mild hallucinations, temporarily blinds others, shows up not only as a headache but as a gastrointestinal disturbance, a painful sensitivity to all sensory stimuli, an abrupt overpowering fatigue, a strokelike aphasia, and a crippling inability to make even the most routine connections. When I am in a migraine aura (for some people the aura lasts fifteen minutes, for others several hours), I will drive through red lights, lose the house keys, spill whatever I am holding, lose the ability to focus my eyes or frame coherent sentences, and generally give the appearance of being on drugs, or drunk. The actual headache, when it comes, brings with it chills, sweating, nausea, a debility that seems to stretch the very limits of endurance. That no one dies of migraine seems, to someone deep into an attack, an ambiguous blessing.

My husband also has migraine, which is unfortunate for him but fortunate for me: perhaps nothing so tends to prolong an attack as the accusing eye of someone who has never had a headache. 'Why not take a couple of aspirin,' the unafflicted will say from the doorway, or 'I'd have a headache, too, spending a beautiful day like this inside with all the shades drawn.' All of us who have migraine suffer not only from the attacks themselves but from this common conviction that we are perversely refusing to cure ourselves by taking a couple of aspirin, that we are making ourselves sick, that we 'bring it on ourselves.' And in the most immediate sense, the sense of why we have a headache this Tuesday and not last Thursday, of course we often do. There certainly is what doctors call a 'migraine personality,' and that personality tends to be ambitious, inward, intolerant of error, rather rigidly organized, perfectionist. 'You don't look like a migraine personality,' a doctor once said to me. 'Your hair's messy. But I suppose you're a compulsive housekeeper.' Actually my house is kept even more negligently than my hair, but the doctor was right nonetheless: perfectionism can also take the form of spending most of a week writing and rewriting and not writing a single paragraph.

But not all perfectionists have migraine, and not all migrainous people have migraine personalities. We do not escape heredity. I have tried in most of the available ways to escape my own migrainous heredity (at one point I learned to give myself two daily injections of histamine with a hypodermic needle, even though the needle so frightened me that I had to close my eyes when I did it), but I still have migraine. And I have learned now to live with it, learned when to expect it, how to outwit it, even how to regard it, when it does come, as more friend than lodger. We have reached a certain understanding, my migraine and I. It never comes when I am in real trouble. Tell me that my house is burned down, my husband has left me, that there is gunfighting in the streets and panic in the banks, and I will not respond by getting a headache. It comes instead when I am fighting not an open but a guerrilla war with my own life, during weeks of small household confusions, lost laundry, unhappy help, canceled appointments, on days when the telephone rings too much and I get no work done and the wind is coming up. On days like that my friend comes uninvited.

And once it comes, now that I am wise in its ways, I no longer fight it. I lie down and let it happen. At first every small apprehension is magnified, every anxiety a pounding terror. Then the pain comes, and I concentrate only on that. Right there is the usefulness of migraine, there in that imposed yoga, the concentration on the pain. For when the pain recedes, ten or twelve hours later, everything goes with it, all the hidden resentments, all the vain anxieties. The migraine has acted as a circuit breaker, and the fuses have emerged intact. There is a pleasant convalescent euphoria. I open the windows and feel the air, eat gratefully, sleep well. I notice the particular nature of a flower in a glass on the stair landing. I count my blessings.

1968

On the Road

Where are we heading, they asked in all the television and radio studios. They asked it in New York and Los Angeles and they asked it in Boston and Washington and they asked it in Dallas and Houston and Chicago and San Francisco. Sometimes they made eye contact as they asked it. Sometimes they closed their eyes as they asked it. Quite often they wondered not just where we were heading but where we were heading 'as Americans,' or 'as concerned Americans,' or 'as American women,' or, on one occasion, 'as the American guy and the American woman.' I never learned the answer, nor did the answer matter, for one of the eerie and liberating aspects of broadcast discourse is that nothing one says will alter in the slightest either the form or the length of the conversation. Our voices in the studios were those of manic actors assigned to do three-minute, four-minute, seven-minute improvs. Our faces on the monitors were those of concerned Americans. On my way to one of those studios in Boston I had seen the magnolias bursting white down Marlborough Street. On my way to another in Dallas I had watched the highway lights blazing and dimming pink against the big dawn sky. Outside one studio in Houston the afternoon heat was sinking into the deep primeval green of the place and outside the next, that night in Chicago, snow fell and glittered in the lights along the lake. Outside all these studios America lay in all its exhilaratingly volatile weather and eccentricity and specificity, but inside the studios we shed the specific and rocketed on to the general, for they were The Interviewers and I was The Author and the single question we seemed able to address together was *where are we heading*.

'8:30 A.M. to 9:30 A.M.: LIVE on WFSB TV/THIS MORNING.
'10 A.M. to 10:30 A.M.: LIVE on WINF AM/THE WORLD TODAY.
'10:45 A.M. to 11:55 A.M.: PRESS INTERVIEW with HARTFORD COURANT.
'12 noon to 1:30 P.M.: AUTOGRAPHING at BARNES AND NOBLE.
'2 P.M. to 2:30 P.M.: TAPE at WDRC AM/FM.
'3 P.M. to 3:30 P.M.: PRESS INTERVIEW with THE HILL INK.
'7:30 P.M. to 9 P.M.: TAPE at WHNB TV/WHAT ABOUT WOMEN.'

From 12 noon to 1:30 P.M., that first day in Hartford, I talked to a man who had cut a picture of me from a magazine in 1970 and had come round to Barnes and Noble to see what I looked like in 1977. From 2 P.M. to 2:30 P.M., that first day in Hartford, I listened to the receptionists at WDRC AM/FM talk about the new records and I watched snow drop from the pine boughs in the cemetery across the street. The name of the cemetery was Mt St Benedict and my husband's father had been buried there. 'Any Steely Dan come in?' the receptionists kept asking. From 8:30 A.M. until 9 P.M., that first day in Hartford, I neglected to mention the name of the book I was supposed to be promoting. It was my fourth book but I had never before done what is called in the trade a book tour. I was not sure what I was doing or why I was doing it. I had left California equipped with two 'good' suits, a box of unanswered mail, Elizabeth Hardwick's *Seduction and Betrayal*, Edmund Wilson's *To the Finland Station*, six Judy Blume books and my eleven-year-old daughter. The Judy Blume books were along to divert my daughter. My daughter was along to divert me. Three days into the tour I sent home the box of unanswered mail to make room for a packet of Simon and Schuster press releases describing me in favorable terms. Four days into the tour I sent home *Seduction and Betrayal* and *To the Finland Station* to make room for a thousand-watt hair blower. By the time I reached Boston, ten days into the tour, I knew that I had never before heard and would possibly never again hear America singing at precisely this pitch: ethereal, speedy, an angel choir on Dexamyl.

Where were we heading. The set for this discussion was always the same: a cozy oasis of wicker and ferns in the wilderness of cables and cameras and Styrofoam coffee cups that was the actual studio. On wicker settees across the nation I expressed my conviction that we were heading 'into an era' of whatever the clock seemed to demand. In green rooms across the nation I listened to other people talk about where we were heading, and also about their vocations, avocations, and secret interests. I discussed L-dopa and biorhythm with a woman whose father invented prayer breakfasts. I exchanged makeup tips with a former Mouseketeer. I stopped reading newspapers and started relying on bulletins from limo drivers, from Mouseketeers, from the callers-in on call-in shows and from the closed-circuit screens in airports that flashed random stories off the wire ('CARTER URGES BARBITURATE BAN' is one that got my attention at La Guardia) between advertisements for *Shenandoah*. I gravitated to the random. I swung with the nonsequential.

I began to see America as my own, a child's map over which my child and I could skim and light at will. We spoke not of cities but of airports. If rain fell at Logan we could find sun at Dulles. Bags lost at O'Hare could be found at Dallas/Fort Worth. In the first-class cabins of the planes on which we traveled we were often, my child and I, the only female passengers, and I apprehended for the first time those particular illusions of mobility which power American business. Time was money. Motion was progress. Decisions were snap and the ministrations of other people were constant. Room service, for example, assumed paramount importance. We needed, my eleven-year-old and I, instant but erratically timed infusions of consommé, oatmeal, crab salad and asparagus vinaigrette. We needed Perrier water and tea to drink when we were working. We needed bourbon on the rocks and Shirley Temples to drink when we were not. A kind of irritable panic came over us when room service went off, and also when no one answered in the housekeeping department. In short we had fallen into the peculiar hormonal momentum of business travel, and I had begun to understand the

habituation many men and a few women have to planes and telephones and schedules. I had begun to regard my own schedule – a
sheaf of thick cream-colored pages printed with the words 'SIMON
& SCHUSTER/A DIVISION OF GULF & WESTERN CORPOR-
ATION' – with a reverence approaching the mystical. We wanted
24-hour room service. We wanted direct-dial telephones. We wanted
to stay on the road forever.

We saw air as our element. In Houston the air was warm and rich
and suggestive of fossil fuel and we pretended we owned a house in
River Oaks. In Chicago the air was brilliant and thin and we pretended we owned the 27th floor of the Ritz. In New York the air
was charged and crackling and shorting out with opinions, and we
pretended we had some. Everyone in New York had opinions.
Opinions were demanded in return. The absence of opinion was
construed as opinion. Even my daughter was developing opinions.
'Had an interesting talk with Carl Bernstein,' she noted in the log
she had been assigned to keep for her fifth-grade teacher in Malibu,
California. Many of these New York opinions seemed intended as
tonic revisions, bold corrections to opinions in vogue during the
previous week, but since I had just dropped from the sky it was
difficult for me to distinguish those opinions which were 'bold' and
'revisionist' from those which were merely 'weary' and 'rote.' At the
time I left New York many people were expressing a bold belief in
'joy' – joy in children, joy in wedlock, joy in the dailiness of life –
but joy was trickling down fast to show-business personalities. Mike
Nichols, for example, was expressing his joy in the pages of *Newsweek*,
and also his weariness with 'lapidary bleakness.' Lapidary bleakness
was definitely rote.

We were rethinking the Sixties that week, or Morris Dickstein was.

We were taking another look at the Fifties that week, or Hilton
Kramer was.

I agreed passionately. I disagreed passionately. I called room service on one phone and listened attentively on the other to people
who seemed convinced that the 'texture' of their lives had been
agreeably or adversely affected by conversion to the politics of joy,
by regression to lapidary bleakness, by the Sixties, by the Fifties, by

the recent change in administrations and by the sale of *The Thorn Birds* to paper for one-million-nine.

I lost track of information.

I was blitzed by opinion.

I began to see opinions arcing in the air, intersecting flight patterns. The Eastern shuttle was cleared for landing and so was lapidary bleakness. John Leonard and joy were on converging vectors. I began to see the country itself as a projection on air, a kind of hologram, an invisible grid of image and opinion and electronic impulse. There were opinions in the air and there were planes in the air and there were even people in the air: one afternoon in New York my husband saw a man jump from a window and fall to the sidewalk outside the Yale Club. I mentioned this to a *Daily News* photographer who was taking my picture. 'You have to catch a jumper in the act to make the paper,' he advised me. He had caught two in the act but only the first had made the paper. The second was a better picture but coincided with the crash of a DC-10 at Orly. 'They're all over town,' the photographer said. 'Jumpers. A lot of them aren't even jumpers. They're window washers. Who fall.'

What does that say about us as a nation, I was asked the next day when I mentioned the jumpers and window washers on the air. *Where are we headed.* On the 27th floor of the Ritz in Chicago my daughter and I sat frozen at the breakfast table until the window washers glided safely out of sight. At a call-in station in Los Angeles I was told by the guard that there would be a delay because they had a jumper on the line. 'I say let him jump,' the guard said to me. I imagined a sky dense with jumpers and fallers and DC-10s. I held my daughter's hand at takeoff and landing and watched for antennae on the drive into town. The big antennae with the pulsing red lights had been for a month our landmarks. The big antennae with the pulsing red lights had in fact been for a month our destinations. 'Out 1–10 to the antenna' was the kind of direction we had come to understand, for we were on the road, on the grid, on the air and also in it. *Where were we heading.* I don't know where you're heading, I said in the studio attached to the last of these antennae, my eyes fixed on still another of the neon FLEETWOOD MAC signs that flickered that spring in radio stations from coast to coast, but I'm heading home.

1977

On the Mall

They float on the landscape like pyramids to the boom years, all those Plazas and Malls and Esplanades. All those Squares and Fairs. All those Towns and Dales, all those Villages, all those Forests and Parks and Lands. Stonestown. Hillsdale. Valley Fair, Mayfair, Northgate, Southgate, Eastgate, Westgate. Gulfgate. They are toy garden cities in which no one lives but everyone consumes, profound equalizers, the perfect fusion of the profit motive and the egalitarian ideal, and to hear their names is to recall words and phrases no longer quite current. Baby Boom. Consumer Explosion. Leisure Revolution. Do-It-Yourself Revolution. Backyard Revolution. Suburbia. 'The Shopping Center,' the Urban Land Institute could pronounce in 1957, 'is today's extraordinary retail business evolvement . . . The automobile accounts for suburbia, and suburbia accounts for the shopping center.'

It was a peculiar and visionary time, those years after World War II to which all the Malls and Towns and Dales stand as climate-controlled monuments. Even the word 'automobile,' as in 'the automobile accounts for suburbia and suburbia accounts for the shopping center,' no longer carries the particular freight it once did: as a child in the late Forties in California I recall reading and believing that the 'freedom of movement' afforded by the automobile was 'America's fifth freedom.' The trend was up. The solution was in sight. The frontier had been reinvented, and its shape was the subdivision, that new free land on which all settlers could recast their lives *tabula rasa*. For one perishable moment there the American idea seemed about to achieve itself, via F.H.A. housing and the acquisition of major appliances, and a certain enigmatic glamour attached to the architects of this newfound land. They made something of nothing. They gambled and sometimes lost. They staked the past to seize the future. I have difficulty now imagining a childhood in which a man named Jere Strizek, the developer of Town and Country Village outside Sacramento (143,000 square feet gross floor area, 68 stores, 1000 parking spaces, the Urban Land Institute's 'prototype for centers using heavy timber and tile construction for informality'), could materialize as a role model, but I had such a childhood, just after World War II, in Sacramento. I never met or even saw Jere Strizek, but at the age of 12 I imagined him a kind of frontiersman, a romantic and revolutionary spirit, and in the indigenous grain he was.

I suppose James B. Douglas and David D. Bohannon were too.

I first heard of James B. Douglas and David D. Bohannon not when I was 12 but a dozen years later, when I was living in New York, working for *Vogue*, and taking, by correspondence, a University of California Extension course in shopping-center theory. This did not seem to me eccentric at the time. I remember sitting on the cool floor in Irving Penn's studio and reading, in *The Community Builders Handbook*, advice from James B. Douglas on shopping-center financing. I recall staying late in my pale-blue office on the twentieth floor of the Graybar Building to memorize David D. Bohannon's parking ratios. My 'real' life was to sit in this office and describe life as it was lived in Djakarta and Caneel Bay and in the great châteaux of the Loire Valley, but my dream life was to put together a Class-A regional shopping center with three full-line department stores as major tenants.

That I was perhaps the only person I knew in New York, let alone on the Condé Nast floors of the Graybar Building, to have memorized the distinctions among 'A,' 'B,' and 'C' shopping centers did not occur to me (the defining distinction, as long as I have your attention, is that an 'A,' or 'regional,' center has as its major tenant a full-line department store which carries major appliances; a 'B,' or 'community,' center has as its major tenant a junior department store which does not carry major appliances; and a 'C,' or 'neighborhood,' center has as its major tenant only a supermarket): my interest in shopping centers was in no way casual. I did want to build them. I wanted to build them because I had fallen into the habit of writing fiction, and I had it in my head that a couple of good centers might support this habit less taxingly than a pale-blue office at *Vogue*. I had even devised an original scheme by which I planned to gain enough capital and credibility to enter the shopping-center game: I would lease warehouses in, say, Queens, and offer Manhattan delicatessens the opportunity to sell competitively by buying cooperatively, from my trucks. I see a few wrinkles in this scheme now (the words 'concrete overcoat' come to mind), but I did not then. In fact I planned to run it out of the pale-blue office.

James B. Douglas and David D. Bohannon. In 1950 James B. Douglas had opened Northgate, in Seattle, the first regional center to combine a pedestrian mall with an underground truck tunnel. In 1954 David D. Bohannon had opened Hillsdale, a forty-acre regional center on the peninsula south of San Francisco. That is the only solid bio I have on James B. Douglas and David D. Bohannon to this day, but many of their opinions are engraved on my memory. David D. Bohannon believed in preserving the integrity of the shopping center by not cutting up the site with any dedicated roads. David D. Bohannon believed that architectural setbacks in a center looked 'pretty on paper' but caused 'customer resistance.' James B. Douglas advised that a small-loan office could prosper in a center only if it was placed away from foot traffic, since people who want small loans do not want to be observed getting them. I do not now recall whether it was James B. Douglas or David D. Bohannon or someone else altogether who passed along this hint on how to paint the lines around the parking spaces (actually this is called 'striping the lot,' and the spaces are 'stalls'): make each space a foot wider than it need be – ten feet, say, instead of nine – when the center first opens and business is slow. By this single stroke the developer achieves a couple of important objectives, the appearance of a popular center and the illusion of easy parking, and no one will really notice when business picks up and the spaces shrink.

Nor do I recall who first solved what was once a crucial center dilemma: the placement of the major tenant vis-à-vis the parking lot. The dilemma was that the major tenant – the draw, the raison d'être for the financing, the Sears, the Macy's, the May Company – wanted its customer to walk directly from car to store. The smaller tenants, on the other hand, wanted that same customer to *pass their stores* on the way from the car to, say, Macy's. The solution to this conflict of interests was actually very simple: *two major tenants*, one at each end of a mall. This is called 'anchoring the mall,' and represents seminal work in shopping-center theory. One thing you will note about shopping-center theory is that you could have thought of it yourself, and a course in it will go a long way toward dispelling the notion that business proceeds from mysteries too recondite for you and me.

A few aspects of shopping-center theory do in fact remain impenetrable to me. I have no idea why the Community Builders' Council ranks 'Restaurant' as deserving a Number One (or 'Hot Spot') location but exiles 'Chinese Restaurant' to a Number Three, out there with 'Power and Light Office' and 'Christian Science Reading Room.' Nor do I know why the Council approves of enlivening a mall with 'small animals' but specifically, vehemently, and with no further explanation, excludes 'monkeys.' If I had a center I would have monkeys, and Chinese restaurants, and Mylar kites and bands of small girls playing tambourine.

A few years ago at a party I met a woman from Detroit who told me that the Joyce Carol Oates novel with which she identified most closely was *Wonderland*.

I asked her why.

'Because,' she said, 'my husband has a branch there.'

I did not understand.

'In Wonderland the center,' the woman said patiently. 'My husband has a branch in Wonderland.'

I have never visited Wonderland but imagine it to have bands of small girls playing tambourine.

*   *   *

A few facts about shopping centers.

The 'biggest' center in the United States is generally agreed to be Woodfield, outside Chicago, a 'super' regional or 'leviathan' two-million-square-foot center with four major tenants.

The 'first' shopping center in the United States is generally agreed to be Country Club Plaza in Kansas City, built in the Twenties. There were some other early centers, notably Edward H. Bouton's 1907 Roland Park in Baltimore, Hugh Prather's 1931 Highland Park Shopping Village in Dallas, and Hugh Potter's 1937 River Oaks in Houston, but the developer of Country Club Plaza, the late J. C. Nichols, is referred to with ritual frequency in the literature of shopping centers, usually as 'pioneering J. C. Nichols,' 'trailblazing J. C. Nichols,' or 'J. C. Nichols, father of the center as we know it.'

Those are some facts I know about shopping centers because I still want to be Jere Strizek or James B. Douglas or David D. Bohannon. Here are some facts I know about shopping centers because I never will be Jere Strizek or James B. Douglas or David D. Bohannon: a good center in which to spend the day if you wake feeling low in Honolulu, Hawaii, is Ala Moana, major tenants Liberty House and Sears. A good center in which to spend the day if you wake feeling low in Oxnard, California, is The Esplanade, major tenants the May Company and Sears. A good center in which to spend the day if you wake feeling low in Biloxi, Mississippi, is Edgewater Plaza, major tenant Godchaux's. Ala Moana in Honolulu is larger than The Esplanade in Oxnard, and The Esplanade in Oxnard is larger than Edgewater Plaza in Biloxi. Ala Moana has carp pools. The Esplanade and Edgewater Plaza do not.

These marginal distinctions to one side, Ala Moana, The Esplanade, and Edgewater Plaza are the same place, which is precisely their role not only as equalizers but in the sedation of anxiety. In each of them one moves for a while in an aqueous suspension not only of light but of judgment, not only of judgment but of 'personality.' One meets no acquaintances at The Esplanade. One gets no telephone calls at Edgewater Plaza. 'It's a hard place to run in to for a pair of stockings,' a friend complained to me recently of Ala Moana, and I knew that she was not yet ready to surrender her ego to the idea of the center. The last time I went to Ala Moana it was to buy *The New York Times*. Because *The New York Times* was not in, I sat on the mall for a while and ate caramel corn. In the end I bought not *The New York Times* at all but two straw hats at Liberty House, four bottles of nail enamel at Woolworth's, and a toaster, on sale at Sears. In the literature of shopping centers these would be described as impulse purchases, but the impulse here was obscure. I do not wear hats, nor do I like caramel corn. I do not use nail enamel. Yet flying back across the Pacific I regretted only the toaster.

1975

In Bogotá

On the Colombian coast it was hot, fevered, eleven degrees off the equator with evening trades that did not relieve but blew hot and dusty. The sky was white, the casino idle. I had never meant to leave the coast but after a week of it I began to think exclusively of Bogotá, floating on the Andes an hour away by air. In Bogotá it would be cool. In Bogotá one could get *The New York Times* only two days late and the *Miami Herald* only one day late and also emeralds, and bottled water. In Bogotá there would be fresh roses in the bathrooms at the Hotel Tequendama and hot water twenty-four hours a day and numbers to be dialed for chicken sandwiches from room service and Xerox *rápido* and long-distance operators who could get Los Angeles in ten minutes. In my room in Cartagena I would wake to the bleached coastal morning and find myself repeating certain words and phrases under my breath, an incantation: *Bogotá, Bacatá*. El Dorado. Emeralds. Hot water. Madeira consommé in cool dining rooms. *Santa Fé de Bogotá del Nuevo Reino de Granada de las Indias del Mar Océano*. The Avianca flight to Bogotá left Cartagena every morning at ten-forty, but such was the slowed motion of the coast that it took me another four days to get on it.

Maybe that is the one true way to see Bogotá, to have it float in the mind until the need for it is visceral, for the whole history of the place has been to seem a mirage, a delusion on the high savannah, its gold and its emeralds unattainable, inaccessible, its isolation so splendid and unthinkable that the very existence of a city astonishes. There on the very spine of the Andes gardeners espalier roses on embassy walls. Swarms of little girls in proper navy-blue school blazers line up to enter the faded tent of a tatty traveling circus: the elephant, the strong man, the tattooed man from Maracaibo. I arrived in Bogotá on a day in 1973 when the streets seemed bathed in mist and thin brilliant light and in the amplified pop voice of Nelson Ned, a Brazilian dwarf whose records played in every *disco* storefront. Outside the sixteenth-century Church of San Francisco, where the Spanish viceroys took office when the country was Nueva Granada and where Simón Bolívar assumed the presidency of the doomed republic called Gran Colombia, small children and old women hawked Cuban cigars and cartons of American cigarettes and newspapers with the headline 'JACKIE Y ARI.' I lit a candle for my daughter and bought a paper to read about Jackie and Ari, how the princess *de los norteamericanos* ruled the king of the Greek sea by demanding of him pink champagne every night and *medialunas* every morning, a story a child might invent. Later, in the Gold Museum of the Banco de la República, I looked at the gold the Spaniards opened the Americas to get, the vision of El Dorado which was to animate a century and is believed to have begun here, outside Bogotá, at Lake Guatavita. 'Many golden offerings were cast into the lake,' wrote the anthropologist Olivia Vlahos of the nights when the Chibcha Indians lit bonfires on the Andes and confirmed their rulers at Guatavita.

> *Many more were heaped on a raft . . . Then into the firelight stepped the ruler-to-be, his nakedness coated with a sticky resin. Onto the resin his priests applied gold dust and more gold dust until he gleamed like a golden statue. He stepped onto the raft, which was cut loose to drift into the middle of the lake. Suddenly he dived into the black water. When he emerged, the gold was gone, washed clean from his body. And he was king.*

Until the Spaniards heard the story, and came to find El Dorado for themselves. 'One thing you must understand,' a young Colombian said to me at dinner that night. We were at Eduardo's out in the Chico district and the piano player was playing 'Love Is Blue' and we were drinking an indifferent bottle of Château Léoville-Poyferré which cost $20 American. 'Spain sent all its highest aristocracy to South America.' In fact I had heard variations on this hallucination before, on the coast: when Colombians spoke about the past I often had the sense of being in a place where history tended to sink, even as it happened, into the traceless solitude of autosuggestion. The princess was drinking pink champagne. High in the mountains the men were made of gold. Spain sent its highest aristocracy to South America. They were all stories a child might invent.

Many years later, as he faced the firing squad, Colonel Aureliano Buendía was to remember that distant afternoon when his father took him to discover ice.

– The opening line of *One Hundred Years of Solitude*,
by the Colombian novelist Gabriel García Márquez.

At the big movie theaters in Bogotá in the spring of 1973 *The Professionals* was playing, and *It's a Mad Mad Mad Mad World*, two American pictures released in, respectively, 1967 and 1964. The English-language racks of paperback stands were packed with Edmund Wilson's *The Cold War and the Income Tax*, the 1964 Signet edition. This slight but definite dislocation of time fixed on the mind the awesome isolation of the place, as did dislocations of other kinds. On the fourth floor of the glossy new Bogotá Hilton one could lunch in an orchid-filled gallery that overlooked the indoor swimming pool, and also overlooked a shantytown of packing-crate and tin-can shacks where a small boy, his body hideously scarred and his face obscured by a knitted mask, played listlessly with a yo-yo. In the lobby of the Hotel Tequendama two Braniff stewardesses in turquoise-blue Pucci pantsuits flirted desultorily with a German waiting for the airport limousine; a third ignored the German and stood before a relief map on which buttons could be pressed to light up the major cities of Colombia. Santa Marta, on the coast; Barranquilla, Cartagena. Medellín, on the Central Cordillera. Cali, on the Cauca River, San Agustín on the Magdalena. Leticia, on the Amazon.

I watched her press the buttons one by one, transfixed by the vast darkness each tiny bulb illumined. The light for Bogotá blinked twice and went out. The girl in the Pucci pantsuit traced the Andes with her index finger. *Alto arrecife de la aurora humana*, the Chilean poet Pablo Neruda called the Andes. *High reef of the human dawn.* It cost the *conquistador* Gonzalo Jiménez de Quesada two years and the health of most of his men to reach Bogotá from the coast. It cost me $26.

'I knew they were your bags,' the man at the airport said, producing them triumphantly from a moraine of baggage and cartons and rubble from the construction that seemed all over Bogotá a chronic condition. 'They smelled American.' *Parece una turista norteamericana,* I read about myself in *El Espectador* a few mornings later. She resembles an American tourist. In fact I was aware of being an American in Colombia in a way I had not been in other places. I kept running into Americans, compatriots for whom the emotional center of Bogotá was the massive concrete embassy on Carrera 10, members of a phantom colony called 'the American presence' which politesse prevented them from naming out loud. Several times I met a young American who ran an 'information' office, which he urged me to visit; he had extremely formal manners, appeared for the most desultory evening in black tie, and was, according to the Colombian I asked, CIA. I recall talking at a party to a USIS man who spoke in a low mellifluous voice of fevers he had known, fevers in Sierra Leone, fevers in Monrovia, fevers on the Colombian coast. Our host interrupted this litany, demanded to know why the ambassador had not come to the party. 'Little situation in Cali,' the USIS man said, and smiled professionally. He seemed very concerned that no breach of American manners be inferred, and so, absurdly, did I. We had nothing in common except the eagles on our passports, but those eagles made us, in some way I did not entirely understand, co-conspirators, two strangers heavy with responsibility for seeing that the eagle should not offend. We would prefer the sweet local Roman-Cola to the Coca-Cola the Colombians liked. We would think of Standard Oil as Esso Colombiano. We would not speak of fever except to one another. Later I met an American actor who had spent two weeks taking cold showers in Bogotá before he discovered that the hot and cold taps in the room assigned him were simply reversed: he had never asked, he said, because he did not want to be considered an arrogant *gringo*.

*   *   *

In *El Tiempo* that morning I had read that General Gustavo Rojas Pinilla, who took over Colombia in a military coup in 1953 and closed down the press before he was overthrown in 1957, was launching a new bid for power on a Peronist platform, and I had thought that perhaps people at the party would be talking about that, but they were not. Why had the American film industry not made films about the Vietnam War, was what the Colombian stringer for the Caribbean newspaper wanted to talk about. The young Colombian filmmakers looked at him incredulously. 'What would be the point,' one finally shrugged. 'They run that war on television.'

The filmmakers had lived in New York, spoke of Rip Torn, Norman Mailer, Ricky Leacock, Super 8. One had come to the party in a stovepipe preacher's hat; another in a violet macramé shawl to the knees. The girl with them, a famous beauty from the coast, wore a flamingo-pink sequinned midriff, and her pale red hair was fluffed around her head in an electric halo. She watched the *cumbia* dancers and fondled a baby ocelot and remained impassive both to the possibility of General Gustavo Rojas Pinilla's comeback and to the question of why the American film industry had not made films about the Vietnam War. Later, outside the gate, the filmmakers lit thick marijuana cigarettes in view of the uniformed *policia* and asked if I knew Paul Morrissey's and Andy Warhol's address in Rome. The girl from the coast cradled her ocelot against the wind.

Of the time I spent in Bogotá I remember mainly images, indelible but difficult to connect. I remember the walls on the second floor of the Museo Nacional, white and cool and lined with portraits of the presidents of Colombia, a great many presidents. I remember the emeralds in shop windows, lying casually in trays, all of them oddly pale at the center, somehow watered, cold at the very heart where one expects the fire. I asked the price of one: 'Twenty-thousand American,' the woman said. She was reading a booklet called *Horós-copo: Sagitario* and did not look up. I remember walking across Plaza Bolívar, the great square from which all Colombian power emanates, at midafternoon when men in dark European suits stood talking on the steps of the Capitol and the mountains floated all around, their perspective made fluid by sun and shadow; I remember the way the mountains dwarfed a deserted Ferris wheel in the Parque Nacional in late afternoon.

In fact the mountains loom behind every image I remember, and perhaps are themselves the connection. Some afternoons I would drive out along their talus slopes through the Chico district, out Carrera 7 where the grounds of the great houses were immaculately clipped and the gates bore brass plaques with the names of European embassies and American foundations and Argentinian neurologists. I recall stopping in El Chico to make a telephone call one day, from a small shopping center off Carrera 7; the shopping center adjoined a church where a funeral mass had just taken place. The mourners were leaving the church, talking on the street, the women, most of them, in black pantsuits and violet-tinted glasses and pleated silk dresses and Givenchy coats that had not been bought in Bogotá. In El Chico it did not seem so far to Paris or New York, but there remained the mountains, and beyond the mountains that dense world described by Gabriel García Márquez as so recent that many things lacked names.

And even just a little farther, out where Carrera 7 became the Carretera Central del Norte, the rutted road that plunged through the mountains to Tunja and eventually to Caracas, it was in many ways a perpetual frontier, vertiginous in its extremes. Rickety buses hurtled dizzyingly down the center of the road, swerving now and then to pick up a laborer, to avoid a pothole or a pack of children. Back from the road stretched large *haciendas*, their immense main houses barely visible in the folds of the slopes, their stone walls splashed occasionally with red paint, crude representations of the hammer and sickle and admonitions to vote *comunista*. One day when I was out there a cloud burst, and because my rented car with 110,000 miles on it had no windshield wipers, I stopped by the side of the road. Rain streamed over the MESA ARIZONA WESTWOOD WARRIORS and GO TIDE decals on the car windows. Gullies formed on the road. Up in the high gravel quarries men worked on, picking with shovels at the Andes for twelve and a half pesos a load.

Through another of our cities without a center, as hideous
as Los Angeles, and with as many cars
per head, and past the 20-foot neon sign
for Coppertone *on a church, past the population*
earning $700 per capita
in jerry skyscraper living-slabs, and on to the White House
of El Presidente Leoni, his small men with 18-inch repeating pistols,
   firing 45 bullets a minute,
the two armed guards petrified beside us, while we had champagne,
and someone bugging the President: 'Where are the girls?'
And the enclosed leader, quite a fellow, saying,
'I don't know where yours are, but I know where to find mine.' . . .
This house, this pioneer democracy, built
on foundations, not of rock, but blood as hard as rock.

— Robert Lowell, 'Caracas'

There is one more image I remember, and it comes in two parts.
First there was the mine. Tunneled into a mountain in Zipaquirá,
fifty kilometers north of Bogotá, is a salt mine. This single mine
produces, each year, enough salt for all of South America, and has
done so since before Europeans knew the continent existed: salt, not
gold, was the economic basis of the Chibcha Empire, and Zipaquirá
one of its capitals. The mine is vast, its air oppressive. I happened to
be inside the mine because inside the mine there is, carved into the
mountain 450 feet below the surface, a cathedral in which 10,000
people can hear mass at the same time. Fourteen massive stone
pilasters support the vault. Recessed fluorescent tubes illuminate the
Stations of the Cross, the dense air absorbing and dimming the light
unsteadily. One could think of Chibcha sacrifices here, of the *conquistador* priests struggling to superimpose the European mass on the
screams of the slaughtered children.

But one would be wrong. The building of this enigmatic exca-
vation in the salt mountain was undertaken not by the Chibcha but
by the Banco de la República, in 1954. In 1954 General Gustavo Rojas
Pinilla and his colonels were running Colombia, and the country was
wrenched by *La Violencia*, the fifteen years of anarchy that followed
the assassination of Jorge Gaitán in Bogotá in 1948. In 1954 people
were fleeing the terrorized countryside to squat in shacks in the

comparative safety of Bogotá. In 1954 Colombia still had few public works projects, no transportation to speak of: Bogotá would not be connected by rail with the Caribbean until 1961. As I stood in the dim mountain reading the Banco de la República's dedicatory plaque, 1954 seemed to me an extraordinary year to have hit on the notion of building a cathedral of salt, but the Colombians to whom I mentioned it only shrugged.

The second part of the image. I had come up from the mine and was having lunch on the side of the salt mountain, in the chilly dining room of the Hostería del Libertador. There were heavy draperies that gave off a faint muskiness when touched. There were white brocade tablecloths, carefully darned. For every stalk of blanched asparagus served, there appeared another battery of silverplated flatware and platters and *vinaigrette* sauceboats, and also another battery of 'waiters': little boys, twelve or thirteen years old, dressed in tailcoats and white gloves and taught to serve as if this small inn on an Andean precipice were Vienna under the Hapsburgs.

I sat there for a long time. All around us the wind was sweeping the clouds off the Andes and across the savannah. Four hundred and fifty feet beneath us was the cathedral built of salt in the year 1954. *This house, this pioneer democracy, built on foundations, not of rock, but blood as hard as rock.* One of the little boys in white gloves picked up an empty wine bottle from a table, fitted it precisely into a wine holder, and marched toward the kitchen holding it stiffly before him, glancing covertly at the *maître d'hôtel* for approval. It seemed to me later that I had never before seen and would perhaps never again see the residuum of European custom so movingly and pointlessly observed.

1974

At the Dam

Since the afternoon in 1967 when I first saw Hoover Dam, its image has never been entirely absent from my inner eye. I will be talking to someone in Los Angeles, say, or New York, and suddenly the dam will materialize, its pristine concave face gleaming white against the harsh rusts and taupes and mauves of that rock canyon hundreds or thousands of miles from where I am. I will be driving down Sunset Boulevard, or about to enter a freeway, and abruptly those power transmission towers will appear before me, canted vertiginously over the tailrace. Sometimes I am confronted by the intakes and some-times by the shadow of the heavy cable that spans the canyon and sometimes by the ominous outlets to unused spillways, black in the lunar clarity of the desert light. Quite often I hear the turbines. Frequently I wonder what is happening at the dam this instant, at this precise intersection of time and space, how much water is being released to fill downstream orders and what lights are flashing and which generators are in full use and which just spinning free.

I used to wonder what it was about the dam that made me think of it at times and in places where I once thought of the Mindanao Trench, or of the stars wheeling in their courses, or of the words *As it was in the beginning, is now and ever shall be, world without end, amen*. Dams, after all, are commonplace: we have all seen one. This particular dam had existed as an idea in the world's mind for almost forty years before I saw it. Hoover Dam, showpiece of the Boulder Canyon project, the several million tons of concrete that made the Southwest plausible, the *fait accompli* that was to convey, in the innocent time of its construction, the notion that mankind's brightest promise lay in American engineering.

Of course the dam derives some of its emotional effect from precisely that aspect, that sense of being a monument to a faith since misplaced. 'They died to make the desert bloom,' reads a plaque dedicated to the 96 men who died building this first of the great high dams, and in context the worn phrase touches, suggests all of that trust in harnessing resources, in the meliorative power of the dynamo, so central to the early Thirties. Boulder City, built in 1931 as the construction town for the dam, retains the ambience of a model city, a new town, a toy triangular grid of green lawns and trim bungalows, all fanning out from the Reclamation building. The bronze sculptures at the dam itself evoke muscular citizens of a tomorrow that never came, sheaves of wheat clutched heavenward, thunderbolts defied. Winged Victories guard the flagpole. The flag whips in the canyon wind. An empty Pepsi-Cola can clatters across the terrazzo. The place is perfectly frozen in time.

But history does not explain it all, does not entirely suggest what makes that dam so affecting. Nor, even, does energy, the massive involvement with power and pressure and the transparent sexual overtones to that involvement. Once when I revisited the dam I walked through it with a man from the Bureau of Reclamation. For a while we trailed behind a guided tour, and then we went on, went into parts of the dam where visitors do not generally go. Once in a while he would explain something, usually in that recondite language having to do with 'peaking power,' with 'outages' and 'dewatering,' but on the whole we spent the afternoon in a world so alien, so complete and so beautiful unto itself that it was scarcely necessary to speak at all. We saw almost no one. Cranes moved above us as if under their own volition. Generators roared. Transformers hummed. The gratings on which we stood vibrated. We watched a hundred-ton steel shaft plunging down to that place where the water was. And finally we got down to that place where the water was, where the water sucked out of Lake Mead roared through thirty-foot penstocks and then into thirteen-foot penstocks and finally into the turbines themselves. 'Touch it,' the Reclamation man said, and I did, and for a long time I just stood there with my hands on the turbine. It was a peculiar moment, but so explicit as to suggest nothing beyond itself.

There was something beyond all that, something beyond energy, beyond history, something I could not fix in my mind. When I came up from the dam that day the wind was blowing harder, through the canyon and all across the Mojave. Later, toward Henderson and Las Vegas, there would be dust blowing, blowing past the Country-Western Casino FRI & SAT NITES and blowing past the Shrine of Our Lady of Safe Journey STOP & PRAY, but out at the dam there was no dust, only the rock and the dam and a little greasewood and a few garbage cans, their tops chained, banging against a fence. I walked across the marble star map that traces a sidereal revolution of the equinox and fixes forever, the Reclamation man had told me, for all time and for all people who can read the stars, the date the dam was dedicated. The star map was, he had said, for when we were all gone and the dam was left. I had not thought much of it when he said it, but I thought of it then, with the wind whining and the sun dropping behind a mesa with the finality of a sunset in space. Of course that was the image I had seen always, seen it without quite realizing what I saw, a dynamo finally free of man, splendid at last in its absolute isolation, transmitting power and releasing water to a world where no one is.

1970

V

On the Morning after
the Sixties

On the Morning After the Sixties

I am talking here about being a child of my time. When I think about the Sixties now I think about an afternoon not of the Sixties at all, an afternoon early in my sophomore year at Berkeley, a bright autumn Saturday in 1953. I was lying on a leather couch in a fraternity house (there had been a lunch for the alumni, my date had gone on to the game, I do not now recall why I had stayed behind), lying there alone reading a book by Lionel Trilling and listening to a middle-aged man pick out on a piano in need of tuning the melodic line to 'Blue Room.' All that afternoon he sat at the piano and all that afternoon he played 'Blue Room' and he never got it right. I can hear and see it still, the wrong note in 'We will thrive on / Keep alive on,' the sunlight falling through the big windows, the man picking up his drink and beginning again and telling me, without ever saying a word, something I had not known before about bad marriages and wasted time and looking backward. That such an afternoon would now seem implausible in every detail – the idea of having had a 'date' for a football lunch now seems to me so exotic as to be almost czarist – suggests the extent to which the narrative on which many of us grew up no longer applies.

The distance we have come from the world in which I went to college was on my mind quite a bit during those seasons when not only Berkeley but dozens of other campuses were periodically shut down, incipient battlegrounds, their borders sealed. To think of Berkeley as it was in the Fifties was not to think of barricades and reconstituted classes. 'Reconstitution' would have sounded to us then like Newspeak, and barricades are never personal. We were all very personal then, sometimes relentlessly so, and, at that point where we either act or do not act, most of us are still. I suppose I am talking about just that: the ambiguity of belonging to a generation distrustful of political highs, the historical irrelevancy of growing up convinced that the heart of darkness lay not in some error of social organization but in man's own blood. If man was bound to err, then any social organization was bound to be in error. It was a premise which still seems to me accurate enough, but one which robbed us early of a certain capacity for surprise.

At Berkeley in the Fifties no one was surprised by anything at all, a *donnée* which tended to render discourse less than spirited, and debate nonexistent. The world was by definition imperfect, and so of course was the university. There was some talk even then about IBM cards, but on balance the notion that free education for tens of thousands of people might involve automation did not seem unreasonable. We took it for granted that the Board of Regents would sometimes act wrongly. We simply avoided those students rumored to be FBI informers. We were that generation called 'silent,' but we were silent neither, as some thought, because we shared the period's official optimism nor, as others thought, because we feared its official repression. We were silent because the exhilaration of social action seemed to many of us just one more way of escaping the personal, of masking for a while that dread of the meaningless which was man's fate.

To have assumed that particular fate so early was the peculiarity of my generation. I think now that we were the last generation to identify with adults. That most of us have found adulthood just as morally ambiguous as we expected it to be falls perhaps into the category of prophecies self-fulfilled: I am simply not sure. I am telling you only how it was. The mood of Berkeley in those years was one of mild but chronic 'depression,' against which I remember certain small things that seemed to me somehow explications, dazzling in their clarity, of the world I was about to enter: I remember a woman picking daffodils in the rain one day when I was walking in the hills. I remember a teacher who drank too much one night and revealed his fright and bitterness. I remember my real joy at discovering for the first time how language worked, at discovering, for example, that the central line of *Heart of Darkness* was a postscript. All such images were personal, and the personal was all that most of us expected to find. We would make a separate peace. We would do graduate work in Middle English, we would go abroad. We would make some money and live on a ranch. We would survive outside history, in a kind of *idée fixe* referred to always, during the years I spent at Berkeley, as 'some little town with a decent beach.'

As it worked out I did not find or even look for the little town with the decent beach. I sat in the large bare apartment in which I lived my junior and senior years (I had lived awhile in a sorority, the Tri Delt house, and had left it, typically, not over any 'issue' but because I, the implacable 'I,' did not like living with sixty people) and I read Camus and Henry James and I watched a flowering plum come in and out of blossom and at night, most nights, I walked outside and looked up to where the cyclotron and the bevatron glowed on the dark hillside, unspeakable mysteries which engaged me, in the style of my time, only personally. Later I got out of Berkeley and went to New York and later I got out of New York and came to Los Angeles. What I have made for myself is personal, but is not exactly peace. Only one person I knew at Berkeley later discovered an ideology, dealt himself into history, cut himself loose from both his own dread and his own time. A few of the people I knew at Berkeley killed themselves not long after. Another attempted suicide in Mexico and then, in a recovery which seemed in many ways a more advanced derangement, came home and joined the Bank of America's three-year executive-training program. Most of us live less theatrically, but remain the survivors of a peculiar and inward time. If I could believe that going to a barricade would affect man's fate in the slightest I would go to that barricade, and quite often I wish that I could, but it would be less than honest to say that I expect to happen upon such a happy ending.

1970

Quiet Days in Malibu

1

In a way it seems the most idiosyncratic of beach communities, twenty-seven miles of coastline with no hotel, no passable restaurant, nothing to attract the traveler's dollar. It is not a resort. No one 'vacations' or 'holidays,' as those words are conventionally understood, at Malibu. Its principal residential street, the Pacific Coast Highway, is quite literally a highway, California 1, which runs from the Mexican border to the Oregon line and brings Greyhound buses and refrigerated produce trucks and sixteen-wheel gasoline tankers hurtling past the front windows of houses frequently bought and sold for over a million dollars. The water off Malibu is neither as clear nor as tropically colored as the water off La Jolla. The beaches at Malibu are neither as white nor as wide as the beach at Carmel. The hills are scrubby and barren, infested with bikers and rattlesnakes, scarred with cuts and old burns and new R.V. parks. For these and other reasons Malibu tends to astonish and disappoint those who have never before seen it, and yet its very name remains, in the imagination of people all over the world, a kind of shorthand for the easy life. I had not before 1971 and will probably not again live in a place with a Chevrolet named after it.

2

Dick Haddock, a family man, a man twenty-six years in the same line of work, a man who has on the telephone and in his office the crisp and easy manner of technological middle management, is in many respects the prototypical Southern California solid citizen. He lives in a San Fernando Valley subdivision near a freshwater marina and a good shopping plaza. His son is a high-school swimmer. His daughter is 'into tennis.' He drives thirty miles to and from work, puts in a forty-hour week, regularly takes courses to maintain his professional skills, keeps in shape and looks it. When he discusses his career he talks, in a kind of politely impersonal second person, about how 'you would want like any other individual to advance yourself,' about 'improving your rating' and 'being more of an asset to your department,' about 'really knowing your business.' Dick Haddock's business for all these twenty-six years has been that of a professional lifeguard for the Los Angeles County Department of Beaches, and his office is a $190,000 lookout on Zuma Beach in northern Malibu.

It was Thanksgiving morning, 1975. A Santa Ana wind was just dying after blowing in off the Mojave for three weeks and setting 69,000 acres of Los Angeles County on fire. Squadrons of planes had been dropping chemicals on the fires to no effect. Querulous interviews with burned-out householders had become a fixed element of the six o'clock news. Smoke from the fires had that week stretched a hundred miles out over the Pacific and darkened the days and lit the nights and by Thanksgiving morning there was the sense all over Southern California of living in some grave solar dislocation. It was one of those weeks when Los Angeles seemed most perilously and breathtakingly itself, a cartoon of natural disaster, and it was a peculiar week in which to spend the day with Dick Haddock and the rest of the Zuma headquarters crew.

Actually I had wanted to meet the lifeguards ever since I moved to Malibu. I would drive past Zuma some cold winter mornings and see a few of them making their mandatory daily half-mile swims in open ocean. I would drive past Zuma some late foggy nights and see others moving around behind the lookout's lighted windows, the only other souls awake in all of northern Malibu. It seemed to me a curious, almost beatified career choice, electing to save those in peril upon the sea forty hours a week, and as the soot drifted down around the Zuma lookout on that Thanksgiving morning the laconic routines and paramilitary rankings of these civil servants in red trunks took on a devotionary and dreamlike inevitability. There was the 'captain,' John McFarlane, a man who had already taken his daily half-mile run and his daily half-mile swim and was putting on his glasses to catch up on paperwork. Had the water been below 56 degrees he would have been allowed to swim in a wet suit, but the water was not below 56 degrees and so he had swum as usual in his red trunks. The water was 58 degrees. John McFarlane is 48. There was the 'lieutenant,' Dick Haddock, telling me about how each of the Department's 125 permanent lifeguards (there are also 600 part-time or 'recurrent' lifeguards) learns crowd control at the Los Angeles County Sheriff's Academy, learns emergency driving techniques at the California Highway Patrol Academy, learns medical procedures at the U.S.C. Medical Center, and, besides running the daily half-mile and swimming the daily half-mile, does a monthly 500-meter paddle and a monthly pier jump. A 'pier jump' is just what it sounds like, and its purpose is to gain practice around pilings in heavy surf.

There was as well the man out on patrol.

There were as well the 'call-car personnel,' two trained divers and cliff-climbers 'ready to roll at any time' in what was always referred to as 'a Code 3 vehicle with red light and siren,' two men not rolling this Thanksgiving morning but sitting around the lookout, listening to the Los Angeles Rams beat the Detroit Lions on the radio, watching the gray horizon and waiting for a call.

No call came. The radios and the telephones crackled occasionally with reports from the other 'operations' supervised by the Zuma crew: the 'rescue-boat operation' at Paradise Cove, the 'beach operations' at Leo Carrillo, Nicholas, Point Dume, Corral, Malibu Surfrider, Malibu Lagoon, Las Tunas, Topanga North and Topanga South. Those happen to be the names of some Malibu public beaches but in the Zuma lookout that day the names took on the sound of battle stations during a doubtful cease-fire. All quiet at Leo. Situation normal at Surfrider.

The lifeguards seemed most comfortable when they were talking about 'operations' and 'situations,' as in 'a phone-watch situation' or 'a riptide situation.' They also talked easily about 'functions,' as in 'the function of maintaining a secure position on the beach.' Like other men at war they had charts, forms, logs, counts kept current to within twelve hours: *1405 surf rescues off Zuma between 12:01 A.M. January 1, 1975 and 11:59 P.M. Thanksgiving Eve 1975.* As well as: *36,120 prevention rescues, 872 first aids, 176 beach emergency calls, 12 resuscitations, 8 boat distress calls, 107 boat warnings, 438 lost-and-found children,* and *0 deaths.* Zero. No body count. When he had occasion to use the word 'body' Dick Haddock would hesitate and glance away.

On the whole the lifeguards favored a diction as flat and finally poetic as that of Houston Control. Everything that morning was 'real fine.' The headquarters crew was 'feeling good.' The day was 'looking good.' Malibu surf was 'two feet and shape is poor.' Earlier that morning there had been a hundred or so surfers in the water, a hundred or so of those bleached children of indeterminate age and sex who bob off Zuma and appear to exist exclusively on packaged beef jerky, but by ten they had all pocketed their Thanksgiving jerky and moved on to some better break. 'It heats up, we could use some more personnel,' Dick Haddock said about noon, assessing the empty guard towers. 'That happened, we might move on a decision to open Towers One and Eleven, I'd call and say we need two recurrents at Zuma, plus I might put an extra man at Leo.'

It did not heat up. Instead it began to rain, and on the radio the morning N.F.L. game gave way to the afternoon N.F.L. game, and after a while I drove with one of the call-car men to Paradise Cove, where the rescue-boat crew needed a diver. They did not need a diver to bring up a body, or a murder weapon, or a crate of stolen ammo, or any of the things Department divers sometimes get their names in the paper for bringing up. They needed a diver, with scuba gear and a wet suit, because they had been removing the propeller from the rescue boat and had dropped a metal part the size of a dime in twenty feet of water. I had the distinct impression that they particularly needed a diver in a wet suit because nobody on the boat crew wanted to go back in the water in his trunks to replace the propeller, but there seemed to be some tacit agreement that the lost part was to be considered the point of the dive.

'I guess you know it's fifty-eight down there,' the diver said.

'Don't need to tell me how cold it is,' the boat lieutenant said. His name was Leonard McKinley and he had 'gone permanent' in 1942 and he was of an age to refer to Zuma as a 'bathing' beach. 'After you find that little thing you could put the propeller back on for us, you wanted. As long as you're in the water anyway? In your suit?'

'I had a feeling you'd say that.'

Leonard McKinley and I stood on the boat and watched the diver disappear. In the morning soot from the fires had coated the surface but now the wind was up and the soot was clouding the water. Kelp fronds undulated on the surface. The boat rocked. The radio sputtered with reports of a yacht named *Ursula* in distress.

'One of the other boats is going for it,' Leonard McKinley said. 'We're not. Some days we just sit here like firemen. Other days, a day with rips, I been out ten hours straight. You get your big rips in the summer, swells coming up from Mexico. A Santa Ana, you get your capsized boats, we got one the other day, it was overdue out of Santa Monica, they were about drowned when we picked them up.'

I tried to keep my eyes on the green-glass water but could not. I had been sick on boats in the Catalina Channel and in the Gulf of California and even in San Francisco Bay, and now I seemed to be getting sick on a boat still moored at the end of the Paradise Cove pier. The radio reported the *Ursula* under tow to Marina del Rey. I concentrated on the pilings.

'He gets the propeller on,' Leonard McKinley said, 'you want to go out?'

I said I thought not.

'You come back another day,' Leonard McKinley said, and I said that I would, and although I have not gone back there is no day when I do not think of Leonard McKinley and Dick Haddock and what they are doing, what situations they face, what operations, what green-glass water. The water today is 56 degrees.

3

Amado Vazquez is a Mexican national who has lived in Los Angeles County as a resident alien since 1947. Like many Mexicans who have lived for a long time around Los Angeles he speaks of Mexico as 'over there,' remains more comfortable in Spanish than in English, and transmits, in his every movement, a kind of 'different' propriety, a correctness, a cultural reserve. He is in no sense a Chicano. He is rather what California-born Mexicans sometimes call 'Mexican-from-Mexico,' pronounced as one word and used to suggest precisely that difference, that rectitude, that personal conservatism. He was born in Ahualulco, Jalisco. He was trained as a barber at the age of ten. Since the age of twenty-seven, when he came north to visit his brother and find new work for himself, he has married, fathered two children, and become, to the limited number of people who know and understand the rather special work he found for himself in California, a kind of legend. Amado Vazquez was, at the time I first met him, head grower at Arthur Freed Orchids, a commercial nursery in Malibu founded by the late motion-picture producer Arthur Freed, and he is one of a handful of truly great orchid breeders in the world.

In the beginning I met Amado Vazquez not because I knew about orchids but because I liked greenhouses. All I knew about orchids was that back in a canyon near my house someone was growing them *in greenhouses*. All I knew about Amado Vazquez was that he was the man who would let me spend time alone in these greenhouses. To understand how extraordinary this seemed to me you would need to have craved the particular light and silence of greenhouses as I did: all my life I had been trying to spend time in one greenhouse or another, and all my life the person in charge of one greenhouse or another had been trying to hustle me out. When I was nine I would deliberately miss the school bus in order to walk home, because by walking I could pass a greenhouse. I recall being told at that particular greenhouse that the purchase of a nickel pansy did not entitle me to 'spend the day,' and at another that my breathing was 'using up the air.'

And yet back in this canyon near my house twenty-five years later were what seemed to me the most beautiful greenhouses in the world – the most aqueous filtered light, the softest tropical air, the most silent clouds of flowers – and the person in charge, Amado Vazquez, seemed willing to take only the most benign notice of my presence. He seemed to assume that I had my own reasons for being there. He would speak only to offer a nut he had just cracked, or a flower cut from a plant he was pruning. Occasionally Arthur Freed's brother Hugo, who was then running the business, would come into the greenhouse with real customers, serious men in dark suits who appeared to have just flown in from Taipei or Durban and who spoke in hushed voices, as if they had come to inspect medieval enamels, or uncut diamonds.

But then the buyers from Taipei or Durban would go into the office to make their deal and the silence in the greenhouse would again be total. The temperature was always 72 degrees. The humidity was always 60 per cent. Great arcs of white phalaenopsis trembled overhead. I learned the names of the crosses by studying labels there in the greenhouse, the exotic names whose value I did not then understand. *Amabilis* × *Rimestadiana = Elisabethae. Aphrodite* × *Rimestadiana = Gilles Gratiot. Amabilis* × *Gilles Gratiot = Katherine Siegwart* and *Katherine Siegwart* × *Elisabethae = Doris. Doris* after Doris Duke. *Doris* which first flowered at Duke Farms in 1940. At least once each visit I would remember the nickel pansy and find Amado Vazquez and show him a plant I wanted to buy, but he would only smile and shake his head. 'For breeding,' he would say, or 'not for sale today.' And then he would lift the spray of flowers and show me some point I would not have noticed, some marginal difference in the substance of the petal or the shape of the blossom. 'Very beautiful,' he would say. 'Very nice you like it.' What he would not say was that these plants he was letting me handle, these plants 'for breeding' or 'not for sale today,' were stud plants, and that the value of such a plant at Arthur Freed could range from ten thousand to more than three-quarters of a million dollars.

I suppose the day I realized this was the day I stopped using the Arthur Freed greenhouses as a place to eat my lunch, but I made a point of going up one day in 1976 to see Amado Vazquez and to talk to Marvin Saltzman, who took over the business in 1973 and is married to Arthur Freed's daughter Barbara. (As in *Phal. Barbara Freed Saltzman* 'Jean McPherson,' *Phal. Barbara Freed Saltzman* 'Zuma

Canyon,' and *Phal. Barbara Freed Saltzman* 'Malibu Queen,' three
plants 'not for sale today' at Arthur Freed.) It was peculiar talking to
Marvin Saltzman because I had never before been in the office at
Arthur Freed, never seen the walls lined with dulled silver awards,
never seen the genealogical charts on the famous Freed hybrids,
never known anything at all about the actual business of orchids.

'Frankly it's an expensive business to get into,' Marvin Saltzman
said. He was turning the pages of *Sander's List*, the standard orchid
studbook, published every several years and showing the parentage
of every hybrid registered with the Royal Horticultural Society, and
he seemed oblivious to the primeval silence of the greenhouse
beyond the office window. He had shown me how Amado Vazquez
places the pollen from one plant into the ovary of a flower on
another. He had explained that the best times to do this are at full
moon and high tide, because phalaenopsis plants are more fertile
then. He had explained that a phalaenopsis is more fertile at full
moon because in nature it must be pollinated by a night-flying moth,
and over sixty-five million years of evolution its period of highest
fertility began to coincide with its period of highest visibility. He had
explained that a phalaenopsis is more fertile at high tide because the
moisture content of every plant responds to tidal movement. It was
all an old story to Marvin Saltzman. I could not take my eyes from
the window.

'You bring back five thousand seedlings from the jungle and you
wait three years for them to flower,' Marvin Saltzman said. 'You find
two you like and you throw out the other four thousand nine hundred ninety-eight and you try to breed the two. Maybe the polleniz-
ation takes, eighty-five per cent of the time it doesn't. Say you're
lucky, it takes, you'll still wait another four years before you see a
flower. Meanwhile you've got a big capital investment. An Arthur
Freed could take $400,000 a year from M-G-M and put $100,000 of
it into getting this place started, but not many people could. You see
a lot of what we call backyard nurseries – people who have fifty or
a hundred plants, maybe they have two they think are exceptional,
they decide to breed them – but you talk about major nurseries,
there are maybe only ten in the United States, another ten in Europe.
That's about it. Twenty.'

Twenty is also about how many head growers there are, which is

part of what lends Amado Vazquez his legendary aspect, and after a
while I left the office and went out to see him in the greenhouse.
There in the greenhouse everything was operating as usual to
approximate that particular level of a Malaysian rain forest – not on
the ground but perhaps a hundred feet up – where epiphytic orchids
grow wild. In the rain forest these orchids get broken by wind and
rain. They get pollinated randomly and rarely by insects. Their seedlings are crushed by screaming monkeys and tree boas and the
orchids live unseen and die young. There in the greenhouse nothing
would break the orchids and they would be pollinated at full moon
and high tide by Amado Vazquez, and their seedlings would be
tended in a sterile box with sterile gloves and sterile tools by Amado
Vazquez's wife, Maria, and the orchids would not seem to die at all.
'We don't know how long they'll live,' Marvin Saltzman told me.
'They haven't been bred under protected conditions that long. The
botanists estimate a hundred and fifty, two hundred years, but we
don't know. All we know is that a plant a hundred years old will
show no signs of senility.'

It was very peaceful there in the greenhouse with Amado Vazquez
and the plants that would outlive us both. 'We grew in osmunda
then,' he said suddenly. Osmunda is a potting medium. Amado
Vazquez talks exclusively in terms of how the orchids grow. He had
been talking about the years when he first came to this country and
got a job with his brother tending a private orchid collection in San
Marino, and he had fallen silent. 'I didn't know orchids then, now
they're like my children. You wait for the first bloom like you wait
for a baby to come. Sometimes you wait four years and it opens and
it isn't what you expected, maybe your heart wants to break, but
you love it. You never say, "that one was prettier." You just love
them. My whole life is orchids.'

And in fact it was. Amado Vazquez's wife, Maria (as in *Phal. Maria
Vasquez* 'Malibu,' the spelling of Vazquez being mysteriously altered
by everyone at Arthur Freed except the Vazquezes themselves),
worked in the laboratory at Arthur Freed. His son, George (as in
Phal. George Vasquez 'Malibu'), was the sales manager at Arthur Freed.
His daughter, Linda (as in *Phal. Linda Mia* 'Innocence'), worked at
Arthur Freed before her marriage. Amado Vazquez will often get up
in the night to check a heater, adjust a light, hold a seed pod in his

hand and try to sense if morning will be time enough to sow the
seeds in the sterile flask. When Amado and Maria Vazquez go to
Central or South America, they go to look for orchids. When Amado
and Maria Vazquez went for the first time to Europe a few years ago,
they looked for orchids. 'I asked all over Madrid for orchids,' Amado
Vazquez recalled. 'Finally they tell me about this one place. I go
there, I knock. The woman finally lets me in. She agrees to let me
see the orchids. She takes me into a house and . . .'

Amado Vazquez broke off, laughing.

'She has three orchids,' he finally managed to say. 'Three. One of
them dead. All three from Oregon.'

We were standing in a sea of orchids, an extravagance of orchids,
and he had given me an armful of blossoms from his own cattleyas
to take to my child, more blossoms maybe than in all of Madrid.
It seemed to me that day that I had never talked to anyone so
direct and unembarrassed about the things he loved. He had
told me earlier that he had never become a United States citizen
because he had an image in his mind which he knew to be false
but could not shake: the image was that of standing before a judge
and stamping on the flag of Mexico. 'And I love my country,' he had
said. Amado Vazquez loved his country. Amado Vazquez loved his
family. Amado Vazquez loved orchids. 'You want to know how I feel
about the plants,' he said as I was leaving. 'I'll tell you. I will die in
orchids.'

4

In the part of Malibu where I lived from January of 1971 until quite
recently we all knew one another's cars, and watched for them on
the highway and at the Trancas Market and at the Point Dume Gulf
station. We exchanged information at the Trancas Market. We left
packages and messages for one another at the Gulf station. We called
one another in times of wind and fire and rain, we knew when one
another's septic tanks needed pumping, we watched for ambulances
on the highway and helicopters on the beach and worried about one
another's dogs and horses and children and corral gates and Coastal

Commission permits. An accident on the highway was likely to involve someone we knew. A rattlesnake in my driveway meant its mate in yours. A stranger's campfire on your beach meant fire on both our slopes.

In fact this was a way of life I had not expected to find in Malibu. When I first moved in 1971 from Hollywood to a house on the Pacific Coast Highway I had accepted the conventional notion that Malibu meant the easy life, had worried that we would be cut off from 'the real world,' by which I believe I meant daily exposure to the Sunset Strip. By the time we left Malibu, seven years later, I had come to see the spirit of the place as one of shared isolation and adversity, and I think now that I never loved the house on the Pacific Coast Highway more than on those many days when it was impossible to leave it, when fire or flood had in fact closed the highway. We moved to this house on the highway in the year of our daughter's fifth birthday. In the year of her twelfth it rained until the highway collapsed, and one of her friends drowned at Zuma Beach, a casualty of Quaaludes.

One morning during the fire season of 1978, some months after we had sold the house on the Pacific Coast Highway, a brush fire caught in Agoura, in the San Fernando Valley. Within two hours a Santa Ana wind had pushed this fire across 25,000 acres and thirteen miles to the coast, where it jumped the Pacific Coast Highway as a half-mile fire storm generating winds of 100 miles per hour and temperatures up to 2500 degrees Fahrenheit. Refugees huddled on Zuma Beach. Horses caught fire and were shot on the beach, birds exploded in the air. Houses did not explode but imploded, as in a nuclear strike. By the time this fire storm had passed 197 houses had vanished into ash, many of them houses which belonged or had belonged to people we knew. A few days after the highway reopened I drove out to Malibu to see Amado Vazquez, who had, some months before, bought from the Freed estate all the stock at Arthur Freed Orchids, and had been in the process of moving it a half-mile down the canyon to his own new nursery, Zuma Canyon Orchids. I found him in the main greenhouse at what had been Arthur Freed Orchids. The place was now a range not of orchids but of shattered glass and melted metal and the imploded shards of the thousands of chemical beakers that had held the Freed seedlings, the new crosses. 'I lost three years,' Amado Vazquez said, and for an instant I thought we would both cry. 'You want today to see flowers,' he said then, 'we go down to the other place.' I did not want that day to see flowers. After I said goodbye to Amado Vazquez my husband and daughter and I went to look at the house on the Pacific Coast Highway in which we had lived for seven years. The fire had come to within 125 feet of the property, then stopped or turned or been beaten back, it was hard to tell which. In any case it was no longer our house.

1976–1978

After Henry

This book is dedicated to Henry Robbins and to Bret Easton Ellis, each of whom did time with its publisher.

Acknowledgments

'In the Realm of the Fisher King', 'Insider Baseball', 'Shooters Inc.', 'Girl of the Golden West', and 'Sentimental Journeys' appeared originally in *The New York Review of Books*. 'Los Angeles Days', 'Down at City Hall', 'L.A. *Noir*', 'Fire Season', 'Times Mirror Square', and part of 'Pacific Distances' appeared originally as 'Letters from Los Angeles' in *The New Yorker*. Most of 'Pacific Distances' and the introductory piece, 'After Henry', appeared originally in *New West*, which later became *California* and eventually folded. I would like to thank my editors at all three magazines, Jon Carroll at *New West*, Robert Gottlieb at *The New Yorker*, and most especially, since he has put up with me over nineteen years and through many long and eccentric projects, Robert Silvers at *The New York Review*.

I

After Henry

After Henry

In the summer of 1966 I was living in a borrowed house in Brentwood, and had a new baby. I had published one book, three years before. My husband was writing his first. Our daybook for those months shows no income at all for April, $305.06 for May, none for June, and, for July, $5.29, a dividend on our single capital asset, fifty shares of Transamerica stock left to me by my grandmother. This 1966 daybook shows laundry lists and appointments with pediatricians. It shows sixty christening presents received and sixty thank-you notes written, shows the summer sale at Saks and the attempt to retrieve a fifteen-dollar deposit from Southern Counties Gas, but it does not show the date in June on which we first met Henry Robbins.

This seems to me now a peculiar and poignant omission, and one that suggests the particular fractures that new babies and borrowed houses can cause in the moods of people who live largely by their wits. Henry Robbins was until that June night in 1966 an abstract to us, another New York editor, a stranger at Farrar, Straus & Giroux who had called or written and said that he was coming to California to see some writers. I thought so little of myself as a writer that summer that I was obscurely ashamed to go to dinner with still another editor, ashamed to sit down again and discuss this 'work' I was not doing, but in the end I did go: in the end I put on a black silk dress and went with my husband to the Bistro in Beverly Hills and met Henry Robbins and began, right away, to laugh. The three of us laughed until two in the morning, when we were no longer at the Bistro but at the Daisy, listening over and over to 'In the Midnight Hour' and 'Softly As I Leave You' and to one another's funny, brilliant, enchanting voices, voices that transcended lost laundry and babysitters and prospects of $5.29, voices full of promise, *writers'* voices.

In short we got drunk together, and before the summer was out Henry Robbins had signed contracts with each of us, and, from that summer in 1966 until the summer of 1979, very few weeks passed during which one or the other of us did not talk to Henry Robbins about something which was amusing us or interesting us or worrying us, about our hopes and about our doubts, about work and love and money and gossip; about our news, good or bad. On the July morning in 1979 when we got word from New York that Henry Robbins had died on his way to work a few hours before, had fallen dead, age fifty-one, to the floor of the 14th Street subway station, there was only one person I wanted to talk to about it, and that one person was Henry.

'Childhood is the kingdom where nobody dies' is a line, from the poem by Edna St Vincent Millay, that has stuck in my mind ever since I first read it, when I was in fact a child and nobody died. Of course people did die, but they were either very old or died unusual deaths, died while rafting on the Stanislaus or loading a shotgun or doing 95 drunk: death was construed as either a 'blessing' or an exceptional case, the dramatic instance on which someone else's (never our own) story turned. Illness, in that kingdom where I and most people I knew lingered long past childhood, proved self-limiting. Fever of unknown etiology signaled only the indulgence of a week in bed. Chest pains, investigated, revealed hypochondria.

As time passed it occurred to many of us that our benign experience was less than general, that we had been to date blessed or charmed or plain lucky, players on a good roll, but by that time we were busy: caught up in days that seemed too full, too various, too crowded with friends and obligations and children, dinner parties and deadlines, commitments and overcommitments. 'You can't imagine how it is when everyone you know is gone,' someone I knew who was old would say to me, and I would nod, uncomprehending, yes I can, I can imagine; would even think, God forgive me, that there must be a certain peace in outliving all debts and claims, in being known to no one, floating free. I believed that days would be too full forever, too crowded with friends there was no time to see. I believed, by way of contemplating the future, that we would all be around for one another's funerals. I was wrong. I had failed to imagine, I had not understood. Here was the way it was going to be: I would be around for Henry's funeral, but he was not going to be around for mine.

The funeral was not actually a funeral but a memorial service, in the prevailing way, an occasion for all of us to meet on a tropical August New York morning in the auditorium of the Society for Ethical Culture at 64th and Central Park West. A truism about working with language is that other people's arrangements of words are always crowding in on one's actual experience, and this morning in New York was no exception. 'Abide with me: do not go away' was a line I kept hearing, unspoken, all through the service; my husband was speaking, and half a dozen other writers and publishers who had been close to Henry Robbins – Wilfrid Sheed, Donald Barthelme, John Irving, Doris Grumbach; Robert Giroux from Farrar, Straus & Giroux; John Macrae from Dutton – but the undersongs I heard were fragments of a poem by Delmore Schwartz, dead thirteen years, the casualty of another New York summer. *Abide with me: do not go away*, and then:

> *Controlling our pace before we get old,*
> *Walking together on the receding road,*
> *Like Chaplin and his orphan sister.*

Five years before, Henry had left Farrar, Straus for Simon and Schuster, and I had gone with him. Two years after that he had left Simon and Schuster and gone to Dutton. This time I had not gone with him, had stayed where my contract was, and yet I remained Henry's orphan sister, Henry's writer. I remember that he worried from time to time about whether we had enough money, and that he would sometimes, with difficulty, ask us if we needed some. I remember that he did not like the title *Play It As It Lays* and I remember railing at him on the telephone from a hotel room in Chicago because my husband's novel *True Confessions* was not yet in the window at Kroch's & Brentano's and I remember a Halloween night in New York in 1970 when our children went trick-or-treating together in the building on West 86th Street in which Henry and his wife and their two children then lived. I remember that this apartment on West 86th Street had white curtains, and that on one hot summer evening we all sat there and ate chicken in tarragon aspic and watched the curtains lift and move in the air off the river and our world seemed one of considerable promise.

I remember arguing with Henry over the use of the second person in the second sentence of *A Book of Common Prayer*. I remember his actual hurt and outrage when any of us, any of his orphan sisters or brothers, got a bad review or a slighting word or even a letter that he imagined capable of marring our most inconsequential moment. I remember him flying to California because I wanted him to read the first 110 pages of *A Book of Common Prayer* and did not want to send them to New York. I remember him turning up in Berkeley one night when I needed him in 1975; I was to lecture that night, an occasion freighted by the fact that I was to lecture many members of the English department who had once lectured me, and I was, until Henry arrived, scared witless, the sacrificial star of my own exposure dream. I remember that he came first to the Faculty Club, where I was staying, and walked me down the campus to 2000 LSB, where I was to speak. I remember him telling me that it would go just fine. I remember believing him.

I always believed what Henry told me, except about two things, the title *Play It As It Lays* and the use of the second person in the second sentence of *A Book of Common Prayer*, believed him even when time and personalities and the difficulty of making a living by either editing books or writing them had complicated our relationship. What editors do for writers is mysterious, and does not, contrary to general belief, have much to do with titles and sentences and 'changes'. Nor, my railing notwithstanding, does it have much to do with the window at Kroch's & Brentano's in Chicago. The relationship between an editor and a writer is much subtler and deeper than that, at once so elusive and so radical that it seems almost parental:

the editor, if the editor was Henry Robbins, was the person who gave the writer the idea of himself, the idea of herself, the image of self that enabled the writer to sit down alone and do it.

This is a tricky undertaking, and requires the editor not only to maintain a faith the writer shares only in intermittent flashes but also to like the writer, which is hard to do. Writers are only rarely likeable. They bring nothing to the party, leave their game at the typewriter. They fear their contribution to the general welfare to be evanescent, even doubtful, and, since the business of publishing is an only marginally profitable enterprise that increasingly attracts people who sense this marginality all too keenly, people who feel defensive or demeaned because they are not at the tables where the high rollers play (not managing mergers, not running motion picture studios, not even principal players in whatever larger concern holds the paper on the publishing house), it has become natural enough for a publisher or an editor to seize on the writer's fear, reinforce it, turn the writer into a necessary but finally unimportant accessory to the 'real' world of publishing. Publishers and editors do not, in the real world, get on the night TWA to California to soothe a jumpy midlist writer. Publishers and editors in the real world have access to corporate G-3s, and prefer cruising the Galápagos with the raiders they have so far failed to become. A publisher or editor who has contempt for his own class position can find solace in transferring that contempt to the writer, who typically has no G-3 and can be seen as dependent on the publisher's largesse.

This was not a solace, nor for that matter a contempt, that Henry understood. The last time I saw him was two months before he fell to the floor of the 14th Street subway station, one night in Los Angeles when the annual meeting of the American Booksellers Association was winding to a close. He had come by the house on his way to a party and we talked him into skipping the party, staying for dinner. What he told me that night was indirect, and involved implicit allusions to other people and other commitments and everything that had happened among us since that summer night in 1966, but it came down to this: he wanted me to know that I could do it without him. That was a third thing Henry told me that I did not believe.

II

Washington

In the Realm of the Fisher King

President Ronald Reagan, we were later told by his speechwriter Peggy Noonan, spent his off-camera time in the White House answering fifty letters a week, selected by the people who ran his mail operation, from citizens. He put the family pictures these citizens sent him in his pockets and desk drawers. When he did not have the zip code, he apologized to his secretary for not looking it up himself. He sharpened his own pencils, we were told by Helene von Damm, his secretary first in Sacramento and then in Washington, and he also got his own coffee.

In the post-Reagan rush to establish that we knew all along about this peculiarity in that particular White House, we forgot the actual peculiarity of the place, which had to do less with the absence at the center than with the amount of centrifugal energy this absence left spinning free at the edges. The Reagan White House was one in which great expectations were allowed into play. Ardor, of a kind that only rarely survives a fully occupied Oval Office, flourished unchecked. 'You'd be in someone's home and on the way to the bathroom you'd pass the bedroom and see a big thick copy of Paul Johnson's *Modern Times* lying half open on the table by the bed,' Peggy Noonan, who gave Ronald Reagan the boys of Pointe du Hoc and the *Challenger* crew slipping the surly bonds of earth and who gave George Bush the thousand points of light and the kinder, gentler nation, told us in *What I Saw at the Revolution: A Political Life in the Reagan Era*.

'Three months later you'd go back and it was still there,' she

wrote. 'There were words. You had a notion instead of a thought
and a dustup instead of a fight, you had a can-do attitude and you
were in touch with the zeitgeist. No one had intentions they had an
agenda and no one was wrong they were fundamentally wrong and
you didn't work on something you broke your pick on it and it
wasn't an agreement it was a done deal. All politics is local but more
to the point all economics is micro. There were phrases: personnel is
policy and ideas have consequences and ideas drive politics and it's
a war of ideas . . . and to do nothing is to endorse the status quo and
roll back the Brezhnev Doctrine and there's no such thing as a free
lunch, especially if you're dining with the press.'

Peggy Noonan arrived in Washington in 1984, thirty-three years
old, out of Brooklyn and Massapequa and Fairleigh Dickinson and
CBS Radio, where she had written Dan Rather's five-minute com-
mentaries. A few years later, when Rather told her that in lieu of a
Christmas present he wanted to make a donation to her favorite
charity, the charity she specified was The William J. Casey Fund for
the Nicaraguan Resistance. She did not immediately, or for some
months after, meet the man for whose every public utterance she
and the other staff writers were responsible; at the time she checked
into the White House, no speechwriter had spoken to Mr Reagan in
more than a year. 'We wave to him,' one said.

  In the absence of an actual president, this resourceful child of a
large Irish Catholic family sat in her office in the Old Executive
Office Building and invented an ideal one: she read Vachel Lindsay
(particularly 'I brag and chant of Bryan Bryan Bryan / Candidate for
President who sketched a silver Zion') and she read Franklin Delano
Roosevelt (whom she pictured, again ideally, up in Dutchess County
'sitting at a great table with all the chicks, eating a big spring lunch
of beefy red tomatoes and potato salad and mayonnaise and deviled
eggs on the old china with the flowers almost rubbed off') and she
thought 'this is how Reagan should sound'. What Miss Noonan had
expected Washington to be, she told us, was 'Aaron Copland and
"Appalachian Spring"'. What she found instead was a populist revolution trying to make itself, a crisis of raised expectations and lowered
possibilities, the children of an expanded middle class determined to

tear down the established order and what they saw as its repressive liberal orthodoxies: 'There were libertarians whose girlfriends had just given birth to their sons, hoisting a Coors with social conservatives who walked into the party with a wife who bothered to be warm and a son who carried a Mason jar of something daddy grew in the backyard. There were Protestant fundamentalists hoping they wouldn't be dismissed by neocon intellectuals from Queens and neocons talking to fundamentalists thinking: I wonder if when they look at me they see what Annie Hall's grandmother saw when she looked down the table at Woody Allen.'

She stayed at the White House until the spring of 1986, when she was more or less forced out by the refusal of Donald Regan, at that time chief of staff, to approve her promotion to head speechwriter. Regan thought her, according to Larry Speakes, who did not have a famous feel for the romance of the revolution, too 'hard-line', too 'dogmatic', too 'right-wing', too much 'Buchanan's protégée'. On the occasion of her resignation she received a form letter from the president, signed with the auto-pen. Donald Regan said that there was no need for her to have what was referred to as 'a good-bye moment', a farewell shake-hands with the president. On the day Donald Regan himself left the White House, Miss Noonan received this message, left on her answering machine by a friend at the White House: 'Hey, Peggy, Don Regan didn't get his good-bye moment.' By that time she was hearing the 'true tone of Washington' less as 'Appalachian Spring' than as something a little more raucous, 'nearer,' she said, 'to Jefferson Starship and "They Built This City on Rock and Roll"'.

The White House she rendered was one of considerable febrility. Everyone, she told us, could quote Richard John Neuhaus on what was called the collapse of the dogmas of the secular enlightenment. Everyone could quote Michael Novak on what was called the collapse of the assumption that education is or should be 'value-free'. Everyone could quote George Gilder on what was called the humane nature of the free market. Everyone could quote Jean-François Revel on how democracies perish, and everyone could quote Jeane Kirkpatrick on authoritarian versus totalitarian governments, and everyone spoke of 'the movement', as in 'he's movement from way back', or 'she's good, she's hard-core'.

They talked about subverting the pragmatists, who believed that an issue could not be won without the *Washington Post* and the networks, by 'going over the heads of the media to the people'. They charged one another's zeal by firing off endless letters, memos, clippings. 'Many thanks for Macedo's new monograph; his brand of judicial activism is more principled than Tribe's,' such letters read. 'If this gets into the hands of the Russians, it's curtains for the free world!' was the tone to take on the yellow Post-It attached to a clipping. 'Soldier on!' was the way to sign off. Those PROF memos we later saw from Robert McFarlane to Lieutenant Colonel Oliver North ('Roger Ollie. Well done – if the world only knew how many times you have kept a semblance of integrity and gumption to US policy, they would make you Secretary of State. But they can't know and would complain if they did – such is the state of democracy in the late 20th century . . . Bravo Zulu') do not seem, in this context, quite so unusual.

'Bureaucrats with soft hands adopted the clipped laconic style of John Ford characters,' Miss Noonan noted. 'A small man from NSC was asked at a meeting if he knew of someone who could work up a statement. Yes, he knew someone at State, a paid pen who's pushed some good paper.' To be a moderate was to be a 'squish', or a 'weenie', or a 'wuss'. 'He got rolled,' they would say of someone who had lost the day, or, 'He took a lickin' and kept on tickin'.' They walked around the White House wearing ties ('slightly stained,' according to Miss Noonan, 'from the mayonnaise that fell from the sandwich that was wolfed down at the working lunch on judicial reform') embroidered with the code of the movement: eagles, flags, busts of Jefferson. Little gold Laffer curves identified the wearers as 'free-market purists'. Liberty bells stood for 'judicial restraint'.

The favored style here, like the favored foreign policy, seems to have been less military than paramilitary, a matter of talking tough. 'That's not off my disk,' Lieutenant Colonel Oliver North would snap by way of indicating that an idea was not his. 'The fellas', as Miss Noonan called them, the sharp, the smooth, the inner circle and those who aspired to it, made a point of not using seat belts on Air Force One. The less smooth flaunted souvenirs of action on the far borders of the Reagan doctrine. 'Jack Wheeler came back from Afghanistan with a Russian officer's belt slung over his shoulder,' Miss Noonan recalls. 'Grover Norquist came back from Africa rubbing his eyes from taking notes in a tent with Savimbi.' Miss Noonan herself had lunch in the White House mess with a 'Mujahadeen warrior' and his public relations man. 'What is the condition of your troops in the field?' she asked. 'We need help,' he said. The Filipino steward approached, pad and pencil in hand. The mujahadeen leader looked up. 'I will have meat,' he said.

This is not a milieu in which one readily places Nancy Reagan, whose preferred style derived from the more structured, if equally rigorous, world from which she had come. The nature of this world was not very well understood. I recall being puzzled, on visits to Washington during the first year or two of the Reagan administration, by the tenacity of certain misapprehensions about the Reagans and the men generally regarded as their intimates, that small group of industrialists and entrepreneurs who had encouraged and financed, as a venture in risk capital, Ronald Reagan's appearances in both Sacramento and Washington. The president was above all, I was told repeatedly, a Californian, a Westerner, as were the acquaintances who made up his kitchen cabinet; it was the 'Westernness' of these men that explained not only their rather intransigent views about America's mission in the world but also their apparent lack of interest in or identification with Americans for whom the trend was less reliably up. It was 'Westernness', too, that could explain those affronts to the local style so discussed in Washington during the early years, the overwrought clothes and the borrowed jewelry and the Le Cirque hair and the wall-to-wall carpeting and the table settings. In style and substance alike, the Reagans and their friends were said to display what was first called 'the California mentality', and then, as the administration got more settled and the social demonology of the exotic landscape more specific, 'the California Club mentality'.

I recall hearing about this 'California Club mentality' at a dinner table in Georgetown, and responding with a certain atavistic outrage (I was from California, my own brother then lived during the week at the California Club); what seems curious in retrospect is that many of the men in question, including the president, had only a convenient connection with California in particular and the West in general. William Wilson was actually born in Los Angeles, and Earle Jorgenson in San Francisco, but the late Justin Dart was born in Illinois, graduated from Northwestern, married a Walgreen heiress in Chicago, and did not move United Rexall, later Dart Industries, from Boston to Los Angeles until he was already its president. The late Alfred Bloomingdale was born in New York, graduated from Brown, and seeded the Diners Club with money from his family's New York store. What these men represented was not 'the West' but what was for this century a relatively new kind of monied class in America, a group devoid of social responsibilities precisely because their ties to any one place had been so attenuated.

Ronald and Nancy Reagan had in fact lived most of their adult lives in California, but as part of the entertainment community, the members of which do not belong to the California Club. In 1964, when I first went to live in Los Angeles, and for some years later, life in the upper reaches of this community was, for women, quite rigidly organized. Women left the table after dessert, and had coffee upstairs, isolated in the bedroom or dressing room with demitasse cups and rock sugar ordered from London and cinnamon sticks in lieu of demitasse spoons. On the hostess's dressing table there were always very large bottles of Fracas and Gardenia and Tuberose. The dessert that preceded this retreat (a soufflé or mousse with raspberry sauce) was inflexibly served on Flora Danica plates, and was itself preceded by the ritual of the finger bowls and the doilies. I recall being repeatedly told a cautionary tale about what Joan Crawford had said to a young woman who removed her finger bowl but left the doily. The details of exactly what Joan Crawford had said and to whom and at whose table she had said it differed with the teller, but it was always Joan Crawford, and it always involved the doily; one of the reasons Mrs Reagan ordered the famous new china was because, she told us in her own account of life in the Reagan White House, *My Turn*, the Johnson china had no finger bowls.

These subtropical evenings were not designed to invigorate. Large arrangements of flowers, ordered from David Jones, discouraged attempts at general conversation, ensuring that the table was turned on schedule. Expensive 'resort' dresses and pajamas were worn,

Pucci silks to the floor. When the women rejoined the men down-stairs, trays of white crème de menthe were passed. Large parties were held in tents, with pink lights and chili from Chasen's. Lunch took place at the Bistro, and later at the Bistro Garden and at Jimmy's, which was owned by Jimmy Murphy, who everyone knew because he had worked for Kurt Niklas at the Bistro.

These forms were those of the local *ancien régime*, and as such had largely faded out by the late sixties, but can be examined in detail in the photographs Jean Howard took over the years and collected in *Jean Howard's Hollywood: A Photo Memoir*. Although neither Reagan appears in Miss Howard's book (the people she saw tended to be stars or powers or famously amusing, and the Reagans, who fell into hard times and television, were not locally thought to fill any of these slots), the photographs give a sense of the rigors of the place. What one notices in a photograph of the Joseph Cottens' 1955 Fourth of July lunch, the day Jennifer Jones led the conga line into the pool, is not the pool. There are people in the pool, yes, and even chairs, but most of the guests sit decorously on the lawn, wearing rep ties, silk dresses, high-heeled shoes. Mrs Henry Hathaway, for a day in the sun at Anatole Litvak's beach house, wears a strapless dress of embroidered and scalloped organdy, and pearl earrings. Natalie Wood, lunching on Minna Wallis's lawn with Warren Beatty and George Cukor and the Hathaways and the Minnellis and the Axel-rods, wears a black straw hat with a silk ribbon, a white dress, black and white beads, perfect full makeup, and her hair pinned back.

This was the world from which Nancy Reagan went in 1966 to Sacramento and in 1980 to Washington, and it is in many ways the world, although it was vanishing *in situ* even before Ronald Reagan was elected governor of California, she never left. *My Turn* did not document a life radically altered by later experience. Eight years in Sacramento left so little imprint on Mrs Reagan that she described the house in which she lived there – a house located on 45th Street off M Street in a city laid out on a numerical and alphabetical grid running from 1st Street to 66th Street and from A Street to Y Street – as 'an English-style country house in the suburbs'.

She did not find it unusual that this house should have been bought for and rented to her and her husband (they paid $1,250 a month) by the same group of men who gave the State of California eleven acres on which to build Mrs Reagan the 'governor's mansion' she actually wanted and who later funded the million-dollar redecoration of the Reagan White House and who eventually bought the house on St Cloud Road in Bel Air to which the Reagans moved when they left Washington (the street number of the St Cloud house was 666, but the Reagans had it changed to 668, to avoid an association with the Beast in Revelations); she seemed to construe houses as part of her deal, like the housing provided to actors on location. Before the kitchen cabinet picked up Ronald Reagan's contract, the Reagans had lived in a house in Pacific Palisades remodeled by his then sponsor, General Electric.

This expectation on the part of the Reagans that other people would care for their needs struck many people, right away, as remarkable, and was usually characterized as a habit of the rich. But of course it is not a habit of the rich, and in any case the Reagans were not rich: they, and this expectation, were the products of studio Hollywood, a system in which performers performed, and in return were cared for. 'I preferred the studio system to the anxiety of looking for work in New York,' Mrs Reagan told us in *My Turn*. During the eight years she lived in Washington, Mrs Reagan said, she 'never once set foot in a supermarket or in almost any other kind of store, with the exception of a card shop at 17th and K, where I used to buy my birthday cards', and carried money only when she went out for a manicure.

She was surprised to learn ('Nobody had told us') that she and her husband were expected to pay for their own food, dry cleaning, and toothpaste while in the White House. She seemed never to understand why it was imprudent of her to have accepted clothes from their makers when so many of them encouraged her to do so. Only Geoffrey Beene, whose clothes for Patricia Nixon and whose wedding dress for Lynda Bird Johnson were purchased through stores at retail prices, seemed to have resisted this impulse. 'I don't quite understand how clothes can be "on loan" to a woman,' he told the *Los Angeles Times* in January of 1982, when the question of Mrs Reagan's clothes was first raised. 'I also think they'll run into a great deal of trouble deciding which of all these clothes are of museum quality . . . They also claim she's helping to "rescue" the American fashion industry. I didn't know it was in such dire straits.'

The clothes were, as Mrs Reagan seemed to construe it, 'wardrobe' – a production expense, like the housing and the catering and the first-class travel and the furniture and paintings and cars that get taken home after the set is struck – and should rightly have gone on the studio budget. That the producers of this particular production – the men Mrs Reagan called their 'wealthier friends', their 'very generous' friends – sometimes misunderstood their own role was understandable: Helene von Damm told us that only after William Wilson was warned that anyone with White House credentials was subject to a full-scale FBI investigation (Fred Fielding, the White House counsel, told him this) did he relinquish Suite 180 of the Executive Office Building, which he had commandeered the day after the inauguration in order to vet the appointment of the nominal, as opposed to the kitchen, cabinet.

'So began my stewardship,' Edith Bolling Wilson wrote later about the stroke that paralyzed Woodrow Wilson in October of 1919, eighteen months before he left the White House. The stewardship Nancy Reagan shared first with James Baker and Ed Meese and Michael Deaver and then less easily with Donald Regan was, perhaps because each of its principals was working a different scenario and only one, James Baker, had anything approaching a full script, considerably more Byzantine than most. Baker, whose ultimate role in this White House was to preserve it for the established order, seems to have relied heavily on the tendency of opposing forces, let loose, to neutralize each other. 'Usually in a big place there's only one person or group to be afraid of,' Peggy Noonan observed. 'But in the Reagan White House there were two, the chief of staff and his people and the First Lady and hers – a pincer formation that made everyone feel vulnerable.' Miss Noonan showed us Mrs Reagan moving through the corridors with her East Wing entourage, the members of which were said in the West Wing to be 'not serious', readers of *W* and *Vogue*. Mrs Reagan herself was variously referred to as 'Evita', 'Mommy', 'The Missus', 'The Hairdo with Anxiety'. Miss Noonan dismissed her as not 'a liberal or a leftist or a moderate or a détentist' but 'a Galanoist, a wealthy well-dressed woman who followed the common wisdom of her class'.

In fact Nancy Reagan was more interesting than that: it was precisely 'her class' in which she had trouble believing. She was not an experienced woman. Her social skills, like those of many women trained in the insular life of the motion picture community, were strikingly undeveloped. She and Raisa Gorbachev had 'little in common', and 'completely different outlooks on the world'. She and Betty Ford 'were different people who came from different worlds'. She seems to have been comfortable in the company of Michael Deaver, of Ted Graber (her decorator), and of only a few other people. She seems not to have had much sense about who goes with who. At a state dinner for José Napoleón Duarte of El Salvador, she seated herself between President Duarte and Ralph Lauren. She had limited social experience and apparently unlimited social anxiety. Helene von Damm complained that Mrs Reagan would not consent, during the first presidential campaign, to letting the fund-raisers call on 'her New York friends'; trying to put together a list for the New York dinner in November of 1979 at which Ronald Reagan was to announce his candidacy, Miss von Damm finally dispatched an emissary to extract a few names from Jerry Zipkin, who parted with them reluctantly, and then said, 'Remember, don't use my name.'

Perhaps Mrs Reagan's most endearing quality was this little girl's fear of being left out, of not having the best friends and not going to the parties in the biggest houses. She collected slights. She took refuge in a kind of piss-elegance, a fanciness (the 'English-style country house in the suburbs'), in using words like 'inappropriate'. It was 'inappropriate, to say the least' for Geraldine Ferraro and her husband to leave the dais and go 'down on the floor, working the crowd' at a 1984 Italian-American Federation dinner at which the candidates on both tickets were speaking. It was 'uncalled for – and mean' when, at the time John Koehler had been named to replace Patrick Buchanan as director of communications and it was learned that Koehler had been a member of Hitler Youth, Donald Regan said 'blame it on the East Wing'.

Mrs Gorbachev, as Mrs Reagan saw it, 'condescended' to her, and 'expected to be deferred to'. Mrs Gorbachev accepted an invitation from Pamela Harriman before she answered one from Mrs Reagan. The reason Ben Bradlee called Iran-contra 'the most fun he'd had since Watergate' was just possibly because, she explained in *My Turn*, he resented her relationship with Katharine Graham. Betty Ford was given a box on the floor of the 1976 Republican National Convention, and Mrs Reagan only a skybox. Mrs Reagan was evenhanded: Maureen Reagan 'may have been right' when she called this slight deliberate. When, on the second night of that convention, the band struck up 'Tie a Yellow Ribbon Round the Ole Oak Tree' during an ovation for Mrs Reagan, Mrs Ford started dancing with Tony Orlando. Mrs Reagan was magnanimous: 'Some of our people saw this as a deliberate attempt to upstage me, but I never thought that was her intention.'

Michael Deaver, in his version of more or less the same events, *Behind the Scenes*, gave us an arresting account of taking the Reagans, during the 1980 campaign, to an Episcopal church near the farm on which they were staying outside Middleburg, Virginia. After advancing the church and negotiating the subject of the sermon with the minister (Ezekiel and the bones rather than what Deaver called 'reborn Christians', presumably Christian rebirth), he finally agreed that the Reagans would attend an eleven o'clock Sunday service. 'We were not told,' Deaver wrote, 'and I did not anticipate, that the eleven o'clock service would also be holy communion,' a ritual he characterized as 'very foreign to the Reagans'. He described 'nervous glances', and 'mildly frantic' whispers about what to do, since the Reagans' experience had been of Bel Air Presbyterian, 'a proper Protestant church where trays are passed containing small glasses of grape juice and little squares of bread'. The moment arrived: '. . . halfway down the aisle I felt Nancy clutch my arm . . . "*Mike!*" she hissed. "*Are those people drinking out of the same cup?*"'

Here the incident takes on elements of 'I Love Lucy'. Deaver assures Mrs Reagan that it will be acceptable to just dip the wafer in the chalice. Mrs Reagan chances this, but manages somehow to drop the wafer in the wine. Ronald Reagan, cast here as Ricky Ricardo, is too deaf to hear Deaver's whispered instructions, and has been instructed by his wife to 'do exactly as I do'. He, too, drops the wafer in the wine, where it is left to float next to Mrs Reagan's. 'Nancy was relieved to leave the church,' Deaver reports. 'The president was chipper as he stepped into the sunlight, satisfied that the service had gone quite well.'

I had read this account several times before I realized what so attracted me to it: here we had a perfect model of the Reagan White House. There was the aide who located the correct setting ('I did some quick scouting and found a beautiful Episcopal church'), who anticipated every conceivable problem and handled it adroitly (he had 'a discreet chat with the minister', he 'gently raised the question'), and yet who somehow missed, as in the visit to Bitburg, a key point. There was the wife, charged with protecting her husband's face to the world, a task requiring, she hinted in *My Turn*, considerable vigilance. This was a husband who could be 'naive about people'. He had for example 'too much trust' in David Stockman. He had 'given his word' to Helmut Kohl, and so felt 'duty-bound to honor his commitment' to visit Bitburg. He was, Mrs Reagan disclosed during a 'Good Morning America' interview at the time *My Turn* was published, 'the softest touch going' when it came to what she referred to as (another instance of somehow missing a key point) 'the poor'. Mrs Reagan understood all this. She handled all this. And yet there she was outside Middleburg, Virginia, once again the victim of bad advance, confronted by the 'foreign' communion table and rendered stiff with apprehension that a finger bowl might get removed without its doily.

And there, at the center of it all, was Ronald Reagan, insufficiently briefed (or, as they say in the White House, 'badly served') on the wafer issue but moving ahead, stepping 'into the sunlight' satisfied with his own and everyone else's performance, apparently oblivious of (or inured to, or indifferent to) the crises being managed in his presence and for his benefit. What he had, and the aide and the wife did not have, was the story, the high concept, what Ed Meese used to call 'the big picture', as in 'he's a big-picture man'. The big picture here was of the candidate going to church on Sunday morning; the details obsessing the wife and the aide – what church, what to do with the wafer – remained outside the frame.

*   *   *

From the beginning in California, the principal in this administration was operating on what might have seemed distinctly special information. He had 'feelings' about things, for example about the Vietnam War. 'I have a feeling that we are doing better in the war than the people have been told,' he was quoted as having said in the *Los Angeles Times* on October 16, 1967. With the transforming power of the presidency, this special information that no one else understood – these big pictures, these high concepts – took on a magical quality, and some people in the White House came to believe that they had in their possession, sharpening his own pencils in the Oval Office, the Fisher King himself, the keeper of the grail, the source of that ineffable contact with the electorate that was in turn the source of the power.

There were times, we know now, when this White House had fairly well absented itself from the art of the possible. McFarlane flying to Teheran with the cake and the Bible and ten falsified Irish passports did not derive from our traditional executive tradition. The place was running instead on its own superstition, on the reading of bones, on the belief that a flicker of attention from the president during the presentation of a plan (the ideal presentation, Peggy Noonan explained, was one in which 'the president was forced to look at a picture, read a short letter, or respond to a question') ensured the transfer of the magic to whatever was that week exciting the ardor of the children who wanted to make the revolution – to SDI, to the mujahadeen, to Jonas Savimbi, to the contras.

Miss Noonan recalled what she referred to as 'the contra meetings', which turned on the magical notion that putting the president on display in the right setting (i.e., 'going over the heads of the media to the people') was all that was needed to 'inspire a commitment on the part of the American people'. They sat in those meetings and discussed having the president speak at the Orange Bowl in Miami on the anniversary of John F. Kennedy's Orange Bowl speech after the Bay of Pigs, never mind that the Kennedy Orange Bowl speech had become over the years in Miami the symbol of American betrayal. They sat in those meetings and discussed having the president go over the heads of his congressional opponents by speaking in Jim Wright's district near the Alamo: '. . . something like "*Blank* miles to the north of here is the Alamo,"' Miss Noonan wrote in

her notebook, sketching out the ritual in which the magic would
be transferred. '"... Where brave heroes *blank*, and where the
commander of the garrison wrote during those terrible last days
blank ..."'

But the Fisher King was sketching another big picture, one he
had had in mind since California. We have heard again and again
that Mrs Reagan turned the president away from the Evil Empire
and toward the meetings with Gorbachev. (Later, on NBC 'Nightly
News', the San Francisco astrologer Joan Quigley claimed a role in
influencing both Reagans on this point, explaining that she had
'changed their Evil Empire attitude by briefing them on Gorbachev's
horoscope'.) Mrs Reagan herself allowed that she 'felt it was ridiculous for these two heavily armed superpowers to be sitting there and
not talking to each other' and 'did push Ronnie a little'.

But how much pushing was actually needed remains in question.
The Soviet Union appeared to Ronald Reagan as an abstraction, a
place where people were helpless to resist 'communism', the inani-
mate evil which, as he had put it in a 1951 speech to a Kiwanis
convention and would continue to put it for the next three and a
half decades, had 'tried to invade our industry' and been 'fought'
and eventually 'licked'. This was a construct in which the actual
citizens of the Soviet Union could be seen to have been, like the
motion picture industry, 'invaded' – in need only of liberation. The
liberating force might be the appearance of a Shane-like character,
someone to 'lick' the evil, or it might be just the sweet light of reason.
'A people free to choose will always choose peace,' as President
Reagan told students at Moscow State University in May of 1988.

In this sense he was dealing from an entirely abstract deck, and
the opening to the East had been his card all along, his big picture,
his story. And this is how it went: what he would like to do, he had
told any number of people over the years (I recall first hearing it
from George Will, who cautioned me not to tell it because conversations with presidents were privileged), was take the leader of the
Soviet Union (who this leader would be was another of those details
outside the frame) on a flight to Los Angeles. When the plane came
in low over the middle-class subdivisions that stretch from the San
Bernardino mountains to LAX, he would direct the leader of the
Soviet Union to the window, and point out all the swimming pools

below. 'Those are the pools of the capitalists,' the leader of the Soviet Union would say. 'No,' the leader of the free world would say. 'Those are the pools of the workers.' *Blank* years further on, when brave heroes *blanked*, and where the leader of the free world *blank*, accidental history took its course, but we have yet to pay for the ardor.

1989

Insider Baseball

1

It occurred to me during the summer of 1988, in California and Atlanta and New Orleans, in the course of watching first the California primary and then the Democratic and Republican national conventions, that it had not been by accident that the people with whom I had preferred to spend time in high school had, on the whole, hung out in gas stations. They had not run for student body office. They had not gone to Yale or Swarthmore or DePauw, nor had they even applied. They had gotten drafted, gone through basic at Fort Ord. They had knocked up girls, and married them, had begun what they called the first night of the rest of their lives with a midnight drive to Carson City and a five-dollar ceremony performed by a justice still in his pajamas. They got jobs at the places that had laid off their uncles. They paid their bills or did not pay their bills, made down payments on tract houses, led lives on that social and economic edge referred to, in Washington and among those whose preferred locus is Washington, as 'out there'. They were never destined to be, in other words, communicants in what we have come to call, when we want to indicate the traditional ways in which power is exchanged and the status quo maintained in the United States, 'the process'.

'The process today gives everyone a chance to participate,' Tom Hayden, by way of explaining 'the difference' between 1968 and 1988, said to Bryant Gumbel on NBC at 7:50 A.M. on the day after

Jesse Jackson spoke at the 1988 Democratic convention in Atlanta. This was, at a convention that had as its controlling principle the notably nonparticipatory idea of 'unity', demonstrably not true, but people inside the process, constituting as they do a self-created and self-referring class, a new kind of managerial elite, tend to speak of the world not necessarily as it is but as they want people out there to believe it is. They tend to prefer the theoretical to the observable, and to dismiss that which might be learned empirically as 'anecdotal'. They tend to speak a language common in Washington but not specifically shared by the rest of us. They talk about 'programs', and 'policy', and how to 'implement' them or it, about 'trade-offs' and constituencies and positioning the candidate and distancing the candidate, about the 'story', and how it will 'play'. They speak of a candidate's performance, by which they usually mean his skill at circumventing questions, not as citizens but as professional insiders, attuned to signals pitched beyond the range of normal hearing: 'I hear he did all right this afternoon,' they were saying to one another in the press section of the Louisiana Superdome in New Orleans on the evening in August of 1988 when Dan Quayle was or was not to be nominated for the vice presidency. 'I hear he did OK with Brinkley.' By the time the balloons fell that night the narrative had changed: 'Quayle, zip,' the professionals were saying as they brushed the confetti off their laptops.

These were people who spoke of the process as an end in itself, connected only nominally, and vestigially, to the electorate and its possible concerns. 'She used to be an issues person but now she's involved in the process,' a prominent conservative said to me in New Orleans by way of suggesting why an acquaintance who believed Jack Kemp was 'speaking directly to what people out there want' had nonetheless backed George Bush. 'Anything that brings the process closer to the people is all to the good,' George Bush had declared in his 1987 autobiography, *Looking Forward*, accepting as given this relatively recent notion that the people and the process need not automatically be on convergent tracks.

When we talk about the process, then, we are talking, increasingly, not about 'the democratic process', or the general mechanism affording the citizens of a state a voice in its affairs, but the reverse: a mechanism seen as so specialized that access to it is correctly limited to its own professionals, to those who manage policy and those who report on it, to those who run the polls and those who quote them, to those who ask and those who answer the questions on the Sunday shows, to the media consultants, to the columnists, to the issues advisers, to those who give the off-the-record breakfasts and to those who attend them; to that handful of insiders who invent, year in and year out, the narrative of public life. 'I didn't realize you were a political junkie,' Martin Kaplan, the former *Washington Post* reporter and Mondale speechwriter who was married to Susan Estrich, the manager of the Dukakis campaign, said when I mentioned that I planned to write about the campaign; the assumption here, that the narrative should be not just written only by its own specialists but also legible only to its own specialists, is why, finally, an American presidential campaign raises questions that go so vertiginously to the heart of the structure.

What strikes one most vividly about such a campaign is precisely its remoteness from the actual life of the country. The figures are well known, and suggest a national indifference usually construed, by those inside the process, as ignorance, or 'apathy', in any case a defect not in themselves but in the clay they have been given to mold. Only slightly more than half of those eligible to vote in the United States did vote in the 1984 presidential election. An average 18.5 percent of what Nielsen Media Research calls the 'television households' in the United States tuned into network coverage of the 1988 Republican convention in New Orleans, meaning 81.5 percent did not. An average 20.2 percent of these 'television households' tuned into network coverage of the 1988 Democratic convention in Atlanta, meaning 79.8 percent did not. The decision to tune in or out ran along predictable lines: 'The demography is good even if the households are low,' a programming executive at Bozell, Jacobs, Kenyon & Eckhardt told the *New York Times* in July of 1988 about the agency's decision to buy 'campaign event' time for Merrill Lynch on both CBS and CNN. 'The ratings are about nine percent off 1984,' an NBC marketing vice president allowed, again to the *New York Times*, 'but the upscale target audience is there.'

When I read this piece I recalled standing, the day before the

California primary, in a dusty Central California schoolyard to which
the leading Democratic candidate had come to speak one more time
about what kind of president he wanted to be. The crowd was listless,
restless. There were gray thunderclouds overhead. A little rain fell.
'We welcome you to Silicon Valley,' an official had said by way of
greeting the candidate, but this was not in fact Silicon Valley: this
was San Jose, and a part of San Jose particularly untouched by
technological prosperity, a neighborhood in which the lowering of
two-toned Impalas remained a central activity.

'I want to be a candidate who brings people together,' the candidate was saying at the exact moment a man began shouldering his
way past me and through a group of women with children in their
arms. This was not a solid citizen, not a member of the upscale target
audience. This was a man wearing a down vest and a camouflage
hat, a man with a definite little glitter in his eyes, a member not of
the 18.5 percent and not of the 20.2 percent but of the 81.5, the
79.8. 'I've got to see the next president,' he muttered repeatedly.
'I've got something to tell him.'

'. . . Because that's what this party is all about,' the candidate said.

'Where is he?' the man said, confused. 'Who is he?'

'Get lost,' someone said.

'. . . Because that's what this country is all about,' the candidate
said.

Here we had the last true conflict of cultures in America, that
between the empirical and the theoretical. On the empirical evidence
this country was about two-toned Impalas and people with camouflage hats and a little glitter in their eyes, but this had not been,
among people inclined to the theoretical, the preferred assessment.
Nor had it even been, despite the fact that we had all stood together
on the same dusty asphalt, under the same plane trees, the general
assessment: this was how Joe Klein, writing a few weeks later in *New
York* magazine, had described those last days before the California
primary:

Breezing across California on his way to the nomination last
week, Michael Dukakis crossed a curious American threshold
. . . The crowds were larger, more excited now; they seemed to
be searching for reasons to love him. They cheered eagerly,

almost without provocation. People reached out to touch him
– not to shake hands, just to touch him . . . Dukakis seemed to
be making an almost subliminal passage in the public mind: he
was becoming presidential.

Those June days in 1988 during which Michael Dukakis did or
did not cross a curious American threshold had in fact been instructive. The day that ended in the schoolyard in San Jose had at first
seemed, given that it was the day before the California primary,
underscheduled, pointless, three essentially meaningless events separated by plane flights. At Taft High School in Woodland Hills that
morning there had been little girls waving red and gold pom-poms
in front of the cameras; 'Hold that tiger,' the band had played. 'Dream
. . . maker,' the choir had crooned. 'Governor Dukakis . . . this is . . .
Taft High,' the student council president had said. 'I understand that
this is the first time a presidential candidate has come to Taft High,'
Governor Dukakis had said. 'Is there any doubt . . . under those
circumstances . . . who you should support?'
   'Jackson,' a group of Chicano boys on the back sidewalk shouted
in unison.
   'That's what it's all about,' Governor Dukakis had said, and 'health
care', and 'good teachers and good teaching'.
   This event had been abandoned, and another materialized: a
lunchtime 'rally', in a downtown San Diego office plaza through
which many people were passing on their way to lunch, a borrowed
crowd but a less than attentive one. The cameras focused on the
balloons. The sound techs picked up 'La Bamba'. 'We're going to
take child-support enforcement seriously in this country,' Governor
Dukakis had said, and 'tough drug enforcement here and abroad'.
'Tough choices,' he had said, and 'we're going to make teaching a
valued profession in this country'.
   Nothing said in any venue that day had seemed to have much
connection with anybody listening ('I want to work with you and
with working people all over this country,' the candidate had said in
the San Diego office plaza, but people who work in offices in San
Diego do not think of themselves as 'working people'), and late that
afternoon, on the bus to the San Jose airport, I had asked a reporter
who had traveled through the spring with the various campaigns

(among those who moved from plane to plane it was agreed, by June, that the Bush plane had the worst access to the candidate and the best food, that the Dukakis plane had average access and average food, and that the Jackson plane had full access and no time to eat) if the candidate's appearances that day did not seem a little off the point.

'Not really,' the reporter said. 'He covered three major markets.'

Among those who traveled regularly with the campaigns, in other words, it was taken for granted that these 'events' they were covering, and on which they were in fact filing, were not merely meaningless but deliberately so: occasions on which film could be shot and no mistakes made ('They hope he won't make any big mistakes,' the NBC correspondent covering George Bush kept saying the evening of the September 25, 1988, debate at Wake Forest College, and, an hour and a half later, 'He didn't make any big mistakes'), events designed only to provide settings for those unpaid television spots which in this case were appearing, even as we spoke, on the local news in California's three major media markets. 'On the fishing trip, there was no way for the television crews to get videotapes out,' the *Los Angeles Times* noted a few weeks later in a piece about how 'poorly designed and executed events' had interfered with coverage of a Bush campaign 'environmental' swing through the Pacific Northwest. 'At the lumber mill, Bush's advance team arranged camera angles so poorly that in one setup only his legs could get on camera.' A Bush adviser had been quoted: 'There is no reason for camera angles not being provided for. We're going to sit down and talk about these things at length.'

Any traveling campaign, then, was a set, moved at considerable expense from location to location. The employer of each reporter on the Dukakis plane the day before the California primary was billed, for a total flying time of under three hours, $1,129.51; the billing to each reporter who happened, on the morning during the Democratic convention in Atlanta when Michael Dukakis and Lloyd Bentsen met with Jesse Jackson, to ride along on the Dukakis bus from the Hyatt Regency to the World Congress Center, a distance of perhaps ten blocks, was $217.18. There was the hierarchy of the set: there were actors, there were directors, there were script supervisors, there were grips.

There was the isolation of the set, and the arrogance, the contempt for outsiders. I recall pink-cheeked young aides on the Dukakis campaign referring to themselves, innocent of irony and therefore of history, as 'the best and the brightest'. On the morning after the Wake Forest debate, Michael Oreskes of the *New York Times* gave us this memorable account of Bush aides crossing the Wake Forest campus:

> The Bush campaign measured exactly how long it would take
> its spokesmen to walk briskly from the room in which they
> were watching the debate to the center where reporters were
> filing their articles. The answer was three and a half minutes –
> too long for Mr Bush's strategists, Lee Atwater, Robert Teeter,
> and Mr Darman. They ran the course instead as young aides
> cleared students and other onlookers from their path.

There was also the tedium of the set: the time spent waiting for the shots to be set up, the time spent waiting for the bus to join the motorcade, the time spent waiting for telephones on which to file, the time spent waiting for the Secret Service ('the agents', they were called on the traveling campaigns, never the Secret Service, just 'the agents', or 'this detail', or 'this rotation') to sweep the plane.

It was a routine that encouraged a certain passivity. There was the plane, or the bus, and one got on it. There was the schedule, and one followed it. There was time to file, or there was not. 'We should have had a page-one story,' a *Boston Globe* reporter complained to the *Los Angeles Times* after the Bush campaign had failed to provide the advance text of a Seattle 'environment' speech scheduled to end only twenty minutes before the departure of the plane for California. 'There are times when you sit up and moan, "Where is Michael Deaver when you need him?"' an ABC producer said to the *Times* on this point.

A final victory, for the staff and the press on a traveling campaign, would mean not a new production but only a new location: the particular setups and shots of the campaign day (the walk on the beach, the meet-and-greet at the housing project) would dissolve imperceptibly, isolation and arrogance and tedium intact, into the South Lawns, the Oval Office signings, the arrivals and departures of the administration day. There would still be the 'young aides'. There would still be 'onlookers' to be cleared from the path. Another location, another stand-up: 'We already shot a tarmac departure,' they say on the campaign planes. 'This schedule has two Rose Gardens,' they say in the White House pressroom. Ronald Reagan, when asked by David Frost how his life in the Oval Office had differed from his expectations of it, said this: ' – I was surprised at how familiar the whole routine was – the fact that the night before I would get a schedule telling me what I'm going to do all day the next day and so forth.'

American reporters 'like' covering a presidential campaign (it gets them out on the road, it has balloons, it has music, it is viewed as a big story, one that leads to the respect of one's peers, to the Sunday shows, to lecture fees and often to Washington), which is one reason why there has developed among those who do it so arresting an enthusiasm for overlooking the contradictions inherent in reporting that which occurs only in order to be reported. They are willing, in exchange for 'access', to transmit the images their sources wish transmitted. They are even willing, in exchange for certain colorful details around which a 'reconstruction' can be built (the 'kitchen table' at which the Dukakis campaign conferred on the night Lloyd Bentsen was added to the 1988 Democratic ticket, the 'slips of paper' on which key members of the 1988 Bush campaign, aboard Air Force Two on their way to New Orleans, wrote down their own guesses for vice president), to present these images not as a story the campaign wants told but as fact. This was *Time*, reporting from New Orleans on George Bush's reaction when Dan Quayle came under attack:

Bush never wavered in support of the man he had lifted so high. 'How's Danny doing?' he asked several times. But the Vice President never felt the compulsion to question Quayle face-to-face. The awkward investigation was left to Baker. Around noon, Quayle grew restive about answering further questions. 'Let's go,' he urged, but Baker pressed to know more. By early afternoon, the mood began to brighten in the

Bush bunker. There were no new revelations: the media hurricane had for the moment blown out to sea.

This was Sandy Grady, reporting from Atlanta:

Ten minutes before he was to face the biggest audience of his
life, Michael Dukakis got a hug from his 84-year-old mother,
Euterpe, who chided him, 'You'd better be good, Michael.'
Dukakis grinned and said, 'I'll do my best, Ma.'

'Appeal to the media by exposing the [Bush campaign's] heavy-
handed spin-doctoring,' William Safire advised the Dukakis campaign on September 8, 1988. 'We hate to be seen being manipulated.'

'Periodically,' the *New York Times* reported in March 1988, 'Martin
Plissner, the political editor of CBS News, and Susan Morrison, a
television producer and former political aide, organize gatherings of
the politically connected at their home in Washington. At such parties, they organize secret ballots asking the assembled experts who
will win . . . By November 1, 1987, the results of Mr Dole's organizing
efforts were apparent in a new Plissner-Morrison poll . . .' The symbiosis here was complete, and the only outsider was the increasingly
hypothetical voter, who was seen as responsive not to actual issues
but to their adroit presentation: 'At the moment the Republican
message is simpler and more clear than ours,' the Democratic chairman for California, Peter Kelly, said to the *Los Angeles Times* on August
31, 1988, complaining, on the matter of what was called the Pledge
of Allegiance issue, not that it was a false issue but that Bush had
seized the initiative, or 'the symbolism'.

'Bush Gaining in Battle of TV Images,' the *Washington Post* head-
lined a page-one story on September 10, 1988, and quoted Jeff
Greenfield, the ABC News political reporter: 'George Bush is almost
always outdoors, coatless, sometimes with his sleeves rolled up, and
looks ebullient and Happy Warrior-ish. Mike Dukakis is almost
always indoors, with his jacket on, and almost always behind a
lectern.' The Bush campaign, according to that week's issue of *Newsweek*, was, because it had the superior gift for getting film shot in
'dramatic settings – like Boston Harbor', winning 'the all-important
battle of the backdrops'. A CBS producer covering the Dukakis cam-

paign was quoted complaining about an occasion when Governor Dukakis, speaking to students on a California beach, had faced the students instead of the camera. 'The only reason Dukakis was on the beach was to get his picture taken,' the producer had said. 'So you might as well see his face.' Pictures, *Newsweek* had concluded, 'often speak louder than words.'

This 'battle of the backdrops' story appeared on page twenty-four of the *Newsweek* dated September 12, 1988. On page twenty-three of the same issue there appeared, as illustrations for the lead National Affairs story ('Getting Down and Dirty: As the mudslinging campaign moves into full gear, Bush stays on the offensive – and Dukakis calls back his main streetfighting man'), two half-page color photographs, one of each candidate, which seemed to address the very concerns expressed on page twenty-four and in the *Post*. The photograph of George Bush showed him indoors, with his jacket on, and behind a lectern. That of Michael Dukakis showed him outdoors, coatless, with his sleeves rolled up, looking ebullient, about to throw a baseball on an airport tarmac: something had been learned from Jeff Greenfield, or something had been told to Jeff Greenfield. 'We talk to the press, and things take on a life of their own,' Mark Siegel, a Democratic political consultant, said to Elizabeth Drew.

About this baseball on the tarmac. On the day that Michael Dukakis appeared at the high school in Woodland Hills and at the rally in San Diego and in the schoolyard in San Jose, there was, although it did not appear on the schedule, a fourth event, what was referred to among the television crews as a 'tarmac arrival with ball tossing'. This event had taken place in late morning, on the tarmac at the San Diego airport, just after the chartered 737 had rolled to a stop and the candidate had emerged. There had been a moment of hesitation. Then baseball mitts had been produced, and Jack Weeks, the traveling press secretary, had tossed a ball to the candidate. The candidate had tossed the ball back. The rest of us had stood in the sun and given this our full attention, undeflected even by the arrival of an Alaska Airlines 767: some forty adults standing on a tarmac watching a diminutive figure in shirtsleeves and a red tie toss a ball to his press secretary.

'Just a regular guy,' one of the cameramen had said, his inflection that of the 'union official' who confided, in an early Dukakis commercial aimed at blue-collar voters, that he had known 'Mike' a long time, and backed him despite his not being 'your shot-and-beer kind of guy'.

'I'd say he was a regular guy,' another cameraman had said. 'Definitely.'

'I'd sit around with him,' the first cameraman said.

Kara Dukakis, one of the candidate's daughters, had at that moment emerged from the 737.

'You'd have a beer with him?'

Jack Weeks had tossed the ball to Kara Dukakis.

'I'd have a beer with him.'

Kara Dukakis had tossed the ball to her father. Her father had caught the ball and tossed it back to her.

'OK,' one of the cameramen had said. 'We got the daughter. Nice. That's enough. Nice.'

The CNN producer then on the Dukakis campaign told me, later in the day, that the first recorded ball tossing on the Dukakis campaign had been outside a bowling alley somewhere in Ohio. CNN had shot it. When the campaign realized that only one camera had it, they had restaged it.

'We have a lot of things like the ball tossing,' the producer said. 'We have the Greek dancing for example.'

I asked if she still bothered to shoot it.

'I get it,' she said, 'but I don't call in anymore and say, "Hey, hold it, I've got him dancing."'

This sounded about right (the candidate might, after all, bean a citizen during the ball tossing, and CNN would need film), and not until I read Joe Klein's version of these days in California did it occur to me that this eerily contrived moment on the tarmac at San Diego could become, at least provisionally, history. 'The Duke seemed downright jaunty,' Joe Klein reported. 'He tossed a baseball with aides. He was flagrantly multilingual. He danced Greek dances . . .' In the July 25, 1988, issue of *U.S. News & World Report*, Michael Kramer opened his cover story, 'Is Dukakis Tough Enough?', with a more developed version of the ball tossing:

The thermometer read 101 degrees, but the locals guessed 115 on the broiling airport tarmac in Phoenix. After all, it was under a noonday sun in the desert that Michael Dukakis was indulging his truly favorite campaign ritual – a game of catch with his aide Jack Weeks. 'These days,' he has said, 'throwing the ball around when we land somewhere is about the only exercise I get.' For 16 minutes, Dukakis shagged flies and threw strikes. Halfway through, he rolled up his sleeves, but he never loosened his tie. Finally, mercifully, it was over and time to pitch the obvious tongue-in-cheek question: 'Governor, what does throwing a ball around in this heat say about your mental stability?' Without missing a beat, and without a trace of a smile, Dukakis echoed a sentiment he has articulated repeatedly in recent months: 'What it means is that I'm tough.'

Nor was this the last word. On July 31, 1988, in the *Washington Post*, David S. Broder, who had also been with the Dukakis campaign in Phoenix, gave us a third, and, by virtue of his seniority in the process, perhaps the official version of the ball tossing:

Dukakis called out to Jack Weeks, the handsome, curly-haired Welshman who good-naturedly shepherds us wayward pressmen through the daily vagaries of the campaign schedule. Weeks dutifully produced two gloves and a baseball, and there on the tarmac, with its surface temperature just below the boiling point, the governor loosened up his arm and got the kinks out of his back by tossing a couple hundred 90-foot pegs to Weeks.

What we had in the tarmac arrival with ball tossing, then, was an understanding: a repeated moment witnessed by many people, all of whom believed it to be a setup and yet most of whom believed that only an outsider, only someone too 'naive' to know the rules of the game, would so describe it.

2

The narrative is made up of many such understandings, tacit agreements, small and large, to overlook the observable in the interests
of obtaining a dramatic story line. It was understood, for example,
that the first night of the 1988 Republican National Convention in
New Orleans should be for Ronald Reagan 'the last hurrah'. 'Reagan
Electrifies GOP' was the headline the next morning on page one
of *New York Newsday*; in fact the Reagan appearance, which was
rhetorically pitched not to a live audience but to the more intimate
demands of the camera, was, inside the Superdome, barely registered. It was understood, similarly, that Michael Dukakis's acceptance speech on the last night of the 1988 Democratic National
Convention in Atlanta should be the occasion on which his 'passion',
or 'leadership', emerged. 'Could the no-nonsense nominee reach
within himself to discover the language of leadership?' *Time* had
asked. 'Could he go beyond the pedestrian promise of "good jobs at
good wages" to give voice to a new Democratic vision?'

The correct answer, since the forward flow of the narrative here
demanded the appearance of a genuine contender (a contender who
could be seventeen points 'up', so that George Bush could be seventeen points 'down', a position from which he could rise to 'claim' his
own convention), was yes: 'The best speech of his life,' David Broder
reported. Sandy Grady found it 'superb', evoking 'Kennedyesque
echoes' and showing 'unexpected craft and fire'. *Newsweek* had witnessed Michael Dukakis 'electrifying the convention with his
intensely personal acceptance speech'. In fact the convention that
evening had been electrified, not by the speech, which was the same
series of nonsequential clauses Governor Dukakis had employed during the primary campaign ('My friends . . . son of immigrants . . .
good jobs at good wages . . . make teaching a valued and honored
profession . . . it's what the Democratic Party is all about'), but
because the floor had been darkened, swept with laser beams, and
flooded with 'Coming to America', played at concert volume with
the bass turned up.

*   *   *

It is understood that this invented narrative will turn on certain familiar elements. There is the continuing story line of the 'horse race', the reliable daily drama of one candidate falling behind as another pulls ahead. There is the surprise of the new poll, the glamour of the one-on-one colloquy on the midnight plane, a plot point (the nation sleeps while the candidate and his confidant hammer out its fate) pioneered by Theodore H. White. There is the abiding if unexamined faith in the campaign as personal odyssey, and in the spiritual benefits accruing to those who undertake it. There is, in the presented history of the candidate, the crucible event, the day that 'changed the life'.

Robert Dole's life was understood to have changed when he was injured in Italy in 1945. George Bush's life is understood to have changed when he and his wife decided to 'get out and make it on our own' (his words, or rather those of his speechwriter, Peggy Noonan, from the 'lived the dream' acceptance speech at the 1988 convention, suggesting action, shirtsleeves, privilege cast aside) in west Texas. For Bruce Babbitt, 'the dam just kind of broke' during a student summer in Bolivia. For Michael Dukakis, the dam was understood to have broken not during his student summer in Peru but after his 1978 defeat in Massachusetts; his tragic flaw, we read repeatedly during the 1988 campaign, was neither his evident sulkiness at losing that earlier election nor what many saw later as a rather dissociated self-satisfaction ('We're two people very proud of what we've done,' he said on NBC in Atlanta, falling into a favorite speech pattern, 'very proud of each other, actually . . . and very proud that a couple of guys named Dukakis and Jackson have come this far'), but the more attractive 'hubris'.

The narrative requires broad strokes. Michael Dukakis was physically small, and had associations with Harvard, which suggested that he could be cast as an 'intellectual'; the 'immigrant factor', on the other hand, could make him tough (as in 'What it means is that I'm tough'), a 'streetfighter'. 'He's cool, shrewd and still trying to prove he's tough,' the July 25, 1988, cover of *U.S. News & World Report* said about Dukakis. 'Toughness is what it's all about,' one of his advisers was quoted as having said in the cover story. 'People need to feel that a candidate is tough enough to be president. It is the threshold perception.'

George Bush had presented a more tortured narrative problem. The tellers of the story had not understood, or had not responded to, the essential Bush style, which was complex, ironic, the diffident edge of the Northeastern elite. This was what was at first identified as 'the wimp factor', which was replaced not by a more complicated view of the personality but by its reverse: George Bush was by late August no longer a 'wimp' but someone who had 'thrown it over', 'struck out' to make his own way: no longer a product of the effete Northeast but someone who had thrived in Texas, and was therefore 'tough enough to be president'.

That George Bush might have thrived in Texas not in spite of being but precisely because he was a member of the Northeastern elite was a shading that had no part in the narrative: 'He was considered back at the time one of the most charismatic people ever elected to public office in the history of Texas,' Congressman Bill Archer of Houston said. 'That charisma, people talked about it over and over again.' People talked about it, probably, because Andover and Yale and the inheritable tax avoidance they suggested were, during the years George Bush lived in Texas, the exact ideals toward which the Houston and Dallas establishment aspired, but the narrative called for a less ambiguous version: 'Lived in a little shotgun house, one room for the three of us,' as Bush, or Peggy Noonan, had put it in the celebrated no-subject-pronoun cadences of the 'lived the dream' acceptance speech. 'Worked in the oil business, started my own ... Moved from the shotgun to a duplex apartment to a house. Lived the dream – high school football on Friday night, Little League, neighborhood barbecue ... pushing into unknown territory with kids and a dog and a car ...'

All stories, of course, depend for their popular interest upon the invention of personality, or 'character', but in the political narrative, designed as it is to maintain the illusion of 'consensus' by obscuring rather than addressing actual issues, this invention served a further purpose. It was by 1988 generally if unspecifically agreed that the United States faced certain social and economic realities that, if not intractable, did not entirely lend themselves to the kinds of policy fixes people who run for elected office, on whatever ticket, were likely to undertake. We had not yet accommodated the industrialization of parts of the third world. We had not yet adjusted to the economic realignment of a world in which the United States was no longer the principal catalyst for change. 'We really are in an age of transition,' Brent Scowcroft, Bush's leading foreign policy adviser, told Robert Scheer of the *Los Angeles Times* in the fall of 1988, 'from a postwar world where the Soviets were the enemy, where the United States was a superpower and trying to build up both its allies and its former enemies and help the third world transition to independence. That whole world and all of those things are coming to an end or have endeed, and we are now entering a new and different world that will be complex and much less unambiguous than the old one.'

What continued to dominate the rhetoric of the 1988 campaign, however, was not this awareness of a new and different world but nostalgia for an old one, and coded assurance that symptoms of ambiguity or change, of what George Bush called the 'deterioration of values', would be summarily dealt with by increased social control. It was not by accident that the word 'enforcement', devoid of any apparent awareness that it had been tried before, kept coming up in this campaign. A problem named seemed, for both campaigns, a problem solved. Michael Dukakis had promised, by way of achieving his goal of 'no safe haven for dope dealers and drug profits anywhere on this earth', to 'double the number' of Drug Enforcement Administration agents, not a promising approach. George Bush, for his part, had repeatedly promised the death penalty, and not only the Pledge of Allegiance but prayer, or 'moments of silence', in the schools. 'We've got to change this entire culture,' he said in the Wake Forest debate; the polls indicated that the electorate wanted 'change', and this wish for change had been translated, by both campaigns, into the wish for a 'change back', a regression to the 'gentler America' of which George Bush repeatedly spoke.

To the extent that there was a 'difference' between the candidates, the difference lay in just where on the time scale this 'gentler America' could be found. The Dukakis campaign was oriented to 'programs', and the programs it proposed were similar to those that had worked (the encouragement of private sector involvement in low-cost housing, say) in the boom years following World War II. The Bush campaign was oriented to 'values', and the values to which it referred were those not of a postwar but of a prewar America. In neither case did 'ideas' play a part: 'This election isn't about ideology, it's about competence,' Michael Dukakis had said in Atlanta. 'First and foremost, it's a choice between two persons,' one of his senior advisers, Thomas Kiley, had told the *Wall Street Journal*. 'What it all comes down to, after all the shouting and the cheers, is the man at the desk,' George Bush had said in New Orleans. In other words, what it was 'about', what it came 'down to', what was wrong or right with America, was not a historical shift largely unaffected by the actions of individual citizens but 'character', and if 'character' could be seen to count, then every citizen – since everyone was a judge of character, an expert in the field of personality – could be seen to count. This notion, that the citizen's choice among determinedly centrist candidates makes a 'difference', is in fact the narrative's most central element, and also its most fictive.

3

The Democratic National Convention of 1968, during which the process was put to a popular vote on the streets of Chicago and after which it was decided that what had occurred could not be allowed to recur, is generally agreed to have prompted the multiplication of primaries, and the concomitant coverage of those primaries, which led to the end of the national party convention as a more than ceremonial occasion. Early in 1987, as the primary campaigns got under way for the 1988 election, David S. Broder, in the *Washington Post*, offered this compelling analysis of the power these 'reforms' in the nominating procedure had vested not in the party leadership, which is where this power of choice ultimately resides, but in 'the existing communications system', by which he meant the press, or the medium through which the party leadership sells its choice:

> Once the campaign explodes to 18 states, as it will the day after New Hampshire, when the focus shifts to a super-primary across the nation, the existing communications system simply will not accommodate more than two or three candidates in each party. Neither the television networks, nor newspapers

nor magazines, have the resources of people, space and time to describe and analyze the dynamics of two simultaneous half-national elections among Republicans and Democrats. That task is simply beyond us. Since we cannot reduce the number of states voting on Super Tuesday, we have to reduce the number of candidates treated as serious contenders. Those news judgments will be arbitrary – but not subject to appeal. Those who finish first or second in Iowa and New Hampshire will get tickets from the mass media to play in the next big round. Those who don't, won't. A minor exception may be made for the two reverends, Jesse L. Jackson and Marion G. (Pat) Robertson, who have their own church-based communications and support networks and are less dependent on mass-media attention. But no one else.

By the time the existing communications system set itself up in July and August of 1988 in Atlanta and New Orleans, the priorities were clear. 'NOTICE NOTICE NOTICE,' read the typed note given to some print reporters when they picked up their credentials in Atlanta. 'Because the National Democratic Convention Committee permitted the electronic media to exceed specifications for their broadcast booths, your assigned seat's sight line to the podium and the convention floor was obliterated.' The network skyboxes, in other words, had been built in front of the sections originally assigned to the periodical press. 'This is a place that was chosen to be, for all intents and purposes, a large TV studio, to be able to project our message to the American people and a national audience,' Paul Kirk, the chairman of the Democratic National Committee, said by way of explaining why the podium and the skyboxes had so reduced the size of the Omni Coliseum in Atlanta that some thousand delegates and alternates had been, on the evening Jesse Jackson spoke, locked out. Mayor Andrew Young of Atlanta apologized for the lock-out, but said that it would be the same on nights to follow: 'The one hundred and fifty million people in this country who are going to vote have got to be our major target.' Still, convention delegates were seen to have a real róle: 'The folks in the hall are so important for how it looks,' Lane Venardos, senior producer in charge of convention coverage for CBS News, said to the *New York Times* about the Republican convention. The delegates, in other words, could be seen as dress extras.

During those eight summer evenings in 1988, four in Atlanta and four in New Orleans, when roughly 80 percent of the television sets 'out there' were tuned somewhere else, the entire attention of those inside the process was directed toward the invention of this story in which they themselves were the principal players, and for which they themselves were the principal audience. The great arenas in which the conventions were held became worlds all their own, constantly transmitting their own images back to themselves, connected by skywalks to interchangeable structures composed not of floors but of 'levels', mysteriously separated by fountains and glass elevators and escalators that did not quite connect.

In the Louisiana Superdome in New Orleans as in the Omni Coliseum in Atlanta, the grids of lights blazed and dimmed hypnotically. Men with rifles patrolled the high catwalks. The nets packed with balloons swung gently overhead, poised for that instant known as the 'money shot', the moment, or 'window', when everything was working and no network had cut to a commercial. Minicams trawled the floor, fishing in Atlanta for Rob Lowe, in New Orleans for Donald Trump. In the NBC skybox Tom Brokaw floated over the floor, adjusting his tie, putting on his jacket, leaning to speak to John Chancellor. In the CNN skybox Mary Alice Williams sat bathed in white light, the blond madonna of the skyboxes. On the television screens in the press section the images reappeared, but from another angle: Tom Brokaw and Mary Alice Williams again, broadcasting not just above us but also to us, the circle closed.

At the end of prime time, when the skyboxes went dark, the action moved across the skywalks and into the levels, into the lobbies, into one or another Hyatt or Marriott or Hilton or Westin. In the portage from lobby to lobby, level to level, the same people kept materializing, in slightly altered roles. On a level of the Hyatt in Atlanta I saw Ann Lewis in her role as a Jackson adviser. On a level of the Hyatt in New Orleans I saw Ann Lewis in her role as a correspondent for *Ms*. Some pictures were vivid: 'I've been around this process awhile, and one thing I've noticed, it's the people who write the checks who get treated as if they have a certain amount of power,' I recall Nadine Hack, the chairman of Dukakis's New York Finance Council, saying in a suite at the Hyatt in Atlanta: here was a willowy woman with long blond hair standing barefoot on a table and trying to explain how to buy into the action. 'The great thing about those evenings was you could even see Michael Harrington there,' I recall Richard Viguerie saying to me at a party in New Orleans: here was the man who managed the action for the American right trying to explain the early 1960s, and evenings we had both spent on Washington Square.

There was in Atlanta in 1988, according to the Democratic National Committee, 'twice the media presence' that there had been at the 1984 convention. There were in New Orleans 'media workspaces' assigned not only to 117 newspapers and news services and to the American television and radio industry in full strength but to fifty-two foreign networks. On every corner one turned in New Orleans someone was doing a stand-up. There were telephone numbers to be called for quotes: 'Republican State and Local Officials', or 'Pat Robertson Campaign' or 'Richard Wirthlin, Reagan's Pollster'. Newspapers came with teams of thirty, forty, fifty. In every lobby there were stacks of fresh newspapers, the *Atlanta Constitution*, the *New Orleans Times-Picayune*, the *Washington Post*, the *Miami Herald*, the *Los Angeles Times*. In Atlanta these papers were collected in bins, and 'recycled': made into thirty thousand posters, which were in turn distributed to the press in New Orleans.

This perfect recycling tended to present itself, in the narcosis of the event, as a model for the rest: like American political life itself, and like the printed and transmitted images on which that life depended, this was a world with no half-life. It was understood that what was said here would go on the wire and vanish. Garrison Keillor and his cute kids would vanish. Ann Richards and her peppery ripostes would vanish. Phyllis Schlafly and Olympia Snowe would vanish. All the opinions and all the rumors and all the housemaid Spanish spoken in both Atlanta and New Orleans would vanish, all the quotes would vanish, and all that would remain would be the huge arenas themselves, the arenas and the lobbies and the levels and the skywalks to which they connected, the incorporeal heart of the process itself, the agora, the symbolic marketplace in which the narrative was not only written but immediately, efficiently, entirely, consumed.

A certain time lag exists between this world of the arenas and the world as we know it. One evening in New York between the Democratic and Republican conventions I happened to go down to Lafayette Street, to the Public Theater, to look at clips from documentaries on which the English-born filmmaker Richard Leacock had worked during his fifty years in America. We saw folk singers in Virginia in 1941 and oil riggers in Louisiana in 1946 (this was *Louisiana Story*, which Leacock had shot for Robert Flaherty) and tent performers in the corn belt in 1954; we saw Eddy Sachs preparing for the Indianapolis 500 in 1960 and Piri Thomas in Spanish Harlem in 1961. We saw parades, we saw baton twirlers. We saw quints in South Dakota in 1963.

There on the screen at the Public Theater that evening were images and attitudes from an America that had largely vanished, and what was striking was this: these were the very images and attitudes on which 'the campaign' was predicated. That 'unknown territory' into which George Bush had pushed 'with kids and a dog and a car' had existed in this vanished America, and long since been subdivided, cut up for those tract houses on which the people who were not part of the process had made down payments. Michael Dukakis's 'snowblower', and both the amusing frugality and the admirable husbandry of resources it was meant to suggest, derived from some half-remembered idea of what citizens of this vanished America had laughed at and admired. 'The Pledge' was an issue from that world. 'A drug-free America' had perhaps seemed in that world an achievable ideal, as had 'better schools'. I recall listening in Atlanta to Dukakis's foreign policy expert, Madeleine Albright, as she conjured up, in the course of arguing against a 'no first use' minority plank in the Democratic platform, a scenario in which 'Soviet forces overrun Europe' and the United States has, by promising no first use of nuclear weapons, crippled its ability to act: she was talking about a world that had not turned since 1948. What was at work here seemed on the one hand a grave, although in many ways a comfortable, miscalculation of what people in America might have as their deepest

concerns in 1988; it seemed on the other hand just another understanding, another of those agreements to overlook the observable.

4

It was into this sedative fantasy of a fixable imperial America that
Jesse Jackson rode, on a Trailways bus. 'You've never heard a sense
of panic sweep the party as it has in the past few days,' David Garth
had told the *New York Times* during those perilous spring weeks in
1988 when there seemed a real possibility that a black candidate
with no experience in elected office, a candidate believed to be so
profoundly unelectable that he could take the entire Democratic
party down with him, might go to Atlanta with more delegates than
any other Democratic candidate. 'The party is up against an extraordinary endgame,' the pollster Paul Maslin had said. 'I don't know
where this leaves us,' Robert S. Strauss had said. One uncommitted
superdelegate, the *New York Times* had reported, 'said the Dukakis
campaign had changed its message since Mr Dukakis lost the Illinois
primary. Mr Dukakis is no longer the candidate of "inevitability" but
the candidate of order, he said. "They're not doing the train's leaving
the station and you better be on it routine anymore," this official
said. "They're now saying that the station's about to be blown up by
terrorists and we're the only ones who can defuse the bomb."'
    The threat, or the possibility, presented by Jesse Jackson, the
'historic' (as people liked to say after it became certain he would not
have the numbers) part of his candidacy, derived from something
other than the fact that he was black, a circumstance that had before
been and could again be compartmentalized. For example: 'Next
week, when we launch our black radio buys, when we start doing
our black media stuff, Jesse Jackson needs to be on the air in the
black community on our behalf,' Donna Brazile of the Dukakis campaign said to the *New York Times* on September 8, 1988, by way of
emphasizing how much the Dukakis campaign 'sought to make
peace' with Jackson.
    'Black', in other words, could be useful, and even a moral force,
a way for white Americans to attain more perfect attitudes: 'His color

is an enormous plus ... How moving it is, and how important, to see a black candidate meet and overcome the racism that lurks in virtually all of us white Americans,' Anthony Lewis had noted in a March 1988 column explaining why the notion that Jesse Jackson could win was nonetheless 'a romantic delusion' of the kind that had 'repeatedly undermined' the Democratic party. 'You look at what Jesse Jackson has done, you have to wonder what a Tom Bradley of Los Angeles could have done, what an Andy Young of Atlanta could have done,' I heard someone say on one of the Sunday shows after the Jackson campaign had entered its 'historic' (or, in the candidate's word, its 'endless') phase.

'Black', then, by itself and in the right context – the 'right context' being a reasonable constituency composed exclusively of blacks and supportive liberal whites – could be accommodated by the process. Something less traditional, and also less manageable, was at work in the 1988 Jackson candidacy. I recall having dinner, the weekend before the California primary, at the Pebble Beach house of the chairman of a large American corporation. There were sixteen people at the table, all white, all well-off, all well dressed, all well educated, all socially conservative. During the course of the evening it came to my attention that six of the sixteen, or every one of the registered Democrats present, intended to vote on Tuesday for Jesse Jackson. Their reasons were unspecific, but definite. 'I heard him, he didn't sound like a politician,' one said. 'He's talking about right now,' another said. 'You get outside the gate here, take a look around, you have to know we've got some problems, and he's talking about them.'

What made the 1988 Jackson candidacy a bomb that had to be defused, then, was not that blacks were supporting a black candidate, but that significant numbers of whites were supporting – not only supporting but in many cases overcoming deep emotional and economic conflicts of their own in order to support – a candidate who was attractive to them not because of but in spite of the fact that he was black, a candidate whose most potent attraction was that he 'didn't sound like a politician'. 'Character' seemed not to be, among these voters, the point-of-sale issue the narrative made it out to be: a number of white Jackson supporters to whom I talked would quite serenely describe their candidate as a 'con man', or even as, in George Bush's word, a 'hustler'.

'And yet . . .,' they would say. What 'and yet' turned out to mean, almost without variation, was that they were willing to walk off the edge of the known political map for a candidate who was running against, as he repeatedly said, 'politics as usual', against what he called 'consensualist centrist politics'; against what had come to be the very premise of the process, the notion that the winning of and the maintaining of public office warranted the invention of a public narrative based at no point on observable reality.

In other words they were not idealists, these white Jackson voters, but empiricists. By the time Jesse Jackson got to California, where he would eventually get 25 percent of the entire white vote and 49 percent of the total vote from voters between the demographically key ages of thirty to forty-four, the idealists had rallied behind the sole surviving alternative, who was, accordingly, just then being declared 'presidential'. In Los Angeles, during May and early June of 1988, those Democrats who had not fallen in line behind Dukakis were described as 'self-indulgent', or as 'immature'; they were even described, in a dispiriting phrase that prefigured the tenor of the campaign to come, as 'issues wimps'. I recall talking to a rich and politically well-connected Californian who had been, through the primary campaign there, virtually the only prominent Democrat on the famously liberal west side of Los Angeles who was backing Jackson. He said that he could afford 'the luxury of being more interested in issues than in process', but that he would pay for it: 'When I want something, I'll have a hard time getting people to pick up the phone. I recognize that. I made the choice.'

On the June night in 1988 when Michael Dukakis was declared the winner of the California Democratic primary, and the bomb officially defused, there took place in the Crystal Room of the Biltmore Hotel in Los Angeles a 'victory party' that was less a celebration than a ratification by the professionals, a ritual convergence of those California Democrats for whom the phones would continue to get picked up. Charles Manatt was there. John Emerson and Charles Palmer were there. John Van de Kamp was there. Leo McCarthy was there. Robert Shrum was there. All the custom-made suits and monogrammed shirts in Los Angeles that night were there, met in the wide corridors of the Biltmore in order to murmur assurances to one another. The ballroom in fact had been cordoned as if to repel late invaders, roped off in such a way that once the Secret Service, the traveling press, the local press, the visiting national press, the staff, and the candidate had assembled, there would be room for only a controllable handful of celebrants, over whom the cameras would dutifully pan.

In fact the actual 'celebrants' that evening were not at the Biltmore at all, but a few blocks away at the Los Angeles Hilton, dancing under the mirrored ceiling of the ballroom in which the Jackson campaign had gathered, its energy level in defeat notably higher than that of other campaigns in victory. Jackson parties tended to spill out of ballrooms onto several levels of whatever hotel they were in, and to last until three or four in the morning: anyone who wanted to be at a Jackson party was welcome at a Jackson party, which was unusual among the campaigns, and tended to reinforce the populist spirit that had given this one its extraordinary animation.

Of that evening at the Los Angeles Hilton I recall a pretty woman in a gold lamé dress, dancing with a baby in her arms. I recall empty beer bottles, Corona and Excalibur and Budweiser, sitting among the loops of television cable. I recall the candidate himself, dancing on the stage, and, on this June evening when the long shot had not come in, this evening when the campaign was effectively over, giving the women in the traveling press the little parody wave they liked to give him, 'the press chicks' wave', the stiff-armed palm movement they called 'the Nancy Reagan wave'; then taking off his tie and throwing it into the crowd, like a rock star. This was of course a narrative of its own, but a relatively current one, and one that had, because it seemed at some point grounded in the recognizable, a powerful glamour for those estranged from the purposeful nostalgia of the traditional narrative.

In the end the predictable decision was made to go with the process, with predictable, if equivocal, results. On the last afternoon of the 1988 Republican convention in New Orleans I walked from the hotel in the Quarter where I was staying over to Camp Street. I wanted to see 544 Camp, a local point of interest not noted on the points-of-interest maps distributed at the convention but one that figures large in the literature of American conspiracy. '544 Camp Street' was the address stamped on the leaflets Lee Harvey Oswald was distributing around New Orleans between May and September of 1963, the 'Fair Play for Cuba Committee' leaflets that, in the years after Lee Harvey Oswald assassinated John F. Kennedy, suggested to some that he had been acting for Fidel Castro and to others that he had been set up to appear to have been acting for Fidel Castro. Guy Banister had his detective agency at 544 Camp. David Ferrie and Jack Martin frequented the coffee shop on the ground floor at 544 Camp. The Cuban Revolutionary Council rented an office at 544 Camp. People had taken the American political narrative seriously at 544 Camp. They had argued about it, fallen out over it, had hit each other over the head with pistol butts over it.

In fact I never found 544 Camp, because there was no more such address: the small building had been bought and torn down in order to construct a new federal courthouse. Across the street in Lafayette Square that afternoon there had been a loudspeaker, and a young man on a makeshift platform talking about abortion, and unwanted babies being put down the Disposall and 'clogging the main sewer drains of New Orleans', but no one except me had been there to listen. 'Satan – you're the liar,' the young woman with him on the platform had sung, lip-syncing a tape originally made, she told me, by a woman who sang with an Alabama traveling ministry, the Ministry of the Happy Hunters. 'There's one thing you can't deny . . . you're the father of every lie . . .' The young woman had been wearing a black cape, and was made up to portray Satan, or Death, I was unclear which and it had not seemed a distinction worth pursuing.

Still, there were clouds off the Gulf that day and the air was wet and there was about the melancholy of Camp Street a certain sense of abandoned historic moment, heightened, quite soon, by something unusual: the New Orleans police began lining Camp Street, blocking every intersection from Canal Street west. I noticed a man in uniform on a roof. Before long there were Secret Service agents, with wires in their ears. The candidates, it seemed, would be traveling east on Camp Street on their way from the Republican National Committee

Finance Committee Gala (Invitation Only) at the Convention Center
to the Ohio Caucus Rally (Media Invited) at the Hilton. I stood for a
while on Camp Street, on this corner that might be construed as
one of those occasional accidental intersections where the remote
narrative had collided with the actual life of the country, and waited
until the motorcade itself, entirely and perfectly insulated, a mechanism dedicated like the process for which it stood only to the maintenance of itself, had passed, and then I walked to the Superdome. 'I
hear he did OK with Brinkley,' they said that night in the Superdome, and, then, as the confetti fell, 'Quayle, zip.'

1988

Shooters Inc.

In August of 1986, George Bush, traveling in his role as vice president of the United States and accompanied by his staff, the Secret Service, the traveling press, and a personal camera crew wearing baseball caps reading 'Shooters, Inc.' and working on a $10,000 retainer paid by a Bush PAC called the Fund for America's Future, spent several days in Israel and Jordan. The schedule in Israel included, according to reports in the *Los Angeles Times* and the *New York Times*, shoots at the Western Wall, at the Holocaust memorial, at David Ben-Gurion's tomb, and at thirty-two other locations chosen to produce campaign footage illustrating that George Bush was, as Marlin Fitzwater, at that time the vice-presidential press secretary, put it, 'familiar with the issues'. The Shooters, Inc. crew did not go on to Jordan (there was, an official explained to the *Los Angeles Times*, 'nothing to be gained from showing him schmoozing with Arabs'), but the Bush advance team had nonetheless directed, in Amman, considerable attention toward improved visuals for the traveling press. The advance team had requested, for example, that the Jordanian army marching band change its uniforms from white to red; that the Jordanians, who did not have enough helicopters to transport the press, borrow some from the Israeli air force; that, in order to provide the color of live military action behind the vice president, the Jordanians stage maneuvers at a sensitive location overlooking Israel and the Golan Heights; that the Jordanians raise the American flag over their base there; that Bush be photographed looking through binoculars studying 'enemy territory', a shot ultimately vetoed by the State

Department since the 'enemy territory' at hand was Israel; and, possibly the most arresting detail, that camels be present at every stop on the itinerary.

Some months later I happened to be in Amman, and mentioned reading about this Bush trip to several officials at the American embassy there. They could have, it was agreed, 'cordially killed' the reporters in question, particularly Charles P. Wallace from the *Los Angeles Times*, but the reports themselves had been accurate. 'You didn't hear this, but they didn't write half of it,' one said.

This is in fact the kind of story we expect to hear about our elected officials. We not only expect them to use other nations as changeable scrims in the theater of domestic politics but encourage them to do so. After the April failure of the Bay of Pigs in 1961, John Kennedy's job approval rating was four points higher than it had been in March. After the 1965 intervention in the Dominican Republic, Lyndon Johnson's job approval rating rose six points. After the 1983 invasion of Grenada, Ronald Reagan's job approval rating rose four points, and what was that winter referred to in Washington as 'Lebanon' – the sending of American Marines into Beirut, the killing of the 241, and the subsequent pullout – was, in the afterglow of this certified success in the Caribbean, largely forgotten. 'Gemayel could fall tonight and it would be a two-day story,' I recall David Gergen saying a few months later. In May of 1984, Francis X. Clines of the *New York Times* described the view taken by James Baker, who was routinely described during his years in the Reagan White House as 'the ultimate pragmatist', a manager of almost supernatural executive ability: 'In attempting action in Lebanon, Baker argues, President Reagan avoided another "impotent" episode, such as the taking of American hostages in Iran, and in withdrawing the Marines, the President avoided another "Vietnam" . . . "Pulling the Marines out put the lie to the argument that the President's trigger-happy," he [Baker] said.' The 'issue', in other words, was one of preserving faith in President Reagan at home, a task that, after the ultimate pragmatist left the White House, fell into the hands of the less adroit.

History is context. At a moment when the nation had seen control of its economy pass to its creditors and when the administration-elect had for political reasons severely limited its ability to regain that control, this extreme reliance on the efficacy of faith over works meant something different from what it might have meant in 1984 or 1980. On the night in New Orleans in August of 1988 when George Bush accepted the Republican nomination and spoke of his intention to 'speak for freedom, stand for freedom, and be a patient friend to anyone, east or west, who will fight for freedom', the word 'patient' was construed by some in the Louisiana Superdome as an abandonment of the Reagan Doctrine, a suggestion that a Bush administration would play a passive rather than an active role in any dreams of rollback. This overlooked the real nature of the Reagan Doctrine, the usefulness of which to the Reagan administration was exclusively political.

Administrations with little room to maneuver at home have historically looked for sideshows abroad, for the creation of what the pollsters call 'a dramatic event', an external crisis, preferably one so remote that it remains an abstraction. On the evening of the November 1988 election and on several evenings that followed, I happened to sit at dinner next to men with considerable experience in the financial community. They were agreed that the foreign markets would allow the new Bush administration, which was seen to have limited its options by promising for political reasons not to raise taxes, only a limited time before calling in the markers; they disagreed only as to the length of that time and to the nature of the downturn. One thought perhaps two years, another six months. Some saw a 'blowout' ('blowout' was a word used a good deal), others saw a gradual tightening, a transition to the era of limited expectations of which Jerry Brown had spoken when he was governor of California.

These men were, among themselves, uniformly pessimistic. They saw a situation in which the space available for domestic maneuvering had been reduced to zero. In this light it did not seem encouraging that George Bush, on the Thursday he left for his post-election Florida vacation, found time to meet not with those investors around the world who were sending him a message that week (the dollar was again dropping against the yen, against the mark, and against the pound; the Dow was dropping 78.47 points), not with the Germans, not with the Japanese, not even with anyone from the American financial community, but with representatives of the

Afghan resistance. 'Once in a while I think about those things, but not much,' the president-elect told a CBS News crew which asked him, a few days later in Florida, about the falling market.

1988

III

California

Girl of the Golden West

The domestic details spring to memory. Early on the evening of February 4, 1974, in her duplex apartment at 2603 Benvenue in Berkeley, Patricia Campbell Hearst, age nineteen, a student of art history at the University of California at Berkeley and a granddaughter of the late William Randolph Hearst, put on a blue terry-cloth bathrobe, heated a can of chicken-noodle soup and made tuna fish sandwiches for herself and her fiancé, Steven Weed; watched 'Mission Impossible' and 'The Magician' on television; cleaned up the dishes; sat down to study just as the doorbell rang; was abducted at gunpoint and held blindfolded, by three men and five women who called themselves the Symbionese Liberation Army, for the next fifty-seven days.

From the fifty-eighth day, on which she agreed to join her captors and was photographed in front of the SLA's cobra flag carrying a sawed-off M-1 carbine, until September 18, 1975, when she was arrested in San Francisco, Patricia Campbell Hearst participated actively in the robberies of the Hibernia Bank in San Francisco and the Crocker National Bank outside Sacramento; sprayed Crenshaw Boulevard in Los Angeles with a submachine gun to cover a comrade apprehended for shoplifting; and was party or witness to a number of less publicized thefts and several bombings, to which she would later refer as 'actions', or 'operations'.

On trial in San Francisco for the Hibernia Bank operation she appeared in court wearing frosted-white nail polish, and demonstrated for the jury the bolt action necessary to chamber an M-1. On

a psychiatric test administered while she was in custody she completed the sentence 'Most men . . .' with the words '. . . are assholes'.
Seven years later she was living with the bodyguard she had married,
their infant daughter, and two German shepherds 'behind locked
doors in a Spanish-style house equipped with the best electronic
security system available', describing herself as 'older and wiser', and
dedicating her account of these events, *Every Secret Thing*, to 'Mom
and Dad'.

It was a special kind of sentimental education, a public coming-of-age
with an insistently literary cast to it, and it seemed at the time to
offer a parable for the period. Certain of its images entered the
national memory. We had Patricia Campbell Hearst in her first-
communion dress, smiling, and we had Patricia Campbell Hearst in
the Hibernia Bank surveillance stills, not smiling. We again had her
smiling in the engagement picture, an unremarkably pretty girl in a
simple dress on a sunny lawn, and we again had her not smiling in
the 'Tania' snapshot, the famous Polaroid with the M-1. We had her
with her father and her sister Anne in a photograph taken at the
Burlingame Country Club some months before the kidnapping: all
three Hearsts smiling there, not only smiling but wearing leis, the
father in maile and orchid leis, the daughters in pikake, that rarest
and most expensive kind of lei, strand after strand of tiny Arabian
jasmine buds strung like ivory beads.

We had the bank of microphones in front of the Hillsborough
house whenever Randolph and Catherine Hearst ('Dad' and 'Mom'
in the first spectral messages from the absent daughter, 'pig Hearsts'
as the spring progressed) met the press, the potted flowers on the
steps changing with the seasons, domestic upkeep intact in the face
of crisis: azaleas, fuchsias, then cymbidium orchids massed for Easter.
We had, early on, the ugly images of looting and smashed cameras
and frozen turkey legs hurled through windows in West Oakland,
the violent result of the Hearsts' first attempt to meet the SLA ransom
demand, and we had, on television the same night, the news that
William Knowland, the former United States senator from California
and the most prominent member of the family that had run Oakland
for half a century, had taken the pistol he was said to carry as

protection against terrorists, positioned himself on a bank of the Russian River, and blown off the top of his head.

All of these pictures told a story, taught a dramatic lesson, carrying as they did the *frisson* of one another, the invitation to compare and contrast. The image of Patricia Campbell Hearst on the FBI 'wanted' fliers was for example cropped from the image of the unremarkably pretty girl in the simple dress on the sunny lawn, schematic evidence that even a golden girl could be pinned in the beam of history. There was no actual connection between turkey legs thrown through windows in West Oakland and William Knowland lying facedown in the Russian River, but the paradigm was manifest, one California busy being born and another busy dying. Those cymbidiums on the Hearsts' doorstep in Hillsborough dissolved before our eyes into the image of a flaming palm tree in south-central Los Angeles (the model again was two Californias), the palm tree above the stucco bungalow in which Patricia Campbell Hearst was believed for a time to be burning to death on live television. (Actually Patricia Campbell Hearst was in yet a third California, a motel room at Disneyland, watching the palm tree burn as we all were, on television, and it was Donald DeFreeze, Nancy Ling Perry, Angela Atwood, Patricia Soltysik, Camilla Hall, and William Wolfe, one black escaped convict and five children of the white middle class, who were dying in the stucco bungalow.)

Not only the images but the voice told a story, the voice on the tapes, the depressed voice with the California inflection, the voice that trailed off, now almost inaudible, then a hint of whine, a school-girl's sarcasm, a voice every parent recognized: *Mom, Dad. I'm OK. I had a few scrapes and stuff, but they washed them up . . . I just hope you'll do what they say, Dad . . . If you can get the food thing organized before the nineteenth then that's OK . . . Whatever you come up with is basically OK, it was never intended that you feed the whole state . . . I am here because I am a member of a ruling-class family and I think you can begin to see the analogy . . . People should stop acting like I'm dead, Mom should get out of her black dress, that doesn't help at all . . . Mom, Dad . . . I don't believe you're doing all you can . . . Mom, Dad . . . I'm starting to think that no one is concerned about me anymore . . .* And then: *Greetings to the people. This is Tania.*

*   *   *

Patricia Campbell Hearst's great-grandfather had arrived in California by foot in 1850, unschooled, unmarried, thirty years old with few graces and no prospects, a Missouri farmer's son who would spend his thirties scratching around El Dorado and Nevada and Sacramento counties looking for a stake. In 1859 he found one, and at his death in 1891 George Hearst could leave the schoolteacher he had married in 1862 a fortune taken from the ground, the continuing proceeds from the most productive mines of the period, the Ophir in Nevada, the Homestake in South Dakota, the Ontario in Utah, the Anaconda in Montana, the San Luis in Mexico. The widow, Phoebe Apperson Hearst, a tiny, strong-minded woman then only forty-eight years old, took this apparently artesian income and financed her only child in the publishing empire he wanted, underwrote a surprising amount of the campus where her great-granddaughter would be enrolled at the time she was kidnapped, and built for herself, on sixty-seven thousand acres on the McCloud River in Siskiyou County, the original Wyntoon, a quarried-lava castle of which its architect, Bernard Maybeck, said simply: 'Here you can reach all that is within you.'

The extent to which certain places dominate the California imagination is apprehended, even by Californians, only dimly. Deriving not only from the landscape but from the claiming of it, from the romance of emigration, the radical abandonment of established attachments, this imagination remains obdurately symbolic, tending to locate lessons in what the rest of the country perceives only as scenery. Yosemite, for example, remains what Kevin Starr has called 'one of the primary California symbols, a fixed factor of identity for all those who sought a primarily Californian aesthetic'. Both the community of and the coastline at Carmel have a symbolic meaning lost to the contemporary visitor, a lingering allusion to art as freedom, freedom as craft, the 'bohemian' pantheism of the early twentieth century. The Golden Gate Bridge, referring as it does to both the infinite and technology, suggests, to the Californian, a quite complex representation of land's end, and also of its beginning.

Patricia Campbell Hearst told us in *Every Secret Thing* that the place the Hearsts called Wyntoon was 'a mystical land', 'fantastic, otherworldly', 'even more than San Simeon', which was in turn 'so emotionally moving that it is still beyond my powers of description'. That first Maybeck castle on the McCloud River was seen by most

Californians only in photographs, and yet, before it burned in 1933, to be replaced by a compound of rather more playful Julia Morgan chalets ('Cinderella House', 'Angel House', 'Brown Bear House'), Phoebe Hearst's gothic Wyntoon and her son's baroque San Simeon seemed between them to embody certain opposing impulses in the local consciousness: northern and southern, wilderness sanctified and wilderness banished, the aggrandizement of nature and the aggrandizement of self. Wyntoon had mists, and allusions to the infinite, great trunks of trees left to rot where they fell, a wild river, barbaric fireplaces. San Simeon, swimming in sunlight and the here and now, had two swimming pools, and a zoo.

It was a family in which the romantic impulse would seem to have dimmed. Patricia Campbell Hearst told us that she 'grew up in an atmosphere of clear blue skies, bright sunshine, rambling open spaces, long green lawns, large comfortable houses, country clubs with swimming pools and tennis courts and riding horses'. At the Convent of the Sacred Heart in Menlo Park she told a nun to 'go to hell', and thought herself 'quite courageous, although very stupid'. At Santa Catalina in Monterey she and Patricia Tobin, whose family founded one of the banks the SLA would later rob, skipped Benediction, and received 'a load of demerits'. Her father taught her to shoot, duck hunting. Her mother did not allow her to wear jeans into San Francisco. These were inheritors who tended to keep their names out of the paper, to exhibit not much interest in the world at large ('Who the hell is this guy again?' Randolph Hearst asked Steven Weed when the latter suggested trying to approach the SLA through Regis Debray, and then, when told, said, 'We need a goddamn South American revolutionary mixed up in this thing like a hole in the head'), and to regard most forms of distinction with the reflexive distrust of the country club.

Yet if the Hearsts were no longer a particularly arresting California family, they remained embedded in the symbolic content of the place, and for a Hearst to be kidnapped from Berkeley, the very citadel of Phoebe Hearst's aspiration, was California as opera. 'My thoughts at this time were focused on the single issue of survival,' the heiress to Wyntoon and San Simeon told us about the fifty-seven days she spent in the closet. 'Concerns over love and marriage, family life, friends, human relationships, my whole previous life, had really become, in SLA terms, bourgeois luxuries.'

This abrupt sloughing of the past has, to the California ear, a distant echo, and the echo is of emigrant diaries. 'Don't let this letter dishearten anybody, never take no cutoffs and hurry along as fast as you can,' one of the surviving children of the Donner Party concluded her account of that crossing. 'Don't worry about it,' the author of *Every Secret Thing* reported having told herself in the closet after her first sexual encounter with a member of the SLA. 'Don't examine your feelings. Never examine your feelings – they're no help at all.' At the time Patricia Campbell Hearst was on trial in San Francisco, a number of psychiatrists were brought in to try to plumb what seemed to some an unsoundable depth in the narrative, that moment at which the victim binds over her fate to her captors. 'She experienced what I call the death anxiety and the breaking point,' Robert Jay Lifton, who was one of these psychiatrists, said. 'Her external points of reference for maintenance of her personality had disappeared,' Louis Jolyon West, another of the psychiatrists, said. Those were two ways of looking at it, and another was that Patricia Campbell Hearst had cut her losses and headed west, as her great-grandfather had before her.

The story she told in 1982 in *Every Secret Thing* was received, in the main, querulously, just as it had been when she told it during *The United States of America v. Patricia Campbell Hearst*, the 1976 proceeding during which she was tried for and convicted of the armed robbery of the Hibernia Bank (one count) and (the second count), the use of a weapon during the commission of a felony. Laconic, slightly ironic, resistant not only to the prosecution but to her own defense, Patricia Hearst was not, on trial in San Francisco, a conventionally ingratiating personality. 'I don't know,' I recall her saying over and over again during the few days I attended the trial. 'I don't remember.' 'I suppose so.' Had there not been, the prosecutor asked one day, telephones in the motels in which she had stayed when she drove across the country with Jack Scott? I recall Patricia Hearst looking at him as if she thought him deranged. I recall Randolph Hearst looking at the floor. I recall Catherine Hearst arranging a Galanos jacket over the back of her seat.

'Yes, I'm sure,' their daughter said.

Where, the prosecutor asked, were these motels?

'One was . . . I think . . .' Patricia Hearst paused, and then: 'Cheyenne? Wyoming?' She pronounced the names as if they were foreign, exotic, information registered and jettisoned. One of these motels had been in Nevada, the place from which the Hearst money originally came: the heiress pronounced the name *Nevahda*, like a foreigner.

In *Every Secret Thing* as at her trial, she seemed to project an emotional distance, a peculiar combination of passivity and pragmatic recklessness ('I had crossed over. And I would have to make the best of it . . . to live from day to day, to do whatever they said, to play my part, and to pray that I would survive') that many people found inexplicable and irritating. In 1982 as in 1976, she spoke only abstractly about *why*, but quite specifically about *how*. 'I could not believe that I had actually fired that submachine gun,' she said of the incident in which she shot up Crenshaw Boulevard, but here was how she did it: 'I kept my finger pressed on the trigger until the entire clip of thirty shots had been fired . . . I then reached for my own weapon, the semiautomatic carbine. I got off three more shots . . .'

And, after her book as after her trial, the questions raised were not exactly about her veracity but about her authenticity, her general intention, about whether she was, as the assistant prosecutor put it during the trial, 'for real'. This was necessarily a vain line of inquiry (whether or not she 'loved' William Wolfe was the actual point on which the trial came to turn), and one that encouraged a curious rhetorical regression among the inquisitors. 'Why did she choose to write this book?' Mark Starr asked about *Every Secret Thing* in *Newsweek*, and then answered himself: 'Possibly she has inherited her family's journalistic sense of what will sell.' 'The rich get richer,' Jane Alpert concluded in *New York* magazine. 'Patty,' Ted Morgan observed in the *New York Times Book Review*, 'is now, thanks to the proceeds of her book, reverting to a more traditional family pursuit, capital formation.'

These were dreamy notions of what a Hearst might do to turn a dollar, but they reflected a larger dissatisfaction, a conviction that the Hearst in question was telling less than the whole story, 'leaving something out', although what the something might have been, given the doggedly detailed account offered in *Every Secret Thing*, would be hard to define. If 'questions still linger', as they did for *Newsweek*, those questions were not about how to lace a bullet with cyanide: the way the SLA did it was to drill into the lead tip to a point just short of the gunpowder, dip the tiny hole in a mound of cyanide crystals, and seal it with paraffin. If *Every Secret Thing* 'creates more puzzles than it solves', as it did for Jane Alpert, those questions were not about how to make a pipe bomb: the trick here was to pack enough gunpowder into the pipe for a big bang and still leave sufficient oxygen for ignition, a problem, as Patricia Hearst saw it, of 'devising the proper proportions of gunpowder, length of pipe and toaster wire, minus Teko's precious toilet paper'. 'Teko', or Bill Harris, insisted on packing his bombs with toilet paper, and, when one of them failed to explode under a police car in the Mission District, reacted with 'one of his worst temper tantrums'. Many reporters later found Bill and Emily Harris the appealing defendants that Patricia Hearst never was, but *Every Secret Thing* presented a convincing case for their being, as the author put it, not only 'unattractive' but, her most pejorative adjective, 'incompetent'.

As notes from the underground go, Patricia Hearst's were eccentric in detail. She told us that Bill Harris's favorite television program was 'S.W.A.T.' (one could, he said, 'learn a lot about the pigs' tactics by watching these programs'); that Donald DeFreeze, or 'Cinque', drank plum wine from half-gallon jugs and listened to the radio for allusions to the revolution in song lyrics; and that Nancy Ling Perry, who was usually cast by the press in the rather glamorous role of 'former cheerleader and Goldwater Girl', was four feet eleven inches tall, and affected a black accent. Emily Harris trained herself to 'live with deprivation' by chewing only half sticks of gum. Bill Harris bought a yarmulke, under the impression that this was the way, during the sojourn in the Catskills after the Los Angeles shoot-out, to visit Grossinger's unnoticed.

Life with these people had the distorted logic of dreams, and

Patricia Hearst seems to have accepted it with the wary acquiescence of the dreamer. Any face could turn against her. Any move could prove lethal. 'My sisters and I had been brought up to believe that we were responsible for what we did and could not blame our transgressions on something being wrong inside our heads. I had joined the SLA because if I didn't they would have killed me. And I remained with them because I truly believed that the FBI would kill me if they could, and if not, the SLA would.' She had, as she put it, crossed over. She would, as she put it, make the best of it, and not 'reach back to family or friends'.

This was the point on which most people foundered, doubted her, found her least explicable, and it was also the point at which she was most specifically the child of a certain culture. Here is the single personal note in an emigrant diary kept by a relative of mine, William Kilgore, the journal of an overland crossing to Sacramento in 1850: 'This is one of the trying mornings for me, as I now have to leave my family, or back out. Suffice it to say, we started.' Suffice it to say. Don't examine your feelings, they're no help at all. Never take no cutoffs and hurry along as fast as you can. We need a goddamn South American revolutionary mixed up in this thing like a hole in the head. This was a California girl, and she was raised on a history that placed not much emphasis on *why*.

She was never an idealist, and this pleased no one. She was tainted by survival. She came back from the other side with a story no one wanted to hear, a dispiriting account of a situation in which delusion and incompetence were pitted against delusion and incompetence of another kind, and in the febrile rhythms of San Francisco in the midseventies it seemed a story devoid of high notes. The week her trial ended in 1976, the *San Francisco Bay Guardian* published an interview in which members of a collective called New Dawn expressed regret at her defection. 'It's a question of your self-respect or your ass,' one of them said. 'If you choose your ass, you live with nothing.' This idea that the SLA represented an idea worth defending (if only on the grounds that any idea must be better than none) was common enough at the time, although most people granted that the idea had gone awry. By March of 1977 another writer in the *Bay*

Guardian was making a distinction between the 'unbridled adventur-
ism' of the SLA and the 'discipline and skill' of the New World
Liberation Front, whose 'fifty-odd bombings without a casualty'
made them a 'definitely preferable alternative' to the SLA.

As it happened I had kept this issue of the *Bay Guardian*, dated
March 31, 1977 (the *Bay Guardian* was not at the time a notably
radical paper, by the way, but one that provided a fair guide to local
tofu cookery and the mood of the community), and when I got it
out to look at the piece on the SLA I noticed for the first time another
piece: a long and favorable report on a San Francisco minister whose
practice it was to 'confront people and challenge their basic assumptions ... as if he can't let the evil of the world pass him by, a
characteristic he shares with other moral leaders.' The minister, who
was compared at one point to Cesar Chavez, was responsible, according to the writer, for a 'mind-boggling' range of social service programs – food distribution, legal aid, drug rehabilitation, nursing
homes, free Pap smears – as well as for a 'twenty-seven-thousand-
acre agricultural station'. The agricultural station was in Guyana, and
the minister of course was the Reverend Jim Jones, who eventually
chose self-respect over his own and nine hundred other asses. This
was another local opera, and one never spoiled by a protagonist who
insisted on telling it her way.

1982

Pacific Distances

A good part of any day in Los Angeles is spent driving, alone, through streets devoid of meaning to the driver, which is one reason the place exhilarates some people, and floods others with an amorphous unease. There is about these hours spent in transit a seductive unconnectedness. Conventional information is missing. Context clues are missing. In Culver City as in Echo Park as in East Los Angeles, there are the same pastel bungalows. There are the same leggy poinsettia and the same trees of pink and yellow hibiscus. There are the same laundromats, body shops, strip shopping malls, the same travel agencies offering bargain fares on LACSA and TACA. *San Salvador*, the signs promise, on Beverly Boulevard as on Pico as on Alvarado and Soto. *¡No más barata!* There is the same sound, that of the car radio, tuned in my case to KRLA, an AM station that identifies itself as 'the heart and soul of rock and roll' and is given to dislocating programming concepts, for example doing the top hits ('Baby, It's You', 'Break It to Me Gently', 'The Lion Sleeps Tonight') of 1962. Another day, another KRLA concept: 'The Day the Music Died', an exact, radio recreation of the day in 1959, including news breaks (Detroit may market compacts), when the plane carrying Buddy Holly, Ritchie Valens, and the Big Bopper crashed near Clear Lake, Iowa. A few days later, KRLA reports a solid response on 'The Day the Music Died', including 'a call from Ritchie Valens's aunt'.

Such tranced hours are, for many people who live in Los Angeles, the dead center of being there, but there is nothing in them to encourage the normal impulse toward 'recognition', or narrative connection. Those glosses on the human comedy (the widow's heartbreak, the bad cop, the mother-and-child reunion) that lend dramatic structure to more traditional forms of urban life are hard to come by here. There are, in the pages of the Los Angeles newspapers, no Crack Queens, no Coma Moms or Terror Tots. Events may be lurid, but are rarely personalized. 'Mother Apologizes to Her Child, Drives Both Off Cliff,' a headline read in the *Los Angeles Times* one morning in December 1988. (Stories like this are relegated in the *Times* either to the Metro Section or to page three, which used to be referred to as 'the freak-death page', not its least freaky aspect being that quite arresting accounts of death by Clorox or by rattlesnake or by Dumpster tended to appear and then vanish, with no follow-up.) Here was the story, which had to do with a young woman who had lived with her daughter, Brooke, in a Redondo Beach condominium and was said by a neighbor to have 'looked like she was a little down':

> A Redondo Beach woman apologized to her 7-year-old daughter, then apparently tried to take both their lives by driving over a cliff in the Malibu area Tuesday morning, authorities said. The mother, identified by the county coroner's office as Susan Sinclair, 29, was killed, but the child survived without serious injury. 'I'm sorry I have to do this,' the woman was quoted as telling the child just before she suddenly swerved off Malibu Canyon Road about 2½ miles north of Pacific Coast Highway.

'I'm sorry I have to do this.' This was the last we heard of Susan and Brooke Sinclair. When I first moved to Los Angeles from New York, in 1964, I found this absence of narrative a deprivation. At the end of two years I realized (quite suddenly, alone one morning in the car) that I had come to find narrative sentimental. This remains a radical difference between the two cities, and also between the ways in which the residents of those cities view each other.

2

Our children remind us of how random our lives have been. I had occasion in 1979 to speak at my daughter's school in Los Angeles, and I stood there, apparently a grown woman, certainly a woman who had stood up any number of times and spoken to students around the country, and tried to confront a question that suddenly seemed to me almost impenetrable: How had I become a writer, how and why had I made the particular choices I had made in my life? I could see my daughter's friends in the back of the room, Claudia, Julie, Anna. I could see my daughter herself, flushed with embarrassment, afraid, she told me later, that her presence would make me forget what I meant to say.

I could tell them only that I had no more idea of how I had become a writer than I had had, at their age, of how I would become a writer. I could tell them only about the fall of 1954, when I was nineteen and a junior at Berkeley and one of perhaps a dozen students admitted to the late Mark Schorer's English 106A, a kind of 'fiction workshop' that met for discussion three hours a week and required that each student produce, over the course of the semester, at least five short stories. No auditors were allowed. Voices were kept low. English 106A was widely regarded in the fall of 1954 as a kind of sacramental experience, an initiation into the grave world of real writers, and I remember each meeting of this class as an occasion of acute excitement and dread. I remember each other member of this class as older and wiser than I had hope of ever being (it had not yet struck me in any visceral way that being nineteen was not a long-term proposition, just as it had not yet struck Claudia and Julie and Anna and my daughter that they would recover from being thirteen), not only older and wiser but more experienced, more independent, more interesting, more possessed of an exotic past: marriages and the breaking up of marriages, money and the lack of it, sex and politics and the Adriatic seen at dawn: not only the stuff of grown-up life itself but, more poignantly to me at the time, the very stuff that might be transubstantiated into five short stories. I recall a Trotskyist, then in his forties. I recall a young woman who lived, with a barefoot man and a large white dog, in an attic lit only by candles. I recall classroom discussions that ranged over meetings with Paul and Jane Bowles, incidents involving Djuna Barnes, years spent in Paris, in Beverly Hills, in the Yucatán, on the Lower East Side of New York and on Repulse Bay and even on morphine. I had spent seventeen of my nineteen years more or less in Sacramento, and the other two in the Tri Delt house on Warring Street in Berkeley. I had never read Paul or Jane Bowles, let alone met them, and when, some fifteen years later at a friend's house in Santa Monica Canyon, I did meet Paul Bowles, I was immediately rendered as dumb and awestruck as I had been at nineteen in English 106A.

I suppose that what I really wanted to say that day at my daughter's school is that we never reach a point at which our lives lie before us as clearly marked open road, never have and never should expect a map to the years ahead, never do close those circles that seem, at thirteen and fourteen and nineteen, so urgently in need of closing. I wanted to tell my daughter and her friends, but did not, about going back to the English department at Berkeley in the spring of 1975 as a Regents' Lecturer, a reversal of positions that should have been satisfying but proved unsettling, moved me profoundly, answered no questions but raised the same old ones. In Los Angeles in 1975 I had given every appearance of being well settled, grown-up, a woman in definite charge of her own work and of a certain kind of bourgeois household that made working possible. In Berkeley in 1975 I had unpacked my clothes and papers in a single room at the Faculty Club, walked once across campus, and regressed, immediately and helplessly, into the ghetto life of the student I had been twenty years before. I hoarded nuts and bits of chocolate in my desk drawer. I ate tacos for dinner (combination plates, *con arroz y frijoles*), wrapped myself in my bedspread and read until two A.M., smoked too many cigarettes and regretted, like a student, only their cost. I found myself making daily notes, as carefully as I had when I was an undergraduate, of expenses, and my room at the Faculty Club was littered with little scraps of envelopes:

> *$1.15, papers, etc.*
> *$2.85, taco plate*
> *$ .50, tips*
> *$ .15, coffee*

I fell not only into the habits but into the moods of the student day. Every morning I was hopeful, determined, energized by the campanile bells and by the smell of eucalyptus and by the day's projected accomplishments. On the way to breakfast I would walk briskly, breathe deeply, review my 'plans' for the day: I would write five pages, return all calls, lunch on raisins and answer ten letters. I would at last read E. H. Gombrich. I would once and for all get the meaning of the word 'structuralist'. And yet every afternoon by four o'clock, the hour when I met my single class, I was once again dulled, glazed, sunk in an excess of carbohydrates and in my own mediocrity, in my failure – still, after twenty years! – to 'live up to' the day's possibilities.

In certain ways nothing at all had changed in those twenty years. The clean light and fogs were exactly as I had remembered. The creek still ran clear among the shadows, the rhododendron still bloomed in the spring. On the bulletin boards in the English department there were still notices inviting the reader to apply to Mrs Diggory Venn for information on the Radcliffe Publishing Procedures course. The less securely tenured members of the department still yearned for dramatic moves to Johns Hopkins. Anything specific was rendered immediately into a general principle. Anything concrete was rendered abstract. That the spring of 1975 was, outside Berkeley, a season of remarkably specific and operatically concrete events seemed, on the campus, another abstract, another illustration of a general tendency, an instance tending only to confirm or not confirm one or another idea of the world. The wire photos from Phnom Penh and Saigon seemed as deliberately composed as symbolist paintings. The question of whether one spoke of Saigon 'falling' or of Saigon's 'liberation' reduced the fact to a political attitude, a semantic question, another idea.

Days passed. I adopted a shapeless blazer and no makeup. I remember spending considerable time, that spring of 1975, trying to break the code that Telegraph Avenue seemed to present. There, just a block or two off the campus, the campus with its five thousand courses, its four million books, its five million manuscripts, the campus with its cool glades and clear creeks and lucid views, lay this mean wasteland of small venture capital, this unweeded garden in which everything cost more than it was worth. Coffee on Telegraph

Avenue was served neither hot nor cold. Food was slopped lukewarm onto chipped plates. Pita bread was stale, curries were rank. Tatty 'Indian' stores offered faded posters and shoddy silks. Bookstores featured sections on the occult. Drug buys were in progress up and down the street. The place was an illustration of some tropism toward disorder, and I seemed to understand it no better in 1975 than I had as an undergraduate.

I remember trying to discuss Telegraph Avenue with some people from the English department, but they were discussing a paper we had heard on the plotting of *Vanity Fair*, *Middlemarch*, and *Bleak House*. I remember trying to discuss Telegraph Avenue with an old friend who had asked me to dinner, at a place far enough off campus to get a drink, but he was discussing Jane Alpert, Eldridge Cleaver, Daniel Ellsberg, Shana Alexander, a Modesto rancher of his acquaint-ance, Jules Feiffer, Herbert Gold, Herb Caen, Ed Janss, and the move-ment for independence in Micronesia. I remember thinking that I was still, after twenty years, out of step at Berkeley, the victim of a different drummer. I remember sitting in my office in Wheeler Hall one afternoon when someone, not a student, walked in off the street. He said that he was a writer, and I asked what he had written. 'Nothing you'll ever dare to read,' he said. He admired only Céline and Djuna Barnes. With the exception of Djuna Barnes, women could not write. It was possible that I could write but he did not know, he had not read me. 'In any case,' he added, sitting on the edge of my desk, 'your time's gone, your fever's over.' It had probably been a couple of decades, English 106A, since I last heard about Céline and Djuna Barnes and how women could not write, since I last encountered this particular brand of extraliterary machismo, and after my caller had left the office I locked the door and sat there a long time in the afternoon light. At nineteen I had wanted to write. At forty I still wanted to write, and nothing that had happened in the years between made me any more certain that I could.

3

Etcheverry Hall, half a block uphill from the north gate of the University of California at Berkeley, is one of those postwar classroom and office buildings that resemble parking structures and seem designed to suggest that nothing extraordinary has been or will be going on inside. On Etcheverry's east terrace, which is paved with pebbled concrete and bricks, a few students usually sit studying or sunbathing. There are benches, there is grass. There are shrubs and a small tree. There is a net for volleyball, and, on the day in late 1979 when I visited Etcheverry, someone had taken a piece of chalk and printed the word RADIATION on the concrete beneath the net, breaking the letters in a way that looked stenciled and official and scary. In fact it was here, directly below the volleyball court on Etcheverry's east terrace, that the Department of Nuclear Engineering's TRIGA Mark III nuclear reactor, light-water cooled and reflected, went critical, or achieved a sustained nuclear reaction, on August 10, 1966, and had been in continuous operation since. People who wanted to see the reactor dismantled said that it was dangerous, that it could emit deadly radiation and that it was perilously situated just forty yards west of the Hayward Fault. People who ran the reactor said that it was not dangerous, that any emission of measurable radioactivity was extremely unlikely and that 'forty yards west of' the Hayward Fault was a descriptive phrase without intrinsic seismological significance. (This was an assessment with which seismologists agreed.) These differences of opinion represented a difference not only in the meaning of words but in cultures, a difference in images and probably in expectations.

Above the steel door to the reactor room in the basement of Etcheverry Hall was a sign that glowed either green or Roman violet, depending on whether what it said was SAFE ENTRY, which meant that the air lock between the reactor room and the corridor was closed and the radiation levels were normal and the level of pool water was normal, or UNSAFE ENTRY, which meant that at least one of these conditions, usually the first, had not been met. The sign on the steel door itself read only ROOM 1140 / EXCLUSION AREA / ENTRY LIST A, B, or C / CHECK WITH RECEPTIONIST. On the day I visited

Etcheverry I was issued a dosimeter to keep in my pocket, then shown the reactor by Tek Lim, at that time the reactor manager, and Lawrence Grossman, a professor of nuclear engineering. They explained that the Etcheverry TRIGA was a modification of the original TRIGA, which is an acronym for Training/Research/Isotopes/General Atomic, and was designed in 1956 by a team, including Edward Teller and Theodore Taylor and Freeman Dyson, that had set for itself the task of making a reactor so safe, in Freeman Dyson's words, 'that it could be given to a bunch of high school children to play with, without any fear that they would get hurt'.

They explained that the TRIGA operated at a much lower heat level than a power reactor, and was used primarily for 'making things radioactive'. Nutritionists, for example, used it to measure trace elements in diet. Archaeologists used it for dating. NASA used it for high-altitude pollution studies, and for a study on how weightlessness affects human calcium metabolism. Stanford was using it to study lithium in the brain. Physicists from the Lawrence Berkeley Laboratory, up the hill, had been coming down to use it for experiments in the development of a fusion, or 'clean', reactor. A researcher from Ghana used it for a year, testing samples from African waterholes for the arsenic that could kill the animals.

The reactor was operating at one megawatt as we talked. All levels were normal. We were standing, with Harry Braun, the chief reactor operator, on the metal platform around the reactor pool, and I had trouble keeping my eyes from the core, the Cerenkov radiation around the fuel rods, the blue shimmer under twenty feet of clear water. There was a skimmer on the side of the pool, and a bath mat thrown over the railing. There was a fishing pole, and a rubber duck. Harry Braun uses the fishing rod to extract samples from the specimen rack around the core, and the rubber duck to monitor the water movement. 'Or when the little children come on school tours,' he added. 'Sometimes they don't pay any attention until we put the duck in the pool.'

I was ten years old when 'the atomic age', as we called it then, came forcibly to the world's attention. At the time the verbs favored for use with 'the atomic age' were 'dawned' or 'ushered in', both of which implied an upward trend to events. I recall being told that the device which ended World War II was 'the size of a lemon' (this was not true) and that the University of California had helped build it (this was true). I recall listening all one Sunday afternoon to a special radio report called 'The Quick and the Dead', three or four hours during which the people who had built and witnessed the bomb talked about the bomb's and (by extension) their own eerie and apparently unprecedented power, their abrupt elevation to that place from whence they had come to judge the quick and the dead, and I also recall, when summer was over and school started again, being taught to cover my eyes and my brain stem and crouch beneath my desk during atomic-bomb drills.

So unequivocal were these impressions that it never occurred to me that I would not sooner or later – most probably sooner, certainly before I ever grew up or got married or went to college – endure the moment of its happening: first the blinding white light, which appeared in my imagination as a negative photographic image, then the waves of heat, the sound, and, finally, death, instant or pro-longed, depending inflexibly on where one was caught in the scale of concentric circles we all imagined pulsing out from ground zero. Some years later, when I was an undergraduate at Berkeley and had an apartment in an old shingled house a few doors from where Etcheverry now stands, I could look up the hill at night and see the lights at the Lawrence Berkeley Laboratory, at what was then called 'the rad lab', at the cyclotron and the bevatron, and I still expected to wake up one night and see those lights in negative, still expected the blinding white light, the heat wave, the logical conclusion.

After I graduated I moved to New York, and after some months or a year I realized that I was no longer anticipating the blinding flash, and that the expectation had probably been one of those ways in which children deal with mortality, learn to juggle the idea that life will end as surely as it began, to perform in the face of definite annihilation. And yet I know that for me, and I suspect for many of us, this single image – this blinding white light that meant death, this seductive reversal of the usual associations around 'light' and 'white' and 'radiance' – became a metaphor that to some extent determined what I later thought and did. In my Modern Library copy of *The Education of Henry Adams*, a book I first read and scored at

Berkeley in 1954, I see this passage, about the 1900 Paris Great
Exposition, underlined:

> . . . to Adams the dynamo became a symbol of infinity. As he
> grew accustomed to the great gallery of machines, he began to
> feel the forty-foot dynamos as a moral force, much as the early
> Christians felt the Cross.

It had been, at the time I saw the TRIGA Mark III reactor in the
basement of Etcheverry Hall, seventy-nine years since Henry Adams
went to Paris to study Science as he had studied Mont-Saint-Michel
and Chartres. It had been thirty-four years since Robert Oppen-
heimer saw the white light at Alamogordo. The 'nuclear issue', as we
called it, suggesting that the course of the world since the Industrial
Revolution was provisional, open to revision, up for a vote, had been
under discussion all those years, and yet something about the fact of
the reactor still resisted interpretation: the intense blue in the pool
water, the Cerenkov radiation around the fuel rods, the blue past all
blue, the blue like light itself, the blue that is actually a shock wave
in the water and is the exact blue of the glass at Chartres.

4

At the University of California's Lawrence Livermore Laboratory, a
compound of heavily guarded structures in the rolling cattle and
orchard country southeast of Oakland, badges had to be displayed
not only at the gate but again and again, at various points within the compound, to television cameras mounted between two
locked doors. These cameras registered not only the presence but
the color of the badge. A red badge meant 'No Clearance U.S. Citizen'
and might or might not be issued with the white covering badge
that meant 'Visitor Must Be Escorted'. A yellow badge meant
'No Higher Than Confidential Access'. A green badge banded in
yellow indicated that access was to be considered top level but not
exactly unlimited: 'Does Need to Know Exist?' was, according to a
sign in the Badge Office, LLL Building 310, the question to ask as

the bearer moved from station to station among the mysteries of the compound.

The symbolic as well as the literal message of a badge at Livermore – or at Los Alamos, or at Sandia, or at any of the other major labs around the country – was that the government had an interest here, that big money was being spent, Big Physics done. Badges were the totems of the tribe, the family. This was the family that used to keep all the plutonium in the world in a cigar box outside Glenn Seaborg's office in Berkeley, the family that used to try different ways of turning on the early twenty-seven-and-one-half-inch Berkeley cyclotron so as not to blow out large sections of the East Bay power grid. 'Very gently' was said to work best. I have a copy of a photograph that suggests the day-to-day life of this family with considerable poignance, a snapshot taken during the fifties, when Livermore was testing its atmospheric nuclear weapons in the Pacific. The snapshot shows a very young Livermore scientist, with a flattop haircut and an engaging smile, standing on the beach of an unidentified atoll on an unspecified day just preceding or just following (no clue in the caption) a test shot. He is holding a fishing rod, and, in the other hand, a queen triggerfish, according to the caption 'just a few ounces short of a world record'. He is wearing only swimming trunks, and his badge.

On the day in February 1980 when I drove down to Livermore from Berkeley the coast ranges were green from the winter rains. The acacia was out along the highway, a haze of chrome yellow in the window. Inside the compound itself, narcissus and daffodil shoots pressed through the asphalt walkways. I had driven down because I wanted to see Shiva, Livermore's twenty-beam laser, the $35 million tool that was then Livermore's main marker in the biggest Big Physics game then going, the attempt to create a controlled fusion reaction. An uncontrolled fusion reaction was easy, and was called a hydrogen bomb. A controlled fusion reaction was harder, so much harder that it was usually characterized as 'the most difficult technological feat ever undertaken', but the eventual payoff could be virtually limitless nuclear power produced at a fraction the hazard of the fission plants then operating. The difficulty in a controlled fusion reaction was that it involved achieving a thermonuclear burn of 100 million degrees centigrade, or more than six times the heat of the interior of the sun, without exploding the container. That no one had ever done this was, for the family, the point.

Ideas about how to do it were intensely competitive. Some laboratories had concentrated on what was called the 'magnetic bottle' approach, involving the magnetic confinement of plasma; others, on lasers, and the theoretical ability of laser beams to trigger controlled fusion by simultaneously heating and compressing tiny pellets of fuel. Livermore had at that time a magnetic-bottle project but was gambling most heavily on its lasers, on Shiva and on Shiva's then unfinished successor, Nova. This was a high-stakes game: the prizes would end up at those laboratories where the money was, and the money would go to those laboratories where the prizes seemed most likely. It was no accident that Livermore was visited by so many members of Congress, by officials of the Department of Defense and of the Department of Energy, and by not too many other people: friends in high places were essential to the family. The biography of Ernest O. Lawrence, the first of the Berkeley Nobel laureates and the man after whom the Lawrence Berkeley and the Lawrence Livermore laboratories were named, is instructive on this point: there were meetings at the Pacific Union Club, sojourns at Bohemian Grove and San Simeon, even 'a short trip to Acapulco with Randy and Catherine Hearst'. The Eniwetok tests during the fifties were typically preceded for Lawrence by stops in Honolulu, where, for example,

> . . . he was a guest of Admiral John E. Gingrich, a fine host. He reciprocated with a dinner for the admiral and several others at the Royal Hawaiian Hotel the night before departure for Eniwetok, a ten-hour flight from Honolulu. Eniwetok had much the atmosphere of a South Seas resort. A fine officers' club on the beach provided relaxation for congressmen and visitors. The tropical sea invited swimmers and scuba divers. There were no phones to interrupt conversations with interesting and important men . . . chairs had been placed on the beach when observers assembled at the club near dawn [to witness the shot]. Coffee and sandwiches were served, and dark glasses distributed . . .

On the day I visited Livermore the staff was still cleaning up after a January earthquake, a Richter 5.5 on the Mount Diablo-Greenville Fault. Acoustical tiles had fallen from the ceilings of the office buildings. Overhead light fixtures had plummeted onto desks, and wiring and insulation and air-conditioning ducts still hung wrenched from the ceilings. 'You get damage in the office buildings because the office buildings are only built to local code,' I was told by John Emmett, the physicist then in charge of the Livermore laser program. When the ceilings started falling that particular January, John Emmett had been talking to a visitor in his office. He had shown the visitor out, run back inside to see if anyone was trapped under the toppled bookshelves and cabinets, and then run over to the building that houses Shiva. The laser had been affected so slightly that all twenty beams were found, by the sixty-three microcomputers that constantly aligned and realigned the Shiva beams, to be within one-sixteenth of an inch of their original alignment. 'We didn't anticipate any real damage and we didn't get any,' John Emmett said. 'That's the way the gadget is designed.'

What John Emmett called 'the gadget' was framed in an immaculate white steel scaffolding several stories high and roughly the size of a football field. This frame was astonishingly beautiful, a piece of pure theater, a kind of abstract set on which the actors wore white coats, green goggles, and hard hats. 'You wear the goggles because even when we're not firing we've got some little beams bouncing around,' John Emmett said. 'The hard hat is because somebody's always dropping something.' Within the frame, a single infrared laser beam was split into twenty beams, each of which was amplified and reamplified until, at the instant two or three times a day when all twenty beams hit target, they were carrying sixty times as much power as was produced in the entire (exclusive of this room) United States. The target under bombardment was a glass bead a fraction the size of a grain of salt. The entire shoot took one-half billionth of a second. John Emmett and the Livermore laser team had then achieved with Shiva controlled temperatures of 85 million degrees centigrade, or roughly five times the heat at the center of the sun, but not 100 million. They were gambling on Nova for 100 million, the prize.

I recall, that afternoon at Livermore, asking John Emmett what would happen if I looked at the invisible infrared beam without goggles. 'It'll blow a hole in your retina,' he said matter-of-factly. It seemed that he had burned out the retina of one of his own eyes with a laser when he was a graduate student at Stanford. I asked if the sight had come back. 'All but one little spot,' he said. *Give me a mind that is not bored, that does not whimper, whine or sigh / Don't let me worry overmuch about the fussy thing called I:* these are two lines from a popular 'prayer', a late-twenties precursor to the 'Desiderata' that Ernest O. Lawrence kept framed on his desk until his death. The one little spot was not of interest to John Emmett. Making the laser work was.

5

Wintertime and springtime, Honolulu: in the winter there was the garbage strike, forty-two days during which the city lapsed into a profound and seductive tropicality. Trash drifted in the vines off the Lunalilo Freeway. The airport looked Central American, between governments. Green plastic bags of garbage mounded up on the streets, and orange peels and Tab cans thrown in the canals washed down to the sea and up to the tide line in front of our rented house on Kahala Avenue. A day goes this way: in the morning I rearrange our own green plastic mounds, pick up the orange peels and Tab cans from the tide line, and sit down to work at the wet bar in the living room, a U-shaped counter temporarily equipped with an IBM Selectric typewriter. I turn on the radio for news of a break in the garbage strike: I get a sig-alert for the Lunalilo, roadwork between the Wilder Avenue off-ramp and the Punahou overpass. I get the weather: mostly clear. Actually water is dropping in great glassy sheets on the windward side of the island, fifteen minutes across the Pali, but on leeward Oahu the sky is quicksilver, chiaroscuro, light and dark and sudden falls of rain and rainbow, mostly clear. Some time ago I stopped trying to explain to acquaintances on the mainland the ways in which the simplest routines of a day in Honolulu can please and interest me, but on these winter mornings I am reminded that they do. I keep an appointment with a dermatologist at Kapiolani-Children's Medical Center, and am pleased by the drive down Beretania Street in the rain. I stop for groceries at the Star Market in the Kahala Mall, and am pleased by the sprays of vanda orchids and the foot-long watercress and the little Manoa lettuces in the produce department. Some mornings I am even pleased by the garbage strike.

The undertone of every day in Honolulu, the one fact that colors every other, is the place's absolute remove from the rest of the world. Many American cities began remote, but only Honolulu is fated to remain so, and only in Honolulu do the attitudes and institutions born of extreme isolation continue to set the tone of daily life. The edge of the available world is sharply defined: one turns a corner or glances out an office window and there it is, blue sea. There is no cheap freedom to be gained by getting in a car and driving as far as one can go, since as far as one can go on the island of Oahu takes about an hour and fifteen minutes. 'Getting away' involves actual travel, scheduled carriers, involves reservations and reconfirmations and the ambiguous experience of being strapped passive in a darkened cabin and exposed to unwanted images on a flickering screen; involves submission to other people's schedules and involves, most significantly, money.

I have rarely spent an evening at anyone's house in Honolulu when someone in the room was not just off or about to catch an airplane, and the extent to which ten-hour flights figure in the local imagination tends to reinforce the distinction between those who can afford them and those who cannot. More people probably travel in Honolulu than can actually afford to: one study showed recent trips to the mainland in almost 25 percent of Oahu households and recent trips to countries outside the United States in almost 10 percent. Very few of those trips are to Europe, very few to the east coast of the United States. Not only does it take longer to fly from Honolulu to New York than from Honolulu to Hong Kong (the actual air time is about the same, ten or eleven hours either way, but no carrier now flies nonstop from Honolulu to New York), but Hong Kong seems closer in spirit, as do Manila, Tokyo, Sydney. A druggist suggests that I stock up on a prescription over the counter the next

time I am in Hong Kong. The daughter of a friend gets a reward
for good grades, a sweet-sixteen weekend on the Great Barrier
Reef. The far Pacific is home, or near home in mood and appearance
(there are parts of Oahu that bear more resemblance to Southeast
Asia than to anywhere in the mainland United States), and the truly
foreign lies in the other direction: airline posters feature the New
England foliage, the Statue of Liberty, exotic attractions from a distant culture, a culture in which most people in Honolulu have no
roots at all and only a fitful interest. This leaning toward Asia makes
Honolulu's relation to the rest of America oblique, and divergent at
unexpected points, which is part of the place's great but often hidden
eccentricity.

To buy a house anywhere on the island of Oahu in the spring of
1980 cost approximately what a similar property would have cost in
Los Angeles. Three bedrooms and a bath-and-a-half in the tracts near
Pearl Harbor were running over $100,000 ('$138,000' was a figure
I kept noticing in advertisements, once under the headline 'This Is
Your Lucky Day'), although the occasional bungalow with one bath
was offered in the nineties. At the top end of the scale (where 'life
is somehow bigger and disappointment blunted', as one advertisement put it), not quite two-thirds of an acre with a main house,
guesthouse, gatehouse, and saltwater pool on the beach at Diamond
Head was offered – 'fee simple', which was how a piece of property
available for actual sale was described in Honolulu – at $3,750,000.

'Fee simple' was a magical phrase in Honolulu, since one of the
peculiarities of the local arrangement had been that not much property actually changed hands. The island of Oahu was, at its longest
and widest points, forty-five miles long and thirty miles wide, a total
land mass – much of it vertical, unbuildable, the sheer volcanic
precipices of the Koolau and Waianae ranges – of 380,000 acres.
Almost 15 percent of this land was owned by the federal government
and an equal amount by the State of Hawaii. Of the remaining
privately owned land, more than 70 percent was owned by major
landholders, by holders of more than five thousand acres, most notably, on Oahu, by the Campbell Estate, the Damon Estate, Castle
and Cooke, and, in the most densely populated areas of Honolulu,

the Bishop Estate. The Bishop Estate owned a good part of Waikiki, and the Kahala and Waialae districts, and, farther out, Hawaii Kai, which was a Kaiser development but a Bishop holding. The purchaser of a house on Bishop land bought not title to the property itself but a 'leasehold', a land lease, transferred from buyer to buyer, that might be within a few years of expiration or might be (the preferred situation) recently renegotiated, fixed for a long term. An advertisement in the spring of 1980 for a three-bedroom, two-bath, $230,000 house in Hawaii Kai emphasized its 'long, low lease', as did an advertisement for a similar house in the Kahala district offered at $489,000. One Sunday that spring, the Dolman office, a big residential realtor in Honolulu, ran an advertisement in the *Star-Bulletin & Advertiser* featuring forty-seven listings, of which thirty-nine were leasehold. The Earl Thacker office, the same day, featured eighteen listings, ten of which were leasehold, including an oceanfront lease for a house on Kahala Avenue at $1,250,000.

This situation, in which a few owners held most of the land, was relatively unique in the developed world (under 30 percent of the private land in California was held by owners of more than five thousand acres, compared to the more than 70 percent of Oahu) and lent a rather feudal and capricious uncertainty, a note of cosmic transience, to what was in other places a straightforward transaction, a direct assertion of territory, the purchase of a place to live. In some areas the Bishop Estate had offered 'conversions', or the opportunity to convert leasehold to fee-simple property at prices then averaging $5.62 a square foot. This was regarded as a kind of land reform, but it worked adversely on the householder who had already invested all he or she could afford in the leasehold. Someone I know whose Bishop lease came up recently was forced to sell the house in which she had lived for some years because she could afford neither the price of the conversion nor the raised payments of what would have been her new lease. I went with another friend in 1980 to look at a house on the 'other', or non-oceanfront, side of Kahala Avenue, listed at $695,000. The Bishop lease was fixed for thirty years and graduated: $490 a month until 1989, $735 until 1999, and $979 until 2009. The woman showing the house suggested that a conversion might be obtained. No one could promise it, of course, nor could anyone say what price might be set, if indeed a price were set at all.

It was true that nothing on Kahala Avenue itself had at that time been converted. It was also true that the Bishop Estate was talking about Kahala Avenue as a logical place for hotel development. Still, the woman and my friend seemed to agree, it was a pretty house, and a problematic stretch to 2009.

When I first began visiting Honolulu, in 1966, I read in a tourist guidebook that the conventional points of the compass – north, south, east, west – were never employed locally, that one gave directions by saying that a place was either *makai*, toward the sea, or *mauka*, toward the mountains, and, in the city, usually either 'diamond head' or 'ewa', depending on whether the place in question lay, from where one stood, toward Diamond Head or Ewa Plantation. The Royal Hawaiian Hotel, for example, was diamond head of Ewa, but ewa of Diamond Head. The Kahala Hilton Hotel, since it was situated between Diamond Head and Koko Head, was said to be koko head of Diamond Head, and diamond head of Koko Head. There was about this a resolute colorfulness that did not seem entirely plausible to me at the time, particularly since the federally funded signs on the Lunalilo Freeway read EAST and WEST, but as time passed I came to see not only the chimerical compass but the attitude it seemed to reflect as intrinsic to the local accommodation, a way of maintaining fluidity in the rigid structure and isolation of an island society.

This system of bearings is entirely relative (nothing is absolutely ewa, for instance; the Waianae coast is makaha of Ewa, or toward Makaha, and beyond Makaha the known world metamorphoses again), is used at all levels of Honolulu life, and is common even in courtrooms. I recall spending several days at a murder trial during which the HPD evidence specialist, a quite beautiful young woman who looked as if she had walked off 'Hawaii Five-O', spoke of 'picking up latents ewa of the sink'. The police sergeant with whom she had fingerprinted the site said that he had 'dusted the koko head bedroom and the koko head bathroom, also the ewa bedroom and the kitchen floor'. The defendant was said to have placed his briefcase, during a visit to the victim's apartment, 'toward the ewa-makai corner of the couch'. This was a trial, incidentally, during which one of the witnesses, a young woman who had worked a number of call dates with the victim (the victim was a call girl who had been strangled with her own telephone cord in her apartment near Ala Moana), gave her occupation as 'full-time student at the University of Hawaii, carrying sixteen units'. Another witness, also a call girl, said, when asked her occupation, that she was engaged in 'part-time construction'.

The way to get to Ewa was to go beyond Pearl Harbor and down Fort Weaver Road, past the weathered frame building that was once the hospital for Ewa Plantation and past the Japanese graveyard, and turn right. (Going straight instead of turning right would take the driver directly to Ewa Beach, a different proposition. I remember being advised when I first visited Honolulu that if I left the keys in a car in Waikiki I could look for it stripped down in Ewa Beach.) There was no particular reason to go to Ewa, no shops, no businesses, no famous views, no place to eat or even walk far (walk, and you walked right into the cane and the KAPU, or KEEP OUT, signs of the Oahu Sugar Company); there was only the fact that the place was there, intact, operational, a plantation town from another period. There was a school, a post office, a grocery. There were cane tools for sale in the grocery, and the pint bottles of liquor were kept in the office, a kind of wire-mesh cage with a counter. There was the Immaculate Conception Roman Catholic Church, there was the Ewa Hongwanji Mission. On the telephone poles there were torn and rain-stained posters for some revolution past or future, some May Day, a rally, a caucus, a 'Mao Tse-tung Memorial Meeting'.

Ewa was a company town, and its identical frame houses were arranged down a single street, the street that led to the sugar mill. Just one house on this street stood out: a house built of the same frame as the others but not exactly a bungalow, a house transliterated from the New England style, a *haole* house, a manager's house, a house larger than any other house for miles around. A Honolulu psychiatrist once told me, when I asked if he saw any characteristic island syndrome, that, yes, among the children of the planter families, children raised among the memories of the island's colonial past, he did. These patients shared the conviction that they were being watched, being observed, and not living up to what was expected of them. In Ewa one understood how that conviction might take hold. In Ewa one watched the larger house.

On my desk I used to keep a clock on Honolulu time, and around five o'clock by that clock I would sometimes think of Ewa. I would imagine driving through Ewa at that time of day, when the mill and the frame bungalows swim in the softened light like amber, and I would imagine driving on down through Ewa Beach and onto the tract of military housing at Iroquois Point, a place as rigidly structured and culturally isolated in one way as Ewa was in another. From the shoreline at Iroquois Point one looks across the curve of the coast at Waikiki, a circumstance so poignant, suggesting as it does each of the tensions in Honolulu life, that it stops discussion.

6

On the December morning in 1979 when I visited Kai Tak East, the Caritas transit camp for Vietnamese refugees near Kai Tak airport, Kowloon, Hong Kong, a woman of indeterminate age was crouched on the pavement near the washing pumps bleeding out a live chicken. She worked at the chicken's neck with a small paring knife, opening and re-opening the cut and massaging the blood into a tin cup, and periodically she would let the bird run free. The chicken did not exactly run but stumbled, staggered, and finally lurched toward one of the trickles of milky waste water that drained the compound. A flock of small children with bright scarlet rashes on their cheeks giggled and staggered, mimicking the chicken. The woman retrieved the dying chicken and, with what began to seem an almost narcoleptic languor, resumed working the blood from the cut, stroking rhythmically along the matted and stained feathers of the chicken's neck. The chicken had been limp a long time before she finally laid it on the dusty pavement. The children, bored, drifted away. The woman still crouched beside her chicken in the thin December sunlight.

When I think of Hong Kong I remember a particular smell in close places, a smell I construed as jasmine and excrement and sesame oil in varying proportions, and at Kai Tak East, where there were too many people and too few places for them to sleep and cook and eat and wash, this smell pervaded even the wide and dusty exercise yard that was the center of the camp. The smell was in fact what I noticed first, the smell and the dustiness and a certain immediate sense of physical dislocation, a sense of people who had come empty-handed and been assigned odd articles of cast-off clothing, which they wore uneasily: a grave little girl in a faded but still garish metallic bolero, an old man in a Wellesley sweatshirt, a wizened woman in a preteen sweater embroidered with dancing cats. In December in Hong Kong the sun lacked real warmth, and the children in the yard seemed bundled in the unfamiliar fragments of other people's habits. Men talking rubbed their hands as if to generate heat. Women cooking warmed their hands over the electric woks. In the corrugated-metal barracks, each with tiers of 144 metal and plywood bunks on which whole families spread their clothes and eating utensils and straw sleeping mats, mothers and children sat huddled in thin blankets. Outside one barrack a little boy about four years old pressed me to take a taste from his rice bowl. Another urinated against the side of the building.

After a few hours at Kai Tak East the intrinsic inertia and tedium of the camp day became vivid. Conversations in one part of the yard gave way only to conversations in another part of the yard. Preparations for one meal melted into preparations for the next. At the time I was in Hong Kong there were some three hundred thousand Vietnamese refugees, the largest number of whom were 'ethnic Chinese', or Vietnamese of Chinese ancestry, waiting to be processed in improvised camps in the various countries around the South China Sea, in Hong Kong and Thailand and Malaysia and Macao and Indonesia and the Philippines. More than nine thousand of these were at Kai Tak East, and another fifteen thousand at Kai Tak North, the adjoining Red Cross camp. The details of any given passage from Vietnam to Hong Kong differed, but, in the case of the ethnic Chinese, the journey seemed typically to have begun with the payment of gold and the covert collusion of Vietnamese officials and Chinese syndicates outside Vietnam. The question was shadowy. Refugees were a business in this part of the world. Once in Hong Kong, any refugee who claimed to be Vietnamese underwent, before assignment to Kai Tak East or Kai Tak North or one of the other transit camps in the colony, an initial processing and screening by the Hong Kong police, mostly to establish that he or she was not an illegal immigrant from China looking to be relocated instead of repatriated, or, as they said in Hong Kong, 'sent north'. Only after this initial screening did refugees receive the yellow photographic identification cards that let them pass freely through the transit camp gates. The Vietnamese at Kai Tak East came and went all day, going out to work and out to market and out just to get out, but the perimeter of the camp was marked by high chain-link fencing, and in some places by concertina wire. The gates were manned by private security officers. The yellow cards were scrutinized closely. 'This way we know,' a camp administrator told me, 'that what we have here is a genuine case of refugee.'

They were all waiting, these genuine cases of refugee, for the consular interview that might eventually mean a visa out, and the inert tension of life at Kai Tak East derived mainly from this aspect of waiting, of limbo, of suspended hopes and plans and relationships. Of the 11,573 Vietnamese who had passed through Kai Tak East since the camp opened, in June 1979, only some 2,000 had been, by December, relocated, the largest number of them to the United States and Canada. The rest waited, filled out forms, pretended fluency in languages they had barely heard spoken, and looked in vain for their names on the day's list of interviews. Every week or so a few more would be chosen to go, cut loose from the group and put on the truck and taken to the airport for a flight to a country they had never seen.

Six Vietnamese happened to be leaving Kai Tak East the day I was there, two sisters and their younger brother for Australia, and a father and his two sons for France. The three going to Australia were the oldest children of a family that had lost its home and business in the Cholon district of Saigon and been ordered to a 'new economic zone', one of the supervised wastelands in the Vietnamese country-side where large numbers of ethnic Chinese were sent to live off the land and correct their thinking. The parents had paid gold, the equivalent of six ounces, to get these three children out of Saigon via Haiphong, and now the children hoped to earn enough money in Australia to get out their parents and younger siblings. The sisters, who were twenty-three and twenty-four, had no idea how long this would take or if it would be possible. They knew only that they were leaving Hong Kong with their brother on the evening Qantas. They were uncertain in what Australian city the evening Qantas landed, nor did it seem to matter.

I talked to the two girls for a while, and then to the man who was taking his sons to France. This man had paid the equivalent of twelve or thirteen ounces of gold to buy his family out of Hanoi. Because his wife and daughters had left Hanoi on a different day, and been assigned to a different Hong Kong camp, the family was to be, on this day, reunited for the first time in months. The wife and daughters would already be on the truck when it reached Kai Tak East. The truck would take them all to the airport and they would fly together to Nice, 'toute la famille'. Toward noon, when the truck pulled up to the gate, the man rushed past the guards and leapt up to embrace a pretty woman. 'Ma femme!' he cried out again and again to those of us watching from the yard. He pointed wildly, and maneuvered the woman and little girls into better view. 'Ma femme, mes filles!'

I stood in the sun and waved until the truck left, then turned back to the yard. In many ways refugees had become an entrenched fact of Hong Kong life. 'They've got to go, there's no room for them here,' a young Frenchwoman, Saigon born, had said to me at dinner the night before. Beside me in the yard a man sat motionless while a young woman patiently picked the nits from his hair. Across the yard a group of men and women watched without expression as the administrator posted the names of those selected for the next day's consular interviews. A few days later the South China Morning Post carried reports from intelligence sources that hundreds of boats were being assembled in Vietnamese ports to carry out more ethnic Chinese. The headline read, 'HK Alert to New Invasion.' It was believed that weather would not be favorable for passage to Hong Kong until the advent of the summer monsoon. Almost a dozen years later, the British government, which had agreed to relinquish Hong Kong to the Chinese in 1997, reached an accord with the government of Vietnam providing for the forcible repatriation of Hong Kong's remaining Vietnamese refugees. The flights back to Vietnam began in the fall of 1991. Some Vietnamese were

photographed crying and resisting as they were taken to the Hong
Kong airport. Hong Kong authorities stressed that the guards
escorting the refugees were unarmed.

1979–1991

Los Angeles Days

1

During one of the summer weeks I spent in Los Angeles in 1988 there was a cluster of small earthquakes, the most noticeable of which, on the Garlock Fault, a major lateral-slip fracture that intersects the San Andreas in the Tehachapi range north of Los Angeles, occurred at six minutes after four on a Friday afternoon when I happened to be driving in Wilshire Boulevard from the beach. People brought up to believe that the phrase 'terra firma' has real meaning often find it hard to understand the apparent equanimity with which earthquakes are accommodated in California, and tend to write it off as regional spaciness. In fact it is less equanimity than protective detachment, the useful adjustment commonly made in circumstances so unthinkable that psychic survival precludes preparation. I know very few people in California who actually set aside, as instructed, a week's supply of water and food. I know fewer still who could actually lay hands on the wrench required to turn off, as instructed, the main gas valve; the scenario in which this wrench will be needed is a catastrophe, and something in the human spirit rejects planning on a daily basis for catastrophe. I once interviewed, in the late sixties, someone who did prepare: a Pentecostal minister who had received a kind of heavenly earthquake advisory, and on its quite specific instructions was moving his congregation from Port Hueneme, north of Los Angeles, to Murfreesboro, Tennessee. A few months later, when a small earthquake was felt not in Port Hueneme but in Murfreesboro, an event so novel that it was reported nationally, I was, I recall, mildly gratified.

A certain fatalism comes into play. When the ground starts moving all bets are off. Quantification, which in this case takes the form of guessing where the movement at hand will rank on the Richter scale, remains a favored way of regaining the illusion of personal control, and people still crouched in the nearest doorjamb will reach for a telephone and try to call Caltech, in Pasadena, for a Richter reading. 'Rock and roll,' the D.J. said on my car radio that Friday afternoon at six minutes past four. 'This console is definitely shaking . . . no word from Pasadena yet, is there?'

'I would say this is a three,' the D.J.'s colleague said.

'Definitely a three, maybe I would say a little higher than a three.'

'Say an eight . . . just joking.'

'It felt like a six where I was.'

What it turned out to be was a five-two, followed by a dozen smaller aftershocks, and it had knocked out four of the six circuit breakers at the A. D. Edmonston pumping plant on the California Aqueduct, temporarily shutting down the flow of Northern California water over the Tehachapi range and cutting off half of Southern California's water supply for the weekend. This was all within the range not only of the predictable but of the normal. No one had been killed or seriously injured. There was plenty of water for the weekend in the system's four southern reservoirs, Pyramid, Castaic, Silverwood, and Perris lakes. A five-two earthquake is not, in California, where the movements people remember tend to have Richter numbers well over six, a major event, and the probability of earthquakes like this one had in fact been built into the Aqueduct: the decision to pump the water nineteen hundred feet over the Tehachapi was made precisely because the Aqueduct's engineers rejected the idea of tunneling through an area so geologically complex, periodically wrenched by opposing displacements along the San Andreas and the Garlock, that it has been called California's structural knot.

Still, this particular five-two, coming as it did when what Californians call 'the Big One' was pretty much overdue (the Big One is the eight, the Big One is the seven in the wrong place or at the wrong time, the Big One could even be the six-five centered near downtown Los Angeles at nine on a weekday morning), made people a little uneasy. There was some concern through the weekend that this was not merely an ordinary five-two but a 'foreshock', an earthquake prefiguring a larger event (the chances of this, according to Caltech seismologists, run about one in twenty), and by Sunday there was what seemed to many people a sinister amount of activity on other faults: a three-four just east of Ontario at twenty-two minutes past two in the afternoon, a three-six twenty-two minutes later at Lake Berryessa, and, four hours and one minute later, northeast of San Jose, a five-five on the Calaveras Fault. On Monday, there was a two-three in Playa del Rey and a three in Santa Barbara.

Had it not been for the five-two on Friday, very few people would have registered these little quakes (the Caltech seismological monitors in Southern California normally record from twenty to thirty earthquakes a day with magnitudes below three), and in the end nothing came of them, but this time people did register them, and they lent a certain moral gravity to the way the city happened to look that weekend, a temporal dimension to the hard white edges and empty golden light. At odd moments during the next few days people would suddenly clutch at tables, or walls. 'Is it going,' they would say, or 'I think it's moving.' They almost always said 'it', and what they meant by 'it' was not just the ground but the world as they knew it. I have lived all my life with the promise of the Big One, but when it starts going now even I get the jitters.

2

What is striking about Los Angeles after a period away is how well it works. The famous freeways work, the supermarkets work (a visit, say, to the Pacific Palisades Gelson's, where the aisles are wide and the shelves full and checkout is fast and free of attitude, remains the zazen of grocery shopping), the beaches work. The 1984 Olympics were not supposed to work, but they did (daily warnings of gridlock and urban misery gave way, during the first week, to a county-wide block party, with pink and aquamarine flags fluttering over empty streets and parking spaces for once available even in Westwood); not only worked but turned a profit, of almost $223 million, about which there was no scandal. Even the way houses are bought and sold seems to work more efficiently than it does in New York (for all practical purposes there are no exclusive listings in Los Angeles, and the various contingencies on which closing the deal depends are arbitrated not by lawyers but by an escrow company), something that came to my attention when my husband and I arranged to have our Los Angeles house shown for the first time to brokers at eleven o'clock one Saturday morning, went out to do a few errands, and came back at one to find that we had three offers, one of them for appreciably more than the asking price.

Selling a house in two hours was not, in 1988 in Los Angeles, an entirely unusual experience. Around February of 1988, midway through what most people call the winter but Californians call the spring ('winter' in California is widely construed as beginning and ending with the Christmas season, reflecting a local preference for the upside), at a time when residential real estate prices in New York were already plunging in response to the October 1987 stock market crash, there had in fact developed on the west side of Los Angeles a heightened enthusiasm for committing large sums of money to marginal improvements in one's domestic situation: to moving, say, from what was called in the listings a 'convertible 3' in Santa Monica (three bedrooms, one of which might be converted into a study) to a self-explanatory '4 + lib' in Brentwood Park, or to acquiring what was described in the listings as an 'H/F pool', meaning heated and filtered, or a 'N/S tennis court', meaning the preferred placement on the lot, the north-south orientation believed to keep sun from the players' eyes.

By June of 1988 a kind of panic had set in, of a kind that occurs periodically in Southern California but had last occurred in 1979. Multiple offers were commonplace, and deals stalled because bank appraisers could not assess sales fast enough to keep up with the rising market. Residential real estate offices were routinely reporting 'record months'. People were buying one- and two-million-dollar houses as investments, to give their adolescent children what brokers referred to as 'a base in the market', which was one reason why small houses on modest lots priced at a million-four were getting, the day they were listed, thirty and forty offers.

All this seemed to assume an infinitely upward trend, and to be one of those instances in which the preoccupations and apprehensions of people in Los Angeles, a city in many ways predicated on the ability to deal with the future at a rather existential remove, did not exactly coincide with those of the country at large. October 19, 1987, which had so immediately affected the New York market that asking prices on some apartments had in the next three or four months dropped as much as a million dollars, seemed, in Los Angeles, not to have happened. Those California brokers to whom I talked, if they mentioned the crash at all, tended to see it as a catalyst for good times, an event that had emphasized the 'real' in real estate.

The *Los Angeles Times* had taken to running, every Sunday, a chat column devoted mainly to the buying and selling of houses: Ruth Ryon's 'Hot Property', from which one could learn that the highest price paid for a house in Los Angeles to that date was $20.25 million (by Marvin Davis, to Kenny Rogers, for The Knoll in Beverly Hills); that the $2.5 million paid in 1986 for 668 St Cloud Road in Bel Air (by Earle Jorgenson and Holmes Tuttle and some eighteen other friends of President and Mrs Reagan, for whom the house was bought and who rent it with an option to buy) was strikingly under value, since even an unbuilt acre in the right part of Bel Air (the house bought by the Reagans' friends is definitely in the right part of Bel Air) will sell for $3 million; and that two houses in the Reagans' new neighborhood sold recently for $13.5 million and $14.75 million respectively. A typical 'Hot Property' item ran this way:

Newlyweds Tracey E. Bregman Recht, star of the daytime soap 'The Young and the Restless', and her husband Ron Recht, a commercial real estate developer, just bought their first home, on 2.5 acres in a nifty neighborhood. They're just up the street from Merv Griffin's house (which I've heard is about to be listed at some astronomical price) and they're just down the street from Pickfair, now owned by Pia Zadora and her husband. The Rechts bought a house that was built in 1957 on San Ysidro Drive in Beverly Hills for an undisclosed price, believed to be several million dollars, and now they're fixing it up . . .

I spent some time, before this 1988 bull market broke, with two West Side brokers, Betty Budlong and Romelle Dunas of the Jon Douglas office, both of whom spoke about the going price of 'anything at all' as a million dollars, and of 'something decent' as two million dollars. 'Right now I've got two clients in the price range of five to six hundred thousand dollars,' Romelle Dunas said. 'I sat all morning trying to think what I could show them today.'

'I'd cancel the appointment,' Betty Budlong said.

'I just sold their condo for four. I'm sick. The houses for five-fifty are smaller than their condo.'

'I think you could still find something in Ocean Park,' Betty Budlong said. 'Ocean Park, Sunset Park, somewhere like that. Brentwood Glen, you know, over here, the Rattery tract . . . of course that's inching toward six.'

'Inching toward six and you're living in the right lane of the San Diego Freeway,' Romelle Dunas said.

'In seventeen hundred square feet,' Betty Budlong said.

'If you're lucky. I saw one that was fifteen hundred square feet. I have a feeling when these people go out today they're not going to close on their condo.'

Betty Budlong thought about this. 'I think you should make a good friend of Sonny Fox,' she said at last.

Sonny Fox was a Jon Douglas agent in Sherman Oaks, in the San Fernando Valley, only a twenty-minute drive from Beverly Hills on the San Diego Freeway but a twenty-minute drive toward which someone living on the West Side – even someone who would drive forty minutes to Malibu – was apt to display considerable sales resistance.

'In the Valley,' Romelle Dunas said after a pause.

Betty Budlong shrugged. 'In the Valley.'

'People are afraid to get out of this market,' Romelle Dunas said.

'They can't afford to get out,' Betty Budlong said. 'I know two people who in any other market would have sold their houses. One of them has accepted a job in Chicago, the other is in Washington for at least two years. They're both leasing their houses. Because until they're sure they're not coming back, they don't want to get out.'

The notion that land will be worth more tomorrow than it is

worth today has been a real part of the California experience, and remains deeply embedded in the California mentality, but this seemed extreme, and it occurred to me that the buying and selling of houses was perhaps one more area in which the local capacity for protective detachment had come into play, that people capable of compartmentalizing the Big One might be less inclined than others to worry about getting their money out of a 4 + lib, H/F pool. I asked if foreign buyers could be pushing up the market.

Betty Budlong thought not. 'These are people who are moving, say, from a seven-fifty house to a million-dollar house.'

I asked if the market could be affected by a defense cutback.

Betty Budlong thought not. 'Most of the people who buy on the West Side are professionals, or in the entertainment industry. People who work at Hughes and Douglas, say, don't live in Brentwood or Santa Monica or Beverly Hills.'

I asked Betty Budlong if she saw anything at all that could affect the market.

'Tight money could affect this market,' Betty Budlong said. 'For a while.'

'Then it always goes higher,' Romelle Dunas said.

'Which is why people can't afford to get out,' Betty Budlong said.

'They couldn't get back in,' Romelle Dunas said.

3

This entire question of houses and what they were worth (and what they should be worth, and what it meant when the roof over someone's head was also his or her major asset) was, during the spring and summer of 1988, understandably more on the local mind than it perhaps should have been, which was one reason why a certain house then under construction just west of the Los Angeles Country Club became the focus of considerable attention, and of emotions usually left dormant on the west side of Los Angeles. The house was that being built by the television producer ('Dynasty', 'Loveboat', 'Fantasy Island') Aaron Spelling and his wife Candy at the corner of Mapleton and Club View in Holmby Hills, on six acres the Spellings had bought in 1983, for $10,250,000, from Patrick Frawley, the chairman of Schick.

At the time of the purchase there was already a fairly impressive house on the property, a house once lived in by Bing Crosby, but the Spellings, who had become known for expansive domestic gestures (crossing the country in private railroad cars, for example, and importing snow to Beverly Hills for their children's Christmas parties), had decided that the Crosby/Frawley house was what is known locally as a teardown. The progress of the replacement, which was rising from the only residential site I have ever seen with a two-story contractor's office and a sign reading CONSTRUCTION AREA: HARD HATS REQUIRED, became over the next several months not just a form of popular entertainment but, among inhabitants of a city without much common experience, a unifying, even a political, idea.

At first the project was identified, on the kind of site sign usually reserved for office towers in progress, as 'THE MANOR'; later 'THE MANOR' was modified to what seemed, given the resemblance of the structure to a resort Hyatt, the slightly nutty discretion of '594 SOUTH MAPLETON DRIVE'. It was said that the structure ('house' seemed not entirely to cover it) would have 56,500 square feet. It was said that the interior plan would include a bowling alley, and 560 square feet of extra closet space, balconied between the second and the attic floors. It was said, by the owner, that such was the mass of the steel frame construction that to break up the foundation alone would take a demolition crew six months, and cost from four to five million dollars.

Within a few months the site itself had become an established attraction, and evening drive-bys were enlivened by a skittish defensiveness on the part of the guards, who would switch on the perimeter floods and light up the steel girders and mounded earth like a prison yard. The *Los Angeles Times* and *Herald Examiner* published periodic reports on and rumors about the job ('Callers came out of the woodwork yesterday in the wake of our little tale about Candy Spelling having the foundation of her $45-million mansion-in-progress lowered because she didn't want to see the Robinson's department store sign from where her bed-to-be was to sit'), followed by curiously provocative corrections, or 'denials', from Aaron Spelling. 'The only time Candy sees the Robinson's sign is when she's shopping' was one correction that got everyone's attention, but in many ways the most compelling was this: 'They say we have an Olympic-sized swimming pool. Not true. There's no gazebo, no guesthouse ... When people go out to dinner, unless they talk about their movies, they have nothing else to talk about, so they single out Candy.'

In that single clause, 'unless they talk about their movies', there was hidden a great local truth, and the inchoate heart of the matter: this house was, in the end, that of a television producer, and people who make movies did not, on the average evening, have dinner with people who make television. People who make television had most of the money, but people who make movies still had most of the status, and believed themselves the keepers of the community's unspoken code, of the rules, say, about what constituted excess on the housing front. This was a distinction usually left tacit, but the fact of the Spelling house was making people say things out loud. 'There are people in this town worth hundreds of millions of dollars,' Richard Zanuck, one of the most successful motion picture producers in the business, once said to my husband, 'and they can't get a table at Chasen's.' This was a man whose father had run a studio and who had himself run a studio, and his bewilderment was that of someone who had uncovered an anomaly in the wheeling of the stars.

4

When people in Los Angeles talk about 'this town', they do not mean Los Angeles, nor do they exactly mean what many of them call 'the community'. 'The community' is more narrowly defined, and generally confined to those inhabitants of this town who can be relied upon to sit at one another's tables on approved evenings (benefiting the American Film Institute, say) and to get one another's daughters into approved schools, say Westlake, in Holmby Hills, not far from the Spellings' house but on eleven acres rather than six. People in the community meet one another for lunch at Hillcrest, but do not, in the main, attend Friars' Club Roasts. People in the community sojourn with their children in Paris, and Aspen, and at the Kahala Hilton in Honolulu, but visit Las Vegas only on business.

'The community' is made up of people who can, in other words, get a table at Chasen's.

'This town' is broader, and means just 'the industry', which is the way people who make television and motion pictures refer, tellingly, to the environment in which they work. The extent to which the industry in question resembles conventional industries is often obscured by its unconventional product, which requires that its 'workers' perform in unconventional ways, for which they are paid unconventional sums of money: some people do make big money writing and directing and producing and acting in television, and some people also make big money, although considerably less big, writing and directing and producing and acting in motion pictures.

Still, as in other entrepreneurial enterprises, it is not those who work on the line in this industry but those who manage it who make the biggest money of all, and who tend to have things their way, which is what the five-month 1988 Writers Guild of America strike, which had become by the time of its settlement in early August 1988 perhaps the most acrimonious union strike in recent industry history, was initially and finally about. It was not about what were inflexibly referred to by both union and management as 'the so-called creative issues', nor was it exclusively about the complicated formulas and residuals that were the tokens on the board. It was about respect, and about whether the people who made the biggest money were or were not going to give a little to the people who made the less big money.

In other words, it was a class issue, which was hard for people outside the industry – who in the first place did not understand the essentially adversarial nature of the business (a good contract, it is understood in Hollywood, is one that ensures the other party's breach) and in the second place believed everybody involved to be overpaid – to entirely understand. 'Whose side does one take in such a war – that of the writers with their scads of money, or that of the producers with their tons of money?' the *Washington Post*'s television reporter, Tom Shales, demanded (as it turned out, rhetorically) in a June 29, 1988, piece arguing that the writers were 'more interested in strutting and swaggering than in reaching a settlement', that 'a handful of hotheads' who failed to realize that 'the salad days are over' were bringing down an industry beset by 'dwindling' profits, and that the only effect of the strike was to crush 'those in the lowest-paying jobs', for example a waitress, laid off when Universal shut down its commissary, who Tom Shales perceived to be 'not too thrilled with the writers and their grievances' when he saw her interviewed on a television newscast. (This was an example of what became known locally during the strike as 'the little people argument', and referred to the traditional practice among struck companies of firing their nonunion hostages. When hard times come to Hollywood, the typing pool goes first, and is understood to symbolize the need of the studio to 'cut back', or 'slash costs'.) 'Just because the producers are richer doesn't mean the writers are right. Or righteous,' Tom Shales concluded. 'These guys haven't just seen too many Rambo movies, they've written too many Rambo movies.'

This piece, which reflected with rather impressive fidelity the arguments then being made by the Alliance of Motion Picture and Television Producers, the negotiating body for management, was typical of most coverage of the strike, and also of what had become, by early summer of 1988, the prevailing mood around town. Writers have never been much admired in Hollywood. In an industry predicated on social fluidity, on the daily calibration and reassessment of status and power, screenwriters, who perform a function that remains only dimly understood even by the people who hire them, occupy a notably static place: even the most successful of them have no real power, and therefore no real status. 'I can always get a writer,' Ray Stark once told my husband, who had expressed a disinclination to join the team on a Stark picture for which he had been, Ray Stark had told him a few weeks before, 'the only possible writer'.

Writers (even the only possible writers), it is universally believed, can always be replaced, which is why they are so frequently referred to in the plural. Writers, it is believed by many, are even best replaced, hired serially, since they bring, in this view, only a limited amount of talent and energy to bear on what directors often call their 'vision'. A number of directors prefer to hire fresh writers – usually writers with whom they have previously worked – just before shooting: Sydney Pollack, no matter who wrote the picture he is directing, has the habit of hiring for the period just before and during production David Rayfiel or Elaine May or Kurt Luedtke. 'I want it in the contract when David Rayfiel comes in,' a writer I know once said when he and Pollack were talking about doing a picture together; this was a practical but unappreciated approach.

The previous writer on a picture is typically described as 'exhausted', or 'worn-out on this'. What is meant by 'this' is the task at hand, which is seen as narrow and technical, one color in the larger vision, a matter of taking notes from a producer or an actor or a director, and adding dialogue – something, it is understood, that the producer or actor or director could do without a writer, if only he or she had the time, if only he or she were not required to keep that larger vision in focus. 'I've got the ideas,' one frequently hears in the industry. 'All I need is a writer.'

Such 'ideas', when explored, typically tend toward the general ('relationships between men and women', say, or 'rebel without a cause in the west Valley'), and the necessity for paying a writer to render such ideas specific remains a source of considerable resentment. Writers are generally seen as balky, obstacles to the forward flow of the project. They take time. They want money. They are typically the first element on a picture, the people whose job it is to invent a world sufficiently compelling to interest actors and directors, and, as the first element, they are often unwilling to recognize the necessity for keeping the front money down, for cutting their fees in order to get a project going. 'Everyone', they are told, is taking a cut ('everyone' in this instance generally means every one of the writers), yet they insist on 'irresponsible' fees. A director who gets several million dollars a picture will often complain, quite bitterly, about being 'held up' by the demands of his writers. 'You're haggling over pennies,' a director once complained to me.

This resentment surfaces most openly in contract negotiations ('We don't give points to writers,' studio business-affairs lawyers will say in a negotiation, or, despite the fact that a writer has often delivered one or two drafts on the basis of a deal memo alone, 'Our policy is no payment without a fully executed contract'), but in fact suffuses every aspect of life in the community. Writers do not get gross from dollar one, nor do they get the Thalberg Award, nor do they even determine when and where a meeting will take place: these are facts of local life known even to children. Writers who work regularly live comfortably, but not in the houses with the better N/S courts. Writers sometimes get to Paris on business, but rarely on the Concorde. Writers occasionally have lunch at Hillcrest, but only when their agents take them. Writers have at best a provisional relationship with the community in which they live, which is precisely what has made them, over the years, such convenient pariahs. 'Fuck 'em, they're weaklings,' as one director I know said about the Guild.

As the strike wore on, then, a certain natural irritation, even a bellicosity, was bound to surface when the subject of the writers (or, as some put it, 'the writers and their so-called demands') came up, as was an impatience with the whole idea of collective bargaining. 'If you're good enough, you can negotiate your own contract,' I recall being told by one director. It was frequently suggested that the strike was supported only by those members of the Guild who were not full-time working writers. 'A lot of them aren't writers,' an Alliance spokesman told the *Los Angeles Times*. 'They pay their one-hundred-dollar-a-year dues and get invitations to screenings.' A television producer suggested to me that perhaps the answer was 'another guild', one that would function, although he did not say this, as a sweetheart union. 'A guild for working writers,' he said. 'That's a guild we could negotiate with.'

I heard repeatedly during the strike that I, as a member of the Guild 'but an intelligent person', had surely failed to understand what 'the leadership' of the Guild was doing to me; when I said that I did understand it, that I had lost three pictures during the course of the strike and would continue to vote against a settlement until certain money issues had been resolved, I was advised that such intransigence would lead nowhere, because 'the producers won't budge', because 'they're united on this', because 'they're going to just write off the Guild', and because, an antic note, 'they're going to start hiring college kids – they're even going to start hiring journalists'.

In this mounting enthusiasm to punish the industry's own writers by replacing them 'even' with journalists ('Why not air traffic controllers?' said a writer to whom I mentioned this threat), certain facts about the strike receded early into the mists of claim and counter-claim. Many people preferred to believe that, as Tom Shales summarized it, the producers had 'offered increases', and that the writers had 'said they were not enough'. In fact the producers had offered,

on the key points in the negotiation, rollbacks on a residual payment
structure established in 1985, when the WGA contract had been last
negotiated. Many people preferred to believe, as Tom Shales seemed
to believe, that it was the writers, not the producers, who were
refusing to negotiate. In fact the strike had been, from the Alliance's
'last and final offer' on March 6, 1988, until a federal mediator called
both sides to meet on May 23, 1988, less a strike than a lockout,
with the producers agreeing to attend only a single meeting, on
April 8, which lasted twenty minutes before the Alliance negotiators
walked out. 'It looks like the writers are shooting the whole industry
in the foot – and they're doing it willfully and stupidly,' Grant Tinker,
the television producer and former chairman of NBC, told the *Los
Angeles Times* after the Guild rejected, by a vote of 2,789 to 933, the
June version of the Alliance's series of 'last and final' offers. 'It's just
pigheaded and stupid for the writers to have so badly misread what's
going on here.'

What was going on here was interesting. This had not been an
industry unaccustomed to labor disputes, nor had it been one, plans
to hire 'journalists' notwithstanding, historically hospitable to outsiders. ('We don't go for strangers in Hollywood,' Cecilia Brady said
in *The Last Tycoon*; this remains the most succinct description I know
of the picture business.) For reasons deep in the structure of the
industry, writers' strikes have been a fixed feature of local life, and
gains earned by the writers have traditionally been passed on to the
other unions – who themselves strike only rarely – in a fairly inflexible ratio: for every dollar in residuals the Writers Guild gets, another
dollar goes to the Directors Guild, three dollars go to the Screen
Actors Guild, and eight or nine dollars go to IATSE, the principal
craft union, which needs the higher take because its pension and
health benefits, unlike those of the other unions, are funded entirely
from residuals. 'So when the WGA negotiates for a dollar increase
in residuals, say, the studios don't think just a dollar, they think
twelve or thirteen,' a former Guild president told me. 'The industry
is a kind of family, and its members are interdependent.'

Something new was at work, and it had to do with a changed
attitude among the top executives. I recall being told, quite early in
this strike, by someone who had been a studio head of production
and had bargained for management in previous strikes, that this

strike would be different, and in many ways unpredictable. The problem, he said, was the absence at the bargaining table of 'a Lew Wasserman, an Arthur Krim'. Lew Wasserman, the chairman of MCA-Universal, it is said in the industry, was always looking for the solution; as he grew less active, Arthur Krim, at United Artists, and to a lesser extent Ted Ashley, at Warner Brothers, fulfilled this function, which was essentially that of the *consigliere*. 'The guys who are running the studios now, they don't deal,' he said. 'Sid Sheinberg bargaining for Universal, Barry Diller for Fox, that's ridiculous. They won't even talk. As far as the Disney guys go, Eisner, Katzenberg, they play hardball, that's the way they run their operation.'

Roger Fisher, the Williston Professor of Law at Harvard Law School and director of the Harvard Negotiation Project, suggested, in an analysis of the strike published in the *Los Angeles Times*, that what had been needed between management and labor in this case was 'understanding, two-way communication, reliability, and acceptance', the very qualities that natural selection in the motion picture industry had tended to eliminate. It was in fact June of 1988, three months into the strike, before the people running the studios actually entered the negotiating sessions, which they referred to, significantly, as 'downtime'. 'I talked to Diller, Mancuso, Daly,' I was told by one of the two or three most powerful agents in the industry. He meant Barry Diller at Twentieth Century-Fox and Frank Mancuso at Paramount and Robert Daly at Warner Brothers. 'I said look, you guys, you want this thing settled, you better indicate you're taking it seriously enough to put in the downtime yourselves. Sheinberg [Sidney Sheinberg of MCA-Universal] and Mancuso have kind of emerged as the point players for management, but you've got to remember, these guys are all prima donnas, they hate each other, so it was a big problem presenting a sufficiently united front to put somebody out there speaking for all of them.'

In the context of an industry traditionally organized, like a mob family, around principles of discretion and unity, this notion of the executive as prima donna was a new phenomenon, and not one tending toward an appreciation of the 'interdependence' of unions and management. It did not work toward the settlement of this strike that the main players on one side of the negotiations were themselves regarded as stars, the subjects of fan profiles, pieces often written by

people who admired and wanted to work in the industry. Michael
Eisner of Disney had been on the cover of *Time*. Sidney Sheinberg of
Universal had been on the cover of *Manhattan, inc.* Executive foibles
had been detailed (Jeffrey Katzenberg of Disney 'guzzled' Diet Coke,
and 'sold his Porsche after he almost killed himself trying to shift
gears and dial at the same time'), as had, and this presented a problem, company profits and executive compensation. Nineteen eighty-
seven net profit for Warner Communications was up 76.6 percent
over 1986. Nineteen eighty-seven net profit for Paramount was up
130 percent over 1986. CBS was up 21 percent, ABC 53 percent.
The chairman and CEO of Columbia, Victor Kaufman, received in
1987 $826,154 in salary and an additional $1,506,142 in stock
options and bonuses. Michael Eisner was said to have received,
including options and bonuses, a figure that ranged from $23 million
(this was Disney's own figure) to more than $80 million (this was
what the number of shares involved in the stock options seemed to
suggest), but was most often given as $63 million.

During a season when management was issuing white papers
explaining the 'new, colder realities facing the entertainment industry', this last figure in particular had an energizing effect on the local
consciousness, and was frequently mentioned in relation to another
figure, that for the combined total received in residual payments by
all nine thousand members of the Writers Guild. This figure was $58
million, which, against Michael Eisner's $63, made it hard for many
people to accept the notion that residual rollbacks were entirely
imperative. Trust seemed lacking, as did a certain mutuality of interest. 'We used to sit across the table from people we had personally
worked with on movies,' I was told by a writer who had sat in on
negotiating sessions during this and past strikes. 'These people aren't
movie people. They think like their own business-affairs lawyers.
You take somebody like Jeff Katzenberg, he has a very ideological
position. He said the other night, "I'm speaking as a dedicated capitalist. I own this screenplay. So why should I hand anybody else the
right to have any say about it?"'

In June of 1988, three months into the strike, it was said around Los
Angeles that the strike was essentially over, because the producers

said it was over, and that the only problem remaining was to find a way for the Guild negotiators to save face – 'a bone', as Jeffrey Katzenberg was said to be calling it, to throw the writers. 'This has largely come down to a question of how Brian will look,' I was told that month by someone close to management. He was talking about Brian Walton, the Guild's executive director and chief negotiator. 'It's a presentation problem, a question of giving him something he can present to the membership, after fifteen weeks, as something approaching win-win.' It was generally conceded that the producers, despite disavowals, were determined to break the union; even the disavowals, focusing as they did on the useful clerical work done by the Guild ('If the Guild didn't exist we'd have to invent it,' Sidney Sheinberg said at one point), suggested that what the producers had in mind was less a union than a trade association. It was taken for granted that it was not the producers but the writers who, once the situation was correctly 'presented', would give in. 'Let's get this town back to work,' people were saying, and 'This strike has to end.'

Still, this strike did not end. By late July, it was said around Los Angeles that the negotiations once again in progress were not really negotiations at all; that 'they' were meeting only because a federal mediator had ordered them to meet, and that the time spent at the table was just that, time spent at a table, downtime. Twenty-one writers had announced their intention of working in spite of the strike, describing this decision as evidence of 'the highest form of loyalty' to the Guild. 'What's it for?' people were saying, and 'This is lose-lose.'

'Writers are children,' Monroe Stahr had said almost half a century before, in *The Last Tycoon*, by way of explaining why his own negotiations with the Writers Guild had reached, after a year, a dead end. 'They are not equipped for authority. There is no substitute for will. Sometimes you have to fake will when you don't feel it at all . . . So I've had to take an attitude in this Guild matter.' In the end, the attitude once again was taken and once again prevailed. 'This strike has run out of gas,' people began to say, and 'This is ridiculous, this is enough,' as if the writers were not only children but bad children, who had been humored too long. 'We've gotten to the end of the road and hit a brick wall,' the negotiator for the Alliance of Motion Picture and Television Producers, J. Nicholas Counter III,

said on the Sunday afternoon of July 31, 1988, at a press conference
called by the Alliance to announce that negotiations with the Writers
Guild were at an end, 'hopelessly' deadlocked. 'I suggest it's time for
Mr Walton to look to himself for the answer as to why his guild
is still on strike,' Jeffrey Katzenberg said that afternoon to Aljean
Harmetz of the *New York Times*. That evening, Jeffrey Katzenberg
and the other executives of the major studios met with Kenneth
Ziffren, a prominent local lawyer who represented several Guild
members who, because they had television production companies,
had a particular interest in ending the strike; the marginally different
formulas suggested by Kenneth Ziffren seemed to many the bone
they had been looking for: a way of solving 'the presentation problem', of making the strike look, now that the writers understood that
it had run out of gas, 'like something approaching win-win'. On the
following Sunday, August 7, 1988, the Guild membership voted to
end the strike, on essentially the same terms it had turned down in
June.

During the five months of the dispute many people outside the
industry had asked me what the strike was about, and I had heard
myself talk about ancillary markets and about the history of pattern
bargaining, about the 'issues', but the dynamic of the strike, the
particular momentum that kept several thousand people with not
much in common voting for at least a while against what appeared
to be their own best interests, had remained hard to explain. The
amounts of money to be gained or lost had seemed, against the
money lost during the course of the strike, insignificant. The 'creative' issues, the provisions that touched on the right of the writer
to have some say in the production, would have been, if won,
unenforceable.

Yet I had been for the strike, and felt toward that handful of
writers who had declared their intention to desert it, and by so doing
encouraged the terms on which it would end, a coolness bordering
on distaste, as if we had gone back forty years, and they had named
names. 'You need to have worked in the industry,' I would say by
way of explanation, or 'You have to live there.' Not until July of
1988, at the Democratic National Convention in Atlanta, did the

emotional core of the strike come clear to me. I had gone to Atlanta in an extra-industry role, that of 'reporter' (or, as we say in Hollywood, 'journalist'), with credentials that gave me a seat in the Omni but access to only a rotating pass to go on the floor. I was waiting for this rotating pass one evening when I ran into a director I knew, Paul Mazursky. We talked for a moment, and I noticed that he, like all the other industry people I saw in Atlanta, had a top pass, one of the several all-access passes. In this case it was a floor pass, and, since I was working and he seemed not about to go on the floor, I asked if I might borrow it for half an hour.

He considered this.

He would, he said, 'really like' to do this for me, but thought not. He seemed surprised that I had asked, and uncomfortable that I had breached the natural order of the community as we both knew it: directors and actors and producers, I should have understood, have floor passes. Writers do not, which is why they strike.

1988

Down at City Hall

Just inside the main lobby of City Hall in Los Angeles there was for some time a curious shrine to Tom Bradley, the seventy-one-year-old black former police officer who was in April of 1989 elected to his fifth four-year term as mayor of Los Angeles. There was an Olympic flag, suspended behind glass and lit reverentially, its five interlocking rings worked in bright satin. There were, displayed in a kind of architectural niche, various other mementos of the 1984 Los Angeles Olympics, the event that remained the symbolic centerpiece not only of Tom Bradley's sixteen-year administration (arriving passengers at LAX, for example, were for some years after 1984 confronted on the down escalators by large pictures of Mayor Bradley and the somewhat unsettling legend 'Welcome to Los Angeles XXIII Olympiad', as if the plane had touched down in a time warp), but of what Bradley's people liked to present as the city's ascension, under his guidance, to American capital of the Pacific rim.

And there was, behind a crimson silk rope, a sheet of glass on which a three-dimensional holographic image of Tom Bradley, telephone to ear, appeared and disappeared. If the viewer moved to the right, the mayor could be seen to smile; if the viewer moved to the left, the mayor turned grave, and lowered his head to study a paper. From certain angles the mayor vanished altogether, leaving only an eerie blue. It was this disappearing effect, mirroring as it did what many saw as a certain elusiveness about the mayor himself, that most often arrested the passing citizen. 'That's the shot on the Jackson endorsement,' I recall a television cameraman saying as we passed this dematerializing Tom Bradley one afternoon in June of 1988, a few days before the California presidential primary, on our way from a press conference during which the actual Tom Bradley had successfully, and quite characteristically, managed to appear with Jesse Jackson without in the least recommending him.

In fact it seemed the shot on the entire Bradley administration, the enduring electability of which was something many people in Los Angeles found hard to define, or even to talk about. 'I don't think Tom Bradley is beatable,' I was told not long before the 1989 mayoralty election by Zev Yaroslavsky, a Los Angeles City Council member who ran an abortive campaign against Bradley in 1985 and aborted a second campaign against him in January of 1989. 'At least not by me. His personal popularity transcends the fact that he has been presiding over a city that in some aspects has been experiencing serious difficulties during his term in office. Most people agree that we've got this traffic, that air quality stinks, that they see a hundred and one things wrong with the quality of life. But nobody blames him for it.'

In part because of this perceived ability to float free of his own administration and in part because of his presumed attractiveness to black voters, Tom Bradley was over the years repeatedly mentioned, usually in the same clause with Andrew Young, as a potential national figure, even a vice-presidential possibility. This persistent white fantasy to one side, Tom Bradley was never a charismatic, or even a particularly comfortable, candidate. His margin in the April 1989 election, for which a large majority of Los Angeles voters did not bother even to turn out, was surprisingly low. His votes never traveled outside Los Angeles. He twice tried, in 1982 and in 1986, to become governor of California, and was twice defeated by George Deukmejian, not himself noted for much sparkle as a candidate.

Bradley's strength in Los Angeles did not derive exclusively or even principally from the black community, which, in a city where the fastest-growing ethnic groups were Asian and Hispanic, constituted a decreasing percentage of the population and in any case had come to vote for Bradley, who was the first black ever elected to the Los Angeles City Council, grudgingly at best. One city official to whom I spoke during the 1989 campaign pointed out that when Bradley last ran for governor, there was a falling off in even those low-income black precincts in south-central Los Angeles that had previously been, however unenthusiastically, his territory. 'He assumed south-central would be there for him,' she said. 'And so he didn't work it. And having been taken for granted, it wasn't there.'

'He is probably less liked in south-central than other elected officials who represent south-central,' another city official conceded. 'I mean they view him as somebody who is maybe more interested in wining and dining Prince Andrew and Princess Sarah or whatever her name is than in dealing with the crumbling floor in the Nickerson Gardens gymnasium.'

Nickerson Gardens was a housing project in Watts, where people may vote but tended not to bid on city contracts, tended not to exhibit interest in the precise location of proposed freeway exits, tended not to have projects that could be made 'important' to the mayor because they were 'important' to them; tended not, in other words, to require the kind of access that generates contributions to a campaign. Tom Bradley was an access politician in the traditional mold. 'We would be rather disappointed if, having supported him, he were inaccessible to us,' Eli Broad, a longtime Bradley supporter and the chairman of Kaufman & Broad, told the *Los Angeles Times* during the summer of 1988. 'It's not really a quid pro quo. [But] there's no question that ... if someone ... wants money for the campaign, and if you want to talk to them six months later and don't hear from them, you just don't give any more.'

Kaufman & Broad was at that time the largest builder of single-family houses in California, the developer and builder of such sub-divisions as California Dawn ('From $108,990, 2, 3, and 4 Bedroom Homes'), California Esprit ('From the low $130,000s, 3 and 4 Bedroom Homes'), and California Gallery ('From $150,000, 3 and 4 Bedroom Homes'). California Dawn, California Esprit, and California Gallery were all in Palmdale, on the Mojave desert, an hour and a half northeast of Los Angeles. According to the final report of the Los Angeles 2000 Committee, a group appointed by Mayor Bradley to recommend a development strategy for the city, the Los Angeles Department of Airports was reviving a languishing plan to build an international airport on 17,750 acres the city happened to own six miles from the center of Palmdale.

The notion of building a Palmdale airport, first proposed in 1968 and more or less dormant since the midseventies, had met, over the years, considerable resistance, not the least of which derived from an almost total disinclination on the part of both carriers and passengers to go to Palmdale. But the possibilities were clear at the outset. There would be first of all the acquisition of the 17,750 acres (which would ultimately cost the city about $100 million to buy and to maintain), and the speculative boom that would accompany any such large-scale public acquisition. There would be the need for a highway project, estimated early on at another $100 million, to link Palmdale with the population. There could even be the eventual possibility of a $1.5 billion mountain tunnel, cutting the distance roughly in half. The construction of a monorail could be investigated. The creation of a foreign-trade zone could be studied. There would be the demand not only for housing (as in California Dawn, California Esprit, and California Gallery) but for schools, shopping centers, aircraft-related industry.

This hypothetical Palmdale International Airport, then, had survived as that ideal civic project, the one that just hangs in there, sometimes a threat, sometimes a promise, in either case a money machine. Here was the way the machine worked: with the encouragement of interested investors and an interested city government, the city would eventually reach Palmdale, and the Palmdale International Airport would reach critical mass, at which point many possibilities would be realized and many opportunities generated, both for development and for the access required to facilitate that development. This has been the history of Los Angeles.

Tom Bradley turned up in June of 1988 at a dinner dance honoring Eli Broad. He turned up in September of 1988 as a speaker at a party celebrating Kaufman & Broad's thirtieth anniversary. Bradley's most useful tool as a campaigner may well have been this practice of turning up wherever a supporter or potential supporter asked him to turn up, an impassive and slightly baffling stranger at bar mitzvahs and anniversary cocktail parties and backyard barbecues. 'It is just something that I do because I enjoy it,' Bradley told the *Los Angeles Times* in the summer of 1988 about another such event, a neighborhood barbecue at the South El Monte home of one of his planning

commissioners. 'I showed up and I tell you, you've never seen a
happier couple in your life than that man and his wife. And the
whole family was there . . . As we were out in the front yard chatting
or taking pictures, everybody who drove by was honking and waving. It was important to him. He enjoyed that. And I enjoyed his
enjoyment. I get a pleasure out of that.'

This fairly impenetrable style was often referred to locally as 'low-
keyed', or 'conciliatory', which seemed in context to be code words
for staying out of the way, not making waves, raising the money and
granting the access the money is meant to secure. Tom Bradley
was generally regarded as a pro-business, pro-development mayor,
a supporter of the kinds of redevelopment and public works projects
that tend, however problematical their ultimate public benefit, to
suggest considerable opportunity to the kinds of people who are
apt to support one or another political campaign. He was often credited with having built the downtown skyline, which translated
roughly into having encouraged developers to think of downtown
Los Angeles, which was until his tenure a rather somnolent financial
district enlivened by the fact that it was also *el centro*, the commercial
core of the Mexican and Central American communities, as bulldoz-
able, a raw canvas to be rendered indistinguishable from Atlanta or
Houston.

Bradley was redeveloping Watts. He was redeveloping Hollywood.
He was redeveloping, in all, more than seven thousand acres around
town. He was building – in a city so decentralized as to render
conventional mass transit virtually useless and at a time when big
transit projects had been largely discredited (one transportation
economist had demonstrated that San Francisco's BART system must
operate for 535 years before the energy presumably saved by its use
catches up with the energy expended on its construction) – one of
the world's most expensive mass-transit projects: $3.5 billion for the
projected twenty miles of track, from downtown through Hollywood
and over Cahuenga Pass to the San Fernando Valley, that would
constitute the system's 'first phase' and 'second phase'. This route
was one that, according to the project's opponents, could serve at
maximum use only 1.5 percent of the work force; most of that 1.5
percent, however, either lived or worked in the heart of the Hollywood Redevelopment. 'You go out to where the houses stop and

buy land,' Bob Hope is supposed to have said when he was asked how he made so much money. This is, in Los Angeles, one way to make money, and the second is to buy land on which the houses have already been built, and get the city to redevelop it.

Metrorail and the Hollywood Redevelopment were of course big projects, major ways of creating opportunity. The true Bradley style was perhaps most apparent when the opportunities were small, for example in the proposal during the spring of 1989 to sell a thirty-five-year-old public housing project, Jordan Downs, to a private developer. Jordan Downs was in Watts, south-central. The price asked for Jordan Downs was reported to be around $10 million. The deal was to include a pledge by the prospective buyer to spend an additional $14 million renovating the project.

Now. When we talk about Jordan Downs we are talking about seven hundred rental units in a virtual war zone, an area where the median family income was $11,427 and even children carried AK-47s. Presented with a developer who wants to spend $24 million to take on the very kind of property that owners all over the country are trying, if not to torch, at least to abandon, the average urban citizen looks for subtext. The subtext in this instance was not hard to find: Jordan Downs was a forty-acre piece of property, only 15 percent of which was developed. This largely undeveloped property bordered both the Century Freeway, which was soon to be completed, and the Watts Redevelopment. In other words the property would very soon, if all went as planned, vastly increase in value, and 85 percent of it would be in hand, available either for resale or for development.

Nor was the developed 15 percent of the property, Jordan Downs itself, the problem it might have seemed at first glance. The project, it turned out, would have to be maintained as low-income rental housing for an estimated period of at most fifteen years, during which time the developer stood in any case to receive, from the federal Department of Housing and Urban Development and the city housing authority, a guaranteed subsidy of $420,000 a month plus federal tax credits estimated at $1.6 million a year. This was the kind of small perfect deal – nobody is actually hurt by it, unless the nobody happens to be a tenant at Jordan Downs, and unable to pay the rent required to make the property break even – that has traditionally

been the mother's milk of urban politics. But many people believed
Los Angeles to be different, and in one significant aspect it was: the
difference in Los Angeles was that very few of its citizens seemed to
notice the small perfect deals, or, if they did notice, to much care.

It was believed for a while during 1988 in Los Angeles that Zev
Yaroslavsky, who represented the largely west-side and affluent Fifth
District in the Los Angeles City Council (the Fifth includes, in the
basin, Beverly-Fairfax, Century City, Bel Air, Westwood, and part of
West Los Angeles, and, in the San Fernando Valley, parts of Sherman
Oaks, Van Nuys, and North Hollywood), could beat Bradley. It was,
people said, 'Zev's year'. It was said to be 'time for Zev'. It was to be,
Zev Yaroslavsky himself frequently said, 'an election about who runs
Los Angeles', meaning do a handful of developers run it or do the
rest of the citizens run it. He had raised almost $2 million. He had
gained the support of a number of local players who had previously
backed Bradley, including Marc Nathanson, the chairman of Falcon
Cable TV, and Barry Diller, the chairman of Twentieth Century-Fox.
He had flat-out won what many saw as an exhibition game for
the mayoralty race: a showdown, in November of 1988, between
Armand Hammer's Occidental Petroleum Corporation, which had
wanted since 1966 to begin drilling for oil on two acres it was holding
across the Pacific Coast Highway from Will Rogers State Beach, and
the many people who did not want – and had so far, through a series
of legal maneuvers, managed to prevent – this drilling.

The showdown took the form of placing opposing propositions,
one co-sponsored by Zev Yaroslavsky and the other by an Occidental
front calling itself the Los Angeles Public and Coastal Protection
Committee, before the voters on the November 8, 1988, ballot. The
Los Angeles Public and Coastal Protection Committee had some notable talent prepared to labor on its behalf. It had the support of Mayor
Bradley. It would have, by the eve of the election, the endorsement
of the *Los Angeles Times*. It had not only Armand Hammer's own
attorney, Arthur Groman, but also, and perhaps most importantly,
Mickey Kantor, of Manatt, Phelps, Rothenberg, and Phillips, a law
firm so deeply connected to Democratic power in California that most
people believed Bradley to be backing the Occidental proposition not

for Armand Hammer but for Manatt. It had Robert Shrum, of Doak & Shrum, who used to write speeches for Ted Kennedy but was now running campaigns in California. It had, above all, $7.3 million, $7.1 million of it provided directly by Occidental.

There was considerable opacity about this entire endeavor. In the first place, the wording of the Los Angeles Public and Coastal Protection Committee (or Occidental) proposition tended to equate a vote for drilling with a vote for more efficient crime fighting, for more intensive drug-busting, for better schools, and for the cleanup of toxic wastes, all of which were floated as part of Occidental's dedication to public and coastal protection. In the second place, the players themselves had kept changing sides. On the side of the anti-drilling proposition there was of course its co-author, Zev Yaroslavsky, but Zev Yaroslavsky had backed Occidental when the drilling question came before the City Council in 1978. On the side of the Occidental proposition there was of course Tom Bradley, but Tom Bradley had first been elected mayor, in 1973, on an anti-Occidental platform, and in 1978 he had vetoed drilling on the Pacific Coast Highway site after the City Council approved it.

During the summer and fall of 1988, when the drilling and the antidrilling propositions were placed fairly insistently before the voters, there were seventeen operating oil fields around town, with tens of thousands of wells. There were more wells along the highways leading north and south. Oil was being pumped from the Beverly Hills High School campus. Oil was being pumped from the golf course at the Hillcrest Country Club. Oil was being pumped from the Twentieth Century-Fox lot. Off Carpinteria, south of Santa Barbara, oil was being pumped offshore, and even people who had expensive beach houses at Rincon del Mar had come to think of the rigs as not entirely unattractive features of the view – something a little mysterious out there in the mist, something a little Japanese on the horizon. In other words the drilling for and pumping of crude oil in Southern California had not historically carried much true political resonance, which made this battle of the propositions a largely symbolic, or 'political', confrontation, not entirely about oil drilling. That Zev Yaroslavsky won it – and won it spending only $2.8 million, some $4 million less than Occidental spent – seemed to many to suggest a certain discontent with the way things were going, a certain desire for change: the very desire for change on which Zev Yaroslavsky was planning, in the course of his campaign for the mayor's office, to run.

There was, early on, considerable interest in this promised mayoralty race between Tom Bradley and Zev Yaroslavsky. Some saw the contest, and this was the way the Bradley people liked to present it, as a long-awaited confrontation between the rest of the city (Bradley) and the West Side (Yaroslavsky), which was well-off, heavily Jewish, and the only part of the city that visitors to Los Angeles normally saw. This scenario had in fact been laid out in the drilling battle, during which Occidental, by way of Mickey Kantor and Robert Shrum, introduced the notion that a vote for Occidental was a vote against 'a few selfish people who don't want their beach view obstructed', against 'elitists', against, in other words, the West Side. 'The euphemism they kept using here was that it was another ploy by the "rich Westsiders" against the poor minorities and the blacks,' I was told by a deputy to Councilman Marvin Braude, who had co-authored the antidrilling proposition with Zev Yaroslavsky and in whose district Occidental's Pacific Coast Highway property lay. 'You always heard about "rich Westsiders" in connection with anything we were doing. It was the euphemism for the Jews.'

Others saw the race, and this was increasingly the way the Yaroslavsky people liked to frame it, as a confrontation between the forces of unrestricted growth (developers, the oil business, Bradley) and the proponents of controlled, or 'slow', growth (environmentalists, the No Oil lobby, the West Side, Yaroslavsky). Neither version was long on nuance, and both tended to overlook facts that did not support the favored angles (Bradley had for years been the West Side's own candidate, for example, and Yaroslavsky had himself broken bread with a developer or two), but the two scenarios, Yaroslavsky's *Greed v. Slow Growth* and Bradley's *The People v. the West Side*, continued to provide, for that handful of people in Los Angeles who actually followed city politics, a kind of narrative line. The election would fall, as these people saw it, to whoever told his story best, to whoever had the best tellers, the best fixers.

*   *   *

Only a few people in Los Angeles were believed to be able to fix things, whether the things to be fixed, or arranged, or managed, were labor problems or city permits or elections. There was the master of them all, Paul Ziffren, whose practice as a lawyer had often been indistinguishable from the practice of politics, but he was by the time of this race less active than he had once been. There was his son Kenneth Ziffren, who settled the Writers Guild of America strike in the summer of 1988. There was, operating in a slightly different arena, Sidney Korshak, who settled the Delano grape strike against Schenley in 1966. There was almost anybody at the Manatt office. There was Joseph Cerrell, a political consultant about whom it had been said, 'You want to get elected to the judicial, you call him, a campaign can run you fifty thousand dollars.' There was Robert Shrum, who worked Alan Cranston's last campaign for the Senate and Representative Richard Gephardt's campaign in the 1988 presidential primaries. There were Michael Berman and Carl D'Agostino, of BAD Campaigns, Inc., who were considered direct mail (most of it negative) geniuses and were central to what was locally called 'the Waxman-Berman machine', the Democratic and quite specifically Jewish political organization built by Michael Berman; his brother, Representative Howard Berman; Representative Henry Waxman; and Representative Mel Levine, who was positioning himself to run for Alan Cranston's Senate seat in 1992. It was Michael Berman who figured out how to send Howard Berman and Henry Waxman and Mel Levine to Congress in the first place. It was Michael Berman and Carl D'Agostino who continued to figure out how to elect Waxman-Berman candidates on the state and local levels.

These figures were not without a certain local glamour, and a considerable amount of the interest in this mayoralty race derived from the fact that Doak & Shrum – which, remember, had been part of Mickey Kantor's team on the Occidental proposition – was working for Bradley, while Berman and D'Agostino, who had been hired by Yaroslavsky and Braude to run their antidrilling proposition, were backing Yaroslavsky. A mayoralty contest between Shrum and the Berman-D'Agostino firm, Bill Boyarsky wrote in the *Los Angeles Times*, could be 'one of the great matchups of low-down campaigning'; in other words a chance, as I recall being told in June of

1988 by someone else, 'for Berman and D'Agostino to knock off Doak & Shrum'.

Then something happened, nobody was saying quite how. One Friday in August of 1988, a reporter at the *Los Angeles Times*, Kenneth Reich, got a phone call from a woman who refused to identify herself but said that she was sending him certain material prepared by BAD Campaigns, Inc. The material – delivered the following Monday with a typewritten and unsigned note reading, 'You should be interested to see this. Government is bad enough without BAD' – consisted of three strategy memos addressed to Zev Yaroslavsky. One was dated March 29, 1988, another was dated May 4, 1988, and the third, headed 'Things to Do', was undated.

Berman and D'Agostino acknowledged that the two dated documents were early drafts of memos prepared by their office, but denied having written the undated memo, which, accordingly, was never printed by the *Times*. The memos that were printed, which Yaroslavsky charged had been stolen from a three-ring binder belonging to one of his aides, had, however, an immediately electrifying effect, not because they said anything that most interested people in Los Angeles did not know or believe but because they violated the local social contract by saying it out loud, and in the vernacular. The memos printed in the *Times* read, in part:

The reason why BAD thinks you [Yaroslavsky] can beat Bradley is: you've got fifty IQ-points on him (and that's no compliment) ... Just because you are more slow-growth than Bradley does not mean you can take anti-growth voters for granted ... many are racially tolerant people who are strongly pulled to Bradley because of his height, skin color and calm demeanor. They like voting for him – they feel less guilty about how little they used to pay their household help ...

Yaroslavsky's vision [should be that] there is no reason on this earth why some flitty restaurateur should be allowed to build a hotel at the corner of Beverly and La Cienega ... The Yaroslavsky vision says 'there is no reason on earth why anyone should be building more places to shop in West L.A.' ... There is no reason for guilt-ridden liberals to vote out of office that fine, dignified 'person of color' except that your Vision is total, unwavering and convincing. You want to hug every tree, stop every new building, end the traffic jams and clean up the Bay . . .

To beat Bradley, you must be intensely, thoroughly and totally committed to your vision of L.A. . . . It is the way you overcome the racial tug many Jews and non-Jewish liberals feel toward Bradley. It is also the way you overcome the possible Republican preference for the conservative black over the Jewish kid friendly with the Waxman-Berman machine . . .

Bradley can and will excite black voters to outvote the white electorate especially if there is a runoff where his mayoral office is seen as jeopardized by a perfidious Jew . . .

What we do know is that Jewish wealth in Los Angeles is endless. That almost every Jewish person who meets you will like you and that asking for $2,000 is not an unreasonable request to people who are both wealthy and like you . . .

The Yaroslavsky campaign becomes the United Jewish appeal . . .

This was not, on the face of it, remarkable stuff. The language in the memos was widely described as 'cynical', but of course it was not: it was just the working shorthand of people who might even be said, on the evidence of what they wrote down, to have an idealized view of the system, people who noticed the small perfect deals and did not approve of them, or at any rate assumed that there was an electorate out there that did not approve of them. This may have been an erroneous assumption, a strategic miscalculation, but the idea that some of Yaroslavsky's people might have miscalculated the electorate was not, for some people who had supported him and were now beginning to back away, the problem.

'Make a complete list of mainstream Jewish charities,' the March 29 memo had advised. 'Find a person in each charity to slip us a list with name, address and phone numbers of $1,000-and-above contributors . . . Zev begins dialing for dollars . . . Make a list of 50 contributors to Zev who have not participated to their ability and who belong to every Jewish country club in the L.A. area . . . Make a list of every studio, Hollywood PR firm and 100 top show business personalities in Jewish Los Angeles ... You cannot let Bradley become the chichi, in, campaign against the pushy Jew ...'

It was this acknowledgment, even this insistence, that there were in Los Angeles not only Jewish voters but specifically Jewish interests, and Jewish money, that troubled many people, most particularly those very members of the West Side Jewish community on whose support the Yaroslavsky people were counting. What happened next was largely a matter of 'perceptions', of a very few people talking among themselves, as they were used to talking whenever there was something to be decided, some candidate or cause to be backed or not backed. The word 'divisive' started coming up again and again. It would be, people were saying, a 'divisive' campaign, even a 'disastrous' campaign, a campaign that would 'pit the blacks against the Jews'. There was, it was said, 'already enough trouble', trouble that had been simmering, as these people saw it, since at least 1985, when Tom Bradley's Jewish supporters on the West Side had insisted that he denounce the Reverend Louis Farrakhan, and some black leaders had protested that Bradley should not be taking orders from the West Side. This issue of race, most people hastened to say, would never be raised by the candidates themselves. The problem would be, as Neil Sandberg of the American Jewish Committee put it to Bill Boyarsky of the *Los Angeles Times*, 'undisciplined elements in both communities'. The problem would be, in other words, the candidates' 'people'.

Discussions were held. Many telephone calls were made. In December of 1988, a letter was drafted and signed by some of the most politically active people on the West Side. This letter called on Zev Yaroslavsky to back off, not to run, not to proceed on a course that the signers construed as an invitation, if not to open ethnic conflict, at least to a breaking apart of the coalition between the black and Jewish communities that had given the West Side its recent power over the old-line Los Angeles establishment – the downtown and San Marino money base, which was what people in Los Angeles meant when they referred to the California Club. On the sixth of January, citing a private poll that showed Bradley to be running far ahead, Zev Yaroslavsky announced that he would not run. The BAD memos, he said, had 'played absolutely no role' in his decision to withdraw. The 'fear of a divisive campaign', he said, had 'played no role on my part'.

This 'fear of a divisive campaign', and the attendant specter of the membership of the California Club invading City Hall, seemed on the face of it incorporeal, one of those received fears that sometimes overtake a community and redirect the course of its affairs. Still, the convergence of the BAD memos and the polarization implicit in the Occidental campaign had generated a considerable amount of what could only be described as class conflict. 'Most of us have known for a long time that the environmentalists are ... white, middle-class groups who have not really shown a lot of concern about the black community or black issues,' Maxine Waters, who represented part of south-central in the California State Assembly and was probably the most effective and visible black politician in Southern California, told Bill Boyarsky when he talked to her, after the publication of the BAD memos, about the drilling issue. 'Yet we have continued to give support . . . I want to tell you I may very well support the oil drilling. I feel such a need to assert independence from this kind of crap, and I feel such a need for the black community not to be led on by someone else's agenda and not even knowing what the agenda was.'

One afternoon in February of 1989 when I happened to be in City Hall seeing Zev Yaroslavsky and Marvin Braude, I asked what they made of the 'divisive campaign' question. The apprehension, Yaroslavsky said, had been confined to 'a very small group of people', whose concern, as he saw it, had been 'fueled by my neighbors here in the mayor's office, who were trying to say we could have another Chicago, another Ed Koch'.

'Some of it started before your candidacy,' Marvin Braude said to him. 'With the Farrakhan incident. That set the tone of it.'

'Let me tell you,' Zev Yaroslavsky said. 'If there's any reason why I would have run, it would have been to disprove that notion. Because nothing so offends me – politically and personally – as the notion that I, simply because I'm white or Jewish, don't have the right to run against a fourth-term incumbent just because he happens to be black.'

Zev Yaroslavsky, at that point, was mounting a campaign to save his own council seat. He had put the mayoral campaign behind him. Still, it rankled. 'Nothing I was talking about had remotely to do with race,' he said. 'It never would have been an issue, unless Bradley brought it up. But I must say they made every effort to put everything we did into a racial context. They tried to make the Oxy oil initiative racial. They tried to make Proposition U – which was our first slow-growth initiative – racial. They pitted rich against poor, white against black, West Side against South Side –'

'It wasn't only Bradley,' Marvin Braude said, interrupting. 'It was the people who were using this for their own selfish purposes. It was the developers. It was Occidental.'

'I think if the election had gone on . . .' Zev Yaroslavsky paused. 'It doesn't matter. At this point it's speculative. But I think the mayor and his people, especially his people, were running a very risky strategy of trying to make race an issue. For their candidate's benefit.'

During the week in February 1989 when I saw Zev Yaroslavsky and Marvin Braude, the *Los Angeles Times* Poll did a telephone sampling to determine local attitudes toward the city and its mayor. About 60 percent of those polled, the *Times* reported a few days later, under the headline 'People Turn Pessimistic About Life in Los Angeles', believed that the 'quality of life' in Los Angeles had deteriorated during the last fifteen years. About 50 percent said that within the past year they had considered leaving Los Angeles, mainly for San Diego. Sixty-seven percent of those polled, however, believed that Tom Bradley, who had been mayor during this period when the quality of life had so deteriorated that many of them were thinking of moving to San Diego, had done a good job.

This was not actually news. On the whole, life in Los Angeles, perhaps because it is a city so largely populated by people who are ready to drop everything and move to San Diego (just as they or their parents or their grandparents had dropped everything and moved to Los Angeles), seems not to encourage a conventional interest in its elected officials. 'Nobody but the press corps and a few elites care anything about the day-to-day workings in city government' is the way this was put in one of the 'cynical' BAD memos.

In fact there were maybe a hundred people in Los Angeles, aside

from the handful of reporters assigned to the city desk, who followed
City Hall. A significant number of the hundred were lawyers at
Manatt. All of the hundred were people who understand access.
Some of these people said that of course Zev Yaroslavsky would run
again, in 1993, when he would be only forty-four and Tom Bradley
would be seventy-five and presumably ready to step aside. Nineteen
ninety-three, in this revised view, would be 'Zev's year'. Nineteen
ninety-three would be 'time for Zev'. Others said that 1993 would
be too late, that the entire question of whether or not Zev Yaroslavsky could hold together Tom Bradley's famous black-Jewish coalition would be, in a Los Angeles increasingly populated by Hispanics
and Asians, irrelevant, history, moot. Nineteen ninety-three, these
people said, would be the year for other people altogether, for more
recent figures on the local political landscape, for people like Gloria
Molina or Richard Alatorre, people like Mike Woo, people whose
names would tell a different story, although not necessarily to a
different hundred people.

1989

L.A. Noir

Around Division 47, Los Angeles Municipal Court, the downtown courtroom where, for eleven weeks during the spring and summer of 1989, a preliminary hearing was held to determine if the charges brought in the 1983 murder of a thirty-three-year-old road-show promoter named Roy Alexander Radin should be dismissed or if the defendants should be bound over to superior court for arraignment and trial, it was said that there were, 'in the works', five movies, four books, and 'countless' pieces about the case. Sometimes it was said that there were four movies and five books 'in the works', or one movie and two books, or two movies and six books. There were, in any event, 'big balls' in the air. 'Everybody's working this one,' a reporter covering the trial said one morning as we waited to get patted down at the entrance to the courtroom, a security measure prompted by a telephoned bomb threat and encouraged by the general wish of everyone involved to make this a noticeable case. 'Major money.'

This was curious. Murder cases are generally of interest to the extent that they suggest some anomaly or lesson in the world revealed, but there seemed neither anomalies nor lessons in the murder of Roy Radin, who was last seen alive getting into a limousine to go to dinner at a Beverly Hills restaurant, La Scala, and was next seen decomposed, in a canyon off Interstate 5. Among the defendants actually present for the preliminary hearing was Karen Delayne ('Lanie') Jacobs Greenberger, a fairly attractive hard case late of South Florida, where her husband was said to have been the number-two man in the cocaine operation run by Carlos Lehder, the only major Colombian drug figure to have been tried and convicted in the United States. (Lanie Greenberger herself was said to have done considerable business in this line, and to have had nearly a million dollars in cocaine and cash stolen from her Sherman Oaks house not long before Roy Radin disappeared.) The other defendants present were William Mentzer and Alex Marti, somewhat less attractive hard cases, late of Larry Flynt's security staff. (Larry Flynt is the publisher of *Hustler*, and one of the collateral artifacts that turned up in the Radin case was a million-dollar check Flynt had written in 1983 to the late Mitchell Livingston WerBell III, a former arms dealer who operated a counterterrorism school outside Atlanta and described himself as a retired lieutenant general in the Royal Free Afghan Army. The Los Angeles County Sheriff's Department said that Flynt had written the check to WerBell as payment on a contract to kill Frank Sinatra, Hugh Hefner, Bob Guccione, and Walter Annenberg. Larry Flynt's lawyer said that there had been no contract, and described the check, on which payment was stopped, as a dinner-party joke.) There was also an absent defendant, a third Flynt security man, fighting extradition from Maryland.

In other words this was a genre case, and the genre, L.A. *noir*, was familiar. There is a *noir* case every year or two in Los Angeles. There was for example the Wonderland case, which involved the 1981 bludgeoning to death of four people. The Wonderland case, so called because the bludgeoning took place in a house on Wonderland Avenue in Laurel Canyon, turned, like the Radin case, on a million-dollar cocaine theft, but featured even more deeply *noir* players, including a nightclub entrepreneur and convicted cocaine dealer named Adel Nasrallah, aka 'Eddie Nash'; a pornographic-movie star, now dead of AIDS, named John C. Holmes, aka 'Johnny Wadd'; and a young man named Scott Thorson, who was, at the time he first testified in the case, an inmate in the Los Angeles County Jail (Scott Thorson was, in the natural ecology of the criminal justice system, the star witness for the state in the Wonderland case), and who in 1982 sued Liberace on the grounds that he had been promised $100,000 a year for life in return for his services as Liberace's lover, driver, travel secretary, and animal trainer.

In this context there would have seemed nothing particularly novel about the Radin case. It was true that there were, floating around the edges of the story, several other unnatural deaths, for example that of Lanie Greenberger's husband, Larry Greenberger, aka 'Vinnie De Angelo', who either shot himself or was shot in the head in September of 1988 on the front porch of his house in Okeechobee, Florida, but these deaths were essentially unsurprising. It was also true that the Radin case offered not bad sidebar details. I was interested for example in how much security Larry Flynt apparently had patrolling Doheny Estates, where his house was, and Century City, where the *Hustler* offices were. I was interested in Dean Kahn, who ran the limousine service that provided the stretch Cadillac with smoked windows in which Roy Radin took, in the language of this particular revealed world, his last ride. I was interested in how Roy Radin, before he came to Los Angeles and decided to go to dinner at La Scala, had endeavored to make his way in the world by touring high school auditoriums with Tiny Tim, Frank Fontaine, and a corps of tap-dancing dwarfs.

Still, promoters of tap-dancing dwarfs who get done in by hard cases have not been, historically, the stuff of which five movies, four books, and countless pieces are made. The almost febrile interest in this case derived not from the principals but from what was essentially a cameo role, played by Robert Evans. Robert Evans had been head of production at Paramount during the golden period of *The Godfather* and *Love Story* and *Rosemary's Baby*, had moved on to produce independently such successful motion pictures as *Chinatown* and *Marathon Man*, and was, during what was generally agreed to be a dry spell in his career (he had recently made a forty-five-minute videotape on the life of John Paul II, and had announced that he was writing an autobiography, to be called *The Kid Stays in the Picture*), a district attorney's dream: quite possibly desperate, quite famously risk-oriented, high-visibility figure with low-life connections.

It was the contention of the Los Angeles County District Attorney's office that Lanie Greenberger had hired her codefendants to kill Roy Radin after he refused to cut her in on his share of the profits from Robert Evans's 1984 picture *The Cotton Club*. It was claimed that Lanie Greenberger had introduced Roy Radin, who wanted to get into the movie business, to Robert Evans. It was claimed that Roy Radin had offered to find, in return for 45 percent of the profits from either one Evans picture (*The Cotton Club*) or three Evans pictures (*The Cotton Club, The Sicilian,* and *The Two Jakes*), 'Puerto Rican investors' willing to put up either thirty-five or fifty million dollars.

Certain objections leap to the nonprosecutorial mind here (the 'Puerto Rican investors' turned out to be one Puerto Rican banker with 'connections', the money never actually materialized, Roy Radin therefore had no share of the profits, there were no profits in any case), but seem not to have figured in the state's case. The District Attorney's office was also hinting, if not quite contending, that Robert Evans himself had been in on the payoff of Radin's killers, and the DA's office had a protected witness (still another Flynt security man, this one receiving $3,000 a month from the Los Angeles County Sheriff's Department) who had agreed to say in court that one of the defendants, William Mentzer, told him that Lanie Greenberger and Robert Evans had, in the witness's words, 'paid for the contract'. Given the state's own logic, it was hard to know what Robert Evans might have thought to gain by putting out a contract on the goose with the $50 million egg, but the deputy district attorney on the case seemed unwilling to let go of this possibility, and had in fact told reporters that Robert Evans was 'one of the people who we have not eliminated as a suspect'.

Neither, on the other hand, was Robert Evans one of the people they had arrested, a circumstance suggesting certain lacunae in the case from the major-money point of view, and also from the district attorney's. Among people outside the criminal justice system, it was widely if vaguely assumed that Robert Evans was somehow 'on trial' during the summer of 1989. 'Evans Linked for First Time in Court to Radin's Murder,' the headlines were telling them, and, in the past-tense obituary mode, 'Evans' Success Came Early: Career Epitomized Hollywood Dream.'

'Bob always had a premonition that his career would peak before he was fifty and fade downhill,' Peter Bart, who had worked under Evans at Paramount, told the *Los Angeles Times*, again in the obituary mode. 'He lived by it. He was haunted by it . . . To those of us who knew him and knew what a good-spirited person he was, it's a terrible sadness.' Here was a case described by the *Times* as 'focused on the dark side of Hollywood deal making', a case offering 'an unsparing look at the film capital's unsavory side', a case everyone was calling just Cotton Club, or even just Cotton, as in ' "Cotton": Big Movie Deal's Sequel Is Murder'.

Inside the system, the fact that no charge had been brought against the single person on the horizon who had a demonstrable connection with *The Cotton Club* was rendering Cotton Club, *qua* Cotton Club, increasingly problematic. Not only was Robert Evans not 'on trial' in Division 47, but what was going on there was not even a 'trial', only a preliminary hearing, intended to determine whether the state had sufficient evidence and cause to prosecute those charged, none of whom was Evans. Since 1978, when a California Supreme Court ruling provided criminal defendants the right to a preliminary hearing even after indictment by a grand jury, preliminary hearings have virtually replaced grand juries as a way of indicting felony suspects in California, and are one of the reasons that criminal cases in Los Angeles now tend to go on for years. The preliminary hearing alone in the McMartin child-abuse case lasted eighteen months.

On the days I dropped by Division 47, the judge, a young black woman with a shock of gray in her hair, seemed fretful, inattentive. The lawyers seemed weary. The bailiffs discussed their domestic arrangements on the telephone. When Lanie Greenberger entered the courtroom, not exactly walking but undulating forward on the balls of her feet, in a little half-time prance, no one bothered to look up. The courtroom had been full on the day Robert Evans appeared as the first witness for the prosecution and took the Fifth, but in the absence of Evans there were only a few reporters and the usual two or three retirees in the courtroom, perhaps a dozen people in all, reduced to interviewing each other and discussing alternative names for the Night Stalker case, which involved a man named Richard Ramirez who had been accused of thirteen murders and thirty other felonies committed in Los Angeles County during 1984 and 1985. One reporter was calling the Ramirez case, which was then in its sixth month of trial after nine weeks of preliminary hearings and six months of jury selection, Valley Intruder. Another had settled on Serial Killer. 'I still slug it Night Stalker,' a third said, and she turned to me. 'Let me ask you,' she said. 'This is how hard up I am. Is there a story in your being here?'

The preliminary hearing in the Radin case had originally been scheduled for three weeks, and lasted eleven. On July 12, 1989, in Division 47, Judge Patti Jo McKay ruled not only that there was sufficient evidence to bind over Lanie Greenberger, Alex Marti, and William Mentzer for trial but also that the Radin murder may have been committed for financial gain, which meant that the defendants could receive, if convicted, penalties of death. 'Mr Radin was an obstacle to further negotiation involving *The Cotton Club*,' the prosecuting attorney had argued in closing. 'The deal could not go through until specific issues such as percentages were worked out. It was at that time that Mrs Greenberger had the motive to murder Mr Radin.'

I was struck by this as a final argument, because it seemed to suggest an entire case based on the notion that an interest in an entirely hypothetical share of the entirely hypothetical profits from an entirely hypothetical motion picture (at the time Roy Radin was killed, *The Cotton Club* had an advertising poster but no shooting script and no money and no cast and no start date) was money in the bank. All that had stood between Lanie Greenberger and Fat City, as the prosecutor saw it, was boilerplate, a matter of seeing that 'percentages were worked out'.

The prosecution's certainty on this point puzzled me, and I asked an acquaintance in the picture business if he thought there had ever been money to be made from *The Cotton Club*. He seemed not to believe what I was asking. There had been 'gross positions', he reminded me, participants with a piece of the gross rather than the net. There had been previous investors. There had been commitments already made on *The Cotton Club*, paper out all over town. There had been, above all, a $26 million budget going in (it eventually cost $47 million), and a production team not noted for thrift. 'It had to make a hundred to a hundred forty million, depending on how much got stolen, before anybody saw gross,' he said. 'Net on this baby was dreamland. Which could have been figured out, with no loss of life, by a junior agent just out of the William Morris mailroom.'

There was always in the Cotton Club case a certain dreamland aspect, a looniness that derived in part from the ardent if misplaced faith of everyone involved, from the belief in windfalls, in sudden changes of fortune (five movies and four books would change someone's fortune, a piece of *The Cotton Club* someone else's, a high-

visibility case the district attorney's); in killings, both literal and figu-
rative. In fact this kind of faith is not unusual in Los Angeles. In a
city not only largely conceived as a series of real estate promotions
but largely supported by a series of confidence games, a city even
then afloat on motion pictures and junk bonds and the B-2 Stealth
bomber, the conviction that something can be made of nothing may
be one of the few narratives in which everyone participates. A belief
in extreme possibilities colors daily life. Anyone might have woken
up one morning and been discovered at Schwab's, or killed at Bob's
Big Boy. 'Luck is all around you,' a silky voice says on the California
State Lottery's Lotto commercials, against a background track of
'Dream a Little Dream of Me'. 'Imagine winning millions . . . what
would you do?'

During the summer of 1989 this shimmer of the possible still lay on
Cotton Club, although there seemed, among those dreamers to
whom I spoke in both the picture business and the criminal justice
business, a certain impatience with the way the case was actually
playing out. There was nobody in either business, including the
detectives on the case, who could hear the words 'Cotton Club' and
not see a possible score, but the material was resistant. It still lacked
a bankable element. There was a definite wish to move on, as they
say in the picture business, to screenplay. The detectives were keeping in touch with motion picture producers, car phone to car phone,
sketching in connecting lines not apparent in the courtroom. 'This
friend of mine in the sheriff's office laid it out for me three years
ago,' one producer told me. 'The deal was, "This is all about drugs,
Bob Evans is involved, we're going to get him." And so forth. He
wanted me to have the story when and if the movie was done. He
called me a week ago, from his car, wanted to know if I was going
to move on it.'

I heard a number of alternative scenarios. 'The story is in this one
cop who wouldn't let it go,' I was told by a producer. 'The story is
in the peripheral characters,' I was told by a detective I had reached
by dialing his car phone. Another producer reported having run into
Robert Evans's lawyer, Robert Shapiro, the evening before at Hillcrest
Country Club, where the Thomas Hearns–Sugar Ray Leonard fight

was being shown closed circuit from Caesars Palace in Las Vegas. 'I asked how our boy was doing,' he said, meaning Evans. 'Shapiro says he's doing fine. Scotfree, he says. Here's the story. A soft guy from our world, just sitting up there in his sixteen-room house, keeps getting visits from these detectives. Big guys. Real hard guys. Apes. Waiting for him to crack.'

Here we had the rough line for several quite different stories, but it would have been hard not to notice that each of them depended for its dramatic thrust on the presence of Robert Evans. I mentioned this one day to Marcia Morrissey, who – as co-counsel with the Miami trial lawyer Edward Shohat, who had defended Carlos Lehder – was representing Lanie Greenberger. 'Naturally they all *want* him in,' Marcia Morrissey said.

I asked if she thought the District Attorney's Office would manage to get him in.

Marcia Morrissey rolled her eyes. 'That's what it's called, isn't it? I mean face it. It's called Cotton Club.'

1989

Fire Season

'I've seen fire and I've seen rain,' I recall James Taylor singing over and over on the news radio station between updates on the 1978 Mandeville and Kanan fires, both of which started on October 23 of that year and could be seen burning toward each other, systematically wiping out large parts of Malibu and Pacific Palisades, from an upstairs window of my house in Brentwood. It was said that the Kanan fire was burning on a twenty-mile front and had already jumped the Pacific Coast Highway at Trancas Canyon. The stand in the Mandeville fire, it was said, would be made at Sunset Boulevard. I stood at the window and watched a house on a hill above Sunset implode, its oxygen sucked out by the force of the fire.

Some thirty-four thousand acres of Los Angeles County burned that week in 1978. More than eighty thousand acres had burned in 1968. Close to a hundred and thirty thousand acres had burned in 1970. Seventy-four-some thousand had burned in 1975, sixty-some thousand would burn in 1979. Forty-six thousand would burn in 1980, forty-five thousand in 1982. In the hills behind Malibu, where the moist air off the Pacific makes the brush grow fast, it takes about twelve years before a burn is ready to burn again. Inland, where the manzanita and sumac and chamise that make up the native brush in Southern California grow more slowly (the wild mustard that turns the hills a translucent yellow after rain is not native but exotic, introduced in the 1920s in an effort to reseed burns), regrowth takes from fifteen to twenty years. Since 1919, when the county began keeping records of its fires, some areas have burned eight times.

In other words there is nothing unusual about fires in Los Angeles, which is after all a desert city with only two distinct seasons, one beginning in January and lasting three or four months during which storms come in from the northern Pacific and it rains (often an inch every two or three hours, sometimes and in some places an inch a minute) and one lasting eight or nine months during which it burns, or gets ready to burn. Most years it is September or October before the Santa Ana winds start blowing down through the passes and the relative humidity drops to figures like 7 or 6 or 3 percent and the bougainvillea starts rattling in the driveway and people start watching the horizon for smoke and tuning in to another of those extreme local possibilities, in this case that of imminent devastation. What was unusual in 1989, after two years of drought and a third year of less than average rainfall, was that it was ready to burn while the June fogs still lay on the coastline. On the first of May that year, months earlier than ever before, the California Department of Forestry had declared the start of fire season and begun hiring extra crews. By the last week in June there had already been more than two thousand brush and forest fires in California. Three hundred and twenty of them were burning that week alone.

One morning early that summer I drove out the San Bernardino Freeway to the headquarters of the Los Angeles County Fire Department, which was responsible not only for coordinating fire fighting and reseeding operations throughout the county but for sending, under the California Master Mutual Aid agreement, both equipment and strike teams to fires around the state. Los Angeles County sent strike teams to fight the 116,000-acre Wheeler fire in Ventura County in 1985. (The logistics of these big fires are essentially military. Within twelve hours of the first reports on the Wheeler fire, which eventually burned for two weeks and involved three thousand fire fighters flown in from around the country, a camp had materialized, equipped with kitchen, sanitation, transportation and medical facilities, a communications network, a 'situation trailer', a 'what if' trailer for long-range contingency planning, and a 'pool coordinator', to get off-duty crews to and from the houses of residents who had offered the use of their swimming pools. 'We simply superimposed a city on top of the incident,' a camp spokesman said at the time.) Los Angeles County sent strike teams to fight the 100,000-acre

Las Pilitas fire in San Luis Obispo County the same year. It sent specially trained people to act as 'overhead' on, or to run, the crews of military personnel brought in from all over the United States to fight the Yellowstone fires in 1988.

On the June morning in 1989 when I visited the headquarters building in East Los Angeles, it was already generally agreed that, as one of the men to whom I spoke put it, 'we pretty much know we're going to see some fires this year', with no probable break until January or February. (There is usually some November rain in Los Angeles, often enough to allow crews to gain control of a fire already burning, but only rarely does November rain put enough moisture into the brush to offset the Santa Ana winds that blow until the end of December.) There had been unusually early Santa Ana conditions, a week of temperatures over one hundred. The measurable moisture in the brush, a measurement the Fire Department calls the 'fuel stick', was in some areas already down to single digits. The daily 'burn index', which rates the probability of fire on a scale running from 0 to 200, was that morning showing figures of 45 for the Los Angeles basin, 41 for what is called the 'high country', 125 for the Antelope Valley, and, for the Santa Clarita Valley, 192.

Anyone who has spent fire season in Los Angeles knows some of its special language – knows, for example, the difference between a fire that has been 'controlled' and a fire that has so far been merely 'contained' (a 'contained' fire has been surrounded, usually by a trench half as wide as the brush is high, but is still burning out of control within this line and may well jump it), knows the difference between 'full' and 'partial' control ('partial' control means, if the wind changes, no control at all), knows about 'backfiring' and about 'making the stand' and about the difference between a Red Flag Alert (there will probably be a fire today) and a Red Flag Warning (there will probably be a Red Flag Alert within three days).

Still, 'burn index' was new to me, and one of the headquarters foresters, Paul Rippens, tried that morning to explain it. 'Let's take the Antelope Valley, up around Palmdale, Lancaster,' he said. 'For today, temperature's going to be ninety-six, humidity's going to be seventeen percent, wind speed's going to be fifteen miles per hour, and the fuel stick is six, which is getting pretty low.'

'Six burns very well,' another forester, John Haggenmiller, said.

'If the fuel stick's up around twelve, it's pretty hard to get it to burn. That's the range that you have. Anything under six and it's ready to burn very well.'

'So you correlate all that, you get an Antelope Valley burn index today of one twenty-five, the adjective for which is "high", ' Paul Rippens continued. 'The adjectives we use are "low", "moderate", "high", "very high", and "extreme". One twenty-five is "high". High probability of fire. We had a hundred-plus-acre fire out there yesterday, about a four-hour fire. Divide the burn index by ten and you get the average flame length. So a burn index of one twenty-five is going to give you a twelve-and-a-half-foot flame length out there. If you've got a good fire burning, flame length has a lot to do with it.'

'There's a possibility of a grass fire going through and not doing much damage at all,' John Haggenmiller said. 'Other cases, where the fuel has been allowed to build up – say you had a bug kill or a dieback, a lot of decadent fuel – you're going to get a flame length of thirty, forty feet. And it gets up into the crown of a tree and the whole thing goes down. That does a lot of damage.'

Among the men to whom I spoke that morning there was a certain grudging admiration for what they called 'the big hitters', the major fires, the ones people remember. 'I'd say about ninety-five percent of our fires, we're able to hold down to under five acres,' I was told by Captain Garry Oversby, who did community relations and education for the Fire Department. 'It's the ones when we have extreme Santa Ana conditions, extreme weather – they get started, all we can do is try to hold the thing in check until the weather lays down a little bit for us. Times like that, we revert to what we call a defensive attack. Just basically go right along the edges of that fire until we can get a break. Reach a natural barrier. Or sometimes we make a stand several miles in advance of the fire – construct a line there, and then maybe set a backfire. Which will burn back toward the main fire and take out the vegetation, rob the main fire of its fuel.'

They spoke of the way a true big hitter 'moved', of the way it 'pushed', of the way it could 'spot', or throw embers and firebrands, a mile ahead of itself, rendering any kind of conventional firebreak useless; of the way a big hitter, once it got moving, would 'outrun anybody'. 'You get the right weather conditions in Malibu, it's almost impossible to stop it,' Paul Rippens said. He was talking about the fires that typically start somewhere in the brush off the Ventura Freeway and then burn twenty miles to the sea, the fires that roar over a ridge in a matter of seconds and make national news because they tend to take out, just before they hit the beach along Malibu, houses that belong to well-known people. Taking out houses is what the men at headquarters mean when they talk about 'the urban interface'.

'We can dump all our resources out there,' Paul Rippens said, and he shrugged.

'You can pick up the flanks and channel it,' John Haggenmiller said, 'but until the wind stops or you run out of fuel, you can't do much else.'

'You get into Malibu,' Paul Rippens said, 'you're looking at what we call two-story brush.'

'You know the wind,' John Haggenmiller said. 'You're not going to change that phenomenon.'

'You can dump everything you've got on that fire,' Paul Rippens said. 'It's still going to go to what we call the big blue break.'

It occurred to me then that it had been eleven years since the October night in 1978 when I listened to James Taylor singing 'Fire and Rain' between reports on how the Kanan fire had jumped the Pacific Coast Highway to go to the big blue break. On the twelve-year-average fire cycle that regulates life in Malibu, the Kanan burn, which happened to include a beach on which my husband and daughter and I had lived from 1971 until June of 1978, was coming due again. 'Beautiful country burn again,' I wrote in my notebook, a line from a Robinson Jeffers poem I remember at some point during every fire season, and I got up to leave.

A week or so later 3,700 acres burned in the hills west of the Antelope Valley. The flames reached sixty feet. The wind was gusting at forty miles an hour. There were 250 fire fighters on the ground, and they evacuated 1,500 residents, one of whom returned to find her house gone but managed to recover, according to the *Los Angeles Times*, 'an undamaged American flag and a porcelain Nativity set handmade by her mother'. A week after this Antelope Valley fire, 1,500 acres burned in the Puente Hills, above Whittier. The temperatures that day were in the high nineties, and the flames were as high as fifty feet. There were more than 970 fire fighters on the line. Two hundred and fifty families were evacuated. They took with them what people always take out of fires, mainly snapshots, mementos small enough to put in the car. 'We won't have a stitch of clothing, but at least we'll have these,' a woman about to leave the Puente Hills told the *Times* as she packed the snapshots into the trunk of her car.

People who live with fires think a great deal about what will happen 'when', as the phrase goes in the instruction leaflets, 'the fire comes'. These leaflets, which are stuck up on refrigerator doors all over Los Angeles County, never say 'if'. When the fire comes there will be no water pressure. The roof one watered all the night before will go dry in seconds. Plastic trash cans must be filled with water and wet gunnysacks kept at hand, for smothering the sparks that blow ahead of the fire. The garden hoses must be connected and left where they can be seen. The cars must be placed in the garage, headed out. Whatever one wants most to save must be placed in the cars. The lights must be left on, so that the house can be seen in the smoke. I remember my daughter's Malibu kindergarten sending home on the first day of the fall semester a detailed contingency plan, with alternative sites where, depending on the direction of the wind when the fire came, the children would be taken to wait for their parents. The last-ditch site was the naval air station at Point Mugu, twenty miles up the coast.

'Dry winds and dust, hair full of knots,' our Malibu child wrote when asked, in the fourth grade, for an 'autumn' poem. 'Gardens are dead, animals not fed . . . People mumble as leaves crumble, fire ashes tumble.' The rhythm here is not one that many people outside Los Angeles seem to hear. In the *New York Times* this morning I read a piece in which the way people in Los Angeles 'persist' in living with fire was described as 'denial'. 'Denial' is a word from a different lyric altogether. This will have been only the second fire season over twenty-five years during which I did not have a house somewhere in Los Angeles County, and the second during which I did not keep the snapshots in a box near the door, ready to go when the fire comes.

1989

Times Mirror Square

Harrison Gray Otis, the first successful editor and publisher of the *Los Angeles Times* and in many ways the prototypical Los Angeles citizen, would seem to have been one of those entrepreneurial drifters at once set loose and energized by the Civil War and the westward expansion. He was born in a log house in Ohio in 1837. He went to work as an apprentice printer at fourteen. He was a delegate at twenty-three to the Republican National Convention at which Abraham Lincoln was nominated for the presidency. He spent forty-nine months in the Ohio Infantry, was wounded at Antietam in 1862 and again in Virginia in 1864, and then parlayed his Army connections into government jobs, first as a journeyman printer at the Government Printing Office in Washington and then at the Patent Office. He made his first foray to Southern California in 1874, to investigate a goat-raising scheme that never materialized, and pronounced the place 'the fattest land I was ever in'. He drifted first to Santa Barbara, where he published a small daily without notable success (he and his wife and three children, he noted later, were reduced to living in the fattest land on 'not enough to keep a rabbit alive'), and struck out then for Alaska, where he had lucked into a $10-a-day government sinecure as the special agent in charge of poaching and liquor control in the Seal Islands.

In 1882, already a forty-five-year-old man with a rather accidental past and unremarkable prospects, Harrison Gray Otis managed finally to seize the moment: he quit the government job, returned to Southern California, and put down $6,000, $5,000 of it borrowed, for a quarter interest in the four-page *Los Angeles Daily Times*, a failed paper started a few months before by a former editor of the *Sacramento Union* (the *Union*, for which Mark Twain was a correspondent, is the oldest California daily still publishing) and abandoned almost immediately to its creditors. 'Small beginnings, but great oaks, etc.,' Harrison Gray Otis later noted of his purchase. He seems to have known immediately what kind of Los Angeles he wanted, and what role a newspaper could play in getting it: 'Los Angeles wants no dudes, loafers and paupers; people who have no means and trust to luck,' the new citizen announced in an early editorial, already shedding his previous skin, his middle-aged skin, the skin of a person who had recently had no means and trusted to luck. Los Angeles, as he saw it, was all capital formation, no service. It needed, he said, no 'cheap politicians, failures, bummers, scrubs, impecunious clerks, bookkeepers, lawyers, doctors. The market is overstaffed already. We need workers! Hustlers! Men of brains, brawn and guts! Men who have a little capital and a good deal of energy – first-class men!'

The extent to which Los Angeles was literally invented by the *Los Angeles Times* and by its owners, Harrison Gray Otis and his descendants in the Chandler family, remains hard for people in less recent parts of the country to fully apprehend. At the time Harrison Gray Otis bought his paper there were only some five thousand people living in Los Angeles. There was no navigable river. The Los Angeles River was capable of providing ditch water for a population of two or three hundred thousand, but there was little other ground water to speak of. Los Angeles has water today because Harrison Gray Otis and his son-in-law Harry Chandler wanted it, and fought a series of outright water wars to get it. 'With this water problem out of the way, the growth of Los Angeles will leap forward as never before,' the *Times* advised its readers in 1905, a few weeks before the initial vote to fund the aqueduct meant to bring water from the Owens River, 233 miles to the north. 'Adjacent towns will soon be knocking on our doors for admission to secure the benefits to be derived from our never-failing supply of life-giving water, and Greater Los Angeles will become a magnificent reality.' Any citizen voting against the aqueduct bonds, the *Times* warned on the day before the election, would be 'placing himself in the attitude of an *enemy of the city*'.

To oppose the Chandlers, in other words, was to oppose the

perfection of Los Angeles, the expansion that was the city's imperial destiny. The false droughts and artful title transactions that brought Northern California water south are familiar stories in Los Angeles, and were made so in other parts of the country by the motion picture *Chinatown*. Without Owens River water the San Fernando Valley could not have been developed. The San Fernando Valley was where Harrison Gray Otis and Harry Chandler, through two interlocking syndicates, the San Fernando Mission Land Company and the Los Angeles Suburban Homes Company, happened to have bought or optioned, before the completion of the aqueduct and in some cases before the aqueduct vote, almost sixty-five thousand acres, virtually the entire valley from what is now Burbank to what is now Tarzana, at strictly dry-land prices, between $31 and $53 an acre. 'Have A Contract for A Lot in Your Pocket When the Big Bonds are Voted,' the advertisements read in the *Times* during the days before the initial vote on the aqueduct bonds. 'Pacoima Will Feel the First Benefits of the Owens River Water and Every Purchaser Investing Now Will Reap the Fruits of his Wisdom in Gratifying Profits.'

A great deal of Los Angeles as it appears today derived from this impulse to improve Chandler property. The Los Angeles Civic Center and Union Station and the curiosity known as Olvera Street (Olvera Street is part of El Pueblo de Los Angeles State Historic Park, but it was actually conceived in 1926 as the first local theme mall, the theme being 'Mexican marketplace') are where they are because Harry Chandler wanted to develop the north end of downtown, where the *Times* building and many of his other downtown holdings lay. California has an aerospace industry today because Harry Chandler believed that the development of Los Angeles required that new industry be encouraged, and, in 1920, called on his friends to lend Donald Douglas $15,000 to build an experimental torpedo plane.

The same year, Harry Chandler called on his friends to build Caltech, and the year after that to build a facility (the Coliseum, near the University of Southern California) large enough to attract the 1932 Olympics. The Hollywood Bowl exists because Harry Chandler wanted it. The Los Angeles highway system exists because Harry Chandler knew that people would not buy land in his outlying subdivisions unless they could drive to them, and also because Harry Chandler sat on the board of Goodyear Tire & Rubber, which by then had Los Angeles plants. Goodyear Tire & Rubber had Los Angeles plants in the first place because Harry Chandler and his friends made an investment of $7.5 million to build them.

It was this total identification of the Chandler family's destiny with that of Los Angeles that made the *Times* so peculiar an institution, and also such a rich one. Under their corporate umbrella, the Times Mirror Company, the Chandlers now own, for all practical purposes, not only the *Times*, which for a number of years carried more full-run advertising linage than any other newspaper in the United States, but *Newsday, New York Newsday*, the *Baltimore Sun*, the *Hartford Courant*, the *National Journal*, nine specialized book- and educational-publishing houses, seventeen specialized magazines, the CBS affiliates in Dallas and Austin, the ABC affiliate in St Louis, the NBC affiliate in Birmingham, a cable-television business, and a company that exists exclusively to dispose of what had been Times Mirror's timber and ranchland (this company, since it is meant to self-destruct, is described by Times Mirror as 'entropic'): an empire with operating revenues for 1989 of $3,517,493,000.

The climate in which the *Times* prospered was a special one. Los Angeles had been, through its entire brief history, a boom town. People who lived there had tended to believe, and were encouraged to do so by the increasingly fat newspaper dropped at their doors every morning, that the trend would be unfailingly up. It seemed logical that the people who made business work in California should begin to desert San Francisco, which had been since the gold rush the financial center of the West, and look instead to Los Angeles, where the money increasingly was. It seemed logical that shipping should decline in San Francisco, one of the world's great natural ports, even as it flourished in Los Angeles, where a port had to be dredged, and was, at the insistence of the *Times* and Harry Chandler. It seemed logical that the wish to dredge this port should involve, since Los Angeles was originally landlocked, the annexation first of a twenty-mile corridor to the sea and then the 'consolidation' with Los Angeles ('annexation' of one incorporated city by another was prohibited by state law) of two entire other cities, San Pedro and Wilmington, both of which lay on the Pacific.

The logic here was based on the declared imperative of unlimited opportunity, which in turn dictated unlimited growth. What was construed by people in the rest of the country as accidental – the sprawl of the city, the apparent absence of a cohesive center – was in fact purposeful, the scheme itself: this would be a new kind of city, one that would seem to have no finite limits, a literal cloud on the land that would eventually touch the Tehachapi range to the north and the Mexican border to the south, the San Bernardino Mountains to the east and the Pacific to the west; not just a city finally but its own nation, The Southland. That the Chandlers had been sufficiently prescient to buy up hundreds of thousands of acres on the far reaches of the expanding cloud – 300,000 acres spanning the Tehachapi, 860,000 acres in Baja California, which Harrison Gray Otis and Harry Chandler were at one point trying to get the Taft administration to annex from Mexico, thereby redefining even what might have seemed Southern California's one fixed border (the Pacific was seen locally as not a border but an opportunity, a bridge to Hawaii and on to Asia) – was only what might be expected of any provident citizen: 'The best interests of Los Angeles are paramount to the *Times*,' Harry Chandler wrote in 1934, and it had been, historically, the *Times* that defined what those best interests were.

The *Times* under Harrison Gray Otis was a paper in which the owners' opponents were routinely described as 'thieves', 'scoundrels', 'blackmailers', 'venal', 'cowardly', 'mean', 'un-American', 'assassinlike', 'petty', 'despotic', and 'anarchic scum'. It was said of General Otis (he had been commissioned a brigadier general when he led an expeditionary force to the Philippines during the Spanish-American War, and he was General Otis forever after, just as his houses were The Bivouac and The Outpost, the *Times* building was The Fortress, and the *Times* staff The Phalanx) that he had a remarkably even temper, that of a hungry tiger. A libel suit or judgment against the paper was seen as neither a problem nor an embarrassment but a journalistic windfall, an opportunity to reprint the offending story, intact and often. In November of 1884, after the election of Grover Cleveland to the presidency, the *Times* continued to maintain for eleven days that the president-elect was James G. Blaine, Harrison Gray Otis's candidate.

Even under Harry Chandler's son Norman, who was publisher

from 1944 until 1960, the *Times* continued to exhibit a fitful willful-
ness. The Los Angeles for which the *Times* was at that time published
was still remote from the sources of national and international
power, isolated not only geographically but developmentally, a deliberately adolescent city, intent on its own growth and not much
interested in the world outside. In 1960, when Norman Chandler's
son Otis was named publisher of the *Times*, the paper had only one
foreign correspondent, based in Paris. The city itself was run by a
handful of men who worked for the banks and the old-line law
firms downtown and drove home at five o'clock to Hancock Park or
Pasadena or San Marino. They had lunch at the California Club or
the Los Angeles Athletic Club. They held their weddings and funerals
in Protestant or Catholic churches and did not, on the whole, know
people who lived on the West Side, in Beverly Hills and Bel Air and
Brentwood and Pacific Palisades, many of the most prominent of
whom were in the entertainment business and were Jewish. As
William Severns, the original general manager of the Los Angeles
Music Center's operating company, put it in a recent interview with
Patt Morrison of the *Times*, there was at that time a 'big schism in
society' between these downtown people and what he called 'the
movie group'. The movie group, he said, 'didn't even know where
downtown was, except when they came downtown for a divorce'.
(This was in itself a cultural crossed connection, since people on
the West Side generally got divorced not downtown but in Santa
Monica.)

It was Norman Chandler's wife, Dorothy Buffum Chandler, called
Buff, who perceived that it was in the interests of the city, and
therefore of the *Times*, to draw the West Side into the power structure, and she saw the Music Center, for which she was then raising
money, as a natural way to initiate this process. I once watched Mrs
Chandler, at a dinner sometime in 1964, try to talk the late Jules
Stein, the founder and at that time the chairman of MCA, into
contributing $25,000 toward the construction of the Music Center.
Jules Stein said that he would be glad to donate any amount to Mrs
Chandler's Music Center, and would then expect Mrs Chandler to
make a matching contribution, for this was the way things got done
on the West Side, to the eye clinic he was then building at the UCLA
Medical Center. 'I can't do that,' Mrs Chandler said, and then she

leaned across the table, and demonstrated what the Chandlers had always seen as the true usefulness of owning a newspaper: 'But I can give you twenty-five thousand dollars' worth of free publicity in the paper.'

By the time Mrs Chandler was through, the Music Center and one of its support groups, The Amazing Blue Ribbon, had become the common ground on which the West Side met downtown. This was not to say that all the top editors and managers at the *Times* were entirely comfortable on the West Side; many of them tended still to regard it as alien, a place where people exchanged too many social kisses and held novel, if not dangerous, ideas. 'I always enjoy visiting the West Side,' I recall being told by Tom Johnson, who had in 1980 become the publisher of the *Times*, when we happened to be seated next to each other at a party in Brentwood. He then took a notepad and a pen from his pocket. 'I like to hear what people out here think.' Nor was it to say that an occasional citizen of a more self-absorbed Los Angeles did not still surface, and even write querulous letters to the *Times*:

Regarding 'The Party Pace Picks Up During September' (by Jeannine Stein, Aug. 31): the social season in Los Angeles starts the first Friday in October when the Autumn Cotillion is held. This event, started over fifty years ago, brings together the socially prominent folks of Los Angeles who wouldn't be seen in Michael's and haven't yet decided if the opera is here to stay. By the time Cotillion comes around families are back from vacation, dove hunting season is just over and deer hunting season hasn't begun so the gentlemen of the city find no excuse not to attend. Following that comes the annual Assembly Ball and the Chevaliers du Tastevin dinner followed by the Las Madrinas Debutante Ball. If you are invited to these events you are in socially. No *nouveau riche* or publicity seekers nor social climbers need apply.

The *Times* in which this letter appeared, on September 10, 1989, was one that maintained six bureaus in Europe, five in Latin America, five in Asia, three in the Middle East, and two in Africa. It was reaching an area inhabited by between 13 and 14 million people, more than half of whom, a recent Rand Corporation study suggests, had arrived in Los Angeles as adults, eighteen years old or over, citizens whose memories did not include the Las Madrinas Debutante Ball. In fact there is in Los Angeles no memory everyone shares, no monument everyone knows, no historical reference as meaningful as the long sweep of the ramps where the San Diego and Santa Monica freeways intersect, as the way the hard Santa Ana light strikes the palm trees against the white western wall of the Carnation Milk building on Wilshire Boulevard. Mention of 'historic' sites tends usually to signal a hustle under way, for example transforming a commercial development into historic Olvera Street, or wrapping a twenty-story office tower and a four-hundred-room hotel around the historic Mann's Chinese Theater (the historic Mann's Chinese Theater was originally Grauman's Chinese, but a significant percentage of the population has no reason to remember this), a featured part of the Hollywood Redevelopment.

Californians until recently spoke of the United States beyond Colorado as 'back east'. If they went to New York, they went 'back' to New York, a way of speaking that carried with it the suggestion of living on a distant frontier. Californians of my daughter's generation speak of going 'out' to New York, a meaningful shift in the perception of one's place in the world. The Los Angeles that Norman and Buff Chandler's son Otis inherited in 1960 – and, with his mother, proceeded over the next twenty years to reinvent – was, in other words, a new proposition, potentially one of the world's great cities but still unformed, outgrowing its old controlling idea, its tropistic confidence in growth, and not yet seized by a new one. It was Otis Chandler who decided that what Los Angeles needed if it was to be a world-class city was a world-class newspaper, and he set out to get one.

Partly in response to the question of what a daily newspaper could do that television could not do better, and partly in response to geography – papers on the West Coast have a three-hour advantage going to press, and a three-hour disadvantage when they come off the press – Otis Chandler, then thirty-two, decided that the *Times* should be what was sometimes called a daily magazine, a newspaper that would cover breaking news competitively, but remain willing to commit enormous resources to providing a kind of analysis and background no one else was providing. He made it clear at the outset that the paper was no longer his father's but his, antagonizing members of his own family in 1961 by running a five-part report on the John Birch Society, of which his aunt and uncle Alberta and Philip Chandler were influential members. Otis Chandler followed up the John Birch series, in case anyone had missed the point, by signing the Chandler name to a front-page editorial opposing Birch activities. 'His legs bestrid the ocean, his reared arm crested the world,' as the brass letters read (for no clear reason, since it is what Cleopatra says about Antony as the asps are about to arrive in the fifth act of *Antony and Cleopatra*) at the base of the turning globe in the lobby of the *Times* building. 'His voice was propertied to all the tuned spheres.' One reason Otis Chandler could property the voice of the *Times* to all the tuned spheres was that his *Times* continued to make more money than his father's. 'The paper was published every day and they could see it,' he later said about his family. 'They disagreed endlessly with my editorial policies. But they never disagreed with the financial results.'

In fact an unusual kind of reporting developed at the *Times*, the editorial philosophy of which was frequently said to be 'run it long and run it once'. The *Times* became a paper on which reporters were allowed, even encouraged, to give the reader the kind of detail that was known to everyone on the scene but rarely got filed. On the night Son of Sam was arrested in New York, according to Charles T. Powers, then in the *Times'* New York bureau, Roone Arledge was walking around Police Headquarters, 'dressed as if for a touch football game, a glass of scotch in one hand, a portable two-way radio in the other, directing his network's feed to the Coast', details that told the reader pretty much all there was to know about celebrity police work. In San Salvador in the early spring of 1982, when representatives from the centrist Christian Democrats, the militarist National Conciliation Party, and the rightist ARENA were all meeting under a pito tree on Francisco ('Chachi') Guerrero's patio, Laurie Becklund of the *Times* asked Guerrero, who has since been assassinated, how people so opposed to one another could possibly work together. 'We all know each other – we've known each other for years,' he said. 'You underestimate our *política tropical*.' A few days later, when Laurie Becklund asked an ARENA leader why ARENA, then trying to close out the Christian Democrats, did not fear losing American aid, the answer she got, and filed, summed up the entire relationship between the United States and the Salvadoran right: 'We believe in gringos.'

This kind of detail was sometimes dismissed by reporters at other papers as 'L.A. color', but really it was something different: the details gave the tone of the situation, the subtext without which the text could not be understood, and sharing this subtext with the reader was the natural tendency of reporters who, because of the nature of both the paper on which they worked and the city in which it was published, tended not to think of themselves as insiders. 'Jesse don't wanna run nothing but his mouth,' Mayor Marion Barry of Washington, D.C., was quoted as having said, about Jesse Jackson, early in 1990 in a piece by Bella Stumbo in the *Los Angeles Times*; there was in this piece, I was told in New York, after both the *New York Times* and the *Washington Post* had been forced to report the ensuing controversy, nothing that many *Post* and *New York Times* reporters in Washington did not already know. This was presumably true, but only the *Los Angeles Times* had printed it.

Unconventional choices were made at the *Times*. Otis Chandler had insisted that the best people in the country be courted and hired, regardless of their politics. The political cartoonist Paul Conrad was lured from the *Denver Post*, brought out for an interview, and met at the airport, per his demand, by the editor of the paper. Robert Scheer, who had a considerable reputation as a political journalist at *Ramparts* and *New Times* but no newspaper experience, was not only hired but given whatever he wanted, including the use of the executive dining room, the Picasso Room. 'For the money we're paying Scheer, I should hope he'd be abrasive,' William Thomas, the editor of the *Times* from 1971 until 1989, said to a network executive who called to complain that Scheer had been abrasive in an interview. The *Times* had by then abandoned traditional ideas of what newspaper reporters and editors should be paid, and was in some cases paying double the going rate. 'I don't think newspapers should take a back seat to magazines, TV, or public relations,' Otis Chandler had said early on. He had bought the *Times* a high-visibility Washington bureau. He had bought the *Times* a foreign staff.

By 1980, when Otis Chandler named Tom Johnson the publisher

of the *Times* and created for himself the new title of editor in chief, the *Times* was carrying, in the average week, more columns of news than either the *New York Times* or the *Washington Post*. It was running long analytical background pieces from parts of the country and of the world that other papers left to the wires. Its Washington bureau, even Bob Woodward of the *Washington Post* conceded recently, was frequently beating the *Post*. Its foreign coverage, particularly from Central America and the Middle East, was, day for day, stronger than that of the national competition. 'Otis was a little more specific than just indicating he wanted the *Times* to be among the top U.S. newspapers,' Nick Williams, the editor of the *Times* from 1958 until 1971, said later of Otis Chandler's ascension to publisher of the *Times*. 'He said, "I want it to be the number one newspaper in the country."'
What began worrying people in Los Angeles during the fall of 1989, starting on the morning in October when the *Times* unveiled the first edition of what it referred to on billboards and television advertisements and radio spots and bus shelters and bus tails and rack cards and in-paper advertisements and even in its own house newsletter as 'the new, faster-format *Los Angeles Times*', was whether having the number one newspaper in the country was a luxury the Chandlers, and the city, could still afford.

It was hard, that fall at the *Times*, to sort out exactly what was going on. A series of shoes had already been dropped. There had been in January 1989 the installation of a new editor, someone from outside, someone whose particular depths and shallows many people had trouble sounding, someone from the East (actually he was from Tennessee, but his basic training had been under Benjamin Bradlee at the *Washington Post*, and around the *Times* he continued to be referred to, tellingly, as an Easterner), Shelby Coffey III. There had been some months later the announcement of a new approach to what had become the *Times*' Orange County problem, the problem being that a few miles to the south, in Orange County, the *Times*' zoned edition had so far been unable to unseat the *Orange County Register*, the leading paper in a market so rich that the *Register* had a few years earlier become the one paper in the United States with more full-run advertising linage than the *Times*.

The new approach to this Orange County problem seemed straightforward enough (the editor of the Orange County edition, at that time Narda Zacchino, would get twenty-nine additional reporters, an expanded plant, virtual autonomy over what appeared in the *Times* in Orange County, and would report only to Shelby Coffey), although it did involve a new 'president', or business person, for Orange County, Lawrence M. Higby, whose particular skills – he was a marketing expert out of Taco Bell, Pepsi, and H. R. Haldeman's office in the Nixon White House, where he had been known as Haldeman's Haldeman – made some people uneasy. Narda Zacchino was liked and respected around the *Times* (she had more or less grown up on the paper, and was married to Robert Scheer), but Higby was an unknown quantity, and there were intimations that not everyone was entirely comfortable with these heightened stakes in Orange County. According to the *Wall Street Journal*, Tom Johnson, the publisher, said in an August 1989 talk to the Washington bureau that the decision to give Narda Zacchino and Lawrence Higby autonomy in Orange County had led to 'blood all over the floor' in Los Angeles. He described the situation in Orange County as 'a failure of mine', an area in which 'I should have done more sooner.'

Still, it was September 1989 before people outside the *Times* started noticing the blood, or even the dropped shoes, already on the floor. September was when it was announced, quite unexpectedly, that Tom Johnson, who had been Otis Chandler's own choice as publisher and had in turn picked Shelby Coffey as editor, was moving upstairs to what were described as 'broader responsibilities', for example newsprint supply. The publisher's office, it was explained, would now be occupied by David Laventhol, who had spent time at the *New York Herald Tribune* and the *Washington Post*, had moved next to *Newsday* (he was editor, then publisher), had been since 1987 the president of the parent Times Mirror Company, and had achieved, mainly because he was seen to have beat the *New York Times* in Queens with *New York Newsday*, a certain reputation for knowing how to run the kind of regional war the *Los Angeles Times* wanted to run in Orange County. David Laventhol, like Shelby Coffey, was referred to around the office as an Easterner.

Then, on October 11, 1989, there was the format change, to which many of the paper's most vocal readers, a significant number of whom had been comparing the paper favorably every morning with the national edition of the *New York Times*, reacted negatively. It appeared that some readers of the *Los Angeles Times* did not want color photographs on its front page. Nor, it appeared, did these readers want News Highlights or news briefs or boxes summarizing the background of a story in three or four sentences without dependent clauses. A Laguna Niguel subscriber described himself in a letter to the editor as 'heartsick'. A Temple City reader characterized the changes as 'beyond my belief'. By the first of December even the student newspaper at Caltech, the *California Tech*, was having a little fun at the *Times'* expense, calling itself the *New, Faster Format Tech* and declaring itself dedicated to 'increasing the amount of information on the front page by replacing all stories with pictures'. In the lost-and-found classified section of the *Times* itself there appeared, sandwiched among pleas for lost Akitas ('Has Tattoo') and lost Saudi Arabian Airlines ID cards and lost four-carat emerald-cut diamond rings set in platinum ('sentimental value'), this notice, apparently placed by a group of the *Times'* own reporters: '*LA TIMES:* Last seen in a confused state disguised as *USA Today*. If found, please return to Times Mirror Square.'

The words '*USA Today*' were heard quite a bit during the first few months of the new, faster format, as were 'New Coke' and 'Michael Dukakis'. It was said that Shelby Coffey and David Laventhol had turned the paper over to its marketing people. It was said that the marketing people were bent on reducing the paper to its zoned editions, especially to its Orange County edition, and reducing the zoned editions to a collection of suburban shoppers. It was said that the paper was conducting a deliberate dumb-down, turning itself over to the interests and whims (less to read, more local service announcements) of the several thousand people who had taken part in the videotaped focus groups the marketing people and key editors had been running down in Orange County. A new format for a newspaper or magazine tends inevitably to suggest a perceived problem with the product, and the insistence with which this particular new format was promoted – the advertising stressed the superior disposability of the new *Times*, how easy it was, how cut down, how little time the reader need spend with it – convinced many people that the paper was determined to be less than it had been. 'READ THIS,' *Times* rack cards now demanded. 'QUICK.'

The architects of the new, faster format became, predictably, defensive, even impatient. People with doubts were increasingly seen as balky, resistant to all change, sulky dogs in the manger of progress. 'Just look at this,' Narda Zacchino, who as editor of the Orange County edition had been one of the central figures in the redesign, ordered me, brandishing first a copy of that morning's *USA Today* and then one of that morning's *Times*. 'Do they look alike? No. They look nothing alike. I know there's been a negative response from within the paper. "This is *USA Today*," you hear. Well, look at it. It's not *USA Today*. But we're a newspaper. We want people to read the newspaper. I've been struggling down there for seven years, trying to get people to read the paper. And, despite the in-house criticism, we're not getting criticism from outside. Our response has been very, very good.'

Shelby Coffey mentioned the redesign that Walter Bernard had done in 1977 for Henry Anatole Grunwald at *Time*. 'They got scorched,' he said. 'They had thousands of letters, cancellations by the hundreds. I remember seeing it the first time and being jarred. In fact I thought they had lost their senses. They had gone to color. They had done the departments and the type in quite a different way. But it stood up over the years as one of the most successful, maybe *the* most successful, of the redesigns. I think you have to accept as a given that it's going to take six months or a year before people get used to this.'

Around the paper, where it was understood that the format change had originally been developed in response to the needs of the Orange County edition, a certain paranoia had taken hold. People were exchanging rumors by computer mail. People were debating whether the Orange County edition should be encouraged to run announcements of local events in column one of page one ('Tonight: Tito Puente brings his Latin Jazz All-Stars to San Juan Capistrano . . . Puente, a giant among salsa musicians, is a particular favorite at New York's celebrated Blue Note nightclub. Time: 8 P.M. at the Coach House, 33157 Camino Capistrano. Tickets: $19.50. Information: (714) 496–8930") and still call itself the *Los Angeles Times*. People were noticing that the Orange County edition was, as far as that

went, not always calling itself the *Los Angeles Times* – that some of its
subscription callers were urging telephone contacts to subscribe to
'the Orange County *Times*'. People were tormenting one another
with various forms of the verb 'to drive', as in 'market-driven' and
'customer-driven' and 'a lot of people are calling this paper market-
driven but it's not, what drives this paper is editorial' and 'this paper
has different forces driving it than something like *The Nation*'. (The
necessity for distinguishing the *Los Angeles Times* from *The Nation* was
perhaps the most arresting but far from the only straw point made
to me in the course of a few days at the *Times*.)

The mood was rendered no less febrile by what began to seem an
unusual number of personnel changes. During the first few days of
November 1989, the *Los Angeles Herald Examiner* folded, and a visible
number of its columnists and its sports and arts and entertainment
writers began appearing immediately in the *Times*. A week or so later,
Dennis Britton, who had been, with Shelby Coffey and two other
editors, a final contender for the editorship of the *Times* (the four
candidates had been asked by Tom Johnson to submit written analy-
ses of the content of the *Times* and of the areas in which it needed
strengthening), bailed out as one of the *Times*' deputy managing
editors, accepting the editorship of the *Chicago Sun-Times*.

A week after that, it was announced that Anthony Day, the editor
of the *Times* editorial pages since 1971, would be replaced by Thomas
Plate, who had directed the partially autonomous editorial and op-ed
pages for *New York Newsday* and was expected to play a role in doing
something similar for Orange County. In the fever of the moment it
was easy for some people to believe that the changes were all of a
piece, that, for example, Anthony Day's leaving the editorial page
had something to do with the new fast read, or with the fact that
some people on the Times Mirror board had occasionally expressed
dissatisfaction with the paper's editorial direction on certain issues,
particularly its strong anti-Administration stand on Central American
policy. Anthony Day was told only, he reported, that it was 'time for
a change', that he would be made a reporter and assigned a beat
('ideas and ideology in the modern world'), and that he would report
directly to Shelby Coffey. 'There was this strange, and strangely
moving, party for Tony last Saturday at which Tom Johnson spoke,'
a friend at the *Times* wrote me not long after Day was fired. 'And

they sang songs to Tony – among them a version of "Yesterday" in which the words were changed to "Tony-day". ("Why he had to go, we don't know, they wouldn't say").'

Part of the problem, as some people at the *Times* saw it, was that neither Shelby Coffey nor David Laventhol shared much history with anybody at the *Times*. Shelby Coffey was viewed by many people at the *Times* as virtually unfathomable. He seemed to place mysterious demands upon himself. His manner, which was essentially border Southern, was unfamiliar in Los Angeles. His wife, Mary Lee, was for many people at the *Times* equally hard to place, a delicate Southerner who looked like a lifetime Maid of Cotton but was in fact a doctor, not even a gynecologist or a pediatrician but a trauma specialist, working the emergency room at Huntington Hospital in Pasadena. 'You know the golden rule of the emergency room,' Mary Lee Coffey drawled the first time I met her, not long after her arrival in Los Angeles. She was wearing a white angora sweater. 'Keep 'em alive till eight-oh-five.'

Together, Shelby Coffey and David Laventhol, a demonstrated corporate player, suggested a new mood at the *Times*, a little leaner and maybe a little meaner, a little more market-oriented. 'Since 1881, the *Los Angeles Times* has led the way with award-winning journalism,' a *Times* help-wanted advertisement read around that time. 'As we progress into our second century, we're positioned as one of America's largest newspapers. To help us maintain our leadership position, we're currently seeking a Promotion Writer.' Some people in the newsroom began referring to the two as the First Street Gangster Crips (the Gangster Crips were a prominent Los Angeles gang, and the *Times* building was on First Street), and to their changes as drive-bys. They were repeatedly referred to as 'guys whose ties are all in Washington or New York', as 'people with Eastern ideas of what Los Angeles wants or deserves'. Shelby Coffey's new editors were called 'the Stepford Wives', and Shelby Coffey himself was called, to his face, 'the Dan Quayle of journalism'. (That this was said by a reporter who continued to be employed by the *Times* suggested not only the essentially tolerant nature of the paper but the extent to which Coffey appeared dedicated to the accommodation of dissent.) During the 1989 Christmas season, a blowup of his photograph, with a red hat pinned above it, appeared in one of the departments at the *Times*. 'He Knows When You Are Sleeping,' the legend read. 'And With Whom.'

This question of Coffey and Laventhol being 'Easterners' was never far below the surface. 'Easterner', as the word is used in Los Angeles, remains somewhat harder to translate than First Street Gangster Crip. It carries both an arrogance and a defensiveness, and has to do not exactly with geography (people who themselves came from the East will quite often dismiss other people as 'Easterners') but with a virtually uncrackable complex of attitudes. An Easterner, in the local view, believes that Los Angeles begins and ends on the West Side and is about the movie business. Easterners, moreover, do not understand even the movie business: they come out in January and get taken to dinner at Spago and complain that the view is obscured by billboards, by advertisements for motion pictures, missing the point that advertisements for motion pictures are the most comforting possible view for those people who regularly get window tables at Spago. Easterners refer to Los Angeles as El Lay, as La La Land, as the Left Coast. 'I suppose you're glad to be here,' Easterners say to Californians when they run into them in New York. 'I suppose you can always read the *Times* here,' Easterners say on their January visits to Los Angeles, meaning the *New York Times*.

Easterners see the *Los Angeles Times* only rarely, and complain, when they do see it, about the length of its pieces. 'They can only improve it,' an editor of the *New York Times* said to me when I mentioned that the *Los Angeles Times* had undertaken some changes. He said that the paper had been in the past 'unreadable'. It was, he said, 'all gray'. I asked what he meant. 'It's these stories that cover whole pages,' he said. 'And then the story breaks to the next page and keeps going.' This was said on a day when, of eight stories on the front page of the *New York Times*, seven broke to other sections. 'Who back east cares?' I was asked by someone at the *Los Angeles Times* when I said that I was writing about the changes at the paper. 'If this were happening to the *New York Times*, you'd have the *Washington Post* all over it.'

When people in Los Angeles talked about what was happening at the *Times*, they were talking about something harder to define, in the end, than any real or perceived or feared changes in the paper itself, which in fact was looking good. Day for day, not much about the *Times* had actually changed. There sometimes seemed fewer of the analytic national pieces that used to appear in column one. There seemed to be some increase in syndicated soft features, picked up with the columnists and arts reviewers when the *Herald Examiner* folded. But the 'new, faster-format *Los Angeles Times*' (or, as early advertisements called it, the 'new, fast-read *Los Angeles Times*') still carried more words every day than appear in the New Testament. It still carried in the average week more columns of news than the *New York Times* or the *Washington Post*. It still ran pieces at a length few other papers would countenance – David Shaw's January 1990 series on the coverage of the McMartin child-abuse case, for example, ran 17,000 words. The paper's editorials were just as strong under Thomas Plate as they had been under Anthony Day. Its reporters were still filing stories full of details that did not appear in other papers, for example the fact (this was from Kenneth Freed in Panama, January 1, 1990) that nearly 125 journalists, after spending less than twelve hours in Panama without leaving Howard Air Force Base, where they were advised that there was shooting on the streets of Panama City ('It is war out there,' the briefing officer told them), had accepted the Southern Command's offer of a charter flight back to Miami.

The *Times* had begun, moreover, to do aggressive local coverage, not historically the paper's strong point, and also to do frequent 'special reports', eight-to-fourteen-page sections, with no advertising, offering wrap-up news magazine coverage of, say, China, or Eastern Europe, or the October 1989 Northern California earthquake, or the state of the environment in Southern California. A week or so before Christmas 1989, Shelby Coffey initiated a daily 'Moscow Edition', a six-to-eight-page selection of stories from that day's *Los Angeles Times*. This Moscow Edition, which was prepared in Los Angeles, faxed to the *Times* bureau in Moscow, and delivered by hand to some 125 Soviet officials, turned out to be sufficiently popular that the Moscow bureau received a call from the Soviet Foreign Ministry requesting that the *Times* extend its publication to weekends and even to Christmas Day.

'Shelby may be fighting more of a fight against the dumbing-down of the newspaper than we know or he can say,' one *Times* editor, who had himself been wary of the changes under way but had come to believe that there had been among some members of the staff an unjustified rush to judgment, said to me. 'That the *Times* is still essentially the same paper seems to me so plainly the case as to refute the word "new" in "the new, faster-format *Los Angeles Times*". What small novelty there is would have received very little promotion had it begun as a routine editorial modification. But it didn't originate in editorial discussion. It originated in market research, which was why it got promoted so heavily. The *Times* needed a way to declare Orange County a new ball game, and this was it. But you can't change the paper anywhere without changing it everywhere. And once the *Times* throws the switch, a colossal amount of current seems to flow through the whole system.'

In a way the uneasiness had to do with the entire difficult question of 'Easterners'. It was not that Shelby Coffey was an Easterner or that David Laventhol was an Easterner but that Easterners had been brought in, that there was no Chandler in the publisher's office, no one to whom the *Los Angeles Times* was intrinsically more important than, say, *Newsday*, no one who could reliably be expected to have a visceral appreciation not just of how far the *Times* had come but of how far Los Angeles itself had come, of how fragile the idea of the place was and how easily it could be lost. Los Angeles had been the most idealized of American cities, and the least accidental. Its development had proceeded not from the circumstances of geography but from sheer will, from an idea. It had been General Otis and Harry Chandler who conceived the future of Los Angeles as one of ever-expanding possibility, and had instructed the readers of the *Times* in what was needed to achieve that future. It had been Otis Chandler who articulated this vision by defining the *Times'* sphere of influence as regional, from Santa Barbara to the border and from the mountains to the sea, and who told the readers of the *Times* that this was what they wanted.

What the *Times* seemed to be telling its readers now was significantly different, and was based not on the logic of infinite opportunity proceeding from infinite growth but on the logic of minimizing risk, on corporate logic, and it was not impossible to follow that logic to a point at which what might be best for the *Times* and what might be best for Los Angeles would no longer necessarily coincide. 'You talk to people in Orange County, they don't want news of Los Angeles,' David Laventhol said one afternoon in late November of 1989. 'We did a survey. Ask them what news they want, news from Los Angeles rates very, very low.'

We were talking about his sense that Southern California was fragmenting more than it was coalescing, about what one *Times* editor had called 'the aggressive disidentification with Los Angeles' of the more recent and more uniformly affluent communities in Ventura and San Diego and Orange counties. This aggressive disidentification with Los Angeles was the reason the Orange County Edition had been made autonomous.

'I spent many years in the New York market, and in many ways this is a more complex market,' David Laventhol said. 'The *New York Times* and some other papers were traditionally able to connect the entire New York community. It's much tougher here. If anything could bind this whole place together – anything that's important, anything beyond baseball teams – it would probably be the *Times*. But people are looking inward right now. They aren't thinking in terms of the whole region. It's partly a function of transportation, jobs, the difficulty of commuting or whatever, but it's also a function of lifestyle. People in Orange County don't like the West Side of Los Angeles. They don't like the South Side of Los Angeles. They don't like whatever. They're lined up at the county line with their backs to Los Angeles.'

Some years ago, Otis Chandler was asked how many readers would actually miss the *Times* were it to stop publishing tomorrow. 'Probably less than half,' Otis Chandler had said, and been so quoted in his own paper. For reasons that might not have been clear to his market-research people, he had nonetheless continued trying to make that paper the best in the country. During the 1989 Christmas season there was at the *Times*, as there had traditionally been, a party, and a Christmas toast was given, as it had traditionally been, by the publisher. In the past the publishers of the *Times* had stressed the growth of the enterprise, both achieved and anticipated. It had been a good year, David Laventhol said at the 1989 Christmas party, and he was glad it was over.

1990

IV

New York

Sentimental Journeys

1

We know her story, and some of us, although not all of us, which was to become one of the story's several equivocal aspects, know her name. She was a twenty-nine-year-old unmarried white woman who worked as an investment banker in the corporate finance department at Salomon Brothers in downtown Manhattan, the energy and natural resources group. She was said by one of the principals in a Texas oil-stock offering on which she had collaborated as a member of the Salomon team to have done 'topnotch' work. She lived alone in an apartment on East 83rd Street, between York and East End, a sublet cooperative she was thinking about buying. She often worked late and when she got home she would change into jogging clothes and at eight-thirty or nine-thirty in the evening would go running, six or seven miles through Central Park, north on the East Drive, west on the less traveled road connecting the East and West Drives at approximately 102nd Street, and south on the West Drive. The wisdom of this was later questioned by some, by those who were accustomed to thinking of the Park as a place to avoid after dark, and defended by others, the more adroit of whom spoke of the citizen's absolute right to public access ('That park belongs to us and this time nobody is going to take it from us,' Ronnie Eldridge, at the time a Democratic candidate for the City Council of New York, declared on the op-ed page of the *New York Times*), others of whom spoke of 'running' as a preemptive right.

'Runners have Type A controlled personalities and they don't like their schedules interrupted,' one runner, a securities trader, told the *Times* to this point. 'When people run is a function of their lifestyle,' another runner said. 'I am personally very angry,' a third said. 'Because women should have the right to run anytime.'

For this woman in this instance these notional rights did not prevail. She was found, with her clothes torn off, not far from the 102nd Street connecting road at one-thirty on the morning of April 20, 1989. She was taken near death to Metropolitan Hospital on East 97th Street. She had lost 75 percent of her blood. Her skull had been crushed, her left eyeball pushed back through its socket, the characteristic surface wrinkles of her brain flattened. Dirt and twigs were found in her vagina, suggesting rape. By May 2, when she first woke from coma, six black and Hispanic teenagers, four of whom had made videotaped statements concerning their roles in the attack and another of whom had described his role in an unsigned verbal statement, had been charged with her assault and rape and she had become, unwilling and unwitting, a sacrificial player in the sentimental narrative that is New York public life.

Nightmare in Central Park, the headlines and display type read. *Teen Wolfpack Beats and Rapes Wall Street Exec on Jogging Path. Central Park Horror. Wolf Pack's Prey. Female Jogger Near Death After Savage Attack by Roving Gang. Rape Rampage. Park Marauders Call It 'Wilding', Street Slang for Going Berserk. Rape Suspect: 'It Was Fun'. Rape Suspect's Jailhouse Boast: 'She Wasn't Nothing'. The teenagers were back in the holding cell, the confessions gory and complete. One shouted 'hit the beat' and they all started rapping to 'Wild Thing'. The Jogger and the Wolf Pack. An Outrage and a Prayer.* And, on the Monday morning after the attack, on the front page of the *New York Post*, with a photograph of Governor Mario Cuomo and the headline *'None of Us Is Safe'*, this italic text: 'A visibly shaken Governor Cuomo spoke out yesterday on the vicious Central Park rape: "The people are angry and frightened – my mother is, my family is. To me, as a person who's lived in this city all of his life, this is the ultimate shriek of alarm."'

Later it would be recalled that 3,254 other rapes were reported that year, including one the following week involving the near decapitation of a black woman in Fort Tryon Park and one two weeks later involving a black woman in Brooklyn who was robbed, raped, sodomized, and thrown down an air shaft of a four-story building, but the point was rhetorical, since crimes are universally understood to be news to the extent that they offer, however erroneously, a story, a lesson, a high concept. In the 1986 Central Park death of Jennifer Levin, then eighteen, at the hands of Robert Chambers, then nineteen, the 'story', extrapolated more or less from thin air but left largely uncorrected, had to do not with people living wretchedly and marginally on the underside of where they wanted to be, not with the Dreiserian pursuit of 'respectability' that marked the revealed details (Robert Chambers's mother was a private-duty nurse who worked twelve-hour night shifts to enroll her son in private schools and the Knickerbocker Greys), but with 'preppies', and the familiar 'too much too soon'.

Susan Brownmiller, during a year spent monitoring newspaper coverage of rape as part of her research for *Against Our Will: Men, Women and Rape*, found, not surprisingly, that 'although New York City police statistics showed that black women were more frequent victims of rape than white women, the favored victim in the tabloid headline ... was young, white, middle class and "attractive".' In its quite extensive coverage of rape-murders during the year 1971, according to Ms Brownmiller, the *Daily News* published in its four-star final edition only two stories in which the victim was not described in the lead paragraph as 'attractive': one of these stories involved an eight-year-old child, the other was a second-day follow-up on a first-day story that had in fact described the victim as 'attractive'. The *Times*, she found, covered rapes only infrequently that year, but what coverage they did 'concerned victims who had some kind of middle-class status, such as "nurse", "dancer" or "teacher", and with a favored setting of Central Park'.

As a news story, 'Jogger' was understood to turn on the demonstrable 'difference' between the victim and her accused assailants, four of whom lived in Schomburg Plaza, a federally subsidized apartment complex at the northeast corner of Fifth Avenue and 110th Street in East Harlem, and the rest of whom lived in the projects and rehabilitated tenements just to the north and west of Schomburg Plaza. Some twenty-five teenagers were brought in for questioning; eight were held. The six who were finally indicted ranged in age from fourteen to sixteen. That none of the six had previous police records passed, in this context, for achievement; beyond that, one was recalled by his classmates to have taken pride in his expensive basketball shoes, another to have been 'a follower'. *I'm a smooth type of fellow, cool, calm, and mellow*, one of the six, Yusef Salaam, would say in the rap he presented as part of his statement before sentencing.

> *I'm kind of laid back, but now I'm speaking so that you know / I got*
> *used and abused and even was put on the news . . .*
> *I'm not dissing them all, but the some that I called.*
> *They tried to dis me like I was an inch small, like a midget, a mouse,*
> *something less than a man.*

The victim, by contrast, was a leader, part of what the *Times* would describe as 'the wave of young professionals who took over New York in the 1980's', one of those who were 'handsome and pretty and educated and white', who, according to the *Times*, not only 'believed they owned the world' but 'had reason to'. She was from a Pittsburgh suburb, Upper St Clair, the daughter of a retired Westinghouse senior manager. She had been Phi Beta Kappa at Wellesley, a graduate of the Yale School of Management, a congressional intern, nominated for a Rhodes Scholarship, remembered by the chairman of her department at Wellesley as 'probably one of the top four or five students of the decade'. She was reported to be a vegetarian, and 'fun-loving', although only 'when time permitted', and also to have had (these were the *Times*' details) 'concerns about the ethics of the American business world'.

In other words she was wrenched, even as she hung between death and life and later between insentience and sentience, into New York's ideal sister, daughter, Bacharach bride: a young woman of conventional middle-class privilege and promise whose situation was such that many people tended to overlook the fact that the state's case against the accused was not invulnerable. The state could implicate most of the defendants in the assault and rape in their own videotaped words, but had none of the incontrovertible forensic evidence – no matching semen, no matching fingernail scrapings, no matching blood – commonly produced in this kind of case. Despite the fact that jurors in the second trial would eventually mention physical evidence as having been crucial in their bringing guilty verdicts against one defendant, Kevin Richardson, there was not actually much physical evidence at hand. Fragments of hair 'similar [to] and consistent' with that of the victim were found on Kevin Richardson's clothing and underwear, but the state's own criminologist had testified that hair samples were necessarily inconclusive since, unlike fingerprints, they could not be traced to a single person. Dirt samples found on the defendants' clothing were, again, similar to dirt found in that part of the park where the attack took place, but the state's criminologist allowed that the samples were also similar to dirt found in other uncultivated areas of the park. To suggest, however, that this minimal physical evidence could open the case to an aggressive defense – to, say, the kind of defense that such celebrated New York criminal lawyers as Jack Litman and Barry Slotnick typically present – would come to be construed, during the weeks and months to come, as a further attack on the victim.

She would be Lady Courage to the *New York Post*, she would be A Profile in Courage to the *Daily News* and *New York Newsday*. She would become for Anna Quindlen in the *New York Times* the figure of 'New York rising above the dirt, the New Yorker who has known the best, and the worst, and has stayed on, living somewhere in the middle'. She would become for David Dinkins, the first black mayor of New York, the emblem of his apparently fragile hopes for the city itself: 'I hope the city will be able to learn a lesson from this event and be inspired by the young woman who was assaulted in the case,' he said. 'Despite tremendous odds, she is rebuilding her life. What a human life can do, a human society can do as well.' She was even then for John Gutfreund, at that time the chairman and chief executive officer of Salomon Brothers, the personification of 'what makes this city so vibrant and so great', now 'struck down by a side of our city that is as awful and terrifying as the creative side is wonderful'. It was precisely in this conflation of victim and city, this confusion of personal woe with public distress, that the crime's 'story' would be found, its lesson, its encouraging promise of narrative resolution.

One reason the victim in this case could be so readily abstracted, and her situation so readily made to stand for that of the city itself, was that she remained, as a victim of rape, unnamed in most press reports. Although the American and English press convention of not naming victims of rape (adult rape victims are named in French papers) derives from the understandable wish to protect the victim, the rationalization of this special protection rests on a number of doubtful, even magical, assumptions. The convention assumes, by providing a protection for victims of rape not afforded victims of other assaults, that rape involves a violation absent from other kinds of assault. The convention assumes that this violation is of a nature best kept secret, that the rape victim feels, and would feel still more strongly were she identified, a shame and self-loathing unique to this form of assault; in other words that she has been in an unspecified way party to her own assault, that a special contract exists between this one kind of victim and her assailant. The convention assumes, finally, that the victim would be, were this special contract revealed, the natural object of prurient interest; that the act of male penetration involves such potent mysteries that the woman so penetrated (as opposed, say, to having her face crushed with a brick or her brain penetrated with a length of pipe) is permanently marked, 'different', even – especially if there is a perceived racial or social 'difference' between victim and assailant, as in nineteenth-century stories featuring white women taken by Indians – 'ruined'.

These quite specifically masculine assumptions (women do not want to be raped, nor do they want to have their brains smashed, but very few mystify the difference between the two) tend in general to be self-fulfilling, guiding the victim to define her assault as her protectors do. 'Ultimately we're doing women a disservice by separating rape from other violent crimes,' Deni Elliott, the director of Dartmouth's Ethics Institute, suggested in a discussion of this custom in *Time*. 'We are participating in the stigma of rape by treating victims of this crime differently,' Geneva Overholser, the editor of the *Des Moines Register*, said about her decision to publish in February of 1990 a five-part piece about a rape victim who agreed to be named. 'When we as a society refuse to talk openly about rape, I think we weaken our ability to deal with it.' Susan Estrich, a professor of criminal law at Harvard Law School and the manager of Michael Dukakis's 1988 presidential campaign, discussed, in *Real Rape*, the conflicting emotions that followed her own 1974 rape:

At first, being raped is something you simply don't talk about. Then it occurs to you that people whose houses are broken into or who are mugged in Central Park talk about it *all* the time . . . If it isn't my fault, why am I supposed to be ashamed? If I'm not ashamed, if it wasn't 'personal', why look askance when I mention it?

There were, in the 1989 Central Park attack, specific circumstances that reinforced the conviction that the victim should not be named. She had clearly been, according to the doctors who examined her at Metropolitan Hospital and to the statements made by the suspects (she herself remembered neither the attack nor anything that happened during the next six weeks), raped by one or more assailants. She had also been beaten so brutally that, fifteen months later, she could not focus her eyes or walk unaided. She had lost all sense of smell. She could not read without experiencing double vision. She was believed at the time to have permanently lost function in some areas of her brain.

Given these circumstances, the fact that neither the victim's family nor, later, the victim herself wanted her name known struck an immediate chord of sympathy, seemed a belated way to protect her as she had not been protected in Central Park. Yet there was in this case a special emotional undertow that derived in part from the deep and allusive associations and taboos attaching, in American black history, to the idea of the rape of white women. Rape remained, in the collective memory of many blacks, the very core of their victimization. Black men were accused of raping white women, even as black women were, Malcolm X wrote in *The Autobiography of Malcolm X*, 'raped by the slavemaster white man until there had begun to emerge a homemade, handmade, brainwashed race that was no longer even of its true color, that no longer even knew its true family names'. The very frequency of sexual contact between white men and black women increased the potency of the taboo on any such contact between black men and white women. The abolition of slavery, W. J. Cash wrote in *The Mind of the South*,

. . . in destroying the rigid fixity of the black at the bottom of the scale, in throwing open to him at least the legal opportunity

to advance, had inevitably opened up to the mind of every
Southerner a vista at the end of which stood the overthrow of
this taboo. If it was given to the black to advance at all, who
could say (once more the logic of the doctrine of his inherent
inferiority would not hold) that he would not one day advance
the whole way and lay claim to complete equality, including,
specifically, the ever crucial right of marriage?

What Southerners felt, therefore, was that any assertion of
any kind on the part of the Negro constituted in a perfectly
real manner an attack on the Southern woman. What they
saw, more or less consciously, in the conditions of Reconstruction was a passage toward a condition for her as degrading, in
their view, as rape itself. And a condition, moreover, which,
logic or no logic, they infallibly thought of as being as absolutely
forced upon her as rape, and hence a condition for which the
term 'rape' stood as truly as for the *de facto* deed.

Nor was the idea of rape the only potentially treacherous under-
current in this case. There has historically been, for American blacks,
an entire complex of loaded references around the question of 'naming': slave names, masters' names, African names, call me by my
rightful name, nobody knows my name; stories, in which the specific
gravity of naming locked directly into that of rape, of black men
whipped for addressing white women by their given names. That, in
this case, just such an interlocking of references could work to fuel
resentments and inchoate hatreds seemed clear, and it seemed
equally clear that some of what ultimately occurred – the repeated
references to lynchings, the identification of the defendants with the
Scottsboro boys, the insistently provocative repetition of the victim's
name, the weird and self-defeating insistence that no rape had taken
place and little harm been done the victim – derived momentum
from this historical freight. 'Years ago, if a white woman said a Black
man looked at her lustfully, he could be hung higher than a magnolia
tree in bloom, while a white mob watched joyfully sipping tea and
eating cookies,' Yusef Salaam's mother reminded readers of the
Amsterdam News. 'The first thing you do in the United States of
America when a white woman is raped is round up a bunch of black
youths, and I think that's what happened here,' the Reverend Calvin

O. Butts III of the Abyssinian Baptist Church in Harlem told the *New York Times*. 'You going to arrest me now because I said the jogger's name?' Gary Byrd asked rhetorically on his WLIB show, and was quoted by Edwin Diamond in *New York* magazine:

> I mean, she's obviously a public figure, and a very mysterious one, I might add. Well, it's a funny place we live in called America, and should we be surprised that they're up to their usual tricks? It was a trick that got us here in the first place.

This reflected one of the problems with not naming this victim: she was in fact named all the time. Everyone in the courthouse, everyone who worked for a paper or a television station or who followed the case for whatever professional reason, knew her name. She was referred to by name in all court records and in all court proceedings. She was named, in the days immediately following the attack, on some local television stations. She was also routinely named – and this was part of the difficulty, part of what led to a damaging self-righteousness among those who did not name her and to an equally damaging embattlement among those who did – in Manhattan's black-owned newspapers, the *Amsterdam News* and the *City Sun*, and she was named as well on WLIB, the Manhattan radio station owned by a black partnership that included Percy Sutton and, until 1985, when he transferred his stock to his son, Mayor Dinkins.

That the victim in this case was identified on Centre Street and north of 96th Street but not in between made for a certain cognitive dissonance, especially since the names of even the juvenile suspects had been released by the police and the press before any suspect had been arraigned, let alone indicted. 'The police normally withhold the names of minors who are accused of crimes,' the *Times* explained (actually the police normally withhold the names of accused 'juveniles', or minors under age sixteen, but not of minors sixteen or seventeen), 'but officials said they made public the names of the youths charged in the attack on the woman because of the seriousness of the incident.' There seemed a debatable point here, the question of whether 'the seriousness of the incident' might not have in fact seemed a compelling reason to avoid any appearance of a rush to judgment by preserving the anonymity of a juvenile suspect; one of the names released by the police and published in the *Times* was of a fourteen-year-old who was ultimately not indicted.

There were, early on, certain aspects of this case that seemed not well handled by the police and prosecutors, and others that seemed not well handled by the press. It would seem to have been tactically unwise, since New York State law requires that a parent or guardian be present when children under sixteen are questioned, for police to continue the interrogation of Yusef Salaam, then fifteen, on the grounds that his Transit Authority bus pass said he was sixteen, while his mother was kept waiting outside. It would seem to have been unwise for Linda Fairstein, the assistant district attorney in charge of Manhattan sex crimes, to ignore, at the precinct house, the mother's assertion that the son was fifteen, and later to suggest, in court, that the boy's age had been unclear to her because the mother had used the word 'minor'.

It would also seem to have been unwise for Linda Fairstein to tell David Nocenti, the assistant U.S. Attorney who was paired with Yusef Salaam in a 'Big Brother' program and who had come to the precinct house at the mother's request, that he had 'no legal standing' there and that she would file a complaint with his supervisors. It would seem in this volatile a case imprudent of the police to follow their normal procedure by presenting Raymond Santana's initial statement in their own words, cop phrases that would predictably seem to some in the courtroom, as the expression of a fourteen-year-old held overnight and into the next afternoon for interrogation, unconvincing:

> On April 19, 1989, at approximately 20:30 hours, I was at the Taft Projects in the vicinity of 113th St and Madison Avenue. I was there with numerous friends . . . At approximately 21:00 hours, we all (myself and approximately 15 others) walked south on Madison Avenue to E. 110th Street, then walked westbound to Fifth Avenue. At Fifth Avenue and 110th Street, we met up with an additional group of approximately 15 other males, who also entered Central Park with us at that location with the intent to rob cyclists and joggers . . .

In a case in which most of the defendants had made videotaped statements admitting at least some role in the assault and rape, this less than meticulous attitude toward the gathering and dissemination of information seemed peculiar and self-defeating, the kind of pressured or unthinking standard procedure that could not only exacerbate the fears and angers and suspicions of conspiracy shared by many blacks but open what seemed, on the basis of the confessions, a conclusive case to the kind of doubt that would eventually keep juries out, in the trial of the first three defendants, ten days, and, in the trial of the next two defendants, twelve days. One of the reasons the jury in the first trial could not agree, *Manhattan Lawyer* reported in its October 1990 issue, was that one juror, Ronald Gold, remained 'deeply troubled by the discrepancies between the story [Antron] McCray tells on his videotaped statement and the prosecution's scenario':

> Why did McCray place the rape at the reservoir, Gold demanded, when all evidence indicated it happened at the 102 Street cross-drive? Why did McCray say the jogger was raped where she fell, when the prosecution said she'd been dragged 300 feet into the woods first? Why did McCray talk about having to hold her arms down, if she was found bound and gagged?
>
> The debate raged for the last two days, with jurors dropping in and out of Gold's acquittal [for McCray] camp . . .
>
> After the jurors watched McCray's video for the fifth time, Miranda [Rafael Miranda, another juror] knew it well enough to cite the time-code numbers imprinted at the bottom of the videotape as he rebuffed Gold's arguments with specific statements from McCray's own lips. [McCray, on the videotape, after admitting that he had held the victim by her left arm as her clothes were pulled off, volunteered that he had 'got on top' of her, and said that he had rubbed against her without an erection 'so everybody would . . . just know I did it'.] The pressure on Gold was mounting. Three jurors agree that it was evident Gold, worn down perhaps by his own displays of temper as much as anything else, capitulated out of exhaustion. While a bitter Gold told other jurors he felt terrible about ultimately giving in, Brueland [Harold Brueland, another juror who had for a time favored acquittal for McCray] believes it was all part of the process.

'I'd like to tell Ronnie someday that nervous exhaustion is an element built into the court system. They know that,' Brueland says of court officials. 'They know we're only going to be able to take it for so long. It's just a matter of, you know, who's got the guts to stick with it.'

So fixed were the emotions provoked by this case that the idea that there could have been, for even one juror, even a moment's doubt in the state's case, let alone the kind of doubt that could be sustained over ten days, seemed, to many in the city, bewildering, almost unthinkable: the attack on the jogger had by then passed into narrative, and the narrative was about confrontation, about what Governor Cuomo had called 'the ultimate shriek of alarm', about what was wrong with the city and about its solution. What was wrong with the city had been identified, and its names were Raymond Santana, Yusef Salaam, Antron McCray, Kharey Wise, Kevin Richardson, and Steve Lopez. 'They never could have thought of it as they raged through Central Park, tormenting and ruining people,' Bob Herbert wrote in the News after the verdicts came in on the first three defendants.

> There was no way it could have crossed their vicious minds. Running with the pack, they would have scoffed at the very idea. They would have laughed.
>
> And yet it happened. In the end, Yusef Salaam, Antron McCray and Raymond Santana were nailed by a woman.
>
> Elizabeth Lederer stood in the courtroom and watched Saturday night as the three were hauled off to jail ... At times during the trial, she looked about half the height of the long and lanky Salaam, who sneered at her from the witness stand. Salaam was apparently too dumb to realize that Lederer – this petite, soft-spoken, curly-haired prosecutor – was the jogger's avenger ...
>
> You could tell that her thoughts were elsewhere, that she was thinking about the jogger.
>
> You could tell that she was thinking: I did it.
>
> I did it for you.

Do this in remembrance of me: the solution, then, or so such pervasive fantasies suggested, was to partake of the symbolic body and blood of The Jogger, whose idealization was by this point complete, and was rendered, significantly, in details stressing her 'difference', or superior class. The Jogger was someone who wore, according to *Newsday*, 'a light gold chain around her slender neck' as well as, according to the *News*, a 'modest' gold ring and 'a thin sheen' of lipstick. The Jogger was someone who would not, according to the *Post*, 'even dignify her alleged attackers with a glance'. The Jogger was someone who spoke, according to the *News*, in accents 'suited to boardrooms', accents that might therefore seem 'foreign to many native New Yorkers'. In her first appearance on the witness stand she had been subjected, the *Times* noted, 'to questions that most people do not have to answer publicly during their lifetimes', principally about her use of a diaphragm on the Sunday preceding the attack, and had answered these questions, according to an editorial in the *News*, with an 'indomitable dignity' that had taught the city a lesson 'about courage and class'.

This emphasis on perceived refinements of character and of manner and of taste tended to distort and to flatten, and ultimately to suggest not the actual victim of an actual crime but a fictional character of a slightly earlier period, the well-brought-up virgin who briefly graces the city with her presence and receives in turn a taste of 'real life'. The defendants, by contrast, were seen as incapable of appreciating these marginal distinctions, ignorant of both the norms and accoutrements of middle-class life. 'Did you have jogging clothes on?' Elizabeth Lederer asked Yusef Salaam, by way of trying to discredit his statement that he had gone into the park that night only to 'walk around'. Did he have 'jogging clothes', did he have 'sports equipment', did he have 'a bicycle'. A pernicious nostalgia had come to permeate the case, a longing for the New York that had seemed for a while to be about 'sports equipment', about getting and spending rather than about having and not having: the reason that this victim must not be named was so that she could go unrecognized, it was astonishingly said, by Jerry Nachman, the editor of the *New York Post*, and then by others who seemed to find in this a particular resonance, to Bloomingdale's.

*   *   *

Some New York stories involving young middle-class white women do not make it to the editorial pages, or even necessarily to the front pages. In April 1990, a young middle-class white woman named Laurie Sue Rosenthal, raised in an Orthodox Jewish household and at age twenty-nine still living with her parents in Jamaica, Queens, happened to die, according to the coroner's report, from the accidental toxicity of Darvocet in combination with alcohol, in an apartment at 36 East 68th Street in Manhattan. The apartment belonged to the man she had been, according to her parents, seeing for about a year, a minor city assistant commissioner named Peter Franconeri. Peter Franconeri, who was at the time in charge of elevator and boiler inspections for the Buildings Department and married to someone else, wrapped Laurie Sue Rosenthal's body in a blanket; placed it, along with her handbag and ID, outside the building with the trash; and went to his office at 60 Hudson Street. At some point an anonymous call was made to 911. Franconeri was identified only after Laurie Sue Rosenthal's parents gave the police his beeper number, which they found in her address book. According to *Newsday*, which covered the story more extensively than the *News*, the *Post*, or the *Times*,

> Initial police reports indicated that there were no visible wounds on Rosenthal's body. But Rosenthal's mother, Ceil, said yesterday that the family was told the autopsy revealed two 'unexplained bruises' on her daughter's body.
>
> Larry and Ceil Rosenthal said those findings seemed to support their suspicions that their daughter was upset because they received a call from their daughter at 3 A.M. Thursday 'saying that he had beaten her up'. The family reported the conversation to police.
>
> 'I told her to get into a cab and get home,' Larry Rosenthal said yesterday. 'The next I heard was two detectives telling me terrible things.'
>
> 'The ME [medical examiner] said the bruises did not constitute a beating but they were going to examine them further,' Ceil Rosenthal said.

'There were some minor bruises,' a spokeswoman for the Office of the Chief Medical Examiner told *Newsday* a few days later, but the bruises 'did not in any way contribute to her death'. This is worth rerunning: A young woman calls her parents at three in the morning, 'distraught'. She says that she has been beaten up. A few hours later, on East 68th Street between Madison and Park avenues, a few steps from Porthault and Pratesi and Armani and Saint Laurent and the Westbury Hotel, at a time of day in this part of New York 10021 when Jim Buck's dog trainers are assembling their morning packs and Henry Kravis's Bentley is idling outside his Park Avenue apartment and the construction crews are clocking in over near the Frick at the multimillion-dollar houses under reconstruction for Bill Cosby and for the owner of The Limited, this young middle-class white woman's body, showing bruises, gets put out with the trash.

'Everybody got upside down because of who he was,' an unidentified police officer later told Jim Dwyer of *Newsday*, referring to the man who put the young woman out with the trash. 'If it had happened to anyone else, nothing would have come of it. A summons would have been issued and that would have been the end of it.' In fact nothing did come of the death of Laurie Sue Rosenthal, which might have seemed a natural tabloid story but failed, on several levels, to catch the local imagination. For one thing she could not be trimmed into the role of the preferred tabloid victim, who is conventionally presented as fate's random choice (Laurie Sue Rosenthal had, for whatever reason, taken the Darvocet instead of a taxi home, her parents reported treatment for a previous Valium dependency, she could be presumed to have known over the course of a year that Franconeri was married and yet continued to see him); for another, she seemed not to have attended an expensive school or to have been employed in a glamour industry (no Ivy Grad, no Wall Street Exec), which made it hard to cast her as part of 'what makes this city so vibrant and so great'.

In August 1990, Peter Franconeri pled guilty to a misdemeanor, the unlawful removal of a body, and was sentenced by Criminal Court judge Peter Benitez to seventy-five hours of community service. This was neither surprising nor much of a story (only twenty-three lines even in *Newsday*, on page twenty-nine of the city edition), and the case's lenient resolution was for many people a kind of relief. The district attorney's office had asked for 'some incarceration', the amount usually described as a 'touch', but no one wanted, it was said, to crucify the guy: Peter Franconeri was somebody who knew a lot of people, understood how to live in the city, who had for example not only the apartment on East 68th Street between Madison and Park but a house in Southampton and who also understood that putting a body outside with the trash was nothing to get upside down about, if it was handled right. Such understandings may in fact have been the city's true 'ultimate shriek of alarm', but it was not a shriek the city wanted to recognize.

2

Perhaps the most arresting collateral news to surface, during the first few days after the attack on the Central Park jogger, was that a significant number of New Yorkers apparently believed the city sufficiently well-ordered to incorporate Central Park into their evening fitness schedules. 'Prudence' was defined, even after the attack, as 'staying south of 90th Street', or having 'an awareness that you need to think about planning your routes', or, in the case of one woman interviewed by the *Times*, deciding to quit her daytime job (she was a lawyer) because she was 'tired of being stuck out there, running later and later at night'. 'I don't think there's a runner who couldn't describe the silky, gliding feeling you get running at night,' an editor of *Runner's World* told the *Times*. 'You see less of what's around you and you become centered on your running.'

The notion that Central Park at night might be a good place to 'see less of what's around you' was recent. There were two reasons why Frederick Law Olmsted and Calvert Vaux, when they devised their winning entry in the 1858 competition for a Central Park design, decided to sink the transverse roads below grade level. One reason, the most often cited, was aesthetic, a recognition on the part of the designers that the four crossings specified by the terms of the competition, at 65th, 79th, 85th, and 97th streets, would intersect the sweep of the landscape, be 'at variance with those agreeable sentiments which we should wish the park to inspire'. The other reason, which appears to have been equally compelling, had to do with security. The problem with grade-level crossings, Olmsted and Vaux wrote in their 'Greensward' plan, would be this:

> The transverse roads will . . . have to be kept open, while the park proper will be useless for any good purpose after dusk; for experience has shown that even in London, with its admirable police arrangements, the public cannot be assured safe transit through large open spaces of ground after nightfall.
>
> These public throughfares will then require to be well-lighted at the sides, and, to restrain marauders pursued by the police from escaping into the obscurity of the park, strong fences or walls, six or eight feet high, will be necessary.

The park, in other words, was seen from its conception as intrinsically dangerous after dark, a place of 'obscurity', 'useless for any good purpose', a refuge only for 'marauders'. The parks of Europe closed at nightfall, Olmsted noted in his 1882 pamphlet *The Spoils of the Park: With a Few Leaves from the Deep-laden Note-books of 'A Wholly Unpractical Man'*, 'but one surface road is kept open across Hyde Park, and the superintendent of the Metropolitan Police told me that a man's chances of being garrotted or robbed were, because of the facilities for concealment to be found in the Park, greater in passing at night along this road than anywhere else in London.'

In the high pitch of the initial 'jogger' coverage, suggesting as it did a city overtaken by animals, this pragmatic approach to urban living gave way to a more ideal construct, one in which New York either had once been or should be 'safe', and now, as in Governor Cuomo's 'none of us is safe', was not. It was time, accordingly, to 'take it back', time to 'say no'; time, as David Dinkins would put it during his campaign for the mayoralty in the summer of 1989, to 'draw the line'. What the line was to be drawn against was 'crime', an abstract, a free-floating specter that could be dispelled by certain acts of personal affirmation, by the kind of moral rearmament that later figured in Mayor Dinkins's plan to revitalize the city by initiating weekly 'Tuesday Night Out Against Crime' rallies.

By going into the park at night, Tom Wicker wrote in the *Times*, the victim in this case had 'affirmed the primacy of freedom over fear'. A week after the assault, Susan Chace suggested on the op-ed page of the *Times* that readers walk into the park at night and join hands. 'A woman can't run in the park at an offbeat time,' she wrote. 'Accept it, you say. I can't. It shouldn't be like this in New York City, in 1989, in spring.' Ronnie Eldridge also suggested that readers walk into the park at night, but to light candles. 'Who are we that we allow ourselves to be chased out of the most magnificent part of our city?' she asked, and also: 'If we give up the park, what are we supposed to do: fall back to Columbus Avenue and plant grass?' This was interesting, suggesting as it did that the city's not inconsiderable problems could be solved by the willingness of its citizens to hold or draw some line, to 'say no'; in other words that a reliance on certain magical gestures could affect the city's fate.

The insistent sentimentalization of experience, which is to say the encouragement of such reliance, is not new in New York. A preference for broad strokes, for the distortion and flattening of character and the reduction of events to narrative, has been for well over a hundred years the heart of the way the city presents itself: Lady Liberty, huddled masses, ticker-tape parades, heroes, gutters, bright lights, broken hearts, 8 million stories in the naked city; 8 million stories and all the same story, each devised to obscure not only the city's actual tensions of race and class but also, more significantly, the civic and commercial arrangements that rendered those tensions irreconcilable.

Central Park itself was such a 'story', an artificial pastoral in the nineteenth-century English romantic tradition, conceived, during a decade when the population of Manhattan would increase by 58 percent, as a civic project that would allow the letting of contracts and the employment of voters on a scale rarely before undertaken in New York. Ten million cartloads of dirt would need to be shifted during the twenty years of its construction. Four to five million trees and shrubs would need to be planted, half a million cubic yards of topsoil imported, 114 miles of ceramic pipe laid.

Nor need the completion of the park mean the end of the possibilities: in 1870, once William Marcy Tweed had revised the city charter and invented his Department of Public Parks, new roads could be built whenever jobs were needed. Trees could be dug up, and replanted. Crews could be set loose to prune, to clear, to hack at will. Frederick Law Olmsted, when he objected, could be overridden, and finally eased out. 'A "delegation" from a great political organization called on me by appointment,' Olmsted wrote in *The Spoils of the Park*, recalling the conditions under which he had worked:

> After introductions and handshakings, a circle was formed, and a gentleman stepped before me, and said, 'We know how much pressed you must be ... but at your convenience our association would like to have you determine what share of your patronage we can expect, and make suitable arrangements for our using it. We will take the liberty to suggest, sir, that there could be no more convenient way than that you should send us our due quota of tickets, if you will please, sir, in this form, *leaving us to fill in the name.*' Here a packet of printed tickets was produced, from which I took one at random. It was a blank appointment and bore the signature of Mr Tweed.

> As superintendent of the Park, I once received in six days more than seven thousand letters of advice as to appointments, nearly all from men in office ... I have heard a candidate for a magisterial office in the city addressing from my doorsteps a crowd of such advice-bearers, telling them that I was bound to give them employment, and suggesting plainly, that, if I was slow about it, a rope round my neck might serve to lessen my reluctance to take good counsel. I have had a dozen men force their way into my house before I had risen from bed on a Sunday morning, and some break into my drawing room in their eagerness to deliver letters of advice.

Central Park, then, for its underwriters if not for Olmstead, was about contracts and concrete and kickbacks, about pork, but the sentimentalization that worked to obscure the pork, the 'story', had to do with certain dramatic contrasts, or extremes, that were believed to characterize life in this as in no other city. These 'contrasts', which have since become the very spine of the New York narrative, appeared early on: Philip Hone, the mayor of New York in 1826 and 1827, spoke in 1843 of a city 'overwhelmed with population, and

where the two extremes of costly luxury in living, expensive establishments and improvident wastes are presented in daily and hourly
contrast with squalid mixing and hapless destruction'. Given this
narrative, Central Park could be and ultimately would be seen the
way Olmsted himself saw it, as an essay in democracy, a social experiment meant to socialize a new immigrant population and to amelior-
ate the perilous separation of rich and poor. It was the duty and the
interest of the city's privileged class, Olmsted had suggested some
years before he designed Central Park, to 'get up parks, gardens,
music, dancing schools, reunions which will be so attractive as to
force into contact the good and the bad, the gentleman and the
rowdy'.

The notion that the interests of the 'gentleman' and the 'rowdy'
might be at odds did not intrude: then as now, the preferred narrative
worked to veil actual conflict, to cloud the extent to which the
condition of being rich was predicated upon the continued neediness
of a working class; to confirm the responsible stewardship of 'the
gentleman' and to forestall the possibility of a self-conscious, or poli-
ticized, proletariat. Social and economic phenomena, in this narrative, were personalized. Politics were exclusively electoral. Problems
were best addressed by the emergence and election of 'leaders', who
could in turn inspire the individual citizen to 'participate', or 'make
a difference'. 'Will you help?' Mayor Dinkins asked New Yorkers, in
a September 1990 address from St Patrick's Cathedral intended as a
response to the 'New York crime wave' stories then leading the news.
'Do you care? Are you ready to become part of the solution?'

'Stay,' Governor Cuomo urged the same New Yorkers. 'Believe.
Participate. Don't give up.' Manhattan borough president Ruth
Messinger, at the dedication of a school flagpole, mentioned the
importance of 'getting involved' and 'participating', or 'pitching in
to put the shine back on the Big Apple'. In a discussion of the popular
'New York' stories written between 1902 and 1910 by William Sidney
Porter, or 'O. Henry', William R. Taylor of the State University of
New York at Stony Brook spoke of the way in which these stories,
with their 'focus on individuals' plights', their 'absence of social or
political implications' and 'ideological neutrality', provided 'a
miraculous form of social glue':

These sentimental accounts of relations between classes in the city have a specific historical meaning: empathy without political compassion. They reduce the scale of human suffering to what atomized individuals endure as their plucky, sad lives were recounted week after week for almost a decade . . . their sentimental reading of oppression, class differences, human suffering, and affection helped create a new language for interpreting the city's complex society, a language that began to replace the threadbare moralism that New Yorkers inherited from 19th-century readings of the city. This language localized suffering in particular moments and confined it to particular occasions; it smoothed over differences because it could be read almost the same way from either end of the social scale.

Stories in which terrible crimes are inflicted on innocent victims, offering as they do a similarly sentimental reading of class differences and human suffering, a reading that promises both resolution and retribution, have long performed as the city's endorphins, a built-in source of natural morphine working to blur the edges of real and to a great extent insoluble problems. What is singular about New York, and remains virtually incomprehensible to people who live in less rigidly organized parts of the country, is the minimal level of comfort and opportunity its citizens have come to accept. The romantic capitalist pursuit of privacy and security and individual freedom, so taken for granted nationally, plays, locally, not much role. A city where virtually every impulse has been to stifle rather than to encourage normal competition, New York works, when it does work, not on a market economy but on little deals, payoffs, accommodations, *baksheesh*, arrangements that circumvent the direct exchange of goods and services and prevent what would be, in a competitive economy, the normal ascendance of the superior product.

There were in the five boroughs in 1990 only 581 supermarkets (a supermarket, as defined by the trade magazine *Progressive Grocer*, is a market that does an annual volume of $2 million), or, assuming a population of 8 million, one supermarket for every 13,769 citizens. Groceries, costing more than they should because of this absence of competition and also because of the proliferation of payoffs required to ensure this absence of competition (produce, we have come to understand, belongs to the Gambinos, and fish to the Lucheses and the Genoveses, and a piece of the construction of the market to each of the above, but keeping the door open belongs finally to the inspector here, the inspector there), are carried home or delivered, as if in Jakarta, by pushcart.

It has historically taken, in New York as if in Mexico City, ten years to process and specify and bid and contract and construct a new school; twenty or thirty years to build or, in the cases of Bruckner Boulevard and the West Side Highway, to not quite build a highway. A recent public scandal revealed that a batch of city-ordered Pap smears had gone unread for more than a year (in the developed world the Pap smear, a test for cervical cancer, is commonly read within a few days); what did not become a public scandal, what is still accepted as the way things are, is that even Pap smears ordered by Park Avenue gynecologists can go unread for several weeks.

Such resemblances to cities of the third world are in no way casual, or based on the 'color' of a polyglot population: these are all cities arranged primarily not to improve the lives of their citizens but to be labor-intensive, to accommodate, ideally at the subsistence level, since it is at the subsistence level that the work force is most apt to be captive and loyalty assured, a third-world population. In some ways New York's very attractiveness, its promises of opportunity and improved wages, its commitments as a city in the developed world, were what seemed destined to render it ultimately unworkable. Where the vitality of such cities in the less developed world had depended on their ability to guarantee low-cost labor and an absence of regulation, New York had historically depended instead on the constant welling up of new businesses, of new employers to replace those phased out, like the New York garment manufacturers who found it cheaper to make their clothes in Hong Kong or Kuala Lumpur or Taipei, by rising local costs.

It had been the old pattern of New York, supported by an expanding national economy, to lose one kind of business and gain another. It was the more recent error of New York to misconstrue this history of turnover as an indestructible resource, there to be taxed at will, there to be regulated whenever a dollar could be seen in doing so, there for the taking. By 1977, New York had lost some 600,000 jobs, most of them in manufacturing and in the kinds of small businesses that could no longer maintain their narrow profit margins inside the city. During the 'recovery' years, from 1977 until 1988, most of these jobs were indeed replaced, but in a potentially perilous way: of the 500,000 new jobs created, most were in the area most vulnerable to a downturn, that of financial and business services, and many of the rest in an area not only equally vulnerable to bad times but dispiriting to the city even in good, that of tourist and restaurant services.

The demonstration that many kinds of businesses were finding New York expendable had failed to prompt real efforts to make the city more competitive. Taxes grew still more punitive, regulation more Byzantine. Forty-nine thousand new jobs were created in New York's city agencies between 1983 and 1990, even as the services provided by those agencies were widely perceived to decline. Attempts at 'reform' typically tended to create more jobs: in 1988, in response to the length of time it was taking to build or repair a school, a new agency, the School Construction Authority, was formed. A New York City school, it was said, would now take only five years to build. The head of the School Construction Authority was to receive $145,000 a year and each of the three vice presidents $110,000 a year. An executive gym, with Nautilus equipment, was contemplated for the top floor of the agency's new headquarters at the International Design Center in Long Island City. Two years into this reform, the backlog on repairs to existing schools stood at 33,000 outstanding requests. 'To relieve the charity of friends of the support of a half-blind and half-witted man by employing him at the public expense as an inspector of cement may not be practical with reference to the permanent firmness of a wall,' Olmsted noted after his Central Park experience, 'while it is perfectly so with reference to the triumph of sound doctrine at an election.'

In fact the highest per capita taxes of any city in the United States (and, as anyone running a small business knows, the widest variety of taxes) provide, in New York, unless the citizen is prepared to cut a side deal here and there, only the continuing multiplication of regulations designed to benefit the contractors and agencies and unions with whom the regulators have cut their own deals. A kitchen appliance accepted throughout the rest of the United States as a basic postwar amenity, the in-sink garbage disposal unit, is for example

illegal in New York. Disposals, a city employee advised me, not only
encourage rats, and 'bacteria', presumably in a way that bags of
garbage sitting on the sidewalk do not ('Because it is,' I was told
when I asked how this could be), but also encourage people 'to put
their babies down them'.

On the one hand this illustrates how a familiar urban principle,
that of patronage (the more garbage there is to be collected, the
more garbage collectors can be employed), can be reduced, in the
bureaucratic wilderness that is any third-world city, to voodoo; on
the other it reflects this particular city's underlying criminal ethic, its
acceptance of graft and grift as the bedrock of every transaction.
'Garbage costs are outrageous,' an executive of Supermarkets General, which owns Pathmark, recently told *City Limits* about why the
chains preferred to locate in the suburbs. 'Every time you need to
hire a contractor, it's a problem.' The problem, however, is one
from which not only the contractor but everyone with whom the
contractor does business – a chain of direct or indirect patronage
extending deep into the fabric of the city – stands to derive one
or another benefit, which was one reason the death of a young
middle-class white woman in the East 68th Street apartment of the
assistant commissioner in charge of boiler and elevator inspections
flickered so feebly on the local attention span.

It was only within the transforming narrative of 'contrasts' that both
the essential criminality of the city and its related absence of civility
could become points of pride, evidence of 'energy': if you could make
it here you could make it anywhere, hello sucker, get smart. Those
who did not get the deal, who bought retail, who did not know what
it took to get their electrical work signed off, were dismissed as
provincials, bridge-and-tunnels, out-of-towners who did not have
what it took not to get taken. 'Every tourist's nightmare became a
reality for a Maryland couple over the weekend when the husband
was beaten and robbed on Fifth Avenue in front of Trump Tower,'
began a story in the *New York Post* during the summer of 1990.
'Where do you think we're from, Iowa?' the prosecutor who took
Robert Chambers's statement said on videotape by way of indicating
that he doubted Chambers's version of Jennifer Levin's death. 'They

go after poor people like you from out of town, they prey on the tourists,' a clerk explained in the West 46th Street computer store where my husband and I had taken refuge to escape three muggers. My husband said that we lived in New York. 'That's why they didn't get you,' the clerk said, effortlessly incorporating this change in the data. 'That's how you could move fast.'

The narrative comforts us, in other words, with the assurance that the world is knowable, even flat, and New York its center, its motor, its dangerous but vital 'energy'. 'Family in Fatal Mugging Loved New York' was the *Times* headline on a story following the September 1990 murder, in the Seventh Avenue IND station, of a twenty-two-year-old tourist from Utah. The young man, his parents, his brother, and his sister-in-law had attended the U.S. Open and were reportedly on their way to dinner at a Moroccan restaurant downtown. 'New York, to them, was the greatest place in the world,' a family friend from Utah was quoted as having said. Since the narrative requires that the rest of the country provide a dramatic contrast to New York, the family's hometown in Utah was characterized by the *Times* as a place where 'life revolves around the orderly rhythms of Brigham Young University' and 'there is only about one murder a year'. The town was in fact Provo, where Gary Gilmore shot the motel manager, both in life and in *The Executioner's Song*. 'She loved New York, she just loved it,' a friend of the assaulted jogger told the *Times* after the attack. 'I think she liked the fast pace, the competitiveness.'

New York, the *Times* concluded, 'invigorated' the jogger, 'matched her energy level'. At a time when the city lay virtually inert, when forty thousand jobs had been wiped out in the financial markets and former traders were selling shirts at Bergdorf Goodman for Men, when the rate of mortgage delinquencies had doubled, when 50 or 60 million square feet of office space remained unrented (60 million square feet of unrented office space is the equivalent of fifteen darkened World Trade Towers) and even prime commercial blocks on Madison Avenue in the Seventies were boarded up, empty; at a time when the money had dropped out of all the markets and the Europeans who had lent the city their élan and their capital during the eighties had moved on, vanished to more cheerful venues, this notion of the city's 'energy' was sedative, as was the commandeering of 'crime' as the city's central problem.

3

The extent to which the October 1987 crash of the New York financial markets damaged the illusions of infinite recovery and growth
on which the city had operated during the 1980s had been at first
hard to apprehend. 'Ours is a time of New York ascendant,' the
New York City Commission on the Year 2000, created during the
mayoralty of Edward Koch to reflect the best thinking of the city's
various business and institutional establishments, had declared in its
1987 report. 'The city's economy is stronger than it has been in
decades, and is driven both by its own resilience and by the national
economy; New York is more than ever the international capital of
finance, and the gateway to the American economy.'

And then, its citizens had come gradually to understand, it was
not. This perception that something was 'wrong' in New York had
been insidious, a slow-onset illness at first noticeable only in periods
of temporary remission. Losses that might have seemed someone
else's problem (or even comeuppance) as the markets were in their
initial 1987 free-fall, and that might have seemed more remote still
as the markets regained the appearance of strength, had come imperceptibly but inexorably to alter the tone of daily life. By April of
1990, people who lived in and around New York were expressing,
in interviews with the *Times,* considerable anguish and fear that
they did so: 'I feel very resentful that I've lost a lot of flexibility in my
life,' one said. 'I often wonder, "Am I crazy for coming here?"' 'People
feel a sense of impending doom about what may happen to them,' a
clinical psychologist said. People were 'frustrated', 'feeling absolutely
desolate', 'trapped', 'angry', 'terrified', and 'on the verge of panic'.

It was a panic that seemed in many ways specific to New York,
and inexplicable outside it. Even later, when the troubles of New
York had become a common theme, Americans from less depressed
venues had difficulty comprehending the nature of those troubles,
and tended to attribute them, as New Yorkers themselves had come
to do, to 'crime'. 'Escape From New York' was the headline on the
front page of the *New York Post* on September 10, 1990. 'Rampaging
Crime Wave Has 59% of Residents Terrified. Most Would Get Out
of the City, Says Time/CNN Poll.' This poll appeared in the edition

of *Time* dated September 17, 1990, which carried the cover legend 'The Rotting of the Big Apple'. 'Reason: a surge of drugs and violent crime that government officials seem utterly unable to combat,' the story inside explained. Columnists referred, locally, to 'this sewer of a city'. The *Times* ran a plaintive piece about the snatch of Elizabeth Rohatyn's Hermès handbag outside Arcadia, a restaurant on East 62nd Street that had for a while seemed the very heart of the New York everyone now missed, the New York where getting and spending could take place without undue reference to having and not having, the duty-free New York; that this had occurred to the wife of Felix Rohatyn, who was widely perceived to have saved the city from its fiscal crisis in the midseventies, seemed to many a clarion irony.

This question of crime was tricky. There were in fact eight American cities with higher homicide rates, and twelve with higher overall crime rates. Crime had long been taken for granted in the less affluent parts of the city, and had become in the midseventies, as both unemployment and the costs of maintaining property rose and what had once been functioning neighborhoods were abandoned and burned and left to whoever claimed them, endemic. 'In some poor neighborhoods, crime became almost a way of life,' Jim Sleeper, an editor at *Newsday* and the author of *The Closest of Strangers: Liberalism and the Politics of Race in New York*, noted in his discussion of the social disintegration that occurred during this period:

> . . . a subculture of violence with complex bonds of utility and affection within families and the larger, 'law-abiding' community. Struggling merchants might 'fence' stolen goods, for example, thus providing quick cover and additional incentive for burglaries and robberies; the drug economy became more vigorous, reshaping criminal lifestyles and tormenting the loyalties of families and friends. A walk down even a reasonably busy street in a poor, minority neighborhood at high noon could become an unnerving journey into a landscape eerie and grim.

What seemed markedly different a decade later, what made crime a 'story', was that the more privileged, and especially the more privileged white, citizens of New York had begun to feel unnerved at high noon in even their own neighborhoods. Although New York City Police Department statistics suggested that white New Yorkers were not actually in increased mortal danger (the increase in homicides between 1977 and 1989, from 1,557 to 1,903, was entirely among what the NYPD classified as Hispanic, Asian, and black victims; the number of white murder victims had steadily declined, from 361 in 1977 to 227 in 1984 and 190 in 1989), the apprehension of such danger, exacerbated by street snatches and muggings and the quite useful sense that the youth in the hooded sweatshirt with his hands jammed in his pockets might well be a predator, had become general. These more privileged New Yorkers now felt unnerved not only on the street, where the necessity for evasive strategies had become an exhausting constant, but in even the most insulated and protected apartment buildings. As the residents of such buildings, the owners of twelve- and sixteen- and twenty-four-room apartments, watched the potted ficus trees disappear from outside their doors and the graffiti appear on their limestone walls and the smashed safety glass from car windows get swept off their sidewalks, it had become increasingly easy to imagine the outcome of a confrontation between, say, the relief night doorman and six dropouts from Julia Richman High School on East 67th Street.

And yet those New Yorkers who had spoken to the *Times* in April of 1990 about their loss of flexibility, about their panic, their desolation, their anger, and their sense of impending doom, had not been talking about drugs, or crime, or any of the city's more publicized and to some extent inflated ills. These were people who did not for the most part have twelve- and sixteen-room apartments and doormen and the luxury of projected fears. These people were talking instead about an immediate fear, about money, about the vertiginous plunge in the value of their houses and apartments and condominiums, about the possibility or probability of foreclosure and loss; about, implicitly, their fears of being left, like so many they saw every day, below the line, out in the cold, on the street.

This was a climate in which many of the questions that had seized the city's attention in 1987 and 1988, for example that of whether Mortimer Zuckerman should be 'allowed' to build two fifty-nine-story office towers on the site of what is now the Coliseum, seemed in retrospect wistful, the baroque concerns of better times. 'There's no way anyone would make a sane judgment to go into the ground now,' a vice president at Cushman and Wakefield told the *New York Observer* about the delay in the Coliseum project, which had in fact lost its projected major tenant, Salomon Brothers, shortly after Black Monday, 1987. 'It would be suicide. You're better off sitting in a tub of water and opening your wrists.' Such fears were, for a number of reasons, less easy to incorporate into the narrative than the fear of crime.

The imposition of a sentimental, or false, narrative on the disparate and often random experience that constitutes the life of a city or a country means, necessarily, that much of what happens in that city or country will be rendered merely illustrative, a series of set pieces, or performance opportunities. Mayor Dinkins could, in such a symbolic substitute for civic life, 'break the boycott' (the Flatbush boycott organized to mobilize resentment of Korean merchants in black neighborhoods) by purchasing a few dollars' worth of produce from a Korean grocer on Church Avenue. Governor Cuomo could 'declare war on crime' by calling for five thousand additional police; Mayor Dinkins could 'up the ante' by calling for sixty-five hundred. 'White slut comes into the park looking for the African man,' a black woman could say, her voice loud but still conversational, in the corridor outside the courtroom where, during the summer of 1990, the first three defendants in the Central Park attack, Antron McCray, Yusef Salaam, and Raymond Santana, were tried on charges of attempted murder, assault, sodomy, and rape. 'Boyfriend beats shit out of her, they blame it on our boys,' the woman could continue, and then, referring to a young man with whom the victim had at one time split the cost of an apartment: 'How about the roommate, anybody test his semen? No. He's white. They don't do it to each other.'

Glances could then flicker among those reporters and producers and courtroom sketch artists and photographers and cameramen and techs and summer interns who assembled daily at 111 Centre Street. Cellular phones could be picked up, a show of indifference. Small talk could be exchanged with the marshals, a show of solidarity. The woman could then raise her voice: 'White folk, all of them are devils, even those that haven't been born yet, they are *devils*. Little *demons*. I don't understand these devils, I guess they think this is *their court*.' The reporters could gaze beyond her, faces blank, no eye contact, a more correct form of hostility and also more lethal. The woman could hold her ground but avert her eyes, letting her gaze fall on another black, in this instance a black *Daily News* columnist, Bob Herbert. 'You,' she could say. 'You are a *disgrace*. Go ahead. Line up there. Line up with the white folk. Look at them, lining up for their first-class seats while *my* people are downstairs behind *barricades* . . . kept behind barricades like *cattle* . . . not even allowed in the room to see their sons lynched . . . is that an *African* I see in that line? Or is that a *Negro*. Oh, oh, sorry, shush, white folk didn't know, he was *passing* . . .'

In a city in which grave and disrupting problems had become general – problems of not having, problems of not making it, problems that demonstrably existed, among the mad and the ill and the underequipped and the overwhelmed, with decreasing reference to color – the case of the Central Park jogger provided more than just a safe, or structured, setting in which various and sometimes only marginally related rages could be vented. 'This trial,' the *Daily News* announced on its editorial page one morning in July 1990, midway through the trial of the first three defendants, 'is about more than the rape and brutalization of a single woman. It is about the rape and the brutalization of a city. The jogger is a symbol of all that's wrong here. And all that's right, because she is nothing less than an inspiration.'

The *News* did not define the ways in which 'the rape and the brutalization of the city' manifested itself, nor was definition necessary: this was a city in which the threat or the fear of brutalization had become so immediate that citizens were urged to take up their own defense, to form citizen patrols or militia, as in Beirut. This was a city in which between twenty and thirty neighborhoods had already given over their protection, which was to say the right to determine who belonged in the neighborhood and who did not and what should be done about it, to the Guardian Angels. This was a city in which a Brooklyn vigilante group, which called itself Crack Busters and was said to be trying to rid its Bedford-Stuyvesant neighborhood of drugs, would before September was out 'settle an argument' by dousing with gasoline and setting on fire an abandoned van and the three homeless citizens inside. This was a city in which the *Times* would soon perceive, in the failing economy, 'a bright side for the city at large', the bright side being that while there was believed to have been an increase in the number of middle-income and upper-income families who wanted to leave the city, 'the slumping market is keeping many of those families in New York'.

In this city rapidly vanishing into the chasm between its actual life and its preferred narratives, what people said when they talked about the case of the Central Park jogger came to seem a kind of poetry, a way of expressing, without directly stating, different but equally volatile and similarly occult visions of the same disaster. One vision, shared by those who had seized upon the attack on the jogger as an exact representation of what was wrong with the city, was of a city systematically ruined, violated, raped by its underclass. The opposing vision, shared by those who had seized upon the arrest of the defendants as an exact representation of their own victimization, was of a city in which the powerless had been systematically ruined, violated, raped by the powerful. For so long as this case held the city's febrile attention, then, it offered a narrative for the city's distress, a frame in which the actual social and economic forces wrenching the city could be personalized and ultimately obscured.

Or rather it offered two narratives, mutually exclusive. Among a number of blacks, particularly those whose experience with or distrust of the criminal justice system was such that they tended to discount the fact that five of the six defendants had to varying degrees admitted taking part in the attack, and to focus instead on the absence of any supporting forensic evidence incontrovertibly linking this victim to these defendants, the case could be read as a confirmation not only of their victimization but of the white conspiracy they saw at the heart of that victimization. For the *Amsterdam News*, which did not veer automatically to the radical analysis (a typical issue in the fall of 1990 lauded the FBI for its minority recruiting and the Harlem National Guard for its high morale and readiness to go to the Gulf), the defendants could in this light be seen as victims of 'a political trial', of a 'legal lynching', of a case 'rigged from the very beginning' by the decision of 'the white press' that 'whoever was arrested and charged in this case of the attempted murder, rape and sodomy of a well-connected, bright, beautiful, and promising white woman was guilty, pure and simple'.

For Alton H. Maddox, Jr, the message to be drawn from the case was that the American criminal justice system, which was under any circumstances 'inherently and unabashedly racist', failed 'to function equitably at any level when a Black male is accused of raping a white female'. For others the message was more general, and worked to reinforce the fragile but functional mythology of a heroic black past, the narrative in which European domination could be explained as a direct and vengeful response to African superiority. 'Today the white man is faced head-on with what is happening on the Black Continent, Africa,' Malcolm X wrote.

> Look at the artifacts being discovered there, that are proving over and over again, how the black man had great, fine, sensitive civilizations before the white man was out of the caves. Below the Sahara, in the places where most of America's Negroes' foreparents were kidnapped, there is being unearthed some of the finest craftsmanship, sculpture and other objects, that has ever been seen by modern man. Some of these things now are on view in such places as New York City's Museum of Modern Art. Gold work of such fine tolerance and workmanship that it has no rival. Ancient objects produced by black hands ... refined by those black hands with results that no human hand today can equal.
>
> History has been so 'whitened' by the white man that even the black professors have known little more than the most ignorant black man about the talents and rich civilizations and cultures of the black man of millenniums ago ...

'Our proud African queen,' the Reverend Al Sharpton had said of Tawana Brawley's mother, Glenda Brawley: 'She stepped out of anonymity, stepped out of obscurity, and walked into history.' It was said in the corridors of the courthouse where Yusuf Salaam was tried that he carried himself 'like an African king'.

'It makes no difference anymore whether the attack on Tawana happened,' William Kunstler had told *New York Newsday* when the alleged rape and torture of Tawana Brawley by a varying number of white police officers seemed, as an actual prosecutable crime if not as a window on what people needed to believe, to have dematerialized. 'If her story was a concoction to prevent her parents from punishing her for staying out all night, that doesn't disguise the fact that a lot of young black women are treated the way she said she was treated.' The importance of whether or not the crime had occurred was, in this view, entirely resident in the crime's 'description', which was defined by Stanley Diamond in *The Nation* as 'a crime that did not occur' but was 'described with skill and controlled hysteria by the black actors as the epitome of degradation, a repellent model of what actually happens to too many black women'.

A good deal of what got said around the edges of the jogger case, in the corridors and on the call-in shows, seemed to derive exclusively from the suspicions of conspiracy increasingly entrenched among those who believe themselves powerless. A poll conducted in June of 1990 by the *New York Times* and WCBS-TV News determined that 77 percent of blacks polled believed either that it was 'true' or 'might possibly be true' (as opposed to 'almost certainly not true') that the government of the United States 'singles out and investigates black elected officials in order to discredit them in a way it doesn't do with white officials'. Sixty percent believed that it was true or might possibly be true that the government 'deliberately makes sure that drugs are easily available in poor black neighborhoods in order to harm black people'. Twenty-nine percent believed that it was true or might possibly be true that 'the virus which causes AIDS was deliberately created in a laboratory in order to infect black people'. In each case, the alternative response to 'true' or 'might possibly be true' was 'almost certainly not true', which might have seemed in itself to reflect a less than ringing belief in the absence of conspiracy. 'The conspiracy to destroy Black boys is very complex and interwoven,' Jawanza Kunjufu, a Chicago educational consultant, wrote in his *Countering the Conspiracy to Destroy Black Boys*, a 1982 pamphlet that has since been extended to three volumes.

> There are many contributors to the conspiracy, ranging from the very visible who are more obvious, to the less visible and silent partners who are more difficult to recognize.

Those people who adhere to the doctrine of white racism, imperialism, and white male supremacy are easier to recognize. Those people who actively promote drugs and gang violence are active conspirators, and easier to identify. What makes the conspiracy more complex are those people who do not plot together to destroy Black boys, but, through their indifference, perpetuate it. This passive group of conspirators consists of parents, educators, and white liberals who deny being racists, but through their silence allow institutional racism to continue.

For those who proceeded from the conviction that there was under way a conspiracy to destroy blacks, particularly black boys, a belief in the innocence of these defendants, a conviction that even their own statements had been rigged against them or wrenched from them, followed logically. It was in the corridors and on the call-in shows that the conspiracy got sketched in, in a series of fantasy details that conflicted not only with known facts but even with each other. It was said that the prosecution was withholding evidence that the victim had gone to the park to meet a drug dealer. It was said, alternately or concurrently, that the prosecution was withholding evidence that the victim had gone to the park to take part in a satanic ritual. It was said that the forensic photographs showing her battered body were not 'real' photographs, that 'they', the prosecution, had 'brought in some corpse for the pictures'. It was said that the young woman who appeared on the witness stand and identified herself as the victim was not the 'real' victim, that 'they' had in this case brought in an actress.

What was being expressed in each instance was the sense that secrets must be in play, that 'they', the people who had power in the courtroom, were in possession of information systematically withheld – since information itself was power – from those who did not have power. On the day the first three defendants were sentenced, C. Vernon Mason, who had formally entered the case in the penalty phase as Antron McCray's attorney, filed a brief that included the bewildering and untrue assertion that the victim's boyfriend, who had not at that time been called to testify, was black. That some whites jumped to engage this assertion on its own terms (the *Daily*

News columnist Gail Collins referred to it as Mason's 'slimiest argument of the hour – an announcement that the jogger had a black lover') tended only to reinforce the sense of racial estrangement that was the intended subtext of the assertion, which was without meaning or significance except in that emotional deep where whites are seen as conspiring in secret to sink blacks in misery. 'Just answer me, who got addicted?' I recall one black spectator asking another as they left the courtroom. 'I'll tell you who got addicted, the inner city got addicted.' He had with him a pamphlet that laid out a scenario in which the government had conspired to exterminate blacks by flooding their neighborhoods with drugs, a scenario touching all the familiar points, Laos, Cambodia, the Golden Triangle, the CIA, more secrets, more poetry.

'From the beginning I have insisted that this was not a racial case,' Robert Morgenthau, the Manhattan district attorney, said after the verdicts came in on the first jogger trial. He spoke of those who, in his view, wanted 'to divide the races and advance their own private agendas', and of how the city was 'ill-served' by those who had so 'sought to exploit' this case. 'We had hoped that the racial tensions surrounding the jogger trial would begin to dissipate soon after the jury arrived at a verdict,' a *Post* editorial began a few days later. The editorial spoke of an 'ugly claque of "activists"', of the 'divisive atmosphere' they had created, and of the anticipation with which the city's citizens had waited for 'mainstream black leaders' to step forward with praise for the way in which the verdicts had brought New York 'back from the brink of criminal chaos':

> Alas, in the jogger case, the wait was in vain. Instead of praise for a verdict which demonstrated that sometimes criminals are caught and punished, New Yorkers heard charlatans like the Rev. Al Sharpton claim the case was fixed. They heard that C. Vernon Mason, one of the engineers of the Tawana Brawley hoax – the attorney who thinks Mayor Dinkins wears 'too many yarmulkes' – was planning to appeal the verdicts . . .

To those whose preferred view of the city was of an inherently dynamic and productive community ordered by the natural play of its conflicting elements, enriched, as in Mayor Dinkins's 'gorgeous mosaic', by its very 'contrasts', this case offered a number of useful elements. There was the confirmation of 'crime' as the canker corroding the life of the city. There was, in the random and feral evening described by the East Harlem attackers and the clear innocence of and damage done to the Upper East Side and Wall Street victim, an eerily exact and conveniently personalized representation of what the *Daily News* had called 'the rape and the brutalization of a city'. Among the reporters on this case, whose own narrative conventions involved 'hero cops' and 'brave prosecutors' going hand to hand against 'crime' (the 'Secret Agony of Jogger DA', we learned in the *Post* a few days after the verdicts in the first trial, was that 'Brave Prosecutor's Marriage Failed as She Put Rapists Away'), there seemed an unflagging enthusiasm for the repetition and reinforcement of these elements, and an equally unflagging resistance, even hostility, to exploring the point of view of the defendants' families and friends and personal or political allies (or, as they were called in news reports, the 'supporters') who gathered daily at the other end of the corridor from the courtroom.

This seemed curious. Criminal cases are widely regarded by American reporters as windows on the city or culture in which they take place, opportunities to enter not only households but parts of the culture normally closed, and yet this was a case in which indifference to the world of the defendants extended even to the reporting of names and occupations. Yusuf Salaam's mother, who happened to be young and photogenic and to have European features, was pictured so regularly that she and her son became the instantly recognizable 'images' of Jogger One, but even then no one got her name quite right. For a while in the papers she was 'Cheroney', or sometimes 'Cheron*ay*', McEllhonor, then she became Cheroney McEllhonor Salaam. After she testified, the spelling of her first name was corrected to 'Sharonne', although, since the byline on a piece she wrote for the *Amsterdam News* spelled it differently, 'Sharrone', this may have been another misunderstanding. Her occupation was frequently given as 'designer' (later, after her son's conviction, she went to work as a paralegal for William Kunstler), but no one seemed to take this seriously enough to say what she designed or for whom; not until after she testified, when *Newsday* reported her testimony that on the evening of her son's arrest she had arrived at the precinct house late because she was an instructor at the Parsons School of Design, did the notion of 'designer' seem sufficiently concrete to suggest an actual occupation.

The Jogger One defendants were referred to repeatedly in the news columns of the *Post* as 'thugs'. The defendants and their families were often said by reporters to be 'sneering'. (The reporters, in turn, were said at the other end of the corridor to be 'smirking'.) 'We don't have nearly so strong a question as to the guilt or innocence of the defendants as we did at Bensonhurst,' a *Newsday* reporter covering the first jogger trial said to the *New York Observer*, well before the closing arguments, by way of explaining why *Newsday*'s coverage may have seemed less extensive on this trial than on the Bensonhurst trials. 'There is not a big question as to what happened in Central Park that night. Some details are missing, but it's fairly clear who did what to whom.'

In fact this came close to the heart of it: that it seemed, on the basis of the videotaped statements, fairly clear who had done what to whom was precisely the case's liberating aspect, the circumstance that enabled many of the city's citizens to say and think what they might otherwise have left unexpressed. Unlike other recent high visibility cases in New York, unlike Bensonhurst and unlike Howard Beach and unlike Bernhard Goetz, here was a case in which the issue not exactly of race but of an increasingly visible underclass could be confronted by the middle class, both white and black, without guilt. Here was a case that gave this middle class a way to transfer and express what had clearly become a growing and previously inadmissible rage with the city's disorder, with the entire range of ills and uneasy guilts that came to mind in a city where entire families slept in the discarded boxes in which new Sub-Zero refrigerators were delivered, at twenty-six hundred per, to more affluent families. Here was also a case, most significantly, in which even that transferred rage could be transferred still further, veiled, personalized: a case in which the city's distress could be seen to derive not precisely from its underclass but instead from certain identifiable individuals who claimed to speak for this underclass, individuals who, in Robert

Morgenthau's words, 'sought to exploit' this case, to 'advance their own private agendas'; individuals who wished even to 'divide the races'.

If the city's problems could be seen as deliberate disruptions of a naturally cohesive and harmonious community, a community in which, undisrupted, 'contrasts' generated a perhaps dangerous but vital 'energy', then those problems were tractable, and could be addressed, like 'crime', by the call for 'better leadership'. Considerable comfort could be obtained, given this story line, through the demonization of the Reverend Al Sharpton, whose presence on the edges of certain criminal cases that interested him had a polarizing effect that tended to reinforce the narrative. Jim Sleeper, in *The Closest of Strangers*, described one of the fifteen marches Sharpton led through Bensonhurst after the 1989 killing of an East New York sixteen-year-old, Yusuf Hawkins, who had come into Bensonhurst and been set upon, with baseball bats and ultimately with bullets, by a group of young whites.

An August 27, 1989, *Daily News* photo of the Reverend Al Sharpton and a claque of black teenagers marching in Bensonhurst to protest Hawkins's death shows that they are not really 'marching.' They are stumbling along, huddled together, heads bowed under the storm of hatred breaking over them, eyes wide, hanging on to one another and to Sharpton, scared out of their wits. They, too, are innocents – or were until that day, which they will always remember. And because Sharpton is with them, his head bowed, his face showing that he knows what they're feeling, he is in the hearts of black people all over New York.

Yet something is wrong with this picture. Sharpton did not invite or coordinate with Bensonhurst community leaders who wanted to join the march. Without the time for organizing which these leaders should have been given in order to rein in the punks who stood waving watermelons; without an effort by black leaders more reputable than Sharpton to recruit whites citywide and swell the march, Sharpton was assured that the punks would carry the day. At several points he even baited them by blowing kisses . . .

'I knew that Bensonhurst would clarify whether it had been a racial incident or not,' Sharpton said by way of explaining, on a recent 'Frontline' documentary, his strategy in Bensonhurst. 'The fact that I was so controversial to Bensonhurst helped them forget that the cameras were there,' he said. 'So I decided to help them . . . I would throw kisses to them, and they would go nuts.' *Question*, began a joke told in the aftermath of the first jogger trial. *You're in a room with Hitler, Saddam Hussein, and Al Sharpton. You have only two bullets. Who do you shoot? Answer: Al Sharpton. Twice.*

Sharpton did not exactly fit the roles New York traditionally assigns, for maximum audience comfort, to prominent blacks. He seemed in many ways a phantasm, someone whose instinct for the connections between religion and politics and show business was so innate that he had been all his life the vessel for other people's hopes and fears. He had given his first sermon at age four. He was touring with Mahalia Jackson at eleven. As a teenager, according to Robert D. McFadden, Ralph Blumenthal, M. A. Farber, E. R. Shipp, Charles Strum, and Craig Wolff, the *New York Times* reporters and editors who collaborated on *Outrage: The Story Behind the Tawana Brawley Hoax*, Sharpton was tutored first by Adam Clayton Powell, Jr ('You got to know when to hit it and you got to know when to quit it and when it's quittin' time, don't push it,' Powell told him), then by the Reverend Jesse Jackson ('Once you turn on the gas, you got to cook or burn 'em up,' Jackson told him), and eventually, after obtaining a grant from Bayard Rustin and campaigning for Shirley Chisholm, by James Brown. 'Once, he trailed Brown down a corridor, through a door, and, to his astonishment, onto a stage flooded with spotlights,' the authors of *Outrage* reported. 'He immediately went into a wiggle and dance.'

It was perhaps this talent for seizing the spotlight and the moment, this fatal bent for the wiggle and the dance, that most clearly disqualified Sharpton from casting as the Good Negro, the credit to the race, the exemplary if often imagined figure whose refined manners and good grammar could be stressed and who could be seen to lay, as Jimmy Walker said of Joe Louis, 'a rose on the grave of Abraham Lincoln'. It was left, then, to cast Sharpton, and for Sharpton to cast himself, as the Outrageous Nigger, the familiar role – assigned sixty years ago to Father Divine and thirty years later to Adam Clayton

Powell – of the essentially manageable fraud whose first concern is his own well-being. It was for example repeatedly mentioned, during the ten days the jury was out on the first jogger trial, that Sharpton had chosen to wait out the verdict not at 111 Centre Street but 'in the air-conditioned comfort' of C. Vernon Mason's office, from which he could be summoned by beeper.

Sharpton, it was frequently said by whites and also by some blacks, 'represented nobody', was 'self-appointed' and 'self-promoting'. He was an 'exploiter' of blacks, someone who 'did them more harm than good'. It was pointed out that he had been indicted by the state of New York in June of 1989 on charges of grand larceny. (He was ultimately acquitted.) It was pointed out that *New York Newsday*, working on information that appeared to have been supplied by federal law-enforcement agencies, had in January 1988 named him as a federal informant, and that he himself admitted to having let the government tap his phone in a drug-enforcement effort. It was routinely said, most tellingly of all in a narrative based on the magical ability of 'leaders' to improve the commonweal, that he was 'not the right leader', 'not at all the leader the black community needs'. His clothes and his demeanor were ridiculed (my husband was asked by *Esquire* to do a piece predicated on interviewing Sharpton while he was having his hair processed), his motives derided, and his tactics, which were those of an extremely sophisticated player who counted being widely despised among his stronger cards, not very well understood.

Whites tended to believe, and to say, that Sharpton was 'using' the racial issue – which, in the sense that all political action is based on 'using' one issue or another, he clearly was. Whites also tended to see him as destructive and irresponsible, indifferent to the truth or to the sensibilities of whites – which, most notoriously in the nurturing of the Tawana Brawley case, a primal fantasy in which white men were accused of a crime Sharpton may well have known to be a fabrication, he also clearly was. What seemed not at all understood was that for Sharpton, who had no interest in making the problem appear more tractable ('The question is, do you want to "ease" it or do you want to "heal" it,' he had said when asked if his marches had not worked against 'easing tension' in Bensonhurst), the fact that blacks and whites could sometimes be shown to have divergent interests by no means suggested the need for an ameliorative solution. Such divergent interests were instead a lucky break, a ready-made organizing tool, a dramatic illustration of who had the power and who did not, who was making it and who was falling below the line; a metaphor for the sense of victimization felt not only by blacks but by all those Sharpton called 'the left-out opposition'. *We got the power*, the chants go on 'Sharpton and Fulani in Babylon: Volume I, The Battle of New York City', a tape of the speeches of Sharpton and of Leonora Fulani, a leader of the New Alliance Party. *We are the chosen people. Out of the pain. We that can't even talk together. Have learned to walk together.*

'I'm no longer sure what I thought about Al Sharpton a year or two ago still applies,' Jerry Nachman, the editor of the *New York Post*, who had frequently criticized Sharpton, told Howard Kurtz of the *Washington Post* in September of 1990. 'I spent a lot of time on the street. There's a lot of anger, a lot of frustration. Rightly or wrongly, he may be articulating a great deal more of what typical attitudes are than some of us thought.' Wilbert Tatum, the editor and publisher of the *Amsterdam News*, tried to explain to Kurtz how, in his view, Sharpton had been cast as 'a caricature of black leadership':

> He was fat. He wore jogging suits. He wore a medallion and gold chains. And the unforgivable of unforgivables, he had processed hair. The white media, perhaps not consciously, said, 'We're going to promote this guy because we can point up the ridiculousness and paucity of black leadership.' Al understood precisely what they were doing, precisely. Al is probably the most brilliant tactician this country has ever produced . . .

Whites often mentioned, as a clinching argument, that Sharpton paid his demonstrators to appear; the figure usually mentioned was five dollars (by November 1990, when Sharpton was fielding demonstrators to protest the killing of a black woman alleged to have grabbed a police nightstick in the aftermath of a domestic dispute, a police source quoted in the *Post* had jumped the payment to twenty dollars), but the figure floated by a prosecutor on the jogger case was four dollars. This seemed on many levels a misunderstanding, or an estrangement, or as blacks would say a disrespect, too deep to address, but on its simplest level it served to suggest what value was placed by whites on what they thought of as black time.

In the fall of 1990, the fourth and fifth of the six defendants in the Central Park attack, Kevin Richardson and Kharey Wise, went on trial. Since this particular narrative had achieved full resolution, or catharsis, with the conviction of the first three defendants, the city's interest in the case had by then largely waned. Those 'charlatans' who had sought to 'exploit' the case had been whisked, until they could next prove useful, into the wings. Even the verdicts in this second trial, coinciding as they did with yet another arrest of John ('The Dapper Don') Gotti, a reliable favorite on the New York stage, did not lead the local news. It was in fact the economy itself that had come center stage in the city's new, and yet familiar, narrative work: a work in which the vital yet beleaguered city would or would not weather yet another 'crisis' (the answer was a resounding yes); a work, or a dreamwork, that emphasized not only the cyclical nature of such 'crises' but the regenerative power of the city's 'contrasts'. 'With its migratory population, its diversity of cultures and institutions, and its vast resources of infrastructure, capital, and intellect, New York has been the quintessential modern city for more than a century, constantly reinventing itself,' Michael Stone concluded in his *New York* magazine cover story, 'Hard Times'. 'Though the process may be long and painful, there's no reason to believe it won't happen again.'

These were points commonly made in support of a narrative that tended, with its dramatic line of 'crisis' and resolution, or recovery, only to further obscure the economic and historical groundwork for the situation in which the city found itself: that long unindictable conspiracy of criminal and semicriminal civic and commercial arrangements, deals, negotiations, gimmes and getmes, graft and grift, pipe, topsoil, concrete, garbage; the conspiracy of those in the know, those with a connection, those with a rabbi at the Department of Sanitation or the Buildings Department or the School Construction Authority or Foley Square, the conspiracy of those who believed everybody got upside down because of who it was, it happened to anybody else, a summons gets issued and that's the end of it. On

November 12, 1990, in its page-one analysis of the city's troubles, the *New York Times* went so far as to locate, in 'public spending', not the drain on the city's vitality and resources it had historically been but 'an important positive factor':

> Not in decades has so much money gone for public works in the area – airports, highways, bridges, sewers, subways and other projects. Roughly $12 billion will be spent in the metropolitan region in the current fiscal year. Such government outlays are a healthy counterforce to a 43 percent decline since 1987 in the value of new private construction, a decline related to the sharp drop in real estate prices ... While nearly every industry in the private sector has been reducing payrolls since spring, government hiring has risen, maintaining an annual growth rate of 20,000 people since 1987 ...

That there might well be, in a city in which the proliferation of and increase in taxes were already driving private-sector payrolls out of town, hardly anyone left to tax for such public works and public-sector jobs was a point not too many people wished seriously to address: among the citizens of a New York come to grief on the sentimental stories told in defense of its own lazy criminality, the city's inevitability remained the given, the heart, the first and last word on which all the stories rested. We love New York, the narrative promises, because it matches our energy level.

1990

Lightning Source UK Ltd.
Milton Keynes UK
UKHW042323200722
406148UK00002B/278

9 780007 204380